THE LONELY
POLYGAMIST

ALSO BY **BRADY UDALL**

LETTING LOOSE THE HOUNDS: STORIES

THE MIRACLE LIFE OF EDGAR MINT: A NOVEL

THE LONELY POLYGAMIST

....

A NOVEL

....

BRADY UDALL

JONATHAN CAPE
LONDON

Published by Jonathan Cape 2010

2 4 6 8 10 9 7 5 3 1

First published in Great Britain in 2010 by
Jonathan Cape
Random House, 20 Vauxhall Bridge Road,
London SW1V 2SA

www.rbooks.co.uk

Addresses for companies within The Random House Group Limited can be found at:
www.randomhouse.co.uk/offices.htm

The Random House Group Limited Reg. No. 954009

A CIP catalogue record for this book
is available from the British Library

ISBN 9780224078061

The Random House Group Limited makes every effort to ensure that the papers
used in its books are made from trees that have been legally sourced from well-managed
and credibly certified forests. Our paper procurement policy can be found at:
www.randomhouse.co.uk/paper.htm

Printed and bound in Great Britain by
Clays Ltd, St Ives Plc

IN MEMORY OF

CAROL HOUCK SMITH

1923–2008

And for my brothers and sisters,
every last one of them:

TRAVIS

SYMONIE

CORD

BOOMER

CAMIE

LINDY

BRIGHAM

KEEGAN

GOLDEN RICHARDS
(The Father, Age: 45)

BEVERLY RICHARDS
(Mother #1, Age: 48)

Em *(Daughter #1, Age: 17)*
Nephi *(Son #1, Age: 16)*
Josephine *(Daughter #2, First Twin #1, Age: 14)*
Naomi *(Daughter #3, First Twin #2, Age: 14)*
Parley *(Son #3, Age: 13)*
Alvin *(Son #4, Age: 11)*
Glory *(Daughter #9, Deceased)*
Martin *(Son #10, Stooge #1, Age: 8)*
Louise *(Daughter #11, "The Tattletale," Age: 6)*
Sariah *(Daughter #14, Age: 4)*

NOLA RICHARDS
(Mother #2, Age: 43)

Helaman *(Son #2, Age: 15)*
Novella *(Daughter #5, Age: 13)*
Sybil *(Daughter #6, Second Twin #1, Age: 12)*
Deeanne *(Daughter #7, Second Twin #2, Age: 12)*
Clifton *(Son #6, Age: 10)*
Boo *(Son #8, Stooge #3, Age: 8)*
Teague *(Son #11, Age: 7)*
Darling *(Daughter #13, "The Family Weeper," Age: 5)*
Jame-o *(Son #13, Age: 4)*
Pet *(Daughter #15, Age: 3)*

ROSE-OF-SHARON RICHARDS
(Mother #3, Age: 40)

Pauline *(Daughter #4, Age: 14)*
Gale *(Daughter #8, Age: 12)*
Rusty *(Son #5, "The Family Terrorist," Age: 11)*
Herschel *(Son #7, "The Buttkisser," Age: 9)*
Wayne *(Son #9, Stooge #2, Age: 8)*
Fig Newton *(Daughter #12, Age: 6)*
Ferris *(Son #12, "The Streaker," Age 4)*

TRISH RICHARDS
(Mother #4, Age: 27)

Faye *(Daughter #10, "The Creepy One," Age: 7)*

Our end drifts nearer,

the moon lifts,

radiant with terror.

The state

is a diver under a glass bell.

A father's no shield

for his child.

—ROBERT LOWELL, "FALL 1961"

THE LONELY
POLYGAMIST

1.
...

FAMILY HOME EVENING

T O PUT IT AS SIMPLY AS POSSIBLE: THIS IS THE STORY OF A POLYGAMIST who has an affair. But there is much more to it than that, of course; the life of any polygamist, even when not complicated by lies and secrets and infidelity, is anything but simple. Take, for example, the Friday night in early spring when Golden Richards returned to Big House—one of three houses he called home—after a week away on the job. It should have been the sweetest, most wholesome of domestic scenes: a father arrives home to the loving attentions of his wives and children. But what was about to happen inside that house, Golden realized as he pulled up into the long gravel drive, would not be wholesome or sweet, or anything close to it.

The place was lit up like a carnival tent—yellow light burned in every one of the house's two dozen windows—and the sound coming from inside was as loud as he'd ever heard it: a whooping clamor that occasionally broke up into individual shouts and wails and thumps before gathering into a rising howl that rattled the front door on its hinges and made the windows buzz. Golden hadn't heard it like this in years, but he knew exactly what it was. It was the sound of recrimination and chaos. It was the sound of trouble.

"Oh crud," Golden said.

Even though he'd just driven over two hundred miles without so much as a pit stop, it was not easy to convince himself to turn off the ignition, to let go of the steering wheel. A need to pee that bordered

on spiritual torment was what finally made him pry his long body out
of the cab of the GMC. He stood bewildered in the dead hollyhocks,
his hair full of sawdust, squinting and rubbing his aching behind
with both hands. He was a large, wide-shouldered man with knobby
hands and a slight overbite that he tried to hide by pursing his lips
in the manner of somebody preparing to whistle. He pursed his lips
now, and surveyed the front yard, which, in the watery moonlight,
had taken on the look of a recently abandoned battlefield: mittens and
scarves and jump ropes hanging in the bushes, parkas and broken
toys and heaven knows what scattered all the way up to the road as if
left there by a receding tide. On the propane tank, in blue crayon, was
scrawled the word BOOGER.

"Nice," Golden said. "Would you take a look at this."

Not only was his bladder set to give out at any moment, but his
bad leg had fallen asleep on the drive home. When he tried to cut
across the lawn and mount the front steps it was as if he had been
afflicted with a sudden palsy. His leg buckled and bowed as he
hopped across the grass and up the steps, grimacing and pivoting on
his good leg in an effort to stay upright, tripping on toys as he went,
until he had to make a blind grab at the rail to keep from going sideways off the porch. He limped up to the front door, a feeling of doom
settling on the back of his neck. His leg tingled painfully and he could
feel the noise of the house in the vibration of the boards beneath his
feet.

A hand-lettered sign next to the front door commanded:

WIPE YOUR FEET

and Golden obediently scuffed the soles of his boots on the rubber
welcome mat. He took a few deep motivational nose-breaths, put his
hand on the doorknob, but couldn't find the will to give it a turn.

There was no getting around it: he was afraid. Afraid that, finally,
the truth had been discovered, that he had been exposed as a sneak, a
cheat, a liar. Look at him: a man afraid to walk into his own house.

Once he'd thumbed his shirttail into his pants, knocked some of the sawdust out of his hair, dug a breath mint from his shirt pocket, and taken a couple toots of Afrin nasal spray, he felt a bit more sure of himself. He put his hand back on the doorknob and closed his eyes.

"Come on," he whispered, "come on, you sissy."

Like a man gathering to jump into an icy pond, he pushed open the door. A wave of heat hit him—the house was as hot as a bakery. The tiled entry was dim and empty, and the rich, sugary smell of something in the oven—hopefully Beverly's pineapple upside-down cake—made his mouth water. He took one stealthy heel-to-toe step, another, stopped to listen. Over the sounds of hollering and pounding feet he could hear the radio and the sound of water chuckling through overhead pipes. Normally there would have been a crush of children waiting at the door, all of them shouting at once, pulling at his clothes and asking him what he'd brought them, the little ones standing on their heads or displaying some new bruise or scab—*Look at me! Look at me!*—and the wives hanging back, waiting for their chance to lay their claims on him, each one of them a burning spotlight of attention and need.

But for the first time in his memory there was no one there to greet him. He was all alone and it unnerved him.

He listened, trying to get a sense of what he might be facing. A door slammed. Muffled voices echoed down the stairway. He willed himself to step forward, out of the dark hallway and into the light of the family room, but Golden kept imagining slipping back out the door, skulking away like a burglar, maybe heading out to the highway and getting a room at the Apache Acres Motor Inn, where he could take a long serious leak, call home to claim engine trouble, and then order some of that good country-fried steak from the all-night diner and watch *Starsky and Hutch* on a color television—but his little fantasy didn't last long because at that moment the children attacked.

Somebody yelled, "Kill the zombie!" and he was grabbed from behind by his belt, from both sides around the calves. They came from behind the couches and the top of the stairs, ten, twelve of them, ramming him with their small heads, clawing at his legs, hooking their fingers in the pockets of his jeans, trying to drag him down. Herschel, Fig Newton, Ferris, Darling, Jame-o, Louise, Teague. There were the second twins: Sybil and Deeanne. And the Three Stooges, yipping like mariachis. They were all sweaty and wild and for a moment it felt like the sheer weight of them might tear him apart.

On another night, Golden might have gone along, moaning like a cartoon mummy, flailing his arms in mock undead rage, falling with them onto the carpet of the living room floor, wrestling and tickling and kissing—but not tonight. No way. He locked his knees and went stiff, hoping to outlast them, but they hung on, screaming with laughter, egging each other on. Eleven-year-old Rusty, who was, as his mother called him, "hefty" and getting too old for this kind of thing, slipped from his hiding place behind the curtains and leapt off the piano bench onto Golden's back, nearly bringing the whole pile down.

"Okay now!" Golden grunted. "Let's try not to overdo it!" He was whacked across the shins with a plastic samurai sword and it felt like someone was trying to take a bite out of his kneecap.

At first he offered no resistance, did little more than stand there and take the punishment as his due. But then Teague, who had developed the habit of trying to slug Golden in the crotch whenever there was an opening, did exactly that and Golden decided he'd had enough. He shrugged off Rusty and started the work of peeling them away, one by one. Several resisted, thinking it was still a game. Two or three were still at his legs and someone had climbed up his back and grabbed hold of his shirt collar. Pet, her silver-pink hair in braids, stood on her tiptoes and squeezed him fervently around the middle, putting a strain on his kidneys.

"Okay, hey, watch it, careful now." Golden hoisted Pet out of the way and several more jumped in to try and take her place. "That's it, oh—ow! Hey, ha, all right, there. Stop. Oh boy. Ouch! Get off! *Now!*"

They fell back, blinking, their faces slack with surprise. Fig Newton was so stunned that tears sprang from her eyes as if she had been struck. Only Louise, who was partially deaf and rarely wore her hearing aid, kept on, gnawing on Golden's boot and growling like a dog.

"Okay, everybody," Golden rasped, pulling his pants back up to their original position. He shook off Louise and pulled Fig Newton, still weeping bitterly, close against his hip. "I'm real sorry, kids, I don't got much of a zombie in me tonight. Another time, that's a promise." He stuck his hand in his hair and sighed, tried to put on a relaxed smile. "Hoo-wee. Now, where are your mothers?"

This question brightened them up instantly. Some shrugged, others shouted, "We don't know!" In twos and threes they scattered, already whooping it up again, most of them off to resume their laps around the racetrack.

When Golden built Big House eleven years before, he had made two mistakes: not enough bathrooms, and the racetrack. The racetrack was a mistake in planning, pure and simple. The house had been built according to a standard floor plan: kitchen at the center, surrounded by the living room, family room, dining room and rec room, each of which opened into the room next to it. How could he have foreseen that such a configuration would create a kind of European-style roundabout, a perfect racetrack oval that would allow the kids to tear through the house in endless, uninterrupted procession? Big House became the scene of an ongoing stampede: kids sprinting through the rooms after each other, banking around corners and accelerating on the straightaways, careening and skidding and bouncing off walls, always, for some reason, in a counterclockwise flow. Sometimes just being in the house made Golden dizzy. There he'd be at his place in the kitchen having a mug of Postum or looking over some blueprints, not paying too much attention to the daily mob circling by, and the next thing he knew he'd get so light-headed he'd have to grab the counter to keep from tipping sideways off his stool.

After only a year and a half, a foot-wide track had been worn in the carpet, down to the matting, and Golden tried to ban all running in the house. He might as well have asked the planets to pause in their orbits. He tried placing a love seat in the dining room entry-way to disrupt the flow even threatened to seal off the dining room completely if that's what it took, but Nola and Rose-of-Sharon—the two wives and sisters who shared this house—convinced him that all the running, despite the noise and carpet damage, was actually a blessing; it was a good release of enthusiasm and kept them out of trouble.

"Enthusiasm?" Golden had asked. "Couldn't they run around the house, *outside*, where kids are supposed to release their enthusiasm? I'm worried about the floor joists in here."

Nola sighed, as she often did when explaining things to Golden. "You know they run out there too, but at least in here they're con-tained," she said. Rose-of-Sharon, working with her sister on a birth-ing quilt, had nodded her agreement. "In here we can keep track of them. At least in here we know they're not running out into the road, getting mowed down by cattle trucks or stolen by criminals."

And that was that. From then on, Big House would be known as a place where running indoors was not only allowed, but encouraged.

It would also be known as a place where it was difficult to find an available bathroom. Golden first tried the one off the back hallway, but found it occupied (it boasted a padded toilet seat and a library of Sears and Roebuck catalogs, which meant it was pretty much always in use, even in the dead of night). The seven-thousand-square-foot house struck him as a bit overdone when he'd built it, but now, as he tried to make his way to the only other first-floor bathroom, way off in the far corner, he found it downright appalling.

He paused near the grandfather clock to get his bearings. When you lived in three separate houses, as Golden did, it wasn't too hard to get confused about little things like where the spare lightbulbs were kept or how to work the alarm clocks, or where, exactly, the bath-rooms were located. A few weeks before, he awoke in the middle of the night and, thinking he was in Old House, walked out to what he thought was the kitchen to get a glass of water, only to end up taking a little spill down the stairs and straining something in his groin.

He was finally able to sketch a picture of the bathroom in his mind—it was at the end of the hall near the garage—and he pushed on with his trek: through the rec room, where a few of the older boys were scaling the rock fireplace all the way up to the ten-foot ceilings, while below the Three Stooges—Martin, Boo, and Wayne—practiced kung fu combinations and beat each other with cardboard wrapping-paper tubes; past the living room, where Pauline and Novella sat cross-legged in the middle of the floor, whispering secrets and shrieking about something written on a sheet of notebook paper; and on to the dining room, where a tinfoil-covered plate was positioned carefully all by itself at the head of the expansive three-sectioned table. One of the overhead track lights was trained on it so that it had the look of an artifact displayed in a museum.

The plate, Golden knew, was a sign, a message. *You are late*, it said. *Dinner is over and, once again, we've eaten without you.*

This was the kind of reprimand he'd been getting a lot lately. His construction business had been going south for more than two years now, and he had to start taking jobs farther and farther out, which meant even less time with the family. Now that he was on a job site two hundred miles away in Nye County, Nevada, he was gone for days at a time, sometimes a full week, and whenever he walked into one of his houses he felt more than ever like a stranger, an outlander unfamiliar with the customs of the place.

By showing up late tonight he'd made a particularly serious error. It was Family Home Evening, the one night of the week when the entire family gathered at Big House (the only one that could accommodate all thirty-two of them), to have dinner and a family meeting consisting of scripture reading, songs, games and maybe lemon bars or chocolate chip ice cream if everybody behaved themselves. No doubt they had cooked an elaborate dinner, cleaned the house and prepared something special for Home Evening, and waited. Waited for a husband and father who was almost never around, who had made a habit out of keeping them waiting. Then, as they had been doing more and more lately, they ate without him.

Just then little Ferris ran by, nude from the waist down, apparently recovered from his father's outburst in the entryway. One of his sisters shouted after him, "Ferris has his pants off again!" and Ferris, as if to confirm this declaration, did a joyous, hip-rolling dance that seemed vaguely suggestive, especially for a four-year-old.

"La la la," he sang. "Do do do."

Too busy enjoying his own nudity to notice Golden, the boy rubbed his butt luxuriously along the pine wainscoting and then shimmied to the other side of the room, where he pressed himself into a potted plant. Only when Novella appeared, threatening to tell his mother, did he gallop off around the racetrack, slapping his haunches as he went.

Alone again, Golden regarded the plate on the table. Despite everything—he could not help himself—he lifted the foil and carefully extracted a barbecued chicken wing, which he slurped at guiltily as he took mincing, sidelong steps down the hall. He turned the corner to find chubby and ever-sweating Clifton at the locked bathroom door, kicking it in rhythm with a kind of plaintive boot-camp chant: "Open up, open up, right now, right now, open up, open up, hey-hey, right now."

When he saw Golden he wailed, "Are we gonna do something about the girls in this place? What are they doing in there all the time? Huh? I hate 'em!"

Golden slumped against the wall, defeated. The boy was right— the girls were bathroom hogs. Even the preadolescents could take half an hour to straighten their clothes and check their hair and perform other cryptic ministrations the boys could only guess at. And when a bathroom did become available they always seemed to get there first, as if they were trading insider information to which the boys—who saw using the bathroom as nothing more than a nuisance—were not party. Golden should have had some genuine sympathy for Clifton, but at this point all he felt was annoyed that the boy had beat him to the punch.

Under the cracking thunder of kids jumping off the bunk beds in the room directly above him, he could hear the ratcheting of a sewing machine and turned to see a sight that made his blood turn to water: Beverly, the first wife, in the all-purpose room across the hall, working intently on a length of sheer fabric. In excruciating slow motion Golden tried to step backward out of sight, but just as he was about to clear the doorway she glanced up at him, stopping him cold. She went back to her sewing without a word.

Until now he had been sure the wives were assembled in an upstairs room deciding his fate, grimly analyzing the evidence against him, united in their desire to see him pay for his lies and transgressions. But here was Beverly, alone, and Golden couldn't decide whether this was bad news or a positive development. Maybe the scheming was already over and they had retired to separate quarters of the house, or maybe there had been no scheming at all and there was something else brewing which he could only guess at. Golden was in no state of mind to be making guesses; he felt fortunate just to have been able to locate the bathroom.

He tried to read something into Beverly's posture, but there was nothing to read; she always kept her back straight, her elbows close to her ribs. Even in her most distracted or carefree moments she never slumped or loafed or dragged, never allowed herself to sit back and take it easy. When she slept she lay with her head just so on the pillow, her hands clasped across her chest on top of the blankets, as if posing for a mattress commercial.

Pressing his thighs together so he wouldn't wet his pants, Golden hobbled across the hall and leaned against the doorjamb in a desperate attempt to look casual. He realized he was holding the half-eaten chicken wing right out in the open and in a moment of panic stuffed it into his pocket.

"Ah, hey, hello." He gave a little wave as if he were talking to her through a pane of glass. He raised his voice so she could hear him above the sewing machine and a round of sustained caterwauling that had started out in the family room. "Sorry I'm late! That darn concrete guy didn't show until four o'clock!"

There was the tiniest rise and fall of her shoulders, but she kept feeding the fabric through the machine. He stepped closer to her and felt a drop in temperature; Beverly was a woman whose moods held sway over the immediate atmosphere, who seemed to be in control of everything, including the weather. She had kinky iron-gray hair she kept in check with an assortment of clips, barrettes, clasps and stickpins. Tonight, as usual, she had her hair up in a barely contained bun, which bristled with what looked like an arsenal of miniature weaponry.

Only after she had hemmed the entire length of the fabric did she get up to deliver a perfunctory kiss on the cheek and tell him that there was dinner waiting for him at the table. She then sat back down and checked her hem under the light of a jeweler's lamp.

"Your drive?" she said.

"Long like always!" he said. "I'm thinking maybe I should trade my pickup for Elwin's old crop duster and do belly rolls all the way home. Least that way I could stay awake."

Out in the hall Clifton gave the closed bathroom door a good kick and sang, "I'm dying out here! I'm *dy-ing*!"

Beverly nodded, didn't look up. Normally he would have waited her out, but Clifton wasn't the only one on the brink of a serious accident.

"I, uh, is there—is there something going on?"

"There's a lot going on, Golden, there always is."

"Everything seems a bit, you know, crazy."

"Well, that's how it is around here, in case you've forgotten."

"Not the normal crazy, that's not what I'm talking about. Something seems, I don't know . . ."

Beverly looked squarely at him for the first time, and his mouth moved silently as he searched for the word he wanted. Words: they were difficult for Golden in the best of times, and nearly impossible when he was under the gun like this.

". . . awry," he said, finally.

"*Awry*." She took special care with the pronunciation. She held his gaze for a second more and went back to her work. "Okay, awry. Awry it is. And you're right, there's a lot that is awry tonight. For example, your dog, who has found it necessary, for the third time in two weeks, to piddle in my shoes."

"Cooter?" Golden said.

"Unless you keep another dog I don't know about. I locked him in the utility closet, and if he's piddled on something in there I'm going to let the neighbors use him for target practice."

For a second or two, Golden felt a twinge of optimism. Could this be what it was all about, Cooter doing a number on Beverly's shoes? Beverly and Cooter had been carrying on a feud for years, but the other wives tolerated the little dog, even had shown a fondness for him, which was probably why he had never piddled in *their* shoes. No, the other wives had no reason to be upset by Cooter's misdeeds, and even mighty Beverly did not have the power, by herself, to make things go *this* awry.

"By the way," Beverly said as she tied off a length of thread, "you've got something on your lip."

THE CLOSET

In the dusty darkness of a closet that smelled like shoe polish and Pine-Sol, and warmed by a fifty-gallon water heater that occasionally released a contented gurgle, he felt buffered, momentarily safe from the perils of the house. He'd come here after talking to Beverly, after wiping the barbecue sauce from his mouth and staring at his boots for a while before finally taking the only good choice available to him, which was to cut and run. He'd mumbled something about having a word with Cooter and, before Beverly could protest, made his escape.

By a stroke of luck the utility closet was only twenty feet down the hall. Golden pulled the door shut behind him and it was like he'd stumbled out of high winds and flying debris into a storm cellar made of reinforced concrete: the noise dropped away instantly and left nothing in his ears but a distant ringing and the sound of Cooter panting at his feet. He wondered why he hadn't discovered this place before—it was downright pleasant in here. When things got out of hand, when everybody was at him and he needed a little peace, he wouldn't have to sneak out to the garage where he kept his tools and a spare army cot; he could slip in here and polish his shoes and keep the water heater company for a while.

None of this, however, changed the fact that he had to pee *right now*. In fact, this unexpected tranquility was having a relaxing effect not only on his state of mind, but also on his bladder (the gurgling water heater wasn't helping either). He felt his buttocks unclenching for the first time in several hours and then a deflating sensation in his bladder and he knew that it had come: the point of no return. He bit his lip and groped in the dark for a light chain—wasn't there a light chain in here?—and when he couldn't locate one he fell into a kind of resigned panic: knocking over brooms and plungers, grappling with an ironing board in the pitch-dark—*Aw, wouldn't you know it, aw, darn it, oh no, no, no, come on, please*—sweeping spray bottles and canisters of Ajax off the shelves, sending Cooter, who had been drowsing against the warmth of the water heater, into blind, scrabbling hysterics. By some miracle Golden's hand settled on what he had been searching for: a five-gallon plastic mop bucket.

Five gallons, Golden thought. *Let's hope it's enough.*

After a frantic battle with his zipper, Golden was finally able to relax and, as his father would have said, "make a bargain with mother nature." The relief was profound, like coming up for air after a long submersion. While the bucket filled, Golden had time to locate the pull chain with his free hand and switch on the light. He figured that if someone happened to open the door on these proceedings it all might somehow appear more legitimate with the light on.

Under the dour yellow light of the forty-watt bulb it took him a second to locate Cooter, who was wearing underpants.

Golden shook his head. "Oh man, she got you again, didn't she. I'm real sorry about this, boy."

Cooter turned away, his damp eyes bulging with resentment, apparently not yet prepared to accept apologies from anyone. Cooter was a skittish, bug-eyed dachshund mix who had been first required to wear undershorts several years ago when he'd suffered a period of obsessive licking, in which he licked his hind end so much it bled. The underwear helped him curb his habit, but when he started peeing on Beverly's belongings she took the tiny jockeys out of retirement and employed them as psychological torment. The dog hated them and would not urinate or defecate with them on unless he had no other choice. They were dainty little things that had once belonged to a baseball doll named Swingin' Baby Timmy (the doll had also sported all the realistic baseball gear: socks, stirrups, cleats, wristbands and a complete baseball uniform) and were all white except for a yellow explosion on the rear, inside of which the words HOME RUN!!! were printed in blue.

Cooter was extremely sensitive to the attention he got while wearing his HOME RUN!!! underwear and Golden decided it was probably a blessing in disguise that Beverly had put him here in the closet, out of public view.

Golden tried giving the dog a friendly nudge with the toe of his boot, but Cooter backed into a bag of rock salt and turned his head as if he'd been the object of a cruel insult.

"Come on now," Golden whispered. "Don't give me that. You deserve what you're getting, you big baby. How many times have I told you about going on Beverly's shoes? Huh? Huh? You're going to get us both tossed out into the cold, you know that? Huh? You think I'm joking? You think this is a joke? You think—"

Golden flinched, struck by the moment he found himself in: standing in a dark closet, knuckles smeared with barbecue sauce, tinkling into a bucket while delivering a lecture about bathroom manners to a dog wearing jockey shorts. Could it get, he wondered, any worse than this? Sure it could. It probably would before the night was over, which was why he couldn't find the wherewithal to laugh at himself, not yet, not until his fate, for better or worse, was decided.

After he finished his business he crouched next to Cooter and proffered his sauce-covered hand. Cooter sniffed at it uncertainly and looked up at Golden for guidance. Golden felt a welling of affection for the little dog; he was a weasel-like creature with bulging Marty Feldman eyes and a hairless butt who had no idea how hideous he was.

"Go on ahead," Golden sighed. "Knock yourself out."

While Cooter snaked his tongue between Golden's fingers in an attempt to get every last bit of sauce, Golden opened the door a crack and hissed at Clifton, who was still on bathroom vigil down the hall. Clifton came up, bobbing and bending at the waist, his face red with indignation.

"There's *two* of 'em in there," he said. "Girls. I can hear 'em giggling and running the water. And Mom told the boys if we went out in the bushes anymore she'd ground us. Why won't somebody help me?"

"I'm going to help you if you keep your voice down." Golden held the door open for him. "Number one or number two?"

"Number one, mainly." Clifton looked from Cooter to Golden. "Did Aunt Beverly lock you in here too?"

Golden took the bucket down from the shelf. "You see this bucket? You can go in this bucket, and forget all about the bathroom or the bushes, if you do one little favor for me."

"Did you go in the bucket?"

"Well. Yes. But you can't tell anybody about this, understand? It's a secret."

"Can I have my own bucket?"

"This is an emergency bucket. There's only one, and it's for emergencies. You can use it if you do this one favor for me and don't mention it to anyone."

"How about I go in the bucket first, and then the favor?"

Golden shook his head. He knew that if he let the boy go in the bucket first he'd likely never see him again. "It'll take just a few seconds. I want you to go upstairs and take a look around and find out where your mother and Aunt Trish and Aunt Rose are. Then come back and tell me. Like a spy mission. Top secret. Don't talk to anybody. Me and Cooter'll wait for you right here."

In practically no time—about fifteen seconds, by Golden's estimation—Clifton was back. "They're in the upstairs kitchen. All three of 'em."

"What? You already went up there?"

The boy shrugged. "I can run fast when I have to."

"What are they doing?"

"Washing stuff and talking. Where's the bucket?"

"Just one more thing. Do they look mad?"

Clifton sighed. "I think they're probably mad at you. I think that's why you're hiding in this closet."

Golden handed Clifton the bucket. "When you're done, put it behind the rag pile. And don't let Cooter out or Aunt Beverly will have your hide."

THE BARGE

Out in the bright lights and noise, Golden was overcome by a wave of dizziness, and suddenly felt vulnerable again. He wished he'd taken more time in the closet to gather himself, to prepare a defense. As he climbed the stairs, a gang of children pulsing around him like a school of fish, he decided he wanted it over with. No more faking it. He would offer no apologies or excuses. He would place himself at their mercy.

The wives were gathered in the upstairs kitchen, all three of them, just as Clifton had said. Golden had installed the upstairs kitchen so Nola and Rose-of-Sharon would have the option of cooking for and feeding their families separately. Not much more than a galley kitchen, it turned out to be too small for even one of their families, and was used only when the kitchen downstairs couldn't accommodate the cooking and cleaning for several dozen people. Slowly, Rose-of-Sharon was converting it into what Golden thought of as Estrogen Ground Zero: its drawers were filled with the tools of womanly crafts, of knitting and needlepoint and tole painting. On every available section of wall space were hung portraits of kittens and poodles and elaborate framed embroideries that declared BLESS THIS HOUSE and LOVE IS SPOKEN HERE. Macramé and beadwork dangled from the ceiling, and the countertops and windowsills were decorated with doilies and little pincushions in the shapes of smiling tomatoes and plump snowmen. The air was thick with rose-petal potpourri and lilac-scented candles, and Rose-of-Sharon had recently plastered the walls with daisy wallpaper so bright it made Golden feel like he was in a room full of popping flashbulbs.

Golden tried to make sense of their conversation, but the constant hiss of water in the sink made the voices blur into one another. His back pressed to the wall, he performed a maneuver that involved craning his neck and holding his head at an extreme angle so he could eyeball the situation without being spotted. Rose-of-Sharon was at the table, sucking on her shirt collar, carefully mapping out a new quilt on a sheet of graph paper. Nola and Trish were out of sight, probably standing at the sink.

Golden took a moment to deliver two generous squirts of Afrin nasal spray into each of his nostrils. All his life he'd had the bad habit of sneezing when he was nervous—anxiety and dread would build like a physical pressure inside his head, and the slightest itch or irritation of the nasal cavity would trigger a great, ripping sneeze, the sound of which could make children cry and adults recoil as if a grenade had gone off. The spray was the only thing he'd found that kept the sneezing in check, and now that he'd made it this far into the heart of enemy territory, he wanted to make sure he didn't give his position away until he was absolutely ready.

He gave himself a quick once-over and found his bootlaces untied, his shirt untucked, and the back of his left hand covered with a residue of barbecue sauce and dog slobber. Doomed, he tied his laces, patted at his hair, and tried to wrestle his shirttail into the tops of his jeans until he gave up, nearly yanking his shirt clean off in a spasm of frustration. The heck with it. No more stalling, he was going in. He started forward, paused, stepped back to check his zipper.

One more toot of nasal spray, one more breath mint for good luck, and he was ready. In what he considered to be an act of reckless bravery, he strode into the kitchen, put his hand on Rose-of-Sharon's shoulder, and, with all the confidence he could muster, croaked, "Hello, girls."

Nola and Trish, who were indeed standing together at the sink in a rising curtain of steam, did not turn around. Rose-of-Sharon's shoulder, soft and pliant when he first touched it, now felt like something made of wood. Trish cast a quick, nervous glance back at him and Nola fished a basting pan out of the dishwater, went to town on it with a ball of steel wool.

"Sorry I'm so late," Golden said. "Had to wait two hours for the darn electrician—"

Rose-of-Sharon slipped from under his hand, ducking, and went to the drawer next to the stove, where she began sorting a collection of embroidered hot pads and oven mitts. Such an act of hostility, even one so mild, was so unlike her that for a few moments Golden's hand hovered in midair as if he really couldn't believe there wasn't a woman's shoulder positioned firmly beneath it.

Now all three women had their backs to him and in the sudden silence of that room he knew that minty breath and tied bootlaces weren't going to make a bit of difference. The wives waited for him to say something but his tongue hung in his mouth like a hunk of old bread. He sat down at the table. Unaccountably, he needed to pee again.

"I've been looking for you downstairs," he said. "The kids didn't know where you were."

There was a drawn-out silence, broken by the clank of dishes, the *whang* of a cookie sheet. Finally, Nola sighed. In a tone that sounded, if you didn't know any better, quite jolly, she said, "Hey, girls, we've been discovered! Ha ha! Wives ahoy!"

Nola could always be counted on to break the silence; she simply didn't have the capacity to keep quiet for long. She was a bosomy, wide-bodied woman with a barroom laugh and the small, pouting mouth of a child. Rose-of-Sharon had her younger sister's freckled skin and pale green eyes, but that was where the similarities ended. She was long-boned and big-jointed, and her face was handsome, sometimes pretty if the shadows fell across it the right way, but her face almost always took a back seat to her hair, which was done in a new style nearly every week. She and Nola ran the Virgin County Academy of Hair Design in town. Nola, the head stylist, used Rose-of-Sharon as a sort of hairstyle guinea pig, and, if the style came out well, a walking advertisement for the academy. Tonight Rose-of-Sharon's hair was done up in a way that made Golden think of the word *milkmaid*. The sisters had shared Big House for the entire eleven years of its existence and Golden had never once seen them argue or disagree.

"You're mad at me," Golden said. "Why don't you yell and get it over with? Throw a plate at me? Something?"

"We're not going to yell at you," Trish said.

"Oh, we'll see about that," Nola said. "And if we hadn't just taken the trouble to wash all these dishes you might have gotten that plate you were asking about." She stepped back from the sink and whapped Golden across the shoulder with a dish towel. Nola was always whacking him with something or other, usually as demonstration of her affection for him, but this dish towel had more of a sting to it than he was used to. He rubbed his shoulder and wondered if everybody in the house was going to take a shot at him before the night was out.

"*Nola*," Rose-of-Sharon said. By the tremor in her voice, he could tell she was about to cry. Golden hoped it was because she felt bad about turning her back on him; he needed any scrap of sympathy he could get.

"I'm sorry," Golden said. "I'm real, real . . . sorry. Terribly. About everything."

"Sorry's nice," Nola said. "Real, real sorry, oh that's pretty good too. But what are you going to do about it? Are you going to leave it where it is or are you gonna make us haul it out back and break it up into kindling?"

Golden looked up. "Kindling?"

"Or maybe we could put it out in the Spooners' pasture," Trish said. "That way their mangy cows could have a seat when they get tired of standing around looking stupid."

All three women laughed, each in her particular way: Nola, loud and hooting; Rose-of-Sharon with her hand clapped over her mouth; Trish, like an evil witch in an old black-and-white movie: *eee-eee-eeeeeeeee*. Golden had nothing to do but sit at the table with his mouth half open.

They were happening more and more lately, these moments of dislocation when it seemed everyone was speaking in a kind of pig latin that he could not quite make sense of. He'd come home and the children would start asking him questions that stumped him, the wives would mention places and names that meant nothing to him, would refer to the children by nicknames he'd never heard, and once in a while everybody'd start laughing, just like now, and Golden lost, the only one not in on the joke.

He said, "I'm, I guess I don't, I didn't—"

This made them laugh harder, and though Golden wasn't happy about being the grinning jackass at the table, it made him hopeful: if they could laugh like this, things couldn't be *that* bad.

Trish wiped her eyes. "I think we could find more than one good use for that junky old couch."

"Ha ha," Golden said, still deeply confused. And then from his slump he straightened up so quickly that he banged his knees on the underside of the table. *"Couch,"* he said. He'd meant to say *ouch*, but *couch*, like a stone dislodged from a hillside, was what had tumbled out of his mouth. And then he knew why: the anger, the noise, the cold looks, the plate covered with tinfoil, all of these things had nothing to do with the whopping lies he'd been telling for months now, the deception that had overtaken his life. It was about a stinky, broken-down, truly wonderful old wreck of a couch.

"Couch!" Golden said again, as if he were delivering the clinching answer on a game show. "Where is it?"

"You're telling me you didn't see it downstairs?" Nola said. "She had her boys bring it in before dinner, acting like she was doing us a great favor, like we'd never had a couch before and were lucky just to be getting a look at one."

Without another word Golden shot out of the kitchen and hobbled as fast as he could down the stairs, eventually taking two steps at a time. He remembered now. Remembered how Beverly had called him at the construction site a few days ago, saying she'd found a once-in-a-lifetime deal on a new Churchill hide-a-bed from Steltzmeyer Furniture in St. George, which was going out of business. She'd been complaining about the old couch for at least two years. Because of its fishy smell and enormous size, the children referred to it as the Barge, and regularly took it on jungle river expeditions, slaughtered bands of pirates and man-eating sharks from its decks, and had contests to see how many of them could crowd onto it at once (the record was eighteen). It slumped in the middle, its ruined springs poking through the burnt-orange plaid fabric, and had been haunted by the smell of fish ever since one of the Three Stooges threw up his tuna casserole dinner all over the cushions.

Golden, in a flustered effort to get off the phone as quickly as possible, told Beverly to get the couch, no problem, go right on ahead. Beverly wondered what she should do with the old one and here was where Golden made his mistake. Just before he hung up he'd mentioned something about the sisters finding a place for it in Big House.

Under their present financial circumstances, allowing Beverly to buy a new couch was bad enough, but telling her to give the old one to the sisters—he really needed to have his head examined. The other wives had become so sensitive over the years at getting Beverly's hand-me-downs and castoffs that even bringing up the subject could result in instant accusation and tears. So it was no wonder how things had turned out: the three sister-wives had gone upstairs to fix their portion of the dinner away from Beverly and the offending couch, and Beverly, for her part, had stayed downstairs, feeling unjustly accused. She was, after all, simply carrying out Golden's wishes.

When Golden couldn't see the couch from the stair landing, he hit the living room at a fast walk, and, before he knew it, was trotting along, only the slightest hitch in his gait; all these years, and he'd never once given the racetrack a try. He took the first bend, following the ratty, worn-down groove, and it was like he was being whipped along by a spontaneous gravitational force. He felt strong and weightless, loping past the dinner table like a lead-off hitter rounding second, children in every room turning to watch him go. He leapt over a tub of wooden blocks—carpentry pencils and his toothbrush bouncing out of his shirt pocket—and felt only the slightest twinge of pain in his knee. He was feeling so fine he missed the couch entirely on the first go-round. Only when he'd nearly completed another lap did he see it—how could he have missed it?—pushed into a corner in the family room, given a wide berth, looking sunken and exhausted, as if it had spent the night sobbing in despair.

Golden went into the kitchen and rang the dinner bell, an eight-inch length of old rail hanging from the ceiling by a chain. "Boys! I need boys!" he called, and they came running. They were sweaty and red-faced and ready for action. "Every available boy—let's see—ages nine through fourteen, I guess. We've got furniture to move. Dee-anne, you go upstairs and tell the mothers in the kitchen that we're going to get them another couch. Boys, let's get this one outside."

Before he could start giving orders they already had it up off the floor, weaving and banging into the doorjamb like a crew of drunken pallbearers. Suddenly Beverly was behind him. "What's this?" she said.

"Well, we decided what we're going to do here is get a different couch, it doesn't really go all that good with the carpet and the, you know, furnishings."

"Right now? We need to be getting these kids to bed. We can discuss the couch tomorrow."

"Won't take but a minute. The boys will help me. Back in two ticks."

Golden felt Beverly's hard glare on his back, but he avoided it as best he could, ducked and sidestepped, told himself not to turn around or he'd never make it out alive. He helped the boys squeeze the couch through the front door and shouted encouragement when their arms started to give out. The sky was clouded with stars and it was cold out, so Golden decided that instead of the pickup he'd better take the old Cadillac, a 1963 hearse he bought from Teddy Hornbeck when Teddy sold his funeral business and moved to Florida, where people were known to be dying on a more steady and dependable basis. The hearse had only four thousand miles on it and was one of the most beautiful machines Golden had ever laid eyes on: ultra-long and sleek, with just a hint of fins at the back and velvet drapes at the windows that concealed an interior so large you could host a bridge tournament inside. Behind the single back seat Golden installed three removable benches he'd made out of welded steel tubing and oak planks, and there you had it: the family man's dream machine, a car that could haul five adults and thirteen children with a certain kind of style. Of course, some people thought it was morbid, even disrespectful to God and the departed, but Golden didn't mind; he loved the profound, vibrating hum of its eight-cylinder and the way it drifted effortlessly down the road like a baby grand launched into a river.

With the couch loaded up and the boys inside, he counted heads; if he didn't have every boy in the proclaimed age range there would be hell to pay later. To make sure he had them all, he resorted to his habit of singing the names of the children, under his breath, to the

tune of "The Old Gray Mare"—*EmNephiHelamanPaulineNaomi
JosephineParleyNovellaGaleSybilDeeanne* . . .—it was the only way he
could come close to remembering them all. After sorting out the girls
and younger boys, he discovered that the Three Stooges were missing. Golden asked if anyone knew where they were and noticed Clifton sliding down in his seat.

"Speak up, Clifton," Golden said.

"Why are you asking me? I don't know anything!"

"No need to shout. You tell me right now or you're staying home
with the girls and the babies." On cue, Pet had come out on the
porch and, with her head thrown back, started up an operatic wail of
anguish at being left behind.

Clifton punched the seat in disgust. "In the closet."

"Closet? What are they doing in the closet?"

The boy pulled himself up, put his mouth next to Golden's ear.
"The *bucket*."

Sure enough, they were in the closet, all three of them, pants
down, jostling for position, trying to fill the bucket at the same time.
Little Ferris was there too, still nude below the waist, patiently waiting his turn. For Golden it was hard not to think that there might be
something wrong about a household in which the dog was wearing
underwear and the children weren't.

"*Boys*," Golden said when he stuck his head in the closet. "What
do you think you're doing?"

They must have sensed their father's good mood because the boys
merely looked up at him, grinned, and continued tinkling. Golden
swore them to secrecy before herding them all out into the hall,
including Cooter, who he smuggled out underneath his shirt. They
snuck past the all-purpose room, where Beverly was back at work on
her sewing, and just as they were about to slip outside, Golden felt a
tug on his shirt from behind, which startled him so badly he squeezed
Cooter under his arm like the bellows of a bagpipe.

It was not Beverly behind him, but Trish. "Are you going somewhere?" she whispered.

"Going to exchange that couch," he whispered back. "Taking the boys here. We won't be too long."

She took a step closer to him so that he could smell the citrus shampoo she favored. "Do you know who you're with tonight?" she said.

The truth was he never knew who he was supposed to be with on any given night. Every weekend the girls convened, and according to some arcane algebraic formula decided in whose bed he would be sleeping on which night of the week. He was always grateful when somebody was thoughtful enough to tell him outright instead of making him guess.

"Let me see," he said. "With you?" He shifted uncomfortably, and she gave a curious look at the lump under his shirt, which was Cooter licking his armpit.

"Good guess, Charlie Chan," she said, taking a step closer. She wore a blue dress he'd never seen before, and had her hair up in a ponytail.

"Boys," Golden said, "you go out to the Cadillac and I'll be there shortly. Go on now." Jostling each other with their elbows, they zig-zagged out onto the lawn, bending at their waists and doing furtive head bobs and kung-fu poses.

Looking over her shoulder, Trish slipped an arm around his waist and seemed to be moving in to attempt a kiss when Herschel came bounding down the hall, shouting, "Hubba-hubba!" A moment later Cooter gave Golden's armpit another lick and he grunted, stifling a laugh.

"Okay," she said, releasing him, looking confused now. "Don't take too long."

He groaned, suppressing the laugh that was like a bubble about to pop in his throat, and turned to follow his boys. From the stable where the hearse was parked he waved and called out, "Back in a flash!"

Once everybody was loaded, Golden pulled onto the highway and aimed the Cadillac in the direction of town. His plan was simple: he would trade the couch in the small waiting room of his real estate and construction office for Beverly's plaid monstrosity. He would return the new couch to Big House and everything to its rightful order. Sister Barbara, the old lady from church who performed the occasional bookkeeping and receptionist duties, was not going to be happy about losing her new couch to a domestic dispute within the Richards clan, but the simple fact was that Golden did not sleep with Sister Barbara on a regular basis.

The moon was now hidden behind a low bank of clouds and the light of the stars overhead seemed to thicken and gather like smoke. Golden drove slowly past the darkened forms of water tanks and outbuildings and sandstone bluffs, piloting the car easily around potholes and darting jackrabbits caught in the triangle of his headlights. With the heater blowing gusts of hot wind and Cooter dozing in his lap and the boys talking drowsily in the back, Golden held his foot steady on the gas pedal and for the first time tonight felt relaxed enough to fully exhale and settle his sore butt into the plush seat. Then he heard whispers and snickering from the back.

"Rusty's acting like a dead man," someone said.

Golden turned to see Rusty laid out on the couch, his eyes closed, his hands crossed over his chest in the official posture of death. Some of the boys were giggling and Rusty himself was working hard not to smile.

Golden stomped on the brakes and the car ground to a hard stop, the back end fishtailing as the tires bit into the road. His teeth ground hard against each other and his voice was raw with sudden anger. "You stop that. Don't you *ever* play like that. *Never*."

Rusty, the weird one, the troublemaker, the one always doing the wrong thing, rolled off the couch and crawled to the very back of the car, whimpering that he was sorry. Golden had hit the brakes harder than he intended, sending Cooter onto the floor and pitching several of the boys on top of each other. They all looked up at him now, frightened, their eyes round as dimes.

Golden turned and gathered Cooter back onto his lap. He sat for a while looking out the windshield, his hands on the steering wheel, until his breathing slowed. The smell of exhaust had entered the car and the only sound was the deep underwater gurgle of the engine. "I shouldn't've—" he said, and shook his head. It was the second time tonight he'd yelled at them, the second time he'd given them a scare. He turned around to face them. "I'm sorry," he said, and for one generous moment allowed himself to feel that he was apologizing not only to these boys, but to their mothers and the rest of the family, for the lies he'd been telling them, for his absences in body and spirit, for the joke of a husband and father he'd become.

And just as he'd hoped, they absolved him. Of course they did; they were boys. "No problemo," one of them said, and the others sighed with relief, nodding their sweaty heads.

He put the hearse into gear and gradually opened her up, let the big car fly over the old blacktop with its tarred creases and sudden dips, the headlights cutting through the darkness like the point of a hurtling plow, tossing the black outlines of windmills and hay sheds and road signs to either side. The boys, their faces pressed to the windows, murmured and hummed their approval. Only when they reached the outskirts of town did Golden tap the brakes. The old hearse slowed reluctantly and as it glided under the still-lit Christmas lights of a quiet main street, the words PEACE and LOVE and JOY spelled out in glowing red and green bulbs overhead, Golden felt, for the first time in what seemed like months, something akin to hope: maybe, just maybe, everything would be all right.

2.

- - - - -

THE POSTCARD

How does a shy, lonely boy from the backwaters of Louisiana become an apostle of God, the husband to four wives, the father to twenty-eight children? Easier than you think.

Golden, it was true, had very little going for him early on. He was born at a rest stop somewhere between Gulfport and New Orleans, and spent the first four years of his life being dragged through a series of jerkwater towns by a father who couldn't stay put and a mother who was losing the will to go on. Golden's father was a wildcatter, a man who claimed he could *feel* oil underground the way certain spiritual types can detect the presence of the Holy Spirit. He spent his days scouting locations, hustling leases from backcountry dirt farmers, driving the caliche roads of Alabama and East Texas in his old paneled Ford, which he had outfitted with a special horn he liked to blow—*ah-ooga!*—to let the locals know he was on the scene.

For the first few years Golden's mother, Malke, dutifully followed; they'd take up at a boardinghouse or rent a room in a bowl-and-pitcher hotel and Royal would head out into the hollows and hill country to chase oil. Malke and Golden spent their days waiting; for a letter from Royal, a telegram, or a phone call, or for that rare, glorious moment when they first heard the truck's horn before it rattled into view.

It was in Bernice, Louisiana, that Malke finally dug in her heels. She and three-year-old Golden had spent a full month in a sour-smelling room in the Hidey Hole Tourist Court on the outskirts of

Haines Delta, Mississippi, and now that they had a private apartment over a dentist's office for the reasonable rate of twenty-five dollars a month, she decided she was set. For two weeks, while Royal
was down south, sinking a test hole in Jackson County, chatting up
lonely, big-busted country women and doing Lord knows what else,
Malke painted the apartment's three rooms a bright blue the color
of swimming pool water, sewed curtains for the windows, got rid of
the roaches and the nest of mice behind the enormous old Chambers
stove, and put a sign on the front door:

> No Vagrants or Salesmen,
> Please and Thank You

Malke believed her husband would grow tired of life on the road
and settle down with them. There were openings at the chicken plant,
and Mr. Ottman, who owned the quarry north of town, needed a new
driver. When Royal came home from his trip to Valentine County,
Malke told him what she had in mind.

"Malke, baby!" Royal said. "Did you really say chicken plant? Get
ahold a yourself."

There ensued a round of shouting and threats, little of which
could be deciphered from either side. Little Golden, now four years
old, wakened from his nap with his hair standing on end as if he'd
just witnessed something highly astonishing, watched from the
kitchen doorway.

At some point Royal took his wife by the wrists, said, "Wait a second, wait one goddanged second."

He was a short man with creamy skin and an easy smile, in evidence even at this tense moment. He was the kind of charmer who,
despite his rough clothes and country ways, glittered. He had pretty
violet eyes and wore Brylcreem to the point of overkill.

He put his arm around his wife's waist. "Baby," he cooed huskily,
"can I sing you a song? Will you let me sing you a song?"

She shook her head, tried to twist away, but he held her tight.

Royal would never admit to it, but singing was his one and only true talent. Despite what he told people, he had no special aptitude for finding oil—had no training in geology, no education at all beyond the third grade, no sixth sense for detecting it underground—but his singing, along with his looks and his devil-may-care charm, helped him secure leases, got him free drinks and invitations to dinner, had people asking his advice for things he knew nothing about. He could do basso profundo and coloratura, and falsetto, could, as he put it, "yodel it up pretty good," could imitate him some birdcall. At this moment he figured yodeling or birdcall weren't going to cut it, so he conjured up a little Perry Como. He cleared his throat and, in his best trembling falsetto, crooned "I Dream of You" into his wife's ear.

Within ten seconds he had her dancing. They glided around the room, her head on his shoulder. An hour later they were all having dinner at the highway diner, Royal and Malke stealing kisses and slapping each other playfully, little Golden squinching his toes with delight over the sight of his mother and father together, happy, and in love.

Two days later his father drove off into the fog-blown Louisiana night to chase down a lead on a gas well in the Black Warrior country. He didn't come back for six months.

THE BOY AT THE WINDOW

Golden grew too fast, his pants at perpetual high water, his shoes pinching his toes. He was a boy at odds with his own body: top-heavy, always stumbling, reeling suddenly like someone on the deck of a storm-tossed ship, breaking things, knocking pictures off the walls and whimpering apologies while his mother shrieked her dismay. He was too big for himself, always—too big to cry, too big to spill his milk. At four he looked six; at six, ten. By the time he was eleven he stood at eye level with his mother. At twelve he could, if he had a mind to, scoop her up in his arms and hustle her around the room.

Prisoner to the small apartment and his mother's black moods, Golden would escape to his attic bedroom and sit at the window that looked out over Givens Street and the town square, which was nothing more than a patch of weedy grass with a couple of elms and a bench where old men in hats liked to sit and hawk loogies onto the sidewalk. He was not interested in the old men or the teenagers who crawled into the bank of lilac bushes to put their hands under each other's clothes, he was watching and waiting for one thing only: his daddy's old Ford to turn the corner at LeJeune Hardware and come rattling past the old men on the bench, startling them with its call—*ah-ooga!*—before coming to a stop under the persimmon tree in front of Darkly Dental. Once, back when he was six and still full of hope, his father did drive up one morning, just as Golden had so often imagined it, and he was so shocked that his voice caught in his throat. He tried to shout, *Daddy's here! Daddy's here!* but all he could get out was the sound a choking person makes: *ack.* He rushed into the kitchen, his face flushed crimson, going, *Ack, ack, ack!* and his mother, who thought he was choking, panicked and could think of nothing else to do but slap him smartly across the face. He fell backward against the refrigerator, his face burning, but finally able to say it, in a whispery squeak, "Daddy's home!"

For the first few years in Bernice, Royal would show up at least once every six weeks, his eyes lit with a wicked and charming light, and would sometimes stay for a week or more, working at his desk, making calls, going on errands into Baton Rouge, taking Malke out to dinner and dancing to get back on her good side. But as the years went on, he would be away for two months, three, without so much as a phone call, a postcard, or a telegraph message.

Golden's mother dealt with her husband's absences the only way she knew how: she suffered. To show him. To get back at him. To find a way, somehow, into that heedless heart of his.

Like the kin of the deceased at a third world funeral, she suffered openly, demonstratively, without shame. For Malke, every look and gesture was an expression of her despair. Though beautiful, with a

head of dark, glossy hair and perfectly cut cheekbones, she did everything she could to make herself unattractive; she used no makeup
and kept from her face every expression except fatigue and bitterness.
She wore, in spite of the closet full of fine skirts and blouses, the same
sleeveless housedress that looked like it had been made from a faded
window curtain. Her eyes were remote and hard and she moved with
the slow, underwater movements of the drugged and demented.

She wasn't shy about her misery. She wept without warning
at church meetings, sighed in the aisles of the dry goods store, and
turned away every kind word, every offer of companionship or charity. When she gave testimony at the Holiness Church of God in Jesus'
Name, in the converted boathouse down by the mudflats, she would
often suggest to the congregation that because of the life of sorrow
and loneliness she led, the trials inflicted upon her by her no-account
husband, she had some notion of the agonies Our Christ Lord must
have endured while nailed to the cross.

The day the postcard came was particularly bad. Goldy's mother
spent the entire morning weeping at the kitchen table because old
widowed Dr. Darkly from downstairs had asked her, the third
time that year, for her hand in marriage. He had offered her a life
of comfort and ease, which included his two-story brick home out
next to the lake, his cranberry DeSoto, his membership at the Oyster
Bay Country Club, and the undying love and devotion of his deepest heart. Already starting to cry, she'd told him, *no thanks, Doctor,
maybe another time.* What she didn't have to say was that she was still
in love with the lousy run-around son-of-a-bitch who didn't have the
decency to write or call or send money for groceries.

Goldy, twelve years old now, didn't care about Dr. Darkly or the
groceries or his mother's weeping, the sound of which had become
as common as the starlings that screeched like lunatics in the persimmon tree. He was mad because it was the first day of school and,
once again, he wasn't going. From the window of his attic room he
watched the old yellow bus grind its way around the town square,
full of children looking gleeful and expectant in new clothes and stu-

pid haircuts. He should have been starting sixth grade, but had not
once set foot inside the school, because his mother kept him home
with her. She was a woman who did not like to suffer alone.

To make things worse, it had begun raining outside, great gouts
of water pouring down so suddenly the old bench-sitters in the square
were caught out in the open. They tried to run, which wasn't a good
idea, as the youngest of them was over seventy. Like men caught in
quicksand they clawed the air with their arms, making slow progress.
They bellowed and cussed each other, trying in vain to keep their cigarettes lit. It was good for a laugh, but that had been two hours ago and
the only pleasure now was in imagining how the rain was ruining the
first day of school for all those worthless happy children on the bus.

Then Golden saw the mailman, Mr. Gay. Mr. Gay skipped along
with his canvas mailbag as if it were seventy degrees and sunny.
Somebody yelled out from the shoe store across the street, "Rain, sleet
or snow, Mr. Gay!" and Mr. Gay gave a hearty salute.

Mr. Gay was as happy as his name, and though Golden had spoken to him only a few times, he thought of him as his best friend. Mr.
Gay would make his way around the square, handing out mail to the
shopkeepers and business owners, and when he got to Golden's side
of the street he always looked up where Goldy waited at the window.
If there was no mail that day, which was almost always the case, he
would give a sad little shake of the head, wave, and walk in solemn
commiseration for ten feet or so before resuming his sprightly gait.
Mr. Gay took the lack of mail personally. But if there was mail, he
would point to his bag and make a face like, *Oh yes!*

Today Mr. Gay, wearing a yellow slicker and the kind of hat the
Gorton's fisherman wore on the box of fish sticks, looked up at Goldy
and gave him the *Oh yes!* expression. Had he seen it right through all
the rain? Had Mr. Gay given him the *Oh yes!* face on a day like this?

He bolted from the window, skidded down the attic stairs past his
mother, who had finished her bout of extravagant weeping for the
day and now looked almost corpselike with her gray skin and sunken
sockets, a woman grown ugly with love. She did not even look his

way as he frantically unchained the safety lock on the front door and went slipping down the slick outside stairs to meet Mr. Gay under the awning of Darkly Dental. Above the awning hung a sign that read:

DARKLY DENTAL

SEDATION EXTRACTION

MODERN TECHNOLOGY

IMMEDIATE RELIEF!

RELATIVELY PAINLESS

"You're going to like this one!" Mr. Gay said over the drumming of raindrops on the canvas awning. He handed over the postcard, reached up to pat Golden's stiff blond hair (by now Golden had a good two inches on him), and marched undaunted out into the squall.

Golden looked at the picture of the hound dog wearing a hat, and turned it over to see his father's writing. Though he could read in a rudimentary way—he had taught himself with a stack of grade school primers donated by some old ladies from the church—he could not bear to waste the precious seconds it would take to sound everything out. Racing back up the stairs, holding the postcard under his shirt to keep it dry, he slipped on the wet wood and, unable to extend his arms, fell face-first onto the landing. He got right up, hardly noticing his split upper lip, and burst into the apartment yelling his head off, "Postcard! Picture postcard!"

As Golden's mother read the back of the postcard an amazing transformation took place: color washed back into her face. Her eyes softened and then clarified, the hint of a smile edging the corners of her mouth. Even in her faded housedress, with her puffy eyes and wet nose, her beauty returned in an instant.

Golden watched, mesmerized, waiting for his mother to read the card out loud, but it took her a full minute to notice her sopping, overgrown son who had split his lip wide open and now had blood running down his chin and neck and soaking the front of his shirt. She cried, "Oh God!" and grabbed a dish towel to press against his face. He fought her off, yelling, "No, read it! Read it first!" So she read it out loud, twice, slower and more luxuriously than she meant to, unable to keep herself from smiling just a little, while her boy, who might have bled to death in the time it took her to read those few lines, squinched his toes joyfully inside his wet shoes.

FOR MY WIFE MALKE AND MY SON GOLDY BOY THIS
IS ROYAL HERE I AM CHANGING MY WAYS BELEVE IT
OR NOT I AM NO LONGER SIMILER TO THE ANIMAL ON
THE FRONT OF THE PITCHER CARD IT WILL BE BETTER
I PROMISE I WONT LEAVE YOU NO MORE YOUR TRUE
HUSBEND AND DEDDY ROYAL

That afternoon, after they went downstairs and had Dr. Darkly put a few stitches in Golden's lip free of charge (he'd nearly swooned at seeing Golden's mother looking so flushed and beautiful), after Golden had bathed, dressed in clean jeans and button-up shirt, after his mother had herself changed into a red skirt and white cardigan, they sat down to a meal of warm milk and bread and ate their fill while taking turns reading the postcard and then finally propping it up against the sugar bowl so it was like they were having dinner with a hound dog in a straw hat. Golden couldn't stop looking at his mother, who had become the most beautiful woman in the world, and she couldn't stop picking up the postcard, looking over it again and again, as if there were something she might have missed. The rain never stopped, and finally his mother said, "I'd like to be alone for a while." He climbed the stairs to his attic room, sat in his place at the window overlooking the square, and waited.

GOLDEN'S DADDY

For three years the postcard hung thumbtacked to the wall above the kitchen table, a place of honor normally reserved for a life-sized tablet-shaped cardboard replica of the Ten Commandments with an inset eight-by-ten photo of the Reverend Marvin J. Peete in his *Let's-all-get-ready-to-cast-out-some-demons!* pose. The postcard, a cruel joke, marked the end of Royal as they knew him; it was the last correspondence they had received, the last sign in the world that Golden's daddy had ever existed.

For a long time Golden had been trying to work up the courage to tear it off the wall. For him, it represented everything that was bad in his life: his stretched-to-their-limit secondhand clothes, his smelly attic room, his lack of friends, his extravagantly depressed mother. Every time their power was shut off, every time the Ladies' Aid Society showed up at the door with a box of donated canned goods, singing hymns coming and going so the entire town knew he and his mother were charity cases, he blamed his daddy. He blamed his daddy for their leaky roof, for the hives that attacked his legs and back, for the mice in the walls, for the sleazy men who often showed up at the door asking if his mother wanted to make a little money on the side.

By the time he was a teenager, he had developed an active imagination, which was devoted almost exclusively to arranging satisfying ways for his father to die: choking on peach pits, toppling off balconies, getting zapped by lightning or torn to tatters by wild boars. And it didn't always happen by accident either; sometimes Golden took him out from a distance with a crossbow or pushed him into the path of an oncoming stampede. When people around town tried to comfort his mother by theorizing that Royal had died under mysterious circumstances (instead of running off on her as everybody, including Golden, assumed), it didn't bother Golden a bit; if his daddy was already dead, then it wouldn't hurt him at all if Golden went ahead and ran over him a few times with a loaded cement truck.

The fall Golden turned sixteen he started both football and school. The new high school coach, Coach Valardi, had seen Golden standing in line at the drugstore and wondered why a boy of such glorious heft and dimension was not on the team. For years, the school board had allowed Golden to stay at home with his mother, had advised the sheriff not to enforce the truancy laws because his mother was a difficult woman with a frail constitution and a mortal case of the nerves and it would serve everyone if her son was allowed to stay home and keep her company. Coach Valardi convinced them that the football team, having won only three games in four years, needed Golden more than his mother did.

Accompanied by Principal Wiggins, and by Reverend Peete for moral support, Coach Valardi sat on the front room couch and made his case while Golden listened from the top of the attic steps. The coach spoke about the thrill of competition, the character-building aspect of sports, etc. When he started to run out of ideas the reverend stepped in and recited a few Old Testament verses that didn't have anything to do with anything. Golden's mother, mostly out of a disinclination to let the reverend down, agreed to let her son go.

Outside, at the bottom of the stairs inside the yellow mist of a streetlamp, Principal Wiggins pulled Golden aside for a just-us-men conversation.

"How old you say you are, son?"

"Sixteen."

"Your mama's kept you well fed, we'll give her that much. Sixteen, I'd guess that'd put you in, oh, tenth grade or so. Can you read?"

"Yessir. A little."

"Can you do your sums?"

"I don't know what that means."

"Well, all right, then," Principal Wiggins said, clapping Golden on the back. "The tenth grade it is."

In the classroom, sitting like a teenager stuck in a first-grader's desk, Golden was no success, but he was happy. He could barely follow the lessons, flubbed assignment after assignment, took his lunch by himself in the cafeteria, walked the hallways gawking like a tourist, hiding his overbite with his hand. He had an acne problem and a wispy blond beard that no one had taught him to shave. He offered friendship to everyone who would speak to him, but found no takers. He was slow, good-natured, and, because of his size, a target of jokes and pranks of all sorts: wet willies, a roadkill armadillo in his locker, fake love notes written by the boys in the back row, Vaseline on the toilet seat. Happily, he moved from one humiliation to the next; anything was better than sitting at home with his mother.

Football wasn't nearly so complicated. He ran where he was told to run, knocked down whoever got in his way. Every night he spent an hour puzzling over the playbook before he moved on to his homework. It was easier now to forget about his father; he had other things to think about. He was way behind, with a lot to learn.

On a Friday night in the fall of his senior year, in the third quarter of a blowout loss to the Gledsden Hellions, Golden broke from the huddle and, as he ran to the line of scrimmage, looked across the cinder track to see his father leaning against the chain-link fence. The man was too far away for Golden to make out his features exactly, but he had the dark hair and flashing smile, the easy slouch with one leg crossed over the other, and even wore the kind of western-style shirt his daddy favored.

Golden stood in the middle of the green field, the lights overhead so bright they cast no shadow, and he felt nothing close to anger or hate, but a burst of adrenalized joy, the same feeling he'd had when he was three, sitting at the upstairs window, the first one to spot his father's pickup come rattling around the square.

My daddy, he thought. *My daddy*.

He was about to raise his hand to wave, but Coach Valardi screamed from the sidelines, "Goddamit, Richards, get up to the line!" When Coach raised his voice he sounded like a housewife yelling at her kids from the back porch. "Get your big ass moving! Ahh! They gonna hit us with delay of game!"

Later, Golden would not remember getting into his three-point stance, or what the play was, or if he had executed his blocking assignment correctly. He would only remember coming out of a pile of bodies and seeing the ball come loose, bounce once, and land at his feet. At that moment it seemed that his life, which had felt like a sour disappointment just a few minutes before, was a long gradual wave cresting at this moment, and he scooped up the ball, held it softly to his chest, and ran like he never had before.

He felt a few bodies bounce off him and fall away and then he was charging down the sidelines toward the end zone, with Coach Valardi shrieking into his earhole and one of the opposing players— a skinny cornerback half his size—running alongside, trying to drag him down by the shoulder pads. He grunted, made an unsuccessful swipe at the cornerback with his forearm, and about eight yards from the orange cone someone came in at him low and hard and his left knee buckled sideways with a snapping sound that traveled through his skeleton like an electric current and reverberated inside his skull. The pain was a bucket of scalding water dowsing his body, but he was able to keep his feet the last few yards, his ruined knee grinding with each lumbering stride, until he tilted forward and fell headfirst into the end zone as if diving into a pond, his face mask digging a furrow in the soft turf.

He turned over on his back, groaning, his face covered in sod. If the crowd was cheering, he couldn't hear it. He tried to prop himself on his elbows to look for his father, but his eyes were full of dirt. Now he could hear shouting, could feel his teammates slapping his shoulder pads, trying to pull him up. He pushed them away, shucked off his helmet, lay back down, and smiled.

My daddy.

A MAN IN A MAGAZINE

The man was not his father, of course, but a college scout from Tuscaloosa who had come to check out Junior Franz, the star tailback from the opposing team. It was a disappointment that struck him as low as he'd ever been: Golden's football career was over and, because of a staph infection he contracted after knee surgery, so was his academic career. He spent the rest of the year either bedridden or in the hospital, and never attended another day of school.

For ten months he hardly left the attic, took a regimen of pain-killers provided by Dr. Darkly, longed for the humiliations and minor thrills of the classroom, and did his best to match his mother's depression with his own. Except for Coach Valardi, who came to get his football gear back, Golden received no visits from classmates or teachers, no cards or letters offering good wishes. It was as if he'd never been to Mount Oxnard High at all, never had a life outside the dark, mildewy apartment. His mother fed him, changed his dress-ings, did not argue with him when he told her he planned never to get out of bed again. When she finally had to take the receptionist job Dr. Darkly had been offering her for years, it was a relief to finally be free of her, at least for a portion of each day.

Boredom, finally, forced him out of his bed, and as his knee grew stronger he began to make forays downstairs, mostly hopping on his good leg and using walls and furniture for leverage, but occasionally putting enough weight on the knee to feel a satisfying dose of pain. One morning, using the beechwood cane Dr. Darkly had lent him, he hobbled into his mother's room, a mysterious space that had been off-limits to him for as long as he could remember.

He stood next to her bureau for a moment, taking in the smell of perfume and cigarette smoke and face cream, and then began opening drawers, where he found unexpected things: candy bars hidden under blouses, a small book called *A Man Came Calling*, and some lacy under-wear, tucked in its own little silk bag, with the price tag still attached, waiting, he would realize years later, for a special occasion that never came. He cast around under the bed, sifted through the linen chest, hungry to find something, he didn't know what. In the small closet, he rifled through dresses, examined shoes, found a sewing kit, an old girdle, a set of pink curlers, a tin of peppermints. Though he could see nothing on the single high shelf, he groped around, standing on tiptoes, until his hand rested on a wooden cigar box. He knew imme-diately that this was what he had come here to find.

Inside the box were letters, five of them, all from his father. Three of the envelopes were addressed to *Malke and Golden Richards*, but the one on top was addressed to *Master Golden Richards* in his father's careless third-grader script.

GOLDEN BOY YOUR MOTHER IS ANGRY AT ME WICH
SHE HAS EVERY RITE SHE TOLD ME NOT TO RITE
OR CALL AGIN BUT I WILL TRY ONE LAST TIME HERE
IS A PLANE TICKIT COME OUT TO UTAH AND I WILL
BUY YOU A MOTOR BIKE OR A ARABIYEN HORSE
THATS IT ROYAL

"What?" Golden said, just to hear his own voice. "What is this?"

He shuffled through the other letters. All of them had money—one a check for a thousand dollars—these much longer than the one addressed only to him, pages of rambling prose without paragraphs or commas, and one of them was folded up with the glossy pages of a cut-out magazine article titled "Striking It Rich!" On the first page was a photograph of a vast desert panorama, and underneath the caption, *Through This Forsaken Land of Towering Buttes and Treacherous Canyons Royal Richards Made His Perilous Way to a Fabulous Discovery!* On the third page was a photo of his daddy, standing atop a boulder in a cowboy hat, holding a rifle in one hand and a bubbling bottle of champagne in the other. The caption read, *He Fought Storms, Rattlers, Poison Water, and Death Itself to Find His Uranium Bonanza!*

In three breathless pages the article detailed how Royal, destitute after losing his shirt on an oil-well venture in Alabama, headed west, taking any job he could find to survive: street sweep and bricklayer, stableman and extra on the set of the feature film *The Conqueror*, where he had a "notable confrontation with screen idol John Wayne." It wasn't too long before he, like thousands of hopeful Americans, caught Uranium Fever and headed into the Utah desert with a Geiger counter and a dream. Three years he hiked the arroyos and slot canyons of the Colorado Plateau, finding nothing but scorpions, thirst, sunstroke and failure. He was cursed with mishaps. He lost his truck to quicksand, faced flash floods, blistering heat and perilous electrical storms, was bit by a rattler and lay for three days in the shade of a mesquite bush, hoping to die. Still he did not give up. He spent his remaining money on a scintillometer, a fifteen-pound gadget that registered radiation to a greater depth than a Geiger counter, and struck out on foot into the most treacherous reaches of the Dirty Devil country, ready to strike it rich or die trying.

The article spared no detail on how many ways Royal came close to death: he ran out of food, then water, and came down with arsenic poisoning from drinking river water polluted by a dead sheep. His feet swelled until his boots bit into his flesh, so he spent days wandering deliriously through the desert, barefoot and sun-scorched, with every step losing the will to go on. One morning he woke up and found that the needle on his scintillometer, an obscenely heavy machine he'd been carrying around in his delirium like a ball and chain, was stuck at high register. He adjusted the dial but the needle wouldn't return to normal. For an instant his head cleared and he looked down at the conglomerate rock beneath his hideously swollen feet. It was ash-gray, instead of the more common rust-red, and riddled with canary-yellow cartonite. The ground he was standing on, the entire ridge as far as he could see, was high-grade uranium ore.

The will to live, which had earlier deserted him, returned in short order. He was without food or reliable water, his boots were useless, and he would never make it back to civilization on foot. So, after piling a series of rock cairns to stake his mining claim, he built a makeshift raft out of driftwood lashed together with his bootlaces, belt, and scintillometer strap and pushed out into the churning Dirty Devil River. He clung to the makeshift contraption for twelve harrowing miles, grinding against canyon walls, bouncing off boulders, swamping in the rapids, foundering in the pools and shallows, until a rancher found him washed up on a sandbar.

The last page detailed the finale of this great adventure: after six months of attempting to excavate the mine himself, Royal Richards

said what the heck and sold out for two million dollars to the Vana-
dium Corporation. On the opposite page was a picture of Golden's
daddy, looking handsome in a tuxedo, holding up a bubbling bottle of
champagne and brandishing a cigar. Underneath it read:

ROYAL RICHARDS, TOGGED OUT IN DINNER JACKET,
CELEBRATES HIS ASTOUNDING
TURN OF FORTUNE!

Golden stood in the dim closet, dust motes swirling in his vision,
unable to do anything but stare at the image of his father, who looked,
amazingly, exactly like the man who had left eight years before and
never returned. He put the glossy paper to his nose, hoping he might
smell his father's cologne.

Golden thought he heard a noise outside, maybe his mother coming up the outside stairs. He stuffed everything back into the cigar
box and hobbled out into the living room, his breath suddenly coming
out of him in gasps. He waited, but heard nothing else. He thought
about stepping into the closet to have another look, to read all of the
letters, to stare at the pictures again, but he was afraid if he went back
into that closet he would take the wooden cigar box down from the
high shelf and find it empty.

He went up to his room, took his place at the window. It's what he
always did when he didn't know what else to do. For so long he had
hated everything he could see from that window, the pathetic little
square with its scrubby oak bushes and defunct fountain, surrounded
by faded storefronts and cobbled streets crumbling at the edges and
cratered with potholes, but now it all seemed alien, strangely beautiful: the fountain and its tattered coat of moss, the broken beer bottles
glinting like treasure in the crabgrass, the old peckerwoods snoozing
in the heat with their bright straw hats and multicolored suspenders,
the leaves of the persimmon tree ticking in the breeze.

The idea rang in his head like a bell: his daddy was alive. His daddy was not only alive, but a hero, a millionaire, a man in a magazine. Everything, suddenly, seemed possible. He rested his chin on the windowsill. *I'm going to leave this place*, he thought, understanding for the first time why it all seemed so suddenly beautiful, *and I'm never coming back*.

3.
· · · · ·

AN AMBUSH

WHEN SHE STEPPED INTO THE VIRGIN COUNTY ACADEMY OF HAIR DESIGN, the first thing she noticed was that the women inside—all five of them—wore western-style handkerchiefs around their faces like bandits. The second thing was the scorched-hair smell of a recently administered permanent, which explained the handkerchiefs. Nola, the establishment's owner and sole licensed stylist, provided hankies spritzed with dime-store perfume to her customers when one of them received a perm.

"Anything," she always said, "to keep my girls happy."

Trish let the heavy glass door rattle shut behind her, and Nola, who was giving an unidentifiable middle-aged bandit a trim, pointed her scissors at Trish and said, "Stick 'em up, chicky! Your money or your life!"

Trish tried to laugh with the other ladies but fumes caught in her throat and she gagged.

"Oh come on," said a flap-eared crone baking under one of the hair dryers, "somebody get her a hankie before she kilts over on us."

Rose-of-Sharon, who was behind the counter studying needle-point samplers, padded across the tiled floor to a drawer on the other side of the room, pulled out a blue cotton handkerchief, spritzed it with a faux-crystal decanter of Night Passion—a perfume that smelled to Trish like something they might use in a funeral home to improve the odor of a corpse—and carefully, almost tenderly, tied it around Trish's nose and mouth.

It was only the second time she'd been in here during the past year and it looked like nothing had changed, not even the identical pair of old ladies with identical perms flipping through old seed catalogs. There were still the ancient Christmas cards and wedding announcements taped to the cracked mirror, the three naugahyde barber chairs in a row next to the black bakelite shampoo sink, the series of white styrofoam heads on a shelf, some of which sported wigs, some of which had gone bald, one of which gazed mysteriously down upon the room through a pair of false eyelashes.

Nola had been running this place for years, even before she became Golden's second wife. She had taken a keen interest in hair at age fifteen when she permanently lost all of her own. Her father, a man who managed to support three wives and eighteen children on a bricklayer's pay, couldn't afford the extravagance of a wig, so Nola had saved up her egg money and bought a book called *The Wig-maker's Art*. With hair donated by her sisters, she practiced making her own extensions, weaves and full-wefted caps, all of which she sold as fast as she could make them. She learned a dozen different styles, even tried her hand at toupees and hairpieces, which turned old bald cowboys into screen idols overnight. The more wigs she made, the more hair she required, and so she began making house calls, offering a cut-and-style free of charge. Plural wives who had not cut their hair in their entire lives were suddenly jumping at the chance to be shorn at the skilled hands of Nola Harrison. Because Nola was engaged in a good cause—there was a significant number of women who had lost their hair to cancer or radiation poisoning or simple old age and needed a good wig—the priesthood council could make only feeble protests. *As long as the hairstyles stay modest, none of them Marilyn Monroe haircuts or dye jobs, and the women don't get into shenanigans like getting their nails painted, then I guess we can go along with it.* Within a year Nola saved enough money to lease the old Anderson Building, which at one time had been the Tender Brothers Drugstore and Café. She dreamed of teaching other women from the valley to cut hair and make wigs, but it turned out she was the only hairstylist and wig-maker this part of the valley needed. Though the academy had never produced a single graduate, it provided, on Tuesdays and Thursdays and an occasional Saturday afternoon, a place where the town women could get a perm, where the plural wives could get a trim or shampoo, where any woman at wits' end could go to get a break from the incessant demands of children and men.

"Oh, we're a bunch of desperadoes, all right," Nola said now, her eyes as bright as brass tacks above her red bandana, her scissors going *snick snick snick*, the hammock of fat under her arm quivering. "But we do like to smell pretty."

Trish sat in one of the folding chairs along the wall to wait her turn. Next to her, a pile of old magazines a foot high threatened to slide to the floor. She flipped through a finger-worn copy of *Life* and wondered if a poisonous cloud of hair chemicals might be preferable to a handkerchief soaked with cathouse perfume. She'd come in wanting only a shampoo and trim for her big night tonight, maybe catch up on a little gossip, but now she felt on the verge of vomiting or passing out or both.

Doing her best to breathe through her mouth, she shuffled through several more magazines until she came upon something unexpected: a *Cosmopolitan* whose cover featured a heavily made-up woman in ultra-tight tennis shorts and halter top standing in the face of a stiff breeze. Next to her head of feathered, windblown hair was the headline:

OBSESSED WITH YOUR BREASTS?
HOW TO DEAL WITH THOSE FEELINGS

And below that:

THE CRUEL LOVER: WHY ARE YOU
DRAWN TO HIM? HOW TO FREE YOURSELF
FROM HIS DEVASTATING ATTRACTION

She wondered how long it had been since she'd seen a magazine like this, and how could such a thing have managed to end up in Nola's reading pile? Flushed with adolescent guilt, she turned the pages filled with underwear advertisements: women in bra and panties having lunch, wearing fur coats, conducting board meetings, gazing thoughtfully out of windows. There was an article called "Alternatives to Bikini Waxing" and a column about the misunderstood affliction known as nymphomania.

Along with the illicit thrill of reading about the newest Cleavage Enhancement Brassiere and the woman from Ohio who claimed to have sex thirty to forty times a week, she felt an unexpected longing for the life she had left behind, the life in which reading a magazine like this wouldn't have caused her a moment of shame, a life where Cleavage Enhancements and bikini waxes were an option if not a necessity, a life she thought she had given up on forever.

She paused at one of the feature articles titled "Advanced Lovemaking Techniques For the Rest of Us." Wearing the casual expression of somebody checking out the newest advances in Tupperware technology in *Family Circle*, she read:

A BIRD IN THE HAND

Pleasuring your man manually—whether it's a prelude to full-fledged sex or an erotic act in itself—is an incredibly sexy sack skill that's sadly overlooked

She felt a touch on her shoulder and nearly leapt sideways off her chair. Rose-of-Sharon was already backing up, saying, "Oh dear, I didn't mean, I just wanted to—" She squeezed her hands against her breastbone, her shoulders braced in an apologetic hunch. She was a woman, Trish thought, who might have been pretty if she didn't look scared to death fifty minutes out of every hour. Trish stood, slipped the *Cosmo* under an old *National Geographic*, and took Rose-of-Sharon by the wrists to calm her. When Trish first met her, Rose seemed shy, unsure of herself in a charming country-girl sort of way, but over the past year her nervousness had come to seem almost pathological—she avoided eye contact, had difficulty finishing a sentence, went skittish around anyone but her sister and her children, framed every conversation in terms of apology and regret. A few years before Trish joined the family, Rose had spent six weeks in a hospital after a nervous breakdown, and while no one spoke about it openly, there was a worry among Golden and the other wives that she might be headed down that path again. Even as Rose grew pale and unsure and small, her sister widened at the waist, added new hips and busts and stomachs, became even more bombastic and full of color, telling jokes, teasing anyone who happened into her sights, yelping with please-don't-kill-me laughter.

"I was wondering if you wanted a shampoo," Rose-of-Sharon said in her choked little powder-soft voice. "I can do it, if you want. But if you want Nola to do it . . ."

"Oh no!" Trish said. "Of course. A shampoo. Thank you. That would be lovely." She practically had to drag Rose-of-Sharon over to the shampoo sink, where she sat back in a swivel chair and placed her neck in the sunken lip, thinking, for some reason, of some famous person she'd read about—was it Sir Thomas More or maybe Louis XVI?—who had asked to be positioned in the guillotine with his face toward heaven so he could meet his doom head-on.

While Rose-of-Sharon wetted down her hair, Trish kept up a stream of questions to keep her sister-wife comfortable. *How were the kids? Who was looking after the younger ones while she was here at the academy? Had Sybil gotten over her flu?* But once Rose-of-Sharon began to massage the shampoo into Trish's hair, the questions dropped off and Rose's answers—if there were any—lost themselves to the gurgling of the spigot, the pleasure of the warm water, the peppermint scent of the shampoo, the soft and steady pressure of Rose's massaging fingertips. For a moment she felt luxuriously alone in her pleasure, the crackling of shampoo suds in her ears blocking out every other sound, her eyes closed to the unforgiving brilliance of midday light slanting in from the window, and the phrase *advanced lovemaking* slipped into her mind, and *full-fledged sex*, and she began to feel oddly relaxed and aroused, a tingling at her chest and inside her thighs, and then she heard a faraway voice:

". . . going to Cedar City tonight?"

"What?" Trish sat up a little, the tingling blood in her chest moving quickly up her neck and into her cheeks.

"Oh. No. I was just—I was just wondering if you knew about my Pauline's recital? In Cedar City? Tonight?"

Blinking, Trish craned her neck to look Rose in the eye. A second ago she had barely been able to formulate one-word answers to Trish's questions, and now she was engaging in what sounded suspiciously like idle chatter. "Yes," she said, settling back in. "Beverly mentioned it." She closed her eyes, hoping that would end the conversation once and for all.

Rose-of-Sharon's hands were still in her hair, but instead of moving across her scalp with a soft kneading motion as before, they had begun to tremble. Trish opened her eyes again and caught Nola and Rose exchanging a look—Nola's encouraging and Rose's full of doubt—and she realized with a start what was going on. This was not an innocent shampoo-and-rinse, a nice moment between sister-wives. Rose-of-Sharon, her shy, sweet sister-wife, had maneuvered her into this compromising position to ask Trish to give up her night with Golden—her first night with him in over two weeks—so he could accompany Rose-of-Sharon to her daughter's recital in Cedar City, so they could stay together in a hotel and sleep in a hotel bed with everything that implied, and eat at a restaurant and have a fine old time while Trish sat at home, alone, throttled with jealousy and loneliness.

This, to put it impolitely, was an ambush.

Not that long ago Trish wouldn't have minded so much. It was normal for the wives to barter and trade their time with their husband, and Trish, a fourth wife with nothing but her goodwill to offer, was always ready to give in, to make allowances. Generosity. Selflessness. Lovingkindness. These were, as the women so often reminded each other, a large part of what living the Principle was about. But not tonight. She hadn't been alone with Golden in two weeks, had hardly seen him at all during that time, and though she didn't like to admit it, she missed him so greedily, was so hungry for him that she wanted nothing more than to attach herself to him like a feral cat.

She had begun at five this morning with a preliminary shower, plucking the two rogue hairs from her chin, taking a pumice stone to her elbows and feet, and finishing up with a regimen of lotions and leave-in conditioner that made her feel like she'd been dipped in lard. Then she moved on to the house: scrubbed the walls and floors spotless, washed and hung out the sheets, vacuumed and dusted. When she couldn't stand to be inside a second longer she had come to town for groceries and a hairdo, all for *him*, for her rumpled Golden, as if he were some kind of visiting dignitary instead of a graying construction contractor with a limp who had three pairs of shoes to his name and demonstrated a persistent inability to keep track of his own wallet.

It amazed her still how quickly, how easily, she had fallen for this man. She had arrived in Virgin a damaged, frightened girl, and though she came with firsthand knowledge of the complications and drawbacks of plural marriage, something in Golden's shy, deferential manner had disarmed her. He represented everything she needed: acceptance, forgiveness, a safe place to land. She loved the soft touch of his large hands, his bright, prominent teeth, the way he paused meaningfully before he spoke, as if each thought were as important as the next. And it didn't hurt that when they first kissed, on a warm fall night in the front seat of the hearse, the moon rising hoary and gold over the far peaks, she felt a sharp little tug in her soul.

Before Trish married into the family, Golden's rotation schedule was simple: three nights a week at Old House, four nights at Big House. But things got complicated when Trish moved into her own place—a two-bedroom duplex at the northern edge of the valley—and suddenly there didn't seem to be enough days in the week to accommodate everyone. They managed with the help of a calendar, a chalkboard overlaid with a grid, and a calculator (which they used to figure out the ratio of Golden's time with each wife in direct relation to the number of children that belonged to her), until these last couple of years Golden began working at distant job sites, spending

four or five nights a week away from home, and his schedule became
so unpredictable a grand council of the world's greatest logistical
minds couldn't have come up with a schedule that made any sense
or satisfied everyone. Every Sunday they met for what had come to
be known as the Summit of the Wives, in which each wife made her
case for the week, claiming Golden for an anniversary or a birthday, a
teacher's meeting or 4-H show.

Of Golden, big as he was (and whose presence at these meetings was considered more or less irrelevant), there was simply never
enough to go around.

Often at these meetings Nola and Beverly, whose relationship
had developed into one long rivalrous dance, would lock horns over
who had been shortchanged the week before, which wife deserved an
extra night that week, which child had been deprived of her father's
presence at something so emotionally formative as the county spell-
ing bee. Trish and Rose-of-Sharon made it a habit to stay out of the
way, occasionally making a point or taking sides in a way that favored
their own particular agenda, taking whatever leftovers they could get.
Never once had they had a run-in until, it seemed very likely, right
now.

Rose-of-Sharon had begun to talk in a way Trish had never heard
before, a kind of breathy, headlong chatter, about Pauline's recent
ascension to first chair in the high school band, and her advances in
the French horn, *which is the most difficult of all the brass instruments
by the way I don't know if you knew that or not and because of its mellow
sound was often included with the woodwinds and anyway Pauline is so
excited about going to Cedar City for regionals that she hasn't slept in two
nights! and oh she's been practicing like MAD for a month and it's going
to be quite a treat to stay in a motel and see the sights without the rest of
the children tagging along . . .*

As she spoke, her trembling hands had begun to grip Trish's head,
her fingertips slowly increasing the pressure until it felt like a bird of
prey had sunk its talons into her skull and was attempting to lift her
bodily out of the chair.

"It's a big deal for her, a very important event," Rose said, her voice thin and distressed.

"Yes—oh, ow—I can imagine," Trish said.

"She'd really like it—it'd really be nice, you know . . ."

Here it comes, Trish thought, hoping it would come very soon, before Rose-of-Sharon's fingernails pierced her scalp.

". . . if she had her *family* there, besides just me . . ."

Come on, Trish thought, *get to it*, please.

"If maybe. If her . . ."—she seemed to hold her breath for a moment and then let it out in a rush of words—*"father*-could-be-there-oh-it'd-be-something-she'd-never-forget."

Trish grabbed Rose's hands, now locked into paralysis, and with some effort pried them from her head. She sat up and tried to look her in the eye, but Rose stared resolutely at the swirl of water disappearing down the sink's drain.

"He hasn't been over in two weeks," Trish whispered, even though now that the dryer had rattled into silence her words carried easily into every part of the room. "I've seen him twice in the past month. If I don't see him tonight, who knows how long it will be, you understand? Rose? I'm beginning to think he won't even recognize me anymore."

She laughed—a pathetic attempt to lighten the mood—but Rose only nodded. Unable to speak or make a gesture of condolence or regret, Trish sat in the sunken chair, a black-hearted villain in her bank-robber's mask, her shameful features hidden from view. Nola, whose scissors had been poised above her customer's springy hair during the entire exchange, sighed and resumed her *snick snick snick*. Rose eased her hands from Trish's grip and gently dried her hair with a towel.

She did not wait for Rose to comb out her tangled hair, did not wait for her turn in Nola's chair. A bitterness had risen in her throat, sudden and hot—that she should have to feel *guilty* for wanting to be a participant in her own life, that she should be *ashamed* of wanting to spend a few hours with her own husband!—and she knew she should leave immediately. She made an excuse about a forgotten appointment at the clinic and on her way out made sure to slip the *Cosmo* from underneath the teetering magazine pile and tuck it under her arm as if it belonged to her. She stepped out into the bright day, the sidewalk scorching white beneath her feet, the sky a pale panel of blue over her head, and walked slowly at first, her hair wet and wild, her face still covered with the handkerchief, and then began to run, making a break for it like the outlaw she was.

4.
·····

THE A-HOLES OF OLD HOUSE

THEY CAUGHT HIM IN THE UNDERWEAR. HE HAD JUST SLIPPED HIS foot into a pair of nylon tights when that little bubble-eyed freak Louise peeked in the room and ran down the stairs screaming her head off, "Rusty! Oh no! Rusty! He's in the underwear! Rusty's in the underwear!" Like she was Paul Revere telling everybody the Russians were coming.

He happened to be wearing some panties over his jeans too, he wanted to see how they looked, kind of like an experiment. They were made of a smooth blue satiny material with a tiny bow on the band and were so small he had a terrible time getting them off. He yanked and pulled and had them down to his ankles when Aunt Beverly walked in and scared him so bad he tipped backward and cracked his head on the edge of the dresser.

Even though his head hitting the dresser had made a noise, and he was now in a lot of pain, Aunt Beverly didn't say, *Are you okay, Rusty, hmm, you want an ice pack or something on that?* She just watched him squirm around on the floor trying to stretch the panties around his feet. Rusty thought, *Aunt Beverly, you old witchy woman*, which made him feel a little less like he might crap his pants in fear.

Someday, when he had discovered his own mysterious personal superpower, which would most likely be chemically radioactive laser beams that shot out of his eyes, he would do battle with Aunt Beverly and blast that witchy stare right off her fat face until her hair caught fire and she had to jump through a window and into the cow trough outside to put out the flames. And all the brothers and sisters would run screaming before him and his deadly laser beams, and he would blast one or two of them in the back before he said, *Come on back, guys, I'm just kidding, ha ha, I won't harm the rest of you as long as Aunt Beverly apologizes for all her wrong actions and crimes against humanity*, and Aunt Beverly would come up to him all wet from the cow trough and her bald head still smoking and say, *I'm sorry, Rusty, please forgive us all, won't you, we will do whatever you say as long as you'll allow us to keep our precious lives.*

Now there was a bunch more girls gathered in the doorway laughing, oh, so insanely happy about what was going on here, it looked like their big white teeth were going to pop out of their mouths. Rusty laughed too, just to show them he understood how funny this underwear situation was, but instead of laughing he snorked, which made them laugh harder, which made his face get hot and itchy. Aunt Beverly trained her witchy-woman stare on them for a second and they ran away howling and giggling, *Hee hee, oh my gosh! Stop it! Shhhhh!* and in about thirty seconds everybody in the family, including the neighbors and other innocent bystanders, would be up to date on the underwear thing. What a gyp.

Aunt Beverly stood right over him and asked what he thought he was doing, creeping around in the Big Girls' room like some kind of pervert, trying on their underwear.

Rusty held his breath and had to concentrate extremely hard not to let her make him cry. When he had to breathe again he tried not to snork, which was what came out anyway.

"This is funny?" she said. "You think any of this is amusing?"

No, Rusty didn't think any of it was funny, especially not the snork. He mumbled that he had been looking for his tube socks in the Big Girls' drawer because they sometimes took his socks just to make him mad.

"Honestly. You want to blame this little abomination of yours on the girls now? You sneaking through their drawers and putting on their intimate items is their fault, is that what you're saying?"

He looked down at his shirt, which was too small with a tear-hole and grease spots on it, not that anybody cared. And come to think of it, weren't his own underwear gross and ratty too? Gray and full of holes and so stretched out the Jolly Green Giant could wear them under his little skirt thing no problem? Of course the girls' underwear was clean and fresh and extremely elastic. If he had good underwear, the nice tight kind that looked sharp and made you feel good about yourself, then maybe he wouldn't have to go trying on other people's intimate items, would he?

Aunt Beverly told him he was to go to his room, where he would stay for the rest of the day, until she and the other mothers decided on an appropriate punishment.

Appropriate. This was Aunt Beverly's favorite word, her power word, the word that granted her her awful destructive might, which she would surely lose forever if she didn't say it at least fifteen times a day.

That sort of talk isn't appropriate. Let's find a more appropriate activity, children. We'll discuss this at an appropriate time. Your shoes, Rusty, do not smell very appropriate.

How about, Rusty thought, *you kiss my appropriate behind?*

"What?" said Aunt Beverly. "What did you say?"

What? He hadn't said anything! Had he? He turned his head away so she could not look into his eyes. The possibility that Aunt Beverly might be able to see deep into his inner brain with her witchy-woman stare did not surprise him at all.

"Not only will you stay in your room for the rest of the day," Aunt Beverly said, "but you will go without dinner tonight. And no dessert for the rest of the week. One more word from you and you will be grounded for the rest of the month. I will not allow this kind of perversion in my house."

At this, Rusty just stood there like a big buttfudge bawling his fat brains out. He thought about his own sorry stretched-out underwear, which made him cry harder, and how everybody would know that he was trying on girl's panties in the middle of the day, and the worst, no dessert for a week. *What a big dang gyp!* He cried so hard he began to cough, and slobber came out of his mouth, which often happened because he had some kind of condition that made him have too much spit in his mouth. But Aunt Beverly did not hug him, or say, *now-now*, or make him a glass of chocolate milk on ice like his own mother would've, she just gave him one last stare and went out the door.

Well, crying like that made him feel a little better, and staying in his room wouldn't be so bad—at least he wouldn't have to do chores. Out in the hall, Parley was waiting for him. Parley was two years older and could run faster and throw farther and make musical armpit farts everyone thought were hilarious. Rusty tried to walk by, but Parley stood in his way with his arm against Rusty's chest, and whispered, *Fag.* Rusty pushed past him, but Parley stayed right with him, doing the musical armpits and singing, *A-Faggety-Fag-Fag-Fee, A-Faggety-Fag-Fag-Foo.*

One of the sorriest things about Old House was that it was really *old*, with squeaking floors and clanking radiators, but the worst part of it was you had to march up about six hundred stairs to get to the Tower, which was where they made Rusty stay, most likely because they wanted him to reduce in size his sizable love handles. So he climbed, huffing and stopping once in a while to let some spit dribble out of his mouth, while Parley was with him step for step calling him the world's most out-of-shape homo.

Rusty spent the next two hours in the Tower bedroom, which was not his bedroom at all, but a room that belonged to Parley and Nephi, who promised to murder him in his sleep if he kept up his snoring, which was why he now slept with a hammer under his pillow. They had sturdy beds with nice fluffy pillows, while he slept on a foam rubber pad on the floor.

For the thousandth time, Rusty read the sign hanging above the dresser. A few months ago Aunt Beverly made a bunch of them and hung them up in everybody's bedroom, even put one in the bathroom. In her flowery, old-style writing it said:

Christ Is the Head of This House
The Unseen Guest
at Every Meal
The Silent Listener
to Every Conversation

See if that doesn't creep you right out.

No, this was not his bedroom, or his house, and Aunt Beverly, no matter what anybody said, was not his mother. His mother was back at Big House, where he belonged with his *real* brothers and sisters, who were all, honestly, a bunch of a-holes too. He had to live in Old House with Aunt Beverly's family because somebody had the big idea to do an interfamily exchange program, where children from the different mothers went to live at the other houses, so they could all love each other and understand each other, and have no divisions or strife among them, which was all a big fat gyp.

People said the exchange program was his father's idea, but Rusty and everybody else knew that all of his father's big ideas were really Aunt Beverly's, and that Aunt Beverly got this idea from the Jensens, a family in the church who were always trying to be cooler than everyone else, with their brand-name clothes and Six Flags vacations. Last year the Jensens signed up for the Foreign Exchange Program and got two Japanese kids: a sister and a brother. You should have seen them dumb Japanese kids! One minute they're back in their little paper house in Japan eating Chinese food with chopsticks, and the next thing they know they're in the Jensen compound with eighteen new brothers and sisters and four mothers and having to stand in line for a bowl of cornflakes! They were only there for a couple of weeks before somebody alerted the authorities, who took them to a regular American family in Colorado where they didn't have to wait half an hour for a chance at the toilet.

So now that Parley was gone, Rusty sat on one of the beds that wasn't his and looked out the window. It was a bright day, the sky blue and without a cloud, but cold enough that there wasn't a lot going on in the side yard or the pastures beyond. He watched a couple of Brother Spooner's cows trying to hump each other, which was fun for a while until he realized that they were doing it only because they were as bored as he was. He watched Raymond the Ostrich strut around in the smaller pasture next to the Spooner home. People said Brother Spooner used to have dozens of ostriches at one time, he was planning to make millions of dollars selling them for ostrich hamburgers, turning what was left over into cowboy boots and those feathery scarf things dancing ladies wear, but it turned out there weren't a whole lot of people interested in eating something that looked like a giant mutant turkey. So Brother Spooner had gotten rid of all his ostriches, except Raymond, who had once attacked a kid from town who was trying to siphon gas from the Spooners' tractor, and because Raymond had run the kid down and kicked the living dookie out of him and defended the Spooner way of life, he was now considered part of the family.

After the cows stopped humping and Raymond disappeared behind the feed bin and Rusty could not look out the window a minute longer, he crossed the room and regarded himself in the mirror on the closet door. His face was still red from crying, and blubber showed through the gaps in his shirt. He was sort of fat all right, and the owner of a shirt so raggedy and stained it looked like he had stolen it off a dead hobo, but he was no fag.

"Fag, you say?" he asked in his Scoundrel accent, which always made him feel better, doing the squinty-eyed thing while taking a drag from an imaginary pipe. "Get a hold of yourself, man, you may be many things to many people, but a *fag*? My dear man, I dare say *not*."

5.

OLD HOUSE

*L*ook closely and you'll see: in this house there is trouble. There has been trouble here for a good many years, though you'd hardly know it by appearances. The children, rambunctious as always, scamper and gossip and play, the mothers busy themselves making dinner, and the father— where is he, anyway?—labors somewhere in the outer precincts of the backyard.

No, nothing obviously the matter. If you didn't know any better you might think: domestic sweetness, familial bliss. But look a little closer, get right up close, and you can't miss the off-kilter rituals, the sorrows nursed in isolation, the back-door transactions, the mini-dramas of dread and anxiety and longing. At this very second, for example, you'll find Daughters #2 and #3 in an upstairs bedroom, hatching a plot of revenge on Daughter #5 for being a kiss-up and a tattletale and exposing their respective crushes on two of the best-looking boys in the valley, while Daughter #5 herself is curled up in her hiding place under the stairs, trying to stanch the most recent of her spontaneous nosebleeds, which she believes to be divine punishment for impure thoughts and questionable intentions, and because of which she has become a tattletale and Miss Goody Two Shoes in hopes of getting on God's good side. In the woodshed you'll find Son #4 weeping bitterly and eating his own earwax. In the front room is Daughter #10, right out there in the open, sitting alone on the lavender Queen Anne divan, talking openly, idly to her dead brother, Son X, while two of her living brothers, Sons #11 and #6, aim their homemade rubber-

band guns at the back of her head and count: one, two, three. And maybe, if you're paying attention, you'll notice Mother #2 slipping into the hall bathroom the second it comes open to give her wig a quick adjustment and stuff her latest and rather unpredictable roll of stomach fat under the band of her pantyhose—she wants to look good for her man tonight!— and coming back into the kitchen, letting out that braying laugh with which she tries to hide large and complicated feelings.

The house, a gothic Victorian with a jagged roofline and a three-story tower fashioned from blond sandstone, makes proud display of its odd-shaped rooms and narrow hallways and tilting staircases—an architecture that, despite Mother #1's every attempt to suppress such things, encourages factionalization and secrecy and disorder. Away from the warm bright center of the house where the mothers try to outdo each other in the kitchen, there is a shadow world of disputed territories and black-market economies, a shifting and complex geography of meeting places and neutral zones and sour little crevices and dusty pockets where children go to steal a few desperate moments of solitude.

Mother #1 has done everything she can to battle such chaos, to sniff out any hint of sloth or insurrection. Not that anyone cares or notices. Not that anyone expresses any gratitude at all for the way she endeavors daily to improve these children's souls, to clean up their diction and straighten out their morals and impart to them an appreciation of their divine legacies, their celestial bloodlines. Not that anyone, including the adults who sometimes share the house, pays any attention to the dozens of placards she has made using her self-taught calligraphy skills, placards that feature suggestions, warnings, reminders, and admonishments placed in strategic locations around the house:

On the front door: Please Remove Shoes
Below the doorbell: Ringing Twice May Be Necessary
In the foyer: Please Place Shoes in Shoe Box—Neatly and Quietly
Above the foyer light switch: Turn Off Light When Not in Use

And so on as you make your way through the house. The upstairs bathroom, known as the Black Hole of Calcutta, requires eight placards all by itself:

On the door: Please Keep Locked When Occupied

And under that one, another: Please Respect the Privacy of Others

Under the toothbrush rack (which features nine toothbrushes lined in a neat row, each plastic handle bearing its owner's name in the same Edwardian script): Remember: Use Only Your Toothbrush and Your Toothbrush Only

Next to the toilet paper holder: No More than Four Squares Per Use, No Fewer Than One

On the wall next to the tub, under a plastic blue egg timer on its own ceramic shelf: Showers Two Minutes Maximum

Above the toilet: Lid Down When Not in Use

And below that: Boys, Lift Seat When Making Water

And below that: Boys, AIM!!! Please and Thank You

At the top of the stairs on the wall of the landing there is a large black-and-white portrait of Brigham Young, his meaty face pressed into a frown of dire warning, as if to say: Don't even think about it.

You cannot take five steps in this house without being reprimanded or corrected or warned, without being reminded that rules and laws are what separate us from the worst aspects of ourselves and are all we have to keep sin and ugliness and anarchy at bay—and that is exactly how Mother #1 would have it. No one in this house has any idea, but Mother #1 is well and personally acquainted with sin and ugliness and anarchy, and she has come to know that rules and commandments and laws, if you hold to them fast and believe in them with your whole heart, can save your life and maybe even your soul.

Likewise, no one in this house would have any idea that Mother #3 has her own inner life, small though it may be. Mother #3, more than anyone in the family, is easy to miss. She speaks, if she speaks, second or third or fourth. You can walk right past her, as her own children often do, without seeing or noticing a thing. One of the children, Daughter #11, has started a rumor that has been picking up steam among the under-seven segment of the domestic population, that Mother #3 is disappearing, fading in and out, flickering into nothing at inopportune and often comical moments, like a ghost in a black-and-white cartoon. For so long she has asked for nothing, required nothing, taken nothing, only given. It is the story of so many mothers in this small valley and, for that matter, in the larger world that she has heard so much about. It's very simple: she has given too much, and now there is very little left of Mother #3.

From the kitchen she calls for someone to bring up some potatoes from the cellar but, as usual, no one pays her any mind. So she goes down herself, and comes upon the Three Stooges in their customary spot next to the old industrial boiler, practicing some native sport that seems to involve kicking each other repeatedly in the behind. Boys, she says, gathering the potatoes from the bin, boys, boys. But they go on as if she weren't there, kicking, guffawing, groaning in mock or possibly real pain. The Three Stooges love each other dearly—anyone can see that—and they demonstrate it by slapping, tripping, and choking each other silly. They are inseparable, these three, except when they are separated, which is most of the time, when Stooges #1 and #3 go home to Big House, and leave Stooge #2 behind to pine after them, jealous of the life they share without him. Stooge #2 is a born worrier, and his worries tend to center on an uncertain future in which he and the other two stooges will be separated for good. He is only seven years old, but he knows about things like jobs and death and marriage, things that could steal him away from his brothers and them from him, and the thought of these things only makes him punch and kick and squeeze them harder, sometimes with such force he worries he might one day truly hurt them.

Upstairs in the kitchen Mother #3 hands Mother #4 a bowl of washed potatoes and wordlessly they begin to peel. After so many quiet nights spent in her small duplex, Mother #4 still marvels at the great wash of sound that never recedes, only falters for a moment and then rushes back like a stiff breeze coming off the sea. Even in the midst of all this commotion she knows none of it really belongs to her, and marvels at the strange fact of her dearest wish: to be part of it, to give in to its distractions, to find herself the owner of a life lived rather than a life endured. And then she looks into the face of Mother #3, worn smooth and almost featureless, with moist eyes that can't settle on anything more than a heartbeat at a time, and she knows this is a very dangerous wish. She could so eas-

ily become Mother #3—or Mothers #2 and #1, for that matter!—and she wonders what it is she wants, exactly, what in heaven's name has brought her here.

Mother #3 takes the peeled potatoes to the stove, leaving Mother #4 to look out the window at the broad gray shapes of dusk. Mother #4 can't help it, she searches the backyard for any sign of her husband. She wants him to be out there in pooling dark, watching her. She wants him to know how lost she is.

Where, then, is this husband, exactly? You can be certain he is not paying any attention to the house. If he were, he'd see that in the dark it looks radioactive, full of careening particles, the chaos of warm bodies. He'd be more than a little threatened, and rightfully so, by so much heat and light.

At this moment the Father is hiding, as usual. His secret lair is the ground floor of the Doll House, a ramshackle two-story playhouse made of plywood and cedar shakes whose construction he abandoned three years ago after the death of Daughter #9. After the funeral he boarded up the windows, except for the small one that faces west, put a padlock on the tiny door, spray-painted several black X's on the walls and ramparts, and condemned it, declared it off-limits, henceforth and forever.

When he's at Old House and wants to be alone, which is most of the time, he sneaks out here (he keeps the key to the padlock on a retractable janitor's key ring) and squats on a milk crate, his head occasionally bumping the splintery ceiling, his face framed by the small window that looks out across the river to the Spooner place. Often, he engages in a long-distance staring contest with an ostrich who patrols his territory with a haughty air, like a retired industrialist who has nothing left to do but admire all he owns. One day—and he has fantasized about this in great detail—he wouldn't mind going over there and breaking the thing's neck.

This spot, this is where he was sitting when it happened. He doesn't know what he's doing here now, doesn't know if it's self-punishment, or escape, or a refusal of time's passage. Some part of him, he knows, will be sitting here all his life.

It used to be that when he was alone like this he talked to God: What am I supposed to do? Please tell me what to do. But since Daughter #9 has been taken from him he has kept his silence.

Now, in this secret place, he allows his mind to go wherever it wants. Tonight, for instance, he is thinking about tomorrow morning, how he will wake early when the house is asleep and load up his pickup and make the long drive to Nevada. He considers how easy it would be to blow right on by the Highway 19 exit to continue on toward someplace where the living is free and easy, where there is no one to please and the obligations are few. He knows he is capable of such a thing; he has done it once already, abandoned one life for another.

He has been engaged in this kind of thinking for many months now, but lately his thoughts have centered on a woman, a dark-skinned stranger, and somehow for him she has come to comprise—in her short, muscled legs and her braided hair and her bright laugh—his desire for release, his dreams of escape. He believes, in a way that he doesn't fully understand, that she might be the one to save him.

Tonight, the darkness has swallowed everything except a bright wire of gold along the horizon. The Father watches the wire grow thinner and finer until it disappears, leaving behind a residue of lavender and blue. Very faintly, as if from some kinder and simpler time, the voices of his children rise out of the murky dusk, reminding him that there are things to do, that he has responsibilities of a certain kind, that he is, whether he likes it or not, the Father. The voices are louder now, calling for him to come in. He loves these children. He does, he loves them so much. He looks out the window. He stays a little while longer.

6.

. . . . .

THE STATE OF HIS SOUL

THE PUSSYCAT MANOR SAT JUST OFF STATE HIGHWAY 19, ITS TINY
patch of lawn a perfect, unnatural green in the middle of this high desert plain. The brothel was an old ranch house with three different mo-
bile homes attached at odd angles, giving the structure the aspect of a
train wreck's aftermath. The sign out front—PUSSYCAT MANOR—GIRLS
GALORE—featured an extremely curvy cartoon cat in lingerie stroking its own tail and purring in blinking pink neon: PRRRRRRRR. Eleven
o'clock in the morning and the parking lot was two-thirds full.

Slumped down in the front seat of his pickup, parked in the back
corner of the lot next to a pair of dumpsters, Golden watched customers of all stripes—sweating tourists, businessmen, a couple of
pimple-faced Marines—come and go. He'd been sitting here half
an hour, wiping the sweat from his brow, taking toots off his Afrin
while Cooter snoozed peacefully against his thigh. "If you're going to
do it, do it," Golden suggested to his reflection in the rearview mirror.
"If you're not, then get back to work." Apparently, this bit of self-
motivation did the trick. He waited until the coast was clear and hustled across the parking lot, wincing at the hard light and clutching at
his thighs to keep his keys from jingling in his pockets.

The parlor of the PussyCat Manor, dim and cool as an underground chamber, smelled like cigarette smoke and money. The only
true light came from a hanging lamp in the corner and the neon beer
signs flickering over the bar. Everywhere you looked, there were

half-dressed women: some lounging on the red velvet sofas, a couple standing in the faint glow of the jukebox, deliberating over the selections as if studying a sacred text, and one, a striking black girl with glitter in her afro, sitting at the white baby grand in the corner and tapping out "Go Tell Aunt Rhodie" with one finger.

Golden walked through the door and all the women looked up at him. He blinked and turned to leave.

"Come back here, honey!" cried the black girl. "We ain't gonna bite you, not less you pay us to!"

The other girls shrieked with laughter, and one of them intercepted him before he could make it outside. "Come on, why don't you give yourself a minute," she said. "We're all very nice and you can take your time deciding." She was a rosy-faced blond girl wearing a pink kimono open to her navel.

Golden took a breath. "I'm not. It isn't. I don't have anything to decide." Defeated, and knowing he would be unable to make himself any clearer than that, he chose a spot on her forehead and stared at it with conviction so as not to risk a glance at her cleavage.

She took him by the elbow and guided him toward a hallway whose entryway was hung with strings of clicking glass beads. They passed through the beads, which raked at Golden's hair and slithered across the bridge of his nose and around his shoulders. With her hand on his arm like that and those breasts swaying at the edge of his vision, he would follow her anywhere.

Finally, at the end of the hallway, after passing a series of doors from behind which came all manner of odd and startling human noises whose nature he didn't care to speculate on, Golden was able to wrest his elbow from her grip. "I'm the contractor on the new building." He held up his yellow hard hat for corroboration. "I'm here to see Miss Alberta."

"Miss Alberta's the matron here," the girl said. "She doesn't see men, not anymore."

Golden sneezed twice, loudly and furiously, and a female voice from behind one of the doors called, "Bless you!"

"I'm not here to *see* her," Golden whispered to the girl. "I'm here to talk. To her. The owner, Mr. Ted Leo, told me she's the one to see when he's away."

"You sure you don't want anything else?" the girl said. "Since you're working for Ted Leo, we'll give you a deal, two for one or throw in something a little extra."

"Oh, thank you, my." Golden's face bloomed into a third stage of heat. "We're in the middle of something out on the site, and I really just came to talk to Miss Alberta."

The girl went in search of the matron and Golden took a leather chair directly across from two women who stared at him openly and whispered to each other without looking away. One wore a garment that looked like it had been made from spare mosquito netting, and the other had on shorts, a cut-off tank top, and glue-on fingernails—each one painted, if Golden was not mistaken, with a miniature likeness of the American flag. Above the couch hung a painting of still another woman, this one fully naked and bigger than life. She was lying on her side on a Persian rug, looking back over her shoulder, a swollen grape between her teeth, her large, old-fashioned behind glowing with an unholy light.

With no safe place to settle his gaze, he looked around the room and pretended to note the sheetrocking job, the doorjambs that were inches out of plumb. He took a pen from his shirt pocket, studied it as if it were an archaeological treasure of profound significance. He turned it over in his hands, clicked the button several times, and when he dropped it, acted for all the world as if it hadn't happened. Thirty seconds passed and the girl in the mosquito netting picked it up and handed it over. "Dropped this," she said.

"I'm sorry. Thanks. I'm truly sorry," he said.

Finally, Miss Alberta showed up, obviously in a sour mood, shouting down the hall at someone named Chester and snapping her fingers at a girl who had fallen asleep on one of the couches. Golden jumped up from his chair with a force that caused it to topple backward.

Except for her showgirl-style fake eyelashes, Miss Alberta looked like any chunky middle-aged woman you might run into at the post office: permed auburn hair, flowery blouse, cheap silver rings on every finger. Behind the eyelashes were hard little eyes like two watermelon seeds.

She leaned back and eyeballed him up and down as if he were a Christmas tree she was considering for purchase. She came right out with an accusation: "You're the inspector, aren't you."

"No," Golden said. "I don't believe so."

"I thought we were dealing with Bennett these days. We have an agreement. You slippery boogers aren't supposed to show up unannounced."

Golden explained he wasn't an inspector, that he disliked inspectors as much as she did. Again, he held out his yellow hard hat as proof.

"Then you're here for business?"

"Yes," Golden sighed. "I—"

"Then go sit down and wait your turn like the rest. Big ones like you make us all nervous."

"Ma'am," Golden said.

"One wrong move from a lumberjack like you and it's off to the emergency room for one of my girls. Don't think it hasn't happened before. I should start charging by the pound with some of you boys."

Golden cleared his throat.

The scowl left her face for a moment and she gave a slight grin. Golden's tongue-tied discomfort, it was clear, was improving her mood immensely.

"So are you going to tell me what you want or should we stand here all day?"

"My name is Golden Richards." He pointed vaguely toward the door. "I'm the contractor on the new building. Mr. Ted Leo told me in his absence I should speak to you."

"You might have mentioned that in the first place, Mr. Richards, before I gave you the business. Every day of the week I have to deal with such a lineup of knuckleheads you wouldn't believe, so you'll forgive me for presuming the worst, which is the only way to manage things around here. Follow me to the office, where we can have some privacy."

The office, a tiny room stacked with papers, files, and ledger books, was just off the main parlor. "Please," Miss Alberta said, gesturing to the only chair in the room, upon which there appeared to be a stack of at least a dozen rubber penises encased in shrink-wrap plastic.

"I generally like to stand," Golden said, stepping to the side. Anyone caught hanging around in a whorehouse, he thought, deserved exactly this.

"Oh, the darn *dildos!*" Miss Alberta cried, as if she'd forgotten to put away her knitting. She scooped them up and dumped them on the counter next to a wall-mounted corkboard filled with thumb-tacked notes, receipts and reminders. Pictures of several chubby children—her grandkids, by the beady-eyed look of them—were taped all over the walls. She put on a pair of bifocals and jotted something in one of the ledger books. "We just got a new order and haven't had time to put things away. Can I get you something? Coffee?"

He shook his head, but not in response to Miss Alberta's question; he was trying to shake loose the word *dildo*, which had lodged in his brain and blocked his flow of thought. *Dildo.* He mouthed the word and looked up with a start to see if Miss Alberta had seen him. He'd heard the word used once or twice around the work site, but it never really meant anything to him. He'd always figured a dildo was some kind of bird.

"I hope Ted Leo is being civil with you, he can be difficult to work for, that man."

Golden shook his head again until a few words found their way out of his mouth: "No. Ted Leo's been good, real good."

"And how's the building going?"

"Fine." Golden nodded. "Going fine." The truth was they were weeks behind schedule, he'd lost one of his electrical contractors, and he was having trouble with his in-house crew, which was why he had ventured into the PussyCat Manor in the first place.

"I was wondering if one of my men, his name is Charles Odlum, has been in here. Most people call him Leonard."

"Can I ask why you'd like to know?"

"I hired all my men on the condition they wouldn't, you know, frequent the establishment. They've been compliant, but I've gotten a report about Leonard—"

"You object to the idea of a brothel, Mr. Richards?" she said, her voice whittled down to a fine point. "Maybe you've forgotten you're building one."

"No, ma'am. I just don't want it to be a . . . distraction for my men. They can do what they want in their spare time, but the fact is we're working on a site with a . . . an operational brothel on it. You can see the difficulty, I hope. It's up to me to draw the line on something like this."

In fact, the brothel had become a bigger distraction than he could have imagined. Though the actual building, just over a shallow rise, could not be seen from the job site, the lighted sign, with its depiction of a busty cartoon cat stroking her fluffed-up tail, was visible at all hours of the day. The brothel, and what went on inside it, was by far the most popular topic of conversation among the men. They referred to it as the Poontang Palace and Ye Olde Nunnery, and speculated endlessly on the girls' names, their various specialties and physical characteristics, and what might be the highest-priced items on the menu (The Full-Body Tongue-Wash? The Interracial Triple-Team?). Naturally, all the sex talk—not to mention the ever-present and extremely sexy cartoon cat—made the men horny. Some of them, in fact, seemed to be suffering from acute horniness, a horniness raised to elevated and possibly unhealthy levels. Golden did not want to admit to himself that the ban on brothel visits was making it worse.

Last week, for example, Golden had come out of the trailer to find Leonard Odlum humping a trash barrel. Leonard was a hyperactive redneck from eastern Oklahoma with the attention span of a kitten. Never without a cheekful of chaw and his trusted companion, the Dixie cup in which to spit it, he was always bouncing on his toes, performing disco dance combinations and yelling incomprehensible phrases at people who were out of earshot. And on this day, it seemed, he was humping a trash barrel.

When Golden asked what he was doing, Leonard said, "Who? Me?"

Holding his spit cup aloft with one hand and grasping the edge of the empty steel barrel with the other, he thrusted and caressed his crotch against it with an air of abject helplessness, the barrel occasionally making a hollow ringing like a broken church bell: *Tong Tong Tong.*

"Come on, get back to work," Golden called, weakly. "Before you hurt yourself."

"I'm on break," Leonard grunted, "and this is what I'm doing."

Down at the gate two drivers from the gravel pit were standing next to their dump truck, pointing at Leonard and laughing. Releasing his grasp on the barrel, Leonard turned to Golden, his hips still twitching slightly, holding his spit cup above the fray. Golden took a step back.

"See here?" Leonard said. He looked down at his pants, appalled by what he saw. "Lookit. It just keeps on like this, you oughta be glad I came across this barrel before you showed up." He walked around in a circle, his twitching crotch leading the way. "You let us at those hookers ever' now and then, this wouldn't be happening!"

Golden couldn't tell if this was all an act or if Leonard was in genuine distress. When Leonard started to reacquaint himself with the barrel again, Golden retreated to his trailer to hide until Leonard was finished. Several other workers had shown up to cheer and whistle. One of them yelled, "I hope the intercourse is consensual, Leonard!"

Now, according to several of the crew, Leonard had moved on from the barrel to the real thing; over the past two days he'd bragged to just about everyone he'd come across that he'd gone over the hill and got himself a hooker named Boutique, who he'd lit up, he'd said, like a High-9 slot machine. He had insisted from the beginning that making red-blooded men like him work in the close vicinity of so much available pay-for-pussy without being allowed to partake was a violation of his basic human rights. "This is America," he'd yell at anybody who'd listen, *"ain't it?"*

"I'm not trying to be a bother," Golden told Miss Alberta, "but I'd like to make sure my man actually came in here before I confront him about it. It would make things easier for me."

"No doubt it would," Miss Alberta said. "But we take privacy very seriously here, Mr. Richards, and we don't make a habit of revealing who our clients are, even when the request has been so politely made by a gentleman such as yourself. If that answer doesn't suit you, you can take it up with the Supreme Court, or the honorable Ted Leo, who will tell you the same thing."

Before Miss Alberta was finished, Golden was already backing out of the room like a crab. When he got to the doorway, he clapped on his hard hat, which was, he realized, the exact color of some of the dildos. "I didn't know there were rules for things like this, or I wouldn't have asked."

Miss Alberta took off her bifocals and slumped into her chair with a sigh. In an instant her tone changed from judgmental and severe to oversweet, as if she were speaking to one of her moon-faced grand-children. "Honey, that's quite all right. Not everybody's up to speed on whorehouse ethics these days. You finish that nice new building for us, and don't worry too much about your men. What we do, it helps men, it relaxes them, makes them happy." She opened a cup-board, pulled out two containers: one a ceramic candy dish full of homemade butter toffee, and the other a blown-glass chalice over-flowing with little disks packaged in shiny foil. Polite gentleman that he was, Golden selected one of each.

"If you'd ever like to come back," said Miss Alberta, "remember to bring that condom with you, we're requiring them now, and we'll take good care of you. If not, might as well have one of my toffees. They're better than sex anyway."

Outside, the bleached afternoon light blinded him; even in March the shock of heat and sun was like being hit across the forehead with a shovel. He walked out into the parking lot, blinking and grimacing, until he could see well enough to locate his pickup. He got behind the steering wheel and Cooter jumped into his lap, wiggled his entire body with excitement.

Golden stared at the shiny package glinting in his hand like a polished doubloon. The only other time he'd seen a condom up close was at the tribal fair in Page, Arizona, several years ago. He'd been waiting in line for snow cones with eight or nine of the kids when Donald Mifflin, a roofing contractor Golden had worked with on a couple of projects, walked up and cried, "Why lookee here! Hey-hey! If it ain't the great Golden R.!"

Donald Mifflin was of the species of construction man for which Golden had little tolerance: the fat and hairy and loud kind, the kind full of hale bravado and endless lines of bullshit.

"So!" shouted Donald, gesturing with his corn dog to the crowd of sweating, impatient children. "All these nippers belong to you?"

Golden gave a noncommittal chuckle; he had learned long ago not to engage strangers or acquaintances about his family situation.

"Seriously now," said Donald. "They all yours?"

Golden looked down at the kids, who stared back up at him, waiting patiently for him to claim or disown them.

"Ehhh." He sighed. "Yep. All mine."

Donald held up his corn dog and, mouth screwed up in concentration, dug into his back pocket for his wallet-on-a-chain, from which he extracted a small square packet of green foil and handed it to Golden. On the packet was printed in ribbons of cursive, *Gentleman's Best!*

"What is this?" Golden said.

Donald looked around meaningfully at the children, stepped forward, and in a whisper just quiet enough for everyone within a fifty-foot radius to hear, said, *"This, my friend, is so you don't go fucking yourself out of a spot at the dinner table."*

With that he gave Golden a clap on the back, a wink and a nod to the kids, and shambled off in the direction of the bumper cars.

Though Golden had never heard anyone in the church address the topic of condoms specifically, The Evils of Birth Control was a subject taken up often and at length. Birth control was high wickedness and pure selfishness, an abuse of mortal agency, a corruptor of men, a destroyer of civilizations. It poisoned the fountains of life, made mockery of God and all His commandments, the most fundamental of which was to multiply and replenish the earth. The condom, then, in its shiny little wrapper, was the embodiment of worldly vice, the antithesis of everything for which the church and its proudly prolific members stood.

That afternoon at the county fair Golden had tossed the thing into the nearest garbage barrel as if it were the maggoty remains of a mouse.

But today, in the hot cab of his GMC, he considered the gold foil package for a long time. On the front it said, A *PleasurePlus Prophylactic*, and on the back, *For the Pleasure of Sensual Living*. After a while he noticed he still held, in his other hand, the toffee he'd sheepishly fished out of Miss Alberta's bowl. He offered it to Cooter, who sucked on it thoughtfully for a few seconds, rattling it around in his teeth, before giving a shudder and spitting it out onto the seat.

Golden took out his wallet. He looked at himself in the rearview mirror; what he saw there offered no encouragement or reproach, no shocking news about the state of his soul. He opened his wallet. Slowly, he slipped the condom inside.

7.
· · · · ·

NUMBER ONE: DANIEL

Born dead and four months premature, weighing all of eleven ounces and no bigger than her own hand. His skin was a deep, startling red covered with fine blond hairs that clustered in a dense little crop at the top of his head.

She delivered him after eight hours of induced labor. They took him away to clean him up and when the young, grimacing nurse brought him back to her, he was not swaddled in a blanket as she'd expected, but laid out on a cold metal pan.

"The doctor said not to touch him," the nurse said, looking away, "or his skin might slip off."

If she had not been so exhausted, so emptied out with anger and bewilderment ever since the moment the doctor had whispered to her, with his papery hand on her arm, that the baby she carried had no heartbeat, she might have climbed off her bed and throttled the dumb girl with her bare hands. She felt herself shaking. *God damn it.* Then she said the words out loud, startling herself. "God *damn* it."

Before this moment she never could have imagined the situation that would cause her to say such a thing out loud, but here it was.

Once the nurse was gone, she cupped him in her hands as if handling an injured bird, and nestled him in the fold of her hospital gown. She could see herself in this boy, tiny and red as a demon though he was: in his prominent forehead and oversized feet. His fingers were tapered—so delicate they were almost translucent—and his miniature lips so cracked and dry that she bent down and pressed her own lips against them as if she might kiss them back into life.

At some point her husband, Billy, came into the room. He was a block of a man, a high school wrestler with a pink cauliflower ear, a sergeant in the National Guard with a fondness for dirt bikes and weaponry, and he practically cowered in the corner behind a meal cart. She remembered what he'd said four days before, when she'd come home from the doctor's office to tell him her news. After he allowed her to sob into his chest, after he squeezed her with his thick arms in a most sensitive way, he'd said, in a flat voice she didn't know if she could ever forgive him for, "It's a stillbirth, Trish. Happens all the time."

A BEAUTIFUL DISCOVERY

This was back in 1972, four years before she would escape life with Billy and find her way down to Virgin, where she would become what she promised herself she would never be: a plural wife, one of many jewels in her husband's crown.

She'd grown up in the Principle, in a Montana polygamist enclave called Pinedale, where her father, sixty-two years old when she was born, presided over his six wives and forty children with the solemn beneficence of a biblical king. They all lived in a single compound in a stand of ponderosas: two log homes and six Western Pacific boxcars that had been converted into bedrooms for the children and a few of the younger wives. They raised their own meat and vegetables, sewed their own clothes, pumped water by hand, and each night gathered, like the inhabitants of some medieval village, in the smoky, bustling great room with its river-rock fireplace and thirty-foot table made from a single massive tamarack cut lengthwise, to sing and eat and thank the Lord for their good fortune.

When her father died, the family disintegrated instantly. Trish was twelve years old. Four of the wives, along with their children, were absorbed into other church families, while the other two, including Trish's mother, disappeared into the world of the gentiles. With nothing but eighty dollars to her name—her portion of the inheritance—she put herself and her four children on a bus to Reno, Nevada, where she would find work as a casino hostess.

In less than a month, Trish had lost her father, five of her mothers (some of whom had fed her, sung her to sleep at night, diapered her, even breast-fed her) and thirty-six of her sisters and brothers, all of whom she missed gravely, reciting their names in a murmuring singsong: "*Michael, Deborah, Ivan, Paul, Sheila, Ricky, Mavis, Joan . . . Timmy, Keith, Caroline . . . Pearl, Millie, Wyatt, Dale . . .*" Unlike her children, Trish's mother did not seem to be grieved by these losses. Though nearly forty years old, she had married into the family as the sixth of six wives and managed to bear only four children, which afforded her the status of a hired maid.

"Really, I don't know how I did it all those years," Trish heard her transformed mother explain to an incredulous, pink-haired neighbor in Reno. "I cleaned, I cooked, I scrubbed, I swept, I peeled, I tended, I talked pretty and ate humble pie all the damn day long, and what did I get for my trouble? Living in a *boxcar*, and sleeping once a week with an old goat and his faulty equipment."

Trish's mother took easily to her new, emancipated lifestyle. She wore heels and skirts, smacked her gum, swore off cooking anything but Swanson tinfoil dinners, and every Saturday night went out dancing with friends from work. But for Trish it wasn't so easy. She had never seen a TV, listened to a radio, read a book other than the Bible and Book of Mormon, spoken directly to a boy who was not her brother. The first time she flushed a toilet she fled the bathroom in a panic.

One of her first and most important discoveries was her own beguiling face. In Pinedale she had been invisible to herself and everyone else, noticed only when she spoke out of turn or did not do her chores fast enough. She wore pioneer-style gingham dresses, hand-me-down work boots, and never felt any compulsion at all to study herself in a mirror (every morning her mother would brush her long black hair and tug it into two stiff braids). In Reno, she was constantly being waylaid by her own reflection: in medicine cabinet mirrors, department store windows, freshly waxed limousines, the chrome toaster on the kitchen counter. Amazed, she'd stand in front of the glass trophy case at school and consider her pert little nose and pouty lips and gleaming blackberry eyes. She was stunning!—why hadn't anyone told her?

She learned clothes and makeup from her mother's friend, Carlotta, who had worked six years as a showgirl and knew how to apply complex combinations of mascara, rouge, and base in ways that would, according to Carlotta, "set the boys' nuts on fire." Every chance she got, Trish ducked into the nearest bathroom to admire her sooty eyelashes and glowing cheeks, to assure the integrity of her painted lips and penciled eyebrows.

At school the girls hated her, of course, but the boys never wavered in their attentions—little packs of them vying for the privilege to lean against her locker—even after the girls spread rumors that she was a slut, that she turned tricks on weekends down by the railyard. She didn't know how to flirt or engage in small talk, and managed to turn down every offer of a date until she was fifteen, which only thickened the ether of mystery that hung around her. It was bullnecked Billy Paddock who first successfully asked her out. Actually, he sat across from her at study hall one afternoon and *told* her that he was going to take her to the Spring Hop on Saturday night, that he would pick her up at seven sharp, and that he would be bringing a pink peony corsage in case she wanted to wear a dress that matched.

It's how she'd been trained for most of her life: she did as she was told.

After Billy there were other boys. He wanted her for himself but she began to exercise the privilege her looks afforded her: she let other boys tell her what to do. She drew the line at French kissing and petting, but Billy didn't know that. He'd find out about her date with Marty Craig, wide receiver and star of track and field, and work himself into a purple-faced rage. He went out with other girls, feigned indifference, but was always there, watching, making sure she was his for Homecoming, Harvest Ball, Prom—all the big ones. She lost herself in the thrill of infatuation, in the pleasure of a boy's cold hand on her breast, but then the guilt would form like a hard bone in her chest and she would feel God watching her, the old God who lived among the tall pines and in the flat pale sky of Montana, and late at night, with the smell of aftershave and cigarette smoke still clinging to her, she would pray, beg His forgiveness and cry until her eyes were aching and dry.

On the last night of her junior year, she let Billy go all the way; a relief, finally, to relent. She closed her eyes and wept the few minutes that it took.

Within a month she discovered she was pregnant. By the time she graduated from high school she was a married woman, the mother of a two-month-old baby girl, washing diapers and ironing shirts in a tract house not much bigger than a Western Pacific boxcar.

NUMBER TWO: MARTINE

Not two years after Daniel, a kindly old German doctor, short and stout as a dwarf, delivered the absurd news: after six months of pregnancy she was, once again, carrying a dead baby.

She was so overcome by what this strange little man in a lab coat was telling her that she laughed out loud. "You're kidding."

"No. Nope." He shook his head. "No kidding."

"You're kidding," she said again, though this time in a whisper, the words dropping from her mouth like faint echoes.

"*No* kidding," the little doctor insisted.

They ran tests and discovered a simple explanation: she suffered from a condition that clotted the blood, cutting off the flow of oxygen and nutrients through the umbilical cord, a condition that could be treated by a daily pill of baby aspirin. But too late for tiny red Daniel, and now Martine.

She asked the doctor why her first daughter, her living daughter, Faye, who was now four years old, had managed to arrive safely into this world at all.

The doctor shrugged and waved his fat little hand. "I haf delifered over two thousand babies, my dear," he said, "and it is a miracle each time one off them has come out alife and stayed that way. You haf successfully birthed one child. Now that we understand your condition, I haf no doubt you can do it again." He raised his eyebrows. "No kidding."

On a snowy winter evening she delivered the fetus in a haze of painkillers (to take the edge off, the nurses had told her) and, once the labor was over, fell into a weeping, half-conscious sleep. She woke to a blur of light and voices, asking to see her baby, and the nurse informed her that her husband had authorized them to take the fetus and properly dispose of it.

"Everything," the nurse said in a professionally kind voice, "has been taken care of for you."

Trish could not speak or move. She imagined her baby with its delicate fingers and nubbed chin, feet tucked together, curled up on top of a pile of medical trash, disposed of. She imagined this pile of trash hauled off in a large truck and dumped in a landfill where rats slithered in and out of sight and seagulls circled and swooped down to snatch whatever they could find.

She tried to ask a question, but no sound came from her mouth. Billy was nowhere to be seen. She tried to get out of the bed, a hoarse growl rising out of her throat, and when the nurse came to try and calm her she kicked and scratched and shrieked until they had to strap her down and tranquilize her.

She went home from the hospital the next day and acted as if nothing had happened. Every morning she made Billy his bowl of oatmeal with brown sugar and raisins, the way Billy liked it. Each day, while he was at work selling hot tubs, she cleaned the bathroom, sanitized with ammonia and boiling water, vacuumed the rugs, dusted, washed clothes, ironed shirts, balanced the checkbook—all in the exact way that Billy required. She wore her matching outfits, put on her makeup and did her hair, and one day, when she thought she might disintegrate in the clean light and sterile odor of her own house, she went across the street, invited her Peeping Tom neighbor, Mr. Ellis, over for a cup of hot chocolate, and let him fuck her.

After Mr. Ellis there was Billy's boss, Ricky Gaines, and then the young man who came to the door asking about donations for the Firemen's Association. The sex offered her relief, made her feel young and heedless for a little while, and when she told Billy what she'd done, he'd given her no response except to take away her checkbook, sell their second car which she used for errands, and explained to her in an eerie whisper that if she tried to leave the house without permission, or allowed anyone inside who he had not authorized, he would kill her.

No wonder, she would think later, that her Faye, who had somehow survived her own corrupted womb, was a haunted child. Faye, who rarely spoke, did not like to play with other children, and spent most of her hours kneeling in the spot beside the fireplace she called her "prayer cave"—a kind of improvised grotto constructed of pillows, blankets and dismembered stuffed animals where she carried on intricate conversations with Jesus and the Holy Ghost and other invisible beings. She seemed to have no affection at all for her remote father, who punished her for minor infractions such as bed-wetting by locking her in a closet or throwing cold water on her in the bathtub while Trish stood by and watched, a mute conspirator. The family was not particularly religious, but somewhere along the line, during one of their few visits to the Mormon church down the street, Faye had been infected by God.

As much as Trish would have liked to, she could not blame Faye's odd behavior entirely on Billy. Needing to talk to someone besides her flaky mother or stone-faced husband, she had told Faye all about

Daniel and Martine, explained in detail how they arrived early into the world and left much too soon, both so perfect in God's sight they were given a pass on the Test of Life and were now living happily with Jesus and His angels up in heaven. The truth of it was that she felt connected to her two dead children in a way she didn't with her living daughter. Trish had no remedy for this, no way to bring them all together except to make Faye an accomplice in this sorrow of hers. Faye, a toddler barely out of diapers, listened to her mother talk about her invisible brother and sister and seemed to understand.

Faye had been carrying on a regular discourse with God and Jesus and several of the Bible prophets since she learned to talk, but gradually she began bringing others into the conversation: the Holy Ghost, Joseph Smith, Abraham Lincoln, Old Yeller, and her two siblings. With Daniel and Martine, she mostly kept them up to date on the news of the Paddock household: the raccoon in the attic, the Fourth of July grass fire on the mountain, the new refrigerator that whistled and moaned when you opened the freezer door. Sometimes she aksed questions, tilting her head and nodding as if receiving answers.

It was hard, sometimes, for Trish not to ask her what they had to say.

Her decision to leave Billy was not particularly painful or even difficult; one sparkling fall morning she felt a rare bit of clarity and the will to put it to use. She asked Faye how she would feel about their going away for a while. Faye sighed as if she'd been waiting a long time to field this particular question.

"We could go away," she said, "and if we like it there, we could never come back."

Trish called her mother, who had taken up with a livestock auctioneer in a trailer park outside Carson City.

"You know I never liked that Billy," her mother said. "Little banty rooster with his head up his you-know-what. We don't have room for you here, honey, but I was talking to Daphne the other day——"

"Hold on," Trish said. "*Aunt* Daphne?" Aunt Daphne had been one of her mother's sister-wives, wife number three, a thoughtlessly kind, chubby woman who hoarded candy at the bottom of her clothes hamper and once gave Trish a whole Big Hunk candy bar, as generous a gift as she had ever received. Trish and her mother occasionally spoke about the family they had left in Montana, and speculated about what had become of them, but as far as Trish knew her mother had never been in contact with any of them.

"She tracked me down, wanted to catch up. She's the same old Daph, sweet and happy all the day long. She's down to Utah, married another plyg there and started to feel lonely once all the kids moved out. That's why she called. A lonely old lady, and I know for a fact she's got all kinds of spare room. She'd be happy to take you and Faye, but you have to promise me, honey. One of those men shows up at the front door with his hat in his hand, looking for another heifer to put in his corral, you turn and run for the hills."

NUMBER THREE: JACK

Eight and a half months along, big as a Volkswagen, she ate heaping portions of kidney beans, pork chops, and spinach greens (all prescribed by her midwife), dutifully took her baby aspirin every morning, after which she would sit on her porch in the sun, dazed with relief. She knew, this time, there would be no tragic replay, no evil doctors casually whispering their horrible news, no nurses absconding with her baby, never to be seen again. She felt this new one, this big baby boy, arch and swim inside her, active as a colt, and she knew that her old life, her old polluted self, was forever gone.

Reno, and everything that had happened there: gone. Billy, the succession of groping teenage boys and rutting men, her vanity and selfishness, her cursed body, her loneliness and hard-packed grief: all gone, cleansed by the sharp hot light of the Virgin River Valley. Reno had been one long detour into a blighted territory, and now she had returned to country in which she belonged, a place filled with women and children and companionship and constant distraction, a place of simple rights and wrongs, a place in which Faye could pray the whole day long and no one think it the slightest bit odd.

She had not heeded her mother's advice, of course. Within a month of moving to Virgin, where she and Faye lived in one wing of Aunt Daphne's six-bedroom rambler, she was attending church regularly and meeting with the Women's Relief Society, an organization that promoted gossip and irreverent female bonding under the cover of quilting bees and seminars on emergency preparedness.

It was on a Saturday afternoon, at something called Service Day, that she first met Golden. Though they worked together only ten minutes or so—he helped her unload flats of tomato sprouts to be planted in the community garden—she was immediately taken by his gentle deference, the sad cast of his eyes. She didn't know it at the time, but a year earlier he had lost one of his young daughters, and Trish would soon come to realize it was the weight of grief she sensed in him, so much like her own, that first drew her to him.

Of course, none of this got past Beverly; nothing ever did. Within a couple of days Trish was being invited to dinner at Old House, to Big House to help with the funeral luncheon for old Brother Billick. Trish thought nothing of it until she got a call one night from Golden himself, who sheepishly inquired if she might like to take a ride with him to Sister Flett's nursery to pick out flowers for the upcoming Easter service. On the phone that night, the cord wrapped around her wrist, she felt herself grinning and spinning in place like the gumsmacking high schooler she had once been: she was being asked out on a date! That her suitor was a man with three wives and twenty-six children didn't bother her nearly as much as it should have.

As the courtship progressed—barbecues and church socials, dinner and a movie in St. George (usually chaperoned by one of the wives), a little chaste nuzzling and kissing in the front seat of the hearse—it became easier and easier to consider living under the protection of this family, to return to the safety of the life she had led as a child, to share her pain with this sweet giant of a man in the hopes that they might find a way to heal each other.

A month before her one-year anniversary in the valley she was baptized and, so quickly it seemed to happen at once, married to Golden and his first three wives, and then pregnant with the child who would make everything right again.

Two days after the midwife stopped by and pronounced her two centimeters dilated, the baby already dropping and loaded for bear, she felt the initial spasm of pain. She was balancing awkwardly on one knee in the corner of the kitchen, searching for the button that had zinged off her overstressed maternity jumper when she'd bent to retrieve a dropped spoon. She winced—her eyes pulled tight at the corners as if someone had grabbed her hair and yanked, making her scalp sing—and then came the hard, torquing jolt, which felt like the baby straightening out all at once and kicking her in the spine. The movement inside her was so violent and sudden she collapsed onto her side and grabbed her belly with both hands as if to keep it from breaking open. She lay on the linoleum, waiting for something else, for a set of aftershocklike contractions, or her water to break, but there was nothing except for a lingering buzz in her nerves.

That night, did she wonder why the baby, such an active little kicker she had nicknamed him Jackhammerin' Jack, had not so much as stirred the rest of the day? After two more days of perfect stillness, as if the child had withdrawn to a distant corner of the womb to ready himself for his initiation into this bright new dimension, did she think to consult the midwife, or at the very least allow herself a moment or two of concern? No. Her faith in this child, in the joy and completion he would give her, was pure. Whenever a sliver of doubt would creep into her peripheral consciousness she resorted to the old childhood chant that dispersed the ghosts and shadow-men who crept out of the woods at night to scratch and whisper under the steel belly of the boxcar: *It'llbeallrightit'llbeallrightit'llbeallrightit'llbeallrightit'llbe allrightit'llbeallright.*

When her water broke early that Wednesday morning, leaking down her legs in slow fingers as she hung a towel on the line, she took it as a confirmation that everything was occurring in its rightful fashion. She called Beverly, who drove her and Faye back to Old House, where Nola and Rose-of-Sharon and some of the older girls had already gathered to set up the master bedroom for birthing. She lay on the expansive king-sized bed, propped up by a bank of pillows, and when the contractions came for real, the pain was sharp and affirming. The old midwife, Sister Meisner, showed up and unpacked her implements like a mobster readying for a hit. Sister Meisner, whose every word and movement suggested a no-nonsense competence, had arthritic old claws and an exquisitely sour face that expressed nothing but irritation at humankind and its shortcomings.

After an intricate hand-washing ritual that included three different cakes of soap and a towel baked for fifteen minutes in the oven, Sister Meisner checked the cervix, timed her contractions, and placed the bell of her old brass stethoscope on Trish's exposed belly. She moved the stethoscope around, tilting her head a little, and quickly her expression changed from one of irritation to one of extreme and wholehearted irritation.

"You've felt the baby move?" she said. "In the last few days? You've felt it kicking?"

Paralyzed, Trish could not so much as open her mouth.

"If you please, young lady, I need your assistance. Maybe you felt a bad pain in the past few days since I last checked you? Like the baby doing a backflip inside you?"

Beverly, who had been undergoing midwife training under Sister Meisner's tutelage, appeared at the foot of the bed, her face gone a shade pale. "I'll call the ambulance in from Hurricane. They'll be here in ten minutes."

"You'll do no such thing," Sister Meisner said. She shook her head, grimaced, and began to bear down against Trish's belly with both hands as if she were trying to push the baby out all on her own. She took up the stethoscope again, glared up at the light fixture as if it had challenged her to a fight, and listened. Her expression never changed, she never looked down, but Trish felt that old gnarled hand, hard and cold as a piece of varnished wood, roughly seek out her own and clutch it tight.

"Your little one is gone," she whispered so that only Trish could hear. "God bless you both."

Then louder, after a few moments: "That's all. No heartbeat, nothing. We'll deliver here, just as planned. Nothing a hospital or ambulance can do. I can feel the cord now. No blood flow. Hasn't been, looks like, for a day or two."

Later, Trish would remember little about the delivery itself, except for her own repeated pleas—as if they were made by somebody else in the room—that she be allowed to hold the baby once it was born. Beverly held her hand and said, *Yes, of course*, and Sister Meisner had nothing to say but, *Not yet, not yet*, and then, *Push, push, push, push.* Trish did not open her eyes the entire six hours, just hunkered down in the trough of sheets and welcomed the pain that came as dazzling yellow flashes across her retinas. And then, all at once, it was over. The years of her life, the months of nausea and expectation, the late-night hours of despair and loss, the hours of sweat and suffering, all funneled into this moment of expectation, only to be met with a ringing silence.

"Hup, crimped cord," said the midwife. "Thirty-eight years and only the third I've seen."

Beverly took the baby and after a few minutes returned with him, cleaned and wrapped in his birthing quilt, which featured bounding lions and frolicking zebras painstakingly hand-stitched in turn by her three sister-wives. Beverly settled the boy into Trish's arms, and when Trish got her first look at him, felt his small compact form sink against her breasts, she cried, not in grief, but in love. He was chubby, with his eyes closed, and his pink jowls gone slack around his mouth, as if he were enjoying a very satisfying nap. Oh, how she loved him! She squeezed him against her chest and pressed her nose into his damp, red-blond hair. His beauty, his smell, obliterated for the moment the monumental injustice of what had happened. She looked at her baby and smiled, unable to contain her mother's pride in his strong features, in his solid heft, in the way his fat little fists tucked neatly under his chin.

She asked for Faye, and against Sister Meisner's protests ("This is not proper," she said. "A viewing, a funeral, that is proper, this is not") the girl was brought in and allowed to hold Jack. Faye went right to her mother and, with no sign of distress or reluctance, picked up the baby, expertly tucking his head into the crook of her elbow, and looked into his face. "Jack, you've been a bad little boy, haven't you?"

"Blessed Savior," Sister Meisner said under her breath.

"Where did you go?" Faye said to the dead baby. "Did you fly away, you bad boy?"

"Heavenly Father forgive us all," Sister Meisner said.

Next, Beverly ushered Golden in, and Sister Meisner, going through her final checkup, mumbled and groused, wondered to herself what this was, a convention? Who was going to be invited in next, the entire extended family? The next-door neighbors? The mayor of San Francisco?

Golden stepped to the side, hulking and sheepish, looking to Beverly, in his eyes a desperate wish for clarification or instruction. Beverly stood next to the door, her hand on the knob, and thanked Sister Meisner for her service. "We can handle things from here, Mavis. Please don't forget the cinnamon cake I made for you on the kitchen table."

Sister Meisner planted her feet in a bowlegged stance, a shoot-this-old-gray-head-if-you-must look in her eye. She glared at Golden as if he were the cause of everything, and he could only nod in apparent agreement. Finally, she took up her satchel and webby shawl and stomped grumbling out the door.

After a nod from Beverly, Golden went to Trish, put his hand on hers. Trish took the baby from Faye and smiled at him. She had forgotten, until this moment, that this baby was as much his as hers. "Here he is." It was all she could say. She knew she was smiling and could hardly understand why. "Look at him."

He nodded but did not glance at the baby.

"Why don't you take him for a minute," Beverly urged.

"No, I don't—" he said.

"You go ahead and hold him for a minute," she ordered calmly, "while I attend to a few things with your wife. Sit in the rocker over there and sing him a lullaby. Go on, Goldy. Every child deserves a lullaby."

Trish had not noticed until now, but outside night had begun to set in. The wind blew and the timbers of the old house shifted and creaked. Golden turned on the bureau lamp and sat down with the baby, cradling it in the manner of someone used to dropping things. He started to rock, blinked hard and swallowed, hummed a few notes. He took his time looking down at the baby, and only when his eyes settled on the child's face did he begin to cry: a small hiccup of a sob and then tears crowding the inner hollows of his eye sockets and tracking down his nose. He cleared his throat, tried another feeble hum. He didn't know any lullabies. So he sang the only song he could think of:

I'm a broken-hearted keelman
And I'm o'er head in love
With a young lass from Gateshead
And I call her my dove.

Her name's Cushie Butterfield
And she sells yella clay
And her cousin's a muckman
And they call him Tom Grey.

He paused. For a second it seemed to occur to him the song might not be appropriate for the occasion, but then he continued on, his voice filling the room like it was no more than a coat closet. Trish had never heard Golden sing before, had always assumed him to be tone-deaf. She'd sat next to him at church, where he'd always mumbled the hymns, as most of the men did, rolled the words in his mouth like used-up chewing gum they didn't know how to get rid of. But now, after a whispery first line, his voice grew full and sweet.

She's a big lass
She's a bonny lass
And she likes her beer
And I call her Cushie Butterfield
And I wish she was here.

Later, after Golden had gone to make arrangements with the funeral home, Nola and Rose-of-Sharon came in, eyes bright with tears, and they wept as they admired the baby and told Trish how beautiful he was. Beverly led them in a prayer and then all four sister-wives sat together on the bed, holding hands and clutching each other for comfort. Trish loved them then as much as she had ever loved her own kin, her own blood.

Once they were gone, she eased herself into a prone position, wincing at the pain between her legs, and closed her eyes. In the coming weeks and months she would feel the weight of this loss, would sit in her bathtub late at night, her nipples sore, her tender breasts engorged with milk, and wonder how much hurt a person could withstand—but not now. Now the wind scoured the windows with dust, the house creaked, and she settled into sleep, contented, her little boy at her side.

8.
- - · · ·

THE BOY AT THE WINDOW

THE BOY WAITS AT THE WINDOW. HE HAS GROWN TIRED OF SCRUTI-nizing himself in the mirror and is now back at his post on the old ce-ramic radiator, stiff-backed and still as if sitting for a portrait, taking in the view: river, fields, road, ostrich, neighbors' house, crow, water tower, and in the far distance the floating blue mountains so familiar and remote his brain no longer registers their existence.

If you were to ask the boy what he is waiting for, he wouldn't be able to tell you. He is waiting for a meteor strike, a tornado, a full-scale zombie invasion, anything to rescue him from this room, this house, these people.

He scans the length of the twisting river and, sure enough, there next to the boulder that looks like a giant snail two young mer-maids cavort in the shallow water, silver scales glinting and breasts a-bobbing, playfully tugging on each other's long red hair. "Dear me," says the boy in an English accent. "Now what do we have here." The mermaids squeal deliciously and slap their tail fins on the water.

Lately, women of the nude and semi-nude variety have been insinuating themselves into the boy's consciousness at every opportu-nity; just about anywhere he looks there are well-oiled bikini chicks winking at him from behind bushes, tall Amazon ladies in leather bustiers making little growling noises at him while they sharpen their spears. If he hears music, even organ music at church, here come the

gyrating belly dancers, and if there is water in the vicinity? Bring on
the mermaids.

His erection, which was making a nuisance of itself even before
the mermaids showed up, is now operating at full capacity, making it
hard for him to think. He sighs, shifts his leg around on the radiator.
This boy, he doesn't know what to do with these minute-by-minute
bodily assaults, these crazed thoughts: he is at a loss. Even though
he has some idea that with a little hands-on manipulation he could
achieve temporary relief, he is careful not to touch himself. Which is
odd, because if he is known for anything it is his lack of restraint; he
is a liar, a loudmouth, a thief, an instigator, a Peeping Tom, a crybaby, a snoop. But in this most private aspect of his life, one that no
one will ever see or know about, he shows the self-discipline of an
anchorite. He understands what sex is, at least in theoretical terms,
and though he is fascinated by its dark and manifold mysteries, it
also freaks him out. Which probably has something to do with his
growing suspicion that sex is behind everything, that it is what drives
adults to act in strange, unpredictable ways, that it lurks in places it
should not belong, in church sermons and evening meals and daily
family prayer, that it is responsible for the unreasonable number of
brothers and sisters he has, and is therefore responsible in some way
for the state of his confusing and miserable life.

Or it may just be that he refuses to touch himself because of the
possibility that an invisible Jesus Christ, with His mournful eyes and
weirdly girlish eyelashes, is somewhere in this room, right now, spying on him.

So how does the boy seek relief? He blurts out swear words and
sings dirty song lyrics he has overheard from the bad kids at school.
He imagines in fine detail the suffering and total destruction of his
enemies. He plays grabass with his siblings in highly inappropriate
ways. He tries on his sisters' underwear.

In church they instruct the youngsters that in order to free themselves from bad thoughts they should recite a scripture or sing a

hymn. The boy doesn't understand scripture, and though he has heard hymns his entire life, he has a hard time remembering them.

Now let us hmm-hmm in the day of salvation, he sings. *No longer deranged on the earth need we roam.*

This is the best he can do. It doesn't help at all.

Downstairs somebody yells something and there is a burst of laughter, like when someone delivers a zinger on TV. They are laughing at him, he knows they are. They are calling him a fag and a pervert, which in the boy's estimation would make them fifty percent correct.

The house is quiet again. The mermaids have gone. He has nothing to do, so he sits at the window. He watches. He waits. For something, anything, to happen.

9.

A NEW FRIEND

ON HIS BIKE NOW, HAULING BUTT DOWN WATER SOCKET ROAD, RUSTY was making a break for it. He had spent all that time looking out the window, distracted by the humping cows and the mermaids and Raymond the Ostrich, and not realizing that escape was at hand: all you had to do was open the window, push off the screen, slide down the old copper gutter, jump down two roof levels, drop ten feet to the top of the detached garage, and from there you were home free. No one had seen him, not even Louise with her great all-seeing bubble-eyes, and in less than a minute he was on his bike, which he had snuck out of the garage, and pedaling down the long driveway thinking, *I am in very big trouble.*

Even worse, he didn't have any shoes on. His high tops, which were honestly just as sorry and worn out as his underwear, were with all the other shoes in the box by the front door because Aunt Beverly had a no-shoes-in-the-house policy, which meant if somebody important like Neil Armstrong or Jesus ever decided to stop by they would have to remove their shoes and place them in the shoe box, no exceptions. It wasn't a big deal for some people who were lucky enough to have regular-smelling feet, but Rusty had been born with foot-odor complications, which caused certain people to gag when he entered the room, or to ask him why his feet smelled like hot garbage.

So because of Aunt Beverly's shoe policy, here he was pedaling down the street in his tube socks like a retard. Where was he going?

He didn't know. He had thought about going home and asking his mother to allow him to stay there, he would tell her all the terrible things Aunt Beverly and her a-hole kids were perpetrating on him, but he had already tried that twice now and it hadn't worked. Today, he decided, he would pedal until he got so far out into the desert nobody could ever find him, except for maybe a bunch of illegal Mexican bandits who had got lost on their way to Las Vegas and formed their own civilization by constructing adobe forts and eating lizards and he would surprise them because of his silent-walking ability, and they would look at him suspiciously and say, *Cómo estás?* and because he had paid attention in Spanish class at school he would say, *Bueno, gracias. Cómo estás bien?* and they would all start jumping up saying, *O mi Dios!,* deeply impressed because not only was he a guy with excellent silent-walking ability, he also spoke their difficult language as well, and they would start asking him questions, most of which he couldn't understand because they spoke even faster than Mrs. Burdick at school, but he would hold up his hand and say, *Sí, Sí, mi nombre llamo Rusty,* and they would fall down and practically worship him and his BMX racer because they'd never seen a person riding such a technological bike and he would be their king.

He would show them how to make fire, and how to get free Dr Peppers from the vending machine in front of Platt's Market in town, and in return they would do his bidding, which would include kidnapping Parley and tying him to a juniper tree and practicing some Mexican torture techniques on his genitals, after which he would look Parley in his face and say, *Who's the faggety-fag now, Señor Muchacho?*

Of course, his father and Aunt Beverly would come out to his desert stronghold and beg him for mercy, asking him to come home, the family needed him, they were falling apart without him, especially his mother, who hadn't eaten a bite of food since his disappearance, and the Mexicans would terrify Aunt Beverly with their sharp spears and painted faces but Rusty would hold out his hand and say, *Please, gentlemen,* and the Mexicans would back away, and with great sadness he would inform them in artistic Spanish that he had to go home because his mother, his *señorita mamacita*, was dying of sadness without him, he hoped they would understand, and as he rode away on his bike they would cry their Mexican eyes out and do some mariachi singing and trumpet-playing and shout, *Adiós, amigo Rusty! Adiós!*

It was about at this point that he forgot to watch where he was going and ended up skidding into the irrigation ditch. His front tire bit into the soft sand at the bottom of the ditch and Rusty went over the handlebars and landed not in the soft sand of the ditch but on the other side where there were rocks and stickers and pieces of broken beer bottles. *Ahrrg*, what a gyp! Look at this: he'd scraped the dookie out of his elbow and there were rocks and glass stuck in his palms and his front tire was all bent up, plus he had bit his tongue. Heck yes, he cried. He jammed his hands into his eyes and did some serious howling.

He was so busy howling he didn't hear the truck pull up.

"Oh wow," somebody said. "You okay, kid?"

He stopped howling and said, "Uh?" There was a guy with his arm hanging out the window of an old green pickup, a young guy with a weird adam's apple and red beard that wasn't really a beard at all but about thirty-five curly red whiskers sticking out of his face. His forehead was so sunburned his skin was peeling off like wallpaper. What an idiot.

"You need a ride home?" the guy said.

Rusty hiccupped and wiped the tears from his cheeks. He didn't need a ride from some sunburned idiot with a sorry red beard. Then he thought about walking all the way back to Old House, dragging his mangled bike and possibly dying from thirst or being ambushed by Mexican bandits.

"Can't go home," he said with a sniff. He explained he was running away from his cruel parents who had locked him in his room for nothing more than being curious and having an inquisitive mind, and if he went home now with a busted bike and blood on his shirt there's no doubt that his mother, an extremely evil and unfriendly person named Beverly, would whip the snot out of him with her lion-tamer's bullwhip, and his father would come home and scream the kind of cuss words that Rusty would rather not repeat out loud.

"Well, uh," the guy said. "I don't know what I can do about that, but yeah, I think I can probably fix that bike."

The guy helped him off the ground and put his bike in the back of the pickup, which was filled with trash and wire and rusty tools and a coyote pelt that looked like it had been taken off a coyote not all that long ago. When they got in the pickup the guy shuddered like a ghost had touched him.

"It's my feet," Rusty said. "You'll get used to it."

They drove for a mile or two, then turned off on a dirt road so full of potholes and boulders they spent more time driving next to the road than on it. The guy didn't say anything, didn't look at Rusty, or even try explaining where they were going, just held his index finger up close to his nose. There was nothing but cedar trees and red-rock cliffs, and just when Rusty became certain the guy was taking him out into the boonies so he could murder him in some freaky way that would end up in the newspaper, they came over a rise where two silver-painted Quonset huts sat side by side like igloos on Mars.

Maybe this was a secret military installation where this mysterious sunburned guy was experimenting with ultra-secret death ray isotopes and was going to use Rusty as a human guinea pig? Or maybe he wanted Rusty as his trusted loyal henchman, which wouldn't be so bad either.

"Home sweet home," the guy said, and made a girly little laugh. He led Rusty into one of the huts, which was decorated something like a house: rugs on the cement floor, an easy chair next to a table with a ham radio, a cowhide couch, an enormous Frigidaire that hummed and shuddered.

The guy washed Rusty's hands and arm in a utility sink and put iodine on his scrapes and a gauze bandage on his elbow.

"I was wondering what your name was?" he said.

"Lance," Rusty said.

"Lance," the guy said. "That's a, uh, pretty good name. Yeah. My name's June Haymaker."

Rusty snorked, which was, for once, appropriate.

"A lot of people don't know that June's a man's name," June said, looking wounded by the snork. "You know there was a general, in the Civil War, named June? Definitely a, uh, masculine name."

"I have a sister named June," Rusty lied. "She's three and a half."

June put away the bandages and iodine, slamming some cupboards in the process, and then led Rusty out to the other Quonset hut, which he called his shop. The shop was filled with tools and machines and shelves stacked with boxes of rusty screws and bolts. Fluorescent lights hung from chains made everything, including June's peeling face, look pale green.

June put the bent bike tire in a bench clamp and yanked on it with a wrench. He said, "I've seen you riding your bike before, I think. On Water Socket Road. You live in one of the houses? By the river?

"No," Rusty said. Even though everybody in the valley knew that the Richardses were a polygamist family, and that anybody who didn't know could tell he was a plyg kid just by looking at his crappy shirt, Rusty, along with his brothers and sisters, had been taught from day one never to talk to strangers about their family situation, never to mention they had more than one mother and more brothers and sisters than any normal person should be allowed to have. They weren't supposed to lie, their parents and teachers taught them, they just weren't supposed to tell the truth either. You figure it out.

They were reminded often there were people out there who did not understand their lifestyle and wanted to do them harm. Rusty figured a weirdo with a name like June had to be one of these people.

"So, uh," June said. "You're from one of the plyg families?"

"Yeah," Rusty sighed. Seriously, what was the use anyway? "My dad's Golden. He builds houses and stuff. Most people around here know him."

June nodded and finished straightening the spokes with a pair of pliers. Once he had the wheel all fixed and back on the bike, and the chain and sprockets greased, he said, "You, uh, hungry, Lance? I keep a mini-fridge out here with, you know, snacks. If you want. Then I'll drive you back home."

"I could maybe eat something," Rusty said. Locked away in the Tower he had gone without lunch, which was bad enough, and now it was getting close to dinner and he was ready to start fainting at any moment. June brought two cans of Pepsi, Slim Jims, a sleeve of crackers, and a box of Ding Dongs to the workbench, all of which Rusty put away while making little murmurs of appreciation. Instead of shoving the last Ding Dong into his mouth as he had the others, he savored it, really making sure he tasted it, knowing that as Aunt Beverly's prisoner he would not be enjoying dessert for a very long time. Once the food was gone and he had a minute to consider things, he decided June Haymaker wasn't too bad after all, even with his screwy name and out-of-control Adam's apple.

"What are you doing out here, anyway?" Rusty said. "You building something?"

"Actually," June said, "I'm . . . yes. Building something. Yeah. Maybe I'll show you sometime."

Rusty pointed at June's head. "I was thinking maybe you should wear a hat, though. A hat helps with the sunburn."

"Oh?" June said, pointing to his own face. "Yeah? This? No. Not sunburn. I had a little accident. Nothing, you know, serious. I should put some lotion on it." He looked around as if searching for lotion, but there was only a grease gun and a can of Lava soap. "Yeah. Okay. Anyway. Before I take you home I'll show you something, though. Real quick." June rummaged around in some drawers and came back with what looked like a cardboard paper towel tube with a string hanging out of it. They went outside, where the sun was down and the sky was purple and pink and the red cliffs in the distance looked like they were on fire.

June dragged some kind of welded metal contraption out from under a tarp and set it up so that a metal pipe, about three feet long and sitting on a base of plate steel, was pointing straight into the dark sky. He took a lighter from his pocket, lit the string on the cardboard tube, which began to spit sparks and was, Rusty realized, a fuse. A fuse. Which meant that the cardboard tube thing was some kind of *bomb*.

"Okay," June said, dropping the bomb into the pipe. "Back up a little why don't we."

You didn't have to tell Rusty—he was already hauling his fat butt around the back of the pickup, hands over his head. He heard a noise that went *thoonk* and then a loud hissing and he looked up to see a flash that seemed to break apart into a thousand pieces overhead. It took him a moment to figure out that it wasn't a bomb but fireworks, like the Fourth of July. Not the rinky-dink fireworks you buy at the roadside stands but the real ones they set off at the rodeo grounds. This one exploded not all that high above them with a bang that Rusty felt in his chest, and shot off fat orange and yellow sparks that lit up everything and trailed down in slow arcs until they landed on top of the Quonset huts and bounced on the ground and one of them landed in June's hair, so that he had to smack himself with his palms to keep his head from going up in flames. Once he was sure his scalp was out of fire danger, he looked at Rusty and said, "Oh boy. You like that? I make them. Yeah. Fireworks. For a hobby."

Rusty said that he liked it very much and would like to see a few more, please. June said, "Oh, yeah, maybe another time. We need to get you home." He gave his smoking head one more whack. "Before your parents. Before they get worried."

A SAFE RETURN

On the ride back home, Rusty imagined he could hear bloodhounds baying in the darkness and helicopters crisscrossing the night sky searching for him with their powerful spotlights and there was his family at home with a dozen police cars parked out front, wringing their hands and talking to the television cameras, *We'll do anything to get him back, anything, a two-hundred-dollar reward for his safe return, why don't we go ahead and make it two-fifty, we'll do whatever it takes, we just want him back,* while his father ran through the willows in the river bottom all muddied and worried-looking, shouting, *Rusty! Rusteeeeee!*

But when they pulled up in front of Old House it was so quiet it looked like nobody was home and Rusty remembered that his father was not even around, but still in Nevada building a home for old fogies where he would hardly notice if Rusty disappeared and was found murdered and decapitated out in the desert by some lonely freako like June here.

June helped Rusty take the bike from the bed of the pickup. "Okay, then," he said. "It was, uh, nice . . ."

"Don't you want to come to the door with me?" Rusty said. "Maybe my mother won't get mad if you're there to explain things."

"Oh? Uh," June said. "All right."

Before they made it up to the porch, Aunt Beverly opened the front door. The light behind her made her look black as a shadow and nine feet tall.

"Ma'am?" June said. "I was helping your boy here, uh, he crashed his bike—"

"And who are you?" Beverly said.

"My name? Yes. Ah. Ju—uh, Mr. Haymaker."

Rusty had to try extra hard to stifle a snork. "I wrecked on my bike," Rusty said. "This guy helped me." Wincing pitifully, he made use of his bandaged arm to point at June, who held up the repaired bike as further evidence. June looked terrified, which was how anybody who had to face Aunt Beverly for the first time looked.

"Then I thank you, Mr. Haymaker," she said. "Rusty, you'll get inside the house right now. I had to call your mother and she's sick with worry." Rusty turned away from her witchy-woman stare, but June, who didn't know any better, was looking right into it. He started to back away but then stopped and patted Rusty on the shoulder. "Lance here, yeah, he seems like a pretty good kid."

Aunt Beverly said nothing, just increased the voodoo wattage of her stare, and finally June turned away and practically ran across the yard to his pickup, leaving Rusty to face the a-holes of Old House all alone.

BEEP BOP BOOP

Later that night his father showed up, as he always did, looking confused. It was after dinner, and Rusty was locked up in the Tower not eating dessert. His father made a little knock on the door, saying, *Hey Rusty? Got a minute?* as if Rusty had anything else to do, sitting up here in the Tower on his crumbly foam mat while downstairs everyone was having a good time and enjoying the heck out of some Apple Crisp Delight and vanilla ice cream.

Rusty's father stepped into the bedroom, looking around as if he'd never seen it before. His eyes were bloodshot and his shirt wrinkled and when he settled his big behind on the bed something inside it broke with a muffled snap. Home from Nevada only half an hour and already Aunt Beverly had sent him up here to tell Rusty things he'd heard many times before: that his actions were disappointing and not even a tiny bit appropriate, that he was trying everyone's patience and was a bad influence on the other children, and why couldn't he just *behave?*

His father put his hands on his knees and shifted his butt around on the broken bed, but didn't say anything. This was only the third time Rusty could remember being alone with his father. The first was when his father took him to the hospital after he'd fallen out of the back of the pickup and split his head open on the asphalt, and the other time was when they'd had a private talk of a serious nature after Rusty went around telling everybody the joke he'd overheard at a high school basketball game, the one involving two midgets, a banana, and somebody named Dolly Parton.

In fact, the only time his father ever spoke to Rusty was when he was in trouble, like when Rusty had acted dead in the hearse and his father had screamed at him with his eyes bugging out, as if acting dead in a hearse were not a pretty normal thing for a kid to be doing.

And there was also the time, the really bad time, when they told Rusty he was going to be the next lucky contestant in the interfamily exchange program, and that he would be going to live at Old House, with Aunt Beverly and all her a-hole children. The day they came to take him to Old House Rusty ran into the bathroom and held on to the towel bar with his invincible Bruce Lee grip. They tried to pull him away, the bigger boys and then some of the sisters and then Aunt Beverly and Aunt Nola, yelling, *Let go, Rusty, let go! Or you're going to be in some very serious trouble!* and trying to pry his hands free, but nobody could deal with his kung-fu power. The night before, his mother had come to say good night and he told her he didn't want to go to Old House, he hated it there and it wasn't fair, and she stroked his hair and was nice to him, which she did only late at night when nobody else could see, and she told him he wouldn't have to go if he didn't want to, but there she was the next day, right there in the bathroom next to Aunt Beverly, sniffing a little and saying, *Please let go, Rusty, you're making a scene, this is for your own good.* Finally, they called his father, who was at a church meeting, and his father tried for twenty minutes to talk Rusty into letting go of the towel bar and then said, *The heck with this,* and pulled the bar right out of the wall, yanked it out by the screws, and Rusty started screaming and kicking while his father picked him up and put him over his shoulder with Rusty still gripping the towel bar like nobody's business and the brothers and sisters clapping and shouting, *Hooray!* And his father took him over to Old House in his pickup and they locked him up here in the Tower like he was some kind of criminal from olden times, like the Count of Monte Cristo or Hitler.

Now his father didn't look mad at all, just tired. He stared at

Rusty for a long time, moving his lips a little like he was trying to come up with a word he couldn't remember.

"Rusty," Rusty said. "My name's Rusty."

"Rusty. I know that. And I think you know why I'm here, Rusty. Aunt Beverly tells me you've been in all kinds of trouble this week. Can you tell me why you were in the girls' underwear?"

"Because I'm curious?" Rusty said. "Because I'm a normal curious kid?"

"All right. Okay. What I'm having a difficult time with is the report that I got from Aunt Beverly that you were, you know, wearing the underwear. That's what I'm having trouble with."

Rusty shrugged. "Maybe because I have bad underwear and theirs is all nice and everything?" He got up and selected a random pair from the cardboard box he kept his clothes in.

The underwear were stretched out. They were full of holes. They were a color that wasn't even close to white. They were what his teacher at school would call a *highly effective visual aid*. His father stared at him and his underwear and sighed. Obviously, his father didn't understand him one bit. Was it because Rusty was not a human at all, but the last survivor of a race of intergalactic robots who had sent Rusty to earth in the form of a human to find out if it was a good planet for starting up a whole new race of robots that would one day blow up the universe? Possibly. And being an intergalactic robot, Rusty was new to earth ways and customs and that's why he was having trouble communicating with the earthlings, especially the Richards family, who were all a-holes?

"Okay, then," his father said. "Why don't you go ahead and put those away. We'll see about getting you some new undershorts, but you've got to try harder to keep the rules and respect other people's property. Aunt Beverly says—"

"Meep meep," Rusty said, which is robot language for, *Aunt Beverly is not my mom, and this isn't my house, and it isn't fair.*

His father's huge eyebrows went up and he opened his mouth to say something but nothing came out.

"Zzzzt zzzzt," Rusty said, which is robot language for, *I'm lonely and I'm mad and why does everybody hate me?*

"What is this?" his father said. "What are you doing?"

"Beep bop boop," Rusty said, which is robot language for, *please help me, you are the only one who can do it, I want to go home.*

His father had a hard time pulling himself out of the broken bed, but when he walked over to where Rusty was sitting, Rusty thought that maybe he had been able to communicate using simple robot language, that maybe his father would let him go back home, or if not, at least he might pat him on the back or give him a hug and say, *It's okay, Sport, don't worry, things are going to be all right.*

What his father said was, "I just don't know why you have to act so dang weird."

His father left, and Rusty stood behind the closed door, listening to him thump down the stairs and then hit his head on the low ceiling at the landing, which happened every time. Then his father was gone and everything was quiet. Rusty stared at the closed door.

"Meep meep," he said.

10.

.....

A PEEPING TOM

O F COURSE, HE HADN'T VENTURED INTO THE PUSSYCAT MANOR TO check up on Leonard Odlum at all. He'd braved the hookers and the piles of dildos and Miss Alberta for one reason only: hoping to catch a glimpse of the woman he'd been carrying on with for most of the past month. Carrying on? He didn't know how else to describe it. Though there had been only limited physical contact, and he wasn't entirely sure what her name was, it was possible that what they were doing could be described as an affair. *Affair.* The word itself made his tongue go thick in his mouth, his heart surge with a strange voltage.

Whatever they were doing together, he knew one thing: it wasn't right.

It had started innocently, as all affairs, Golden assumed, do. The first time he'd seen her was at Salt Pond, a spring-fed watering hole circled by basalt boulder fields and stands of cattail. Ted Leo had told Golden he wanted to incorporate the pond into the overall plan of the new brothel, call it Lovemakers' Lagoon or Cuddlers' Cove or something equally corny, and string some lights and build a little dock for fishing and canoeing and moonlit orgies, but for now it was still a shallow pond where foxes drank and cows wallowed in the summer.

The pond was where he most often liked to take his walks after a long day of work. He had little interest in spending time with the crew—who generally hung around their motel playing cards or spending all their money at one of the two bars in town—and his own home away from home, a twenty-year-old snail-back Airstream travel trailer parked on a rise a half mile from the construction site, was so small he could not lie in its lumpy berth without bending his knees or stand up in its six-by-eight kitchen without knocking his head. So he walked, usually following the game trails and up around the pond or down into the sandy arroyos until the charcoal twilight came on and clouds of bats emerged from unseen caves and crevices in the earth to take over the sky.

For several days in a row he'd been seeing the same coyote at the pond—bushy with a distinctive rust-colored pelt and a slight limp— and he had taken to leaving it an offering of food on top of the same boulder before going back to his trailer. That first night the coyote went nowhere near the piece of jerky he'd left, keeping a close eye on him as it trotted off into the lowering dusk, but when he came to check the next morning the jerky was gone. Anything could have swiped it, he knew, a bobcat, a fox, an owl, another coyote, but he liked to think it was his special coyote. A few days afterward, when he spotted the coyote making its way along the ridgeline, he left two Slim Jims on the same boulder and retreated to a stand of junipers three or four hundred yards to the south. It took nearly half an hour for the thing, after much sniffing the air and indecisive pacing, to race up, snatch the meat sticks in its jaws, and go streaking across the sage plain toward the test site, occasionally looking back over its shoulder, a definite spring in its step, as if it had gotten away with something.

So on this particular late February day, after a long afternoon of haggling with a pair of shrill, finger-jabbing county inspectors over a misplaced sewer line, he hiked up the shallow rise to the pond, hoping for nothing but some solitary quiet and the possibility of a glimpse of his coyote. Instead of a coyote, what he found was a woman, a small, dark-skinned woman, up to her thighs in the water of the pond. The sun had just gone down and the sky was a murky silver darkening to lavender near the horizon. The air was still and cool and the pond was like a perfect little mirror under the greater mirror of the sky, and the woman stood ten feet from the shore, in the middle of her own reflection.

Golden, a hundred yards away, hunkered next to a boulder furry with orange lichen, could only see her black hair and brown arms, but something about the way she stood, her fingertips brushing the pond's surface, the tilt of her head, made him hold his breath. Though it was a warm day, he imagined how cool the water must have been, the oozing silt of the pond bed covering her feet. He imagined her feet: little brown feet with perfect toes. He embraced the boulder and held it tight.

She moved just out of view and Golden stood, looking side to side like an outlaw, and crept across a field of smaller boulders, hoping for a better look. Anyone seeing him there, burly and furtive in the half-light of dusk, might have been put in mind of a bear lurking at the edge of the watering hole to see what might come to drink.

It seemed she was talking to herself. She shrugged, held her hands out as if to say, *Who knows?* and then turned suddenly to look behind her as if she knew someone was there. He ducked, fell backward on his butt and scuttled in reverse until he was sure he hadn't been spotted. He jogged back to his trailer, feeling as if he were on the brink of something.

Every day after work he took the same walk, loitered nervously behind the same stand of boulders.

She came again a few days later. This time she did not go into the water but stayed at the edge, trying to skip rocks, yelping with pleasure when she succeeded. She wore some kind of traditional white dress with pineapples and bananas stitched onto it with yarn. It was not sandal weather—a cold front had moved in, kicking up a persistent breeze—but here she was in leather sandals, the first day of March, her brown legs exposed. He found the sandals unaccountably alluring. For over twenty years now he'd lived in the Virgin Valley, a place of summer heat and constant sunshine, and had not once in his memory seen an adult woman or man there wear sandals or high heels or clogs—he had never seen so much as a flip-flop. People there, even in the worst heat, wore sensible, blocky shoes or boots that covered up, if there were such things, the comeliness of ankles, the sexuality of toes.

For a moment he indulged in a sour pang of shame. He was spying on a woman, probably a prostitute, and thinking about her *feet*. That she was likely a prostitute, he decided, made her less threatening. She was not someone he would ever find reason to talk to or be around, no one he could feel anything for except a safely distant fascination.

One warm Tuesday evening, the thick clouds suspended over the eastern horizon gone bronze with the disappearance of the sun, he decided to take a walk. There would be no more spying, no more entertaining questionable thoughts about this poor woman's toes. If he happened to see her, he would say hello and move on, an upstanding citizen out for an evening stroll, a man of pure heart and clean mind.

Instead of creeping and ducking as before, he walked casually, openly, around the largest boulder, on which was spray-painted WEED MAKES ME HAPPY, and looked down to find her there, kneeling at the water's edge, the pond purple with dusk. His blood surged and in a panic not to be seen he toppled forward, groaning, on top of a mesquite bush.

Even though he was poked all over by the stickery branches of the bush, he kept still. Her back was to him, and she was hunched forward, pushing and pulling at something in the water. She straightened up and in a single motion peeled the T-shirt she was wearing over her head, revealing a smooth expanse of skin divided by a white bra strap. The bush stabbed him unmercifully along his chest and neck, his bad knee began to throb, but he did not move. Each breath came long and shallow, and his mind did not register a single impulse until the thought came, *No, this is not right*, and that was when he felt a hand rest firmly on his shoulder—a hand that, as far as Golden knew, might have belonged to a vengeful and very unhappy God.

"What we lookin at here 'zactly?" Leonard whispered into his ear.

"Leonard!" Golden said through clenched teeth, craning his neck around.

"Billups said you's wantin' a talk to me. Saw you come out this way, so I followed. When I saw you fall in this bush I thought you'd had some kind of, you know, *fit*, I'd come over here to find you swallowin' your *tongue* or someth— Now *wait* a *second* here." Leonard seized as if he'd swallowed his plug of tobacco. "Is this a nude woman we're looking at?"

"You need to leave right now, Leonard. I'll talk to you tomorrow."

"Damn me and my shitty eyesight!" he cried, trying to blink his eyes into better focus. "There is a nude *lady* down there!"

Golden tried to shush him, but it was too late. The woman had turned around, holding her arms against her chest.

"She see us?" Leonard said. "Does she have nice titties?"

Golden grabbed Leonard just above his skinny elbow, a sudden anger in him that blurred his vision, and squeezed so hard that Leonard opened his mouth wide in grimace, his silver fillings flashing.

"Watch the spit cup!" Leonard cried.

"Go on now!" Golden said with false cheer, as if talking to a child.

"All right, damn!" Leonard shook his arm loose and rubbed it tenderly. He stood slowly, backing up, and waved in the direction of the woman by the pond.

"Hello there, ma'am!" he called. "We're just out here mindin' our own business!"

Golden stood too, made a halfhearted wave, and began to shuffle down the hill toward the other side of the pond. "Out for a walk!" he called. "Didn't mean to startle you." He was looking intently at his own feet, but out of the corner of his eye could see the woman grabbing the shirt to cover her chest and then straightening up as if she might run. She looked so frightened he felt compelled to say something.

"I was just, ah, walking, out for a walk," he said, pointing up the hill from where he'd come. "I didn't know anybody'd be here. Please don't be scared."

Using one hand to hold her shirt against her chest, she used her other to scoop up a pile of wet clothes at her feet, but when she turned to step off the rock several items peeled off and fell in the water.

"Ay!" she cried, stomped her foot once, and let the rest of the clothes drop at her feet.

"Can I help you?" Golden said, moving cautiously forward, his palms out, to show her he meant her no harm. "I'm sorry for scaring you."

She looked him in the eye for the first time, and he was close enough to see her broad Indian face and small, flat nose, her full lips. She was short—at least an inch or two under five feet—and sturdily built, her skin a swirling of brown shades, as if her pigment had not been properly mixed. He slowly, nonchalantly covered his overbite with his hand—from her angle his front teeth must have hung over her like a store awning.

She turned her back to him and quickly pulled her T-shirt back on. He automatically cast his eyes downward and noticed a pink brick of soap at the edge of the rock, and ribbons of suds separating on the surface of the water, and it finally occurred to him that she was not here to bathe, as he'd first thought, but to wash clothes.

When she turned around and gave him another hard look, he said, "My name is Golden Richards. I'm a nice man."

To show her just how nice he was, he stepped out into the pond, the water up to his calves, to retrieve an article of clothing that was threatening to float away. It turned out to be a bra, a beige, industrial-sized thing with heavy-duty straps and half a dozen hook-and-eye fasteners—the kind of bra worn by grizzled triage nurses in war zones. He held it up for a moment, at a loss, and solemnly handed it over.

Something moved at the base of the boulder field and he looked over the woman's shoulder to see Leonard hiding behind a mesquite bush. He was grinning like a maniac and giving Golden the thumbs-up.

Despite Leonard's poor eyesight, he must have seen the hot glare

Golden directed his way; spit cup held high, he immediately jumped up and began tiptoeing up the path in the exaggerated pantomime of a burglar.

Golden turned his attention back to the woman, who, luckily, had not noticed Leonard but was fixated on Golden's feet. His size-sixteen work boots, full of water and covered in gray muck, were leaking all over the ground like two foundered oil tankers. He shifted in them and they made a rather lewd noise: *squitt.*

"My shoes," he said. "They're wet."

She looked up at him and her face seemed to open wide for a moment, her nostrils flared, and she laughed.

That laugh. It made his skin tingle with heat, gave him the taste of something sweet in his mouth. It was an easy laugh, high-pitched and musical, a sound people would pay to hear.

He helped her collect the rest of her clothes and, with nothing left to do or say, gave her an awkward version of a military salute and staggered up the slope toward the boulders, the sound of his wet boots heard long after his lumbering form had melted away into the dim landscape: *squitt, squitt, squitt, squitt.*

THE ONE MIGHTY AND STRONG

He had been caught spying on a strange woman and had attempted to redeem himself by handling her personal underthings. Any way he looked at it, it was a relationship that should have ended before it started. And yet, there they were, the next evening, trading shy waves from a distance, and the next, wandering along parallel game trails that meandered through the creosote and rabbit brush, as if it were a normal thing for the two of them, in all this limitless space, to come across each other time and again.

Twice he'd stopped and tried to make conversation, asking how her day was going, what she thought of the rain last night, but she wouldn't look him in the face, much less speak to him. He tried out his limited Spanish, which seemed to get her attention, and after a complicated Tarzan-Jane routine she finally spoke a word: Weela. Her name: Weela. Or that's what Golden deduced, anyway. It felt like he'd won a prize to get this much out of her. The moment she said it she seemed to blush and quickly turned to walk back in the direction she'd come.

At night, locked in the coffin of his little trailer, he would say it aloud, and the sound of it—*Weeeeeeeela*—panged him with pleasure and dread.

He did everything he could to stop what was happening. He quit going to the pond every day, tried not to plan his day around her—he certainly had more important things to think about—but the fact was that thinking about her was a luxury, a bliss. It pushed all the important things out of his mind, made him, for a few minutes out of every hour, happily distracted.

It was true: he'd had about all he could stand of important things. He was tired of the big decisions required of him every day, the momentous, life-altering occasions that happened, in this family, at least once a week: the baptisms and birthdays and anniversaries and graduations and band recitals and church plays and 4-H shows. He didn't want to hear about whose junior league basketball game he'd forgotten, or what parent-teacher conference had been missed. He didn't want to see another overdue utility bill or tax notice, didn't want to take any more phone calls regarding feuding wives or love-sick teenage daughters or biblical plagues of chicken pox or pinkeye or flu that were always lurking just out of sight, waiting to bring the family to its knees. More than anything, he was at his limit with the strain of keeping the entire enterprise a secret. For eight months he'd told his wives and everyone at church that he was building a senior citizens' center out in Nevada—a senior citizens' center!—and every time he went back home, he was sure the word had gotten out, the jig was up, he'd been discovered; for the last six months he'd come home every week, stepping delicately, head bowed, waiting for the hammer to come down.

And it wasn't as if his job—building a brothel on the edge of nowhere for a man prone to ugly temper tantrums and bouts of hysterical grandstanding—was doing anything to reduce his anxiety. Ted Leo had hired him, Golden found out after his bid was accepted, because Ted knew his father back when Ted was an army corporal stationed at the Nevada Test Site and Royal Richards was a minor Las Vegas celebrity, the humble uranium miner from Louisiana who'd struck it big. Though Ted had characterized the relationship as a friendship, it became clear to Golden, as time went on, that Ted resented Royal for his unearned fortune and renown, and was now, almost thirty years later—with Royal dead of a brain tumor and Ted still very much on this side of the grave and living what he called his "great God-given American dream"—taking it out on Royal's son, who wanted nothing to do with any of it.

At first Ted was friendly in his loud, despotic way, but it wasn't long before he'd show up at Golden's work trailer in a screaming, hair-tearing rage over why the septic tank was being put where the swimming pool was supposed be (Ted had not mentioned a swimming pool until that moment) or berate Golden over the phone for twenty minutes about the price of copper pipe. He was fond of calling Golden a "big old pussy" or a "horse's ass" and had once taken his most prized possession—a German Luger he claimed to have been owned by Al Capone—from its special drawer in his office desk and brandished it all over the work site, apparently because he wasn't happy with the way one of the framing crew had taken the Lord's name in vain. He would yell and carry on, demean Golden in every conceivable way, and then return ten minutes later and, as if none of it had ever happened, regale Golden with tales of spiritually fulfilling days as a Christian missionary in Guatemala, or invite him out for an afternoon of male bonding in the form of carp fishing.

Though Golden outweighed him by seventy pounds and was fifteen years his junior, Ted was not at all averse to giving Golden the occasional shove, ripping blueprints or building specs out of his hands, or jabbing his finger into the big man's chest as if trying to draw

blood. It didn't matter if incidents like these happened in private or
in front of an entire framing crew, Golden did what he always did
when someone pushed or elbowed or attempted to punch him (all of
which seemed to happen with disturbing regularity, ever since he was
a boy): he smiled politely and removed himself from harm's way, as if
in apology for the offense of being at once large and sweet-natured.

All of it—Ted Leo and the job itself and the stress of keeping it a
secret and the pressure of supporting a family, the very size and com-
plexity of which he could no longer fully encompass in his head—
all of it was bearing on him with such an inexorable weight that the
notion occurred to him, once or twice each day, that he might be losing his mind.

Which was why, back in Virgin, he had stopped Uncle Chick
after sacrament meeting on a Sunday afternoon, asked him if he had
a moment.

"I got moments, but fewer every day," Uncle Chick said. "Let me
help the girls get Dad loaded up and on his way and then I'll be with
you."

They decided to go for a drive, and Uncle Chick eased up to the
hearse, touching the hood with both hands. He gave the roof of the
car a smart slap. "You want me to take the wheel?"

Golden chuckled, as he had the last dozen times Uncle Chick had
made the same joke. Over the past couple of years Uncle Chick's eyesight had been going steadily downhill due to a degenerative eye condition that made him legally blind. He wore spectacles with smoked
lenses that helped a little, and got by the rest of the way on touch,
memory, and sheer cussedness.

They took the old state highway that followed the Virgin River,
the sun so high in the sky it seemed to be invisible, a wall of dust
kicked up by rising low-pressure winds, purple and solid, toward the
west. Cooter, who had been penned up in the back of the hearse during the three-hour service, sat between them, vibrating with nervous
energy and occasionally attempting a trial lick at one of Uncle Chick's
nicked and battered hands.

"Don't know why you'd keep a dog in your vehicle," Uncle Chick said. "Smells like a pig's lunch in here."

He rolled down the window and stuck his nose out, the moving air lifting his stiff, Brylcreemed hair like a lid. "There, now I can think a little. Aside from the gassy dog, I'm glad we can talk. You haven't been around much."

"Work," Golden said. "It's bad."

Uncle Chick nodded approvingly. "Course it's bad. It always is." Uncle Chick preached a single philosophy that guided his own life and the congregation he was responsible for: *Whenever you have to choose between the easy way and the hard, choose the hard, and things will end up all right*. It was a simple but surprisingly effective way to live, Golden had discovered, but it didn't allow for a whole lot of sympathy or brotherly compassion. Things are going terribly for you? Well, great, congratulations: you must be on the right track.

"I got something I been meaning to talk to you about," Uncle Chick said. "Maybe you seen it coming, but it's time I brought it up. Maureen Sinkfoyle."

Golden couldn't help it: he groaned and let go of the steering wheel to grind his knuckles into his eyes. He *had* seen it coming, had taken the time and initiative to worry about it, but then six dozen other worries had crowded his mind and he'd promptly forgotten about it. Maureen, a buxom and not-unattractive woman with a voice that sounded like tearing sheet metal, was one of the ex-wives of the now-notorious Richard Sinkfoyle, who eight months ago had abandoned his three wives and twelve children to take up with some sort of new age fortune-teller he'd met on one of his sales trips to California. The other two wives, both younger and still of childbearing age, had married into other families, but Maureen, who had two teenage boys, both of whom were certified vandals and hell-raisers, lived in a trailer out by Cut Creek, surviving on welfare and the good graces of the Church. As one of a handful of faithful, middle-aged priesthood holders with anything close to financial security in these difficult economic times, Golden knew he was a leading candidate to take in Maureen and her boys. Maureen herself had been making her case in her own subtle ways over the last few months. She had dropped off gifts of sheet cake and canned peaches at Old House, was known to be spending a lot of time with Nola and Rose at the hair academy—surely in an effort to secure tactical allies for her cause—and had occasionally engaged in what was, by Church standards, blatant flirting: significant looks in sacrament meetings, occasional phone calls to his office, asking for help with her hinky furnace or a priesthood blessing for one of her accident-prone boys. In short, he should have been anticipating this; he should have had a defense ready.

"Has Beverly talked to you about it?" Golden said. He did have a single line of defense, and it was a good one. Beverly did not like Maureen, did not like the way she displayed her large bust with snug-fitting dresses, did not think highly of the way she, the matriarch of the family, hadn't so much as put up a fight to keep her husband from running off with a ditzy blond twenty-five-year-old slut. Beverly had arranged Golden's marriage to Nola—and by extension to Rose—and more or less forced him to marry Trish. So her vote was the one that truly counted, in marriage and just about everything else.

Uncle Chick snorted. "No, she hasn't said a word about it to me. It's not up to her. It's up to you and nobody else."

"It's never been up to me," Golden said, unable to hide the resentment in his voice. "Not since the day I got here."

Uncle Chick seemed to accept this mild rebuke. He nodded, his milky gaze fixed on some point out the passenger window where a cloud of blackbirds lifted off a stand of Russian olives. "All right. You're correct. And it shouldn't be up to you. It's up to God, when it comes down to it, every time. God ain't going to wait forever on this, and neither is Maureen. She's a good woman who knows a good man when she sees one."

"Don't forget she married Richard," Golden said.

"Yes, she did, poor thing. We all thought pretty highly of that damned fool, too, until he gave us all sorts a reasons to think otherwise."

Brother Sinkfoyle would be forever reviled in the Church because he'd done the unthinkable: he'd taken the easy way out. And what did he have to show for it? A cute blonde at his side, a life of peace and quiet in the carefree California sunshine. It was hard for Golden not to feel jealous.

"Anyway, forget about that jackass and take this one to the Lord. Difficult times we're in, I know. But somebody's got to step up, and I'm getting too old."

Golden looked over at Uncle Chick, who was busy working a handkerchief out of his vest pocket. The old man gave off an aroma of leather and horse liniment, mingled with a minty old-fashioned cologne that he referred to as "dog water." It was a smell that had never changed in the twenty-plus years Golden had known him, and now that Uncle Chick's eyes were failing and arthritis was twisting his fingers into swollen hooks, Golden had to face the idea that Chick might not be around forever. Ever since his own father had died, had up and run out on him one final time, Uncle Chick had been there to offer advice and encouragement, to take an interest in Golden in a way his father never had. He watched the old man honk lustily into his handkerchief and felt his throat tighten with anticipatory grief.

Uncle Chick put his hand on Golden's shoulder and gave it a gentle shake. His voice was soft and rough. "I know what you've suffered these past few years, how hard your losses have been on you. But there comes a time when you have to move forward, to take care of what you got."

His losses. These he didn't talk about, not with his wives, not with Uncle Chick. He knew there was something in him that needed to talk them out, but he didn't have the necessary vocabulary, much less the courage. So he set his jaw and stared out the windshield until the building silence required Uncle Chick to speak.

"We're all waiting on you, that's all. I'd do anything for you, any of us would."

Not yet ready to speak, Golden acknowledged this with a nod. His eyes had gotten a little moist, which was not helping matters.

He knew he was a disappointment to Uncle Chick, and to just about everyone else who knew him, for that matter. It had not always been this way. There had been a time when he was widely considered a success: a prosperous businessman, a good husband and provider, a pillar of the church. Now it was clear to Golden—as it was, no doubt, to a good many others—that this had all been a mirage, an illusion fabricated, in part, by Beverly, who managed the family and its everyday affairs with the exactitude and logistical expertise of a field marshal, and by his own father, who had left Golden a profitable business as well as a small inheritance to get him through the lean times, and by Uncle Chick himself, who, after Royal's death, took Golden under his wing, installed him, at the green age of thirty-four, into the Council of the Twelve as one of the apostles of the church.

For a time, there were even whispers among some of the members that Golden Richards was the One Mighty and Strong, the man who, according to scriptural prophecy, was to be delivered from on high to set in order the house of God. The polygamists of the Virgin Valley, along with Mormon fundamentalists of all stripes, had been waiting a long time for the One Mighty and Strong. At the turn of the century the official Mormon church had bowed to political pressure and renounced the sacred and fundamental practice of plural marriage, and yet had inexplicably prospered, spreading to all the nations of the world and producing famous politicians and athletes—not to mention the charming and toothy Donny and Marie—while the hardscrabble little fundamentalist groups were reviled by their neighbors, scorned by the larger public, and so harassed by law enforcement that many had taken refuge in Canada and Mexico. Still, they waited in the shadows, building their compounds so far out in the desert no one could find them, meeting in garages and barns and basements, safeguarding the only thing of worth they owned: their pearl of great price, the Principle, which would one day transform the world and bring about the Second Coming of Christ.

These were a people who had every reason to hope for a champion, someone who could redeem their suffering and deliver them from bondage. And for the polygamists of the Virgin Valley, it seemed that Golden Richards just might be the one.

It did not hurt at all that he was a craggy six-foot-six, blond and blue-eyed, and named *Golden*. Nobody was expecting the One Mighty and Strong to be a short and pudgy fellow by the name of Irv.

Golden had an especially good recollection of the day, nearly ten years ago, that established him as an official candidate for the office of divine emancipator. It was a snowy Sunday just before Christmas, and in the middle of the afternoon sacrament service a green Buick Skylark pulled up outside the church, revving its engine. A man wearing a well-oiled pompadour and white undershirt got out of the passenger side and began to stalk the periphery of the small church house, barking out biblical nonsense and clapping his chest with great force, like an irate gorilla.

The congregation murmured and Uncle Chick stopped his sermon to have a look out the window. He stepped back from the pulpit, spoke in a low voice to the prophet, and then motioned all the apostles in attendance—only six on that day—to the back room.

"Well, we knew he'd show up sooner than later, and here he is," Uncle Chick said.

Golden, always a little behind and trying to catch up, said, "Who is it?"

"Ervil LeBaron," said Apostle Barrett, peering out the window. "Look at him. Nutty as they come. And I think that's his brother driving."

Golden had heard the name. The LeBarons were an infamous bunch: violent, scheming, and backward, they gave their fellow polygamists a bad name, which was saying something. When they weren't attacking or killing their enemies, who included the Mexican and American governments, the Mormon church, other polygamist clans, and pretty much anyone else who declined to bow before their claims of divine and absolute authority, they were attacking and killing each other. Ervil would eventually become the most notorious LeBaron of all for sending one of his wives—chosen because she was

the prettiest of the lot—to murder an influential and beloved polygamist leader in Salt Lake City.

"He's been making the rounds, trying to get everybody to pledge
obedience to him and his people," said Apostle Coombs, loosening his
tie. "Up to Manti, Jonas Silber told me, they had to run him off with
shotguns. Anybody got a shotgun?"

"No, no shotguns," said Uncle Chick. "That's the last thing we
need."

Outside, Ervil LeBaron was barking out scriptural condemnations
at an astonishing rate, calling the folks watching from the windows a
perverse and stiff-necked people, going on at length about abomina-
tions and whoredoms and bilious cankers on the holy church of God.
He was getting hoarse, and a little impatient, if the tone of his voice
was any indication.

"Got my thirty-ought-six in my Chevy," said Apostle Throckmorten. "Might take me a minute to find some shells, though."

"Am I talking to myself here?" asked Uncle Chick. "No shooting.
My cripes. He's not carrying a firearm. He's a bully, here to intimidate. So we'll just send him on his way."

He turned to Golden, gave him a long measuring look, seemed to
settle on something. "I got an axe handle in the back of my Ford out
front. I want you to go get it and invite this gentleman to peddle his
papers elsewhere."

Golden blinked. "Axe handle?"

"Right, nice hickory one, up front by the hay bale."

Was this a joke? Golden registered the mood of his fellow apostles, who appeared to have about as much confidence in this plan as
he did. He said, "*Me?*"

"There's that movie where that southern deputy fella goes around
beating up the hillbilly riffraff with a axe handle," offered Apostle
Lambson, nodding. "Worked pretty good for him."

"You're a servant of God, remember that," said Uncle Chick. "Pay
attention, let the Spirit guide you. Now go. We've got a service to finish up."

Like a bride left at the altar, Golden walked the center aisle alone, head bowed, every eye in the congregation following his progress. He made it a point not to let his gaze wander to the left, where his wives and children sat. Outside, the air was cold, sharp. He went to Uncle Chick's pickup, found the axe handle. New snow, frozen overnight, crackled under each step. Ervil LeBaron fell quiet as Golden approached. He stretched out his arms as if waiting for the big man to walk into them.

"Every knee shall bow!" he barked hoarsely, his face a deep, chapped red, his eyes shining with wonder at the truth and power of his perceptions. "And every tongue confess!"

"Please, you need to go," Golden said, stepping forward. He had to concentrate to hold the man's gaze and could barely hear himself over the thump of blood in his ears. "We're trying to have our services here."

Ervil LeBaron moved a half step back but continued to carry on with his nonsense. He pulled a large sheaf of parchment paper from his jeans pocket, claiming he was not leaving until everyone within the sound of his voice put their name to it. Golden stood in the snow, bewildered, waiting for a prompting from the Holy Spirit, some guiding voice that would tell him what to do. But the only thing he could hear was Ervil LeBaron popping himself on the chest and shouting about everlasting burnings and the blood of the lamb.

He knew one thing: he could not hit this man. Intimidated by his own size, he had always kept himself from everything but the mildest gestures; right now he doubted he could so much as raise the axe handle in a threatening manner. While he reviewed his options, trying not to think about the crowd watching from the church windows, his gaze fell on the car, which had obviously been well cared-for. Even though it was several years old, it had been freshly painted a glittering, medieval green, and appointed with swirling white pinstripes along the fenders and door panels. The engine rumbled and the brake lights blinked on and off. Golden ducked his head to get a look at the smirking driver, who was obviously impatient to be on his way.

This was a man, he thought, who didn't want to get involved. This was a man happy to let his brother do the dirty work while he waited safely behind the wheel. Golden stared for a few seconds at the throbbing passenger-side brake light and then, with a quick, almost surreptitious motion, gave it a slight chop with the axe handle. The glass housing broke with a tinkling crunch, leaving a mosaic of bright red shards in the snow.

Golden had to admit: that had felt pretty good. The thought occurred to him that maybe he could do this.

"My car!" shouted the driver. "He hit my car!"

Ervil LeBaron fell quiet. Golden stepped up to address the remaining brake light and by the time the driver understood what was happening it was too late. He'd just gotten it into gear, the tires starting to spin, when Golden took a swing like somebody who knew his way around a baseball bat, and nearly separated the whole assembly from the body of the car.

The driver screamed as if he himself were being bodily assaulted. The car started forward with Golden close behind. Ervil LeBaron had grabbed his arm by this time, hanging on like a man trying to board a moving trolley and shouting some decidedly unbiblical phrases into his ear, but Golden was not going to be denied: he wanted to know what it would feel like to put a nice clean dent in the lid of the car's trunk, and it turned out to feel very, very good.

The car spurted forward and then slowed, the driver giving his brother one last chance to jump in before abandoning him once and for all. Ervil, it appeared, had a choice: he could accept the humiliation of retreat or be left here in the cold with a whole congregation of extremely unsympathetic people and one unpredictable giant and his axe handle. He chose retreat, but as the car roared off, he hung on to the still-open door, bellowing for all to hear that, like the Son of Man in the fullness of times, he would be back.

When Golden entered the chapel after replacing the axe handle where he'd found it, there was no cheering—these were not the kind of people who cheered—but there was a burbling of excitement well

beyond the great good luck of having a drab church meeting interrupted by an episode involving cursing, violence, and a hot rod car.
There was the collective feeling that *something*—and everyone would
have their ideas about exactly what—had just happened. Some felt
merely grateful they had been able to stand up for themselves against
the forces of evil, others that a defining blow had been struck for
righteousness and truth, and there were the few who would suggest
that they had all witnessed a transforming moment, like Moses' slay-
ing of the Egyptian slave master, that would betoken the rise of a new
prophet who would bring about the liberation of God's chosen on the
earth.

This was nearly ten years earlier, which was more than enough
time for everybody to get over their disappointment; Golden was
not the One Mighty and Strong—any fool could see that now—and
what occurred on that December day had no special value except as
an anecdote to be repeated and occasionally reenacted for the amuse-
ment of children and strangers. Even so, it had been a high point
in Golden's life—he'd traded for several years on the goodwill that
single episode had earned him—and everything since had felt like a
bumpy downhill slide.

Now, in the hearse next to Uncle Chick, he dug at his eyes with
the pad of his thumb and did what he always did when faced with
evidence of his failures: he apologized. This habit, of continually
expressing regret and asking forgiveness, had been irritating his wives
for years, so much so that Nola had started calling him, in a Pepe Le
Pew–style French accent, *Monsieur Pardonnez-moi*.

"I'm sorry," Golden said. "For everything."

"Stop that," Uncle Chick said, back to his gruff self. "You got
nothing to be sorry for. Now, what are we really here to talk about?"

"I've got something to tell you," Golden said. "Something I should
have told you some time ago."

Uncle Chick rolled down the window, spat. He said, "This a
confession?"

"Something like that."

"Well good. I'm glad someone in this group of ours has actually committed a sin worth mentioning. I was worried everybody'd turned perfect while I wasn't paying attention."

"All right then." Golden said. "I guess I'm real embarrassed by this, that I didn't come to you with it in the first place—"

Uncle Chick held up one crooked finger and shook his head. "Now. I've got pork roast and potatoes waiting for me at home. And Jell-O, the particular kind I like, with the whipped topping mixed in. So if you please."

"Sorry, I'm sorry." Golden bit the inside of his cheek, gritted his teeth. "You know the project I've been working on . . ."

"The old folks' home."

"I'm not building an old folks' home, Chick. That's what I'm trying to say. I'm building something else."

"The cathouse."

After a moment of mild shock, Golden allowed himself a smile; he was surprised only by the fact that he was not in the least surprised. "How long have you known?"

"Long enough, you dummy. I was hoping you'd fill me in on something I didn't know about. That would've been something. Now how 'bout we turn this rig around. I'm hungry."

"You're the only one who knows?"

"My dad, course. Barrett. Bill knows. He's the one found out. Half of us are in construction, Gold, my cripes, word gets around. I've sworn them boys to secrecy. They won't talk about it, not if they're smart."

"So you don't think it's a problem?"

Uncle Chick turned, seemed to fix Golden with a hard look through the smoked lenses. "Oh, it's a problem. Your Beverly finds out, it's a real serious problem. For you and me both. Anybody else in the church finds out, why, it's a problem. Your church status has been slipping lately—you've been missing your share of meetings, which I can tell you Nels Jensen isn't shy about pointing out. I wish you was putting up a hospital for kindhearted old widows and orphaned kitty-cats, but I know what it's like. I don't like that you went off and did this thing alone—it ain't like you, but I respect it. You've got a family to take care of. This church relies on you. You want me to tell you God's with you on this one? Can't do it, but I don't know that it matters. No turning back now anyhow. Times are bad wherever you decide to look. We do what we have to."

We do what we have to. Those words should have offered him comfort, lifted his burden, but he felt nothing except the same tension that locked up his insides, ruined his ability to concentrate or feel. True: he had taken the job because he had no choice. His contractor's business was barely paying the bills, rents were down on his units, and without a big job like the PussyCat Manor—the biggest single job he'd ever worked on—he'd be filing for bankruptcy before the year was out. Yes, he was risking his church status, his good name, maybe his everlasting soul on behalf of his family, but there was something else, something that could not be rationalized or explained away: he was doing it to escape. To get away four or five days out of every week from feuding wives and the ever-circling mob of little ones, from the jealousies and long-term resentments, from church meetings, from the dentist bills that arrived with horrifying regularity, from the darkness that fell on his heart whenever he walked through the halls of one of his homes, looking in on the children tangled in their bedsheets, thinking, *Whatever happens, I am responsible. They all rely on me.*

For going on three years now, he'd had difficulty sleeping, pitching fitfully in whichever bed he'd found himself on that particular night, until there was nothing left for him to do but wander the house—a jumble of angles and corners to hurt himself on—checking and rechecking the children, staring out of windows, pervaded with a nameless dread. And when he was finally able to drift off, usually laid out on a couch or propped up in a rocking chair, it was with the knowledge that he would be up before dawn, feeling nothing of his old appetites for the bright hours of the day, for the surprises his overcrowded life had come to provide.

Being away and alone seemed the only solution. So he'd jumped at the chance to work on location in Nevada, where he enjoyed the freedom to eat all the beef jerky and canned food he desired, to spend his off hours alone wandering the desert or confined in a travel trailer that smelled like the inside of a lunch box. He had not found the peace and perspective he'd hoped for, but more of the same strangling anxiousness, the unnerving nighttime quiet, and the knowledge he had made a mistake. This sense of desolation was not part of his life in Virgin, but part of *him*; he would take it with him wherever he might go.

Had he the courage or the words, he would have explained all this to Uncle Chick. He would have told him that the only thing that gave him a moment's peace was not the comforting touch of his faithful wives, or the sweet sight of his children come to meet him at the door, or his faith in his God. It was the thought of a woman—a dark-skinned stranger, probably a whore, with round calves and wide feet, whose image pulsed brightly and often in the foggy reaches of his mind.

"I don't like lying to my girls," Golden said.

"It's a miserable thing."

"I'm thinking I should quit the project. I know several people who'd be willing to take over . . ."

"Let's don't go that far."

"I'm all twisted up with it. I don't know what to do anymore."

"You'll finish that job," the old man said, something new and hard entering his voice, "and you won't complain about it or speak of it again. There's hard things we have to do in this life. We bite our lip and do 'em. And we pray to God to help us along the way."

Golden slowed the pickup down along the shoulder, gravel pinging on the oil pan, and swung it back around toward town. "You don't think I should go ahead and tell Beverly about the whole deal, just get it over with?"

"Don't be a dummy," Uncle Chick said. "You do that, and you'll deserve everything you get. We don't need to say another word about it, except this: be careful. You know what I'm talking about. Get away from your family too long, the church, you forget who you are, what's important."

"I'll be careful," Golden said. "I always am."

ON SALT POND

Despite his best intentions to commit himself to God and family, to get through this construction project without conceding another thought to Weela and her fascinating calves, the following Tuesday there he was at Salt Pond after work, innocent as a child, throwing a ball around with his dog.

He'd brought Cooter along even though recent experience had proven it to be a bad idea. Cooter didn't like being cooped up in the trailer or in the cab of the pickup (left outside he would quickly become lunch for an enterprising coyote), he was terrified of the loud machinery, and fast became lonely for the dozens of children who, at any one moment out of the day, vied for his attention. Bored and homesick, he would sulk for the remainder of the work week like a teenager on a family trip to the Smithsonian.

But Golden decided Cooter was exactly what he needed: a distraction, a chaperon, a sidekick, a reminder of who he was and what his commitments were. When Weela didn't show up that evening he went home feeling just a little virtuous, as if he'd passed some sort of test, as if he'd been saved from temptation by virtue of his good intentions alone. But the next day, he sat on his favorite boulder, sulking. The sun was going down, and the shadows of the peaks moved incrementally up the rocky slopes, filling the wide basin like water in a bathtub. A fever of disappointment had come over him; he'd been waiting an hour and a half and there'd been no sign of her.

If only he could figure out his attraction to this woman, he decided, maybe he could liberate himself from it. But the more he thought about it, the more convinced he became that freedom itself was to blame; for the first time in his life he had been left to his own devices, free from the restrictions of church and family, free to do and think and choose as he saw fit. Ever since he was a boy all his choices had been made for him, and now that they had been given a little latitude, where had his questionable instincts led him? To a dark-skinned prostitute with a strange name who liked to wash her clothes in a pond.

To clear his head he picked up a chunk of rhyolite, hucked it over the pond. It would be dark soon. She had not missed him in his absence, who was he kidding, she had no interest in him at all, she was just being polite to the big goofy guy who'd horned in on her private oasis in the desert. He ought to go home, he decided. He ought to go home and never come back.

That's when he saw the top of her head moving over the sagebrush. She wore a red handkerchief that in the last angle of light glowed like a hot coal. He waved his arms. Much too loudly he cried, "Weeeela!" and ducked his head, wincing; he sounded like a kid on a Tilt-A-Wirl.

He clambered down and waited for her, trying not to look pleased. As usual, she did not look directly at him, but stood a few feet away—out of wariness or simple propriety, he couldn't tell—looking out into the distances, occasionally sending a glance his way. Cooter, who had been making his rounds, peeing on as many bushes as possible, trotted up with his ball.

"This is my dog," Golden said. "Cooter."

She squatted and received Cooter with one hand under his chin and the other stroking his side. Immediately he twisted onto his back and offered his belly for rubbing, a lascivious look on his face, his eyes bulging, his tongue hanging out, his hind legs spread wide. Golden was hoping maybe Cooter would draw some words out of her, but she only murmured low nonsense noises and gave Cooter such a thorough rubbing that one of his legs pumped like a piston as he groaned in ecstasy.

To put an end to this embarrassing display, Golden took the ball—a gray mass of wet dirt and hair that at one time may have been

used for a game of tennis—from Cooter's mouth and tossed it high
in the air. The ball bounced twice before caroming off a rock into the
pond. Cooter, who an hour ago had given up a game of fetch after
two or three throws because he'd decided there were better things
to do, now raced to retrieve the ball, kicking up dust as he went. To
Golden's surprise he leapt into the water, stretching for air like a Lab-
rador. Cooter hated water, cried pitifully through his weekly baths,
but the show-off in him had taken over; he paddled out toward the
ball, woofing and kicking like he knew exactly what he was doing.

He made it to the ball without difficulty, but could not seem to get
his mouth around it. He pushed it forward with his nose, snapped
at it, kicked harder, eyes bulging with effort. Weela and Golden
laughed together—he knew it had been a good idea to bring Cooter
along! But then the dog began to tire. He had lost interest in the ball
and now seemed to be paddling in place, the tip of his tail sinking out
of sight until there was nothing but eyes and a snout.

Golden ran to the water's edge, made a frantic attempt to pull off
one of his boots, failed, and splashed out into the shallows. With a
reluctant groan he launched his long body out into the water. At first
he slid forward almost gracefully, like a great fish returned to its element, but then his momentum stalled, his boots filled with water, and
he began to sink. He did not know how to swim, made evident by
the way he slappped at the pond's surface with his palms and choked
on the water that flowed easily into his open mouth as if it were a
bathtub drain. He did his best to churn his legs, all the while casting his arms about in the hopes of locating Cooter, or anything else
to hold on to, but there was only water and more water, bubbling
up everywhere, pushing its way up his nose and down his throat.
He felt something on top of him, a tug at his collar, and instinctively
twisted his body and grabbed handfuls of cloth and hair. As he did so
his boots touched the bottom of the pond and he pushed up with all
he had. He broke the surface almost immediately and, after coughing out a mouthful of dank pond water, was amazed to find himself
standing in the soft muck of the pond's bottom, the water just cover-

ing his shoulders, and Weela clinging to his back, one hand with a firm grip on his collar. She had tried to save him and if the pond had been deeper than five and a half feet he would have certainly dragged her down with him.

He pulled her around to his front and they held on to each other, coughing and gasping. He wasn't sure if he was a coward or a hero. She grasped him tightly around the neck with both arms as if to hold him up, to make sure he didn't try to dive back in.

"Thank you!" he shouted, his ears plugged with water. "I'm sorry! I don't think I know how to swim!" And coughed some more.

Cooter, who had somehow made it to the other side, pulled himself onto the gravelly shore and with a thin wheeze flopped on his side. Golden hardly noticed. He asked Weela if she was okay and she made a noise—he wasn't sure if it was a laugh or a sob—and pressed her cheek against his. Even in the cold water, he could feel the heat of her, could feel every part of her body that touched his: her thigh clamped with a rigid strength around the top of his hips, her breasts against his chest, her cheek against his, her breath hot on his ear.

Golden started forward, tried to walk them out of the pond, but found that his feet were firmly planted in the clayey silt, which was just as well. He was happy to stay right here, wet and cold in the insistent embrace of this strange woman. He asked her again if she was all right; he wanted a response from her, he didn't care if it was in English or Italian or Martian, he wanted to hear words, warm and moist, come out of the lips grazing his ear.

Cooter wheezed out a bark and they both turned to look. He was on his feet now, dripping and quivering, half covered in mud, his bloodshot eyes blinking furiously, his fur slicked down over his bony frame, whining at the ball still bobbing just out of reach.

Weela put her face back against his, her mouth next to his ear. This small gesture of intimacy flooded him with a tingling warmth, a sense of events trembling in the balance. He could feel her lips as she opened her mouth to speak.

She said, "That is a very ugly dog."

11.

. . . . .

ADVANCED LOVEMAKING TECHNIQUES FOR THE REST OF US

ONIGHT TRISH PACED AT THE FRONT WINDOW IN NOTHING BUT A towel, her razor-nicked ankles smarting with every step. Even though she'd showered twice, scrubbed and soaped herself silly both times, the lingering odor of Night Passion perfume trailed her around the room. It was now nine—two hours after Golden had promised he'd be home—and the darkness outside had consumed everything but the lit windows of the houses across the street. Inside, her elaborate dinner of jerked pork and sweet potatoes sat hardening on the kitchen table. Faye had fallen asleep in the back room and the house was so quiet it hummed.

Early this morning she had been awakened by the familiar pain deep within her abdomen that told her she was ovulating—a series of hard cramps followed by a sensation like a token dropping into a slot. As a teenager she'd gone to her mother, who not only told her what it was, but gave it a name: *Mittelschmerz*, a German word meaning "middle pain." It was such a ridiculous-sounding word, Trish used to say it over and over again in the midst of her cramps—*Mittelschmerz! Mittelschmerz! Mittelschmerz!* (using an exaggerated German accent, of course)—as a way to distract herself from the pain.

But there was nothing to distract her from the situation she found herself in now: showered, lotioned, and perfumed to within an inch of her life, the owner of a body as ready and willing as it would ever be— and no man in sight. She kept telling herself that she was being absurd, that she should get herself dressed, that waiting around wantonly in an undersized towel was an obvious and tired tactic if there ever was one. But she couldn't deny the truth: she was out of fresh ideas, out of patience, nearly out of hope. She and Golden had made love only twice since Jack died, and she was beginning to believe that if it didn't happen tonight they might never make anything together again.

Two weeks ago, after the dust-up over Beverly's old couch, Golden had come home as happy and loose as she'd seen him in months, and she was sure it would be their night. Wearing a dress she'd cut and sewn herself and the slippery lip gloss of a teenager, she massaged his shoulders while he ate a few leftovers from the fridge. They chatted for a while, he made polite inquiries about Faye and her schoolwork, she stroked his neck and ears suggestively a few times, and after he put away three bowls of ice cream he went out to his pickup to get his overnight bag. When he didn't come back after five minutes she went out to find the driver's door open and Golden slumped facedown on the vinyl bench seat, which he apparently found quite comfortable. In the yellow glow of the cab light, his fingers wrapped around the handle of his bag, he slept, innocent as a babe. She came this close to taking the bag from his hand and clouting him over the back of the head with it. She woke him and, staggering under his weight, guided him inside the house to the bathroom, where she helped him brush his teeth, scrubbing his big chompers with an angry sawing motion until he begged for mercy through a mouthful of foam. She dragged him to the bed, yanked off his boots, peeled his clothes from his body as if in preparation for emergency surgery . . . but by then he was gone, a huge loaf of dead weight sinking into the mattress, smacking his lips and snoring even before she could get to his socks. She dumped a comforter over his head and went out onto the porch to cry.

Tonight she would show him no such mercy. Already she had spent two hours tucked into what amounted to a hand towel, occasionally wetting her hair so it would look like she had emerged steaming fresh from the shower. She had shaved her legs and, because she was five years out of practice, had lost a few bits of ankle flesh in the process. But it didn't matter. Her calves were smooth and buttery, her hair damp and fragrant, and if all else failed, she had her backup: waiting innocently in the bed table drawer, a twenty-pack of Wrigley's Spearmint gum.

After coming home from the hair academy, she had read her pilfered *Cosmopolitan* cover to cover between peeling potatoes and revacuuming the rugs. It was the hyper-peppy article called "Advanced Lovemaking Techniques for the Rest of Us" that received more of her attention than any other. Under the subheading "Oral Fixations" it read:

Many women are understandably apprehensive about striking out on their first oral adventure. Some are worried about the taste or smell, others are nervous about doing it "the right way." So for all you nervous nellies and old pros alike, here's a tip: keep it minty fresh! Before your lovemaking session, just pop in a cough drop, some Tic Tacs, or your favorite brand of mint gum, and you'll give your man a cool, tingling sensation that will leave him begging for more. You'll not only have fresh, minty breath, but a grateful partner forever in your debt!

Despite her extended detour on the worldly byways of Reno, Trish had very little experience with Advanced Lovemaking Techniques; Billy had always been the traditional, three-frantic-minutes-in-the-pitch-dark sort of man, and Golden, sweet Golden—she'd made love with Golden only enough to know that he was entirely too gentle (worried that he was going to smother or otherwise damage her with his unmanageable bulk) and liked to be kept up to speed on her comfort and pleasure ("Okay? Ah? Right? There?"). Sex was one thing she and the other wives never spoke of, and though she knew there was very little in the way of advanced lovemaking going on with them or with other members of the church (the unspoken law was that sex was meant for procreation and nothing but), she couldn't help but wonder.

The life of a plural wife, she'd found, was a life lived under constant comparison, a life spent wondering. Sitting across from her sister-wives at Sunday dinner, the platters and serving dishes floating past like hovercraft, the questions were almost inescapable: Who of us is the most happy? Which of us is his one true love? Who does he desire most? Who does he open himself up to in the middle of the night? And the one that, lately, crossed her mind most often: Am I the only one he won't have sex with?

To her sister-wives, she knew, she was the new one, the young one, the pretty one (if only they'd seen her in her makeup days!), the free-and-easy one. But beneath the jokes about her movie-starlet bone structure and carefree days ran a cross-current of deep pity. That *look* in their eyes sometimes, they might as well have said it out loud: *Poor Trish, cursed and lonely Trish, banished to her sad little duplex on the other side of the valley. Trish the afterthought. Trish the fifth wheel.*

She was sick of their pity, sick of waiting, sick of sorrow, sick of standing here half nude at the window, vulnerable with wanting. Her hand had cramped from holding the corners of the towel tight against her chest, and it felt good to let go, to stand naked before the entire darkened world. The cold coming off the glass of the window hardened her nipples and made the skin on her arms and shoulders prickle with goose pimples. *I don't give a damn if anybody sees me*, she thought, and not two seconds later a pair of headlights swung around the corner, coming directly at her. She yelped, dropped to the carpet and crawled across the hallway to the safety of the bathroom.

She heard the sound of tires on gravel, the creak of the pickup's door. Frantic, she stuck her head under the shower, gave it a blast of freezing water, and dug around under the sink for the only other available towel, a beach towel that bore a colorful life-sized likeness of Bozo the Clown.

She came dripping and shivering out into the hall and found Golden at the front door with his overnight bag, holding the screen door open, hesitant, as if reluctant to tread on the carpeting. He looked like he might have spent the last few weeks as the subject of a sleep-deprivation experiment: hair tangled and mashed to one side, face pallid and drawn, eyeballs so swollen and bloodshot they looked on the verge of bursting.

The sight of him made her temporarily lose her resolve. "Oh honey, are you tired?"

"Me?" he said. "Oh no, no." He seemed to concentrate intently for a moment, shaking his head as if to ward it off, but it came anyway: a great, cracking yawn that temporarily rearranged his face. Finally, he stepped inside and pressed his cheek against hers, delivering the smallest of electric shocks, and kissed her clumsily on the ear. She felt the crackling rasp of his whiskers, his large hands on her back, and she held him against her in a clutch that lasted several beats too long.

"You're wet," he said, standing back, a damp spot on the front of his shirt.

"Just got out of the shower," she explained. "I wanted to be . . . clean."

He looked from her face down to her body, and she was sure he was taking note of her barely covered breasts, the statements being made by her naked shoulders and smooth thighs.

"Hey, all right!" He nodded, grinning tiredly. "Bozo the Clown!"

She bit her lip, resisted the urge to make some childish remark along the lines of, *Takes one to know one.* She led him through the kitchen, and once she'd ascertained that he needed no dinner, conversation, or shower of his own, she pulled him toward the bedroom. He went happily, eagerly, and with a sigh toppled stiffly and slowly onto the bed like the oldest tree in the forest.

Quickly, she turned off the lamp; the thing she was about to attempt, she was sure, should happen only in the dark.

She helped him off with his shirt and lay beside him, her face close to his, until he kissed her: a chaste kiss, a closemouthed kiss, but a half-naked bedroom kiss nonetheless. She let her mouth linger on his, and he gave in, moving his lips and tilting his head for a better angle. Emboldened, she kissed his neck and chest, making her way down across the smooth plain of his belly, abandoning her towel as she went. The length and breadth of him seemed edgeless. The room was as dark as a cavern and she could hear his every breath, every rustle of fabric, every watery thump her heart made against the bones of her chest. She felt desirable, capable of anything.

She unbuckled his belt, fumbled for a moment with button and zipper, positioned her hands, and then, with the sudden, sure motion of a magician yanking a tablecloth out from under an elaborate dinner setting, pulled down his underwear and pants, all the way to the ankles, shackling him. He made a small surprised noise in the back of his throat and was quiet again.

In the pitch-black she groped for the bedside table, but it was out of reach. She stretched across the bed, opened the drawer and fished around blindly until she came up with the packet of gum. With her other hand, she found Golden's thigh, rubbed it so lightly and sensuously that she touched hair but no skin. She kept this up, one leg and then the other, though the package of gum was giving her trouble. She tried to open it one-handed, went at it with her teeth, gnawing at the smooth, hopelessly impenetrable paper, all the while trying to keep Golden reassured with her stroking fingers, and it became like a juggling act she couldn't quite manage. She gasped in frustration, strangled the packet of gum with one hand and clawed at it with the other, puncturing the paper with her nails, ripping and biting, until she fumbled two pieces out of their foil wrappers and into her mouth. To her ears it sounded as if she had just torn open a giant Christmas present in the dark.

"Trish?" Golden inquired. "You okay?"

"Um, yesh," she said, her mouth packed with gum now, and groped to locate him on the bed once again. Gnashing fiercely, trying to break the wad of gum down to a manageable size, she bought time by slow-massaging his chest and arms with the heels of her hands. She discovered that simultaneously chewing gum and giving a sensual massage in the dark required a form of advanced muscle coordination she had apparently been born without; she ended up kneading the skin of his chest and ribs with the same quick rhythm of her gum-chewing so that he began to gasp like he was being held down and tickled.

"Hey—" he said, and tried to roll over, but she was on top of him, pinning him in place, trying to find a way to position her mouth near his crotch, chewing, chewing, chewing that damn gum, desperately trying to move her hands against him with some sort of erotic intent, kissing his breastbone and belly, moving down down down, raising her head for an instant to gather herself and then plunging back in, skimming her face along the smooth skin of his lower abdomen until her lips found and touched him *there*, and he jerked sideways in surprise, his hipbone butting her jaw and knocking the gum out of her mouth.

"Oh!" he cried. "I'm sorry, I didn't mean . . ."

"No," she said, "it's okay, shush, lie back down."

"Okay," he said. "Yes. I will."

Letting out a small wail of distress, she cast around on the bedspread for the lost wad of gum, and when she couldn't come up with it, set herself again to her task. But as she touched his body again, found it tense and rigid, heard the hard pulse of his breathing, she knew she couldn't go on. As much as she wanted him, as much as she loved him, as much as she wanted to have another child with him, a child that would forever connect her to him and to his, she would not lower herself to this. She would not terrorize him any more.

She got up, stumbled down the hall, and locked herself in the bathroom. She heard the coils of the mattress creak as he stood up and the reverberating *whump* of his large body hitting the floor, tripped up by the pants around his ankles. He recovered quickly, groaning and leaning for balance against the walls.

The bathroom doorknob rattled. "Trish?" he said.

She told him she wasn't feeling well, to go back to bed.

"Is there something wrong? Let me in and we'll talk."

"Just a little stomach thing, I'll be fine. Please leave me alone now."

He waited at the door for ten minutes, occasionally calling her name. She wanted to open the door to him, to fall into his arms and be carried back to the bedroom, where they would make slow, tender love, but some bit of pride, left over from who knows where, prevented her. She ignored him until finally he went plodding back to the bedroom, the carpeted floor squeaking under each step.

She waited in the dark bathroom, her mind blank, until there was no more sound, not even of the bed complaining under Golden's nearly three hundred pounds. She opened the door and walked through her compact house, her eyes wide, as if new rooms might miraculously present themselves. When finally she slid into bed next to her husband—asleep, of course, sputtering, whistling through his nose—he stirred, rolled over, and rested his hand on her hip.

She waited, poised for a change in his breathing, for him to move closer, to press his body against hers, but his breathing slowed and he began to snore. His hand was warm and heavy, and though it wasn't much, she knew she was going to have to learn to accept what she was given, no matter how small.

12.

·····

DRIVING LESSONS

WHEN GOLDEN RICHARDS WAS NINETEEN AND BY EVERY MEASURE STILL a boy—one who built model battleships and took a glass of warm milk every night before bed—he made the first real decision of his life: he abandoned his mother. That was how he would always think of it: a betrayal, a defection, an escape. One May morning he woke up before dawn and snuck away, limping across the town square in the muggy dark, with nothing but a knapsack of clean underwear and a plane ticket to Las Vegas.

Upon his arrival, he did not receive the hero's welcome he had expected. A small, dour Mexican man met him at the airport with a cardboard sign that read ROYAL SON and drove him, without a word, to the house in Utah, where he waited two days for his father to return from a business trip. The Mexican man's wife, a cheerfully fat woman named Tita, fixed his meals and cleaned up after him, and he did little but sleep and wake occasionally to stumble around the house and its grounds, his eyes raw and full of grit, trying to acclimate himself to the dry air, the alien landscape, the constant blast of light.

The house was like nothing Golden had ever seen: a red-brick Victorian with steep gables, mullioned windows, blond limestone detailing and a three-story turret that looked like it had been transplanted from the castle of an Austrian duke. The house was more museum than domicile, filled with booty from Royal's desert expeditions: giant glittering geodes, moqui marbles, amethyst cathedrals and back-lit fluorescent minerals lined up along oak shelves. Early-man spearheads and Fremont rawhide shields, meteorites and Anasazi baskets filled with beads. A beaver skull half encrusted with rose quartz. The jawbone of a megalodon. And the pièce de résistance: the calcified femur of a *Tyrannosaurus rex* weighing half a ton and displayed on a giant table carved from yellow sandstone embossed with fossils of whiskered prehistoric fish.

If the interior of the house confused him, he could make even less sense of what lay outside: a huge, blank sky hovering over a landscape of wild chockablock colors: flat-topped mesas of black basalt, the white, crosshatched elephant hide of Navajo sandstone, ocher cliffs streaked with desert varnish, distant trembling blue mountains covered with pygmy forests of piñon and juniper, the gypsum-rich hills, candy-striped red and yellow and orange.

After a few expeditions into the backyard and over to the river, which at this time of year was a silver ribbon cutting a channel through a bed of crimson sand, he admitted to himself that this place scared him. He preferred to stay inside and, when he wasn't asleep, positioned at the window way up in the tower where he could see everything, watching and waiting—this feeling of clenched expectation so familiar he almost welcomed it—for his father to come home.

When Royal arrived, he did so piloting a shiny new car. It was the morning of Golden's third day out West, the sun edging over the eastern cliffs, drawing long shadows that moved like living things across the knurled landscape. From his window, Royal watched his father get out of the car and stand next to the lilac hedge that flanked the gravel driveway.

"Where is he?" Royal shouted at the house. "Where's my Goldy?"

Golden didn't move. He was almost nauseous with the confusion and uncertainty of what he had done, of this sudden turn his life had made.

Besides the gray cowboy hat tipped back on his head, his father looked, from this distance, like the person who had left him ten years before: a short man who made himself large with a sharp, flashing smile, every word accompanied by dramatic gestures of arms, hips and head.

"Hey!" he cried, moving toward the house. "Wake up! Goldy! Look what I brung!"

When they met on the front porch his father took a step back and laughed. "Whoa, hold on now, lookit here. Make way for the Jolly Green Giant."

It was the kind of thing one of the bullies at school might have said.

"Come on," Royal said, his arms held wide. "Come on now, right here."

Golden went to his father, bent down to embrace him. He smelled his cologne—something sharp and musky—could feel the pleasant rasp of his whiskers against his own soft cheek, and decided that even though it wasn't the reunion he'd planned or hoped for, it was good enough.

This sudden wash of satisfaction caused him to squeeze too hard and he felt the air go out of his father with a wheeze, and then came a faint popping sound. His father fell away from him, clutching his side. Doubled over, he coughed and raised his head, wincing.

"*Hoooh*," he said, blowing out his cheeks. "Hah. Guess you could say I deserved that."

From his shirt pocket he took a ring with a key on it and tossed it into Golden's chest. "See that car? It's yours. Just drove it in from St. George. Let's go see what she can do."

It was a beautiful thing, a black 1956 Ford Thunderbird with portholes in its white detachable hardtop. Golden slid in behind the wheel and held the key up to his face as if the tiny letters engraved on it might offer some instruction. He turned to his father in the passenger seat, who was still gently palpating his ribs. He said, "I don't know how to drive."

"How now?" Royal said.

Golden knew the key was to be inserted into a hole or slot somewhere within arm's reach but he couldn't locate a likely spot.

"You're telling me you're eighteen, a southern boy, and you don't know how to get it down the road?"

"Nineteen," Golden said. "I'm nineteen."

"Okay then, right," Royal said. "Yep. I get it. I get it now. Son don't know how to drive because Daddy's not around to instruct him. See? Even a fool like me will come around eventually. Well, let's do it, then. That key, it goes in the ignition. There on the steering column. No, other side. Now the clutch. Right there on your left. Push down. With your foot, goddamn it. Now give the key a turn."

The starter whinnied and screeched, and after Golden negotiated what amounted to a seven-point turn in order to get the car out of the driveway, they lurched out into the road, gears grinding, engine revving frightfully, new tires chirping with every touch of the brakes. Royal was a terrible teacher and Golden a worse student; the father's instructions started out as firm suggestions that turned quickly to mild cursing and then to shouts of "No, oh no goddamn no!" when the car swerved off the road and nearly took out a couple of boys waiting for the school bus. The son, so big he looked like a teenager stuffed into a child's pedal car, rode the brake and grew damp with sweat, flinching and jerking the steering wheel every time his father called, "New gear, new gear!"

Eventually, the road straightened out and Golden managed to keep the car from drifting off it. Royal took advantage of this lull to fill Golden in on the things his letters had left out. "You know how I got rich and famous and all that, but I didn't write what happened afterwards, I didn't want to upset your mama." He told Golden that after he'd made his fortune he'd carried on a life of such base sin and debauchery he couldn't bring himself to talk about it in the light of day. "Let's just say I was a hot-blooded man with too much money living in Las Vegas and leave it at that," he said, staring out the passenger window with what might have been a touch of wistfulness, as if his past life continued on in some parallel trajectory beyond the clouds. After two solid years of drinking and women and not much else, he'd hit bottom, and that's when Uncle Chick found him drunk and bloodied and stumbling along the crumbling margins of High-way 89 after losing control of his prized 1949 Vincent Black Light-ning and running off the road into a thicket. "It was God's doing, see, I was wandering in the desert, literally and, you know, otherwise, and Uncle Chick saved me. Good Samaritan, et cetera. Brought me home where I belonged."

Golden risked a glance at his father, who was staring at him intently, and he realized that besides the deep creases in his tanned neck and the thinning hair of his temples, there *was* something differ-ent about him: he had a look in his eye. A spark, a glint that gave him the aspect of someone moved by forces beyond his control.

After Golden pulled the car back toward the center line—it was like it was *trying* to run itself into a ditch—Royal went on, explain-ing how he'd accepted God's call, how he'd read the Book of Mor-mon ("sorta like the Bible, only with more sword fights"), and eventually become baptized and dedicated to the plan of salvation, which included the holy covenant of plural marriage, the only means by which man might ascend to the highest levels of the Celestial Kingdom.

Even though Royal's letters had mentioned finding God and becoming a new man, it was still disconcerting to hear his father, a person who'd always considered God a nuisance and killjoy, talk-ing like this. But Golden wasn't listening very closely, anyway; his focus was on keeping the car between the white and yellow lines. He found this was easiest to do by keeping it in second gear and holding a steady rate of speed of fourteen miles per hour.

When the road turned from asphalt to chalky red dirt, Royal, increasingly annoyed at his giant son's skittishness, had Golden turn the car around.

"Now," he said suddenly, "tell me about your mama, how she's doing and all that."

"She's fine," Golden said. He thought of her sitting at the kitchen table, completely alone now, that ashen, lost look on her face, and he wanted to cry.

Royal didn't press for any details, just nodded, pointed out a hawk at the edge of the road, peeling the coat off a roadkill jackrabbit. Like somebody asking a neighbor how their weekend had gone, Royal said, "And how 'bout you? How you been?"

Golden looked at himself in the rearview mirror. He was sitting in a spectacular new car with his rich and reformed daddy at his side, the sun coming up to expose the wild beauty of a place he once believed existed only in books and magazines, and yet he felt unaccountably sad, gripped with a desolation he could barely comprehend. He turned away from his father and with his voice breaking said, "I haven't had much of a life so far, Daddy."

His father was silent for a few moments, which Golden was grateful for. Then he said, "Well come on, you big fucking crybaby, Jesus, stop feeling sorry for yourself why don't you, you're on your way up."

Golden only nodded at this rebuke, though he felt something pulse through him, an urge to take his cramping hands off the wheel and give his father a violent shake. For some reason, this made him think of something his father had said a few minutes earlier.

"What's plural marriage?"

"Now there's a good question," Royal said. "Don't be afraid to ask more when you feel like it. It means marrying more than one wife. That's what men in the church are expected to do. And by the way, sorry for the cursing. That's one of the hooks the devil's still got in me."

"You have other wives?" Golden said, his focus diverted from his oversized right foot, allowing it to weigh on the accelerator. "Besides Mama?"

Royal laughed. "No, not till the church thinks I'm ready, and your mama has to give a divorce, which she's not being altogether cooperative about. I haven't told her about all this church business, so this is between you and me, understand."

The engine was revving again, pulling the car forward with an almost animal impatience.

Royal pointed to the house coming up on the left. "This'll be our stop. Might want to slow her down a little."

Distracted, and still a little fuzzy on the finer points of turning, Golden yanked the wheel hard without so much as touching the brake pedal. The Thunderbird skidded sideways across the gravel driveway and Golden overcorrected, sending the car over a shallow berm and into the lilac hedge. There was the painful shrieking of branches against the car's windows and new paint job, and a throng of sparrows lifted off in a single chittering cloud. The engine died and Golden looked blankly at the windshield, which showed a tangle of flattened leaves, while Royal gently investigated his nose with both hands.

"Well," Royal said, "that'll have to be the end of that."

"Why do they want you to marry more than one wife?" Golden said, still gripping the steering wheel as if the car might decide on its own to start up and take off again at any second. A cloud of dust from the driveway had rolled in through the open windows and stung his eyes. "Why would God want somebody to do that?"

"Ah son," Royal said, eyeing the spot of blood he had wiped from his nostril, "it's *complicated*. Most folks think it's about sex, but that ain't it at all. If a man wants sex, well, I don't have to be the one to tell you there's easier ways to do it than *marrying* someone. God wants us to live the Principle, mostly because it's a hard thing to do and it makes us better for it. And one other thing. This world is full of righteous women, good-hearted women, am I right? But how many good men? Righteous men? Just about none. Couple here and there, maybe. The numbers are outta whack, and that shouldn't mean all the good women out there should have to settle for a bad man. It's basic arithmetic is all it is. "

Golden thought again of his mother, saw in his mind the image of her that defined his childhood: tucked between the wall and kitchen table, gray-faced in her faded housedress, staring into space, paralyzed with bitterness and loss. Was she simply a good woman who settled for a bad man? Was she nothing more than a victim of arithmetic?

He looked at his father, who stared meaningfully back, his scorching violet eyes lit with a mysterious voltage.

"So . . ." Golden hesitated. "You're one of the *good* men?"

A smile spread across his daddy's face. He said, "I am now."

ALL IS WELL

The Virgin Valley: two crumbling volcanic ridges between which a series of small, no-account towns hugged the river, each with its single Mormon chapel and scattering of pioneer homes and failing businesses surrounded by alfalfa fields and orchards of peach and apricot, the entire valley crisscrossed with barbed wire separating neighbor from neighbor, herd from herd, irrigated farmland from giant dusty squares of unwatered ground. To the west the Pine Mountains floating blue and cold in the distance, and to the east the fanged and scalloped horizon of the Vermillion Peaks, shifting color and shape with the motion of sun and clouds.

Golden, drinking water by the gallon and rubbing his sun-stung eyes, worked up and down the valley, framing, rough masonry, ditch work, you name it—anything that required a strong back and no skill. He lived in his daddy's house, worked for his daddy's construction company, but saw very little of him; Royal was a busy man. Having burned through most of his uranium profits during his Las Vegas years, he used what was left to buy real estate all over the valley and to start up Big Indian Construction, named after his first uranium claim. He worked all day negotiating contracts and submitting bids, and in the evenings would attend something called School of the Prophets, where the male hierarchy of the church would meet to discuss doctrine, read scripture and debate vital matters such as the exact date of the Second Coming and whose responsibility it was to pump out the church house's outdoor toilet. Even though Royal had been baptized only a year, he had been ordained a member of the Melchizedek priesthood and, once he began taking wives, would be called to the Council of the Twelve, an order of apostles of which there were currently a grand total of nine.

The only thing Royal and Golden did together, besides an occasional meal and attending church, was bomb-watching. Every few weeks before dawn they would drive up to Royal's favorite overlook on Egyptian Butte and wait for the great white-green flash to expose in an instant the whole broken desert plain, horizon to horizon. Once the mushroom cloud had gone up, lit from within by extraterrestrial fires, Royal would give his head a slow shake, overcome. "Oh look at her," he'd say, his voice moist with reverence, as if looking into the sweet face of a long-awaited newborn. "Isn't she a *beaut*."

At his own expense, Royal had gutted and renovated the sixty-year-old sandstone church where the group's meetings were held, and his tithing amounted to more than that of all the other members put together. Unlike the valley's Mormons who peopled the towns along the river, the members of the Living Church of God, who mostly lived on farms and compounds at the eastern edge of the valley, did not hold positions of power, sat on no boards or councils, had nothing but their little church on the hill and each other. They were generally poor, hardscrabble, and suspicious of outsiders of any stripe—so suspicious there was wide consensus among them that Royal was a spy from the government, somebody sent by Hoover to take notes, write names, and call down an FBI raid that would send the men to prison and the women and children into the care of Social Services. But with Uncle Chick's assurances, and Royal's easy southern manners and open wallet, the people came to believe he was exactly what Uncle Chick said he was: an angel, of sorts, sent from on high. There even began a whispering that this strange little man with the bright eyes might be the One Mighty and Strong, come to redeem them all.

Which left Golden at a loss to explain his own presence. Who was

the giant with the sunburn, and what did he want? He was obviously
no government agent—too big to blend in, with the openmouthed
expression of an idiot—and nothing about him suggested he had
been sent by a higher power; truly, there was something more disturbing than suspicious about a six-foot-six man whose pants were
too short. Shoulders hunched apologetically, strangled by the checkerboard polyester tie his father knotted for him, he would sit in the
back of the chapel those first few Sundays with the latecomers and
crying babies, and do his best to make sense of Uncle Chick's sermons, which seemed to be dedicated to a single central theme: that
this world, and most of the people in it, were all going to hell in a very
large handbasket.

In late July, Golden helped his father and some of the other men
erect an old canvas circus tent on the grass field next to the church.
Uncle Chick had bought it from a bankrupt Hungarian circus that
had washed up in St. George, and while it wasn't exactly the holy tab-
ernacle of Old Testament times, it served well enough as the main
meetinghouse for a few months while the renovations were under
way. Now, on Pioneer Day, which celebrated the arrival of the first
Mormon pioneers to the Salt Lake Valley, it would serve to shelter a
congregation of double the usual 150: family and friends come from
afar to help celebrate, and some of the independent polygamists who
lived in the surrounding country: families who lived by their own
theologies and rules, but who liked to escape their desert compounds
and socialize once in a while.

The circus tent was not an ideal venue for a spiritual meeting; it
was almost unbearably stuffy and smelled of moldy hay and ancient
elephant farts. The canvas walls, which bore the ink-stamped name
of the manufacturer—*Sarasota Tent and Sail*—every ten feet, were
mildewed and stained, the fiber ropes frayed and untrustworthy, and
in the smallest breeze the whole thing flapped and creaked like a sail-
boat gone to seed. But on this particular summer Saturday evening,
filled to bursting with freshly scrubbed worshipers and lit up with the
low sun like a giant Chinese lantern, it seemed almost too exotic and

far-fetched a place for the dour fundamentalist proceedings about to take place under its roof.

A low plywood dais had been built, upon which sat the solemn elders of the church and rat-faced Sister Pectol, who played her portable organ with a funereal air. Golden could see the top of his father's head just behind the row of apostles; he was there to attend to the Prophet, who sat in the place of honor just to the right of the pulpit in his old-fashioned oak and leather wheelchair. The Prophet, an old man made mostly of thin skin and sharp bones, was recovering from what would be the first of many strokes. By grumbling out one side of his mouth he communicated the will of God through his son, Uncle Chick, who had reluctantly taken over leadership of the church, even though the keys of priesthood authority and mantle of true leadership would not be passed down until the Prophet's death.

When the Prophet drooled, Golden's father was on the job to tidy up his chin with a white handkerchief folded into a square.

Uncle Chick gave the signal and the organ fell silent. A prayer was offered and Uncle Chick stood, not behind the pulpit as was his normal practice, but next to it, as if to show he had nothing to hide. He cleared his throat violently, *"Hargh-arrhmgh!"* and in his gruff way welcomed all present and began reciting scripture in a gravelly monotone that sent Golden's mind immediately to wandering. He looked at his hands, pleasantly callused and nicked from the shingling work he'd been doing all month, and at his tanned arms and the new aluminum Timex watch he'd bought with his earnings, and his thoughts turned to Sylvia Anderson, the chubby seventeen-year-old with braided blond hair and a wet, red mouth who was the talk of the church for her open refusal to marry Brother Billet, a grease monkey and part-owner of Virgin Tire and Automotive.

Sylvia Anderson had walked up to Golden after church last Sunday and asked him if he'd give her a ride in his new car. Thinking she had a destination in mind—maybe her family had left for home without her—he asked where she wanted to go. She shrugged and licked her lips in a way that commanded Golden's full attention.

"How about San Diego?" she said. "You get some of your dad's money and we'll drive all the way to California, maybe go to the beach."

Golden sneezed and nodded agreeably, but found himself unable to form words or even sounds; he just nodded and smiled with his lips pursed—*Don't let her see your overbite!*—until Sylvia finally turned to leave. Only after she'd gone out the back door of the church was he able to call out after her, "Well, I guess I'd have to get my license first!"

The humiliation of that moment did not stop him from fantasizing all week about the road trip to San Diego and the possibilities it presented, the potential sleeping arrangements in motel rooms, maybe a little motel-pool skinny-dipping, who could say? He liked to imagine Sylvia in the motel shower innocently asking Golden if he might bring her a towel, and the curving form of her body readily apparent behind the semitransparent curtain . . .

"*Argh-argh-harrghk. . . ahgrrrrrhk!*" Uncle Chick fell into an apocalyptic coughing fit only to surface suddenly and rap the pulpit in a way that dislodged Golden from his reverie. "Who do you think you are?" he called in a near-shout, and at first Golden thought Uncle Chick was speaking directly to him, had divined not only that Golden was an interloper, a faithless imposter who had no business in this place, but also that he had been entertaining questionable thoughts about innocent girls taking showers while all around the Lord's servants worshiped and prayed. "Have you looked into your own heart? Have you asked yourself: *Am I worthy?* Have you asked yourself: *Am I blameless before God?*"

Maybe Golden had missed something, because this seemed like an altogether different Uncle Chick than the one who started the meeting. Uncle Chick, an old doghole miner and part-time scrubland rancher who'd spent some wild years in the navy before coming back into the fold, had never been much of an orator, but tonight he was actually rocking the pulpit, speaking in cadences vaguely Shakespearean, looking down into the audience as if measuring the faith and conviction of each member in turn, including Golden, who tried to hide behind the bobbing gray-haired head of Sister Comruddy. Uncle Chick declared what all in the audience already knew: that these were the last days, that the Second Coming of the Lord was fast upon us, and when it happened, would we be ready?

Then Uncle Chick paused, shifting gears a little, and in a hushed voice began to tell of those they had gathered to celebrate: the pioneers who had sacrificed everything to leave their comfortable lives in Albany and Liverpool and Oslo, who sold all their belongings to cross the vast plains in wagons and handcarts in search of a place where they could practice their religion without fear of torment or persecution; men, women and children who had suffered and died, who *had* given their lives for the gospel that we, today, took for granted. He told of thirst and disease and women dying in childbirth in the back of jouncing wagons; he told of shallow graves dug next to rutted trails and of starving handcart companies forced to boil and eat their own shoe leather; he told the story of his own great-grandmother, whose youngest boy—nicknamed Penny for his bright brown eyes—died of pneumonia one blizzarding January day in eastern Wyoming, and the terrible howling and snarling, late that night, as wolves dug up the small body and tore it to pieces, the grieved mother in the meager protection of her covered wagon tearing batting out of a quilt and stuffing it in her ears to ward off the sound.

Uncle Chick went still, and in the sudden quiet there were a few sniffles, a stifled sob.

"And what about us?" he demanded, so loudly and suddenly that a child in the front whimpered. "What have *we* sacrificed? What have *we* given? Nothing, that's what. We complain about our lot. We gripe. Ah, it's so darn hard, we say, to live this gospel, to bear the burden of the Principle. Well, when you begin to feel sorry for yourself, remember those good saints, hundreds, thousands of them died for you. Died for me. Died for us all. Gave up their lives, just like Christ in Gethsemane, blood coming from His every pore with the agony of the sins of this world, my sins, your sins, each and every one, the agony of a million sins worse than any death could ever be."

Uncle Chick glanced at Sister Pectol, who began to play "My Saviour's Love." And the congregation sang uncertainly, with quavering voices,

He took my sins and sorrows,
He made them His very own;
He bore the burden to Calvary,
And suffered and died alone.

There is something wrong with him; Golden tries to sing, but his throat has gone dry and his chest hurts, he can hardly breathe. His head throbs and a strange prickling sensation runs up his legs and hovers at the back of his neck.

Nearly every Sunday of his childhood he had spent hunkered down next to his mother at meetings like this one, with this same talk of hell and damnation, of the sin and sorrow of this life, and even though he'd occasionally felt the urge to stand up and wave his arms over his head like a nutcase and offer his soul up to Jesus, somehow he'd managed to resist what Reverend Peete had called the promptings of the Spirit; he'd decided church was just another opportunity for his mother to flaunt her misery before the world. He realizes that since coming here she has crossed his mind less and less; he has left her behind with barely a passing thought. But tonight, sitting among this throng of strangers in their starched homemade dresses and ostentatious neckties, some of them dabbing furtively at their eyes, some tearing up outright, Golden feels a portion of his mother's misery, feels her shoulder shaking next to his as she weeps for her own barren life, hears her singing this very hymn as she has a hundred times, and suddenly, his eyes brimming with his own tears, he has a vision of her death, lonely and desperate in some empty room, and though he can't know it at the time, he is at least partly prescient: five and a half years from now in the middle of a hard January freeze, Dr. Darkly will call with the news that his mother, having suffered lately from some vague medical maladies, has passed away, quietly, in her sleep. There will be no funeral, no service of any kind, according to his mother's wishes. But he will fly back to Louisiana to do his filial duty, which will entail little more than paying his last respects at the crematorium in Lafayette and hauling his mother's meager possessions to the local Goodwill. He will spend the next two days comforting a bereft Dr. Darkly and wandering around Bernice in a misty winter rain, trying to connect to something, to some meaningful sorrow, to translate his own history in a way that will make it possible for him to cry for his mother's passing, but he won't find what he is looking for and will board the plane feeling nothing but relief.

No, he will not cry after his mother's death, but he does now, he is a confused boy shamed at his recent betrayal, so sorry for the happiness he could not give her, for the worthless bits and scraps that make up his pitiful existence, his every weakness and sin, and by the time the hymn is over, he knows too—don't ask him how—that his father will die soon, will leave him again for good, and now he begins to weep in earnest.

Golden cannot hear Uncle Chick speaking anymore. The sun has gone down behind the distant mountains and left behind only shadow, everything cast in shades of charcoal, and Uncle Chick goes on with his tales of death and sadness until a few children begin to whimper and even some of the apostles, men who'd rather run naked down Main Street than cry in public, sniffle and rub their eyes.

Though Golden's weeping is contained, it seems to him there are gusts of fouled air escaping his mouth and nose, sludge water leaking from his eyes, and only when it is all gone, when he is spent and emptied out enough to be allowed a single thought, does he understand that he is a changed person; his old self, that tattered, shitty thing he never knew he so much despised, has been tossed aside. Now Uncle Chick is finishing his testimony, affirming his faith in the gospel, in the saving Principle they hold so dear, and just before he finishes he smiles, as if apologizing for all the dramatics, and says, "Remember, brothers and sisters, God loves you," and Golden knows it is true.

Uncle Chick lets go one last series of hacking coughs and, without missing a beat, comes up for air to remind everyone of the Pioneer Day Dance and Family Social to be held directly after the meeting. "Sister Maxine's made her famous brownies, the kind with walnuts in 'em. And we'll brew us up a kettle of homemade root beer."

Sister Pectol hits the opening chords to "Come, Come, Ye Saints," the official church anthem, a hymn sung at every funeral, sacrament meeting, and family gathering, and in showers and gardens all over the Virgin Valley. Though Golden has already heard it enough to last a lifetime, he has never really listened to the words, sung as if by the pioneers themselves trudging their way through the ordeal of their cross-continental trek and keeping hope alive with nothing but their faith and this song.

The congregation stands, relieved that their own ordeal is over, and sings:

> *And should we die, before our journey's through;*
> *Happy day! All is well!*
> *We then are free, from toil and sorrow too;*
> *With the just we shall dwell!*
> *But if our lives are spared again*
> *To see the saints their rest obtain;*
> *Oh, how we'll make this chorus swell—*
> *All is well! All is well!*

Afterward, they stand together in the dry grass under a fully colored sky, a few bright planets showing themselves overhead, shaking hands and chatting quietly, the mothers calling for the children to stay close. At the refreshment table Golden steps aside to let the ones behind him pass, filled with affection for all of them, for the smelly old farmers and their red-cheeked sons and daughters and hard-faced women, and for his grinning father, who hams it up a little as he wheels the prophet between rocks and gopher holes, and for the God who has touched him tonight, who has given him new life.

13.

THE DUPLEX

*I*n this house there is silence: dust on the curtains, the smell of stale sunshine, a hush in the rooms like a suspension of breath. Mother #4 gets up from the dining room table and goes into the kitchen for no reason she can think of, maybe to hear the chatter of her shoes on the pine floor. She turns on the tap, shuts it off, pulls out a chair, and sits. She checks the rooster clock on the wall—but this room and its objects refuse to acknowledge her, to bring her comfort or offer the feeling of home. She pulls the toaster off the counter and looks for her reflection in its polished chrome, knowing she will not like what she sees.

What does she see? A neglected woman, a woman scorned. A woman with crazy eyes and ridiculous hair.

You would never know it by the mundane quality of the light in the windows, the stifled, sterile air, but today is a special day: the eighteen-month anniversary of Son X's birth and death. Though he arrived fully formed, so beautiful and pink-cheeked, because he died before birth (a mere technicality!) he is not included in the family's tally of children, and therefore does not merit a number. When someone asks, as someone always does, How many children are there? the answer comes, Twenty-eight! at which point Mother #4's brain cannot help but sing out a correction: Twenty-nine! Twenty-nine!

Though there is a child here, a living one, she makes almost no noise, only the occasional murmur or cough, the small house hoarding the sound like a just-rung bell.

When Mother #4 looks at the clock again she is startled to see more than an hour has passed. She calls down the hall to Daughter #10 (lucky enough to be numbered on the family list) that it's time to go to the cemetery, and Daughter #10 pokes her head out of her bedroom and shouts, Hooray!

Given the gravity of the occasion, the Mother thinks, she should be bereft and solemn, filled with the dark wine of grief, but all she feels is a buzzing irritation and the beginnings of a headache, maybe a migraine, like a thumbtack pressed into the back of her eye.

At the cemetery, a soft wind rattles the withered flowers, the dried stalks of baby's breath. It's spring, though only the weeds have started to grow in earnest. The Mother comes here once a week, sometimes twice, to tend her son's grave. Every time, as a matter of principle, she invites the Father to come along and every time, as a matter of principle, he refuses. After Son X's burial he has expressed his intention more than once never to return to this place again.

Once, when Mother #4 was a small girl, she asked her own mother what heaven was like. She described a house, a mansion, spacious and ornate beyond imagination. For someone who had been born and raised in a boxcar there could not have been a more compelling description of the place. Even now, when she pictures heaven she sees a house at dusk, a big white midwestern house with deep porches and elaborate gables, wheat fields in the distance pulsing green. The shapes of bodies move across the bright windows and she knows that these shadows are her lost children, watching, waiting for her to come home to them.

Now she is sad again—it hits her just like that—and she allows herself a short, messy cry. She tries to tell herself it is nothing but a fantasy, this heaven, this house of dreams, but she can't deny it is more real to her than the small, quiet duplex in which she eats her meals and lies down to sleep every night.

Sniffling, she pulls up morning glory that has begun to web itself over the grave while Daughter #10 wanders through the stones and monuments like a cruise ship hostess, chatting up the dead. Mother #4 is not comfortable admitting it to anyone, especially herself, but coming out here is, without a doubt, the highlight of the girl's week.

Mother #4 removes from her bag a clean cloth and a bottle of Windex and gives the black granite stone a good polish, taking special care to swab out the red dust from the letters of her son's name and the dates of birth and death, which are the same. She takes great pride in this grave and this marker, beyond the fact that her child is buried here. The day after Son X's death, Mothers #1–3 sat with Mother #4 on her bed and explained, with great kindness and sisterly forbearance, that there should be no funeral for the boy, no marker or grave. Among the three of them, they said, they had suffered a total of seven miscarriages and two stillbirths and none of those babies were given a name or laid to rest in a cemetery; they were angels, these children, spirit beings too pure for the ugliness and iniquities of this world. They belonged to God and God only, and He would name and consecrate them as He saw fit.

With nothing remotely close to kindness or sisterly forbearance Mother #4 let Mothers #1–3 know exactly what she thought about such nonsense. In fact, Mother #4 threw something of a tantrum. Tossing her blankets aside and burying a fist in a pillow, wild in her white nightgown, she said she didn't give a good goddamn what the other Mothers had done or what God thought about the whole thing, she would name her son, just as she had her other two lost ones, and he would be buried with dignity in a place where she could go to visit, to make sure he knew he was remembered and loved.

If Mothers #1–3 thought this might be some kind of postpartum, trauma-induced dementia, they were mistaken. Driven by a mother's protective instinct and a hot, gusting grief she could hardly contain, she shrieked, she raved, she made a fool of herself. In the face of the other Mothers' mild protests and the wary counsel of the Father and the church elders, Mother #4 would not back down. And so, two days later in a quiet ceremony with only the immediate family in attendance, Son X was laid to rest in the oversized family plot in the Virgin City Municipal Cemetery.

Which goes to show that occasionally, if she throws a big enough fit, even the fourth of four wives can get what she wants.

It is getting dark now, the spring light thickening into a weak broth. Mother #4 calls out to Daughter #10 that it's time to go. She stands up, knocks the dust from her knees, and gives the grave one last, proprietary glance. Daughter #10 protests, as she always does, shouting from the far corner of the cemetery, Ten more minutes, just ten more, okay, five, five more!

On the way back across the valley Daughter #10 sets her chin and pouts bitterly, asks where they're going. Mothers #2 and #3 might need help with the desserts for the church social, Mother #4 explains, so they're going to make a stop at Big House. Daughter #10 whines: she's hungry, she's tired, and besides, she hates going to Big House. Daughters #6 and #8 tell lies about her, Son #11 likes to pinch her arms and behind, and Daughter #8 calls her Casper the Not-So-Friendly Ghost. They are bad, bad kids, Daughter #10 concludes, and they are all going to hell.

Mother #4 isn't listening, doesn't hear a word of her daughter's litany. She is thinking of the Duplex, dark and anonymous as a cell, and how she can't face the idea of going back there, not right now.

She pulls up into Big House's driveway and is comforted by the signs of life: most of the windows lit, shouting from the backyard, two bicycles abandoned at the edge of the lawn—no, it isn't her house of dreams, but for now it will do. To get her daughter to release her grip on the handle of the glove box and exit the car, she has to promise a root beer float afterward at the TommyHawk Drive-in. They step onto the porch together, hand in hand. As she reaches for the knob the door swings open to a swell of voices, and with a sigh she lets herself fall forward into the light.

14.

THE FAMILY TERRORIST

Because she liked the company, because she wanted to be of use, on Monday and Wednesday afternoons Trish gave piano lessons. That she barely knew how to play the instrument herself seemed to bother no one.

Today was her first day with Rusty, who plinked out "The Volga Boatman," sweating and blinking, as if someone were holding a gun to his head. He was a wide-faced boy who had inherited his father's heft and his mother's dark hair. He had a reputation in the family as a problem child, a troublemaker—Nola had even taken to calling him the "family terrorist" (which to Trish seemed more than a little severe, but Rose, his mother, freely admitted he could be "something of a handful"). Really, though, he hardly seemed remarkable; like some of the other kids in the family he'd decided that negative attention was better than no attention at all. But there *was* something different about him, she was noticing now. Maybe it had to do with the way he sat so close to her, allowing his thigh to touch hers, or the way he lost interest in the notes on the page and began to play his own sour little song with something like confidence, his fingers producing a series of remorseless sounds. A stranger walking by outside might have heard the noise and imagined a cat stalking a wounded housefly across the keys.

With a slight bow of his head he launched one last haunted-house chord of his own invention. He looked up at her. "Can we be done n—" Before he could finish the question she was already saying, "Okay then, why don't we call it quits for today."

The boy gave a contented sniff, slapped his lesson book shut, and leaned back a little so he could get a good look around the room. He took in the bookcase on the far wall, the small desk with its small typewriter, the water stain on the ceiling a series of yellow, nearly perfect concentric circles. He wasn't interested in this stupid house, he just liked sitting here next to Aunt Trish, easily the prettiest of the mothers, who smelled nice, whose leg was touching his in a way that was making some things happen in his pants. He was eleven years old and full of a need so large and overwhelming that he wasn't sure exactly what it was he needed.

"I like this house," he concluded. "It's quiet."

Trish said, "That's one way to describe it."

Together they listened to the house: the groan of the old refrigerator, the kitchen faucet dripping with a dull *tap-tap* into the sink, Faye murmuring in her prayer cave around the corner. Out the side window the tall red cedar, which had started its existence as a potted plant next to the front porch steps, gently swiped at the window. Rusty sighed. Compared to this, Big House sounded like the prison cafeteria in *Escape from Alcatraz,* which he had never seen, but had heard about in great detail from the bad kids at school.

She asked the boy if he liked Kool-Aid, and in what might have been an attempt at a British accent, he said, "I don't see why not."

In the kitchen she was taking the sugar from a cupboard when she turned to see he had followed her, and was now standing in the doorway, staring at her intently with both hands positioned over his groin. His eyes were a cool green, his skin touched with tiny freckles, and he regarded her openly, his face wide and beseeching. He wanted something—that was clear—but what? Did he need to use the bathroom? Was he hungry? Maybe, after being separated from his own mother these last weeks, all he wanted was a kind word, maybe a hug?

Rusty didn't need to go to the bathroom, though he was hungry and would have accepted a hug, no questions asked. What was on his mind was something else entirely: *tits*. Aunt Trish was framed by the window over the sink, a window full of late afternoon radiance that penetrated her old-fashioned loose-knit sweater so that he could make out, just barely, the silhouetted profile of her breasts suspended in a nimbus of light. This almost holy image released a profane stream of tit-related phrases in his brain: *Keep Your Tits On* and *Tit for Tat* and *Tough Titties* and *Texas Titty Twister* and *Titty-Titty Bang-Bang*.

"How about some cookies with your Kool-Aid?" she asked.

"Keep your tits on," he murmured under his breath, to relieve some of the pressure.

"What's that?"

"Yes ma'am," Rusty said, almost out of breath. "I would like some"—he almost said *titties* but corrected himself in time—"*cookies* with my Kool-Aid."

Aunt Trish dragged Faye away from her prayer cave so she could sit in the backyard with them for lemonade and macaroons. The day was bright and cool, with a breeze that stirred the grass. Faye, who had a ghostly complexion and hair the color of apple juice, sat in her lawn chair and regarded Rusty with open suspicion. When Rusty tried to take a sip of his Kool-Aid, the girl piped up, "We need to say grace."

Rusty, feeling uncharacteristically confident, wondered aloud why they had to say a lousy prayer every time they ate or drank something, why couldn't they just have some danged lemonade once in a while without making a big deal out of it? Aunt Trish, who was quickly becoming Rusty's favorite person in the world, gave him a sympathetic smile and started to say something but was interrupted by Faye, who shushed them both and launched into a prayer that lasted a solid minute and a half and touched on a range of topics, including the lonely old people of the world, the starving orphans of Peru and the fern in the bathroom whose leaves were turning yellow. She forgot to bless the Kool-Aid and cookies, but remembered to include a special request that Rusty get home as safely and as soon as possible.

Technically, Aunt Trish was one of his mothers, but Rusty didn't know her very well, which made it a little easier to think about her without feeling weird about it. When she first came into the family she lived in Old House, and then she had the dead baby, who totally ruined the annual family camping trip, and now she spent most of her time here at the duplex taking care of creepy Faye and being sad.

After he had single-handedly dispatched half the macaroons, which he didn't really care for, Trish went into the house for more. For a minute, Faye stared at him, which was like being stared at by a curly-haired doll possessed by a demon.

The other kids were scared of creepy Faye, but not Rusty. He stared right back.

"It's time for you to go home," she said.

"Says who?"

"Heavenly Father and His only begotten son Jesus Christ."

"You're talking to them right now? And that's what they're telling you, that it's time for me to go home?"

"Yes."

"What else are they telling you?" Rusty had to admit it, he was curious.

"That you're a weak and bad person who is full of sin."

Rusty blinked. Maybe she really *did* talk to them. "Well, you can tell Heavenly Father and his only begotten son Jesus Christ they can go suck eggs, for all I care."

You should have seen the look on her face! She got all her power from talking about God, saying she knew what God and Jesus wanted. So all you had to do was tell God and Jesus to take a flying leap into a garbage heap and where was her power now?

"Thou *shalt not* take the name of the Lord thy God in vain," said Faye, which was exactly what you would expect her to say.

"Or what?" Rusty said. "Heavenly Father and his hippie son Jesus Christ are gonna come down out of the sky and give me a noogie?"

Rusty snorked. He hadn't really tried it before, but taking the Lord's name in vain was kind of enjoyable.

Faye sat back in her chair looking sad. "God have mercy."

"God have mercy on you too. With those huge nostrils of yours."
He snorked again. "Good luck getting a date in high school."

And that was when Aunt Trish came back with more cookies. Faye got up and went somewhere, probably back to her prayer
cave to ask God and Jesus to inflict Rusty with a bad case of cancerous leprosy or smite him with boils. Aunt Trish asked him how he
was liking it over at Old House. She had heard about the underwear
incident, which everyone thought was appalling, but to her seemed
comical.

"Stinks, pretty much," he said. "It's not fair that I'm still doing it
when no one else is."

Trish could not argue with the boy. The family exchange program had been instituted with noble designs and high hopes: to
unify a family that was, like so many overextended empires before
it, coming apart along the seams. Trish kept her own little outpost,
lived by her own rules, and was not much more than a spectator to
the ongoing hostilities between the houses. As the children grew and
the wives became more set in their ways, the differences between Old
House and Big House were clearly deepening, becoming harder and
harder to reconcile. Nola and Rose-of-Sharon, after years of trying
to compete with Beverly's high standards and regimented approach,
had largely given up. In fact, much of their hands-off parenting
style seemed designed to spite Beverly, to let her know her control
and influence had their limits. Five years ago they took the drastic
step of sending their children to public school, thumbing their noses
at Beverly's cherished home-schooling policy, which, she believed,
kept God's most precious souls from the evil influences of relativism,
evolution, communism, feminism, and amoral hippies masquerading
as teachers. The sisters not only released their children out into the
impure world, they allowed the impure world inside: on any given
day you could walk through Big House and find the kids inside
reading comic books, playing ping-pong, eating generic-brand fud-
gesicles and listening to Satanic music by the likes of Bread and Cap-
tain & Tennille. While the Old House children lived according to an

exhaustive master schedule—twice-daily family prayer and scripture study, five hours of home instruction, two hours of chores, recitations of Shakespeare and Frost every Wednesday night, annual performances of *The Sound of Music* or *Fiddler on the Roof*—the children of Big House slept and ate according to their whims, hollered and fought and caroused, listened to the radio and conducted impromptu boxing tournaments in the basement, and took great pleasure in corrupting the children of Old House.

During her first year in the family, she'd noticed these divisions—all families had them in one way or another, but lately they had become acute. More and more, the children were closing ranks according to their allegiances to the respective houses; even the younger children, sensing something beyond their understanding, were not mixing and playing together as readily as they once had. And now poor Rusty here seemed to be the last hope. If he, family terrorist and resident troublemaker, could be brought in line using traditional Old House methods (the prevailing sentiment seemed to go), then maybe there was hope for the family. If the experiment failed, and Rusty was sent back to Big House in disgrace, it would only reinforce the notion that the two families did not belong together, that their values could not be reconciled. Yes, it did seem a little unfair to put all of this on the head of an eleven-year-old boy.

Even though Nola and Rose were suspicious of Beverly's motives in instituting the Exchange Program, Trish thought it was a wonderful idea, supported it wholeheartedly—she wished that she'd thought of it herself. Her first exchange child was Deeanne, who was supposed to be a playmate for Faye, to show Faye by example how a normal girl should act, to bring Faye out of her shell. Deeanne lasted two days. Faye, the girl insisted, gave her the willies. She begged to be allowed to go back to Big House, cried herself to sleep at night, claimed that Faye pinched her when Trish wasn't looking and whispered into her ear that God was unhappy with Deeanne's bad singing voice and secret nose-picking habit. One afternoon, while Trish was doing the dishes, Deeanne ran out into the street, hailed a passing pickup, and claimed she had been kidnapped by a drifter and needed a ride home.

Things went better, at least initially, with the next one. Em, Beverly's oldest, bonded with Trish immediately. The poor girl had spent most of her life as little more than an indentured servant, a nanny and washmaid and cook, a lieutenant-mother who never had the chance to be a true teenage girl. In the first couple of days with Trish her earnest demeanor and industrious habits dropped away and she became another person entirely: a teenager who slept in, took extra-long showers, stayed up late eating Oreos and playing Uno and gossiping with Trish, giggling into the night like sixth-graders on a sleepover. There was no scripture reading or poetry reciting or hymns sung around the piano for them; they pretty much let Faye pray on their behalf. Eventually Trish gave in, dragged her toiletry case out from under the bed and instructed the girl in Makeup 101: how to mix and apply base for proper skin tone, the basics of rouge and mascara and eyeliner. Trish loved the way Em's eyes grew wide when she saw her own face in the mirror. Somewhere along the line, Trish realized, she was closer in age to Em than to any of her sister-wives.

For both of them it was like a three-week vacation that came to an end a week and a half early. One Saturday afternoon in July, Trish and Em were cleaning the kitchen and listening to the Bee Gees on the radio. They had been out back on the deck sunbathing, and they were both wearing clothes from Trish's suitcase: ribbed tank tops and cut-off jeans. The kitchen smelled like Pine-Sol and coconut oil.

Trish was doing a little microphone twirl with her sponge mop and straining to hit the high notes of "How Deep Is Your Love" when out of the corner of her eye she saw Em make a sudden lunge across the counter and pull the plug on the radio. Trish turned around to find Beverly standing in the kitchen doorway, holding Em's clarinet case, and taking in everything with a demeanor that said, *Well isn't this nice*. Reflexively, Trish saw the scene as Beverly surely saw it: Em, sweet and innocent Em, dressed up like a slut and cavorting to perverted music made by grown men hee-hee-heeing like prepubescent girls.

Beverly quietly told Em to gather her things and get in the car.

"We're having a little fun, cleaning the kitchen," Trish explained, even though she knew there was no use. Beverly gave her a long, sad look while Trish's hips, despite everything, still twitched in disco-time.

It took Em only a minute to change back into her own clothes and to pack her bag, and it hurt Trish somehow that the girl didn't share a secret look with her, that she wouldn't glance her way. Even now, three months later, Em treated Trish with the polite deference she reserved for any other adult.

Out on the deck in the cool winter sun, Trish watched Rusty survey her yard and the fields beyond. He picked up his glass and pretended to take a sip from it even though there was no sip left.

He asked if he could use the bathroom. He didn't really need to use the bathroom but he wanted to go back inside the house, snoop around a little and take a look at things, maybe slip something into his pocket he could later claim to have found, which would give him an excuse to come back to return it before his next lesson.

"We've got a little problem on that end," she said. "Toilet's backed up. I was watching the second twins over the weekend and I think one of them dropped something in there."

"You plunger it? I can plunger it for you."

"I plungered it all right." She smiled. "Plungered the living heck out of it. Your dad was supposed to come over to fix it on Monday, but he didn't have time and now he's gone again—"

"He's *always* gone." Rusty popped his lips and gave his head a little shake.

"Well, not to worry, the place next door's vacant and I've got the key, so we've been using the bathroom over there."

"It's all right," Rusty said. "I can hold it."

"It's no problem at all." Trish stood. "The key's right in the kitchen."

Rusty shrugged and squinted for a moment into the low sun. "I'm fine. I've been practicing my self-control. I can hold my breath for like five minutes, and sometimes I don't eat breakfast."

He gave her a quick look to gauge her reaction, walked to the edge of the deck and toed the tufted head of a dead thistle.

"If you want," he said, "I could, you know, do some work for you. For free."

"What kinds of things do you know how to do?"

"I can mow your lawn." He shrugged, and his voice seemed to tighten. "I could, you know, trim your bushes."

She thanked him, told him she was sure she could use his help in the future, when summer came and the lawn and bushes actually required attention. "You probably ought to get going, Aunt Beverly will be on the lookout for you."

"She doesn't care where I am, not really."

"I think she does. She seems to get rather upset when you're not where you're supposed to be."

"Everybody over there, they act like I don't even exist, it's like a big game. When I try to talk they say, *Did you hear something? I didn't hear anything, did you? It must be the wind.* Like that."

"That's terrible," Trish said. "They shouldn't do that."

Rusty shrugged, stuck out his lower lip and said that he didn't care. Trish couldn't tell if it was eleven-year-old bluster or if he really meant it.

"Maybe I should tell Aunt Beverly what's going on."

"She knows. They all do it, even the little ones. And Aunt Beverly does it except when I break the rules, and then all the sudden I'm not invisible anymore. So being invisible isn't all that bad."

Trish wanted to tell him that, despite its immediate rewards, invisibility was not anything to aspire to; it got old very quickly.

She asked him if he wanted a ride home and he told her he'd ride his bike. He picked up a macaroon from the plate and walked to the barbed-wire fence. The turkeys, who where pecking their way along the irrigation ditch by the road, hustled over in one big mob, stood in front of Rusty, gave him their undivided attention.

"Will they eat a cookie?" he asked.

She told him they would eat pretty much anything, including newsprint and styrofoam peanuts.

With a sidearm motion he winged the macaroon over their heads and they made a mad dash for it, gobbling and thrashing their bony, clipped wings, climbing over each other to peck at the cookie with violent stabs of their heads.

Rusty put his hands on the fence wire and watched. He cleared his throat as if he had something important to say. He said, "What a bunch of stupid turkeys."

RUSTY TO THE RESCUE

She washed her tea mug in an otherwise empty sink, looked out the window at a flock of sparrows wheeling and diving over the Gunthers' hay barn in the dawn-pink sky and thought, *I am getting along fine.* She was discovering the only way to make it through each day was to hunker down and wait it out, like in a hurricane or high drought, something to be survived. It had been, what, ten days since she had been alone with Golden, since he'd stepped foot in this house? She could handle it, she knew she could. She knew how to wait. She knew how to be alone.

In those ten days there had been only three or four nights when she'd slept badly and only one when she'd curled herself against the headboard and given in to a fit of whimpering. Mostly bearable nights visited occasionally by the same dream: Trish sleeping exposed on the edge of a rocky precipice, knowing somewhere in her sleeping mind that if she rolled over or shifted her weight even a little, she'd go over the edge into the bottomless dark.

And then last night a real curveball: a prolonged sexual dream that woke her suddenly with its sweaty fervency, leaving her limp and trembling—and curious about who could have broken into her dreams and brought her to such a pitch.

She set the mug in the drainer and went to check on Faye, who slept with such an eerie stillness, her pale skin nearly the color of the sheets, her features so sweetly serene, that no matter how much Trish tried to tell herself, *She's fine, stop your worrying,* she could not restrain herself from putting her hand against the girl's neck to feel for the delicate vibration of blood under the skin.

She waited another hour for Faye to wake up, spent too much time preparing a three-course breakfast the girl hardly touched. She started the laundry, fed the breakfast leftovers to the grateful turkeys, and read scripture with Faye, only because Faye would become agitated if they didn't.

After lunch she vacuumed the hallway, folded the laundry, and sat down at the table to wait—she didn't know what she was waiting for. She had no idea. She thought—and it was not a thought that bothered her as it probably should have—that she might be losing her mind.

Around two o'clock she heard a faint clanking sound out front. She ignored it, but it continued, softly, a chorus of metal clanking, like someone rustling through a cupboard of pots and pans. She opened the door to find Rusty climbing the steps on the porch, wearing an overburdened tool belt and a rusted plumber's snake coiled crossways around his torso like a Mexican bandolier.

"Hey, there," she said, and he said, "Hey, there," back, huffing a little with the exertion of riding his bike across the valley loaded down as he was. He took a big breath and gave her a terse, professional-style nod. She couldn't have been happier to see anyone.

He said, "I've come to fix the, you know, the john."

She let him in and he moved purposefully across the room, holding the head of the long framing hammer that hung from his belt so it wouldn't bang his knee while he walked.

In the bathroom he put his hands on his hips and regarded the toilet.

"This the one?" he said.

He took out his tape measure, experimentally pressed its lock button several times, put it back into its little holster.

"Okay then," he said, "this might take a while."

The only reason he had any idea what to do about a clogged toilet was because he'd seen his father trying to unclog the one in the bathroom on the second floor of Old House, the bathroom that Aunt Nola called the Black Hole of Calcutta. He wasn't sure why it was called the Black Hole of Calcutta, all he knew was that it was damp and dark and smelled like mildew, and that the toilet had a mind of its own. His father had tried to fix it many times, but there was something about the gigantic ceramic water tank that you emptied by pulling a chain, and the old pipes in the house that made it belch and mumble and groan, sometimes in a way that sounded like talking.

At least Aunt Trish's toilet, Rusty was pretty sure, didn't have anything to say, which would make it a whole lot easier to deal with. He uncoiled the plumber's snake and fed the end of it into the hole. He'd seen his father do this at least twice, but he couldn't remember how far the snake was supposed to go down the hole. He fed it in slowly, delicately, as if he were feeding something that might try to bite him.

Faye stood next to her mother and said, "What's he doing here?"

"He came to fix the toilet."

"That's Dad's job."

"If only Dad were here to do it."

Rusty looked at Faye and she stared him down until he had to glance away. He laughed and made a huge snork, which he tried to cover up by pretending to cough, which made him cough for real.

Aunt Trish asked him where he got the tools and he told her from the service truck his father kept in the old chicken pens. "That truck is full of tools, you should see it. There's like some kind of huge jackhammer in there."

"Well," Aunt Trish said, "I'm glad you didn't have to bring *that* with you."

He laughed again, which produced another snork, but this time he didn't care.

He'd fed the snake in about two feet and it didn't seem like it would go any farther. The water, now exactly level with the lip of the bowl, trembled ominously. He said, "I think we've got something here."

"That's a nice shirt," Aunt Trish said, and Rusty couldn't think of anything to say, so he said, "Indeed." He stole a glance at Faye, who had managed to disappear without a sound.

Because he didn't have a nice shirt of his own, before coming over here he had swiped one of Parley's, a long-sleeved button-up with a big collar and prints of motocross riders doing wheelies all over it. Where Parley had ever gotten such an incredible shirt Rusty had no idea. It was made of some kind of silky material that rubbed against his belly and produced instant static electricity that crackled all around him every time he moved.

He rotated the handle on the crank twice, giving off a slight crackle. He paused dramatically, as if listening for something only an FBI agent could detect. He gave it two more violent cranks and . . . nothing. What a gyp! He looked at his tool belt, which was starting to pull his pants down to dangerous levels, wondering if there was something in it that could help him. Maybe he could stick his hand down the hole? Pull out whatever was in there with some pliers? Would that be an act of bravery or something a stupid dickhole would do? He looked at Aunt Trish, whose arms were folded in a way that made it hard to get a good idea what her boobs might be doing. She was smiling at him in a nice way and he had to look down because he knew he was staring. He put a little more pressure on the snake and cranked the handle like crazy, again and again, giving it everything he had until he was sweating from his butt crack and generating enough electricity to power a Christmas tree.

"All right, then!" Aunt Trish called, which made him stop. "Looks like we're going to plan B."

"Plan B?"

"A plumber. Our only choice."

Rusty looked at her dumbly, as if the word *plumber* were foreign to him, which was entirely possible. Though she'd meant it as a joke, she wondered if there was even such thing as a plumber in this valley. Generally, the people here did not rely on professionals; they *were* the professionals. They fixed their own cars, machined their own parts, raised their own food, birthed their own babies. If they didn't know how to do something, there was always a neighbor, someone down the road, who did. She imagined the scandal it would cause if she paid some bumbling fatso to do a job her husband could do in two minutes, if only he came around once in a while, if only he acted like he cared. She imagined the outrage, the gossip, the attention: Beverly's indignation, Nola's amazed delight, Golden's bewilderment, his slow recognition that she would not be taken for granted, that she had needs, that she mattered. Such a pathetic little fantasy, but she couldn't deny the small spasm of pleasure it gave her.

"Ee-yep," Rusty said, assuming the casual stance of a professional: hip out, thumb hooked into tool belt. "I think I might know somebody who can help. I think I can probably take care of it."

"Really, honey, it's all right. Your dad will be home in a few days . . ."

"I'll take *care* of it," he said and shrugged immediately, as if to excuse himself for being rude. He didn't like her to call him honey; it was a word she used for four-year-old Sariah or one of the Three Stooges.

He pulled the snake out of the toilet, wrapped it around his torso, checked his tools. Aunt Trish put her hand on his shoulder. "Thanks so much for your help, Rusty, you're a true gentleman. If you'd like to hang around for a few minutes I'll make us some instant pudding. I think I've got some graham crackers."

As far as Rusty was concerned, instant pudding and graham crackers with Aunt Trish was as good as it could possibly get, better than cherry popsicles on a yacht with Wonder Woman, plus she had touched his shoulder and called him a true gentleman. But some kind of romantic instinct, maybe one he had picked up from his favorite book, *To Love a Scoundrel*, told him that it would be best not to wear out his welcome. The Scoundrel never hung around for instant pudding and graham crackers. He always gave the sexy duchess a quick kiss on the mouth and then jumped out the window, holding on to his wig and landing safely on a haystack going by in a cart.

"I have things I have to do," he said as mysteriously as possible. It was true: he had plans, people to talk to. "Maybe a rain check on the pudding?"

"A rain check," Aunt Trish said. "You can cash it in anytime."

15.
· · · · ·

CIRCLING BACK

TWO MILES NORTH OF HIS LITTLE AIRSTREAM HOME AWAY FROM HOME lay the Nevada Test Site, fourteen hundred square miles of emptiness, a void on the map: swales of sagebrush that went on forever, alkaline flats and deep arroyos and strange accretions of glassy slag in the distance, fields of crater-pocked hardpan edged by yellow sandstone bluffs streaked white with the guano of raptors and bats. On his late afternoon walks he would often climb the big north hill to a hummock of broken rock and look out over the expanse, a tingle in his legs as if he were standing at the edge of a cliff. When the clouds were right, low and moving fast, the heat rippling up off the mineral-green dust and bending long bands of smoky sunlight, the desert looked like what it had once been not so long ago: the bottom of a vast prehistoric sea.

At night he heard strange atmospheric whisperings, saw impossible lights that gathered and skittered across the surface of the darkness. The government had banned open-air testing years ago, but continued in its cheerful, efficient way to set off blast after blast underground. More than once he'd been brought out of sleep by a welling tremor, a roar that could be felt more than heard, clutching his pillow in terror, the blood stalled inside his heart.

It was hard not to be reminded of those early mornings he had spent with his father watching the bomb tests: a single flash against the dark sky, the incandescent cloud with its roiling platinum core, the delayed thunderclap. More and more, walking the game trails just a few miles from the wasted ground where these blasts were unleashed, he was taken by the feeling that things were spiraling in on him, everything he had left behind was in front of him again, his old life, his old self, it was all circling back.

And yet nothing was familiar, everything strange. He had ten thousand things to think about, a worry for every second of the day, but the only subject that truly interested him was Weela, and why he hadn't seen her since their embrace in the pond.

He'd spent what little spare time he had after work scouring the gullies and cracked riverbeds, venturing far out into the rocky wastes, but there was no sign of human life, only the obnoxious ravens, the coyotes who barked at him from distant ridges and then sat on their haunches and stared, as if waiting for him to leave. During his lunch break he would take up a position in a copse of dense mesquite behind the PussyCat Manor, where he spied on hookers sunning themselves topless in deck chairs or barbecuing with a hibachi, laughing and carrying on, once chasing each other through the brush screaming and arguing over, as best Golden could gather, a blow-dryer. He had even gone so far as to venture into the mysterious confines of the Pussy-Cat Manor itself, hoping to catch the glimpse of Weela—he wanted only to know that she was okay, that nothing bad had befallen her—but all he'd gotten for his trouble was a piece of hard toffee and a condom, which, against all his better judgment he kept tucked safely behind his Visa card: a symbol of hope or self-delusion, he didn't know which.

Strangely, not seeing any sign of Weela in or around the Pussy-Cat Manor had cheered him. Maybe she was not avoiding or ignoring him, maybe she was sick or on some kind of vacation (prostitutes took vacations, didn't they?). He told himself he didn't care if she didn't like him or had no interest in him anymore, he only wanted to know that she was safe and that he might have the chance, once more in his life, to hear that laugh of hers again.

To Golden, it seemed that Weela's sudden disappearance was one more in a series of strange events precipitated and possibly created by that not-so-innocent embrace in the pond. First was his reckless foray into the forbidden confines of the PussyCat Manor, and then there was the long weekend at home in which he'd had some kind of argument or standoff with every one of his wives, in which the kids came at him in relentless waves, and everything he did or said seemed exactly and perfectly wrong, though he couldn't have said why. And then, driving back to Nevada early Tuesday morning after spending an awkward night with Trish, he'd felt a strange pulling sensation in his groin. The more he shifted in his seat, the worse it got, and he stopped off at a truck stop near Littlefield to see what the problem was. Standing in front of the urinal in the men's room he pulled down his underwear to find that he had an unreasonably large *something* tangled in his pubic hair. "The heck?" he said, prodding the object, which appeared to be a wad of gum. He was spreading the hair with his fingers, trying to make sense of this new development, when he felt a presence next to him.

Two urinals over a sunken old geezer in a Hawaiian shirt regarded Golden through a pair of thick-lensed glasses. He gave Golden a good once-over, shook his head and, holding up his unbuckled pants with both hands, shuffled sideways to the farthest urinal down the line.

Golden said, "Hey, no, I'm just—"

"Minding my own business here!" the man called, careful not to look Golden's way again. "Let's just all mind our own business, why don't we!"

Golden faced the wall and fiercely attempted to urinate so as to demonstrate he was here to use the facilities for their intended purpose, but on such short notice couldn't work up a stream.

On the drive to the construction site he scoured his faulty memory, but couldn't come up with a likely scenario by which a huge wad of gum might have ended up in his pubic hair. Sure, he'd had an odd encounter with Trish the night before, in which she'd fed him leftovers, taken him to bed, gotten naked, pinned him down, tickled him and pulled his pants around his ankles, only to get upset and lock herself in the bathroom. Just one more baffling episode in a life that had become full of them. Strange as it was, it didn't explain where the gum had come from (Trish, as far as he knew, didn't chew gum, and he was sure she didn't have any in her mouth when they'd kissed). He decided the gum's origins didn't matter nearly as much as what it represented: that he was not in control of his life, that at any given moment of the day he had no idea what was happening to him. He was a man with a crush on a prostitute, a condom in his wallet, and gum in his pubic hair—what could it all mean?

All he could say for sure was he had come to Nevada to escape, to embrace a solitary life, but with Weela gone, he had been overtaken with a loneliness that verged on desperation. At home, his children and wives gathered around for scripture reading, he felt, more piercingly than ever, that his existence was a sham, something quickly assembled for the sake of a photograph. During the long weekend in Virgin he was not allowed an idle moment: he spent several foggy hours in priesthood council before and after church, changed out the shocks on Trish's Volkswagen, drained silt from all three of Big House's water heaters, suffered through a Rose-of-Sharon Sunday dinner (her special undercooked chicken with a side of Ritz-cracker-and-cauliflower casserole), chopped wood, took in three junior league basketball games and two band concerts, attended the Sunday afternoon Summit of the Wives, in which he had to referee a complex dispute over the yearly distribution of hand-me-down clothing and which lucky children might be in the running for a new pair of shoes, failed to repair a broken heat pump in one of his rental houses despite two hours of knuckle-busting, lost a forty-five-minute-long argument with Nola at midnight, in bed, about Beverly's handling of the family finances—and over that entire long weekend there was not a single minute in which the dark-skinned woman of mystery did not assert herself into his waking mind. Even as he conjured her face and replayed her laugh over and over again in a looping reel, another line of thought ran like a crackling cross-current against the flow: Was it possible that right now, somewhere far away and lost in the particulars of her own life, she could be thinking of *him*?

Of course, all of this *thinking*—an activity he was not widely known to engage in on such an intense or extended basis—did not go unnoticed. Beverly seemed always to be nearby, *noticing*, the whole of her formidable radar on duty. At Sunday dinner he sat at the head of the table lost in a memory of Weela's wet cheek against his, when he looked up and saw Beverly standing in the kitchen doorway, watching him. He looked away and thought, *Am I smiling? I'm not smiling, am I?* Of course he was, and what was worse, he had no right to be: he had just sampled a forkful of Rose's casserole. He sifted the food in his mouth—and with little effort composed a suitably pained expression—but when he glanced up again, Beverly had disappeared into the kitchen.

That night, they prayed together, kneeling at the foot of the bed, Golden, in his plaid plus-sized pajamas with a split in the inseam, saying, *Hmm,* and, *Uh-hm,* and thanking and blessing what- or whoever wandered into his mind. Beverly laid out her own prayer like a lawyer presenting closing arguments; she outlined the family's many problems, the financial difficulties and spiritual malaise, the sibling rivalries, the strife among sister-wives, and finished up with a plea: "Give this family, Heavenly Father, the leadership and guidance it has been sorely lacking of late, to bring us through our trials, to make us happier and safer, and to one day bring us, together, into Thy care, In the name of Jesus Christ, Amen." After which she looked Golden straight in the eye, climbed into bed, and proceeded to ignore him.

It was one of those moments he had become all too familiar with: she was mad at him, and he wasn't sure exactly why. She'd even involved God, which meant she was deadly serious. He'd learned that actually asking her to tell him what was wrong never got him anywhere in instances like this. It was best to say nothing, to cut his losses, to maintain the dignity of the ignorant. He turned off the lamp, pulled the sheet up to his neck, and waited for the good-night kiss. Just like their double-prayer at the foot of the bed, the good-night kiss was a two-decades-old custom that never varied: she'd roll over, give him a kiss on the cheek, say, "Good night, Goldy," and he'd wait a beat or two before rolling over to kiss her and say, "Good night, Oldie," which at one time had been funny enough to make them giggle—Beverly having three years on him as she did—but was now bedrock ritual and no laughing matter. He listened to coyotes yipping somewhere far up the canyon, settled his large behind into its crater in the mattress, wondered when was the last time they had forgone the good-night kiss, and could not remember it ever happening.

He did remember some of the other jokes they'd had between them, how she used to tease him gently and he would respond like a bashful, happy child. Sometimes when she was feeling frisky Beverly would turn off the lights and say, *Where is my big man, the One Mighty and Strong?* She would grope for him in the darkness, until she found him and remarked upon how mighty and strong he truly was. It was unlike her to be irreverent about something so sacred, and this Golden found enormously arousing. It had been years, five or six at least, since they had played that game.

While he stared at the patterns on the dark ceiling, he decided if he did not pee right now he would be up in the middle of the night; his bladder, like every other part of him, was not what it used to be. He slipped into the small master bath, flipped the light, and with an inaudible sigh read the sign above the toilet tank:

Golden, Please Take a Seat

He would admit it, urinating neatly and accurately was not easy for a man of his considerable height and occasional lack of focus, but did that mean he had to sit down when he did it? As always, he took a moment to consider disobeying the placard. Why shouldn't a man, in his own bathroom, in his own house, be able to pee any way he saw fit? He sighed again, lowered his pajama bottoms and took a seat.

When he settled back into bed, he noticed Beverly had not moved.

He listened to the clock tick, the ponderous workings of his own lungs. Finally, he gave in. He turned over and spoke meekly into the darkness, "Is there something wrong?"—but her eyes were closed, her breathing even, her arms tucked neatly at her sides.

He watched her for a solid minute, waiting for movement, any sign at all, and then put his mouth to her ear. "Good night, Oldie," he whispered. She didn't grin, she didn't so much as flinch.

A HOLE IN THE GROUND

Out at the job site, Golden called Nola to inquire how best to get gum out of hair. He had thought the gum would have disintegrated on its own, but now, a week after he'd discovered it, it seemed to have hardened into a lump of glassy plastic that yanked on the sensitive hairs of his groin with every step he took.

"So you have gum in your hair," said Nola in her playful, let's-have-a-little-fun tone. Nola, of all his wives, was the easiest to talk to; she was rarely jealous or needy and never failed to say exactly what she meant. For the last two or three years—ever since Glory's death, really—she'd been trying every trick in her considerable book to jolly him out of the funk he was in.

"Yeah," Golden said. "A little. In my hair. In the hair on top of my head."

"Now how'd that happen? You don't chew gum, do you?"

"Me? No. Somebody else. A kid in a car . . . I was out by the highway and a kid in a car, in a convertible, threw his gum at me and it stuck in my hair."

Nola let out a honk of laughter that made him wince. "Why was there a kid throwing gum at you?"

For a moment he did nothing but listen to the sound of the bad connection, the squeaks and hisses of the ionosphere. What had ever possessed him to call Nola? He could have talked to Rose-of-Sharon, who had become so remote and withdrawn lately her whispery voice barely registered over the phone line, but certainly she would have given him a few tips without any fuss, and Beverly would have lectured him, but probably would have kept it to herself.

"I don't know," Golden said. "Kids these days. Terrible. I'm glad it was gum and not something else."

"What kind of gum is it?"

"Well, you know, Dubble Bubble or one a them, I think. Juicy Fruit. Something along those lines. Why does it matter?"

"It doesn't, honey, it doesn't." She laughed again. "You know I just like to have the facts."

After several more rounds of questioning having to do with the age and attitude of the gum-thrower and what kind of car he was driving, she finally got down to the important stuff. "The first thing you can try is ice. It never works, but try it anyway. The next thing is peanut butter. That works sometimes, but almost never. Rub it in there and see what happens. The foolproof method is get out your scissors and start cutting. Works every time."

"I don't have any scissors."

"You've got peanut butter, don't you?"

"I think so."

"Then break out the Skippy, buster, and get to it."

There was a knock at the door of the trailer and Golden looked up to see the smiling face of Ted Leo framed in the dusty glass panel. In his early sixties, Ted had a nearly full head of unnaturally chestnut hair and a chest-and-belly combination that jutted out over his belt like a threat: *Clear the way or get dumped on your ass*. On his fingers and wrists he wore the gaudy ornamentation of a once-poor man who now considered himself a person of means.

Though Golden was grateful to Ted Leo for giving him a job when he most needed one, it was often hard to overlook the fact that the SOB and his unpredictable moods made his working days a misery. He had a brittle, childlike temper that showed itself at the most unlikely or trivial moments, and when he wasn't angry, an overbearingly chummy style that made you nostalgic for the temper tantrums. He had once taken an eight-pound sledge and knocked down most of a framed-in wall because he wasn't happy with a door placement, but when Golden once called him, hands trembling, to tell him their electrical contractor had fled the country under threat of arrest for statutory rape, delaying the whole project by at least a month, Ted Leo simply told Golden to take care of it, he had more important things to do.

As Leonard had once observed, the only thing you knew you were going to get from Ted Leo was that you never knew what you were going to get from Ted Leo.

A few days after Golden won the bid for PussyCat Manor II, Ted Leo had taken him on a driving tour of his many land and business holdings: the PussyCat Manor I; the local weekly, called *The Valley Cryer*, which was mostly letters to the editor, advertisements and brothel coupons; a small ranch that seemed to feature nothing but miniature horses; the Stop-n-Drop Truck Stop; a defunct copper mine that one day, Ted Leo claimed, would produce a fortune in gold.

Ted Leo told Golden he had one last thing to show him, a secret, so long as Golden could keep a secret, *wink wink*. They took a vague dirt road heading north along the eastern boundary of the Nevada Test Site. The man driving was Ted Leo's hulking henchman, an Arizona Papago named Nelson Norman. Golden, as a member of the relatively exclusive Fraternity of Very Large Men, welcomed Nelson as a brother and equal; though he had barely met the man and knew almost nothing about him, he was inclined to like anyone who knew what it was like to move through life so conspicuously. And Nelson was nothing if not conspicuous. With his expansive, neckless torso and powder-barrel legs, he had the bursting, overgrown quality of a prizewinning pumpkin. His head alone, topped with a neat black brush cut, must have weighed in at forty pounds, and Golden had to wonder, as they drove along the fence that stretched north and south into separate infinities, how Nelson ever managed, with those stubby dinosaur arms sticking out of his torso at a forty-five-degree angle, to button his own pants.

Without warning, Nelson gave the steering wheel—which was

partially buried in the cushion of his belly—a hard yank to the left and expertly surfed the big Chevy cross-country over swales of sand and rabbit brush. To Golden it felt very much like fighting through rough seas, and to keep the nausea at bay he focused on the picture of a little girl attached to a string of rosary beads and hung from the rearview mirror. She had a full head of glossy black hair and big liquid eyes so bright and full of wonder that to look into them gave him a warm ache in his throat.

"Yours?" Golden asked over the roar of the engine, and Nelson nodded. "Marjorine. Three years old." He glanced at the picture and Golden caught a split-second expression of intense fatherly pride that disappeared as quickly as it had come, replaced by the default mask of professional boredom.

Nelson slowed a little to guide the truck down into a sand wash and then they were driving along the dry, rock-littered riverbed, bouncing against each other like dice in a cup, Ted Leo in the middle and taking the worst of it. They stopped when they came to the Test Site fence, a standard chain-link ten-footer topped with three rusted strands of barbed wire that spanned the steep banks of the arroyo just above their heads.

Nelson rolled out of the cab to pull away piles of dead brush and they drove directly under the fence, the snipped-off ends of the wire *screek*ing on the pickup's roof, and proceeded up the wash for another mile or so. They climbed out of the wash onto a broken plain of creosote and biscuit-colored sand and walked a few hundred feet until Ted Leo gave the order to stop.

"Isn't this place restricted or top secret or something?" Golden said.

"For some people," Ted Leo said, checking his watch. "A patrol comes along that ridge every thirty minutes, so don't get your undies tied up just yet. Years ago I did a tour here, back in my GI days, saw a good number of the big ones, you know, Hardtack, Dirty Harry, Upshot-Knothole. Got friends up and down the chain of command, and if they ain't my friends, well, more likely than not they owe me a favor or two. So there's nothing at all to worry about. Now." He stepped back and gestured to the expanse of sand and brush that curved away toward every horizon. "See anything?"

Golden made a show of looking around and said that he didn't see anything of note.

"Try again," Ted Leo said.

This time Golden made no effort to humor the man. "I'm not seeing anything."

"Take your time."

"Nothing. I don't see anything."

"Give you a hint. Look under those pontoons you call your feet."

Golden looked down. Under his boots was nothing but the pebbly outer territories of a defunct anthill.

Ted Leo accepted a shovel from Nelson, who had it at the ready like a bored nurse assisting a routine surgery. Ted Leo nudged Golden aside with his hip and began pushing sand around with the shovel. There was a scrape and a clink, and Ted Leo made a delicate eight-step ritual out of hitching up his avocado polyester golf slacks and lowering himself to his knees. With the reverential patience of a dedicated archaeologist he pushed and dusted and flicked away the crumbling clumps of sand until he had revealed a steel hatch door fitted with a crude latch-handle fashioned from one-inch rebar.

Ted Leo offered to let Golden open it but Golden, sensing a practical joke, declined. Ted Leo yanked open the hatch with such a scripted flourish that Golden stepped back despite himself, but no paper streamers or joke-store snakes flew into the air, no one in a werewolf mask leapt out growling and waving his arms.

Assuming something of a professorial air by elevating his diction and occasionally gesturing with a stick, Ted Leo explained what they were standing on was a buried test bunker, constructed of reinforced concrete and filled with animal subjects and scientific equipment meant to record the response of these animals to the shock waves and radiation of one nuclear test, dubbed Shot Priscilla ("Seven megatons of pure persuasion," Ted said wistfully), detonated twenty years ago, exactly a thousand feet from this spot. "The blast collapsed the ven-

tilation system and the dogs and all the other little critters they had
in here suffocated, bless their souls. The average person like yourself looks out across this landscape and sees nothing, but underneath
our feet are miles and miles of bunkers and shelters and tunnels and
elevator shafts, depots and storehouses and control centers. It'll put a
chill down your spine to see it all, to know it's there, like something
out of a science fiction movie. Most of it never to be used or seen
again, like this one here."

Golden gestured to the hole. "What's down there now?"

Ted Leo accepted the flashlight that Nelson had been patiently
holding in his pillowy fist.

"Why don't you take a look yourself?"

Choosing not to reveal himself as an unredeemable pansy, Golden
edged toward the mouth of the bunker and caught a whiff of its cold,
iron-tainted breath. In the beam of his flashlight he couldn't make out
much more than a mass of hanging wire that threw writhing shadows against a concrete wall covered with faint equations and cryptic
instructions scribbled in oil pencil.

"Boo!" shouted Ted Leo, giving Golden a poke in the behind with
his stick. Golden jumped as if something had bitten him. Ted Leo
roared with laughter and looked back at Nelson to gauge what he
thought of this wonderful bit of leg-pulling; if his expression was any
guide, Nelson thought nothing of it at all.

Golden forced a smile, to show what a good sport he was. "Looks
like lots of wire in there."

"Pretty much, and some leftover equipment, plus the mortal
remains of those dogs and rabbits and whatnot. The shitbird scientists
—I don't think I have to tell you how little respect I have for
scientists—decided their little tests were compromised, so they salvaged the expensive equipment and had the rest buried. Tidy up,
move on to the next fiasco and forget about it, that's how your tax
dollars work around here. Or maybe you folks don't pay taxes, I don't
know. Anyhow, as far as the brass here is concerned, this little mass
grave no longer exists."

Golden nodded with somber understanding even though he had no earthly idea why they were out here or what Ted Leo was trying to tell him. Ted Leo, who claimed to have once been a devout Christian and a minister of the word, believed in the power of parable, of the well-illustrated metaphor. He was always trying to send a message of some kind or another—he wouldn't have wasted his valuable time driving Golden out here just to give him a history lesson—and Golden decided it would be best just to wait it out and hope he spotted the message when it decided to show itself.

"Sad," Golden said. "A real shame."

"No it isn't," Ted Leo said. "Not for me. Of all the real estate I own or will own in the future, this might prove to be the most valuable. Because I'm the only one—besides you and big boy here, and maybe a couple a guys who mustered out years ago and forgot about it—who know it's here. You with me now?"

Now Golden was really starting to get confused. He said, "Sure. I see what you mean."

"See, if a place is secret, if you're the only one knows about it, doesn't that place belong to you? It's *yours*, you can do with it whatever you want, you can put anything you want in it, and nobody will ever know. *Poof*, disappeared, like something on *The Twilight Zone*. Bugsy Siegel? Would have given his little Jewish soul for a place like this. No more dumping bodies out under a bush for some hunter or forest ranger to find. This place right here is a Mafioso's wet dream."

Golden said, "Bugsy Siegel?"

Ted Leo gave Golden a hard look. "You telling me you don't know who Bugsy Siegel is."

Golden shook is head.

"Bugsy Siegel. The man who built Las Vegas."

"Sorry," Golden said.

"Lefty Rosenthal, heard of him?"

"Nope."

"Anthony 'The Ant' Spilotro? The Fischetti brothers?"

Golden could see that Ted Leo was starting to get worked up; this time he just shrugged.

"Amazing!" Ted Leo cried. "Your own father, I saw with my own eyes, had dinner one night with Lefty at the Bellagio. I would have given my own left fucking arm to have a sit-down with Lefty Rosenthal, but who was I? Just another little guy, dreaming what it would be like to be a big shot like your old man. Your own father, you see what I'm saying, having words with Lefty Rosenthal, one of the greats. And you don't even know who any of these people are."

"My father never talked about that kind of thing."

"Even so!" Ted Leo was fairly shouting now. "How can you not know who Bugsy fucking Siegel was? How! You people just sit around reading your funny Mormon Bible, is that what you do?"

Golden shrugged again. Short of jumping into the hole at his feet, he couldn't figure out how to make himself less of a target.

"Didn't your father teach you anything?"

"Not really."

This answer seemed to please Ted Leo, at least. He looked at the bunker hole and sighed. "Dear Jesus. Anyway, the point I'm trying to make here is that for somebody like Bugsy or Lefty or Frank, a place like this would be invaluable, see what I mean?" He squatted, still shaking his head, and patted the steel hatch with a kind of wistful fondness. "Nobody could find anything here, because there's no here here, see? Nothing to find. You've got enemies, a place like this could come in handy."

He gave Golden a long steady look, waiting to see if his message was having the intended effect. Golden thought about it and said, "I'm not your enemy, Mr. Leo."

"Course not!" said Ted Leo brightly. "But things change, we both know that, Brother Richards. And we both know that we have to do everything to protect what is ours. The world, especially this part of it, is full of cheats and liars. And that's why I chose you to build my palace. I believe you're a person who, in his own nutty little way, believes in God and doing right by his fellow man. I believe we're two of the same kind. I believe *I* can trust *you*."

Golden Richards, as a general contractor, had had many strange dealings with his clients: he had been sued and countersued, he had been bribed and stiffed and conned, he had been asked to accept a flea-bitten male lion in exchange for a three-thousand-dollar debt, but nobody had ever threatened, even in the most oblique way, to murder him and hide his body in a secret nuclear testing bunker full of dead animals if he didn't mind his manners. He wondered if there weren't already one or two unfortunates interred with the dogs and rabbits somewhere under his feet. If he weren't so desperate for work, he might have thought twice about working for a man like this.

"You'll have nothing to worry about, Mr. Leo," Golden said.

"I know, Brother Richards. Why do you think I brought you out here?"

A LOVELY EVENING

So while Golden was on the phone with Nola getting tips on gum removal, Ted Leo was sticking his head inside the work trailer, shouting, "Brother Richards!" in his croaking voice. Ted Leo had promised from the beginning he wouldn't mention Golden's secret lifestyle to anyone, but yelling "Brother Richards!" every time he saw him did not seem like the height of discretion.

Golden motioned him in, told Nola that he'd call her back, and hung up. Ted Leo made himself comfortable on the dusty love seat across from Golden's desk, picked up a roll of blueprints, looked at them upside down before tossing them aside. He wore a yellow guayabera, beige gabardine pants and polished Top-Siders that matched his artificially chestnut hair with their otherworldly shine.

"Looks like you've got somebody working out there, at least," he said. "With all the mess and equipment you'd think we were trying to rebuild the Colosseum."

The man was in as good a mood as he'd ever seen him, but Golden knew to keep his guard up; Ted Leo's good moods, he knew from experience, could go south very quickly.

"You can see we're getting there, Mr. Leo," Golden said. "We've got the new trusses in, and Ratlett is sending a crew back to fix the window casings I was telling you—"

"Brother Richards," Ted Leo said, holding up both hands as if to stop an oncoming car, "let's forget the professional talk for a minute, which we'll get to soon enough. Do you know why I'm here?"

Golden said that he didn't.

"Do you know how long it's been since you and I had a nice one-on-one conversation?"

Golden shook his head. This was one of the things that annoyed Golden most about Ted Leo: this asking of questions, one after the other, in a way that seemed incomprehensible until Ted Leo finally got to the point. Before he bought the brothel and became what amounted to a glorified pimp, Ted Leo had run a successful evangelical ministry somewhere in the jungles of Central America. Golden imagined this was how Ted Leo converted the locals: asking a series of seemingly unrelated yes-or-no questions until they had unwittingly agreed to be baptized.

"Do you enjoy a good lasagna?" Ted Leo asked.

Golden had to admit that he did.

"And do you have big plans on your social agenda for this evening?"

With a pained look on his face Golden said, "Don't think so."

"Then why don't you come over to my place for dinner. Seven o'clock. My private residence is in the back, as you know. Don't go through the front door or my girls'll jump your bones and not let go." He winked. "Been a slow week."

That night, Golden sat in Ted Leo's living room, hair plastered to his forehead and fingernails scrubbed clean, doing his best to carry on a polite conversation with two hookers. Janine, a disturbingly thin woman with huge silver hoop earrings and ribs like lobster traps, sat to Golden's left sipping wine and adjusting her wig, while Chalis, the plump blond girl who looked no older than sixteen, was telling them how living next to a feedlot in New Mexico her whole life had turned her into a dedicated vegetarian.

"God, those poor cows!" she cried. "Do you know how much they suffer so we can enjoy our burgers and hot dogs and all that?"

Golden allowed that he didn't.

"I mean, lying around in their own filth, waiting to *die*."

"Life in a nutshell!" said Janine, already drunk, raising her wine-glass to the ceiling.

The two women were there, Golden had learned, because they were top performers for the month of February—they had hosted more "parties," as they called them, brought in more money than any of the other girls that month. Their reward was a $500 bonus, a brass plaque, and a private homemade dinner with the great Ted Leo himself. The girls had asked what Golden had done to deserve this honor and he allowed, once again, that he had no idea.

Golden sat on an ostentatious wicker chair shaped like the throne of an Oriental monarch, waiting patiently for his ass to break through the seat. The room was carpeted in deep maroon shag and appointed with oversized furniture that seemed to have ambitions beyond the faux-wood-paneled walls that confined it. Above the fireplace was a framed picture of Ted Leo, wearing aviator shades and smiling like a madman into the camera while putting a hard squeeze on one of Billy Graham's hands. He had arrived late from his round of golf and was now in a hall bathroom with the door open, audibly slapping at himself in the shower and singing "To dreeeeeam, the impossible dreeeeeam," in a way that brought to mind the screeching of a saw blade.

Golden sipped his warm 7UP—he had turned down offers of whiskey, vodka and champagne—and tried not to think about how he was missing his walk to Salt Pond. It seemed to him now that if he could see Weela one more time—hear her laugh again, just once—he could find the strength to endure the unpleasant situations of his life, such as this one.

"To fiiiight," Mr. Ted Leo strained above the spray of hot water, "the impossible fiiiiiight!"

"Sheez," said Chalis. "You think he needs a lozenge or something?"

One of the things adding to his discomfort—beyond Mr. Ted Leo's singing and the ominous creaking of his chair and the way the two women were speaking past him and giving each other looks as if he were a wino who had wandered in from the railyard—was that his privates were covered in peanut butter. Before he'd come to dinner he'd decided to shower first—a big mistake, it turned out—and then spent twenty minutes applying slippery ice cubes to the lump of gum in his pubic hair, which had hardened, finally, to the consistency of prehistoric amber. After he'd melted six ice cubes with no effect except to shock his genitals into puckering submission, he moved on to the peanut butter. He worked a large dollop into the area, his giant blunt fingers making a mess of it, and as he stood hunched over in the kitchen of his tiny trailer, the lightbulb on a wire knocking around his head, his pants around his ankles, performing an act that suddenly seemed deeply deviant, he felt a stab of shame, wondering what string of bad decisions in his life could have led to a moment such as this.

He'd barely had time to wipe the excess peanut butter off with paper towels before he had to leave to be able to make it on time for dinner, and now, trying with the concentration of an acrobat to keep his weight perfectly distributed so the wicker would not give way, it felt as if everything in his groin, including his thighs, was stuck together with glue.

When Ted Leo finally emerged from the bathroom, he did so in a towel held tight at the waist. He had a perfectly round belly and skin evenly covered in thick gray fur still sparkling with drops of moisture. "Girls, you being nice to Brother Richards out here?"

Both girls shrugged and continued to ignore Golden. Clearly, they were not happy about him crashing their exclusive dinner.

Ted Leo winked at the girls, winked at Golden. This was another thing Golden didn't like about the man: he was always winking at everyone, and Golden couldn't understand why.

"These girls," Ted Leo said, "look at them. This one"—he gestured toward Janine—"sexy and mean as a wildcat, and this one"—he held both arms out to Chalis—"just like the girl next door."

"Yeah," said Janine, giving her cigarette a single, delicate puff, "if you happen to live next door to a whorehouse."

"Ha-ha!" Ted Leo roared. "Yes, yes, yes!"

He gave Golden a good-natured slap on the back and then turned back down the hallway, singing, "To fiiiggght the, impossible fiiigght—"

He'd taken only two or three steps before he stopped, pivoted, and lifted his nose to the air.

"Hey now," he said, "what smells like peanut butter?"

A NONTRADITIONAL MAN

Dinner was already on the table by the time Ted Leo, aglow in a green kimono embroidered with tiny Japanese lords and geishas engaged in complicated sex acts, ushered his guests into the dining room. Without a word he bowed his head and held out his arms until everyone joined hands and he proceeded to say grace. During the prayer, which Golden hardly heard a word of, Ted Leo absently rubbed the knuckles of Golden's left hand with his thumb, while on the other side, Janine gripped Golden's left index finger, squeezing in rhythm as if milking a cow.

"Ah, yes, thank you for these good young girls, Lord, for their hard work and positive attitudes, keep them fresh and pretty and free of disease, and the same goes for Brother Richards here, in a manner of speaking, you know what I mean, who is honest and works hard just like the rest of us."

The table was laid out with an impressive spread: lasagna and baked ziti, breaded eggplant, cucumber salad and slabs of steaming garlic bread. Golden wondered where it all came from; though there'd been no sign of a cook, he thought he'd heard pots banging and running water in the kitchen.

While Ted Leo launched into a one-man conversation about one of his favorite topics—the unusually high number of coyotes in the area, and the many interesting and enjoyable ways to kill them— Golden dedicated his full attention to the food. Even though he'd spent most of last weekend at home, he'd gone without a decent home-cooked meal for at least a week. Last Saturday night had been Rose's turn to cook. This time, she had decided to try a dish that had become fashionable among the women of the church: meat loaf with Lipton onion soup mix. Rose, who did not have any of the Lipton mix and figured soup was soup was soup, mixed several cans of Campbell's chicken noodle into the ground beef. The result looked and tasted like a mass of earthworms encased in a brick of steaming industrial sludge. Golden, at the head of the table and always the first served, had gagged a little when a lump of it was spooned onto his plate, but the children sighed and went at it.

This meal, though, was so good he made a grateful low whimpering with every bite. He had become so intimately involved with the food he caught only the tail end of Ted Leo's story about a group of university feminists from Seattle who picketed the brothel and protested the exploitation and degradation of women by lining up at the entrance of the brothel parking lot and chanting, *Hey you! Hey! Hey! Get a date the regular way!*

"Brother Richards," Ted Leo said. "Folks in the outside world and their traditional lifestyles, they just don't understand people like you and me, am I right?

Golden, whose mouth was busy with two forkfuls of ziti, nodded, though he wasn't sure what Ted Leo might be referring to.

Janine gestured with her drink at Golden and asked Ted Leo, "So is he a brothel guy too?"

Ted Leo laughed. "Not exactly, my dear," he said, giving Golden a double-wink. "Not exactly."

After Golden had cleaned up half a pan of lasagna, most of the ziti and the last heel of garlic bread in the time it took the two girls to drink a glass of wine and pick at their salads, Ted Leo asked, with something of a skeptical tone, if Golden wanted any dessert.

"*Well*," Golden said, leaning back in his chair in a show of reluctance, and then giving up on the act immediately, "I think I could go for some, yes, some dessert, I think I definitely want some dessert. For sure."

"That reminds me," Ted Leo said, "there's somebody I'd like you all to meet." He clapped his hands at the side of his head like a flamenco dancer, and shouted, "*Querida!* Dessert for everybody!"

A woman appeared in the entryway holding a pan of orange custard. She was short, almost stocky, wearing a simple white dress and her hair in a bun. Golden had sneaked another bit of eggplant, which was now lodged securely in his throat. He held his breath and resisted the urge to cough or choke.

It was Weela, looking shyly around the room, her gaze about to alight on Golden. Ted Leo stood and gave her a fatherly kiss on the forehead.

"Say hello to Huila," he said, "my lovely wife."

16.

. . . . .

APOCALYPSE TOMORROW

INSTEAD OF RIDING HIS BIKE ALL THE WAY TO JUNE'S HOUSE, WHICH would have taken a long time and given him a serious case of butt pain, he let the air out of his back tire and started walking along the road looking sad. A flatbed pickup blew right by and he knew he wasn't trying hard enough, so he thought about his own funeral, which he often did to make himself feel better. He could see his family gathered around his shiny, complicated coffin, his mother sobbing and kissing his handsome face with his hair all nice and slicked back, his father shaking his big head and saying, *Why? Why? Why?* while all around the mothers and the brothers and sisters wailed and wept and asked each other how they could go on after treating him so badly, how could they ever forgive themselves? He got a lump in his throat and his eyes got a little watery, and wouldn't you know it, right then an old bat in a station wagon stopped and said, "Need a ride?"

Luckily the old bat, who had yellow-white hair and smelled like a cigar, didn't know him. He gave his flat tire a sad look and sniffed a little and told her he lived out on Water Socket Road and she said, "Get in, you poor little duffer." And just like that she'd loaded up his bike and dropped him off at June Haymaker's mailbox. Because of the flat tire he had to walk his bike down the dirt road to June's place, but it was all downhill, and when he got to the Quonset huts he called out, "June! June! Wherefore art thou, June?"

But no June. He knocked on the door of Quonset Hut #1 and

when nobody came to the door he let himself in. It looked pretty much the same as the last time he'd seen it, except there were two bananas on the table, which he took his time eating. He opened the drawers and cabinets in the kitchen, checked out the bathroom and the bedroom, where he discovered a small stack of magazines under the clock radio. "Mmm," he said, "and what do we have here?" *Russian Bride. Thai International. A Foreign Affair. Ukrainian Lovelies.* Magazines packed with hundreds of black-and-white photos of women craning their necks and pooching their lips out: *Name: Alanska Age: 41 Height: 5'9" Weight: 110 lbs Hometown: Minsk. Hobbies: Cooking, Cleaning, Sexy Cuddling.* Not all the pictures had boring statistics next to them. Some of the women had questions next to their pictures like, *Where is the Masculine Man of My Dreams?* or *Will I Offend the North American Women Because I Am Not Overweight?*

Rusty liked the cover of *Ukrainian Lovelies* the best because it showed a woman wearing a bikini and fingerless leather gloves. He felt a little sorry for the woman because the bikini did not fit her very well, and there was a bruise on her thigh, and what were those gloves for? Even so, the picture made things happen in his pants, which wasn't saying much because just about everything made things happen in his pants.

He slipped *Ukrainian Lovelies* down the back of his underwear against his rear end. This was how he often stole comic books from Platt's Market and he knew from experience that his sweat would make the cover stick to his skin and eventually leave a smeared image of the Ukrainian chick on his butt cheeks, the thought of which made some things happen in his pants.

He was going through June's sock drawer when there was a *boom* from somewhere outside and the whole Quonset hut vibrated.

"Holy sweet Jesus Christ," Rusty said. He was really starting to enjoy taking the Lord's name in vain.

From the porthole window he could see smoke rising into the air above the red sandstone cliffs. He ducked out the back door and climbed up the hill until he could see June leaning against his pickup, watching dust and smoke pour out of a huge black hole at the bottom of the cliff. About thirty feet from the first hole was another hole, bigger and rounded on top, shaped like a cave in a cartoon.

Rusty walked right up next to June, who was still watching the smoke with his mouth open, and said, "*Excelente!*"

June's elbow slipped off the hood of the pickup, and he did a hilarious herky-jerk move and nearly fell on his face. He backed up, staring at Rusty, his eyes wide. "Jeez, man! You scared me. Jeez! What are you doing?"

"Stopped by for a visit," Rusty said.

"I don't think you should be here."

"Why not? Are you going to blow up the whole mountain?"

"What? No. I'm building a— It's private."

"I'm not going to tell anyone."

"No, I don't think it's a good idea—"

"Come on, June," Rusty said. "Don't be such a fag."

June, in a straw cowboy hat and an old-fashioned flannel shirt, gave Rusty a worried look. Then his face changed, and he started breathing hard through his sunburned nose. "Okay," he said "*Okay*. But you can't tell anybody. Right? It's going to be my home when I'm finished with it, but yeah, it's also a shelter. A *bomb* shelter. It'll withstand a direct hit from a five-ton warhead or the fallout from a nuclear blast. When I'm done, there'll be three thousand square feet of living and storage space with a filtered ventilation system, all at a constant sixty-eight degrees."

"Sweet holy Jesus Christ Almighty," Rusty said.

June just stood there with a stupid look on his sunburned face.

"Okay," Rusty said. "What do you say we go have a look around?"

So June showed Rusty the first room, already blasted out of the rock, which would one day, he said, in the event of worldwide nuclear cataclysm, serve as the main storage area, the arsenal and ammunition depot, the staging area to repel any and all enemy attacks, if that, heaven forbid, was what it came to. Inside it was damp and cold and smelled like dirty snow. The second chamber would be the main living area, with a large common room and four smaller ones. They scrambled around on piles of busted rocks and June explained how he drilled the boreholes, filled them with explosives, and brought twenty tons of rock down with the press of a button.

"It's a lot of work for one guy," June said, slapping the dust out of his pants, "but I'm making pretty good, you know, pretty good progress."

"Seriously, June, this is the greatest house anybody has ever thought of," said Rusty. "This would be a great place for a family to live, right?"

"That's the idea, I guess. It's a little much just for me."

"It sure is. If you want, I could help you and you won't have to pay me, I work for free." He began picking up pieces of the broken rock and hucking them toward the mouth of the cave.

"Okay, hey, watch out." June had to duck to keep from being clocked by one of the rocks Rusty was pitching between his legs like a dog digging a hole. "That's good! That's fine! Okay there!"

Rusty stood up, huffing. He had one more rock in his hand and, why not, lobbed it over June's head, making him flinch. He said, "I could do this all day. You don't even have to give me water."

"Yeah, that's great, but I've got an old D9 out there that I can move this stuff around with, it's a lot easier that way. But sure you can help me. Sure. We'll find something for you, Lance. No problem. Come on out of here why don't we?"

"One other thing," Rusty said. "I've changed my name. Don't call me Lance anymore. My name is Rusty."

"You changed your name?" With June's mouth hanging open like that you could count the fillings in his teeth. Rusty counted at least five. "Can a kid do that?"

"It's just my new nickname, okay? People change their names all the time. Maybe it's something you should think about."

June stared at his feet. He picked up a small sledgehammer leaning against the rock wall and tossed it toward his truck.

"I sort of like your name, though," Rusty said. "Seriously. If your name was Cynthia or something, you know, *that* would be bad." He scratched his head and looked around. "So what do you say we get a bunch of your dynamite and blow something *up*? Do you have, like, a washing machine you're not using, or an old cow?"

"We're not blowing up a cow," June said. "I don't use dynamite anymore, anyway. Too expensive. Ammonium nitrate, a blasting cap, and some wet newspaper down the borehole and you get the same result at half the price."

"So why don't we get some of that stuff right now and go find something and blow it up? Just you and me, June. Seriously."

June's forehead got all creased like a teacher's and he started to explain about how all explosives, even small ones, are not only dangerous but potentially lethal and should only be handled by trained professionals like himself.

"Wait," Rusty said. "Remember the fireworks you showed me that first time? You said you'd show me more. You *promised*."

"Well, fireworks, sure," June said. "That's different. Fireworks are meant for entertainment purposes, but you still have to be very careful . . ."

Rusty pinched the bridge of his nose between his thumb and finger, which was what Aunt Beverly did to show she was running out of patience. He said, "Did I tell you my birthday's coming up? Do you think we could stop talking maybe and go blow up some fireworks in celebration of my birthday?"

"Wow," June said. "Your birthday? Yeah. Okay. Let's go see what we've got."

They went back to the shop, where June pulled out a ring of keys from his pocket and opened two metal storage lockers. Inside the first were rows of plastic containers marked with boring scientific names like *Potassium Nitrate* and *Ammonium Oxalate* and *Red Magnesium Flash Powder* and in the next one spools of wire and green fuse and bottles of glue and boxes that said *Industrial Blasting Caps*.

Rusty didn't know what any of this was, really, but he knew it was all meant to start things on fire and blow things up, which made him want to spin around singing happily in the mountains like the blond lady in *The Sound of Music*.

On the shelf next to one of the lockers was a row of books with titles like *The Do-It-Yourself Gunpowder Cookbook* and *Surviving Global Slavery* and *Apocalypse Tomorrow* and *How to Derail a Train with Common Household Items*. Rusty thought if they had books like this at the library, maybe more people would stop by to check something out once in a while. Little paperback books such as *Improvised Explosive and Incendiary Devices for the Guerrilla Fighter*, which he shoved in the back pocket of his jeans while June wasn't looking.

"Let's see now," June said, gazing at his collection of explosive materials as if they were his beloved children sleeping peacefully in their cribs. "We could do one of my aerial bombs, but since it's light outside it'll be hard to see. So let's try a little combination setup I've been experimenting with. Yeah. We'll try the two-scale Thunder Flashes, with a bunch of Whistling Chasers, and then a string of big ol' German Knallkörpers that sound like the end of the world. I think maybe you'll enjoy it."

Rusty bowed his head. "I know I will enjoy it, June. Very, very much."

"But first, if you want, real quick, I'll show you how to make a basic American Cannon Cracker, yeah, an all-time classic. Would you like to see that?"

"Please," Rusty said. "Please and thank you."

June started filling a cardboard tube with some kind of gunpowder, explaining everything he was doing like the guy in the boring science filmstrips at school. "Now I am mixing the composition, which is mostly potassium chlorate with powdered charcoal . . ." and even though it was somewhat informative, Rusty wished he would hurry so they could go outside and blow something *up*.

While June was off to the other side of the shop searching for safety glasses, saying, "Safety First!" like Mrs. Alcustra, the playground monitor at school, Rusty went over to the storage cabinets, where all the explosives seemed to be crying out in tiny cartoon voices, *Take me, take me, please!* and so took one small canister labeled *Green Magnesium Flash Powder*, which he slipped into his front pocket. Because he wanted to be fair and not show favoritism or racist behaviors, he grabbed another marked *Red Magnesium Flash Powder*. Red and green, like Christmas. And then, what the hey, a couple of blasting caps from the box and a plastic baggie that said *Potassium Nitrate* and a leftover piece of green fuse, because what if one day in the future he was fighting the Russians or a horde of Killer Bees and needed to build his own American Cracker or German Knock-Popper to ensure the safety of all mankind? Exactly.

He got back on his stool and sighed contentedly. When June came back, he let Rusty help him, which nobody had ever done before. Rusty's father, who knew all kinds of things, like how to mix concrete or build entire houses out of nothing but a bunch of wood, had never let him help or shown him anything. But here was some red-bearded weirdo named June letting him glue the cap on the end of the tube and then he was holding Rusty's wrist steady while Rusty inserted the fuse, June saying, *Right there, that's it, good, just like that*, and it made Rusty's face get all warm having somebody that close to him, telling him how good he was doing, even though June's beard was kind of tickling his ear and his breath smelled like soup.

When they were done, June set up the fireworks on a rusted metal plate outside. Before he lit the fuse June said, "In honor of Mr. Lance Richards—"

"Rusty. Call me Rusty."

"Okay, in honor of Rusty Richards's birthday— How old will you be again?"

"Fifteen."

"Fifteen? Really?"

"Seriously, June."

"Eleven?"

"Twelve. I'm going to be twelve."

"In honor of Mr. Rusty Richards's twelfth birthday! Huzzah!"

"Huzzah!" Rusty cried, even though shouting *huzzah* seemed the tiniest bit gay.

Firecrackers started popping and then a few were spinning on the flat metal plate, glowing red and blue and whistling so loud he had to put his hands over his ears, which was good because he was ready for the last firecrackers, big ones, that went *Blam! Blam! Blam! Blam!* and sent up showers of silver sparks that made him cover his head with his arms and fall backward laughing.

It *was* better than Christmas. It was better than the end of the world.

"You like that? Yeah?" June said. June helped him up off the ground and he felt a little dizzy, grabbing June around the waist for balance, and then kind of gave him a hug, holding on tight, and said, "Thanks, June, you're the best," and June patted him on the back, saying, "Okay, how 'bout not so tight there, buddy, okay, yeah, why don't we let go there, okay, and I'll go get us a snack."

THE GRAND MASTER PLAN

In Quonset Hut #1 June asked what kind of snack Rusty might like and Rusty said, "Do you have any bananas?"

June looked around. "I just had some here, I swear," and turned around again.

"Kinda had a craving for bananas, that's all," Rusty said.

After a complete search of the kitchen, June came up with some Ritz crackers and cheese and a newly mixed batch of Tang.

"Do you mind if I ask if your parents know that you're out here?" June asked. Rusty could tell he was worried about Aunt Beverly. What a sissy! After seeing her that one time he was still probably having nightmares.

"They don't care where I am," Rusty said.

"Well, here," June said, and took a cherry bomb from his shirt pocket. "This is for your birthday. But you have to promise to use it in a safe place under adult supervision."

"Oh yes!" Rusty said. "Huzzah!" He took the cherry bomb but his pants were full of stolen items so he carefully set it on the counter it front of him. He felt bad for stealing from June, who was possibly, except for Mrs. Tollison at school and Aunt Trish, the least jerky person he'd ever met, and definitely the only person who had ever given him an exploding device for a birthday present. Luckily, the guilty feeling went away fast and he cut eight squares of cheese, carefully stacking them interspersed with nine crackers, and crammed the whole cracker-sandwich in his mouth at once. After he'd washed it down with a refreshing glass of Tang, he said, "That whole bomb shelter thing, is that just for you?"

"Well, for now, but I've got plans, this is for the future. This is only stage one."

"Is stage two to get, like, a girlfriend or a wife or something, I hope? Because seriously, June."

June shrugged, cleared his throat, sipped his Tang. "Eventually, yes. But a guy can only do so many things at once." He gave a little laugh and Rusty joined him and after a few seconds said, "Indeed."

Rusty took out his wallet and removed a four-by-six photo, folded twice, of a beautiful smiling woman wearing a festive scarf and holding a pumpkin. He handed it to June. "You want to see what my mom looks like?"

The woman was not his mom, but some stranger whose picture happened to be in the frame he had bought for his mother as a Christmas present. He'd taken the picture of the pumpkin woman out and put in his own picture, which depicted him at the county pool, wet and squinting into the camera. It was not the greatest picture, he admitted it, he was standing knock-kneed with his suit all bunched up in the crotch and his arms sticking out because he was wearing his water wings—but it was the only picture of himself he could find. When his mother opened it up on Christmas morning, Clinton said, "Ha ha! Look at his engorged nipples!" and everybody laughed, but his mother said she loved it, she would cherish it, and she put it on the nightstand next to her bed, behind the clock radio.

Looking at the picture of the pumpkin woman now, June said, "She's, yeah, she's very nice-looking."

She was even better than nice-looking, Rusty thought, she was beautiful, which was why he had kept the picture, because the pumpkin woman reminded him of his mother, who would be beautiful too, if only she had festive scarves to wear and nice clothes, if only she could hang around in pumpkin patches instead of having to change diapers and scrub bathtubs, if only Aunt Nola let her get a word in once in a while and Aunt Beverly didn't ignore her all the time and then suddenly ask her why she didn't have any opinions about anything important, if only his father paid her any attention at all.

"I think you'd like her," Rusty said. "She has a great personality. Plus she's *American*."

June tried to hand the picture back but Rusty told him he could keep it. "I have more where that one came from," he said.

"So you know how to fix stuff, right?" Rusty said.

"Like what?" June said, putting the folded picture in his shirt pocket, taking it back out again and placing it carefully on the table.

"Like, you know, a leaking roof or a broken refrigerator or whatever."

"Are you kidding me?" June said, sitting up a little in his chair. "You give me the right tools, I can fix anything, I can build anything, I could build us a spaceship that would take us to Mars. I could build the space station once we got there. It's all about the money, and having the right tools."

"Well," Rusty said, "you think you could unclog a toilet?"

17.

.....

SACRIFICE

IT WAS NOLA ON THE PHONE, HER VOICE BUFFED TO A HIGH SHINE of satisfaction, to see if Trish had seen Rusty. Nobody had heard from the little son-of-a-bee since he got home from school.

After a moment's hesitation, Trish let go a bald-faced lie: "Haven't seen him since two days ago, I think it was. Piano practice."

"Oh, this one's a goody," Nola said. "The second time in two weeks he's gone missing. Ol' Bev is so irate I could hear her panties wadding up over the phone. She thinks it's all part of a Big House conspiracy to make her look bad."

"People shouldn't get so worked up," Trish said. "I bet he'll be home in the next few minutes." Which wasn't merely an idle bit of hoping on her part; Rusty had, in fact, left her house just a few minutes ago. Earlier he had shown up with someone named June Haymaker, who, with nothing more than a bucket filled with water, had unclogged her toilet. June was a shy, sad-eyed young man in his mid-twenties, skinny as a greyhound, who smelled like recently applied aftershave. When Rusty had introduced him by saying, "This is June, which we all know is a girl's name," June had blushed so fiercely his ears looked like they might catch fire.

He'd carefully explained the physics of what he was doing—something having to do with suction and air pressure—and then dumped the bucket into the toilet bowl from shoulder height. The pipes rang inside the wall and the toilet drained with a satisfying sucking noise.

Faye, who never let herself go over anything, yelped and clapped her hands.

"Learned this in the army," June said. "Guns and ammo galore, but you couldn't find a plunger to save your life."

"June used to shoot guns," Rusty explained, gazing at June with bald admiration. "And blow things *up*."

"Did you kill people?" Faye asked.

"Oh, not . . . not too many," June said, and gave Trish a quick grin.

"People who kill other people," Rusty advised Faye sternly, "don't like to talk about it. It's, like, bad manners, right, June?"

"If you say so," June said. "Though if I'd ever killed somebody, yeah, I'd probably want to brag a little."

Before she knew what she was doing, Trish had improvised dinner of leftover pork chops and instant mashed potatoes. It hadn't even occurred to her to ask if Rusty was expected home—maybe she'd assumed he checked in with Beverly, or maybe she just didn't care. It was so good to have company—someone to eat her food, to ask her about the messy watercolors she'd painted and framed on the dining room wall, to defeat the silence that had begun to overtake her house like a mold.

"I don't think being at Beverly's is doing that boy any good," Trish said now. "He belongs at home with his mother."

"Where do you think he's been the first eleven years of his life? In the state pen? With the circus? That boy's a piece of work and Rose and I have done the best we could. Look, Trishie, I know as well as you do that Beverly's not going to turn him around. He's just a couple of inches off center, our boy Rusty. But it's sure fun for the rest of us to see her try."

"And Rose is all right with this?"

"Rose might not be all that happy about it, but it's the best thing for her. You know she's been going downhill lately, it's worrying is what it is. With Rusty out of the house, daily hostilities—at least here in Big House—are down. A little extra peace and quiet while we watch Beverly bang her head against the wall. Ha! And the beauty of it is that Bev thinks she's pulling one over on us, going to show the world that she can do a job that we couldn't manage. Oh what a hoot."

Trish hadn't been off the phone twenty seconds when Beverly called. Unable to go back now, she produced the same lie she had passed off on Nola. She looked up from her place at the table to find Faye in the doorway of her bedroom, condemning her with a chilly stare.

"I'm giving him ten minutes and I'm calling the police," Beverly said. "Who knows what he's up to?"

"I don't think that's a good—" She cut herself off, tried to remove the pleading from her voice. "He probably just lost track of time, out playing somewhere."

Beverly let her know what she thought of that observation with a long, reproachful silence—a Beverly specialty.

"It's nearly seven o'clock," she said finally. "Nobody's seen him since he got home from school. He is being willfully defiant, and if he's not willing to abide by the rules everybody else does, some harsh measures are in order."

In the background Trish could hear voices, the slamming of a door. Beverly said, "Well. Here he is now. And look at that, wearing his brother's shirt."

There was a muffled scratching, which was, Trish assumed, the sound of Beverly's hand covering the receiver while she ordered Rusty up to bed without his supper. Trish's chest tightened with a pang of genuine sympathy for the boy. It was not easy to face Beverly's wrath, and yet he'd risked exactly that on her behalf. Even though she herself now risked being discovered a liar and Rusty sympathizer, she was glad she'd fed him—and hoped he had the good sense not to confess where he'd been.

She sighed. "Well, thank goodness."

"We're going to have to find a new way to fight this." Beverly's tone had shifted from exasperated to something harder and more insistent. "This kind of a behavior is a symptom of a bigger disease. You know exactly what I'm talking about."

"He's just a boy," Trish said, "he's eleven—"

"I'm done talking about him, do you understand? Done worrying about him and fighting with him. I've got bigger worries. I'm talking about the way we're falling apart, giving up on each other. We're not taking responsibility for one another anymore. Things get difficult and we all retreat to our separate corners. Maybe it's harder for you to see from where you are, but this is a crisis, Patricia. It's not like I haven't been talking about this for months now. I believed that bringing you into the family would bring balance to things, but that obviously hasn't happened."

Trish took a breath. It didn't take Beverly to tell her that she'd failed at her calling of family savior, the one ordained by God to complete the broken circle. What Beverly would never admit was that she had arranged to bring Trish into the family not because her personality was a perfect complement to those of her sister-wives, or because God had led her to them because she was the last piece of the puzzle, the final, binding ingredient. No, what she would never say aloud was that she had brought Trish on as a political ally and nothing more. With Nola and Rose moving out of Old House to pursue their own domestic and spiritual agendas, Beverly had lost her near-universal influence and control. What she needed was simple: someone vulnerable and therefore pliant enough to do her bidding, to stand next to her on every issue. Though Trish did not have a full understanding of this at the beginning, it started to become clear to her when she made the decision to move out of Old House. Not only had she thought she wanted her independence, the commotion had terrified Faye and the odd and unpredictable smells of the house itself had made Trish, three months pregnant with Jack, a swooning, nauseous mess. Beverly was indignant, of course, did everything she could to persuade Trish to stay, and when Trish proved more stubborn than any of them could have predicted, Beverly made sure she ended up in this isolated duplex on the other side of the valley, like some exiled daughter of a Prussian czar.

Though she resented Beverly for using her in such a way, she had learned a few things from the woman, and now turned some of Beverly's own signature icy silence right back in her direction. Then, with a trembling hint of menace, she said, "If you want to blame me for something, maybe you better do it directly."

"I'm not blaming you." Beverly's voice softened into a whisper. "I know how you're still grieving, dear. I know, better than anyone, what you've been going through." And just like that, with the mere suggestion of her loss, she was able to bring tears to Trish's eyes. Though Beverly might not have known it, she still had Trish's loyalty and respect for all she had done for her in the first terrible days after Jack had gone. Still, she hated her sister-wife for knowing her so well.

She held the phone away from her mouth for a moment, swallowed back the little lump of sorrow that seemed to reside permanently at the base of her throat. Sooner or later, she was going to have to get a grip on herself.

"Then what is this about?"

Beverly began to talk, but was overtaken by a fit of coughing.

"Are you okay?" Trish said.

"It's nothing," Beverly said. Though she seemed to have been suffering from some kind of respiratory infection for a while now, she wouldn't admit to it. Beverly did not get sick, did not show weakness; her role was to point out the weakness in others.

Beverly continued, "I've been having some conversations with Uncle Chick, and I've been praying." Trish closed her eyes, considered hanging up. She knew that something bad was coming and that there would be nothing she could do to stop it.

"He knows how this family needs to grow, to evolve. We've become stagnant."

Trish didn't know if the "he" Beverly was referring to was Uncle Chick or the Almighty, but it didn't matter, it all came to the same thing. Everything she felt at that moment—the anger she'd worked up to a nice, jagged point, the familiar weight of sadness on her chest, the sting of shame brought by Beverly's suggestion that she had failed in her most basic obligation as a mother (to bring children into the family and thereby glorify God and His kingdom)—all of it dispersed in an instant, leaving behind only the light, trembling emptiness of fear.

"I have to go," Trish said. "I have a lot to do."

Beverly continued on as if she hadn't heard anything. "We're not thriving, and you know why? Because we're not living the Principle as it should be lived. We've become selfish."

"Please," Trish said, "either say what you're going to say or let's forget about it."

"You have to understand, it's just talk at this point, nothing more. No need to get worked up. Are you listening to me? We all have to pray about it, to see if she's the right one."

"She? You already have somebody picked out?"

"*I* didn't pick out anyone. The prophet, through Uncle Chick, is the one who brought all this up."

"Auberly Stills? Is that who it is?" Trish was trying hard to keep the hysteria out of her voice. "Tell me. Is it Sister Fendler's niece, the redhead?"

Beverly sighed. "It's Maureen. Maureen Sinkfoyle."

Trish laughed: a weird, three-octave cackle. "*Maureen?* But you can't *stand* Maureen."

"I've my difficulties with her, but I'll have to get over them."

"And does Golden know about any of this?" She couldn't imagine, with the way he had been acting of late, that taking on a new wife could be anywhere on his list of priorities. Oh sure, Trish knew that by adding a new wife Golden would improve his spiritual standing and his power and influence in the church, and like most plural wives she had been schooled to be ready for the time when a new wife would join the family, because while it might sound nice in theory, it was always much more difficult in practice. The key to plural mar-

riage, she'd been admonished more than once, was not to take any of
it too personally.

But *Maureen Sinkfoyle*? The same Maureen Sinkfoyle who sometimes shelled and ate peanuts during sacrament meeting? The one
with the juvenile delinquents? The one who used so much Aqua Net
you could hear her hair crackle from across the room?

"Uncle Chick has talked to him about it, but remember, he's not
alone here. We're a family, and we're going to have to make the decision together. I'm bringing it up to you now because you're new at
this, and you're going to have to get used to the idea of sacrifice—"

All at once her anger returned in the form of a white-hot star
expanding behind her eyes, and she slammed the receiver into its cra-
dle. *Sacrifice.* As if Beverly had any right to lecture her on that subject. She turned to find Faye watching from her bedroom doorway
and her anger doubled. She found herself screaming hoarsely at the
girl, and hating herself as she did, to get back into her room and not
come out for the rest of the night.

The phone began to ring and she stepped onto the back porch
to escape the sound of it. It was a cloudy night, the far-off lights of
farmhouses suspended like drifting motes in the void. She went to
the back fence and waited there. When the turkeys didn't appear she
made a cooing sound to announce her presence, but there was nothing except the smell of wet earth, and a fitful breeze in the grass.
Please come, she thought, *please*, and she was startled at how much she
needed them, to be the object of their steadfast attention. They must
have gone back to their pen to roost, she realized, and anyway she had
nothing to offer them, but she waited a little longer, just in case.

When the phone stopped ringing, she went back inside to check
on Faye, who had already fallen asleep on top of her bedcovers. When
Trish lay down next to her, the girl woke up and said in a froggy
voice, "I was having a nightmare about giant rats."

"There are no giant rats," Trish said. "Just me. Go back to sleep
now."

And the girl did, instantly, as if she had never been awake at all.

For the better part of an hour Trish lay next to her daughter's hot, thrumming little form, remembering what she had almost forgotten: the shadow-men and devil's agents of her childhood, the tangled forests full of whispering crows, the rain and distant thunder of restless sleep, the dark weather now edging back into her own muddled dreams.

18.
·····

THE BOY AT THE WINDOW

THE BOY WAITS AT THE WINDOW. FOR THE THIRD TIME IN AS MANY days he has been grounded, confined to his room except to eat his meals and go to school. Though he hates this house and everyone in it, he has come to enjoy sitting on the old radiator, no one but him, waiting and watching.

His father was supposed to have been home for dinner, but dinner is over and he is nowhere to be seen. The house is in a state of anticipation, the children monitoring the windows, checking and rechecking, wanting to be the first to spot the pickup coming up the drive. Up here, the boy has an advantage. He will be able to see the father before anyone else—if he wanted, he could be the first at the door to greet him.

Unlike the others, the boy doesn't usually get worked up over his father's infrequent homecomings, but today he has something to show. The children of the house always have something to show: a piano solo or a poem about clouds, crocheted mittens or a dolphin carved from soap. The boy never has anything except dumb art projects from school or his report card, which he generally prefers to keep to himself. But today, for once, he has something.

PRESIDENT'S COUNCIL ON FITNESS
—

HEREBY CERTIFIES THAT *Rusty Richards* HAS ATTAINED THE PHYSICAL FITNESS AND PROFICIENCY STANDARDS OF THE 7TH-GRADE AGE GROUP AND HAS CONTRIBUTED TO THE PHYSICAL WELL-BEING OF OUR NATION.

To earn such a certificate, seventh-grade boys are required to run a mile in fewer than ten minutes, do fifteen push-ups and sit-ups and at least one pull-up. The boy cheated on the mile (ran three laps instead of four), only did push-ups while the coach was watching, and did thirty sit-ups just for the heck of it because even though he is a blubber-gut, the boy can do sit-ups all day long. It was the pull-up that was the problem. Because everyone in the gym made a point of coming to watch, you could not cheat the pull-up. Apparently there was something terribly entertaining about watching fat boys and weaklings nearly kill themselves to perform a single pull-up. And even worse, as far as the boy was concerned, Coach had declared that if you failed to earn your certificate you wouldn't pass gym, which meant you would fail the seventh grade and be forced to relive its miseries all over again.

The boy was third to last. The only two behind him in line were two extreme fatties who had hung back until the bitter end, hoping to be saved by the end-of-period bell or a miracle fire drill.

To save himself the humiliation, the boy said to Coach, *Can't do it*, and Coach cupped his hand behind his ear as if he hadn't heard correctly. *CAN'T?* Coach boomed, giving everyone a crazy, wide-eyed look as if this were the most astounding word he'd ever heard. *CAN'T*, Coach said, was not in his personal dictionary. *CAN'T* was a word for Democrats and war deserters. *CAN'T*, Coach said, *has no place in his gym, or in the US of A and its sovereign territories, for that matter. So get your goldarned butt up to the bar and give it your best goldarned shot.*

The boy stepped up on the little stool and grabbed the bar with both hands and hung there for a few seconds, doomed. He decided he wouldn't even try, would just hang there feeling sorry for himself until Coach told him to get off. But something happened: he started to get mad. He was mad, of course, about Coach turning his pull-up into a larger spectacle than it otherwise would have been, but then he started to think about his sorry life, his bad haircut and foot odor problem, about how everyone in Old House teased and badgered him, called him names like Busty Rusty or whispered, *Ree-Pul-Seeeevo!* whenever he came into the room, how Aunt Beverly wouldn't talk to him or look at him for an entire day and then during family prayer would make a special point to ask Heavenly Father to help the boy come closer to Christ and improve his self-control. He thought about his father, who barely knew his name, who not only ignored him but his mother as well, his mother who was spending more and more time up in her dark bedroom instead of trying to bring the boy back to Big House where he belonged, and right there, hanging from a bar in front of everyone with his gym shorts threatening to slide down, the boy nearly wept with rage, his head hot, his mouth filling with spit, and he realized he was pulling himself up, nearly halfway already, his arms burning and fingers cramped, and somebody cried, *Go! Go! Go!* and somebody else shouted, *Don't strain your girdle!* because this was Coach's favorite saying and it was one of the few insults you could use in class without getting into trouble. And then, for some reason, an image of his Aunt Trish passed through the boy's mind, her long neck and shampoo smell and full bust stretching the fabric of her sweater, and he began to plead with himself, *No boner, please, please, no boner*, because of all the bad things that had ever happened to him, a boner while attempting a President's Council on Fitness pull-up just might be the most tragic. He was able to fight off the boner successfully but in the process lost some of his momentum, which only made his face get redder, his whole body shaking as if electrified, his eyes bulging dangerously from his head, and, lifted by hot gusts of fury and lust and frustration, he made one last pull, groaning and grimacing and straining his girdle so badly it felt like his intestines might fly out of his butt like paper streamers.

Coach, who never cursed in front of the students, shouted, *Holy Christ, son, that's enough!* and the boy let go of the bar and flopped to the mat. People clapped him on the back, saying, *Good job, good job,* and Thor Erickssen, the third-most-popular kid in the seventh grade, nudged him with his toe and said, *Nice going, whatever-your-name-is.*

Now, only a few hours later, the boy has nearly forgotten all those twisted, uncontrollable feelings, remembers only the glory of the moment, sees only the certificate in his hands, signed by Jimmy Carter, President of the United States of America.

He goes to the closet and, from his hiding spot at the back of the unused and difficult-to-reach top shelf, takes down some of his secret things. This is where he keeps his notebooks, into which he empties the messy contents of his head, as well as his other special items, most of them stolen or salvaged: comic books and magazines and canisters of black powder, a crucifix taken from a roadside memorial, a railroad spike, and piece of jasper that in the boy's mind is a miniature planet over which he presides like a jealous but benevolent god. In this family, nearly all of the children have appropriated some niche or hidey-hole where they can squirrel away their treasured objects, the talismans that embody their most vulnerable selves and so must be protected from the obliterating crowd.

The boy's notebooks are full of doodles and scribbled observations and endless pages of lists (*7 Favorite Ice Cream Toppings, 12 Best Insect Monsters of All Times*), the longest by far his comprehensive *LIST OF REVENGE*, which he revises at least twice a week and comprises, at the present time, thirty-nine names. One entire notebook is reserved for blueprints and strategies and plans, some minor:

Fake Blood Recipes
1. Katchup + water
2. Elmers + food coloring
3. Melt red crayons in pot

some slightly more ambitious:

How to Get More Popular at School
1. take a shower
2. bell bottoms
3. hand out candy
4. mustash?

and the one, of course, he has been developing lately, his Grand Master Plan, which he has already put into motion by giving June the picture of his fake mother, and which will take care of his troubles once and for all:

GRAND MASTER PLAN

Rose-of-Sharon + June

$$+ \qquad = \text{Good Times Forever}$$

Rusty + Aunt Trish

To the boy, this makes perfect sense. It is simple and yet complicated, which he believes all good plans should be. He also believes, despite all evidence to the contrary, that he can bend the world to his will, that he can manufacture a place in it where he will be happy.

Once the boy saw a commercial that begins with a father and mother and their two children walking around the house stiff-legged and grimacing, in obvious discomfort. They each fix themselves a big glass of Metamucil, drink it down, and the next thing you know they're sitting around the kitchen table, cheerful and unconstipated, eating waffles and having a good laugh. And then the deep, mellow voice of the narrator comes on: *Metamucil: Just One More Regular Family*.

The boy can't get the commercial out of his head. A regular family. That's all he's ever wanted. A regular family that can sit around a regular-sized kitchen table drinking some refreshing Metamucil and having a good laugh. But when he tries to picture his ideal regular family, things get a little odd. His mother is there, of course, happy and full of life in the morning sunshine, and June whistles an old-fashioned melody while making waffles and bacon for the boy, who is dressed, for some reason, in full Royal Canadian Mountie regalia and is grooming his noble steed, right there in the dining room, while he waits for his secret admirer, Aunt Trish, to come downstairs for breakfast in her gauzy nightgown.

That his father does not appear in his fantasy or in his plans for a happier life is not lost on the boy. He tries not to, but most of the time he hates his father, blames him for the sorry state of his life, wants to hurt him in ways that make him scared of himself. Sometimes he has no choice but to put him right up at the top of his *LIST OF REVENGE* at #2 behind Aunt Beverly. But tonight, for these few hours, he is willing to forgive, to suspend his plans and schemes and give his father a chance. For the boy, it is terribly simple: all his father needs to do is come home and remark kindly on the boy's certificate. It won't take much, maybe a smile, a squeeze of the shoulder, and the boy will go to bed happy and all will be well.

It is full dark now. When a car comes down the road he can't be sure if it's his father's pickup because all he can see are the glare of headlights. He must wait for the headlights to reach the turnoff into Old House's driveway, and each time they pass by, keep going over the hill toward town, the bubble of anger in his stomach quivers and swells. Downstairs the other children are madly practicing their piano solos and reciting their poems and arguing over who will get to open the door when the big moment comes. Cars pass, one after another, but the boy keeps his position on the radiator until his butt is sore and his head hurts.

It is bedtime now and he has lost count of the cars that have passed—his best guess is six thousand—and his vision is blurry, the lights sprouting strange rainbow colors, and when one more passes, the bubble in the boy's stomach pops and he is seized by a spasm of rage so intense and electrifying that he misses it when it's gone. On shaking legs he goes to his closet and from his secret hiding spot takes down a plastic canister, the one with *Green Magnesium Flash Powder* written on the side. He opens it and taps out some of the powder—black, not green—onto the face of the certificate. He opens the window, letting in cool air and the smell of new grass. He can hear a dog barking, the quiet murmur of the river. He takes a match from the book he keeps in his nylon wallet and waits for a staggered line of cars to pass, *one . . . two . . . three*. He waits for one more car, only one, he will give his father one final chance, and when the headlights pass by he strikes the match and touches the flame to the corner of his certificate.

It doesn't burn well at first, so he tilts it down a little and when the sifting powder reaches the flame he is blinded for a moment by the bright green flash. Jerking back, he lets the certificate go into the night, where it catches a cushion of air, flaring and spinning for a moment, and softly the boy says, *Huzzah,* as he watches it circle in the breeze, burning until it is just a husk of glowing ash spiraling into the dark bushes below.

19.

·····

NO ORDINARY SLEAZEBALL

THE FIRST TIME SHE CAME, GOLDEN WAS ASLEEP ON THE BARGE. HE
liked to stretch out on the old orange and brown plaid dinosaur and
doze for a while before retiring to his trailer, which was about as
roomy and comfortable as an iron lung. He brought the Barge out
here after Sister Barbara, his part-time secretary at the office back in
Virgin, refused to come to work unless he got rid of it. The couch's
signature tuna smell, she claimed, was activating her migraines.
So instead of hauling it out to the dump where it belonged, he'd
brought it to Nevada and set it out in the dry desert air, which so far
had done very little to dispel the fishy odor. Made with enough lumber and hardware to construct a footbridge across a Peruvian cre-
vasse, the Barge had been rained on once, suffered a few direct hits
from the local crow population, but had held up nicely otherwise.
Golden figured that if he left it in this isolated spot and someone
came across it, say a couple of centuries hence, it would be in much
the same shape, though one could hope the fish smell might be gone
by then.

Tonight, he had himself spread out the entire length of it, with his
head on one arm and his toes touching the other. Still damp from his
evening shower and with nothing to do but watch the sun set golden
and smoky over the distant mountains, he closed his eyes to listen to
the mild desert breeze, napped a little, woke up briefly at the call of a
mockingbird.

He'd hardly slept since learning Weela was Ted Leo's wife. He'd been puzzling it out, going over every angle, and he'd been able to convince himself, mostly, that this new development was a good thing, a blessing. Maybe even God's way of looking out for him. She was off-limits to him now, even more so than when he thought she was a prostitute, and he would have to forget about her and get back to the things that mattered: finishing this job, getting his business out from under the threat of bankruptcy, and focusing on his family.

And so, feeling just a little bit virtuous and exceptionally clean— he had succeeded, finally, in washing every trace of peanut butter out of his private area—he had sunk into the worn springs of the couch intent on a round of fitful dozing under the wide Nevada sky before retiring to his bunk for the night.

He woke up to the sound of footsteps. He was sure it was Leonard, who sometimes got bored with perusing pornographic magazines and playing poker down at the motel with the other men, and showed up at Golden's trailer wanting to throw a Frisbee or show off a few of his self-taught tae kwon do katas. It had turned dusky, the sky still molten at the edges, and in the gray light he could make out a shadowy form about a hundred yards off, coming up the shallow rise.

Golden sat up, yawned. "Leonard," he called. "That you?"

Not until she stepped out of the sagebrush about thirty yards off could he see who it was.

"*Allo?*" she said.

"Yes?" he said. "Weela?" The word sounded ridiculous in his mouth, and he said it again under his breath as a kind of practice. He got to his feet, then sat back down, unsure of how to receive her. He was wearing an old work T-shirt, cut-off sweats, and his hideous flipperlike feet—malformed from years of wearing too-small shoes, covered in bunions and terrifying to look upon, especially for the unprepared—were in plain view.

She smiled and held out an aluminum pan covered in tinfoil. He jammed his feet as far into the fine desert sand as they would go. She wore a denim skirt, a rough green hand-knit cardigan, and her hair in a single thick braid. "The other night, I made too much food," she said, eyes lowered. "So I bring this."

He made swimming motions with his arms in the struggle to extract himself from the collapsed cushions of the Barge, and once he'd made it onto his feet there was an awkward exchange involving the transfer of two potholders along with the pan. To be this close to her made him a little dizzy, and he tried to come up with something to say, something that would keep her from turning around and going back home.

Suddenly he needed to sneeze, and his nasal spray was nowhere in sight. He rubbed his nose, looked back at the trailer, grimaced, and then made a reluctant gesture toward the Barge. "Would you like to have a seat?"

Like just about everything else in his life, the Barge embarrassed him, but once they'd settled down on it (she took the middle cushion, which seemed significant), he felt grateful to have it; its generous proportions offered ample space for two respectable people to sit and converse comfortably without having to worry over questions involving propriety or decorum. Even better, they could accomplish this out in the open, nothing to hide, for God and all the world to see.

The pressure continued to build inside his head, and he tried to ward it off by studiously refusing to think about it and then shaking his head in abject denial, but it came anyway: a big, furious chop of a sneeze that rocked him backward and sounded out over the quiet hills like a gunshot. Weela flinched, but seemed to recover herself quickly.

"God bless you," she said.

He rubbed his nose. "Sorry about that, Weela, I didn't mean to scare—"

"My name," she said. "Huila. Weela, no. Ooo-*eee*-la, yes." She crouched and wrote it out with her finger in the sand. *HUILA*

"Ooo-eee-la." It sounded like the call of a bird. "It's pretty. I'm sorry I've had it wrong all this time."

She pointed at the trailer. "This is your home?"

"Oh, this thing," Golden said. "It's my home away from home, I guess."

And just like that they were making small talk. For so long he'd gotten little more than silence out of her, and hearing her speak felt like a privilege. They talked about the construction project, about what it was like to live in a brothel ("Not good," she said, shaking her head). He asked her why she sometimes washed her clothes in the pond and she explained that Ted Leo, instead of buying her a washer and dryer of her own, insisted she use the community appliances in the brothel's common area, where she was always running into the hookers with their extravagant underwear and shrieking laughter. So she went up to the pond every once in a while to get away, to wash a few clothes in peace, even though the water of the pond was not exactly clean.

"Ted Leo," she had said, laughing, "he says sometimes, 'Why do I have this dirt in my pockets?'" and Golden felt an undeniable stab of pleasure at hearing her mimic her husband's froggy voice.

And then she said something that flummoxed him: "Your wife. Does she miss you all the time you are here?"

He'd assumed Ted Leo had told her about his lifestyle, which was one of the reasons he felt so gratified for the kindness she had shown him; most women outside the church, he'd found out over the years, were not at all agreeable to the idea of polygamy, or those who practiced it. Men, on the other hand, never failed to be intrigued.

Six years ago he'd been audited by the IRS, and his case agent was a plump, flirtatious woman from the Phoenix field office, who touched his arm when she talked and made him feel giddy and uncomfortable at the same time; the entire process seemed more like a date with an old girlfriend than an IRS audit. At the end of their first meeting she went over his list of deductions, and she spoke with the tone of a mother scolding a naughty child.

"Sixteen dependents, Mr. Richards! My *goodness*, you've been quite a busy man!"

Golden bunched up his shoulders. "Hee," he said.

"But I'm having a problem with some of the birth dates here. Three of them fall within two weeks of each other, in the very same year. There must be a mistake?"

"No mistake, ma'am." He knew the three birthdays she was referring to. They belonged to Wayne, Martin, and Boo, aka the Three Stooges, whose births marked a grim and trying chapter in the Richards family history. They had all moved into Big House together for a few weeks with the idea that a mass consolidation would make everything easier, but with all the wives in either the last stages of pregnancy or the aftermath of a difficult birth, Golden, with the reluctant assistance of a couple of the older girls, was left to be nanny, cook, maid and disciplinarian. Instantly the place fell apart. Children ran wild, scavenging whatever food they could find and splitting up into guerrilla factions that carried out raids on each other, finally sectioning off and declaring different parts of the house their own sovereign territories. The Three Stooges, it turned out, were all cranky, colicky, insomniac, or some perfectly evil combination of the above, and the never-ending late-night shriek-a-thon was enough to break the most hardened prisoner of war. To escape the noise, the other children called a temporary truce and set up camp in the basement, leaving Golden to make bottles, change diapers, and spend hour after midnight hour with one newborn or another braced against his shoulder, doing anything and everything—sometimes including taking one or two of the little buggers out back to set them on top of the vibrating swamp cooler—in the all-out quest to induce a burp.

The IRS agent pushed her reading glasses onto the bridge of her nose and had a closer look at his return. She said, "Then how on earth . . . ?"

"I'm the husband to the, you know, mothers."

She peered at him over her reading glasses, and it began to dawn on her: he was not just some ordinary sleazeball off the street who'd fathered sixteen children by several different women and had the unbelievable brass to list them all on his tax return. He was actually *married* to these different women, at the same time. You could tell by looking at him: the homemade chinos, the flannel shirt, the believer's haircut. He was one of *those*.

She gripped her pen like a weapon and pushed away from the table as if he might make a move to grab her. He leaned back and put his hands in his pockets to show her he was just as harmless as the next guy, but she fled the room, and the next thing he knew he had a new agent, a man with a bristle cut who gave Golden the hairy eyeball and said he wanted only one-sentence answers to his questions and no lip. By the time the audit was over Golden owed the IRS an extra three thousand dollars.

But Huila, apparently, had not yet been given any reason to view him as a sexual maniac or an exploiter of women. As far as she was concerned he was just your average guy with one wedding ring and one wife to go with it. He was *normal*, was what he was, and for him *normal* was a condition so rarely experienced it felt exhilarating, maybe even a little naughty.

So when she asked if his wife missed him, he answered like any normal man with normal thoughts and a normal life might: "Oh, she misses me to *death*, you know, but I guess she'll have to find a way to make do."

Huila laughed—a cute, childish sound like a burst of hiccups—and Golden was beginning to think this business of being normal was highly underrated.

He asked her where she'd been the previous week—he hadn't seen her on his daily walks. She explained that they had gone to Las Vegas, which meant that Ted Leo went out and conducted business and gambled while she stayed in their condominium watching soap operas.

"I would rather be here, I think, but Ted Leo is the husband, you know."

"Yes, I know. I mean, I think I know."

There ensued the awkward silence of strangers in an elevator. She patted the cushion a couple of times and stood up. "So I will go. Ted Leo will be back soon."

He stood, still holding the pan, grinning like an idiot. Before he could think of anything to say, she said, "Bye-bye," turned, and walked back down the hill.

When the idea struck him that he should at least say goodbye in return, it was too late, she was much too far away, already dissolving into the winking dusk.

He took the pan into his miniature kitchen, where he studied the potholders—both handmade and decorated with cross-stitched roosters—and then peeled away the tinfoil to find baked ziti on one side and lasagna on the other. Though she'd said these were leftovers, the pasta looked and smelled freshly made. He found the only clean utensil available—a splintery wood mixing spoon—and took three or four bites of the still-warm, delectable ziti before he realized, with a small zing of terror in his heart, that he couldn't eat any more: for the first time he could remember, he had lost his appetite.

THE COUNCIL OF THE TWELVE

At home that weekend Golden attended Council Meeting for the first time in two months. Traditionally it was held on Wednesday nights, but because of Golden's difficult out-of-town schedule Uncle Chick had given the okay for a special session on Sunday afternoon. Even though the special meeting was billed as a favor to Golden, for him to be able to get up to speed on church business and fraternize with his fellow apostles, Golden knew the truth: Uncle Chick was worried that Golden was losing his standing and influence among these men and—because Golden was Uncle Chick's staunchest supporter and, by the reckoning of some, his heir apparent—that Uncle Chick was losing something as well.

The meetings were held in the narrow, cramped room behind the chapel, and the men all gathered around a rickety banquet table, hunched over their arms as if the ceiling were slowly lowering itself upon their heads. Weak afternoon light filtered through the single small window, giving the room, with its rough stone walls and subterranean chill, the feel of a monastery prayer chamber or a cell on death row. Generally they took care of church business in the first half hour, spent another half hour debating doctrine and scripture, and spent the rest of the time commiserating—which is to say, complaining in communal fashion—about their exhausting and absurdly complicated lives. More than anything, coming to council meeting was the best excuse available to get away from the wives and children for a couple of hours.

Though these meetings had never been the highlight of Golden's week, he had begun to miss them. It was reassuring to be among men who understood the daily struggle of keeping mouths fed and bodies clothed, of being forever and always on the spot, of bearing up under the weight of their dubious authority with any grace at all.

On this Sunday afternoon, as he ducked under the doorway, his nose suddenly assaulted by the competing aromas of at least half a dozen aftershaves, the first thing he heard was, "The Golden One!" This from Apostle Coombs, a jolly little man prone to outbursts of good-natured shouting. Apostle Coombs hollered this greeting at every opportunity and Golden had yet to pin down whether the man was using it sarcastically—in reference to Golden's widely known failure to become the One Mighty and Strong—or if he was simply being friendly in his obnoxious way. Along with Uncle Chick, it looked like the rest of the apostles were already in attendance. Mostly they were men of a certain age, chapped by the weather and dressed in snap-button shirts and suspenders, who looked like they should have been hanging over the rail at a cattle auction rather than fidgeting in this gloomy room, preparing to discuss the sacred business of God's one true church upon the earth.

Every time they gathered, it was hard not to notice that they were a Council of the Twelve who numbered—since Apostle Barrett passed on last year—only eight.

Because he'd been playing hooky for two months it was, naturally, Golden's turn to offer the opening prayer. Even as he called on God to bless them with His spirit, to guide them in their deliberations, images of Huila flashed into his mind: smiling shyly as she sat next to him on the Barge, close enough to touch, or picking her way through the glowing rabbit brush toward home, stealing a look back over her shoulder. Even as he thanked God for His generous bounty, for the truth of the Principle that guided their lives, he was in his heart thanking his lucky stars for the aluminum pan and cross-stitched pot-holders that sat on the kitchen counter in his Airstream, for all they represented, for the excuse they provided him to see Huila again.

No matter how hard he tried, he could not summon the will to pay attention during the meeting. Nels Jensen, as always, was doing most of the talking. Nels was a smiling second-generation Swede who was so thoroughly and annoyingly friendly that no matter how hard you might try it was impossible to work up any real dislike for the guy. He had left the Short Creek church after a doctrinal dispute with the elders there, and after showing up in Virgin only seven years ago he had already established himself as a political and spiritual force. His humble ambitions—to make more money than any single person in America, to marry as many wives and father as many children as the good Lord would allow, to one day lead the church into the latter days and help usher in the Second Coming of Christ—never seemed calculated, but just a natural part of his person, like his cheerful, rub-bery accent or big velvety ears. He was deeply dedicated to Principle, believed in priesthood lineage and direct revelation and the infal-libility of God's sacred texts, none of which, according to him, was anything to be ashamed of. "Do we have to dress like bumpkins and hide out in the weeds like criminals?" he would ask in the reasonable, Scandinavian manner that never seemed to offend any of the bumpkins or criminals in question. "We should be candles on a hill, yes? How can we be ashamed of the truth?"

As the successful salesman of a broad range of chemical fertilizers and pesticides, he knew the importance of advertising, of spreading the word. During council meetings he often wondered aloud why they weren't more missionary-minded, why they weren't bringing the world around to their way of thinking instead of worrying all the time what the world thought of them. Someone, usually Apostle Lambson, would bring up the fact that their lifestyle was, technically, illegal, and to go out proselytizing might induce the authorities, as they had in the past, to swoop in, throw the men in jail and leave the women and children at the mercy of Social Services. Apostle Jensen would inquire agreeably if this wasn't fear and doubt talking, and would Jesus have brought His truth to the world if He had given in to fear and doubt? Apostle Lambson would remind Nels that for all the wonderful things Jesus had accomplished, He did, let's all remember, wind up getting Himself into some fairly serious trouble.

Uncle Chick, in his smoked-lens glasses and chambray work shirt, always listened to these exchanges with an air of weary patience, as if he had heard it all before, which he had. Patience, along with hard work and obedience and long-suffering, were the virtues Uncle Chick preached, and there wasn't much point in arguing about any of it. God worked in His own way, in His own time. It was up to you to watch, to wait, and if you were faithful and obedient, His will would be revealed. Uncle Chick was the most practical of men, living in a most unpractical way, and so it was not difficult at all for him to abide Nels Jensen—an obvious threat to his authority, a man who viewed patience as a weakness rather than a virtue—for the simple reason that Nels Jensen paid more in tithing than all of them put together.

The only thing Golden could hold against Nels Jensen was that Nels, in nearly every way, made him look bad. He had a successful business, four happy wives and eighteen children who lived in a single three-story mansion with all the latest in features and design, including a restaurant-style kitchen and an intercom system that allowed the inhabitants of the cavernous house to keep track of each other's whereabouts at all times. The house even had a complaints box in the foyer, all tricked out with a tidy pile of scrap paper and a pencil affixed to a string.

Whenever Beverly praised the Jensen family—which she seemed to be doing on a regular basis these days—Nola would always be sure to remind Beverly that she was sure Nels Jensen had room in that big mansion of his for another wife, and Beverly would always give Nola a look that said, *I would love to join the Jensen family, if only to get away from you*, and Golden would find himself thinking that if he ever became delusional or foolhardy enough to outfit one of his houses with a complaints box, it would need to be about the size of a refrigerator.

Before the closing prayer that afternoon, Uncle Chick asked if Golden had any questions, seeing as how he had been out of the loop for a while. At first, Golden shook his head, and then he thought of something. "Does anybody know how to get gum out of hair?"

The apostles looked at him with their mouths open: could he be serious? This was a question for homemaking day at Relief Society, not for the esteemed members of the Council of the Twelve. Apostle Russell nudged Apostle Throckmorten and wondered aloud if maybe this was the sort of thing that filled your head when you stopped coming to council meetings.

"Little crankcase grease'll get gum outta just about anything," mumbled Apostle Dill, suddenly screwing his face up in embarrassment at having revealed himself as a man who might know such a thing. He sighed, added, "But then, you know, you got the problem of what to do with the crankcase grease."

On their way out, Uncle Chick appeared next to Golden, asked him how the job was going, how close he was to finishing. They stepped from the chapel doors into a cool wind scented with sage and ozone that rifled their clothes like a hundred expert hands.

"Getting there," Golden said, praying Uncle Chick would not

bring up the subject of Maureen Sinkfoyle and her unresolved marital status. "Next month or two, looks like."

"We miss you around here, you know," Chick said.

Though Golden wasn't sure what "we" Uncle Chick was referring to, he started to say that he missed being here too, but Uncle Chick launched into one of his coughing fits, each cough a dull axe biting into wet and rotted wood. Chick, who had spent much of his twenties and thirties underground breathing the bad air in gypsum and molybdenum mines, had been fighting emphysema for thirty years, but only now did it seem to be taking a toll on him. Up close, in the clear afternoon light, it was difficult to miss the pallor of his skin, the bruised eye sockets behind the dark glasses, the shaking hand that pressed a handkerchief to his lips. In the week since Golden had last seen him he seemed to have developed a slight tremor of the head.

Seeing Uncle Chick like this only made the realization hit harder: he was letting the man down. With the Prophet incapacitated and confined to a wheelchair, Uncle Chick had spent the last two decades doing everything in his power to keep the church together and thriving, but the job seemed to be getting the better of him: membership was down, many of the faithful having defected to more strident sects or succumbed to the temptations of the world, and the few newcomers were mostly like Nels Jensen, who came in wanting to change everything, who wanted fresh leadership, a new vision for new times.

"You'd think an outfit like ours could only get *bigger*," Uncle Chick had said once, a wisp of sadness in his voice, "but this one just keeps on shrinking."

And where had Golden, Uncle Chick's most reliable ally, been during such difficult days? Locked away inside his own grief and guilt, and lately, off in the wilds of Nevada, mingling with lowlifes and prostitutes and pining after his boss's wife.

Uncle Chick, it seemed, had made the mistake so many others had when it came to Golden Richards: he'd given him his faith and trust.

In a gesture of sympathy, Golden attempted to pat the old man on the back, but Uncle Chick tried to push Golden's arm away and the two men ended up temporarily entangled, and both, for their own reasons, too tired to do anything about it. They stood like that for a moment, gazing out over the valley toward black cliffs in the distance, leaning on each other like two prizefighters in the clinch, looking to buy a little time. Uncle Chick let go a gargling sigh, releasing his hold on Golden's wrist, and pushed himself toward the dirt parking lot, where one of his wives was waiting to drive him home.

Over his shoulder he said, "You just finish that job, all right? You finish it fast as you can, and come back where you're needed. We can't wait on you much longer."

FATHER AND DAUGHTER

After the drive home from church, Golden pulled up next to Old House. He circled around back, hoping to steal a few minutes of solitude in the Doll House before the Summit of the Wives commenced at four o'clock sharp.

He found four-year-old Sariah, still in her Sunday dress, in the backyard alone. She was squatting next to the back steps, carefully scooping gravel into piles with an old spatula.

"My daddy," she said matter-of-factly, without looking up at him. She picked up a pebble, considered it closely, tossed it aside as if it didn't match her expectations.

"Your mama know you're out here?" Golden said. "It's cold for you without your coat."

"I'm *fine*," she said, exasperated. "I'm trying to get these rocks together, if you don't mind." Four years old and had her mother down to a T. She was Beverly's youngest, brown-eyed and feisty, even more self-possessed, it seemed, than the rest of Beverly's girls. He tried not to think about what kind of trouble she might cause in the coming years.

She looked up at him. "Are you going to stay here with us?"

"I'm staying tonight. Tomorrow I have to go back to work."

"Yes," she sighed. "I know."

"I don't like going away, honey, but I have to."

"I have to do things too," she said, indicating her piles of rocks, "and it makes me so *tired*."

Golden eased down into a squatting position and helped Sariah get her gravel piles arranged just the right way. From the very beginning he'd always played with the kids. Wooden blocks, mud pies, pillow forts, it didn't matter, he was always in the middle of it, especially during those early years, living the childhood he'd never had.

It seemed that she forgot about him for a good minute or so, singing a jumble of songs and making spit bubbles, as she created her own gravel configurations with the spatula. He felt a slight sting of resentment about being so blatantly ignored, but then she looked up, smiling as if she'd gotten the better of him, her fine brown hair falling down over one eye, and he was struck by how much she looked like her older sister Glory, dead now almost three years. He shook his head, trying to clear his thoughts, but his eyes watered anyway and his daughter sensed something. She stood up, staring intently at him, and rested a chubby hand on his knee.

"Daddy?"

"Yes, honey?"

"Are you mad at me?"

Pierced to his heart, he said, "Oh no, honey. No. Your daddy loves you."

"I know," she said, wiping her mouth with the back of her hand. She held out the ruffles of her dress, snagged with dead leaves and sticks, and tilted her head. "It's because I'm so pretty."

He wanted to pull her to him, to feel the compact heft of her against his chest, to smell her sweet breath, to tell her that he would never let her come to harm, but he held still, paralyzed by his love for her.

"I'm not mad at you either, Daddy," she said. "Mama's not mad either, too."

"Well, I hope not." He stood and, as he did so, stole the briefest of kisses, brushing his lips against her shining hair. She glanced around and batted at her head as if bothered by a fly.

He held out his hand to her. "You want to come in with me? I don't think you should be out here all alone."

She took her time deliberating. She looked up at the sun, placed her finger in her nostril for a moment. Finally, she said, "Where's Cooter?" It was a stalling tactic all the smart ones learned; when you didn't want to do something, ask a question. When confronted with a question that has no good answer, change the subject.

"Cooter's in the back of the pickup eating his food," he said. "We can go see him after dinner." Though Beverly had not gotten around to putting up a sign about it, it had recently become official: Cooter had been permanently disinvited from Old House.

Sariah sighed again. It was clear she believed her existence to be an especially difficult one.

Golden held out his hand. "You coming in with me?"

She blew a raspberry of disgust, took his hand, and they went inside together.

TWO UNHAPPY PEOPLE

The following Wednesday night, in the darkened cell of his Airstream, he had nothing better to do than stand next to the three-quarter-sized refrigerator with his pants at his ankles and a flashlight trained on his penis. A half hour ago the generator had run out of gas, which meant he had no lights, no stove, no radio—nothing but darkness and a flashlight. After a long drive from Vegas and an entire afternoon spent fighting with the drywallers over who was responsible for the two thousand dollars in leftover gypsum board, he did not have the energy to do anything about it. Instead, he felt happy enough to stand in the dark and consider the gum in his pubic hair, which had not broken down and crumbled away after repeated shower scrubbings, but now had separated into three separate pellets, shiny and grayish and connected with threads of gum as hard and brittle as spun glass. Lately, this had become a habit: pants down, staring at the gum, wondering at the mystery of it and trying to come to a conclusion as to its symbolic significance. He had been taught, and he tended to believe, that there was meaning in everything, that God's will could be found in the details too often missed by the inattentive —but this detail, and God's part in it, had him stumped. He took the largest part of it between his fingers and was thinking about pulling it out with one mighty rip, once and for all, when something scraped against the side of the trailer.

He started, dropping the flashlight and falling back against the refrigerator, which caused the entire trailer to rock to the side. He pulled up his pants and opened the door, but it was a cloudy night with the rumble of thunder in the far distance, and he could make out nothing except the humps of sagebrush and mesquite against the faint radioactive glow of the PussyCat Manor on the other side of the hill. He found the flashlight and pointed it out into the night, but its dim beam had little effect beyond a few feet.

"Mr. Golden?" came a voice.

He swung the beam around and aimed it south, where Huila, half concealed behind a juniper tree, peered into the light and turned, poised as if to run.

"Huila!" Golden said. "Yes, it's me."

She walked up, clutching the collar of her sweater to her throat. "*Ay mi Dios!*" she said. "I thought you was gone, and I was walking and saw a light in there, in your little house. I thought somebody was stealing—"

"Oh no, it's just me," Golden said. "The generator went off, so I don't have any light, just this flashlight."

For some reason—maybe it had to do with the darkness—they were whispering at each other.

"I threw a stick," she said. "To scare the thief!"

"Well, you scared me," Golden said.

She stood near the bottom of the steps and he was bent at the waist to be able to stick his head out the trailer door, like someone about to disembark a plane. Because he'd had no time to button them, he was holding his pants up with his hand. He asked her to give him a moment and he shut the door, fastened his pants and cast around frantically in the dark for his boots. When he met her again outside and inadvertently shone his flashlight into her eyes, the look on her face, carved into simple planes by the yellow light, told him there was something wrong. He could not be sure, but it looked like she had been crying.

He asked her if she would like to sit down. He took his place at one end of the Barge, she at the other.

"I needed to get out," she said, "but I'm sorry to be always coming here."

"I'm glad you came," he said. "I like the company."

They were quiet for a time, on their opposite ends of the couch. Because he could not really see her, he had to suppress the urge to point the flashlight at her and click it on, to be able to know what to say, to read something in her face.

"It's dark out here, isn't it?" he said. "I wish—" And then he had an idea. A fire. He would build a fire. He didn't know why he hadn't thought of it before. With his failing flashlight he ventured out into the scrub, breaking off twigs and snapping branches from stunted piñon pines that were more like bushes than trees. If she wondered what he was doing, she had the good manners not to ask. Wood-gathering made him feel useful and manly and every branch he picked up he broke over his knee with a splintery *cracktch!* whether it needed breaking or not. The flashlight batteries completely dead now, he wandered in the dark, tripping over rocks and groping along the ground for dead wood, fighting with the bushes not yet ready to give up their branches. It took him only a couple of minutes to get a good fire going, but when he looked behind for Huila's reaction, he found the Barge empty.

"Huila?" he said, his voice tinged with panic.

Just then she moved into the ring of firelight dragging a large juniper branch, which she dumped unceremoniously into the middle of his carefully constructed Boy Scout–style campfire. She sat back on the couch and now, in the flickering glow, he could see that something clouded her face; she kept her chin tucked into her neck and would not look at him.

"Are you okay?" he said.

She wore the same green sweater from last week and she wrapped it more tightly around her chest. Her wet eyes reflected the firelight and she made an almost imperceptible shrug.

She said, "I am not happy."

I am not happy. Those four words formed what had to be the clearest and sanest sentence he had ever heard anyone utter in all his life. For so long he'd been living and working among unhappy people—in the last few years, after what might have been a decade-long renaissance of flummoxed contentment, he had once again become one of those people—and yet none of them, himself included, had ever had the grace or courage to express it as a simple truth, rather than as an excuse for something, or a complaint.

She told him that earlier today she had spoken by phone with her aunt in Guatemala. From the few things that Ted Leo had offered at dinner the other night, Golden knew Ted Leo and Huila had met in the hill country north of the capital, where Ted Leo was a Christian missionary and Huila, as Ted Leo put it, "a simple peasant girl, barefoot and beautiful." What Golden didn't know, and what Huila told him now, was that she had left behind her only child, a then-two-year-old boy named Fredy, whose father had run off to the gold mines of Brazil, leaving Huila in the middle of the night without so much as a goodbye, never knowing that he'd conceived a son. Fredy—her voice quavered when she said his name—was nine years old now, and sick: tuberculosis, the doctors at the clinic said. He would need six months of treatment at a sanatorium to have a chance at recovery.

She produced a wallet-sized snapshot from somewhere inside her sweater and handed it to Golden. The boy in the picture was chubby-cheeked, straining not to smile, with the sweet eyes of a girl.

"He's beautiful," Golden said. "You can't go be with him?"

She shook her head. "Ted Leo won't allow it."

She told him that she and Ted Leo had an arrangement: he gave her a monthly allowance of four hundred dollars, a sum that not only cared for Fredy and the aunt who looked after him, but also her bed-ridden grandfather, her uncle's family, and her cousin, Leti, who was attending secretarial school. In return he asked only the undying devotion of a pet dog; she cooked his meals, cleaned his house, kept his bed warm, and, most importantly, never complained, never required anything of him except an occasional thank-you, and *doesn't that taste wonderful*. She was, as Ted Leo liked to tell people, the perfect Christian wife: pure, faithful and not the slightest bit uppity. The kind of servility only to be found in the third world anymore, and such a relief after a long day spent dealing with a pack of smart-mouthed American hookers.

Golden said, "If you need money . . ."

She shook her head. "Ted Leo will pay, he always pays." She looked at the picture and her eyes clarified with tears. "But Fredy is sick. I am his mother."

In just a few minutes the fire had burned down to a pile of coals that flared and smoked with every slight breeze. Golden felt the urge to inch his way across the Barge, to offer a word of comfort or a hand on her shoulder, but he didn't dare. They sat in silence until she said, "You have children?"

Golden thought about it for a long time. The only truly appropriate response to that question was a big dumb grin and a *Do I ever!* But with Huila, he was supposed to be playing the part of a normal man, a man who lived in a single house with one wife and no more children than could fit comfortably in the back seat of a Buick.

He tried to think of a reasonable number. "Five," he said, which sounded about right, even though five kids in the back of a car, even a big one, might be pushing it. But then he said something that was not in any way reasonable, that came as a complete surprise to him. "Five, and one who died a few years ago."

Even as he said it, he felt himself freeze, felt the blood drain from his face and the tips of his fingers. It was bad enough to mention a dead child to a woman whose own son had just fallen sick, but to bring up his daughter, at a time like this, out of nowhere . . . Ever since she had died, Glory, for him, was not a subject open to discussion. Ask him about her, and he would turn his eyes elsewhere. Mention the strange story of her death, and he would leave the room.

Together, they both stared into the pulsing coals, and then Huila stood up and with a slow deliberateness took three short steps and sat down beside him.

"I'm sorry," Huila said.

"It's okay." He shrugged, looked off into the darkness.

"No," she said, with stern kindness. "Not okay."

He wanted to look at her, but couldn't bring himself to. "It's not okay, you're right." It felt good to be corrected, especially by her.

"She was six years old." And then, as if it were the easiest thing in the world, he told her about Glory. He told her everything.

20.

· · · · ·

ROW OF ANGELS

ONE SPARKLING WINTER DAY NEARLY TEN YEARS EARLIER HE'D COME home for lunch to find out the good news: number fifteen had been born, and even better, number fifteen was a girl. The excitement at Old House was palpable, as if somebody had won a large cash prize. "A girl!" Nola boomed from down the hall as Golden stomped snow off his boots. "We got a handy-dandy girl!"

Lately, the Richards family, especially the mothers in particular, had seen just about enough of boys; the family already sported seven of them and had suffered a dispiriting run of four in a row. Though boys were prized for their potential to one day bear the holy Melchizedek priesthood, to be leaders in the church and soldiers for Christ, they had a significant downside: they were *boys*. Until they turned twelve or so, the mothers agreed, they were as inconvenient and as thoroughly useless as a pack of feral cats. Girls were better in just about every way: more helpful, calmer, more responsible, smarter. A series of distinctions which, unfortunately, didn't seem to change all that much as girls turned into women and boys to men. Though they discussed it only among themselves, and more often than not treated it as a joking matter, the women of the church considered it one of God's great mysteries: why He, in all His wisdom, had ever decided to put the boys in charge.

Little number fifteen, then, was a remedy, a balance-maker, a step in the right direction. She was a healthy, robust baby girl and a cause for celebration.

Or so it seemed for the first few months, until her mother, Beverly, began to notice things. The way her head lolled; her little hands caught in fists that never seemed to unclench; bouts of crying that would make her go instantly stiff with rage. With the first fourteen the mothers had seen it all—jaundice, colic, pinkeye, chicken pox, mumps, ear infections, chronic flatulence—and they were sure these abnormalities, these minor episodes, were nothing little Glory couldn't outgrow. There wasn't so much as a mention of a doctor. Instead, they prayed for her and asked Golden to invite Uncle Chick and some of the priesthood council over to lay their hands on her head and bless her with consecrated oil.

The very night of the blessing, just as Beverly was putting her to bed, Glory went stiff, her face turning red, then a mottled purple as she stopped breathing altogether. When the paramedics arrived, she was breathing again, but still unconscious. The doctors at the Las Vegas children's ward delivered the bad news: spastic cerebral palsy. As she grew, her left arm bent and drew up into her chest, her feet extended so that when she learned to walk with forearm braces, at age four, she did so teetering on her tippy-toes like a clumsy ballerina. She had a lopsided face and long, double-jointed fingers that fluttered and nearly hyperextended themselves when she became excited. She could not speak or gesture or make her intentions known except with garbled barks and moans, while her tongue, thick as an overstuffed wallet, probed and punched at her cheeks.

For the first three years of her life, Golden kept his distance. Something in him was disgusted, even frightened, by this broken little creature, and when he watched her crawl across the floor, using her bent wrists for support like an impaired chimpanzee, or spastically spooning mashed potatoes all over her face with her special utensil with its special orthopedic grip, he felt shame settle on his chest. He knew that somehow or another he was responsible for her condition, and he could do nothing about it. He could do nothing about the bleak future she faced, or the attention she drew in public; he could do nothing about his own juvenile embarrassment when she made wet, lewd noises during the sacrament prayers at church.

None of this was lost on Beverly: nothing ever was. She made it Golden's job to feed his daughter, to hold her in church, to massage her legs, exhausted from their daily marathons of flexing and scissoring, and when she turned four, to drive her to her sessions at the clinic in St. George. It was on these long drives that something began to change. She would sit tucked against the pickup door—held tight by the lap belt, a specially made C-shaped cushion around her neck to keep her from sliding and hitting her head—and talk to him. For minutes at a time she would hold him in an unwavering stare and gurgle and coo and squeal insistently and tirelessly, as if trying to communicate with a drooling dullard or someone in a coma. When he didn't respond with a look or a nod of his head or a word or two of his own, she would bark at him—*Ahnk! Ahnk! Ahhhhnk!*—until he acknowledged her in a way that met her satisfaction.

For so long he had been so distracted by her flailing limbs, her restless, predatory tongue, the alien noises broadcast out of her toothy and crooked mouth—and more importantly by his embarrassment and fear of these things—that he'd failed to notice the brightness in her eyes, the sly, satisfied looks she gave when something went her way. At the clinic, he began to help the aides—three cheerful overweight women in matching pink polyester blouses—with her therapy, a slow straightening of her accordioned left arm, a rolling of wrists and ankles, fine motor skills involving wooden rings and beanbags and buttons, and walking practice between two parallel steel bars. Like a great big kid, kneeling on the green carpet amid the rubber balls and pillows and harnesses, he helped to sing the verses that coincided with each stage of her reflex training:

Gallopy, gallopy, gallopy trot,
Gallopy trot to the blacksmith shop.
Shoe the horse, shoe the mare,
And let the baby colt go bare.

or

Up, down, up, down,
This is the way we go to town.
What to buy, to buy a fat pig,
Home again, home again, jig-a-jig-jig.

At the clinic, for his Glory, he was a different man, one who didn't think twice about acting out nursery rhymes or pretending to flit around the room like a butterfly. At home, when her legs hurt and she would cry until no one else could console her, he would take her into a dark room and sing her these little songs, kneading her thighs and calves, no one else but him and her, and every time it would do the trick.

It had taken only a few weeks before the hard knot of revulsion that lodged in his throat at the very sight of her began to unravel itself, giving way to a welling tenderness so abiding and acute that now, three years after her death, he wondered how he managed to withhold any love for his other children. For so long, he had kept his affection in reserve, parceling it out in scraps and carefully broken-off pieces, and usually in secret so others could not see and become jealous. When he hugged one child, or gave out a stick of gum, there had to be hugs and gum for everyone, even if it meant driving to the Shell station on a Saturday night to buy more gum. He had to be cautious with compliments and kisses and gifts of any kind; over time, he developed a noncommittal stone-faced countenance he employed in the presence of his family so he couldn't be accused of *looking* differently upon one child or wife, of loving one over another, of harboring favorites. Even the smallest gesture of regard had to be planned out well in advance and executed with the discipline and skill of a jewel thief.

Not so with afflicted Glory, who was by her condition exempt from all laws of jealousy and preference. He could love her openly and without restraint, as if she were an only child, the one person in the world who mattered to him, his little heart of hearts—and that's exactly what he did.

He involved himself in every aspect of her therapy, built ramps for her wheelchair, talked shop with the lady therapists about the newest advancements in treatment. His father's love, sealed off for so long by his own insecurities and weaknesses, gushed out of him. He took her to his work sites, showed her off to the roofers and the excavating crews. Every time he stopped in at Old House he would stand at the door and call, "Where's my little chicken?" and wherever she was in the house, his little chicken would respond with a high-pitched squawk. Whenever she caught sight of him, even if he left the room for a minute and returned, her eyes would go wide and she would flap her arms ecstatically, her fingers fluttering and her tongue doing its ardent calisthenics until he picked her up.

He was her sidekick, her protector, her tireless advocate. He was so dedicated to her he took the drastic step of defying Beverly over where she should sit during church meetings. By the time she turned five, and could sit up well on her own and walk a few steps with the aid of forearm crutches, Beverly decided it was time she sat in the front row at church, the pew designated as the Row of Angels where the damaged innocents sat: the two mongoloid brothers; a mute-and-blind girl with eyes that never stopped blinking; a wilting kindergartner who'd been diagnosed with fatal leukemia two years prior but had so far refused to die; a retarded, obese adult named Gordon Thune, who was thirty-eight but had the mind of a five-year-old; the beautiful, ever-smiling teenager, Bettie, who had been born with half a brain.

Every Sunday they sat up front, angels all, to remind the other members what it was like to have one foot in heaven, to be blameless before God. Sometimes the angels acted up, especially the talkative mongoloid brothers, and Uncle Chick had to cough in their direction to shush them.

But Golden didn't want Glory to be an angel, or anything close to it. He didn't want her sitting up in front, part of a spectacle that often provided distraction to the congregation, and sometimes even laughs, such as when the mongoloid brothers, cued by the opening chords of a certain hymn, began an extemporaneous duet of "La Cucaracha" or when the leukemia boy, in the midst of one of Uncle Chick's sermons about godly comportment and reverence, fell asleep and dropped his stainless steel vomit bowl.

Glory would not be part of such a sideshow, he told Beverly, with a ring of authority in his voice that surprised him. He would keep her with him during sacrament meetings, on his lap, safe, as far away from God and heaven as he possibly could.

In honor of her sixth birthday, he built her a playhouse, with leftovers from his construction projects. It would have ornamented brackets and pilasters to match those of Old House, a wooden walk-way connected directly to the front porch, and a window facing west, so she could have a good view of the true love of her life, Raymond the Ostrich.

Since she was a toddler she had adored Raymond. Every time she caught sight of him, even at the distance of two hundred yards from Old House, she let loose unique ululations of delight, a special language of love reserved for Raymond and no one else. Golden had made it a habit of wheeling her out through the west pasture, in any and every kind of weather, and parking her chair at the banks of the river that divided their property from Brother Spooner's next door, so she could watch him strut around occasionally pecking at the ground like a chicken, blinking those extravagantly long eyelashes.

One late fall afternoon, after he'd finished shingling the Doll House roof with expensive Virginia slate skimmed off a trophy home he'd been working on, he hefted her out of her wheelchair and carried her to the river, which was not much of a river at all this time of year, but a trickling stream a few inches deep tracking its way around jut-ting boulders and rippling swells of coarse red sand. Before crossing, he sat them both down on a flat rock and together they removed his work boots and socks. (The boots were a birthday present from Bev-erly and had to be treated with the utmost care.) With her twittering

fingers, she methodically untied the laces—a skill she'd been working on in therapy—and helped him remove the boots. She peeled off
his socks, and tucked them into the boots, which she arranged neatly,
side by side, just as she did with her own shoes every night before bed.

He carried her across the wide riverbed with an exaggerated tiptoeing motion that made her laugh. On the far bank he set her down
in some dry grass next to the barbed-wire fence, where she could lean
on her crutches and watch the ostrich through the wire. Raymond,
though, would not cooperate. He was hiding behind an old Tiplady
feed bin, his trembling tailfeathers the only visible part of him.

"Hey bird!" Golden hollered. "Come here, bird! Lookee here!"
He knew that Brother Spooner would not be happy about him tres-
passing on his property and shouting at his prized bird, but Brother
Spooner and his wife were gone for the weekend, off to visit one of
their daughters in Tucson, and therefore would be none the wiser.
He held out a handful of Cooter's dog food, the kind Spooner had
told him Raymond favored. "Come over here you big stupid bird, get
some of this Alpo! Hey bird!"

Raymond swiveled and poked his head out from behind the
bin, blinked his enormous glossy eyes. At this, Glory screeched, and
because her arms were locked into her crutches and supporting most
of her weight, and she could not clap her wrists together or flap her
hands as was her way, her excitement showed in the severe craning of
her neck, the swaying of her body over the fulcrum of her crutches,
her gaping mouth. Afraid she might topple forward into the barbed
wire, Golden put his hand on her humped back to steady her.

"Come on, bird!" he called to Raymond, who was hesitating again.
"Don't look at me that way. We've got prime dog food for you. Get
your big bird behind over here. Hey, bird!"

There was a silence while they both waited for Raymond to make
a move, and that was when she said it, "Mmmmbbbbirrrr."

He looked down at her. Had he just heard what he thought he'd
heard? His daughter, his own little Glory, uttering what sounded
very much like a word, something you could look up in a dictionary?

Though she could form individual sounds, and had her own special ways of communicating—excited nose-breathing that meant she was hungry, a gurgle at the back of her throat that signified contentment, a siren whine that told you she was in pain—she had never made any sound that, when placed in context with a particular situation, could have been characterized as an actual word. The ladies at the rehabilitation center told him that if she had not learned to talk by the time she turned three or four, she most likely never would.

He watched her out of the corner of his eye, but her attention was locked on Raymond. "Bird?" he called out experimentally. "Hey bird?"

She closed her mouth, screwed her face into a mask of almost frightening concentration, and said it, "Mmmbbbiiirrrddtt."

"Yes!" he cried, so loudly a couple of cows that had come over to see what was going on bolted in panic. "*Bird!*"

He thought about picking her up and taking her back to Old House so she could show off to the rest of the family, but then he had a better idea. He told her not to worry, he'd be right back, he was going to get the others so they could all see Raymond too. "Bird," he said to her, and kissed her freckled cheek. "Bird!"

He skipped through the water and sprinted across the pasture to the house, barefoot and heedless as a hippie maiden. He'd watched his two oldest kids take their first steps, but he couldn't remember being present to hear any of his children utter their first word; he was always at work, at another house, at church, always somewhere else. Too often he'd come home to find one of the babies who was fluent, as far as he knew, in nothing but standardized infant gibberish, sitting in her high chair and carrying on in simple but very plain English, "Baby drink! Please! Baby drink!"

"Since when can Sybil talk?" he'd ask.

"Oh jeez, Goldy, she's been talking for a good three weeks," Nola would tell him.

"Wait. Three weeks?"

"Maybe more than that. Where've you been?"

The thing was, he had no idea where he'd been. He often wondered if he wasn't suffering from some mental disease characterized by memory loss and intermittent blackouts: whole chunks of his life fallen away into some dark swirling hole in his mind. Sometimes it felt like he was living in an ongoing time warp, the hours collapsing on themselves, days and weeks speeding ahead of him, and he'd have to claw his way forward through the chaos and fatigue just to catch up, and always, without fail, to lose his focus and fall behind again. But Glory slowed things down for him, moved along at a pace that matched his own. He did not miss anything with her: her self-feeding program and color recognition and toilet training, every minor progression in motor skills and range of motion, her first steps with the parallel bars, then the weighted buggy, then the crutches. He spent eight months teaching her to put on and remove her orthopedic shoes. And now, her first word. His daughter was six years old, doomed to a life without language, and he'd been there to hear it: *bird*.

As he loped across the lawn he was feeling so elated, his chest filled with the bubbling gasses of fatherly pride, that he tried something he'd never so much as considered before: taking the porch steps, all five of them, in one great leaping stride. His big toe caught the top of the last riser and he went down, elbows and knees clapping hard against the wood, but he felt nothing. He scrambled to his feet and yelled, "Bird!"

It did not take him long to gather the whole family and hustle them out through the west pasture and across the river, the children stumbling bewildered and shoeless before him like prisoners on a death march, splashing through the river, stopping to catch tadpoles and splash-bomb each other with rocks. Beverly came behind, clutching a crying baby against her breast, and, in between shouted promises of bodily harm if the children so much as got their pants cuffs wet, demanded to know what he, Golden, had been *thinking* leaving Glory outside *all alone*, not *twenty feet* from a *wild animal widely known for attacking and injuring defenseless young people.*

Golden did what he always did when Beverly scolded him: he smiled mildly and did his best to move out of earshot.

Glory was where he'd left her, perfectly safe, in a staring contest with Raymond across the fence, her knees knocking together in delight. The kids, normally forbidden from going near the river, much less crossing it, even when it was only inches deep, called out to the ostrich, offered him pebbles and blades of grass to eat, tossed dirt clods at him when Beverly wasn't looking. Even the baby had stopped crying, mesmerized by Raymond's unlikely shape and wet, hypnotic eyes.

"All right, now," Golden coached, "be quiet for a minute everybody and listen to this."

He glanced at Glory, who was completely absorbed with Raymond's come-hither stare, and said, "Glory. Come on, Glory, look! Bird!"

She seemed to grin a little, and tilt her head, but said nothing.

"Say it, Glory. Bird! Bird!"

"She can't talk," said Parley, who was nine years old at the time and seemed offended by the very thought. "She's *handicapped*!"

"She said it," Golden said, "just a minute ago." He knelt down in front of her and said it right into her face, whispering this time, "Bird."

She cocked her eyebrows and opened her mouth. She said, "*Ahhhhnk*."

The kids laughed and the baby clapped her hands.

"No!" Golden said, almost shouting now. "Bird! Remember? You just said it."

"Maybe she said something that *sounded* like bird," said Beverly in her carefully cadenced mother's voice, the one she normally employed with grocery cashiers and children under the age of five. "She does that sometimes, Golden."

"One time I heard her say *bazooka*," Clifton offered.

"No." Golden stood and pointed at Raymond. "She said it twice.

I was standing right here." He positioned his mouth next to her ear. "Bird," he said with a husky emphasis, as if trying to hypnotize her. "*Biiirrrd.*"

Glory turned and looked directly at him now, offered a lopsided smile. She said, "Uhhngg."

The children laughed again—even Beverly grinned—and Alvin grabbed his belly in a pantomime of hilarity and fell backward into the grass. Raymond himself seemed to shake his head in disbelief and Josephine shouted, "I think she just said, 'Uhhngg'!"

At that moment, the object of high ridicule by an ostrich and nine of the people he loved most in the world, he felt the hot wash of disappointment at the back of his throat, along with a tinge of irritation at Glory for letting him down. Only later, after turning it over in his mind, would he understand the memory in a way that rescued it from his colorful and extensive collection of shameful and embarrassing moments. That day, with the family gathered around and expectation in the air like an audible buzz, he hadn't understood the look in Glory's eyes, the same sly, knowing look he had noticed for the first time on their drives to the clinic. He'd been too addled to see it then, but he was sure of it now: she had set him up, played a little joke at his expense. His own little girl, bless her heart, had pulled one over on him good.

THE RIVER'S EDGE

That winter it snowed, it rained, it froze, it blew. The sun came out hot one day, melting the snow off the cliffs and mesas, sending ropes of red water twisting down sandstone walls, and the next day a three-week pocket of cold settled in and killed the locust saplings along the driveway, burst the water pipes on the Old House's north side. For five months he'd made almost no progress on Glory's Doll House, so when he had some downtime in the first warm days of April, he dedicated an entire week to its completion. He built the miniature stairway to the second level, covered the exterior plywood with cedar shakes, trimmed the windows and door. On the second day, with the temperature pushing into the seventies, he decided that, for the first time all year, it was warm enough for Glory to sit outside and do some Raymond-watching. He situated her in her wheelchair the way she liked it, unbuckled, with a foam pillow and blanket on each side to keep her tucked in place, her feet planted firmly against the canted steel plates, her crutches across her lap.

He told Beverly that he was taking Glory out to work with him, and wheeled her across the muddy pasture to a firm, gravelly spot twenty feet from the river, which was moving deep and fast and quiet with snowmelt, cutting new banks along the far edge of the bow. Most of the other kids had escaped Old House for the outbuildings and willow thickets and muddy yard. They spied on and chased and attacked each other, shooting their rubber band guns and lobbing mudballs, pausing to hatch plots and form alliances which were exposed and broken in frantic whispering sessions behind the old chicken pen.

Golden locked Glory's wheels and waited with her until Raymond, taking his time like a star of stage and screen, made his appearance, still shaggy with his coat of winter feathers. Glory squealed, clanged her crutches together, called to Raymond in a way that made him strut and puff out his chest a little more.

Golden told her he'd be back in a minute, and because the older boys were avoiding him in an effort to avoid conscription into the Doll House construction crew, he had to go himself to the detached garage for more finishing nails and his carpenter's square. He couldn't find the square, ended up searching the cab and bed of his work truck, without luck. Back inside the Doll House, he knelt to cut two pieces of oak molding before he looked out the window to check on Glory. From this angle he could only see the back of her chair—a square of black naugahyde and two glinting chrome push-handles—and Raymond, just beyond the chair in his line of sight, standing against the fence now and really putting on a show: bobbing his head wildly, flexing his pygmy wings, as if trying to will them to flight. He had taken up the next length of molding, made two back-and-forth passes with the miter saw, when he felt shaken, as if by a large, cold hand. His ears rang, his throat caught, his heart seemed to stop and clench painfully for several beats before starting up again, allowing him to breathe. He struggled to his feet to look out the window. Something was wrong: in Raymond's weird behavior, in the stillness and silence of the chair—it should have been rocking and shaking with Glory's spastic jerks. Even from this distance he should have been able to hear her squeals, the clanking of her crutches.

He threw down the saw and ran. The chair was empty. He stood next to it and turned in place, scanning every horizon for an explanation, trying to make himself believe that maybe the kids had carried her off as a joke, stowed her behind the old chicken coop just to give their old gullible dad a fright, or maybe, in the two or three minutes he'd left her, she'd managed to crutch-walk herself down to the willows, fifty yards south, to hide. Still turning slowly, as if suspended from a wire, he looked down and was met with a sight that would stay lodged in the edge of his vision until the day he himself would go to meet his Maker: Glory's tiny orthopedic shoes, placed side by side, a few feet from the river's edge.

STILL WATERS

It took them three days to find her. Though the Mormons in the valley were suspicious, even openly antagonistic toward their polygamist brethren, a child had gone missing; they formed search parties, set up a command center at the chapel in Hurricane, shut down their farms and shops and businesses to comb miles of riverbank, probing the water with poles and grappling hooks, investigating culverts and fishing holes for any sign of the missing girl. Golden, wandering in a fog of loss, allowed himself a small measure of hope he sipped at greedily, like a secret flask of whiskey, until the second day when a boy found one of her crutches snagged in some tamarisk at the mouth of Dutch Creek. On the third day, the Prophet, who had been fasting and praying in seclusion, had a vision: he saw an angel of God sitting in a willow tree, presiding over still waters.

The word went out and a flotilla of dusty pickups was dispatched to look for willow trees along the river. Golden rode in an old black Packard that brought up the rear, with Uncle Chick at the wheel and the Prophet dozing in the back seat, his gurgling colostomy bag keeping him company. When the men clambered out of their pickups to search, Golden stayed behind, pacing along the side of the highway, looking up with terror at every shout or unexpected sound, biting the margins of his thumbnails until they bled. It went like this all afternoon, one stop after another until they'd worked all the way down to Martin's Point, where the river descended into a narrow gorge. The light was failing and the men were starting to give each other questioning looks. They had parked next to the old trail bridge, and were picking their way through boulders and wild oak to the river below, when the Prophet made a noise and motioned for Golden to stay in the car.

"Going to bless you," he said. After his strokes years ago, the prophet had regained some of his ability to speak, though the words came out rasping and sideways, as if through a mouthful of sawdust. His face was smooth and colorless, obliterated by the weather, worn pale like an old stamp.

He leaned forward and said, "Your head."

Golden slumped all the way down in the front seat so the old man could place his hands on the sides of his head, just above his ears. The prayer was short, but came out with such a deliberateness, a gulf of one or two seconds between every crackling word, that it took a good minute to deliver: "Dear Father. Give this man comfort. You took his sweet baby from him and he don't understand. Comfort him. Bless him with thy Spirit. Bless him with the strength to keep on."

Inside that old car that smelled like leather and Uncle Chick's chewing tobacco, Golden absorbed every word; a liquid warmth in his scalp washed down his neck and shoulders, unlocking the muscles strung tight with relentless hours of worry and grief, and he slumped deeper into the seat until it felt like the only thing holding him upright were the ten blunt fingertips pressed into the sides of his head. When the Prophet finished his blessing he released Golden and, with his black locust walking cane, reached over the seat and pressed on the button in the steering wheel to sound the horn. Uncle Chick, sweating and covered in red dust, came up the bank and helped his father out of the car. The Prophet stood at the passenger-side window and bent down to whisper to Golden, who did not have the strength to open his eyes or acknowledge the old man in any way, "You stay here, son. We'll bring her back to you."

Uncle Chick, getting to be an old man himself but whipcord-strong, hefted his father into his arms, cradling him in the manner of a ventriloquist with his wooden dummy, and they went like that down to the river, heading east, away from the others. By the time the men caught up with him, the Prophet was tottering ankle-deep in the water and shuffling from side to side, investigating the water with his cane. It was a wide spot in the river, a good spot for fishing carp and catfish, and the water, deep and black in the grainy light of dusk, was speckled white with cottonwood fluff and tufts of foam. Nighthawks chittered, and a few sluggish bats wove invisible patterns in the cooling air. Picking their way upstream, the men whispered: in this part of the river there was no willow in sight, only a single enormous cottonwood split in half by lightning.

Maybe the Prophet had confused a willow with a cottonwood, but to those men, it didn't matter. This old man, standing in the water with his cane, this was why they lived the way they did, this was why they believed in the hard truths of the Principle. The Mormons—who had abandoned the Principle a hundred years ago, and who were at this very minute out conducting their own searches with their well-organized search parties, with their maps and grids and hot meals prepared by their women—had many things the fundamentalists did not: they had their expensive modern chapels, their temples and their worldwide bureaucracy and millions of clean-cut members, they had their Donny and Marie. But they did not have this priesthood authority, the ancient biblical power, borne by men of God like the Prophet, who spoke the hard truth, who conversed directly with God and had the ability, like Jesus of old, to release a dead child from her watery grave.

Golden was not there to see it, but they said that the Prophet picked around the bank for a good ten minutes, muttering and bent, searching with his cane. All at once he pushed out into a small hole choked with pussy willow stalks, as if he'd decided to go for a little swim, the water rising to his thighs, his waist, and then he reached down. Some said it was as if the small pale hand rose up through the green murk to grasp the old man's. Some went so far as to say that in the dim light, as the body was pulled to the surface with Uncle Chick on one side and the Prophet on the other, that the dead girl's skin appeared white and unblemished, her left arm straight, her body without handicap or flaw, as perfect as it would be come the morning of the resurrection when she rose from her grave to greet her Savior.

When they brought her back to Golden, wrapped in a wool horse blanket that smelled of dust, she was not perfect anymore. Her hair was knotted with grit and debris, her teeth broken, her nostrils plugged with greenish mud, her skin punctured and abraded from the twelve-mile journey downriver, her china-white body blackened at the edges like the porcelain of an old sink. He would see her like this later, when he carried her into the house to her mother, but for now he slept, his head lodged between the seat and the door, his face still pinched with suffering. The men shushed each other and, like parents of a colicky child who had finally nodded off, tiptoed on the gravel, wincing with every sound, sliding into their pickups and shutting the doors with quiet clicks. Exhausted, they switched on their headlights and in a single procession drove through the lowering darkness to their families to tell of the miracle they'd seen, to hug their own children tight.

RAYMOND THE OSTRICH

He stood under a bright full moon, the grass cold with dew beneath his feet. He wasn't entirely sure how he'd come to be standing out in front of Old House barefoot, the fly of his jeans undone. The last thing he remembered was dozing in the parlor armchair, exhausted after a long day: visitors and mourners streaming through the house for Glory's wake, and Glory in her coffin next to him in her frilly white dress, bows in her hair. Except for his little nap in the car on the way home from Cuttels Bridge, he himself had not slept since she'd gone missing. Tonight he couldn't stand the thought of leaving her there alone in the parlor, of going up to bed as if it were just another ordinary night, as if tomorrow were not her funeral and burial, the last time he would ever see her on this earth.

Beverly had gone to bed hours ago, at ten-thirty sharp, as if it were any ordinary night, and he resented her for it. Resented her for her calmness in the face of this calamity, for her lack of tears, for her allegiance to routine and the maintenance of order at all costs. Most of all, he resented her for not openly blaming him for their daughter's death, for the shocked fury she choked back when he delivered the terrible news, for the three words she whispered as he clutched at her, spoken so quietly he could barely make them out: "How could you."

He was heartsick and tired, his whole body a pulsing ache, but he could not stand the thought of going back and sitting in the chair for the rest of the night. His legs twitched as if they wanted to run, his hands flexed with the desire to break something. He had felt this way all day, jumpy, and since this morning, when he had gone to retrieve Glory at the new funeral home, an old pioneer brick-and-sandstone mansion on the main drag in Hurricane. George Baugh had taken over for Teddy Hornbeck after he sold everything—including his hearse to Golden—and moved to Florida. Mr. Baugh, a chubby pink man in an emerald-green suit that made him look like an artichoke, had a pointy head from which a wisp of gray hair rose like a curl of smoke. When Golden had arrived to take Glory, Mr. Baugh, standing next to a desk in the richly appointed parlor busy with fern stands and overstuffed furniture and heavy velvet draperies, explained that his "people" would deliver Glory to Big House, it was part of the services he offered.

Golden told the man that he had come to take his daughter, he had the perfect car to do so, and he needed her home for the wake that was to begin soon. He looked at his shoes so Mr. Baugh could not see his puffy, wept-out eyes. He said, "Just tell me how much I owe, please, and we can settle this now."

Mr. Baugh shuffled his papers. Mr. Baugh sighed. Mr. Baugh explained, with a thick layer of condescension sugaring his voice, that Golden needn't pay right now, that along with the casket, and the embalming and preparing of the body, there was also the delivery of the body to the residence for the wake, the delivery of the body to the funeral site, and finally, of course, the burial.

"It's all one package deal, sir," the man said, smiling with a false charm. "You go on home now, why don't you, be with your family, and let us take care of everything."

Golden shifted his weight, felt both his fists clench. After those initial hours of violent, wracking grief, every muscle and nerve alive with pain, he'd felt numb. All through the hours of last night and this early morning he'd been floating on vapors, his insides gone cold and still, his mind a whistling void; when he walked, he could not feel his own feet touch the ground. But hearing Mr. Baugh talk in his smug way about delivery and package deals, while his daughter lay dead somewhere in the rooms of this house, sparked a flame inside him. All at once his hands itched with the urge to punch Mr. Baugh's smug little face.

"I'm going to take her now, please," Golden said. "Show me where she is and that'll be it."

Mr. Baugh reassembled a professional smile and, gathering the last of his patience from deep within, repeated his explanation about the embalming, the delivery, the burial, the package deal. Before he could finish, Golden stepped around the desk and started down a hallway toward the back of the house. Mr. Baugh hooted and tried to get in front of him, but Golden gave the little man a slight hip check that sent him pedaling sideways into a potted palm. The first room Golden looked in was full of chairs, the other an office, and then there was the room with four caskets, each of them gleaming in the morning light like sleek automobiles freshly washed and waxed. A thick chemical smell made Golden's eyes water.

From a safe distance, Mr. Baugh shouted that he was calling the police.

"Which one is she?" Golden called, but he already knew. She was in the small one, the one Beverly had picked out, the one that was not a boxy casket, but an actual coffin, shaped to accommodate the human body, built with a rich cherrywood, winged angels carved into the lid. He lifted the casket off its stainless steel bier and was surprised by how light it was: it felt like he was carrying a box of pillows. Out in the parlor, Mr. Baugh barked into the phone and waved a letter opener in Golden's direction to make it clear he was not incapable of defending himself. In the distance, a siren started up—it was the siren the Hurricane fire department set off every day at noon, but Golden didn't know that. He imagined red lights, police cars racing in from every direction, unholstered pistols and bullhorns. He paused for a moment, considering his options and then tucked the coffin under one arm, pushed open the heavy oak door with the other, and sprinted across the lawn to his car.

To arrive home only to find that he'd stolen an empty coffin— Glory's body was back at the funeral home, laid out on a porcelain table in the embalming room, waiting to be transferred to the casket with which Golden had absconded—only made the burn of shame and anger spread inside him like a fever. Beverly had to go back to the funeral home, smooth things out with Mr. Baugh and the responding sheriff's deputy, while Golden stayed home, locked himself in the unfinished Doll House and wept with a hot, incoherent rage.

It had stayed with him all day, that anger, and he didn't know what to do with it. It rose and receded in his throat, smoldered and bunched under the surface of his skin. Now, in the dark hours of morning, he seethed, hot tears leaking down his face like water running over the sides of a boiling pot. He stalked around the west side of the house, past the Doll House, where the moon's reflection stretched and purled on the blue-black surface of the slow-moving river. Something white, hanging suspended in the air on the other side of the river, caught his eye. In a spasm of hope, his mind leapt to the thought that it was an apparition, the spirit of his little girl come back to offer what comfort she could, to let him know that she continued to exist in some peaceful beyond, that she still loved him, that wherever she was, she waited for him there. He moved closer, squinting, his heart turning over in his chest, until he realized what he was looking at was not a spirit presence of any kind, but the white breast feathers of Raymond the Ostrich.

He squeezed his head between his forearms and heard himself make a small choking noise of despair. When he looked up, the big bird was still standing at the fence, lifting one foot into the air, then the other. It stretched its long neck and let out a short, guttural squawk that sounded like a challenge. Golden stumbled forward, his rage returning to him in an instant, and it occurred to him that this bird was the last creature to have seen his girl alive. He found a rock in the mud of the pasture and, with a clumsy three-part motion, heaved it in the general direction of the ostrich. He waited for the sound of its landing, which never came. He moved closer, pitched a jagged hunk of white sandstone that landed with a splash in the middle of the river. Once at the river's bank, with ammunition in the form of round river stones on all sides, he found his range, throwing rock after rock, while Raymond stood at the fence, unperturbed and none the wiser, mocking Golden with a healthy display of feathers, staring him down with his yellow pearl of an eye.

"*Bird!*" Golden growled, his voice broken and raw. "You stupid *bird!*"

He stepped out into the river, the water cutting against his legs with a cold that burned. He splashed across with the idea of pegging that bird with a rock from point-blank range, just to give him a little dose of pain, to startle him from his privileged position at the fence, to make him consider his own mortality for a moment, but by the time he had struggled out of the cold grip of the river, had felt the full force of its merciless pull, there was only one thought in his head: to kill the animal who had done this to his daughter, to him.

Even as he clambered up the wet bank and struggled to squeeze himself through the strands of barbed wire, Raymond did not budge. Maybe the bird, who had carried on a serene and unmolested existence after his infamous encounter with the teenage gasoline thief, could not believe someone was actually violating his sovereign territory. With something like idle curiosity Raymond watched Golden wrestle with the barbed-wire fence, finally pulling himself free of it by allowing the back of his shirt to tear in half, and only when the huge man turned and lunged at him did he think to run. Just as Raymond pivoted, Golden was on him, throwing an arm over his back and hanging on. With surprising power the ostrich surged suddenly to his left and Golden ran alongside him, the acrid smell of the thing full in his nostrils, his feet paddling wildly underneath him until he tripped over a tin feed trough and went down hard in the dirt, still clutching a handful of gray feathers in each fist. In a panic, the bird fled into the small enclosure behind the feed bin while Golden picked himself up and rushed in behind him, hoping to corner him there, but the bird skirted along the back perimeter of the fence, bobbing and skipping wildly, and when Golden tried to cut him off he turned and delivered a deft kick to the outside of Golden's upper thigh, which felt like a blow from the blunt end of a billy club. Holding his leg, Golden tottered and fell backward against the empty feed bin, which made a hollow gonging noise and prompted several cows out in the pasture to moo in sleepy alarm.

The windows of the Spooner house were already lit and Brother Spooner clopped out onto the back steps in unlaced boots, wearing long underwear and armed with a .30-30, calling, "Who's out here? I'll shoot you, whoever you are!"

Golden kept still, hoping Brother Spooner might miss him there in the shadow of the feed bin, but no such luck. Golden watched Brother Spooner's bald head bob along the fence line until he came around the other side of the bin where Golden lay. Brother Spooner looked down and said, "What . . . in . . . the . . . *hell?*"

Golden knew there was no explanation that made any sense, so he offered none. He allowed himself to be helped to his feet and led to the back porch, where Sister Spooner paced in her white flannel nightgown, meat cleaver at the ready.

"As I live and breathe!" she said, clutching her nightgown at the throat as women in nightgowns tend to do. "Oh, he doesn't look very good, Newell, does he? Check to see if he's hurt."

As was customary, Brother Spooner ignored his wife. To Golden he said, "You want to tell me what you think you're up to tonight?"

Golden was barefoot and wet, covered in dust and ostrich feathers and bits of straw, and shuffled along with a halting double-limp that made him look like someone trying to get by on two wooden legs. He shook his head. "My daughter," was all he could say. Unable to stand any longer, he slumped onto the porch step.

"He get you?" Brother Spooner said. "He got you, didn't he."

"He got me."

"He also got your watch, looks like," Sister Spooner said, peering at Raymond, who was pressed into the far corner of his enclosure, looking back over his shoulder with something silver glinting in his beak.

Golden looked at his wrist, which was bare. Sister Spooner said, "He likes shiny things, old Raymond. Watches are his favorite."

"And I'd forget about getting it back, I was you," Brother Spooner said. "As far as he's concerned that watch is now his personal property."

"He'll probably swallow it soon," said Sister Spooner, "but sometimes he likes to wait awhile."

While Golden waited for the feeling to return to his leg, the Spooners had a brief argument over whether or not Brother Spooner should call the sheriff. Sister Spooner, who gripped the meat cleaver like she knew how to use it, prevailed, arguing that Golden was in a state of shock and couldn't be blamed for wading across the river and attacking their prized ostrich in the middle of the night like some kind of lunatic. Once her husband had gone inside to get dressed and find his keys so he could drive Golden home, Sister Spooner took several mincing sideways steps toward him, to put a comforting hand on his shoulder and pick a few of the larger feathers from his hair. His shirt was slashed all the way down the back, he smelled like a manure pile, and his face was striped with the evidence of tears. Even now, his eyes shone wetly, ready to flow at any moment.

He was thinking that he should get up right now, before Brother Spooner came out. He should walk back home on his own power, preserve whatever scraps of dignity he might have left, but the thought of wading back into the cold grasp of that river a second time was too much for him. Sister Spooner, who had always maintained a soft spot for Golden, for his honest, sad face, his addled sweetness in comparison to her husband's hard ways, let herself go and in a surge of pity took his head in her hands, pressed it firmly into the twin ottomans of her breasts.

"You poor thing," she said, "you poor, poor man."

SAFETY IN NUMBERS

Two hours later, dozing at his post next to Glory's coffin and rousing himself twice to check on the other children sleeping soundly in their beds, he put on his work boots and drove his pickup through the pink dawn to the Virgin City Municipal Cemetery, which sat on a broad shelf at the foot of Widow Mountain and overlooked the small town below. Though the sun was not yet up, the ambient light of dawn made the fine red sand that passed for soil in these parts seem to burn like bedded coals against the black volcanic rock of the mountain. There was the usual clamor of birds, excited out of their limited wits by the prospect of a new day.

Golden pulled in and drove slowly over the groomed gravel lane to the northeast corner, where his father, in a fit of optimism, had purchased sixteen burial plots assembled four abreast in a perfect rectangle. He'd bought them only a few months before he died, when he had no reason to doubt he would require these plots, and many more, for all the wives and children who would one day bear his family name.

The sight of his father's grave had always given Golden the oddest feeling; there was something sad and maybe a little funny both about the single polished marker alone in such an expanse of hopeful red dirt.

ROYAL JOSEPH RICHARDS

Light of the Lord

The carved image, which everyone took to be a tree, probably the tree of life, was actually an atomic mushroom cloud—Royal had drawn it on a scrap of paper in the days before his death, and

Golden had delivered the drawing to the stone carver, who had
done an admirable job of replicating it. "I want my marker to be
one of a kind," father had told son in his last hours of lucid thought.
"I want folks to know I went out like I came in, with a big fuckin'
bang."

Golden eased himself delicately out of the pickup and took a
shovel out of its bed. Right away he ran into trouble. The earth was
porous and sandy but littered with basalt cobbles—some small, some
as big as bowling balls. Time and again his shovel rang out against
the stones, sometimes with a flash of sparks. The work was hard and
what he'd hoped for: it obliterated all thought. He dug around each
stone, probing and scraping with the blade of his shovel, and when
one finally was pried loose he felt the relief that comes with pulling
a splinter from under a fingernail. He was two feet down, the sun
climbing against the mountain, sweat dripping steadily out of his
hair, when the sheriff pulled up in his cruiser.

Golden did not stop digging, did not look up while the sheriff
took his time getting out of the car. If he noticed Golden's torn shirt,
his mud-caked pants and the fact that he was covered in feathers, he
didn't mention it.

"Morning," the sheriff called. "Up early, I see."

Golden pulled out a grapefruit-sized cobble and tossed it onto the
pile near the sheriff's boots.

"Got a call," the sheriff said, holding his creased face to the sun.
"Grave robbery in progress. After the mischief you've been up to
these past twenty-four hours, I figured it might be you."

Under the sheriff's gaze, Golden worked harder and faster than
he had when alone, tossing up half-shovelfuls of dirt in random
directions.

"They got a guy with a backhoe does this," said the sheriff, settling into a stance that suggested he would be content to watch
Golden dig for a good long time. "Tellis Blackmore, I think you
know him. Highlight of his day, to come out and dig a grave. Squares
off the corners, makes a tidy pile a dirt, throws them rocks over the

fence so they don't make noises on the casket when he pushes the dirt back in. Hangs around for the burial, sometimes, sheds a tear or two along with the next of kin. You don't plan to put Tellis out of a job, I hope."

Exhausted, Golden let his shovel drop and sat on the edge of the hole. He didn't want to talk to the sheriff, but was glad for the break. He looked at his hands: blisters at the base of every finger. Just as he was entertaining a thought about how thirsty he'd become, the sheriff reached into the front seat of his car and came out with a thermos. He poured something into the lid and handed it to Golden. Orange juice, sweet and cold. Golden downed the cup in one gulp and the sheriff handed over the thermos so he could dispatch what was left of it.

The sheriff was a slight, deeply tanned man with the blown-out face of a dedicated alcoholic. Fifteen years ago he'd lost his wife and two young sons in a car accident and had taken to drink, which cost him his teacher's position at the local high school. With nothing left to lose, he ran for sheriff, made his own pathetic hand-lettered signs, which ended up, after a particularly fierce windstorm, caught in weeds and hedges and plastered against chain-link fences all over the county:

FONTANA FOR SHERIFF
A BRAND NEW START!

The standing sheriff's signs were glossy and professionally printed, but not all that more compelling:

ELECT HOUNSHELL FOR SHERIFF
DIFFERENT MOUSTACHE
SAME VALUES

Everyone was surprised when Fontana won the election, apparently on sympathy alone. Even more surprising was how he took to the job. He controlled his drinking and, because he had no family left, dedicated his every moment to his work. When a paranoid widow called in to say there were burglars whispering in the bushes outside her bedroom window, he spent the night in his cruiser in front of her house so she'd feel safe. He put every county prisoner on work detail and cleaned up the park, refurbished the rodeo grandstands, and used leftover yellow highway paint to paint several of the decrepit houses in Mexican Town, which now gave off a ghostly mustard-yellow aura in the dark of night. He cracked down on teenage hot-rodders and did not tolerate hippies or drifters or drunks (though he spent an occasional night drinking himself into oblivion) and had become something of a legend for giving Frank Sinatra, who was driving through on his way to Las Vegas, a firm lecture and a two-hundred-dollar ticket for speeding, reckless endangerment and driving without a license.

Now he stood next to Golden and creaked. Golden wasn't sure if it was the sheriff himself who was creaking, or if it was his leather holster, but the sound never stopped, even though the sheriff was standing absolutely still.

Golden handed back the thermos. He said, "So you going to arrest me?"

"Maybe later," the sheriff said. "Right now, I'd like you to tell me where I might find an extra spade."

Golden pointed to his pickup and the sheriff retrieved a rusty number nine shovel from the bed. He removed his jacket, along with his holster and two-tone beige polyester shirt, and started digging. At first the arrangement was awkward, but they discovered that if they stood back to back at an angle and worked in rhythm, the deepening hole could accommodate them both. For the first twenty minutes or so, they worked without speaking, but gradually the sheriff, in his immaculate white T-shirt, started to talk. He told a few bad jokes, let slip a little gossip about the mayor's wife, Neda Handley, who was caught shoplifting a pair of high-heel shoes. Golden was grateful to him for never mentioning Glory, or the details of her disappearance or the massive search effort the sheriff had helped to organize. Golden knew that this was a man who understood a father's grief, knew how hard it was to negotiate it in the light of day, to bear it with any dignity at all; not thirty yards from where they were working, near an old black currant bush, were the graves of his wife and two sons.

Later that day at the funeral, sitting on the front pew with his wives, Golden would barely be able to hold himself together, gripping Beverly's hand in his and swallowing back the sobs rising in his throat. Afterward, he would pilot the old Cadillac hearse the five miles from the church to the cemetery. He would ask Beverly this one favor: to be able to make the last drive with his Glory, nobody but the two of them. The sheriff in front with his lights flashing, the line of mourners behind, headlights on, they would roll along, slow as a Fourth of July parade, down the state highway, then across the county cutoff, passing houses and farms where people stepped out onto their porches, cut off their Rototillers and idled their tractors, removed their hats and head scarves, until the full procession passed. For a moment he would see himself as they saw him: a hulking shadow in the long black car, sagged with grief. As the cemetery came into view, he would forget to breathe, the pain in his chest too much, flashes of yellow and red across his vision, and slowly, almost gently, he would pass out, holding on to the steering wheel for dear life, the big hearse crawling slowly onto the shoulder and down the embankment, snapping through dead brush and scraping along a barbed-wire fence, the noise of which would startle him back into consciousness in time for him to swing back, as if nothing had happened, to take his rightful place in line.

But in the soft air of this early morning, numbed by the labor of digging and the sheriff's casual talk, he felt blessed with a bit of peace. The sheriff, who liked a good story, was telling Golden about some of the more colorful polygamists he'd met in his time. There was Calvin Eyre, who declared his desert compound its own sovereign nation and asked the sheriff to set up a one-on-one summit with President Johnson. "And then there was ol' Ross Sudweeks, you remember him, never held a regular job, hardly a dime to his sorry name, but he's got five wives and four thousand children and they all live on welfare and daily trips to the dump. Happiest herd a potlickers you ever seen. One time I was out there delivering Christmas turkeys for the Kiwanis Club—I took nine of 'em out there and I swear I don't think it was enough—and come to find out Ross had married him another one, a cross-eyed single lady with three kids. I had to ask. 'Why do you do it, Ross? What in God's name you thinkin'?' You know what he said?" Here the sheriff paused to heave a stone over the lip of the grave. " 'Safety in numbers.' That's what he told me, winking like it's the best secret in the world. I never forgot that. Safety in numbers."

Another half an hour and they had dug so deep they were having a hard time pitching the dirt out without having it slide right back in. The earth down here was clayey and moist and riddled with pockets of white quartz. "So," said the sheriff, measuring the top edge of the grave, which was just about even with his eyebrows. "We got an escape plan or what?"

"You go on ahead," Golden said. "I'll help you out and then I can finish up. I'm taller than you, I'll get myself out one way or another."

"If not," the sheriff said, "we'll know where to find you." He tossed his shovel out and turned to face Golden. Their eyes met and they stood like that for a moment, two men in a hole. Golden felt his throat thicken, the backs of his eyes sting with tears, and the old sheriff stepped forward and gave him a quick, hard squeeze on the forearm to prevent any unnecessary blubbering. "You're gonna make it, bud, I know you will."

Golden nodded, took the sheriff by the belt and the back of his T-shirt, and with a grunt and a heave pitched him gently out of the hole.

The sheriff buttoned up his shirt, put his holster back on. He clapped the dirt off his hands and knees. Creaking, he gazed around at the red cemetery dirt bristling with markers and stones. He gave Golden one last look and sighed before turning away.

"Safety in numbers," he said. "Ain't no such thing."

21.

· · · · ·

THE MONKEY NET

EVERY DAY NOW HE DID BATTLE WITH AUNT BEVERLY. FROM HER HEI-
nous chambers in the laundry room she made her plots, denying him
dessert and assigning him extra chores and forcing him to wash his
feet daily, plus the house was full of her spies. She grounded him for
the dumbest little things anybody ever heard of and made him read
the longest scriptures during Book of Mormon Hour, but like the
guerrilla fighter he was, he resisted her at every turn, sneaking out
when she wasn't looking and not washing his feet even when he said
he had. When she grounded him for writing

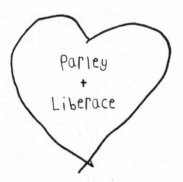

on the wall above the toilet in perfectly erasable pencil, did he stay
grounded? No way. He snuck out, using his silent walking ability, until
her spies discovered him hiding out in the bushes by the river. When

she banished him to the Tower for a whole Saturday for the cherry bomb episode, and posted guards by the door so he couldn't escape, did he cry and pound the walls and beg to be let out? Not likely. He just sat up there watching everything, drawing in his secret notebooks, making his secret plans, his leg jiggling like crazy, laughing at all the dumb a-holes down below, waiting for his moment to strike.

Sometimes, to get him to behave like a normal person—good luck, Sherlock!—she came all the way up to the Tower to talk to him, alone. Which was, seriously, the worst. She read scriptures to him and talked about sin and righteousness.

"The Bible tells us that good can only come from good, and evil from evil," she said. "Do you understand what I'm saying?"

"That I'm evil?"

"No, that's not what I'm saying."

"Maybe I'm evil and I can't help it." Already his leg was jiggling like crazy.

"No, you're not evil. My point is that you have to try to be good."

"Maybe *you're* evil, and you don't even know it."

Aunt Beverly turned her head and coughed into her hand. "Rusty, please, could you listen to me for one minute?"

Even though he drove her crazy like this, she tried to talk to him in a nice way and kept her witchy-woman stare turned down low, and sometimes even put her hand on his shoulder, which should have burned like the saliva of a she-demon, but felt kind of nice. Her voice would go all soft and her eyes kind of shiny and she would tell him how very good it would be for him to repent of his sins, how happy he could be if he would give up his bad self and dedicate his soul to God. Rusty would nod and say, *Yes, hmm*, and sometimes even pray with Aunt Beverly, but after she was gone he would laugh his Scoundrel laugh—*ha! ha! haaaa!*—and go right back to making his plans.

At church, when his mother had asked Rusty what he wanted for his twelfth birthday, he said all he wanted was to come back to Big House. *I don't want any other presents*, he told her, making his saddest funeral face, giving the inside of his left cheek a hard bite to make his eyes water, *I just want to come home*. She smiled and looked away, which she always did before she told him no. When she explained that he couldn't come home yet, because his father and the mothers had agreed he needed more time to show he could behave properly, especially since the cherry bomb in the dryer a few nights ago.

Rusty regretted the cherry bomb, even though it made the most incredible sound ever, you should have heard it—*Ka Wong!!!* He did it because his scientific mind had always been intrigued with this question: *What would a cherry bomb sound like if it blew up inside a dryer?* And since Aunt Beverly had made her famous Raspberry Trifle Dessert that night, and because he wasn't allowed to have any because he had called Nephi a dickhole in Sunday School, and because he needed to create a diversion so he could get himself some without anyone seeing, well, the cherry bomb. The only problem was that after it went off and everybody was running into the laundry room to see what the amazing noise was, Louise and her bubble-eyes spied him scooping some of the Raspberry Trifle Dessert into a bowl and hauling butt up the stairs with it. By the time they caught him he'd already finished it off, scooping it into his mouth with his hands because he had forgotten to grab a spoon.

With the cherry bomb, he hadn't been thinking ahead. He had forgotten it was his special birthday coming up. So he cried a little, to show his mother he was sorry, and said if he couldn't come home this week, then he'd have to settle for having his birthday party at Skate Palace. Skate Palace was in St. George, and if you were a cool person it was where you went, which was why Rusty had never been there. But he knew all about the row of pinball machines and the loud music and the hot mamas on roller skates. Rusty did not know how to play pinball, or to skate, but he knew one thing: he had disco fever. He had it so bad! Lately he'd been listening to *Disco Week with Stu Barrett* on his transistor at night, which was how he'd learned that Disco Fever had been sweeping the nation for all these years. And the only cure for disco fever was the Skate Palace in St. George, where you could glide around with sweaty long-haired chicks listening to "Lovin' Touchin' Squeezin'" and doing risky disco dance combinations.

Already, Rusty had learned one of the most death-defying disco dance moves of all time. Royce Ramirez at school was the one who told him about it, and because it was super-secret and known only by certain disco experts, Royce showed him for the reasonable fee of a ham sandwich and two apples. It was called the Honk Job, and involved two leg kicks, a bunch of crazy finger-snapping, a knee bend, and then several quick spins that brought you right up next to your dance partner so you could reach out at the last second and squeeze her boobs with both hands.

"This is probably the most dangerous move there is," Royce warned. Royce was an eighth-grader but because of his mossy teeth and B.O. complications hung out mostly with sixth-graders. They were behind the dusty curtains in the auditorium that doubled as the school cafeteria. "Seriously, man. You do it wrong, it's gonna be a *real* problem. You execute it right, though, with the finger-snapping in all the right places, and you'll, like, *mesmerize* your lady, and she'll let you honk her boobs all night long."

When his mother found out it would cost twenty-five dollars to rent the Skate Palace for two hours, she said it was a "luxury we can't afford," something Aunt Beverly had started saying about eighteen times a day. Rusty said he would start mowing lawns to pay it off, that he didn't want presents or a cake or anything, that a party at Skate Palace would be good enough for him.

There was no way his mother could say no. For his twelfth birthday, Parley got to have a bonfire picnic, and for Helaman's, Sasquatch rented the county swimming pool for an entire afternoon.

Because there were so many people in this family, and all of them had to have birthdays every year no matter what, everyone could not have their own birthday party—that was the family rule. Aunt Nola said if everybody in the family was going to get their own party they would have to start their own birthday cake factory and sleep in their party hats. So they doubled up. Sometimes tripled. The Three Stooges always had their birthday party together and the two sets of twins, and sometimes one of the kids got paired with one of the mothers. Even this way, honestly, you kind of got sick of all the birthday parties.

Like everything else in this family, birthdays were complicated. In this family, you were never free, you couldn't do anything on your own, because there was always somebody who had a dentist's appointment or volleyball practice or Deeanne would have one of her epileptic seizures and there went everybody's Labor Day picnic down the tubes. It was like they were all connected by the same invisible string, this was how Rusty thought of it, and when one person wanted to do a certain thing or go a certain way, they yanked on all the others, and then another person tried to go in another direction, and so on, and pretty soon they were all tangled up, tied to each other, tripping and flailing, thrashing around like a bunch of monkeys caught in a net.

But the twelfth birthday party, for a boy, was not supposed to be complicated. For one day, you were free of the monkey net. You got your own party. You got to choose what to have for dinner. People were supposed to be nice to you. You didn't have to do chores. You got good presents, instead of the usual ones, such as the plastic croquet set he had received for his eleventh birthday, croquet being the game, according to Helaman, played only by elderly homosexuals and people from France. Twelve was when you received the priesthood, when you became a deacon in the church and were supposed to do things like pass the sacrament on Sunday, paint the houses of the less fortunate, and start being a man. The prophet would put his hands on your head and give you power from God. Rusty wanted to see if he could use this power to cure lepers or control people with the holy power of his mind.

The girls, they didn't get any power, they could not have the priesthood. For them, their special birthday was when they turned eight, the age they could be baptized in the church. As far as the church went, that was the best they could do.

So he made invitations. You weren't supposed to invite nonfamily members to birthday parties—"friends are a luxury this family can't afford," Aunt Nola always said—but when the kids from school showed up at Skate Palace, hopefully with a present for him, he would shrug like it was impossible to keep all his many friends at bay and say, "Come on in, guys, grab yourself some skates and a root beer!"

At night in the Tower, when he was supposed to be doing his homework, he cut letters and pictures of fire from magazines and pasted them on notebook paper.

R. Richards!!!
B-Day BASH!!!
Disco Inferno!!!
Presents and Gift Certificates Gladly Excepted!!!

Rusty knew that such fiery and mysterious invitations would attract kids from school who wouldn't normally be caught dead around him, mostly because he was a plyg kid and was bad at sports and had once, in fourth grade, tripped on his traditional Mongolian skirt and fallen off the stage during the performance of *Dances of Foreign Peoples* and landed on the piano player, Mrs. Biedris, who was something like seventy years old and wore a neck brace for the rest of the year, saying brave things like, "Take your pity elsewhere!" and "Don't worry about me!"

While he made the invitations he listened to the radio and occasionally got up to practice the Honk Job in the mirror.

Satisfaction, uh-huh, came in the chain reaction
I couldn't get enough, uh-huh, so I had to self destruct
Burn baby burn, Disco Inferno
Burn Baby Burn, Burn that mother down!

The week before his party, Aunt Beverly had called him into the kitchen and told him that there was going to be no party at Skate Palace.

"*Honk job*," Rusty whispered.

"What?" said Aunt Beverly.

"*Titty twister*," Rusty said, under his breath. "*Witchy woman.*"

"I can't hear a thing you're saying."

Rusty raised the volume. "You're not my mother."

"I'm well aware of that." She looked up from the dishes, trying to burn a hole in his forehead with her witchy-woman lasers. "You remind me of that nearly every time we speak. I thought, though, that I'd do you the courtesy of letting you know what the plans are for your birthday."

"You're not my mother," he said again, mostly because he knew how much it chapped her behind. "And you don't decide what the plans for my birthday are. It's my special birthday, and it's going to be at Skate Palace."

"You're lucky you're going to have a party at all, young man. You'll get your special party, it's just not going to be at Skate Palace. It will be better than that."

Somewhere better than Skate Palace? For seconds Rusty had a crazy hope. What could be better than Skate Palace? Wacky Waters in Salt Lake City? The deck of a battleship?

Aunt Beverly dried her hands. "You're going to share your birthday party with your father, at Big House."

"How is that special?" he said. "I'm supposed to have my *own* party."

"You're going to have to think of the family before yourself sometimes—"

His head felt hot and surplus spit was beginning to form in his mouth. "But it's supposed to be my own party! My own special party!"

"Most people would consider it a great honor to share their birthday party with their father. He's been away so much that we couldn't schedule his party on his real birthday, so he's been very gracious to share with you. No one has ever shared a birthday with Daddy before, so this is a real honor—"

"I am not happy!" Rusty cried. "This is not an honor! This is a major gyp!"

"No need to yell," said Aunt Beverly. "I can already sense your displeasure."

"A gyp!" Rusty cried.

"Stop talking to my mother that way!" cried Louise, who had been spying on them from the doorway.

"A gyp!"

Rusty made a break for it down the hallway. At the front door he stopped at the PLEASE REMOVE SHOES box but his shoes were nowhere to be found and Aunt Beverly and Louise and probably several other Old House a-holes were breathing down his neck, so he picked up the box, opened the front door and took off across the front lawn to his bike. The box was heavier than it looked, and he spilled a few shoes on the way, but he was able to prop it up on the handlebars. Even though he couldn't see over the box, he set off down the drive-way weaving like crazy and dropping more shoes until he got to the road. Both his socks were coming off and he kept veering off into the weeds and bumping over rocks, but he was feeling better now and he looked back where Aunt Beverly and Louise and Parley and Teague were standing on the front porch barefoot with their big fat mouths hanging open like a bunch of helpless babies—*Help me, I'm helpless!*—watching him ride away with their shoes. *Buenos tarde, amigos!* He reached into the box and one by one started chucking the shoes this way and that like a blind brain-damaged paper boy.

"Disco Inferno, suckers!" he shouted at them as he tore down the road toward Big House. "Burn that mother down!"

THE DEPUTY MARSHAL

Big House smelled like vitamins and basement and hamster cage. It was a smell that gave Rusty a weird feeling in his stomach, like homesickness, which was stupid, because how could you be homesick in your own dumb house?

He had sneaked in through the garage and laundry room with its three angry dryers clicking and rumbling and buzzing away, and there was no one there to stop him. On his way he came across the Second Twins fighting in the hall with Gale, who was dangerous because she kept her nails long and always went for the eyes.

He started up the stairs when Aunt Nola came in behind him, like she'd been waiting for him all along. "And what do we have here?"

"Nothing," he said.

She told him that Aunt Beverly had called to see if Rusty had shown up at Big House yet. Smiling, she shook her head and said, "In hot water yet again, I see."

"Indeed," he said.

"And how are things at Old House these days?"

"Aunt Beverly," Rusty said, which was all he needed to say.

"Don't let her get to you, Rusty-boy. Keep your chinny-chin-chin up."

"I'm trying my best."

"Of course you are. Now look. Your mother is having one of her spells, so no more than thirty seconds up there. Be calm and don't get her excited."

"Promise."

"Well, carry on," she said, going back to the kitchen. "For the record, I haven't seen hide nor hair of you."

He stopped off in his old bedroom and found Herschel playing Chinese checkers by himself. Herschel was the little doughboy who had taken Rusty's spot in his bedroom, who'd been promoted to the Older Boys' room even though he was only nine. A house full of kids and you can't find somebody to play Chinese checkers with? That was Herschel.

So Rusty sat down for a quick game and Herschel said, "You're not supposed to be here, are you?" and Rusty said, "Do you want to play or not?" and Herschel said that he did but he had forgotten the rules, which was the other thing about Herschel: he was dumb as a stick. But unlike Rusty, he was nice and knew how to give people compliments, so nobody minded him.

After Rusty beat him two games in a row and Herschel said, "Hey, you're really pretty good at this game!" Rusty got him in a headlock and gave him an Apache head burn, just for old times' sake. He then told Herschel he'd give him a dollar if he'd stand guard outside the door while he conducted some private business. Once Herschel was gone, he lifted up the mattress of the top bunk, the one Herschel now slept on, where he had hidden his paperback copy of *To Love a Scoundrel.* He kept it here, along with a few other special items, so if his secret hiding place in Old House was discovered he wouldn't lose everything. He was, unlike Herschel, not dumb as a stick.

On the cover were two people in front of a castle at midnight, grabbing at each other under a tree. The man was wearing black riding boots and insanely tight purple pants and for some reason, even though it looked like it was a pretty cold night, he didn't have a shirt on. The woman was wearing what appeared to Rusty to be a shiny pink curtain, and her head was dangling backward so you could get a load of her dewy cleavage.

Dewy cleavage! That's what it said in the book. *Their eyes met, and slowly, sensuously his gaze drifted downward, lighting for the briefest moment on her dewy cleavage.* This was one of many lines in the book that Rusty had committed to memory. He had already made a secret vow his firstborn son would go by the name of Dewy Cleavage Richards.

He'd first seen *To Love a Scoundrel* at the swap meet a few months ago. It was just sitting there with piles of other junk and a cardboard sign that said,

Everything On Table
25¢
No Haggling PLEASE

Of course, Rusty didn't have twenty-five cents, so when the codger was distracted by a crazy-eyed hag who claimed there was no
way in shinola she was going to pay good American coin for a plastic
spatula with a crack in it and the codger responded by picking up the
sign and jabbing at each word with his finger as if he were leading a
bunch of preschoolers in a sing-along, Rusty swiped the book off the
edge of the table and stuffed it down his pants.

He had meant to give it to his mother for her birthday, but he
started reading it and before you knew it his mother's birthday had
passed. Sir Nigel Mountcastle and Lady Jane Welshingham were
secretly in love, even though she was married to the Earl of Buckington, who was away most of the time hunting pygmies in the jungles
of Siam. Even though Sir Nigel was kind of an a-hole, and the book
was confusing, with words Rusty didn't understand and people saying things like, "Unhand the marchioness this instant!" it was easily
the best book he'd ever read.

Rusty had stolen the book for his mother because he knew about
her secret; not only did his mother read books like *To Love a Scoundrel* but she had a collection of them hidden in her closet. Rusty discovered this one Sunday last summer when he claimed he was sick so
he didn't have to go to church, and while he was home alone and had
nothing better to do he went snooping around in her bedroom, where
he found dozens of these books, the kind with half-naked ladies and
long-haired muscle-guys wrestling each other on the covers—a couple under her bed, a lot more stacked up behind clothes in her closet,
one in her nightstand drawer under the Book of Mormon. *Comanche Bride*, and *A Stranger Comes Calling, A Cowboy of My Own, The
Impostress, Slightly Married, The Damsel in This Dress*.

The first time he saw these books, he was scared. He picked up the
first one—*Tropical Fever*, with a picture of a pirate trying to mount
a hula chick—and whispered, "Oh my holy *fudge*." These were his
mother's? His mother, who never cussed, who blushed when the old
fart on PBS said *social intercourse*, who hated nakedness so much she
duct-taped Ferris's clothes to keep him from streaking, who clapped

her hands over her eyes and screamed homicidal murder when she saw Cooter trying to impregnate the neighbor's old blind cat, Mr. Sugar? Though Rusty was feeling weak from looking at all these ladies and their gigantic bosoms, it made him a little sick to think about his mother looking at them too.

But after reading *To Love a Scoundrel* he thought maybe he understood. His mother read these books because she wanted to be like Lady Jane Welshingham or Pollyanna Dansforth or the Comanche Bride, ladies who were beautiful and had adventures and boyfriends who loved them and only them, guys like Sir Nigel Mountcastle, who was ravishing and said things like, "Oh, Jane, you possess me, you enrapture my very soul." As far as Rusty could tell, none of the ladies in these books had seven children and had to share a husband with three others, the husband being a Sasquatch who smelled like Ben-Gay and stumbled around blinking like he didn't know where he was, who was never around, who paid almost no attention at all to Rose-of-Sharon Richards, his very own wife.

It took him a while, but in his studies of all those books Rusty figured out another of his mother's secrets. She had named her children after people in the books. The mothers got to name their own children—this was one area where they could do what they wanted and nobody, not even Sasquatch, had a say—and while the other mothers were going around naming their kids after Book of Mormon prophets and historical people from olden times, Rose-of-Sharon named hers after the beautiful newspaper reporter in *Scoop of a Lifetime* or the secretly lonely millionaire in *A Gentleman in My Bedroom*. Rusty was named after Deputy Marshal Rusty McCready in *Ride the Fire*, which was kind of a gyp, because Gale got to be named after some kind of wizardess of Nature who controlled the wind, and Ferris was an Irish warrior with a braided red beard who went around smashing people's brains in with a stone club.

Before he went to see his mother, to give her his gift and convince her once and for all that it was time for him to come home, that he could repent and act like a normal righteous person if only she would let him come home and have his party at Skate Palace, he had to really quick read his favorite part, where Sir Nigel and Lady Jane get locked up in the dungeon by the Earl of Buckington and escape by covering each other with lamp oil and squeezing through bars. *He boosted her up and stood back for a moment to admire her plush and glistening bottom clamped tight between two rusty iron rods.*

Rusty sighed and shut the book. He counted to ten to allow his pants to settle. When he got out into the hall Herschel said, "Where's my dollar?"

Rusty reached into his pocket, and pretended to put something in Herschel's sweaty palm.

"What's that?" said Herschel.

"An invisible dollar," Rusty said. "Don't lose it or you might not be able to find it again."

At his mother's bedroom door he made a little knock. "Mom?" He thought he heard her say something, so he let himself in.

The room was dark, the drapes glowing at the edges, and the mirror on top of the dresser shimmering next to the big block of blackness that was his mother's bed.

At first he was sure she wasn't there, but then he heard breathing and took a step closer.

His mother was on the bed, half under the covers, asleep. And here was the thing: she was wearing her earmuffs. Blue plastic earmuffs, like the ones guys on aircraft carriers wear to keep their eardrums from breaking. Which meant things were bad. Which meant his mother had given up, she was sick, she couldn't take it anymore.

It wasn't supposed to be like this. They said they had sent him away to Old House for the Family Exchange Program, but he knew it was really because he was a troublemaker who needed to learn how to behave, because he was a pain in everyone's butt, especially his mother's, who had a fragile psychology and needed her rest. But here she was hiding in her room with her earmuffs on, which meant it hadn't worked. Even with him out of her hair, he was still causing trouble, plus his father was still gone all the time, the mothers were still fighting, which meant the kids fought even more, and his mother couldn't stand it, she just wanted everyone to be good and love each other, which definitely wasn't happening, so she stayed up here in her room, trying to disappear.

He took a few steps back. "Mom?" he said. "*Mom?*" He nudged the mattress with his knee.

She lifted her head and blinked. "What happened?"

He said, "It's me."

"Who?" She pulled a muff off one ear.

"Rusty." He reached out to touch her foot under the covers, pulled his hand back. "I came here to give you something."

"What are you doing?"

"I brought you something."

"You can't be here. You can't. I'm sorry about your party but there's nothing I can do."

All he wanted to do was lie down next to her; if he could just lie down next to her for a second it would be all right. When he was little, she used to let him crawl into bed with her and put his face into her neck, which smelled like Dove soap, and sing "Eidelweiss" and "Jesus Wants Me for a Sunbeam." But now he was older and sort of fat, his leg was always jiggling and his feet smelled like old hamburger. He wanted to ask her if she wouldn't mind if he lay down with her for a few seconds, just one second, but the only thing he could say was, "Skate Palace."

She turned her face away. "I tried. I'm sick. I can't do it anymore. Please leave me alone now."

"I came to *give* you something," he whined. He didn't want to whine. He didn't want to think about how his special birthday was going down the tubes, or about his mother being sick again like this might ruin all of his plans forever. If he could learn to control himself and behave, then maybe his Grand Master Plan wouldn't be in very serious trouble, and his mother wouldn't be getting sick again. He had figured that if he could get June fixing Aunt Trish's toilet and roof, then June could start doing some of the work around Big House

and Old House that Sasquatch wasn't around to do, and that way
June and his mother could meet, and of course fall secretly in love,
just like in one of his mother's books, and then Rusty and his mother
and his new stepdad June Haymaker could go live in a bomb shelter, happily ever after. If it were one of his mother's books it would
have a cool title like *Atomic Love Bombs* or maybe *World War Lust*,
and it would feature Rose-of-Sharon, the sad and overlooked housewife who only needed a sensitive and semi-handsome stranger with
a bomb shelter to bring out her inner beauty, and once the stranger
whisked Rose-of-Sharon away to the bomb shelter, along with her
clever and brave son Rusty, who she could not bear to leave behind,
World War III would come and blow the living crap out of civilization as they knew it. Except before the bombs crashed down, Rusty,
with his extra-perception abilities, would detect the sound of the missiles coming on their way over Greenland and he would jump on his
bike and pedal like a madman to Aunt Trish's house, where he would
find Aunt Trish doing some gardening in cut-offs and some kind of
tight top that made her boobs stand out, and he would tell her the
end of the world was at hand and if she wanted to live she better hop
on the back of his bike pronto. She would say, "What about Faye?"
and he would hold out his hand and say, "I'm sorry, but there's no
time," and she would take his hand and hop on the bike and hold him
tight around the waist with her chin on his shoulder as the missiles
screamed overhead, and they would make it to the bomb shelter with
only seconds to spare.

Afterward, they would venture out into the deadly apocalyptic
wasteland, everything black and smoking and burnt to a crisp, and
Rusty would say, "It's really sort of beautiful in its own way, don't
you think?" and Aunt Trish would squeeze his hand, which was her
secret way of agreeing with him. They would visit Old House and
Big House and the Duplex, which were all just piles of ashes now,
and Rusty would bow his head and say, "Such a terrible shame," and
they would all nod their heads and take a moment of silence and then
go back to the bomb shelter and play Monopoly and drink alcoholic

beverages until way after bedtime, because what did rules matter now, anyway? After a few days, when Aunt Trish had gotten over her daughter and everybody else getting blown to bits, she and Rusty would take off their clothes until they were nude and start doing some serious kissing and maybe even sexual relations in their own private section of the bomb shelter, because they loved each other and then there was the survival of the human race to think about, wasn't there?

He took the book from the waistband of his jeans and held it out to his mother. "It's a present. For you. I didn't have time to wrap it, but I got it special, it was hard to get, but I wanted to give you a present, because you never get good presents." He wiped the book on his jeans because his hands had gotten it all sweaty.

"I know you're upset—" his mother started to say, but he held the book out to her so she had to take it. She put it right up to her nose to see it in the dark and when she read the title and got a good look at the cover, she said, "Where did you get this?" Her voice was suddenly all high and crazy. "Why did you give this to me?"

Something had happened to his mother's face. Her eyes were black and shining and her lips shook. He took a step back. He raised his arm to point at the closet, let it drop back against his side. "It's a present?" he said. "I got it for you."

"You take this," she said, waving it at him. She wouldn't look at him now. "You get it out of here. You're not supposed to be here. You want me to call your father? You want me to tell Aunt Beverly?"

His face stung and his throat closed up. He swallowed and tried not to cry, but it was already coming. What a gyp! He started to do the hiccup thing where he could hardly breathe.

"I'm not, *uh . . . uh . . . uh . . . taking* it," he cried, shuddering and gulping. "It's not *fair*." He was really bawling now. Trying to stop only made it worse, and he started making the snorking sound every two seconds and going *uh-huck uh-huck uh-huck*. Why was he such a big effing bawlgut? Why did he have so much spit in his mouth?

"Please, Rusty, please," his mother said. "I don't want you to get into more trouble."

"It's a *present*!" he choked.

"Don't," she said. "Please."

He said, "It's my special *birthday*!" but it sounded more like some-body gargling a bucket of spit.

She put her head back on the pillow. "I can't anymore."

He backed up to the doorway. He waited, but she didn't say any-thing. "It's me, Rusty," he said. "The deputy marshal?"

He waited, but she was quiet. "Mama?"

"Okay," she said, as if she'd just been woken up. "I'll see you . . . soon."

He stood in the doorway and waited some more but she had put the earmuffs back on and closed her eyes. He let the door shut and looked at it for a while. He sniffed, he gulped, he went, *uh-huck, uh-huck*.

He stopped crying when he thought he heard his mother say something, but it was only Aunt Nola downstairs yelling at some-body. He put *To Love a Scoundrel* down his pants. He went down the hall, past Herschel, who was still holding his invisible dollar, down the stairs and past the clicking dryers and then he was outside and on his bike and pedaling like a madman, but at the place where the driveway met the road he stopped. He looked around. There was nowhere for him to go.

22.

·····

JUST MARRIED

IT ALL STARTED ON A SWEET SUMMER DAY IN THE MIDDLE OF THE twentieth century, a perfect day for a picnic. The unblemished sky, the stand of fragrant ponderosas stirred by a mountain breeze as warm and steady as an oceanic current. The day was perfect, and so was the picnic, which Beverly had planned to the last detail: a broad gingham cloth spread with cinnamon bread, fresh-squeezed orange juice from a thermos, croissants, sugared ham, slices of melon, a few wilting sunflowers arranged in a porcelain vase. Golden in his silk tie and gabardine suit jacket, she in her tea-length gown of cream *peau de soie*. The whole thing a vision, a scene from a movie, just as she had always wanted.

They had been married less than an hour. Down the mountain, in a small opening in a stand of old ponderosas, a piece of black basalt stone thrust up at an angle out of the pine needles, furry at the base with lichen, long and flat on top like a narrow table. According to the Prophet, this was a sacred place where Book of Mormon prophets had come to make their blood sacrifices and hold counsel with the Lord. Though it was a rough forty-minute drive from Virgin, this was where many of the binding church ceremonies were held, and despite the bullet-riddled NO HUNTING sign that had come to look like an antique cheese grater, the place felt as hushed and spiritual as any chapel built by human hands.

The ceremony had been simple: in his guttural, failing voice, the

Prophet had instructed the couple to hold hands, facing each other across the stone, which he called the altar. Then he pushed himself up out of his wheelchair, Uncle Chick at his side, and found a sturdy spot in the dirt with his cane. His body trembled like a tuning fork, lightly and without cease. He proclaimed his authority, granted by the ancient priesthood of Melchizedek that stretched back to Moses and Adam. It was just after dawn, and sunlight came through the trees in broad, dusty bands. As he pronounced them man and wife, almost growling with the effort of it, Beverly stared hard into Golden's eyes, as if daring him to blink. He smiled apologetically, sighed, and blinked several times in succession. His face, stark in the morning light, was the picture of terror.

There was no ring, no vows. It was over before it began.

For a fundamentalist wedding, it had been a sparsely attended affair: Uncle Chick and the Prophet and a few chosen church members who'd been coerced to make the drive. Beverly had no family to speak of, and none of Golden's had come. His father had passed away eight months earlier, and his mother, back in Louisiana, had no idea what was happening because he'd had the good sense not to mention it to her.

Though Golden was famished now, he didn't want to disturb the carefully presented food. He nudged a slice of cantaloupe off its plate, nibbled at it in a way he thought might be appropriate. He tried not to yank at his wool trousers, which were making his thighs itch. The sun was in his eyes. He could hear bees buzzing in the grass. He was married now, to a woman he hardly knew, and he was at a loss for words.

He tried again to situate himself comfortably on the cloth, but ended up in an awkward position with his elbow underneath his ribs and one leg bent at an odd and revealing angle. He groaned a little, rolled sideways; he wasn't sure how one was supposed to recline on a picnic blanket while wearing a suit.

"So what do you think?" Beverly asked him. "About how everything has gone?"

"I don't know." His answer came out so quickly she looked startled.

"You don't *know*?"

"I wish I did. I haven't had time to think about it. Sorry." He involuntarily sang out this last word.

As if to shut him up, she began to feed him. To Golden, this seemed an immensely charitable gesture. She put half a strawberry in his mouth, a wedge of tangerine. As far as he could remember, he had never been hand-fed by anyone, and he was surprised by how pleasurable it was. He was even more surprised by the way Beverly knee-walked her way behind him, peeled his jacket down his arms and began to knead his shoulders and neck. Golden was a deeply virginal human being, one whose first kiss came at the age of twenty with a woman he was already engaged to, one who was so ignorant of sex in general, and his own body specifically, that he had never once masturbated to a successful conclusion, despite several valiant attempts. But even he could tell there was something sexual going on here. He had assumed they would consummate their marriage—he imagined something solemn and brief, like the wedding ceremony he'd just been a part of—in the Polar Bear Inn in Page, Arizona, where they would stay on the first night of their honeymoon trip to the Grand Canyon, but the thought of doing it here, right now on this blanket under the beautiful sky, suddenly seemed like an excellent idea.

Beverly was so busy with her ministrations, and Golden so busy receiving them, they didn't notice the smudge of dark cloud that rose slowly over the tops of the trees from the west and began seeping across the pure expanse of sky like an oil slick.

GROUND ZERO

Exactly two hours and twenty minutes earlier, two hundred thirty miles to the west, a bomb named Roy had waited for the radio signal that would bring it to glorious fruition. Roy was an atomic bomb, a seventy-kiloton device five times more powerful than the sorry little firecracker that obliterated Hiroshima. He waited in a corrugated steel cab at the top of a heavily lighted four-hundred-foot tower that looked, in the predawn dark, as cheery as a Christmas tree.

Cradled in a nest of multicolored wires and encased in an aluminum shell about the size of a washtub, Roy hummed expectantly. In those last moments the surrounding desert was hushed except for the plaintive squeal of a young male guinea pig—one of fifty stuffed into small mesh tubes and placed at measured intervals around the tower. The one making the racket had good reason to complain; not only had it been hauled out of its cage and stuffed headfirst into a mesh tube without its customary breakfast, it was the closest of its brethren to Roy, close enough to hear the insistent and deadly hum.

Over loudspeakers, a droning countdown. Far away, in the blastproof control complex, a series of levers were thrown, a button pushed, and from the tower came a mundane mechanical click—and silence. Inside that silence grew a strobing fluorescence that infused the broken landscape with a soft lavender glow, and then came the great shearing flash, a light so wildly bright and alien it seemed not like light at all but something from deepest space: a cold, brute element, the birth-matter of stars, the silvery essence of every created thing. Soundlessly the glare expanded, lighting up the desert horizon to horizon in a single stark exposure, and in the same instant collapsing on itself, breaking up into a billion needles of light blown outward by a concussion that punched a hole in the atmosphere and shifted the plates of the earth.

The detonation tower was vaporized instantly, leaving a ghost image of itself standing like a three-dimensional shadow inside the roiling smoke. Everything within a quarter mile of ground zero: a fleet of obsolete tanks; several domed concrete bunkers inhabited by dogs bought from an animal shelter for a dollar apiece (a sedated German shepherd bristling with shunts and wires, a mutt chained in a tub of salt water, a whining Beagle suffocating inside a gas mask); various smiling dummies crucified on poles and postured behind the

wheels of ammunition transport vehicles; a half-mile-long train tres-
tle built for the occasion; twelve rabbits entombed in an experimental
lead box; a World War II submarine half buried in the sand; and, of
course, unlucky guinea pig number one—all ceased to exist in that
single bright moment, leaving behind only their anonymous particles
sucked up, along with thousands of tons of superheated sand, into a
corkscrewing vortex that hung like a tail from the ascending fireball.

A drone carrying a capuchin monkey named Alice and a dozen
white mice flew too low into the boiling cloud and was flash-burned
in a cartoon puff of smoke.

The scientists, miles away behind bombproof glass, knew immediately they had severely miscalculated; Roy was more awful, more
viciously destructive than any of their most liberal predictions. They
didn't cheer—they were scientists—but one of them called out,
"Raises all around!" and another stepped behind a file cabinet and did
a weird little feet-shuffling dance.

On the desert floor halfway between Roy and the scientists who'd
made him, sixty soldiers hunkered down in a trench, bent at the waist
like supplicants. They had been instructed to hold blast position for
ten seconds after detonation—down on one knee, head bowed, right
arm hooked tight across the eyes—but a private, a young Lithuanian
boy from Scranton with a pronounced widow's peak, would submit
himself to none of this bullshit. His life had been fuck-all since day
one and he had no reason to believe it would get any better; he had no
plans, no future, only ugly memories, regrets. He decided that now
was as good a time as any to stand up and look eternity in the eye.

While the other men were hunched against the embankment,
muttering prayers or elbowing each other like boys in church, the
young private stood up out of the trench at the moment of detonation and took it all in: the flash, the fireball, the great luminous X-ray
that expanded like a bubble from a child's wand and showed him his
own bones glowing red, the storm of beta particles and emancipated
neutrons and other cosmic debris that passed through him as if he
were made of vapor. The radiation was a warm, blessed bath, cleans-

ing him so deeply, down to the marrow of his glowing bones, that he
thought he might weep: this lovely, helpless euphoria, the warm light,
his genitals tingling pleasantly, his heart, so full, stalling in midcon-
traction—and then the shock wave hit. He had been so enchanted by
the healing light, the vision of the rising cloud surrounded by a halo
of fire—Terrible and Magnificent Roy!—that he hadn't noticed the
desert floor tilting toward him in a buckling wave, spitting up rocks
and dust as it came.

He was upended, the jolt starting his heart again. A wall of compressed air slammed him in the back as he fell and pressed him face
first into the ground while sand and debris rained down in torrents.
He heard screaming, and then a roar that obliterated everything, and
he believed, hoped, he was dying.

When he came to he was in pain; his balls ached, his skin tightened with a prickly heat. His head rang. He tried to move and came
to find he was partially buried under a drift of hot dust and cin-
ders. He pushed himself up to his feet, swaying, knuckling his eyes.
He blinked, and the fear that had eluded him a few seconds earlier gripped him tight. The desert was ablaze: thousands of acres of
Joshua trees, creosote and mesquite bushes lit like candles floating on
a dark sea. He saw three individual flames moving slowly up a distant
hill, but he thought his eyes were playing tricks on him. His eyes were
fine; what he saw was a coyote and her two yearling pups stumbling
up a ridge, their backs on fire.

Even with his ears plugged with dirt, he could hear an inhuman
wailing from somewhere close by.

What a terrible person he'd been, what a truly sorry life he'd led.
He resolved right then: he would be a better man, he would clean up
his act, no more boozing and brawling, no more cheap whores. Oh,
how his balls hurt! If he'd known any prayers, he would have said
one and he would have meant every word.

Behind him his comrades were picking themselves up, coughing
and spitting the taste of burnt metal from their mouths. Someone
next to him was sobbing or vomiting. Above their heads the cloud

rose steadily on a blue raft of ionized air, the sky behind it billowing like a black curtain. What had seemed so beautiful a few minutes before now struck the private as vile, even wicked: a monstrous Portuguese man-of-war suspended against the dark sky, waiting to sting.

The sergeant stood in front of them, his eyes wild, shouting incoherently. The private didn't have to hear well to know what the sergeant was saying: he was telling them to get their squad lines ready, they were moving out. They were to speed-march to ground zero and secure it. These were their orders. The private quailed at the thought, but he was one of the first to line up; from here on he was going to be the type of man who obeyed all orders, who lived by the rules.

"Stop your fucking blubbering and move out!" the sergeant cried. The sergeant was bleeding from both nostrils, which nobody volunteered to mention.

They looked out across the scorched expanse in front of them. The desert sand had melted into a glassy green crust that glinted dimly with firelight. If only they could have looked into that dark glass and seen their own futures: sterility, neuromuscular degeneration, paralysis, depression, cancer of brain and bone, the thousand indignities of prolonged suffering, their deaths, much too soon.

Ignorant as they were, they hesitated. The sergeant ordered them onward and they stepped gingerly, as if out onto a frozen pond, wincing at the delicate cracking noise.

A LONE GIRL

Roy, meanwhile, was just getting started. The crest of his robust cloud, still lit from within by pink and amber nuclear fires, had ascended to thirty thousand feet—five and a half miles—into the atmosphere. He moved quickly west across the lunar hills of the great desert, borne aloft by warm air currents, spreading in slow-bloom like a drop of ink in tap water, blocking out the light of dawn. Over the flat-pan playas and crumbling cinder cones burning orange with the new sun, the cloud flattened out as it butted against a rogue cross-wind that sent it diving into the canyons and sand washes where wiry free-range cattle smelled something foul on the air and went bucking crazily into the brush. Over Ely and Buck Valley, across the broad Lincoln County Range laced with its ancient, wandering game trails that had been appropriated by humans and their livestock, ever-deepening grooves that crisscrossed the surface of the land like the creases in the palm of an old sheepherder's hand.

Walking one of these trails on her way home was a lone girl, nearly lost in the expanse of empty landscape: Nola Harrison, fifteen years old, cold, thirsty, sick with fear and guilt. Nola was a good girl, but last night she had decided to be bad. Everett Eckles had invited her to drive out to Snow Pass to watch the bomb go off. *A secret*, he'd whispered to her after seminary study, *just you and me. It's going to be a big one.*

Nobody had ever invited her to do anything, especially not a boy, especially not in the middle of the night. She was chubby, with a sweet, honest face and eyes that creased shut when she smiled.

Her sister's fancy Christmas sweater, which bore the crocheted likeness of a winking puppy, was still twisted around her chest, and she'd managed to lose one of her shoes. The night before had started so promisingly: she had snuck out of her house and waited by the stop sign, where Everett picked her up in his father's old International. They'd driven around for a half an hour in the dark, .30-30 shells and empty antibiotic bottles rolling around on the floor. They listened to the radio. She stole sideways glances, trying to catch his eye. Though she hadn't paid much attention to him before, she decided that she liked him, that she had all along. He was not the most popular or good-looking boy around—he had protuberant eyes and he smelled like horse liniment—but he was popular and good-looking enough for her.

He had pulled the truck over in a stand of junipers and they'd stared out the windshield together, listening to each other breathe. When he talked, he stuttered, and his hands kept themselves busy folding and refolding an old ag brochure until it fell apart in tatters. It took him a good five minutes to ease over the seat next to her. "I guess we'll kiss," he announced, and that was what they did, awkwardly butting heads and arranging themselves so he could take one of her breasts in each hand and rotate his wrists like he was calibrating dials. She heard a noise from the bed of the pickup, but assumed it was a ranch dog, and anyway she was busy wondering how far she would let this boy take her. He reached up under her sweater which, to her surprise and his, brought not so much as a mild protest. Just as he was figuring out the double clasp on her bra she heard what sounded like suppressed giggling. The truck rocked on its springs and two faces appeared at the back window, leering and hooting.

Two boys, Noel Cotcherly and LaVagen Humphries, bounced and howled in the pickup bed, and by the way Everett scooted away from her instantly, sneering and grinning back at his buddies, she knew this was some kind of joke, these boys had been watching everything.

"Wabba zabba!" shouted Noel Cotcherly, flexing his eyebrows. "Nyuk nyuk nyuk!"

She was too shocked for anger or embarrassment. Everett was backed up against the driver's-side door, blinking at her in terror or glee, she couldn't tell. She wanted to say something but her throat had closed tight. She reached around on the floor and threw the first thing she found—an empty Copenhagen can—at Everett's grinning face. Then she got out of the pickup and slammed the door behind her; it was all she could think to do.

The truck pulled away into the darkness, wheels spinning, and the boys in back mooed like cows.

She had been walking for hours now, eyes closed, listening to the rasp of her feet against the fine red dust of that place. Behind her eyelids dim shapes billowed and swelled. She was feverish, disconnected from her body, which seemed to contract and shrink until she felt herself inside it once again, bitter and small.

She did not see Roy's great flash that lit up the heavens, did not hear the boom minutes later, did not notice the growing light of dawn or the malignant cloud that came over the horizon and tailed her like a slinking dog. Only when she felt a prickling on the back of her neck did she open her eyes and look back, and when she saw the cloud, already on top of her, it seemed nothing more than a manifestation of the dark churnings inside her head.

She thought nothing of it at all until her skin began to burn. She was already coated with a layer of fine ash that had gotten into her eyes and mouth. She tried to run her way out of it, moaning and digging at her stinging eyes, until she skidded into a ditch and covered her head with her arms, praying out loud for forgiveness, begging God to spare her, to let this avenging angel pass her by.

When she got home, she ignored her mother who frantically called up the stairs after her, wanting to know what had happened, where she'd been. In the washroom she looked at herself in the mirror: still covered with soot, black as a demon, her eyes so frighteningly white. With a bar of soap she scrubbed her face and neck and then worked at her scalp and her hair. Her hair—brown-red and lustrous, always her best feature—sloughed off like wet cardboard in her hands.

Nola had always been known as a serious, even secretive girl, but from that day on she would play the clown, wearing her funny homemade wig, hamming it up, deflecting attention by inviting it, taking nothing seriously ever again.

THE CURSE OF THE FATHER

Roy continued on, stalking the countryside, sowing his swarms of radioisotopes like seeds: cesium 137, which infiltrates the fleshy tissues; strontium 90, which masquerades as calcium and goes directly to the bones; iodine 131, which has a particular fondness for the thyroid glands of children. Born of raw cataclysm, the ruin he would deliver now was of a variety more delicate, sophisticated: he would coat the roads and pastures and reservoirs with his radioactive powder, cling to homemade undergarments drying on clotheslines, drift like dream-dust through open windows to settle in bassinets and couch cushions and cracks in the floorboards. He would inhabit this place and its people like a ghost. He would insinuate himself into the food chain and into the bodies of the hapless tenants of this land, and he would hide there, in their muscles and brains, breaking them down with exquisitely measured patience, day by day sipping at their bones' marrow, setting their nerves to smoldering and fouling their blood, allowing them all the while the privilege of watching their poisoned children wither to nothing, and only when he had his fill of their suffering would he usher them quietly, mercifully, from the precincts of the living.

Such sorry little towns and their rugged, hopeful people! So brave in their suffering, so proud of their ruined offspring, lined up each Sunday in the Row of Angels, each one a visible punishment for a thousand hidden sins.

Of course, he wasn't going to waste all his charm on these rocky backwaters; Roy had places to go. Salt Lake City, Fort Collins, Rock Springs, Gillette, and over the border into Alberta, where he would drop a nice dose of fallout on the Fort Defiance Wiener Roast and Founders Day Parade. Apparently unimpressed with Canada, he would circle back, buzzing the outskirts of greater Duluth, taking on moisture on his tour down the Mississippi River and releasing a thunder burst of irradiated rain over Chicago's South Side. Nearly two days after his detonation, Roy would leave the continent with one last gift; in an irony that would be lost on history, he would unload three minutes' worth of radioactive hail on Washington, D.C.

But of all Roy's victims, Golden Richards and his new bride were special. Like Nola Harrison and a few hundred other unfortunates, they found themselves in Roy's path when he was young, his cloud still dense and potent and close to the ground. As he swept over the crest of Mount Pennell, the newlyweds were in the preliminary stages of consummating their marriage. Beverly had thoroughly fed Golden, reduced him to jelly with an expert massage, and was now nibbling at his downy earlobe. Somewhere in the middle of the massage Golden had noticed the cloud overhead, but it didn't seem worth bringing up, really, it would have been impolite to interrupt Beverly, intent as she was on her work.

The wind picked up, rustling the grass, lifting up the edges of picnic cloth. Only when the cloud moved across the sun, blotting out its light like an eclipse in high speed, did she look up. Golden assumed it was just another summer mountain thunderstorm, nothing at all to worry about, let's try to ignore it why don't we, but Beverly knew better. This cloud was not the dull-metal gray of a thunderhead, but composed of several shifting colors: purplish black at the center bleeding to red and brown and then dull ocher around the edges. It boiled over the last ridge, full of strange, sparkling bits of light, and came in low through the trees.

"My God," Beverly said, words that startled Golden, both because it was a sin to use the Lord's name in vain—a sin he had never once heard a church member indulge in—and because she said them so naturally.

She stood and pulled at his arm, but he resisted, he was enjoying this picnic way too much, couldn't they just wait it out?

"Get," she said, yanking hard on his wrist, "*up!*"

Just then they both smelled something chemical and the air turned to acid in their noses and throats, making them gasp. A gust of wind pelted them with dust, blinding them for a moment. Mostly by feel, Golden scooped up the blanket with all the food in it and they ran. Down the hill, through the stand of ponderosas, and along the narrow two-track in the grass, the wind coming in hard bursts, pushing the swirling smoke on top of them, covering them instantly with ash. They stumbled along, coughing and waving their arms as if under attack by insects, until they found the car.

Golden could not locate his car keys. Typical Golden. Pawing at his pockets at the most critical moment. Everything went black and for several seconds he could no longer see the car or the ground itself.

He was overwhelmed by an intense heat, an instant fever on the skin, and Beverly called out, "Oh God, hurry!"

They could not have been in a more unfortunate spot: inside the cloud's dense core, a cloud within a cloud thronging with billions of careening microparticles throwing off gamma and beta rays with celebratory abandon: Roy's dark, hot little heart.

Golden managed to get the door open and they tumbled together into the front seat. Inside, the car was calm, deep-cushioned, cool. Even though they were out of the cloud, Golden's skin continued to burn, and he clawed at his shirt and hair. "What is this?" he said, and they looked at each other: both covered head to toe with a pewter soot. Despite themselves, they laughed. Golden rubbed his eyes. His mouth was full of a gritty paste that caked around his teeth and heated the back of his throat. He croaked, "What the heck is it?"

"It's the bomb test," Beverly said, already removing her precious, ruined dress. "We need to clean ourselves off." Beverly knew there was some danger from the bomb fallout; she had heard rumors about dead sheep and AEC government men roaming the area with Geiger counters. What she couldn't have known was that in those few seconds it took for Golden to find his keys, she had inhaled thousands of particles of plutonium oxide, some of which had already settled into the lining of her lungs and begun their slow, steady assault, radiating the surrounding cells until one day, twenty years from now, those cells would begin to mutate and multiply, growing inside her like a secret wish.

Once she had helped Golden off with his shirt and pants, she dipped a clean portion of the picnic blanket in a jug of melted ice and went to work wiping the dust from his body. First, she went at the nooks and crannies of his face, the hollows of his eyes and his nostrils and the fine creases of his neck, and then moved down to his chest and arms. The cold water on his skin brought him out of his shocked state and it struck him that they were both in their underwear and she was touching him. He had never seen her body before, not like this, and he was pleased with what he saw: generous breasts and that curve of hip and the shallow dimples above her knees.

He did what he could to reciprocate, making awkward swipes at her chest and ribs with the cloth and soon she was on top of him and he couldn't distinguish the hot blush on his skin from the fever-warmth rising in his blood. She was kneeling now, facing him, and he knew there was a very good chance they might kiss, which he wanted to be prepared for: he fumbled the water jug into his hands and took a swig to wash down the grit in his mouth. What he swallowed then was not simple dust and sand, but dust and sand infused with microparticles of magnesium and cobalt and iron—the radioactive remnants of Roy's detonation tower—that would eventually be absorbed through the walls of his intestines and into the bloodstream, where they would circulate through the body and finally set up camp in the outer wall of the prostate. There they would linger for most of his life, irradiating his reproductive cells even as they were produced, splitting a chromosome here and there, warping his genes. Golden and his compromised DNA would produce twenty-six healthy children, it was true, but also seven miscarriages (the first only five months into their marriage), three stillbirths, and one broken little girl named Glory, the apple of her daddy's eye.

The damage wouldn't end there, of course; when it comes to humans, pain and suffering are passed through the generations like that unfashionable Christmas gift nobody wants: disease and mutation, anger and despair, failures of intellect and character, all of it genetic damage in one way or another, all of it nothing less than the curse of the father upon the child, a curse inevitably repaid in kind.

Of course, Golden was in no condition to entertain even the most basic existential questions—he was about to have *sex*. Beverly was straddling him now, moving against him, her rising breasts giving him little chucks on the chin. He was back in a state of shock: the only breasts he had seen before were the overworked dugs of tribal women in *National Geographic*. His back itched and he was burning up and his balls ached, which he decided was probably normal in a situation like this. Though he didn't know it, he had waited his entire life for this moment: nearly two decades' worth of suppressed libido and rage, a stark loneliness made all the worse by a deficit of human touch: he was ready to explode.

With a practiced motion, Beverly guided him inside her. For Golden, the feeling was of complete dislocation, the collision of pleasure and pain resulting in something close to oblivion. He went faint for a second, and then came to, his mouth open in an expression of blind awe. His body stiffened and he managed to whimper two words that would later cause him to grind his teeth with embarrassment: "Oh jeez."

It lasted only a few shuddering moments: over, like their wedding ceremony, before it began. But that didn't matter, they would have their entire lives together to get things right. Roy was already moving on, lifting off the mountain and into the low jet stream, leaving the windows coated with soot and the interior of the car in grainy darkness. Golden and Beverly listened to each other breathe, to the sound of the wind rocking the car on its springs. He let his large hands roam all over her and she kissed him tenderly on the mouth. They were young and pretending to be in love. This was all a very long time ago.

23.

BIG HOUSE

In this house there is chaos. Not your everyday sort of entropy, the kind that swells and intensifies before inevitably settling back into orderliness—the warehouse fire that rages and dies, the storm that blows itself out—but chaos of the endemic variety, the kind that expresses itself not only in the full-throated shouts and erratic movement of children who refuse to be counted, in the snarls of will and purpose of the husband and wives, but in the very walls of the house itself, dented and pocked as if someone had gone after a renegade mouse with a hammer, in the finger- and face-smudged windows, the knots of hair clogging every drain, the beds in disarray, the broken clocks and temperamental doors that only the initiated can open, in the poor, swaybacked piano with the half-eaten apple secretly rotting inside its case, in the burned-out lightbulbs and hidey-holes that offer protection to the scam artists and gossipmongers who ply the halls, and in all the broken spaces of the house, ragged and piebald and worn, littered with stacks of paper and battered toys and drifts of unidentifiable objects that speak of the vast and sometimes terrifying manyness of things.

The kind of chaos that begets itself, over and over again, until it becomes a kind of order, a way of life.

Today it is Sunday afternoon, the Summit of the Wives, and there is the Father, in the middle of it all. The wives have just gotten started arguing about something—powdered milk, by the sound of it—and at least half of the children are swooping around the racetrack like a tribe of Visigoths on the attack.

Mother #2: Oh, gag.

Mother #1: We can at least give it a try.

Mother #2: You ever tried it? Horrible. You never know when you're going to get a lump, and when you do, you think you've swallowed a cockroach.

Mother #1 gives Mother #2 a cold stare, which Mother #2 returns, as she always does, with an aggressively cheerful smile.

Mother #1: It's not that bad. You have to mix it well.

Mother #3, whispering into her lap: It's pretty bad.

Mother #1: It is not that bad.

Mother #4: And the kids won't like it, there'll be a revolt.

Mother #1: The kids will do as we tell them.

The Father, in a stupor at the head of the table, has missed the last two summits and is paying dearly for it now. The wives are angry at him, which is evident in the way they have agreed, despite their innumerable differences, to ignore him. He sits forward in his chair, straining to arrange the muscles of his face into an expression that suggests attentiveness, wondering how he'll make it through the next two hours. Nodding meaningfully at nothing in particular, he sneaks a glance at the Official Summit Agenda, which informs him there are sixteen items still up for discussion, and he can't help it, he closes his eyes and whimpers a little in anticipation of the suffering ahead.

For weeks the wives have been telling him the family has reached a crisis point, and though he has been gone enough that he doesn't know every detail, he knows things have gotten bad. In the past couple of months, especially, the houses have grown increasingly clannish, their grudges and rivalries dragged into the open for all to see. The ongoing feud between Mothers #1 and #2 has escalated into a series of almost daily skirmishes waged at meetings like this one, during Sunday dinners and Family Home Evenings, through the channels and byways of church gossip, along telephone lines. The children of the respective houses, never terribly fond of one another in the first place, have followed their mothers' leads, needling and teasing each other, closing ranks and marking off territory, even the young ones taking sides in disputes beyond their understanding.

By increments they are approaching an agreement: to abandon the mass illusion of themselves as a happy, God-fearing family, bound together for all eternity by obligation and love.

Today, in protest against a series of slights and insults from some of the girls of Big House, Daughters #2 and #3 have refused to show up for Sunday dinner, which is precedent-setting, and made all the more remarkable by the fact that Mother #1 has allowed it. In response, Mother #2 has released a few of her oldest from Summit babysitting duty and allowed them to watch TV in the basement (an enormous no-no on the Sabbath) with the volume cranked high, mostly because she knows how much it will annoy Mother #1.

It will only get worse, the Father knows, this is only the beginning. At the moment the wives are bickering about carpooling and the cost-to-pleasure ratio of powdered milk, but another quick glance at the Summit agenda tells him that shortly they will be moving on to more serious matters, such as how to apportion the family's dwindling finances or whether they should continue sharing weekly meals or celebrate birthdays and holidays together, which is simply another way of asking themselves if they want to go on pretending to be a single loving family or give up the charade and move on. Because the Father is in attendance (for once!) they're planning to put it all on the table: the impossible scheduling conflicts, the out-of-control sibling rivalries, the lack of leadership and example, the separate laws of engagement, the spousal fatigue. They're going to try to force him to make decisions, to take sides, which will only focus the spotlight on him more brightly, bringing them around, of course, to the same, irrefutable conclusion: that he is the one responsible for this mess they're in.

The Father, knowing he is probably already a little pale, holds his stomach and assumes the posture and stricken countenance of a sick person, looking to his wives for pity, but they pay him no mind. Some of the older children continue watching TV in the basement, dinosaur screams

*and torture-chamber noises wafting up the stairs, and the younger ones,
having already splintered into various bands, come whooping around the
racetrack, slapping the walls and speaking in tongues. Mother #2 laughs
too enthusiastically at one of her own jokes, Mother #4 presses her temples
with her thumbs and Mother #1, coughing into her fist, looks around the
table as if deciding who to kill first. And where is Mother #3? There she
is, holding her blue earmuffs carefully in her lap, ready to clap them on at
a moment's notice.*

*And here, at the head of the table, impossible to miss, is the Father,
catalyst to an explosion he can't control.*

*For some time the Father has been trying to suggest to his wives that
they have been exaggerating the family's problems, that they are too close
to the action and with the benefit of distance and perspective they would
see, as he does, that their family is no different than any other. It has its
struggles, sure, its ups and downs, a rough patch here and there, but if
they keep persevering there will be better times ahead. He's repeated these
clichés so often he's nearly convinced himself, but he knows the truth: the
family is coming apart.*

*The proof of which he witnessed up close last Saturday afternoon.
He had been upstairs, fiddling with the broken heat register in the Little
Kids' room, when he heard a shriek he mistook for the distressed cry of a
bird, possibly a wounded chicken. He went down the hall to investigate,
thinking one of the kids had brought their 4-H project into the house.
He paused in the doorway of the Big Girls' room, confused. What he
saw, mostly, was hair. An overturned bureau, a torn lampshade, scattered
notebooks, and a lot of hair. Under all the hair were two of his daughters, he wasn't sure which ones, kneeling on the bed facing each other,
grunting and clutching each other's hair in great double-fistfuls. One of
them—Daughter #2, it appeared—reared up, teeth flashing, and dragged
the other, who appeared to be Daughter #5, backward with her off the
bed. There was more breathy screeching and when they rolled toward
him, limbs flying, he backed up to get out of their way. From the safety of
the hall he called on them to cut it out.*

Daughter #2 didn't surprise him—she had always been a bit aggres-

sive and unpredictable, ready to mix it up with the boys or any neighbor girl who dared look at her funny or say the wrong thing. But Daughter #5, Mother #2's oldest girl, was pure sweetness, a girl who loved everyone openly, without shame, a paragon of generosity and Christ-like love, who was now attempting to ram her sister's head into the bedpost.

By now Dog #1 and several of the younger kids had crowded in the doorway to spectate, and the Father was reminded of his fatherly obligations. He pushed past the kids, grabbed Daughter #2 under the armpits, and hoisted her, bucking and kicking, onto the bed.

Cow! *she screamed.* Ugly mudhole pig!

Daughter #5 made a sudden, catlike lunge at her sister, screeching, WITCH! *with such ferocity that Daughters #11 and #14 began to cry and Dog #1 bolted for the bathroom. The Father cut her off, herded her toward the door while she tried clawing her way past him. There was a moment of silence, the girls glaring at each other with naked hate, their faces flushed and slick with tears, their hair wrenched into otherworldly shapes: snags and horns and gnarls.*

For a moment the Father believed he had everything under control, but when he tried to speak the girls started screeching in unison as if he'd cued them. Now the little ones were really crying and Dog #1, down the hall, began to howl, which made it difficult for the Father to make out what the shouting was about, something having to do with Mother #1 withholding money, about Mothers #2 and #3 spreading lies about Mother #1, about Mother #1 trying to control the children of Big House in any way she could, and the Father understood then just how bad it had gotten, that his sweet daughters, on their mothers' behalf, could be acting out the long-standing conflict between the houses in this way.

Gently, he tried to shush them. This has always been his role: peacemaker. Since the beginning he has displayed a singular talent for absorbing criticism and nagging, has even become, over the years, something of a punching bag for the wives and children alike, and now that he'd been away so much it looked as if they'd gotten used to taking out their aggression on each other. The girls kept at it, as if he were not in the room at all, and he clapped his huge hands in quick succession—the same thing he did when he caught Dog #1 in the act of urinating on a pile of clean laundry—but this only made them turn their attention his way, and they went from lobbing accusations and threats at each other to shouting rationalizations and explanations at him—who had said what to whom, who had been wronged and how badly—but he stopped them. He didn't want to hear it, didn't want to be responsible for hearing any of it. It was one of the first pieces of advice the Leader offered after he'd married Wife #2 and officially entered the covenant of plural marriage: don't get involved. Getting involved, the old man advised, means getting more involved, which inevitably leads to further involvement. Let them work out the little things, he said, your job is to keep your eye on the big picture.

At the time, the advice had meant very little to the Father, but now it makes perfect sense. Except, honestly, the part about the big picture. He has no idea what the big picture is. At the moment, the only picture that matters is the one in front of him: his children in riot, his wives preparing to roast him on a spit.

Here is the big picture:

1.   *The Father has feelings for his boss's wife.*
2.   *His own wives are giving up on him.*
3.   *His family is falling apart.*
4.   *His finances are drying up.*
5.   *He has a condom in his wallet and large clump of gum in his pubic hair.*
6.   *He has no idea what to do about any of it.*

As the children flow past, he tries to name them as they go, a game that distracts him a little, calms his mind. In this house, naming has become something of an obsession; the naming disease, as Mother #4 calls it, this is where it began. First, there had to be a way to differentiate it from the original house, so it became Big House, which immediately created the need to designate the original; this sort of naming and setting apart, this is how languages begin. As the family grew, they required a new lan-

guage to distinguish groups and territories: the First and Second Twins,
the Three Stooges, the Pink Bathroom and The Black Hole of Calcutta,
the Big Kitchen and the Small, the trio of Big House washing machines
which, for some reason, work under the aliases of Winken, Blinken and
Nod.

In a life so vast, in a family so forbidding, there must be ways to cut
things down to their proper size. Such a life cannot abide individuals,
only groups, and if you are not a member of a group, if you are on your
own, well then, God help you.

Mother #2 gives the Father a smart slap on the shoulder, which star-
tles him out of his trance. The wives are all looking at him, wanting his
input. He lets his attention wander for a few seconds and suddenly they
are terribly interested in him, in what he has to say. He rubs his eyes and
asks them to repeat the question, he didn't hear it clearly as he would have
liked. Mother #4 gives him a look and Mother #2 puts her two index fin-
gers behind her head like donkey ears, a secret sign the Mothers have been
using for years to indicate when the Father is being a Jackass.

Mother #1 asks the Father what's wrong and he shrugs, and when
Mother #2 asks him why he is moping he says he is not moping, which is
what people who are moping tend to say. He glances down at the agenda,
hoping to come up with a pertinent comment, when, in answer to a
prayer he had not yet found the courage to offer, the phone rings. It is Sis-
ter Barbara, bless her soul, informing him there is a problem with one of
his rental houses, a real emergency.

An emergency? the Father prompts, loud enough that the wives can
hear.

Sister Barbara tells him it's the old Victorian in Mexican Town, and
the renter said the house was collapsing and if someone doesn't show up
right away he is going to call the fire department.

Collapsing? *the Father says.* Oh dear.

He thanks Sister Barbara a little more effusively than the situation
may warrant, then hangs up the phone, which he holds out to his wives as
if to say, What do you want me to do?

Mother #1 tells him that he can't go, no way, that they have to finish this, that it can wait until they're done, but the father keeps repeating the word emergency *as he searches the mantel for his keys.*

Mother #1 orders him to sit down and the Father says, But it's collapsing!

Our house is collapsing! *shouts Mother #1, and though everyone knows she's speaking metaphorically, a couple of the wives and a few of the children glance nervously toward the ceiling. Mother #1 stands up as if to block the door, and the father has his keys now and is edging toward the foyer, saying he'll just go check things out real quick, he'll be right back, they should go on without him. He steps into his loafers and scoops up Dog #1, who from somewhere in the basement heard the jingle of keys and has arrived at the Father's side as if by teleportation. All the wives are standing now and the Father turns quickly, almost in a panic, and fumbles with the doorknob. Outside he bounds down the porch steps, a weird little laugh rising in his throat, and hustles across the gravel driveway to his pickup.*

24.

· · · ·

NESTOR AND THE OLD LADY

Golden's rentals consisted of six houses, a couple of duplexes and an old glassworks that at any one time housed between three and eleven illegal immigrant families. His father's real estate empire, bought with the last of his uranium money, had once been vast, at least three times as big as what he had now, but one by one Golden had sold off a house or commercial building when things got a little tight, such as the year when four babies were born, Josephine had to be flown to Los Angeles to have surgery on her fused spine, and Rose-of-Sharon totaled the family van. Over the past year and a half he had been tempted to sell any or all of his remaining units, but the real estate market was so bad he would have been throwing money away. These days rent money was all that kept his family fed.

The house in question was the one his father used to call, with a certain smirk in his voice, the Old Lady: an 1896 Victorian built by a criminally optimistic Mormon businessman who intended to turn southern Utah into the citrus and cotton capital of the world. In its time it was as opulent as any house in these parts, with a steeply pitched roof, gingerbread bracketing and high mullioned windows. Along with a few other houses, an old glassworks and a quaint but useless gristmill, it made up a pleasant little settlement once known as Jericho, but which now was known to the imaginative locals as Mexican Town.

Golden drove slowly down Mexican Town's single dirt road, hitting the brakes whenever he saw a child, even if the child happened to be sitting on the front step or looking out a window. To the mangy dogs, and there were a lot of them, he paid no attention.

He passed several tarpaper shacks, long featureless houses that had once served as turkey coops, a couple of old red sandstone bungalows, a scattering of travel trailers in a barren cornfield, the brick glassworks surrounded by broken plastic toys and defunct vehicles, and at the very end on a small rise the Old Lady, who, thankfully, was still standing. At one time this had been a lush spot at a bend in the river, but after the floods of 1938, the river jumped its banks and began to carve a new channel nearly half a mile away, leaving the cottonwoods and Navajo willows to wither and the inhabitants to abandon the settlement for the comforts of St. George.

Golden pulled up into the front yard next to an old Wonder Bread truck with the words ¡LOS JODIDOS! painted bright and violent red on one side. There was no one out on the lawn wringing their hands, no smoke rising, nothing to indicate a catastrophe of any sort. He felt the distinct twinge of pleasure at having gotten away with something.

He turned to Cooter, who had regressed with his obsessive licking, and was back in his Swingin' Baby Timmy underwear. "You stay here," he said. "If you're good maybe I'll come back and let you out."

A pack of frisky renegade dogs, which had followed the truck down the road, circled and yipped at him as he made his way up to the house. He was about to knock on the side door when he heard a noise out back, where Nestor and several of his cohorts—mostly Mexican men with long hair and colorful clothing—were lounging on creaky antique chairs and an old bleached-out horsehair divan. To Golden's eye they looked like a scaled-down Mexican version of the Hell's Angels, with a Caucasian hippie and a chubby Ute thrown in for good measure. Across the yard, another group of men with their T-shirts rolled up to their chests stood smoking and affectionately patting their own bellies.

"Jefe!" Nestor called. "El Jefe has arrived, just as we knew he would." Nestor stood and received Golden with a formal stiff-armed hug and a firm handshake. For as long as Golden had known him, Nestor had been this way: polite as an Englishman.

"Jefe and his many disciples," Nestor said, gesturing to the dogs. Golden made a little kick at one of the dogs, which ducked out of the way with a nonchalant expertise. He said, "I got a call."

"Yes, certainly," Nestor said, sitting back down, and taking a sip of something from a jelly jar. "Yes, I see."

Nestor was short and stocky, the only one of the lot with his hair oiled back in the traditional style. He had a handsome, dour face that shone like a full moon when he smiled. Nestor was a musician, and an intermittently successful one, apparently. He was on the road much of the time, with his own band or sitting in with other musicians, and when asked what kind of music he played, he would say, "Every kind. All kinds. The people ask for it? Nestor will play it." Along with being a vocalist of some range and power, Nestor played the drums, the steel guitar, and, on special occasions, to the delight of certain drunken crowds, the chain saw.

"A drink?" He gestured with his jelly jar. "Sit down and enjoy a nice day in the out-of-doors?"

From somewhere in the house came muffled shouting, followed by a sustained banging.

"There's nothing wrong with the house?" Golden said.

Nestor looked back at the house as if he had forgotten it was there. "Oh yes," he said, giving one of the dogs a rub on the head. "Hmm. Yes." He drew back his hand and looked at it. "I believe this dog has fleas."

"*Digalo!*" cried the blind keyboard player, who went by the name of Blind Emilio. "*No tenemos todo el dia!*"

"*Joda a tu madre, Emilio!*" Nestor called back, and they all commenced to curse each other in Spanish. Nestor sidled up and spoke to Golden in a hushed, confidential way. "These are bad men. These are very stupid men with small penises. You know their kind."

The men went from shouting to laughing in an instant and Nestor shouted back at them, "*Mujeres sin nalgas!*" and they all laughed some more.

"I don't want you to be angry," Nestor said to Golden.

"Angry?" Golden said. "Have you ever seen me angry?"

Nestor thought about it. "There is always a first time."

He led Golden into the kitchen and down the stairs into the dim, windowless basement, where there was a pool table and a collection of dinged aluminum kegs turned over for use as chairs. From above came the shouting and banging he had heard earlier.

"So you see," Nestor said.

At first Golden didn't see much of anything. Possibly he was distracted by the hundreds of beer cans and bottles stacked on every horizontal surface, or maybe it was the posters and calendars, dozens of them, of women in bikinis and tube tops, oiled up and smudged with grease and clutching wrenches or blowtorches, ready to go to work. It took him a moment to notice the way the entire ceiling sagged low over the pool table, as if some great weight were pressing down from above. Then he saw that the ten-by-ten wood beam that was supposed to bear the weight of much of the house had been cut in two, half still bolted to the floor, the other on the floor in a thin bed of sawdust.

"It's bad?" Nestor ventured a glance at Golden, his hand on his chin. "Maybe?"

Golden put his arm across Nestor's chest and backed them slowly toward the stairs. The house creaked and shifted slightly, releasing a small shower of dust.

"Who?" Golden said, the word itself a plaintive, confused sound. "Who would cut the beam?"

"Oh, those *putos* outside, of course," Nestor said. "They are playing pool, and you know, the beam is in the way, it has been in the way for some years and sometimes you have a shot in your brain, a beautiful shot that is prevented by that beam, it has happened to me on many occasions, but today it happened to that fucking *culero* Richard, he wanted to make the most beautiful shot of his life, the shot of all time, so he cut the beam. With my performance chain saw, no less. I think he was probably, you know, a little drunk."

Carefully, they made their way back up the stairs. "We have to get everybody out of the house," Golden said. "Is there anybody in here?"

"Maybe that is a small problem," Nestor said. "Please follow me."

Just off the kitchen was a narrow hallway, down which they carefully tiptoed. They stopped in front of a closed door. Nestor put his lips to the door and inquired, "Lardo?" and suddenly there was a pounding, and somebody shouted, "*Sacarme de aqui pinche idiotas malditos!*" Which, translated loosely, means, "Get me the fuck out of here, you motherfucking idiots!"

"Lardo." Nestor offered Golden a thin smile. "He is not happy."

Golden tried the doorknob but the door wouldn't budge.

"You see the problem," said Nestor. "All the rooms on this side, all the doors are stuck."

Golden stood back. "The house has shifted a little, I think, pushed the doorframes out of plumb. Can't he get out the window?"

"It's the bathroom. Lardo was in the tub doing sexual relations with his lady when this bad thing happened. There is only one small window and Lardo is not a thin man." He lowered his voice and made a face. "*His lady, she is not thin, also. I do not want to think about how they managed in the tub.*"

Golden pushed on the door again. "Are they okay in there?"

Nestor shrugged. "I told them to have some more baths, do some sexual relations, it does not have to be a bad time. Why so much yelling and hitting things? Just tell us what we need to do, Jefe, and we will do it. We do not want the house to fall down. It's a good house. You will not have to raise a finger. And we will forever thank you from our hearts."

Outside, where it was safe, Golden explained what they needed: a ten-ton jack, two if they could get them, and a steel beam at least eight feet long.

With a felt-tip pen Nestor wrote these items carefully on the smooth skin of his forearm. He tapped his head with the pen. "I see how you are thinking, Jefe. A steel beam that can withstand the *pinches Mexicanos* and their chain saws. Very good."

After Nestor sent his men away for the jacks, the beam, and a case of beer, he invited Golden to sit with him under an enormous dead cottonwood that offered no shade. Soon they were joined by the town dogs, who lay at their feet and lolled around, sniffing each others' genitals and snarling occasionally. Golden asked about Nestor's latest shows (*Why does everybody love the accordion? No matter how much they ask, Nestor will never play the fucking accordion!*) and Nestor asked after Golden's wives and kids (*Fine, Fine, everybody's doing real good, fine*).

Nestor knew all about Golden's lifestyle and it did not upset him in the slightest. Nestor had a wife and family back in Michoacan, a mistress with two children in Las Vegas, any number of one-night tour groupies-in-waiting, and a select rotation of local girlfriends. Golden had discovered that he could talk to Nestor about things in a way that he couldn't with the other men of the church, even Uncle Chick. There was no judgment in Nestor, no belief in anyone or anything but himself.

"The work?" said Nestor. "The work is good?"

"Oh, fine, it's fine, pain in the behind, you know, but going good."

Nestor grimaced. "Holy God, Jefe, you are a bad liar. You think I can't see? Look at you. You know you can tell your friend Nestor."

Golden balanced himself carefully on his rusty lawn chair and breathed out a great soul-purging sigh. He had not come with the intention of talking to Nestor about Huila, but he could feel it building in him, a confession, a release that he sorely needed.

After that strange firelit night, the night she had told him about her son, Fredy, the night he had poured out his heart about Glory, something had given way, some dam had broken. Now, while he was in Nevada, they had been meeting nearly every day. Like giddy teenagers, sneaking around, setting up secret rendezvous under the cover of darkness, driving out into the desert to look at the stars and talk

into the early morning. Even so, they'd managed a minimum of physical contact: their thighs touching as they sat on the Barge, her head
against his shoulder in the cab of the pickup, his right hand brushing
her hip as they walked side by side along the south ridge, his knuckles
scorched by the briefest touch. He didn't know if it was the fear of
Ted Leo, the fear of Beverly, or the fear of the Almighty God Who
Knew and Saw All, but it took Golden another week and a half, after
all that build-up, to kiss her.

The previous Friday night, with Ted Leo away in Las Vegas and
Golden set to drive home the next morning. They had spent most
of the night together sitting on the Barge, staring into the fire, talking. Golden was so drunk with exhaustion he'd taken off his boots
and socks, allowed his beastly feet out into the open. He had been
rambling on about his fictional wife—a Frankenstein monster constructed from carefully selected negative attributes of each of his
four wives (he wanted Huila to understand that, except for when he
was with her, he was the owner of an unhappiness to match hers)—
when he paused, looked out into the dark night as if he'd lost his
train of thought, and said, "All this time, it's been so hard not to kiss
you."

He felt her go stiff next to him. He'd been repeating this sentence
in his head for days, sometimes daring to say it out loud, experimenting with it as if it were his only line in his first Hollywood movie,
his one chance at the big time, alternating tone and testing inflection,
pursing his lips in a certain enigmatic fashion, knowing all the while
he'd never have the guts to utter such a preposterous thing out loud.
But here he'd gone and blurted it out like an idle thought that had
come to him in passing.

While he waited for a response he felt himself lifting out of his
own body, as if in a dream. After what seemed like a long time, she
said, "Why don't you?"

He stared into his lap, anchored to the couch by his own sinking
weight. He could not look at her. She had practically given him permission and still he couldn't do it, couldn't muster the simple cour-

age, for the first time in his whole damned life, to take a chance, to act without explicit permission.

His problem was simple: he had never learned to take what he wanted, to make the first move. His very life, including his marriages to his wives, his children, his church position, was none of his own doing. His father had brought him to Virgin, set him up in the church and arranged his marriage to Beverly, who, in turn, invited Nola into the family, who then brought Rose-of-Sharon along in a package deal. Only with Trish—who had been more or less forced on him by Beverly—had there been any intimate contact before marriage, and she was the one who had initiated it, wrestling him into submission in the cab of the hearse one night after prayer meeting.

Huila was different simply because he—*he*—had chosen her and she, by some miraculous coincidence, had chosen him.

Which only increased the pressure on him, somehow. He felt like he might lose her forever, might lead a sad life full of regret if he couldn't do this small thing, a brief kiss on a romantic moonlit night by the light of the fire. It was Huila, in the end, who rescued him. She took his hand in hers, gave it an affectionate squeeze as if to say, *It's okay, don't worry about it*, and that was all he needed; he forgot about his buck teeth and his possibly stale breath and his propensity for producing too much saliva when he was nervous: he leaned in and kissed her for a good long time.

FIRST DRINK

Golden leaned back in his chair and wondered how he could formulate any of this in a way Nestor might understand.

"I've got a problem," he said. "A pretty big one."

"Very good." Nestor rubbed his hands together. "I like the big ones."

"You can't tell anyone, Nestor. It would ruin me. Forever."

Nestor frowned the frown of someone deeply offended. "I can't tell anyone, that's what you say? Who? Who I am going to tell? Lardo and his lady? These dogs? Nobody here cares about your problems Jefe, I promise you, except for me."

"I have been seeing . . . another person. A woman."

"Yes, a woman, good." Nestor nodded encouragingly.

"I mean, you know, somebody my wives don't know about."

Nestor raised his eyebrows, and then abruptly threw out his hands as if to dismiss the whole thing. "We are sexual people, where is the harm? We are *men*! Do not apologize for being a man."

"I'm not really talking about sex here."

This appeared to confuse Nestor. "We're not talking about sex?"

"No."

"But we're talking about a woman?"

"Yes."

Nestor pooched his lips, only marginally reassured. "And now, what is the big problem?"

"This woman," Golden said, "is my boss's wife."

"Oh my shit." Nestor put his face in his hands.

Golden toed the dirt with his boot. "And I think I love her."

Through his hands Nestor groaned, "Oh my fuck. Big, big fuck."

"And she's from Guatemala."

"Oh-my-fucking-God-shit."

Nestor smacked himself on the forehead, stood up, walked around in a tight circle and sat back down. "She's from Wah-teh-*ma*la?"

Golden nodded.

"And she's your boss's woman, and you love her?"

Golden shrugged.

"Oh my *shit*." Nestor shook his head, both impressed and dismayed, which was more or less how Golden felt about it himself.

"Maybe you are right," Nestor said. "Maybe this is a big problem."

"For me it is."

Nestor looked up and smiled. "You know what they say about the *hijas* from Wah-teh-mala?"

"No."

"Hmm, maybe you don't want to know."

"Maybe not."

"They say they can fuck the stink off the devil himself. That's what they say." He smiled to himself, quickly glanced up at Golden. "But probably this does not apply to your particular lady."

Nestor left for a moment and returned with two jelly jars filled with amber liquid. Immediately Golden held up his hands to decline but Nestor slapped the hands away and pressed the drink into one of them. "You drink a little, there is no harm. You are sneaking about with your boss's woman and you won't have a little mescal? Come on, Jefe, please. You are helping us with our big problem"—he gestured to the house, which, from this angle, seemed to have shifted on its foundation the tiniest bit—"and we will help you with yours. This is the first step, to relax. You are sitting there like you have something very unpleasant up your *culo*."

Golden took the jar; he was not one to say no twice. He sniffed its contents: not too bad. In fact, it smelled like nothing at all. He had never had a drink, not so much as tasted alcohol of any kind. It was a little late, he thought, to be thinking about all the things he'd not done in his life.

He took an experimental sip, which went down as smoothly as a mouthful of liquid Drāno. His throat clenched and he shuddered with the burn of it.

"Aha!" said Nestor. He gave Golden a questioning look. "Ah?"

Golden blinked and opened his mouth to let out some of the fumes. He croaked, "It's terrible."

"Yes!" said Nestor, grinning brightly, taking another enthusiastic drink. "Yes it is."

FAMILIES ARE FOREVER

Forty minutes later a small Toyota pickup arrived, transporting five Mexicans and a long steel beam, which Golden was brought around to inspect. Though he had had maybe three tiny sips of the mescal, barely enough to register in the jelly jar that he had drunk any at all, the ground felt soft under his feet. He could see immediately the beam was at least four feet too long. He grabbed a hacksaw from his work truck and told them they would have to cut it to eight feet. He then went inside to double-check the measurement, and he realized that the beam, even cut to eight feet, would not fit down the narrow back-and-forth stairs. He skirted the outside of the house, looking for a window or some kind of opening, though he knew there was none. How had they ever gotten a pool table down there? He came around the south end and, sure enough, there was a patched-up section of the sandstone-block foundation, about six feet long.

"Who knocked out the foundation here?" he yelled, but he was all alone on that side of the house. Feeling bold, he stalked around to the front and, with a slightly shrill schoolmarm timbre to his voice, shouted, "Who on *earth* busted out the foundation back here?"

Everyone stopped talking and laughing, Jorge stopped hacksawing, and they all looked at each other. "What foundation?" Nestor said. "We didn't bust no foundation."

"Then how did you get the pool table into the basement?"

They all looked at each other again, eyes wide, and started to laugh. Blind Emilio, who was holding an extended tape measure, had a high, sharp laugh—*ah-hee-ah-heeeeee!*—which caused everyone else to laugh that much harder.

"He is Sherlock Holmes!" Jorge said. "He has discovered our lies!"

"Or Kojak!" said somebody else, which made everyone laugh harder.

Golden had to admit it: he liked these people. He liked them a lot. And he didn't care that they'd knocked out part of the foundation or that the Old Lady might collapse on herself at any moment. He told them to get a pick and punch out a hole in the patched-up section so they could get the beam through, and hurry up about it.

He had meant to supervise the cutting of the beam, but five minutes later he was back on his chair under the dead cottonwood, jelly jar tucked between his thighs, eating some kind of spicy stew from a pie tin. With the oncoming dusk the place had taken on a carnival atmosphere: children chased a soccer ball and Blind Emilio played a child-sized accordion, which induced much third-party harmonizing and crooning, and Cooter, who someone had let out of the cab of the pickup, raced wild circles around the town dogs, nipping at their ankles and showing his teeth, oblivious that he was the only one among them wearing underwear.

"What are we eating here?" Golden asked Nestor, who was dancing with a stout middle-aged woman in apricot spandex tights.

"*Chivo!*" Nestor called over the music. "You know, goat! Perlita here, her recipe!"

Golden held up the pie tin to indicate how much he was enjoying it. In fact, it was a little too spicy for him—sweat had beaded up across his forehead and temples—but it was so delicious he couldn't stop shoveling it down. As he scooped up the last bite, he took a moment to consider how far afield he'd come: not four hours ago he had been in church, blessing the sacrament and reading scripture in suit and tie, and now here he was drinking homemade liquor and eating goat with a bunch of devil-may-care Mexicans.

Some of the men called to him to inspect the hole they'd made in the foundation, and he carefully sat forward in his chair, feeling around with his feet to locate the ground before he tried to stand on it. After a deliberate trek across the backyard, what he found was not the small, inconspicuous hole he might have preferred, but one nearly three feet wide and two feet high.

"*Bueno?*" said Guillermo with a workingman's pride.

"*Muy bueno,*" Golden sighed. "Let's go ahead and get the beam in there."

They went around to the front, where a crowd had gathered next to the ¡LOS JODIDOS! tour bus. At first Golden thought, because of the yelling and whistling, that it was a fight of some sort, but it turned out to be Cooter attempting to mount one of the female dogs. This particular dog was smaller than the others, but still larger than Cooter, who had given up his mounting attempt and now had his forelegs locked around the dog's hips, his muzzle pressed into her hindquarters, his hips pumping away at one of her back legs. There was much applauding and encouragement, and Cooter began to look around, bug-eyed and clearly embarrassed at this turn of events, but unable to stop himself.

"Behold," said Jorge, "life in its glory."

"Who took off his underwear?" Golden said. He considered going in and pulling Cooter away, sparing him this public shame, but at this point he really didn't want to get involved.

"He was in distress," Nestor said. "Perlita thought he needed to relieve himself." He motioned toward Cooter. "Clearly, she was correct."

Grinning shyly, Perlita handed Golden the Swingin' Baby Timmy undershorts, which he stuffed like a handkerchief into his shirt pocket. Perlita's flashing smile, her lustrous black hair, brought Huila to mind in a way that made him go light-headed.

Nestor came up and stood next to Golden. "Hmm," he said under his breath, "you think the girl-dog might be from Wah-teh-mala?"

Together they checked on the hacksawing, which was progressing slowly because Jorge and the thin drummer—Golden thought his name might have been Ronnie—spent most of their time arguing about what kind of saw stroke was the most efficient, and who had been guitarist for Three Dog Night before Al Cinder.

"Come sit back down," Nestor said. "Have some more food and drink while we wait."

"I've got to get home," said Golden, making a sour face.

"You can't go now, before we're finished." He pointed at the house. "You leave now and it will be on your head."

Golden didn't bother to argue—he followed Nestor around to the back, took up his spot under the cottonwood. Evening was falling and you could hear the cooing of doves who sat at equidistant intervals on the telephone wires. Even Lardo—placated by goat stew and a bottle of mescal passed through the high bathroom window—had quit his banging and complaining. Golden sighed and settled in. How lovely to sit under the lowering sky, the dead grass whisking his ankles, with springtime coming on and a feeling in his heart of imminent disaster.

Such a feeling could not last; as hard as he tried not to, Golden pictured his family back at Big House, waiting for him around the dinner table, faces pinched with expectation, the wives grim and perfunctory in their duties, the younger children circling back to the front window so as to be the first to spot him coming up the drive. He could see the framed needlepoint above the mantel, *Families Are Forever*, and wondered if the slogan was meant as a promise or a threat.

He took up his jelly jar from its place under the chair and held it up to the pink western sky, took a small sip from it, shuddered. He really ought to go—they were waiting for him, they always would be. He sat back. He took another sip.

25.

· · · · ·

TO LOVE A SCOUNDREL

OGETHER THEY WATCHED IT BURN ALL THE WAY DOWN. JUNE HAY-maker, wearing a starched and pressed flannel shirt under his Dickies overalls, held on to the top wire of the fence with both hands and gave the fire his full and solemn attention, as if watching a ritual of profound cultural significance. Trish stole a few card-player glances at him, noticing the way the distant flames burnished his sharp cheekbones and flickered in miniature across the tear layer of his eyes.

Twenty minutes before she had been in the house reading her trashy book, so fully entranced she didn't notice the wind whipping up, the sky deepening, the old red cedar at the side of the house creaking at its roots. Only when her eyes began to ache from the words on the page dimming and bleeding into each other did she look around. Thunder rumbled. A handful of rain spattered against the window. Trish liked thunderstorms, but she was annoyed at this one for rousing her from the dream (a ridiculous dream, but a dream nonetheless) of the book she was reading, for depositing her squarely back into her life. The phone rang once, a fretful little ring, and she was further annoyed by the way her heart rose at the sound—somebody was calling!—and at the way it then seized with disappointment when she realized it was only a phantom call, electricity on the lines. Quite suddenly she was angry—not merely annoyed—at her self-pitying self, at the circumstances that brought her to be so easily angered and annoyed and susceptible to self-pity, at the shiny absurd book in her hands as well as the fact that she was enjoying it so much, and when she heard the thunderbolt hit, the walloping crack that registered like a blow to the skull and the small bones of the spine, she thought for a moment it was the sound of her accumulated frustration and anger being released into the world in a single charge.

For a moment she didn't breathe. She tried to turn on the lamp but the power had gone out. Only when the city fire station blared its distant siren and was answered on cue by the entire local dog population did she get up to have a look around. The fire was already well on its way, edging along the roof line of the old swaybacked barn that sat in a fallow, weed-choked field a few hundred yards to the north of the duplex, the same barn she looked at every day while doing the dishes. It had become such a familiar part of her surroundings she had stopped noticing it at all, except once in a while on Friday or Saturday nights when it filled with the laughter and catcalls of drunken teenagers—sounds that made her nostalgic for a wild, heedless adolescence that had never belonged to her. She always assumed the teenagers and their cigarettes would eventually burn the thing down, but it appeared God had beat them to it.

Brother Gunther, her widower neighbor, informed her one day over the fence that the barn was not a barn at all but a turn-of-the-century winery. "They called it the wine house back then, and for miles around, see, there was nothing but orchards and vineyards." Brother Gunther, well past eighty and about as talkative and social as a department store mannequin, was brought instantly to life by the subject. His left eye caught a spark—his right was hidden behind a flesh-colored adhesive bandage —and he waved his arthritic hands along the horizon. "Can you see what I'm saying? Climate and soil were perfect for it and Brother Brigham, a practical man if ever there was, told them not to worry about the Word of Wisdom, just go ahead and make wine. Good wine. Grape wine, plum wine, pomegranate wine, we made it all. I was a boy then. Picked the fruit of the vine. Had a nip or two of the good stuff, I won't lie to you. A paradise, it was, like Palestine in Bible times. And now look. Weeds and empty fields and garbage and young people using Brother Brigham's wine house for making whoopee and smoking their drugs." He let out a quick, rattling sigh as if he'd taken a weak punch to the belly. "We're a sad, sorry bunch, the lot of us."

She had wanted to reach over the fence and give his shoulder a commiserative pat, to show just how much she empathized with his view of things, but as fast as it had come the light dimmed in his good eye and he turned without a word and shuffled across the dead grass to his empty house, his flock of hopeful turkeys trailing behind.

Today, when she'd come out to watch the fire, Trish had looked for Brother Gunther at the back of his house. He was nowhere to be seen, but his turkeys, who'd been hiding in the coop during the thunderstorm, spotted her and headed over to see what she might have for them. She had turned to go into the house to get them some potato chips when she noticed June Haymaker standing at the garden gate at the side of the house. He took a half step back as if she'd caught him at something, and gave a shy half wave. The sight of him made her heart leap the way it had when the phone rang.

Though she'd waved him in, he stayed where he was. He explained he'd been in his shop working when the fire call went out over the police band. He'd come as quickly as he could. Watching his hand fiddle with the latch on the gate, he'd said, "I guess I was worried about you—about your house, I mean." And she stood there smiling bashfully, energetically, her face grown hot with the simple pleasure of being the object of someone else's concern.

"Well. Glad you're okay, then." He jerked his thumb toward his truck. "I should probably be getting home."

"*June*," she had said, amazed to hear a slightly coquettish tremolo in her voice. "Why don't you come on back for a minute? It's not every day you get to watch something burn to the ground."

So now they stood at the fence watching the volunteer firefighters turn valves and unspool their hoses. There was a casual, prankish note to the proceedings; the men, most of whom looked, from this distance, to be no more than high school students themselves, shouted good-naturedly and threatened to spray each other before turning the hoses on the fire, which was now burning through the gaps in the partially collapsed roof. The men were in no hurry—this was clear—believing, no doubt, that the loss of this old barn in a weedy field would have no victims. If only they knew about poor Brother Gunther, Trish thought, and the local teenagers he so despised, who would be forced to find a new spot for making their whoopee and smoking their drugs.

"What a bunch of rank amateurs," June said.

Apparently bored with spraying water on the burning barn, the firefighters began to congregate at the front of it, bunching in together while one of them stood off to the side and pointed.

"The heck are they doing?" June said. "Are they . . . ?"

"Yes, they are, they're having their picture taken."

Sure enough, a chorus of *Cheese!* lifted across the field and a flashbulb went off, and then one more.

"You gotta be kidding me," June said. "Seriously. I mean. What if that place was somebody's house?"

"Then that somebody would be looking for a new place to live," Trish said.

"I'm just glad it wasn't your house," June said.

"With this house," Trish said, tipping her head toward the dumpy old thing, "a raging inferno and a crew of inept firemen might be the best thing that could ever happen to it."

In fact, Trish's house, and its dubious state of repair, was what had brought June by several more times after he'd first come over with Rusty to unclog the toilet. He'd rigged up a new motor for the ventilation fan in the bathroom and repaired every leaking faucet in the place, including the outdoor spigots. He was quiet, intense, and almost superhumanly competent when it came to fixing things and improvising mechanical solutions. At first she had him pegged as one of those socially hamstrung introverts with self-administered haircuts who could not connect with the living and breathing world except through their relationship with inanimate objects. But he'd turned out to be sweet, a little goofy, the owner of a sense of humor that showed itself at the most unexpected moments.

No, she had not expected to like him so much. She liked the way he watched her when she spoke, with the humble intensity of a foreign student in a remedial English class, feverishly jotting mental notes, striving, as if his life depended on it, to absorb every rule and nuanced particular of his subject. He was twenty-seven—their birthdays only two weeks apart—but his angular head and sharp Adam's apple seemed to suggest an older person, one compacted and honed by the trouble of years.

She liked the way he smelled, like old-fashioned talcum powder. She liked how his voice broke when he got excited. She liked, probably more than any one thing, that he so obviously liked her.

And he was not the only one paying her extra attention of late; Rusty had been stopping by the duplex every other day even though he'd been grounded for going AWOL from Old House last week. Beverly had essentially placed the boy under house arrest: he had fifteen minutes to make it to and from school and was not otherwise allowed outside except to do his chores. And yet there he was this past Monday, just before noon, sweating like a coal miner and giving her front door a hearty knock.

"I'm just stopping by to say hi," he said. It was his lunch hour at school, and he'd ridden his bike the entire three miles, most of the way along the graveled margins of Highway 86, apparently just to say hi. Instead of the standard hand-me-downs, he was wearing a red-and-green checkerboard sweater—which was soaked with sweat down the sides and back—and what appeared to be his Sunday shoes, freshly polished. She didn't want to imagine the teasing he had endured for showing up at school in such a getup.

"Do they let you leave the grounds for lunch?" she asked.

"Nah, not really, but nobody cares as long as I get back to class on time." He shrugged, made a swipe with his sleeve at his dripping forehead. "I just came by to say hi." She invited him in and they shared a quick lunch of cheese toast and leftover pasta salad. He spoke very little but regarded her with a steady, forthright stare. He asked her if she planned on attending his special birthday at Skate Palace next Friday and she told him she wouldn't miss it for the world.

She shuttled him and his bike back to school, breaking the speed limit the whole way to get him there on time, and let him off at the corner so as not to be seen by the pertinent authorities. Before she drove away he looked up and down the sidewalk, then stuck his head in the passenger window. He said, with utter earnestness, "This should be our little secret, don't you think?"

They shared a look, she and this boy, and she had to bite her lip to keep from erupting into a giddy, girlish laugh.

Once she was back on the highway, she let the laugh go into the confined space of her car and was a little surprised at how loud and jubilant it was. She knew the whole thing was absurd, of course she did, but she couldn't deny how such a harmless little caper gave life to an otherwise lifeless day.

And then two afternoons ago she had nearly finished her twice-a-week walk with Faye—except for trips to the cemetery, the girl had to be forced into the out-of-doors—when Rusty appeared at the end of the block on his bicycle. Without ever really thinking about it she had always considered bicycle riding to be an innately frolic-some activity, one that couldn't be undertaken without at least the appearance of good cheer, but Rusty, head hung low, one arm loosely maneuvering the handlebars while the other hung limp at his side, was doing his best to disprove this theory. He was despondent; his posture said so. His hair was an unholy mess, his shoes were missing and his dirty tube socks flapped freely.

Faye put up a hand to shield her eyes against the lowering sun. "Here *he* is again."

At first he refused to speak. When she asked him what was wrong, what had happened to his shoes, he shrugged and shook his head with the mild desperation of someone who had good reason to believe if he opened his mouth the only thing likely to come out was a whimper or a sob—a feeling she knew all too well.

She led him into the house and seated him at the table. Faye sighed and retired to her prayer cave. It was clear he had already done his share of crying; there were the telltale streaks on his smudged cheeks and the remnants of tears sparkling in his eyelashes. When she asked him if Aunt Beverly knew where he was, he found the wherewithal to speak: "That witchy woman is *not* my mother."

For some reason this brought a loud, derisive snort from Faye down the hall.

"*Faye*," Trish said.

"All *right*," Faye called.

"Rusty, honey, I don't want you getting into any more trouble than you already have. If you want, I'll drive you home right now and talk to Aunt Beverly. We'll get this worked out."

"Oh no we won't," Rusty said. "I'm not afraid of Aunt Beverly. Everyone acts like she's, you know, Genghis Kong or somebody." He snorted and shook his head. "She's just a bully, that's all, that's all she is. I don't need any help with her."

He set his jaw and stuck out his lower lip, attempting a defiant look, but he couldn't control his sniffing and hiccuping, which undermined the overall effect. Even so, Trish had to admire the boy: no one had ever challenged Beverly this directly, this openly; not Nola, who had been fighting a war of attrition with Beverly for years; not Golden, who received his orders with a *Thank you, ma'am,* and a curtsy; not Uncle Chick, whose decisions and exhortations were widely accepted as the direct and final word of the Lord Almighty—except when they involved Beverly, in which case they were taken as polite recommendations. And certainly not Trish, who was going on twenty-eight and had yet to learn the elementary skill of standing up for herself.

Rusty took a big, shuddering breath and asked to use the bathroom. When he emerged a couple of minutes later he was a new person, his face freshly washed and his hair wetted down and combed straight back in the style of a fifties Hollywood gangster. He had turned both his T-shirt and socks inside out to produce the illusion of cleanliness.

"I was wondering if we could have a word in, you know, private," he said.

They stepped into the kitchen and he reached around behind his back with both hands and for a moment it appeared he might be trying to pull down his pants. He grimaced, and after some involved tugging and pulling he eventually produced a ratty paperback, which he had apparently been carrying around somewhere inside his underwear. He held it out to her.

"It's a present," he said, blushing hard. "To you from me."

There was a couple seconds' hesitation before she took it and carefully turned it over in her hands as if checking it for booby traps; like a sweet bun just out of the oven, it was warm and a little sticky. *To Love a Scoundrel*. By the frayed, dog-eared look of it, it had been consulted often and at length.

She stared at it for a moment, attempting to arrange the appropriate expression on her face, and then she knew: he'd taken the book from his mother. It was a badly kept secret that Rose had an addiction to romance novels. How many times had she come upon her sisterwife hiding in the laundry room or the upstairs kitchen at Big House, her face pressed so deeply into a book it looked like she was trying to *taste* the thing? Trish had never called her on it, never asked what she was doing; she had a pretty good idea why Rose liked such books, aside from their questionable entertainment value. Rose read them because she wanted to know how the other half lived. The half who insinuated themselves into palace politics of the opulent high courts of Prussian royalty and danced away the blossom-scented nights at Civil War–era cotillions and patrolled the woodlands of Normandy in the company of brigands and knaves. The half who, instead of settling for a life of subservience and boredom and disappointment, were not afraid to reach for the forbidden fruits of adventure and passion. The half who, on occasion, were known to have *sex*.

Trish took a good look at the cover, which featured a busty bimbo being wrestled into submission by a shirtless ne'er-do-well. She smiled. "Well, I suppose a sincere thank-you is in order."

Rusty made a grandly dismissive wave. "And you don't have to get me a present or anything, even though my special birthday is coming up. I just wanted to get you something. Because I like to get people things, that's all."

"You didn't have to, but thank you anyway."

"I think you'll enjoy it. After the dictionary and the Bible, it's probably my favorite book."

The crunch of tires on gravel outside brought them to the front window, where they could see June pulling up in his old pickup.

Rusty said, "What's *he* doing here?"

"Got me," Trish said, sliding *To Love a Scoundrel* behind one of the couch cushions. "He's been so nice, though, fixing up whatever needs fixing."

"He was just supposed to fix the toilet and that's all."

Trish held open the door for June, who came in cradling some kind of mechanical contraption with wires hanging off it.

"Hey, everybody," he said. "Oh, hey there, Lance."

"It's Rusty," Rusty said, an edge to his voice. "I already told you."

"Rusty? Right, yeah, sorry." He turned to Trish and grinned. He held up the contraption. "A little present for you."

June's presence, and that shy, aching smile of his, had made blood rush to her face and to hide this fact she covered her cheeks with her hands in a show of mock, blinking gratitude, saying, "You shouldn't have, June! Really now!" Then she noticed Rusty, who had fixed June with a murderous glare.

"You were only supposed to fix the *toilet*." He made an indignant snort. "You weren't supposed to keep coming back."

June turned to him, surprised. "I'm just, uh, helping fix a few things around here. Yeah, this is a fan motor for the swamp cooler."

"As if," Rusty said darkly.

"What? I came across it today at the salvage yard."

"Oh *come on*," Rusty said.

"What?" said June. He looked at Trish for help. "What?"

Watching these two, Trish was taken back to her high school days, when young suitors had shadowed her in the halls, asked her on dates, plied her with gifts, and competed awkwardly for her affections. She had forgotten just how good those days were.

"Rusty, honey, please," she said. "He came to fix the swamp cooler, before it gets too hot around here. He's trying to do us a kindness."

She tried to put a hand on his shoulder but he pulled away and made for the front door. His voice breaking, he shouted, "And what about Big House? Huh? Everything there needs fixing, and who's going to do that? Huh, June? Doesn't anybody care about that?"

He pushed open the screen door, letting it slap shut behind him, and mounted his bike. "I hope you're all happy!" he cried as he pedaled into the scarlet remnants of a sunset, socks flapping. "I hope everybody's happy!"

A WOMAN WITH NOTHING TO LOSE

The old winery had disappeared; now there was nothing but a single bowl of flame feeding on what seemed to be the faint memory of a building, a ghost-image traced in glowing, white-hot lines. The low, flat-bottomed storm clouds had passed and now hovered on the eastern horizon, as if pausing to watch the spectacle, roiling and grumbling and throwing down the occasional stick of lighting.

Because the power had not yet been restored and it was too dark to continue on with her afternoon séance and scripture-reading session, Faye had come out to watch the fire and feed the turkeys a bag of Fritos.

Moving with the caution of a man approaching a poisonous snake, June took a couple of sideways steps and squatted down next to the girl, to meet her at eye-level.

"Stay back," she said, without looking his way.

Slowly, he retreated a few feet. "How's this?"

"That's okay."

"So," he said, "you like turkeys, then?"

"No," she said.

"I don't either," June agreed.

"You're just saying that."

June gave Trish a quick, uncertain glance. "No, I'm—"

"Yes, you are," said Faye. "All grown-ups lie to children, you included."

Trish knew that June had absolutely no chance of getting into Faye's good graces—nobody did, nobody ever had—but it was sure nice, she thought, to watch someone giving it a try.

It didn't take long for everybody to become bored with the fire, including the turkeys, who were more interested in Fritos, and the volunteer firemen, who now appeared to be sitting on top of their water truck playing cards.

Trish turned toward the house, and as if a spell had been broken, the turkeys began to disperse. June looked up at the purple sky as if noting the weather. He nodded. "I should probably be getting going . . ."

"You're welcome to stay," Trish said. "At least let me get you something to drink. I haven't offered you anything."

"If you want I could go ahead and install the fan motor I brought by the other day." He kicked at the dirt beneath his boots, gave the fire one last look. "I've got a couple hours free."

"Nonsense," Trish said, guiding him by the arm toward the house. "It'll be dark soon and the power's still out. And I can't let you go tromping around on top of the house in this weather."

June looked down at his boots as if consulting them. "All right. Maybe I'll stay a minute or two."

He stayed most of the evening. The electricity still off, they roasted hot dogs over the stove's gas burner and popped popcorn in an industrial-sized pot. At some point there was a knock at the front door, which Trish opened to reveal a nervously grinning Maureen

Sinkfoyle. Trish took up a territorial stance in the doorway and had to fight off the urge to slam the door in the poor woman's face.

"Hello, there!" cried Maureen, who wore a wrinkled windbreaker and was cradling something in her arms. Her hair, normally poufed to the limit, had collapsed in the bad weather, which gave her the sad, flopping aspect of a deflated hot-air balloon.

"What can I do for you, Maureen?"

"Oh! Well, I was just stopping by to see if you and your girl were doing all right. I brought some candles"—she showed Trish the bunch of emergency candles she was clutching against her chest—"just in case you needed some, looks like the power might be off through the night, I already dropped off some at Rose and Nola's, my husband—*ex*-husband, I mean! I keep forgetting that!—he used to be big into emergency preparedness, I mean before he abandoned me and the boys, which was an emergency none of us were prepared for! Ha! So we had a whole box of these things lying around and I thought—"

To put a stop to this speech Trish stepped out from behind the screen door, accepted the candles, and quickly retreated to her original position. Maureen was a pitiful figure, abandoned and desperate, pathetic in her ill-fitting clothes and dismantled hairdo, who reminded Trish, in altogether too many ways, of herself. So why couldn't she work up any empathy for this person? Why did she view her as nothing but a threat to the contentment and security she didn't really possess? Why did she want to wrench the screen door off its hinges and scratch the poor woman's eyes out?

"I'll help you light them . . . if you want," Maureen said haltingly, no doubt unsettled by the look on Trish's face. "I'm not doing anything else right now."

Trish took a quick glance into the family room, where June's work boots were visible from the entryway.

Maureen said, "Is somebody here?"

"What? No." Trish crowded the door and lowered her voice. "No, no. It's just me. Me and Faye."

"Would you have a minute or two to chat, then? All this time, and we've never really had the chance to talk—"

"I'm so sorry," Trish said. As she spoke, she gradually nudged the door with her foot, as if it were closing on its own accord and there was precious little she could do about it. "I've got things on the stove and Faye, she isn't feeling very well, and thanks so much for these candles, Maureen, it was really kind of you . . ." Then the latch clicked shut, and Trish waited, holding her breath, until Maureen stepped off the porch and could be seen crossing the lawn toward her car.

Sighing, her arms full of candles, Trish stepped back into the family room. June was on the couch, studying *To Love a Scoundrel*, which, in her hurry to get out of the house earlier this afternoon, she had left on the coffee table, right out in the open. It was past dusk and the room was filled with an eerie dimness tainted with the smoky glow of the still-smoldering fire, and in the semidarkness June was holding the book right up next to his face, reading the back cover.

Trish dropped the candles. "That thing," she said. "That's not really mine, it was a gift . . ."

"I'm sorry," June said, putting the book back down on the table and then quickly picking it up and offering it to her, his face turned to the side. "I didn't know it was anything . . ." She took it from him and tried to think of a good place to put it—maybe toss it in the trash, act like it was something that had blown in with the storm and needed to be disposed of. She looked at the ridiculous cover and then at June, whose eyes were open wide with alarm, and she laughed. She said, "You ever read one of these things?"

"Which things do you mean?"

"Trashy romance novels. Like this one here."

"Only—only every day," June said. "Usually, you know, right before knitting club."

"Oh, so I guess you've probably read this one, then?"

"Probably. Yeah. Which one is that again? I've read so many I get confused."

"*To Love a Scoundrel* by Alice M. Montbeclaire."

"Oh yeah, yes, a classic. Up there with *Beowulf* and, uh, *Gone with the Wind*. Remind me what *Scoundrel* is about."

"Well, you have Sir Nigel Mountcastle, of course . . ."

"Oh my gosh, Sir Nigel Mountcastle! How could anyone forget him?"

She put a hand on her hip. "Do you want me to tell you or not?"

June inserted an imaginary key into his lips and turned it. "Please proceed, yeah, I cease to interrupt."

She filled him in on the basics: how Sir Nigel Mountcastle, the Scoundrel of the title, had freed Lady Jane Welshingham from an Irish insane asylum, in which she had been confined under mysterious circumstances, with the agreement that she would become his personal maidservant for a year. Of course, Lady Jane falls for Sir Nigel's rakish charms, even though he humiliates her at every turn, requiring her to feed him by hand, powder his wigs, and give him his weekly milk bath.

"Ah yes," June said, eyes closed, trying not to laugh, "the milk bath. It's all coming back now."

"The milk bath is for his constitution, of course." She described how during one of the weekly baths Lady Jane simply couldn't help herself and ended up stealing a sip of milk from the hollow of Sir Nigel's collarbone. They were locked in their first passionate kiss, sloshing around wantonly in a tub of milk, when the Earl of Buckington, Lady Jane's husband, burst in and had them arrested on trumped-up charges of adultery and treason. By the time she had finished the explanation about how Sir Nigel and Lady Jane escaped from Newgate Prison by covering themselves with lamp oil and squeezing through the bars, Trish and June were both laughing so hard their eyes watered and June was punching a pillow with his fist.

Once she had come up for air, Trish held out the book. "You know where I got this thing?"

"*Where?*" June said, his voice pitched and girlish, and for some reason this sent them into another round of laughter that had them grasping at their stomachs and gasping for air.

"Rusty," she said, finally, breathing hard. "That's why he went away so mad the other day. He gave me this as a present and then you stopped by and one-upped him with the motor for the swamp cooler."

June sobered considerably. He sat up on the couch and wiped his face. "I did? I didn't mean to."

"I know," Trish said. "Don't worry about it. I think he may have a little bit of a crush on me."

"Well, that's . . ." June nodded and inhaled deeply. "That's completely understandable."

The moment the words came out, June stiffened and there was a sudden increase in atmospheric pressure: the easy hilarity drained away in a second, leaving behind a wire of tension pulled tight, waiting to be plucked. June stood, looking around, patting at his pockets as if searching for a way to tactfully withdraw.

"I should really . . ." He pointed to the door. "Thanks for the hot dogs and everything. Good popcorn!"

"You mean you're going to leave us here all alone in the dark?" Trish had meant this in a playful way, an attempt to bring back the banter of a minute ago, but there was a reproachful edge to the words that made June look up, eyes wide, as if she had accused him of something.

"What?" June said. "No. Let me help you with those candles. I'll stay as long as you want me to—or until the power comes back."

She tried to tell him she was only joking, that he was free to go whenever he pleased, but he was already on his knees, scrambling to pick up the scattered candles. Watching him, it struck her that he had every reason to feel awkward, even guilty; here he was passing time in the darkened home of a married woman, sitting on her furniture, eating her food, even flirting with her while her husband was away. In their few brief conversations she and June had avoided any discussion of her marital situation, and while he may not have known if she was a plural wife or the more standard variety, he certainly had enough sense to guess that her husband, the hairy giant in the wedding picture prominently displayed on top of the piano, might not take kindly to the idea of a single man spending so much time alone with his wife.

The question was: Why didn't *she* feel guilty? She was the married one, after all, the one with commitments and obligations, the one with a daughter upon whom very little was lost. Shouldn't it have bothered her, just a little, that all evening long she'd been considering—and surely this had everything to do with *To Love a Scoundrel*—how it might feel to slip her arms around June's sharp, bony shoulders and put her cheek against his chest? It hadn't occurred to her until now, but lately she had begun to think of herself as single again—Golden was around so little, and even when he was she felt like a married woman in title only. And not just single, but *old* and single, a withered, buttoned-up spinster giving off the spinster scents of cedar chest and sachet and laundry starch, filling the empty hours reading silly romance novels, a woman with nothing to lose.

"We'll be fine, June, thank you," she said, not wanting to come across as *too* desperate. After a beat, she added, "If you'll come back and install that fan motor in a day or two I promise I'll make you something better than hot dogs and popcorn."

Before going, he helped her place and light the candles: on the mantel and the piano and the dining room table. It had grown fully dark and the walls of the house wavered and pulsed in the flickering light. Trish placed the last candle on the sideboard next to the front window, and June, following behind, lit it with a fresh match. For a moment Trish stood still, taken by the warped image reflected in the glass: a man and woman, one of each, standing side by side, looking for all the world as if they belonged together. And then her eye caught a movement outside, and she stepped forward, straining to peer through the reflected image into the night beyond.

"What," said June, "something out there?"

She shook her head. "Nothing, it's nothing." But she had seen something that had passed across the field of her vision so quickly and unexpectedly, she at first took it to be an apparition or a trick of the mind: a boy, riding his bike slowly down the middle of the road, peering balefully into the dimly lit house as he floated by, his pale face and white, flapping socks ghostly against the darkness, there and then gone.

26.

- - - - - -

A SPECIAL BIRTHDAY

SITTING ALONE AT THE TABLE, THE RUBBER BAND ON HIS PARTY HAT
biting into the fat under his chin. The hat said HAPPY BIRTHDAY,
PODNER!!! with a drawing of a cowboy and Indian with their arms
around each other, blowing out the candles on a cake. Gay. Very, very
gay. The cowboy looked like Howdy Doody and the Indian like a
Chinese lady with a feather in her hair. Everyone in the family had
on the same hats, recycled from Clifton's birthday two months ago.

At the head of the table, Rusty stared at his cake, which was not
really his because he had to share it with Sasquatch. The cake was a
big lumpy chocolate thing with fifty-seven white candles sticking out
of it. It looked like a porcupine if the porcupine had been run over by
a truck and left at the side of the road. Fifty-seven was the number
you'd get if you added Rusty's age to his father's. Rusty was twelve
and his father was forty or fifty or something—it was his birthday
and he didn't have to do math if he didn't feel like it.

He was alone because everyone else had gone outside to eat hot
dogs and take whacks at the piñata. Rusty and his father had already
blown out the candles on the cake and opened their presents, which
took forever because his father got a present from each and every
person in the family, it didn't matter if it was a back-scratcher made
from a wire coat hanger or a bunch of macaroni glued together in the
form of a horse, his father had to open each one and go, *wow, boy,*

isn't that great, what is it, oh I see, yeah, isn't that wonderful! What a Sasquatch. What an a-hole.

Rusty got three presents. Let's see—it was his special birthday, the only one he would ever have, he wasn't allowed to have it at Skate Palace, he had to share his party with Sasquatch, and these were the presents he got: a set of scriptures with his name engraved on the front, a kite, a light blue turtleneck sweater his mother had knitted back when she was in her crazy-obsessive knitting phase. When he opened up the turtleneck everyone told him to put it on and he said, "I don't think so."

"Come on, put it on!" they shouted.

"No."

"Put it on," someone said, "you'll make your mother feel bad."

"My mother's not even here!" He almost shouted it.

"We're taking pictures," said Aunt Nola. "She'll want to see."

So he put it on. "It's choking me," he said in the voice of someone being choked.

"It is not," his father said. "It looks great."

What did Sasquatch the a-hole know? The truth was, it was choking him badly. He was having trouble swallowing. And it was made out of wool or cotton or something that was making him itch. And it did not look great—it looked like crap. It looked like something you could buy from Goodwill for a nickel.

Four days ago, Aunt Beverly had come up to the Tower where he was being held for his crimes against humanity to tell him that his mother had checked herself into the hospital for a few days.

"It's nothing serious," she said, "she just needs a little rest. She's feeling run-down. She's had a lot to deal with."

"She can rest in her bed," Rusty said. "She does for most of the day anyway."

"There are people at the hospital who can help her feel better."

"Will she be back for my birthday?"

"We don't know. You'll need to pray for her. She needs your help to feel better."

He thought about it for a few seconds, and then he said it: "Did she have a nervous breakdown?"

Rusty didn't know what a nervous breakdown was, exactly, but when he was little Aunt Nola used to shout at him when he was acting up, *Stop that right now or you're going to give your mother another nervous breakdown!* Her first nervous breakdown had happened when he was little and he couldn't remember it but he had always understood that he was the one who gave it to her.

"I don't think we should call it that," Aunt Beverly said. "You pray for her. You focus on improving your behavior, and she'll be back feeling better."

And now his mother was gone again and he was smiling so hard for Aunt Nola's camera that his face hurt.

When everybody went outside for the hot dogs and the piñata, he stayed at the table. Aunt Trish put her hand on his shoulder. "Coming out? I know you like hot dogs."

He turned away. He didn't want to talk to her, or for her to be nice to him. He wanted her to go away.

"Rusty," she said. "You have every right to be upset."

Yes, yes he did. And it wasn't only because his mother was gone and he was having the cruddiest birthday party since the beginning of Roman civilization. A few nights ago when the power went out and nobody was paying attention to him he rode over to Aunt Trish's house because she always made him feel better. And that's when he saw June and Aunt Trish standing in the window together and he knew. June liked Aunt Trish, who was definitely a fox, and Aunt Trish liked June. You could just see it. Which meant June would never like his mother, especially now that she was in the hospital, and Aunt Trish would never like Rusty, which was a stupid thing to think anyway. So his Grand Master Plan was right down the toilet and he was stuck in Old House until the end of time and he didn't know what he was going to do, and so yes, Aunt Trish, yes, he had every dang right to be upset.

Aunt Trish put her hand on his shoulder and the way she was

looking at him, all nice and sweet, was going to make him cry. What a gyp! His mouth was already filling with spit. He blinked a lot and told her he had to use the bathroom.

Instead of going to the bathroom he walked around Big House, jogged around the racetrack a couple of times, and then up the stairs, where he lay down in his old bed, but it didn't make him feel any better. He went into the Big Girls' room, rustled through their drawers a little, noted that Pauline was now wearing bras—it was about time, in Rusty's opinion. He stood at the big window that looked onto the front yard. They were all down there stuffing their chow-holes, running around and ha-ha-haing like a gang of out-of-control retards. His father was wearing one of his birthday gifts, a yellow trucker's hat with DAD spelled in decal letters on the front, and hoisting Dwight Eisenhower by the neck into a tree. Dwight, whose enormous papier-mâché head was as big as a television and twice the size of his body, had been made by Novella for her ninth-grade civics class project, and now somebody had filled his head with candy and in a few minutes he was going to get the dookie beaten out of him by kids with sticks.

Dwight Eisenhower? Just one more gyp, that's what Rusty thought. If you could have one president to hang from a tree and beat to a pulp for your birthday party, you'd want Albert Einstein or Abraham Lincoln, it wasn't even a contest.

Nobody had noticed that the birthday boy, the one who was supposed to get the first hot dog off the grill and take the first crack at Dwight Eisenhower and who for one stinking day was supposed to be the most important and special in the family, was nowhere to be seen. Nobody cared, not the little boys who kept head-butting Sasquatch's legs and tugging at his belt or the girls who were doing cartwheels and end-overs, saying *Daddy, Daddy, watch this!* or the mothers who kept bringing Sasquatch food even though he already had mustard on his nose and half a hot dog sticking out of his mouth. Not the older boys and girls who were at this minute sitting around in their little groups having a hearty chuckle about how hilarious he'd looked in his turtleneck and gay party hat, nearly slipping sideways off his chair after he'd gotten dizzy from trying to blow out all fifty-seven candles with one giant breath.

At the top of his lungs he shouted, "I'm not feeling *ap-PRE-ciated*!" But nobody heard him.

He went downstairs, and instead of going outside to feel bad for himself and eat four or five hot dogs with a big plate of potato salad and make himself sick on piñata candy, which was sorely tempting, he stood at the front door and stared at it for a while, waiting for someone to come through saying, *Come on, Rusty, where have you been, we've been wating for you, you get to go first on the piñata!*

Nobody came. He reached out and turned the latch on the deadbolt.

For a long time he waited, staring at the door until his eyes blurred, until somebody tried to open it, giving it a good shake and then pounding on it. "Hey!" It sounded like Parley. "Hey! What the . . . ? The door's locked!"

Rusty waited. There was a lot of shouting and he knew they were going to try to get in through the door off the garage, so he took the racetrack through to the laundry room and got to the garage door, just in time. He went into the kitchen and locked the back door and waited. Suddenly there was Josephine's big round face in the back door window with its mouth open wide so he could see the terrifying braces with their mildewy rubber bands and crusty bolts and wires coated with liquefied hot dog. She shouted low and loud like a man, "It's Rusty! He's the one! It's Ruuuuusssssteeeeee!"

He put his hand down his pants, poked his finger through the open fly of his jeans, and she screamed and fell away from the window.

He heard something in the family room. Teague was outside clawing through a rosebush, trying to get at the open window. Rusty shut it and Teague started yelling, tapping hard on the glass, his arms and neck all scratched up, and though his heart wasn't really in it Rusty turned, pulled down his Toughskins, and showed Teague the moon.

This wasn't nearly as fun as it should have been. He sat on the bottom stair and listened to the pounding on the back door, the faraway rattle of the garage doorknob. Somewhere Aunt Nola was laughing and Cooter was barking and Aunt Beverly was shouting orders.

Suddenly the front door shook and his father was yelling, "Rusty! Open this door now! Rusty! Just open it up and there won't be any trouble! Rusty!"

Good one, Sasquatch. It didn't take long for his father's hairy arm to come through Cooter's doggy door and start groping around for the doorknob. Rusty had not considered this possibility. The doggy door was designed to keep burglars and rapists from reaching the lock, but Sasquatch had arms like Too Tall Jones and to Rusty's surprise he was just able to reach it with the tips of his hairy fingers. Suave as the Scoundrel, Rusty went into the dining room and got the wire back-scratcher his father had gotten for his birthday off the table. Just when the hand had figured out how to turn the latch by gripping it between the tips of its middle and ring fingers, Rusty nudged it away with the back-scratcher. This happened twice more until the arm lashed out like a python and tried to snatch Rusty by the ankle but Rusty was ready: he jumped back and swatted the hand hard across the knuckles. There was a yelp and the arm disappeared through the doggy door and a few seconds later Cooter came through it, barking and wagging his butt.

Rusty gave the dog a squeeze, let him lick his face, which was a charitable act on Rusty's part because Cooter had serious dog-breath that smelled even worse than Rusty's feet. He pushed a sofa end table in front of the doggy door, and took Cooter upstairs to see what was developing outside.

They were attacking the house. There were kids at every first-floor window he could see, and Nephi and Parley were dragging an extension ladder from under the porch. Aunt Beverly stalked around with her best witchy-woman face, while Sasquatch dug around in this work truck, probably looking for an extra house key, and Dwight Eisenhower swayed gently in the breeze.

On this ruined planet he was the last human left and they were vampires, all of them, women, children, and men, and they would do anything to drink his precious blood, they would die without it. He saw them get excited about something, mumbling in their weird vampire language and then they were swarming over to one end of the house. He hustled downstairs and realized the voices he was hearing were coming from the basement. Holy Sweet Jesus Lord God Almighty, he'd forgotten about the basement.

Naomi was crouched in one of the window wells, prying open the window with her fingers. By the time he reached her, she had her arm and shoulder through, and he whipped at her with the cord from the blinds, but she had the bloodlust and she scratched at him and two more vampires squeezed down into the well, trying to reach through the window. He made a big production of hawking up a fat loogie in an attempt to give them fair warning, but they kept on coming, so he launched the loogie directly at Naomi's vampire heart and she shrieked and flailed back, smacking another vampire across the face. Rusty gave her one last shove and shut the window, turned the latch, and ran upstairs to make sure everything was secure.

He heard somebody softly calling his name from the other side of the doggy door. He moved the sofa table out of the way and there, in the doggy door, was Jame-o's face. "Let me in," whispered Jame-o. "I'm on your side."

For some reason, looking at little Jame-o's face stuck in the door, that's when it came over him: he started to bawl. Tears ran down his cheeks and he shuddered with chills.

"What's wrong?" said Jame-o.

Rusty hiccupped and took a breath. "Nothing. Go away."

"Let me in and I'll be on your side."

"You're a vampire," Rusty said. "You can't be trusted."

"I'm not," said Jame-o.

"You are," Rusty said, "I'm sorry, but you are."

"Okay," said Jame-o.

He had to admit it, Rusty liked Jame-o, sort of. Of all the brothers and sisters, Jame-o was the only one who was nice to him. Maybe it was because Jame-o was a weirdo too, whose best friend was a vacuum cleaner, who was ignored by everybody but Rusty and the vacuum cleaner. And maybe it was because Jame-o would do just about anything that Rusty told him, such as the time Rusty convinced him that he had to wear a paper bag over his head to keep out bad thoughts, which he did for most of the day, bumping into walls and tripping over everything, until Aunt Nola made him take it off.

"They've got a ladder," Jame-o whispered. "They're gonna get you."

"Thanks, but I can't let you in," Rusty whispered. He sniffed and wiped at his eyes with the hem of his gay sweater. "I'm on my own here."

He went into the dining room and cut off a big hunk of cake. "Take this." He held it out to Jame-o. "And good luck to you."

There were some complications getting the cake through the doggy door without it crumbling all over the place, but Jame-o got most of it, cupped in his little raccoon hands, and started eating it right away. Rusty went back upstairs to check the windows. A vampire was at one of them in the Little Boys' room, at the top of a ladder, working at the latch with a screwdriver, which was weird, because did vampires use hand tools? Rusty thought about opening the window and giving the ladder a push, but decided that would only make them madder.

He went down the hall and stood at the door of his mother's room. He hadn't planned on going in there to snoop. A little while ago, before he had tried to blow out all the candles in one breath, they told him to make a wish, and this was what he had wished: that he could learn to be a good person, that he could improve his behavior so that he could come back to live in Big House, that his mother would come home soon. And now look what had happened. Look where he was now.

He stepped into the dark room and crawled onto the bed and smelled his mother's pillow for a while. He listened to the shouts outside, the pounding of doors and rattling of windows. If it weren't for all the noise, and for his heart going crazy in his chest and the pain in his stomach and his jiggling leg and the tears running down the sides of his face into his ears, he might have been able to take a nap.

Since becoming a good person and improving his behavior was down the tubes for today, he got up and snooped around in the closet looking for *Tropical Night* or *A Stranger Comes Calling* or, he hoped, *Lust on the Moors*. He wanted to do a quick read of some of the good parts, to cheer himself up, but the books were gone. All of them. He looked in the lamp table and under the bed, wondering if she took all the books with her, if it meant somehow she wasn't coming back, and the pain in his stomach got stronger. He went through his mother's drawers, the tears really coming now, and for one second and one second only thought about trying on her underwear.

He heard a scraping noise and a shriek, which he figured was somebody falling off the ladder. He went into the Big Girls' room and looked out the window. Most of them were still attacking the house, but a few of the little ones had lost interest and were throwing rocks at Dwight Eisenhower. After a minute somebody saw him and shouted, "There he is!" and they all looked up at the same time like a bunch of monkeys tangled in a net.

Just look at them: Aunt Beverly with her witchy-woman stare turned on full blast (which was having no effect on him whatsoever), the bucktoothed Sasquatch in his dumb DAD hat with his mouth hanging open, Aunt Nola having her fifth or sixth hot dog, Aunt Trish looking as mysteriously beautiful as the Comanche Bride, and all the kids laughing and jostling, having the time of their lives.

As much as Rusty hated to say it, these were not vampires, these idiots were his family. They were his family and they were the reason he wasn't at this very moment doing the Honk Job at the Skate Palace. They were why he was being held against his will at Old House. They were why he sat by himself at the cafeteria in school. They were why the kids in his class had started calling him Piggy the Plyggy, and ruined his self-esteem. They were why he was mad all the time.

They were why his mother had a nervous breakdown and disappeared. And they were why he was not the good and nice and honest and handsome person he was supposed to be.

He opened the window, he had something to tell them, but right away they started yelling at him.

"What do you think you're doing?"

"You're a dead man!"

"*Ree-pul-seeee-vo!*"

"Open the door or we're calling the *sheriff*!"

"You're ruining the party!" (To which Rusty replied in a whispered voice only he could hear, "Am I? Am I *really*?")

"Hurry, I gotta use the bathroom!"

Rusty looked down at them sadly. He shook his head. He said, "Forgive them, for they know not what they do."

He didn't know why he said this, only that it was what a good person who was trying to improve his behavior might say. He could have shouted at them the phrase Old Man Ridnour with the eye patch used to yell at them from his front porch when they walked home on their way from the bus stop, *Gaze, you sons-a-bitches, gaze!* He could have thrown things out the window at them, such as Aunt Nola's wigs or all their toothbrushes or Pauline's new bras, or maybe he could have pretended to toss Cooter out the window, just to hear them gasp. But he didn't do any of these things. He was going to tell them something. He was going to tell them that he was sorry. That it had been just a big birthday joke, no hard feelings. He was tired of fighting Aunt Beverly, tired of fighting everyone. He was going to tell them that he was sorry and that he was going to try harder to be a good person and improve his behavior, but just as he was clearing his throat and swallowing back the tears that were rising again, Parley and Nephi, who had finally managed to get the window open with their screwdriver, tackled him from behind.

27.

· · · · ·

FOR THE PLEASURE OF SENSUAL LIVING

I will take you to the secret place tonight?
10:00? Maybe bring flashlight.

besos,

H

H E HAD FOUND THE NOTE SLIPPED UNDER THE DOOR OF THE AIRSTREAM
and read it six or seven times before he nudged shut the door with the
heel of his boot. He drew the heavy brown paper, torn from a grocery
bag, under his nose. He thought he could detect next to the smell of
old lettuce a faint whiff of her sandalwood perfume. Except for the
time she had jotted her name in the sand, he had not seen her writing
before. The letters were blocky and slanted to the left, with hooking
flourishes at the end of every stroke. Her lush penmanship, like everything else about her—the way she tasted, smelled, spoke—was an
enthralling and novel loveliness, something he wondered how he had
ever lived without.

He read the note twice more. The word *besos* gave him a little
tingle of delight, and the *H*, an endearing stroke of intrigue, gave
him a sense of deep privilege to be playing a role in the kind of high
drama the rest of the dull and indifferent world could not possibly
understand.

He got back in his GMC, drove the half mile to the office trailer, and called Trish. He had promised her he would be home by dinner-time; if he left right now he would arrive only three hours late.

"Trish," he said, and before he could formulate a likely excuse she cut in with a sharp, vehement, "*Damn* you."

He waited; it was one of the many good pieces of advice Uncle Chick had given him: *In moments of aggravation, wait 'em out. Don't engage. Don't get mad. Don't look 'em in the eye. Let 'em calm down, say your piece, and then run for it.*

He waited, but it became increasingly apparent that she was not going to give in. The silence on the line was hard, aggressive, and he felt the weight of it as a hand against his chest, pushing him back.

"Trish?" he said. "It's not as bad as you think. I'll be there noon tomorrow. I promise. I'll reschedule with Nola. We'll go out to eat tomorrow night. You and me. I promise."

The silence deepened. Golden bided his time by guessing how long decorum required him to wait before he could hang up.

"I can't stand it anymore," she said, finally, in a cold whisper. "I'm not going to sit around waiting for you like this. Okay? Okay. That's it. So I'll see you soon." A click, and the line went dead.

On his way back to the trailer Golden puzzled over the conversation for only a minute; after all, he had a date tonight, and he would need to get ready.

Along with excitement at the delicious prospect of meeting Huila in a few hours, he felt a hot little pellet of anxiety expanding in the pit of his stomach: it was here. They had been working up to it all week and now Huila, with an invitation to the secret place she had mentioned to him a time or two before, had made it more or less official: they were going to have sex. Over the past week, with Ted Leo away on a business trip and Huila giddy with freedom, her eyes like two sparkling lights, they had progressed from chaste kissing and nuzzling in the cab of his pickup, parked in the shadows behind the Frostee Kween down the road, to teenage-style groping and rolling on the Barge.

"Making out," Golden had told her, almost in wonder. "That's what we call it, that's what we're doing. Making out."

"Making out?" she said, the single line between her brow deepening. "Not making love?"

"Technically," he said, temporarily befuddled by his native tongue, "making *out* is, you know, what you do *before* you . . . make . . . or it depends, really, you don't have to—" and she gave him a quick kiss to put an end to such a useless lecture.

"I like what we are making," she said. "I don't care what it is."

Golden was also quite satisfied with all they were making—the whispering and kissing, the light petting, the weight of her breasts against his chest, her fingers in his hair. All the tenderness and affection he had found increasingly impossible to give his wives, he offered to her.

But it was becoming obvious that Huila was not satisfied with mere tenderness. Last night, during a ten-round bout of snuggling and French-kissing on the aft decks of the Barge, she had swung one leg over his hip, her foot locked behind his knee, her skirt pushed up on her thighs, and the heat of her crotch pressed against his. He stiffened, turned to the side just a little, and she immediately relaxed her grip on him, put her cheek against his neck, and there was an embarrassed silence in which they each waited for the other to move, to make some apology or explanation.

Golden was too mortified to say anything, ashamed of his own cowardice. He wanted her so much, hated for her to think that he might not want her, but he was afraid. If he made love with Huila his life, as he knew it, would be gone. He would be stripped of his priesthood, his good name. His wives would leave him and be joined to righteous men of God who took their covenants seriously, who were strong and resolute, men like Nels Jensen, who could handle the Godlike responsibilities that came along with multiple wives and dozens of children. He would be left with nothing, and he wondered why the thought of this did not bother him nearly as much as it should.

Now he removed from his wallet the condom Miss Alberta had given him a few weeks ago: *A PleasurePlus Prophylactic*. He had kept it well hidden, swaddled in a car wash coupon and sandwiched between two defunct credit cards. Out in the light, its gold wrapper glinted balefully like a ring in a fantasy novel, imbued with the power of ancient and obscure gods. This weightless trifle in his hand, he knew, could tame the potency of sex, limit its consequences, which to Golden's way of thinking deserved nothing less than awe. He didn't know if he had the courage to make love to Huila, didn't even know, exactly, how a condom might be put to use in the event that the big moment came, but he did know this: he liked the slogan written on the back. *For the Pleasure of Sensual Living*. Yes, he liked that very much.

He returned the condom to his wallet and stepped into the tiny bathroom, took up his razor and the can of cream, and began to ready himself. For the moment, in his cozy home away from home, he felt safe, but there was calamity ahead, and he was already nostalgic for what he had, for what he would surely lose.

TWO FOR COURAGE

The scissors—enormous heavy-duty all-purpose shears, salvaged from the rusty dregs of his pickup's panel toolbox—had never been intended to cut hair, but they would have to do. He sat on top of the toilet seat, deliberating, talking to himself in terse murmurs, the bathroom so small his jutting knees prevented the door from shutting. After experimenting with ice, peanut butter, and Crisco, he had decided to allow nature and time, which he had been led to believe could obliterate anything, to take care of the gum in his pubic hair. But nature and time, as always, had not been cooperative: there was still a large and very obvious wad tangled on the left side, along with several nasty satellite nuggets, like Jupiter and its moons (which he had created by trying to tease the gum apart) embedded at different depths in the left quadrant of his pubic zone. The right quadrant was bushy and robust, possibly in need of a trim as long as the scissors were out and his pants were down, but the left looked like it belonged to a diseased sexual deviant, or possibly a leper.

He held his breath and snipped carefully around the largest gum pellet, which came away with some difficulty, snarled in its own bed of hair. He had never really noticed before how appallingly hairy he was, or how the hair on his head and arms was a coppery blond while the fur of his torso and legs was reddish brown, and darker as you got closer to the center of things. He began cutting out the smaller pieces, having to go deep here and there, all the while giving himself a running pep talk: *Okay, right there, yes, you got it, watch it, watch it, careful, darn it, easy, easy, okay, there it is, nice one, nice, yes, good, good, good.*

With all the curly tufts of hair drifting to the linoleum you might have thought he was shearing the wool off a buffalo.

Knowing it would be bad, he checked his work with a hand mirror: he looked like he'd contracted a case of the mange. He stood up, tossed the mirror into the sink, shuffled in a circle (nearly tripping over the pants bunched around his ankles) to release some tension, sat back down. He was going to have to trim *all* of it down, even it out so that the bald spots wouldn't be so noticeable. He went back to work, grimacing with strain, the shamefulness of it, taking extreme care not to inflict on himself an injury for which he would be hard-pressed to come up with an explanation.

He finished, took up the mirror again, and his mouth sagged open, releasing a sad little groan. Instead of camouflaging the bald spots, the aggressive trimming had only made them more evident. He reached for the razor and can of Barbasol. He regarded both items as a suicidal man might a loaded pistol. *No choice*, he told himself. *You have no choice.*

He had only made a few passes with the razor when he realized that he had done what he always seemed to do when presented with a bad situation: he had made it worse. Much worse. Sure, he could go ahead and shave his entire pubic area, nice and neat, why not, but what would he do with the rest of the thick fur that started at the knuckles of his toes and ended at the top of his back, the hollow of his throat? Either he would have a strange little clean-shaven circle around his genitals, circumscribed by the dark hair of his belly and thighs, or he would have to shave himself entirely smooth, an activity, he imagined, homosexuals and certain Hollywood actors engaged in all the time. In a sudden fit of optimism he resolved to go ahead with the second option—he still had an hour before he was to meet Huila, didn't he?—until it occurred to him that there was no way he would be able to reach around and shave the coarse pelt off his back or the hairs, which he had never devoted a single thought to until now, on his large sagging behind. And besides, he had only one razor, and it was already going dull.

He hung his head, indulging in a sweet moment of self-pity, and with some difficulty resisted the urge to cry.

Holding his pants up around his thighs so that he could walk without tripping, he shuffled out to his pickup, cast around behind the seat, and came up with the mason jar of moonshine Nestor had pressed on him before he'd driven away from Mexican Town a week and a half ago. "Take it!" Nestor had urged when Golden tried to decline. "You take it, Jefe, you will thank me. But only for emergencies! One sip for comfort, two for courage. Three and down the hole you go."

Was this an emergency? Golden decided that it was: one in a string of so many that he was becoming accustomed to the alarm bell rattling relentlessly inside his chest. He took a sip, gasped, and then one more. Courage, that was what he needed. He assumed his position on the toilet and grimly went to work.

A quarter of an hour later he had an oval bald spot, glaring white and nicely symmetrical, that shone like a skating rink in a stand of dense undergrowth under the light of a full moon.

through and clamber down a series of natural steps until he felt mud under his feet and nothing but air within arm's reach.

"Now turn off your light for one *momentito*," she said, cutting hers. In the thick darkness he felt his heart rate begin to rise, and then Huila struck a match, the sudden small flame such a shock that he stepped backward, spangles of color floating across his vision.

She lit a series of five kerosene lamps, section by section revealing a cavern the size of a small house whose ceiling was hung with formations of thin white stalactites glittering like crystal chandeliers suspended over a small black pool steaming like a cauldron. At the far end of the room long draperies of reddish flowstone seemed to move and furl in the glow of the lamps. The surface of everything was slick with a moisture that already clung to his skin and hair, and the sound of dripping water echoed with such insistence it was impossible to tell if there was only one drip or ten thousand.

Huila explained that Ted Leo had paid very dearly for the land surrounding the cave—the old sheep rancher who owned the place had kept it secret, believing that if its whereabouts became public the hippies and Californians and sodomites of the world would come in droves to smoke their dope and perform their perverted sex rituals and generally ruin his peaceful Christian existence. But when Ted Leo bought the adjoining land for development, the rancher realized he might have a valuable commodity. Despite paying twice the land's estimated value, Ted Leo believed he had made a steal; he could charge his brothel clients steep sums for the chance to spend an hour with a hooker in an otherworldly lava tube with a natural jacuzzi fed by mineral hot springs, or he could take a different route and fleece health nuts and religious zealots for the opportunity to stew their pasty selves in its mysterious healing waters. Or both, he was still deciding.

Huila dimmed the two closest lamps to give full effect to the alien shapes, the glistening skin of formations like great rising columns of hardened glue. She kicked off her sandals and dipped a toe into the small pool. "Ay!" she cried. "Hot, hot!" She showed him the channel that had been chiseled out of the rock, allowing cool water from an overhead spring to flow into the pool so as to regulate the temperature. She removed several round stones from the mouth of the channel and the trickle of water expanded into a steady flow that purled over the smooth rock and into the pool without a sound.

She grabbed the hem of her shirt as if to pull it over her head. She nodded at the pool. "We go in?"

He stayed where he was, backed up against a stalagmite that looked like a massive yellow dog's tooth. "I don't . . ." he said. "I didn't bring my swimming trunks."

She gave him a look and he averted his eyes—*I didn't bring my swimming trunks*. Was he serious? Could he be any more ridiculous? What could someone like Huila see in an ass like him?

"No swimming," she said, now straining just a little to maintain her good mood. "No swimming. Only sitting. It's nice. Are you . . ." —she searched for the word—"bashful? It's okay. I'm bashful too. You cover your eyes for me, and I cover my eyes for you."

Like the monkey who sees no evil, he covered his eyes with both hands and took those few moments in his own little dark world to figure out what to do. He couldn't refuse Huila—this was a special occasion, one she'd put some thought into, and he simply could not disappoint her. He considered stripping down to his underwear, but underwear was only one small step from naked, and naked was what he would give anything right now to avoid; he was certain that if she got a load of his weird little shaved zone she'd want nothing to do with him ever again.

In what seemed like no more than five seconds she called, "Ready!" and he looked through his fingers to find her up to her chin in the steaming water, her hair spread out over the water, a sheet of black satin. Through the clear water her naked body appeared two-dimensional, furling and unfurling like a flag.

"Okeydokey!" he said. "Here I come!"

So fast that she couldn't question or stop him, he advanced toward her over the slick cavern floor with the seesawing carriage of a bear on roller skates, tossing aside his wallet and keys, kicking off his boots and peeling away his socks as he went. At the last moment, in a gesture of wild abandon, he yanked off his shirt, popping a few buttons, and slid into the pool still wearing his pants, as if in his rush to join her he had forgotten this minor detail. His mouth opened involuntarily in a childlike expression of rarefied pain when his brain registered the extreme heat of the water.

"Oh-ah-ah-ha," he gasped. "It's *hot!*"

"Hot!" she agreed, her eyes wide.

Once he was satisfied that the water would not boil the skin off his flesh, he slid the rest of the way in, and they regarded each other from across the small pool, their chins just touching the trembling surface of the water. The heat had made her lips flush pink, her skin glow, and he couldn't imagine her being any more beautiful than she was at that moment.

"It's nice," he said. "This is nice."

"Mmm," she said.

She watched him with a rapt scrutiny and he knew she was wondering what kind of oddball she had taken up with. *She has no idea*, Golden thought, with a trace of bitterness. As far as she was concerned, he was a regular American guy with one wife and five kids and a full complement of pubic hair. If only she knew. He almost laughed. If she had even the smallest inkling of what she was dealing with, she would climb out of this cave, run for home and never look back.

Her face softened just a little and she held her hand out to him. He took it, and she pulled herself over to him, put her hand on his chest and her head against his shoulder.

"Are you afraid?" she said.

"Afraid?" he said.

A long silence. She said, "Afraid of me?"

"What? No. I'm not—I would never be afraid. Of you." To show her just how unafraid he was, he slid down against her and kissed her on the mouth, put his palm against her wet neck. She grabbed hold of him and suddenly they were unmoored, rolling and tumbling like otters, nothing to hold on to but each other, the water sloshing over the lip of rock. He'd never felt anything like it: the buoyant heat, the absence of friction and gravity, the steam that left a salty condensation on her upper lip. He didn't know what would ever become of him, but he wanted this moment to last.

Her skin was as slick as if it had been covered in oil and he struggled to hold on to her, gripping her thigh on one side, locking his leg around hers on the other. He felt the bones of her hips pressing against him, like a pair of small fists, and he was seized with the kind of mindless desire he hadn't experienced in years, an arousal so strong his body shivered trying to contain it. He did a splashing scissor kick, trying to press himself closer, his face getting tangled in her hair, a shuddering thrill in his stomach as he realized that this was the end and the beginning of everything he knew.

She found some leverage and pressed him up against the other side of the pool, and as they kissed he could feel her hand make its way down his belly. Her fingers found one of his belt loops, then the buttons of his pants, but as she began to work at them, jerking a little at the wet denim, something happened to him: he went cold. Some presence, forgotten in the dark back rooms of his mind, had come forward to wake him from this feverish delirium into the reality of what he was about to do. At the time he couldn't have said what it was, but something made him put his hand on hers and say in quavering apology, "I don't think I can."

She made a little groan, let her mouth slip away from his. He tried to pull back from her but she held tight to him.

"It's okay," she said. She was still gasping a little, her eyes bright, her hair twisted over her shoulder in thick wet ropes. He looked away but she put her face in front of his. "I understand. Don't worry. Ted Leo has the same problem. Many times."

"Okay," he said. "I'm so sorry." He had no idea what she was talking about.

"We can still have a nice time, don't worry, please don't worry. It's no problem with me."

He plunged his head into the water in an attempt to hide his face from her, to escape the sting of embarrassment for denying all that she had so willingly offered, the disgust at himself for turning something beautiful and rare—the kind of moment men would trade their lives for—into something awkward and strained. He wondered if the day would ever come when he would be able to make a simple decision, take a single step without this sad, mealymouthed second-guessing, this self-doubt. She held tightly to his hand and he was shamed by her kindness. Only when his head began to throb from the heat of the water did he let himself surface. He stood, thinking he might grab his clothes and make some sort of dramatic, self-flagellating gesture, such as stalking off into one of the cavern's dark grottos to sulk, but he felt a light-headed fizziness as the blood drained all at once from the heat-dilated capillaries in his brain and he began, slowly, to tilt backward. His vision went dim and he was falling, he knew, but there was precious little he could do to stop it. Huila tried to hold him up; he could feel both her hands tightly gripping his wrist, but he swung sideways like a big wooden doll and went down.

When he opened his eyes Huila's face was so close to his he felt her breath on his skin.

"You okay?" she said.

"Just fine, yes," he said.

"You hit your head."

He placed his hand on the back of his skull, where a small goose egg was already forming.

"I can't feel a thing," he said, which was true. "I got light-headed because I stayed under the water too long, that's all."

She sighed, and the worry line between her eyebrows eased away. Suspended in the water he felt weightless, warm and secure, and he realized she was cradling him in her arms, all of him, like a baby. This he liked. This he liked very much.

"I'm sorry," he said.

"For what?" she said with a little laugh. "You didn't try to fall."

"No, I mean about before. I don't know what's wrong with me."

She put three wet fingers across his lips. "Stop. There's nothing wrong. It's common, yes? For a man your age."

"It is?" he said.

"Many men have this problem, men everywhere, it's nothing to think about."

Finally, it hit him. Even though he didn't know what his problem was and never really had, she did: he was *impotent*. Of course that's what she thought. He felt an immediate rush of relief, which, he realized, was probably not the most common of reactions under such circumstances. He decided, right there, that he liked the idea of being impotent. Somehow it was less shameful and complicated than all of the possible versions of the truth—it was nothing more than a physical malady, something he couldn't be blamed for or required to explain. Why hadn't he thought of it before?

"It's really kind of hit and miss—" he started to say, but she shushed him again.

"Don't worry," she said. "We do not need to give it a thought."

"Ted Leo has the same problem?" he said. This was an idea that pleased him deeply.

"Oh yes," she said. "Very bad. You don't know."

"That's a real shame," he said.

"No more talk of this." She bent down to give him a full, deep kiss that rendered him as pliant and insubstantial as the water he floated in.

"But let's remove your pants, yes?" she said, as if to a toddler in need of a diaper change. "So we can enjoy ourselves, with no worries. We can make out, okay? It will be nice."

"Okay," he said in a meek child's voice. He had no strength or inclination to protest anything she wanted of him. He could reveal himself completely to her, he believed, all his quirks and secrets, and she would still love him.

He smiled dreamily, all of him except his face submerged, while she unbuttoned his pants and began to tug them down around his hips.

There was a noise—he heard it inside the water first—a vibration somewhere above them. The report of a car door slamming shut, stamping footsteps and then the echoing *screak* of rusty hinges.

Huila's weight came suddenly forward and he went under for a moment, inhaling water through his nose. He came up coughing, snorting, and she put a hand over his mouth to muffle the noise.

"Huila!" came a voice. "You down there?"

"*Dios, dios*," she whispered, frantically pulling him out of the water and pushing him toward the edge of the pool. "Go hide, now. Please, go."

He lurched out of the pool and hit the floor with a wet slap. He struggled the rest of the way out of his wet pants, which were tripping him up, yanking out one leg and shaking them off with the other as if they were a small, snarling dog that had attached itself to his ankle. He took a moment to look around and skidded and slid toward a rockfall at the back of the cavern.

"Yes!" Huila called, "I'm down here, please come down!" doing her best to cover up the sounds as she splashed out of the pool to retrieve his pants, shirt and shoes and toss them into the shadows. The sound of Ted Leo grunting and scraping his way down the narrow passageway reverberated through the chamber with a sound like thunder from on high, making Golden flinch. He hunkered down, pink and steaming as a boiled shrimp, behind the pile of rocks and tucked his head between his knees. He clamped his nostrils tightly between his thumb and forefinger to prevent a catastrophic sneeze.

"What are you doing!" Ted Leo bellowed. "I get home and nobody's there and I go driving around, worried sick—"

"I'm enjoying myself!" Huila shot back with a vigor that Golden never would have been able to conjure under the circumstances. "Where do you go? When do you come home? I never know!"

For a good two minutes they argued. Mostly it was Ted Leo complaining about Huila's recent abdication of her wifely duties. He couldn't understand what had gotten into her, why she felt like she had to go wandering the hills like John the Baptist, washing her clothes in mud puddles and bathing in caves when they had all the modern facilities back at the house. Most of Huila's protests where in Spanish, so that Golden couldn't really follow, but at some point she made mention of "*putas prostitutas*" and Ted Leo's voice took on an edge of real menace. "You *do not* talk about them that way! Those girls buy the clothes you wear, the food you eat! Now get your behind out of there and get dressed *now*."

Huila tried to tell him she'd be home soon, to go ahead without her, and Golden could hear splashing and Huila's sharp little swear words—*cabrón* and *mierda* and *huevón*—as Ted Leo pulled her bodily out of the pool. The muscles in his legs clenched, and he reached around for a good-sized rock, wondering what he might do with it once he had it in his hand. There was no more splashing or talking, only the echoing *tap-tap* of footsteps and the small, sharp sounds of the kerosene lamps, one by one being blown out.

Golden peered over the rockfall, watched the waggling flashlight beam disappear into the passageway, listened with great interest to the ominous dungeon sound of the door clanging shut. Half crouched, he remained frozen in place, hoping that by keeping perfectly still and not breathing he could suspend this nightmare or make it go away altogether. Through the layers of rock overhead filtered the sound of a motor starting and then dwindling into nothing. He felt the cold, moist darkness being absorbed into his body, like ink into a sponge, and he began not so much to shiver as to shake, his jaw rattling.

"Hello?" he called out experimentally.

He didn't know who he hoped would answer—maybe some kind of forest ranger or a Good Samaritan who had wandered in from an adjoining catacomb.

"Anybody?"

28.
· · · · ·

RULE NUMERO UNO

I**T FELT STRANGE, CROSSING THE BORDER. SHE HAD DONE IT THREE** years before, made the same passage but in the opposite direction, in search of something or someone to save her from the nasty little string of disasters her life had become. Now, moved by a similar desperation, she steered her clackity VW Rabbit down a wide, sweeping descent onto a scrubland plain as flat as the bottom of a skillet, leaving behind the glowing sunset cliffs of Utah and Arizona, her foot steady on the accelerator, both hands fixed tightly to the wheel. The sign, red and white and perforated with shotgun pellets, backlit by a theatrical sky packed with iridescent clouds, said WELCOME TO BEAUTIFUL NEVADA! It gave her a juvenile thrill, as if she had left home for the first time to arrive in the exotic, spice-scented land of her dreams.

Less than two hours ago she had been at home, getting ready for Golden's arrival. June Haymaker was there (as she had so carefully arranged him to be) to take a look at the leak in the roof and to accept her offhand invitation (as she knew he would) to dinner. More importantly, he was there to illustrate to Golden, in the plainest way possible, that if Golden did not want to take care of her, to look after her most fundamental needs, then maybe there was someone else who would.

When Golden called to tell her, once more, that he wouldn't be home when he promised, she had just taken the chicken out of the oven and June was in the attic, creaking and clanking like a ghost,

trying to trace the water stain on the ceiling to its source in the
roof. Even before she hung up, something possessed her. It wasn't
anger so much as a feeling of abandon, the hard snapping *twang* of
release—she was letting go of all that had, for so long, been holding
her back. What *was* it that had been holding her back? she wondered
now. Why had she given in so fully to this idea of patience and long-
suffering? The *hell* with patience. She was done with waiting, with
standing around and wringing her hands.

She called June down from the attic and quickly packed overnight
bags for Faye and herself. While June sat at the head of the table,
befuddled, with clots of gray insulation caught in his beard, she laid
out the dinner she'd prepared: ginger chicken and wild rice and sau-
sage dumplings. She told him something had come up and she had
to leave, but that he should stay and eat his fill. Then she grabbed
Faye by the wrist, who was demanding to know what was wrong and
where they were going, and pulled her out to the car.

After getting Faye buckled in, she went back into the house,
where June seemed not to have moved a muscle, except there was
now a fork in his hand where there hadn't been one before. "I'm
sorry for this," she told him. "I'll call you when I get back." Realizing
that this spasm of abandon might not last, she went with it. She put
her hands on June's bony shoulders, bent down, and gave him a peck
on the cheek.

She drove into town and pulled up in front of the Academy of
Hair Design, where, it being the first Thursday of the month, Nola
spent the afternoon and sometimes the evening giving free cuts and
perms to the ladies of the Snow Canyon Senior Center and Retreat.
The place was half-filled with women in various stages of decline,
a couple in wheelchairs, all wearing their colorful smocks and new
hairdos, which had them in high spirits; they chattered and laughed—
mostly to themselves, it was true—with Nola in the middle of it all,
pointing and flourishing her comb and scissors like an auctioneer.

It took a few seconds, but when the women detected Trish and
Faye standing in the doorway, they hushed. None of them gave Trish

any notice; they all focused on the girl, as if a child were something that had not been seen or heard from in years and whose existence was now a matter of question.

A couple of the more spry ones got up to get a closer look. "Oh dear," one said reverently, "look at this, look at this."

Faye glared at the advancing women and said, "Don't either of you touch me."

"People forget how mean children are," called one of the crones from the back.

"Ladies," Nola said, "this is Trish and her daughter, Faye."

Another one, who had the translucent skin and hooked claws of a wraith, commented, "Nothing better for a child than a nice juicy plum."

Trish asked Nola if they could talk in private and Nola looked around at the women, who had already gone back to talking to themselves or were absorbed with what drama might unfold if Elenore Peele gave the girl a pat on the head, as she was so clearly angling to do. "This is about as private as it gets, don't you think?"

"All right. I'm going somewhere and I'm wondering if you could look after Faye until tomorrow. You're the only one she likes."

Nola gave Trish her famous arched-eyebrows look. "You're going *somewhere*."

What was the use in hiding it? It would be widely known soon enough. "I'm going to Nevada, to see Golden."

Nola opened her mouth wide with genuine surprise. She released a high cackle that one of the women answered reflexively, as one bird answers another. Nola said, "You're *not*."

She was. Yes, she was, though she could understand Nola's incredulity. She was about to break, as Nola herself called it, Rule Numero Uno, which stated that the wife does not go to the husband, she must wait for the husband to come to her. While Trish wasn't sure if it was *the* most important rule of plural marriage, it was a vital one; it kept the more aggressive or needy wives from making unfair demands of the husband's time and attention, and put nearly all the burden of portioning himself—and of managing the jealousy and acrimony if he didn't do a good job of it—on his shoulders.

Two years ago the wives had taken the drastic and, for some in the church, controversial step of scheduling Golden's weekly sleeping arrangements, but when Trish married into the family he was still a free agent, allowed to drift from wife to wife, house to house, like the town drunk bar-hopping on a Saturday night, every decision made out of convenience or faulty memory or according to some otherwise questionable whim.

Nola plied a lock of woolly hair between her fingers and snipped it off at the ends. She was swallowing a grin, enjoying in advance, Trish knew, all the talk and trouble this indiscretion of hers was bound to cause. Not only was she about to break Rule Numero Uno, but she was going to visit Golden on the job site, which had always been expressly off limits, even before he'd taken the project in Nevada; one wife bothering her husband at work was bad enough, but four wives—a workingman's good name could never survive such an assault.

"So this expedition you're about to take," Nola said, "it wouldn't have anything to do with Maureen Sinkfoyle now would it?"

"It might," Trish said, "and it might have to do with all kinds of other things. Rose just checked herself into the hospital, Nola, and what does he do? Runs right back to Nevada as if nothing happened. And now he's not even coming home when he's supposed to. I don't know what to think anymore."

Nola nodded, serious now. "Go on ahead, then, we'll take good care of your girl, right Miss Faye? We'll trim your bangs nice and neat, maybe give you a little bob at the back."

Keeping Elenore Peele at bay with a malevolent glare the way a hiker might use a stick to fend off a bear, Faye said, "Oh no you won't."

THE IMPORTANCE OF BEING IMPOTENT

When she finally found the Airstream on top of the hill, she was nearly at her wits' end: cranky, blinking with fatigue, and nearly out of gas. After the three-hour drive across Nevada she had spent another hour driving up and down a ten-mile stretch of Highway 19, nosing across broken-down cattle guards and investigating private driveways and dirt roads that seemed to lead nowhere. Before leaving the Academy, she had called Sister Barbara to get directions to the construction site and Sister Barbara had informed her, in a tone of polite reproach, that such information was highly confidential and to release it would require Golden's explicit approval. Trish informed Sister Barbara, in a threatening and slightly hysterical tone that could not be construed as polite in any way, that she was Golden's wife, and if Sister Barbara didn't give her the information she needed she would break into the Big Indian Construction office—smash the window if she had to—and get it herself.

Sister Barbara didn't have the exact address on hand, but knew that the site lay on the stretch of highway between Indian Wells and the interstate—it was a major construction project, *gotta be bulldozers and dirt piles everywhere*, she said, *no way you could miss it, dear*. Well, miss it Trish had, at least fifteen times passing by in one direction or the other, hidden as it was two hundred yards off the road in the half-moon dark, a dark made all the more profound by the salaciously bright lights of the PussyCat Manor so close by. The brothel, doing a brisk business at this hour, was the only sign of life she had seen since Indian Wells, and though the idea of a brothel didn't shock her—she had spent much of her life in Reno, after all—the last thing she wanted was to have to step inside one of them to beg directions.

She was saved by a man jauntily pedaling a bicycle down the double yellow line in the middle of the highway, apparently in the direction of the PussyCat Manor. She stopped to ask if he knew where the new senior center was being built and he said, "Senior cen-

ter? Around here?" Wet hair slicked back and gleaming, he had the
freshly scrubbed look of someone on his way to a church service or a
court proceeding.

"A big construction site," she said, "somewhere along this highway."

He pointed. "You mean the brothel."

She shook her head; apparently, the brothel was the only thing on
his mind. Quickly she tried to explain again and he made a broad,
wide-armed shushing gesture, the kind a rock star might make to
quiet down an unruly crowd. "Easy," he said. "Slow up now. Tell me
this: Are you looking for anybody in particular?"

She told him, and after the slightest hesitation he gave her the simple directions. One left, one right, and then up a little rise. "You'll see
the trailer, no problem, a light upon a hill, just like the Bible says."

She thanked him and he gave her a smart, military-style salute
before pedaling off toward the blinking fairy lights of the PussyCat
Manor.

The sight of the Airstream, sitting in the middle of all that sagebrush, its windows darkened, spiked her through with a pang of
guilt. All those nights alone at home she had imagined Golden living
it up, eating junk food and playing cards with his hairy, good-natured
construction buddies. But this sad little thing, it was no bigger than a
cell in a South American prison—she couldn't imagine how he could
fit in there to sleep, much less have a meal or take a shower or host
a game of rummy. She pictured him now, tucked in like a dog in a
passenger crate, sleeping off a long day's work, and she had to shake
her head to keep from being waylaid by feelings of affection and sympathy. She had not come here to sympathize, she reminded herself.
She had come here for answers, explanations—an apology or two at
minimum. She promised herself she wasn't going to leave until she
got them.

She rapped on the flimsy door and waited. Golden was renowned
for his ability to sleep, nap and doze through every sort of clamor
and unrest, from the shrieking scales played by an amateur obo-

ist to the sneak attacks of three-year-olds, so she gave the door a good pounding that somehow degenerated into a jaunty version of *shave-and-a-haircut*.

When no response came, she opened the door, stuck in her head and knew by the silence, the deadness of the air, that nobody was there. The trailer's atmosphere had the musty tang of the inside of an old work hat. It smelled like belt leather and Bag Balm talcum powder —Golden's smell. To take the full tour required only a few steps: a platform double bed with a Golden-shaped crater in the middle, an eat-in kitchen littered with tin cans and crusty Tupperware bowls; a phone-booth-sized bathroom whose floor, quite disturbingly, was covered with drifts of dark hair.

Baffled, she stepped outside to stare blankly at Golden's pickup, parked parallel to the Barge, which looked surprisingly at home out under this big night sky, in front of the blackened remains of a campfire.

Where on earth was he? She tried not to think about the PussyCat Manor, pulsing lasciviously just over the hill. Having twenty prostitutes as next-door neighbors was one of the details of his workaday life he had wisely kept to himself. She plopped herself down on the Barge, wallowed and sulked in its lumpy depths before sitting up to assume the defiant, straight-backed posture of someone braced for bad news and prepared to wait as long as it took for it to arrive.

It didn't take long. She heard it first: the sound of something dragging itself across sand, the rattle of dry brush. She stood, straining to see into the darkness, and then came a strange, low-throated groan, which gave her the encouragement she needed to abandon her post on the Barge for the relative security of her Rabbit, where she locked the doors, snatched the ice scraper from the passenger-side floor and switched on the headlights. Caught in the beams, not fifty yards away, stumbled a pale, ghastly figure that squinted into the light and made a quick squatting motion, as if readying to flee. It took a step back, lowering its head to shield its eyes, and in that small, almost bashful gesture she recognized Golden. She had a harder time making sense of the huge body, pale and glowing, naked except for some kind of dark cloth held bunched around its hips.

She gave the horn a short beep and Golden flinched as if it were a gunshot. He called out, "Who is it?"

She turned off the headlights and got out of the car. "Golden," she called, "it's Trish."

"Who?" As if this were a name he'd heard for the first time in his life.

"Trish, you idiot. Your wife." With the headlights off she could not see him anymore, but she had no problem hearing the crashing and snapping of juniper twigs and dry sagebrush as he thrashed his way toward her. "Trish! Where are you? What happened?"

Once they located each other, she helped him into the trailer, where the sixty-watt bulb confirmed it: except for the flannel shirt whose arms were tied at one hip in a loose knot, he was naked. The dusty, pink skin of his shoulders and forearms was painted with scrapes and scratches and his feet, never much to look at in the first place, were rough with salty grit and spotted with blood. When he moved he gave off a sulfurous brimstone smell.

In that small kitchen they shared a few moments of blinking incomprehension. And then something seemed to wake him and he began to talk: the water system in the trailer had gone on the fritz, he said, and so he had walked down to the little cow pond to bathe—he'd had a long, dirty day—and somehow had managed to drop his flashlight in the pond, which ruined it, and then he couldn't find his clothes and shoes and got lost on the way back to the trailer. He gave a tired bleat of a laugh. "Look at me, got a few scratches here, don't I." He displayed his palms, which looked like they had been used to gather broken glass. "And my feet sorta hurt."

He looked at her expectantly, and Trish knew that it was her turn to explain herself, to make some excuse for her presence, but she told herself not to give in. Tonight, she had already decided, all the explanations were going to be his.

"What—" he said, leaning against the stove, forcing a smile, straining to bring a casual air to the proceedings. "So what brings you out here?"

"I came to talk to you," she said.

He took a breath, let it out slowly. "Okay," he said, "what about?"

"It might take a little while. Why don't you get cleaned up first."

He looked at his wrist and, when he did not find his wristwatch there, nodded as if that's what he'd suspected all along. "So you're going to—to spend the night?"

"If you don't mind," she said. "If you'd rather, I could sleep outside on the couch."

"What? No. I'll go—I'll see if I can get the water running in here and I'll be right with you. There might be something to drink in the fridge." He limped into the bathroom, closed the door, and made a series of banging sounds. "Would you look at that!" he shouted. "Got the water going! Be right out!"

While he showered she tried to make the place habitable—picked clothes off the floor, swiped dirty dishes into the sink, straightened the bed. When she heard the water shut off, she shucked off her own clothes and crawled under the old quilt, pieced together from scraps by a pioneer ancestor long since forgotten, that was Golden's favorite; for many years, until it became too much of a hassle, he had dragged it with him from house to house, marriage bed to marriage bed, unable to sleep soundly without the smell of it in his nose, the soft worn fabric tucked under his chin.

When he came out of the bathroom—now clutching a towel around his waist instead of a torn flannel shirt—he approached her warily, walking tenderly on his damaged feet. With the dust washed off, the scrapes and scratches stood out painfully bright on his pale skin, and it was difficult to resist the urge to get up and tend to him, to rustle up some band-aids and hydrogen peroxide and in the manner of a good frontier wife nurse his wounds. Instead, she calmly watched as he put on a spectacle of ridiculous modesty: he found an old pair of sweat pants in his duffel bag, turned his back to her and struggled into them while still wearing the towel, so there was no absolutely no chance of exposing himself.

He put on a clean T-shirt, filled a large glass with water from the tap, drank it down in three hard swallows. He stared into the empty glass and, after a long pause, said in a low voice, "Whatever you wanted to talk about, it must be important, coming out all this way."

"It's important. To me it is."

"Where's Faye?"

"Nola's got her. She's fine."

"I'm going home tomorrow, we could have talked then."

"I was tired of waiting for you. I don't want to sit around any-more, waiting for you to show up."

"I'm sorry—"

Her words had the sound of an argument rehearsed at length, of grievances nursed in the dark hours of morning: "I don't want to hear how sorry you are. I'm sick of all the excuses. I just want things to change."

He nodded, risked a quick glance at her, resumed the staring con-test with the bottom of his glass. She lifted a corner of the quilt. "Do you want to lie down next to me? I won't bite. I won't even touch you if you don't want me to."

With his eyes downcast, his head turned to the side like a bash-ful toddler, he walked slowly over to the bed and eased, grimacing, under the quilt next to her. The entire trailer groaned and reballasted under this sudden weight shift.

They lay there for a few minutes, Trish pressed against the wall with its tiny window, Golden on his side, facing away from her, the quilt pulled tightly over his shoulders as if for protection from the elements.

Trish said, "I have two simple questions, and I want you to answer me as honestly as you can. I don't care if you hurt my feelings or tell me something difficult. I just want you to tell me the truth."

"Okay," he whispered.

"Why have you been avoiding me? Why don't you want to make love to me?"

"I haven't—"

"You promised," she cut in, "the truth. You *have* been avoiding me. I get to see you once every two weeks, which isn't a whole lot less than the others, but every time you're too tired, or there's some excuse—" She stopped herself. She didn't want the bitterness she felt, the anger, to scare him into silence. "It's been so long now, Golden, a whole year we've been going like this. For a while afterwards, you know, I didn't care, but now, what am I supposed to think? I don't know how to make sense of it."

"It's kind of hard to explain," he said.

"Then try," she said. "We have all night."

"Well, it's . . ."—there was a long silence in which he took two deep breaths and repositioned himself on the bed—"I'm . . . im*po*tent."

"You're what?"

"Im*po*tent," he said.

"You're important?"

"What? No. Im*po*tent. It means—"

Something sparked in her head and she said, "*Im*potent. You mean you're *im*potent."

"*Im*potent. Yes. Isn't that what I said?"

She choked out a laugh, which might have been the cruelest response possible under the circumstances, but she had no other way of expressing the countervailing impulses she felt: the first was relief, verging on elation, that it was not disgust or disinterest that had kept him from her, but a simple bodily breakdown, a health condition that, as far as she knew, was as common among men as dandruff or athlete's foot. And the second impulse, which came like a cold wind on the heels of the first, was fear, that his condition might not be temporary—he was a middle-aged man, after all— and that she would remain trapped in the life she lived now, unfulfilled in every way that mattered, a woman cursed to go without in a land of so much plenty.

He turned over to look at her. "Is it funny?" He said this without bitterness or anger, but with genuine curiosity, as if he were not at all sure whether *impotence*, pronounced correctly or not, implied comedy or tragedy.

"No," she said, "not at all. Just unexpected." Maybe, she thought, it shouldn't have been all that unexpected, not by her or anyone else. But back in the days when they were intimate, he'd never shown any signs of failure or breakdown, and she'd always assumed, without ever consciously thinking about it, that if he was having difficulties— especially *those* kind of difficulties—the subject would have come up, in some way or another, among the wives. Surely, at the very least, Nola would have made a comment or two.

"How long?" she said.

"I don't know," he said. "Kind of off and on, and lately it's got worse."

"Why didn't you tell me?"

He shrugged. "It's not the easiest kind of announcement to make."

His bristly blond hair, for which he'd been named, was still wet and plastered to his forehead. Even though he had just showered she could detect a light perfume of sulfur on him, underneath which was something flowery and sweet. He looked at her earnestly, worriedly, as if waiting for her to pronounce some sort of judgment upon him. She was quiet for a while, trying to enjoy this moment while it lasted, trying not to think what it might mean for her future.

"I don't care," she said finally, and it had felt good, somehow, to tell this lie, to act as if she meant it. "Try not to worry about it. We'll figure something out. It'll be okay." His mouth sagged open a little with relief and she kissed him. Just like that. Even gave him a little tongue, which he readily accepted. She was used to waiting on him, to seducing him into kissing her, but she had already broken Rule Numero Uno; she might as well assert herself a little.

"I'm not done with you now," she said, pulling away. Suddenly she felt like she might begin to cry. "Still one more question to go."

His face clouded with worry again. He said, "Shoot."

She said, "Is it true you're planning to marry Maureen Sinkfoyle?"

He exhaled, and shook his head energetically. "No, no, no—no way." He put his big hand on her shoulder. "Uncle Chick brought it up with me a while ago, but I told him no, I had all I could handle already."

"Beverly said it was already in the works."

"Beverly's always trying to arrange things, you know that. But believe it or not, I'm the one who has to make the decision about who I marry. And I'm done. You're the last. After you, no one else could compare." He blushed a little at the uncharacteristic bit of flattery, but she was so grateful for it she kissed him again.

"Just one more question, then," she said.

"You said only two questions. This makes three."

"Indulge me."

"Only if I can ask you a question first."

"Fair enough."

"Did you call me an idiot a while ago?"

"I think I did."

"Is that really how you feel about me?"

"Most of the time."

For the first time that night his lips looked ready to work themselves into a smile. "Well, all right. What's your last question?"

She looked out window. "Why would anybody want to build an old folks' home right next to a whorehouse?"

A MAN AND HIS WIFE

He watched her sleep, wondering if he'd ever seen her this way before; he had the feeling that as long as he'd known her he'd done most of the sleeping while she'd done most of the watching. The only illumination inside the trailer came from the glowing face of the alarm clock, which cast its weak green light onto the top half of the bed and painted a dull shine on her hair, drew a soft luster from the skin of her cheeks and forehead. She was beautiful: this was his thought. She was beautiful and he couldn't remember the last time he'd noticed.

The warm, heavy hand of exhaustion pressed down on the back of his neck, but sleep wouldn't come. His head hurt—the lump at the back of it had contracted into a hard little stone under the skin and the scrapes and scratches on his feet itched and stung with an insistence that occasionally made him want to whimper and thrash inside the sheets like an infant.

He heard a noise outside—what sounded like the crunch of footsteps—but when he looked out the window he could see only the dark humps of sagebrush.

He squeezed shut his eyes, hoping to force himself into some passing pocket of sleep, and listened to Trish snore. Her snore, which he was sure he had never heard before, had the throaty quality of a reed instrument, an old clarinet played by someone in a secondhand shop. Her breath pulsed softly against his face and he found himself looking at her again, watching the small twitch at the corner of her lip, following the shadowed maze of her ear, and at this bitter hour, with morning beginning to harden like frost in the window, he couldn't escape the thought that he had betrayed her. She had come to him during the worst part of his life—just when the entire family seemed to have agreed as one to end their mourning of Glory's death, leaving Golden behind in his close-fisted sorrow. Unlike the other wives, who in their own ways urged him to move on, to return his attention to his living sons and daughters, Trish had a ready reservoir of sympathy that she could tap at any time. She didn't judge him or require him to be strong. During the first year of their marriage she had been his only reliable source of comfort; her joy in a new pregnancy, the possibility that it offered both of them, helping to brighten his days. And then they had lost Jack, and what had he done? Run away without apology or explanation, afraid or unable to add the weight of that loss to the grief he already carried. He had abandoned her: there it was. He had let her shoulder that pain—and he knew too well the desperate, clawing ache of it—all alone.

He wanted to rest his hand against her cheek, to tell her how sorry he was, to remind himself of everything he owed her. He wanted—in the most selfish and carnal of ways—to press himself into her. He wanted to gather her against him and take comfort in the faint heat of her skin. He wanted to slip his arms around her. He wanted to touch her. He didn't dare.

29.

· · · · ·

THE HUNT

Whenever Golden finished a job, even a small one, it was his habit to celebrate. He was not one for merrymaking, but when it was all over—the haggling, the unreliable subs and the thugs and ex-cons who worked for them, the rotten weather and the soil tests and the asshole inspectors with their freshly sharpened pencils, the nitpicking clients and their bounced checks and threats of litigation and late-night calls about a stain color or the price of a box of roofing nails—when all of that was over, yes, it was time to have a party. His men never failed to invite him to the bars or a kegger out in the sticks, but he always declined. Instead, he bought tubs of ice cream or maybe a case of Twinkies and brought them home, let the kids go nuts. Once, he'd loaded up the whole family and treated them to dinner at a nice sit-down Italian place in St. George called Fat and Swifty's—a mistake he would never repeat. In the past couple of years he'd taken to celebrating by himself: he'd do some shopping—a little something for the wives—or go see an afternoon matinee, depleted and happy, dazed with relief.

Today, there would be none of that; he would go home and act as if everything were normal, as if the job were still on, and try to figure out his next move. But he couldn't deny the relief he felt now. Driving the winding course between the ramparts of the Virgin River Gorge, the Airstream bumping unwillingly along behind the GMC, it was as if everything inside him had turned to tar. He slumped in the seat and barely had the strength to keep his foot pressed on the gas.

Early this morning, not long after Trish had left for Virgin, Ted Leo had pounded on the Airstream's flimsy door, waking Golden from a drooling stupor. Wearing white loafers, a dark green shirt patterned with neon-pink martini glasses, and plaid polyester slacks, Ted Leo had informed Golden that they were going out to do a little coyote hunting before breakfast, and wanted Golden to come along. In contrast to his peppy getup, Ted Leo's face showed nothing but grimness and exhaustion, and Golden was certain he could detect on the man the sour scent of booze. Golden ducked his head under the doorframe to get a look at Nelson sitting at the wheel of Ted's pickup, staring glumly into space. In the bed of the pickup two wedge-headed dogs hung their snouts over the tailgate, watching a jackrabbit lope casually through the brush. Golden had done his best to refuse Ted's invitation, saying he had a lot of work to get to today, but Ted Leo insisted. "We'll have you back in an hour and a half. Get some pants on."

On the drive into the desert there was a minimum of talk. Golden sat in the middle, trying to stay calm, as if he were perfectly happy to be going on an extemporaneous hunting trip with his two good buddies, Nelson and Ted. But it was not easy to hide the unease, percolating like swamp gas from deep in his gut. He had never seen Ted Leo like this: propped against the passenger door, head sunk down between his shoulders, his face a wooden mask, speaking not a word. Even Nelson looked a bit troubled, giving his boss the occasional sideways glance.

They circled around the western edge of a hummock topped with pitted lunar sandstone and suddenly the fence of the Test Site came into view, stretching east and west in a perfect black line like the demarcations on a compass. Golden saw in his mind the abandoned bunker Ted Leo had shown him last summer, felt the heavy, almost animate darkness of the cave he had escaped from only last night, imagined his body stuffed through the bunker's steel hatch and interred there forever among tangles of old wire and the carcasses of dogs. A wet rag of claustrophobic panic pressed against his face and he began to squirm.

"Where we going?" he managed to say. There was no way to keep himself from asking it, just as there was no way to accept, without protest or at the very least a polite inquiry, the emerging possibility that they were all on their way to see him meet his mortal end.

Nelson looked over at Ted Leo as if he had the same question but lacked the appetite to put it into words. Ted Leo didn't speak or move for a good ten seconds. Finally, he said, "Take us up the way, Nelson, and get the guns and dogs ready."

They drove half a mile or so north and Nelson parked the pickup under the negligible protection of an ancient Joshua tree with two sagging arms and a fat trunk bulging with odd-shaped tumors and burls. He gave a piercing whistle, which sent the dogs leaping from the tailgate, circling and sniffing, throwing long, frenetic shadows in the early morning light.

All three men got down on their bellies, the dogs hunkered next to them, and Nelson blew through a wooden cylinder to produce a plaintive, high-pitched howl, followed by a series of sharp, barking yips. Nelson and Ted scanned the hills with binoculars until the dogs began to whine and make low growling noises in their throats.

"There in that shallow draw," said Nelson. "Male, prob'ly."

The dogs raised their heads and both men trained their binoculars in the same direction, but Golden could see nothing.

"Do your thing, girls," Nelson whispered, and the dogs jumped up and scrambled down the slope, ears flapping, cropped tails vibrating with excitement. At first Golden could see only the two dogs racing neck and neck, wide-eyed and grinning like two kids trying to settle a bet, but then a coyote came into view, a big shaggy gray thing with bone-white legs, going hard along the top of the ridge to cut them off. Just when it seemed their paths would inter-sect, the dogs veered away, weaving through the chaparral, tongues wagging, appearing to have the time of their lives. The coyote was clearly faster than the dogs, and occasionally it would put on a burst of speed, stretching out to take long leaping double-strides, and would close in to bite at their flanks as if to hamstring them. One dog would always slow to make a few slashing feints, distracting the coyote, sometimes drawing it into a spinning, growling tangle until the coyote would race away, dragging its hindquarters to protect itself, and the whole dance would start again, their long swinging shadows performing a parallel drama along the brush and sand.

While this went on, the dogs circling ever closer, luring the coyote in, Ted Leo spoke: "The coyote, he can't help it, see. We're upwind and he's probably already picked up our scent, but he just can't help himself. Those pretty dogs come racing through his line of sight, he can smell 'em, and he's stumbling all over himself to go after 'em. He's got a mate and probably a litter of pups up them rocks, every reason to be cautious, but it's in his nature, his blood. He chases after what ain't his, not paying enough attention to his own, and just you watch, he's going to get himself killed."

Golden turned to look at Ted Leo and what he saw made his skin prickle; instead of watching the chase, as Golden had been, Ted Leo was up on one knee, staring at Golden with a carefully controlled malevolence, a glint of cold mockery in his eyes.

Golden pressed his face into the dirt and took a breath, smelled salt and dust and sage and the sour taint of the gun's steel on his hands. "Mr. Leo, I want to explain—"

"You be quiet. I'm doing the talking."

"Yessir." Golden deposited his face back into the dirt, and began reciting names—*EmNephiHelamanPaulineNaomiJosepineParleyNovella GaleAlvinRustyClifton* . . .

"You praying?" said Ted Leo, who seemed amused by this idea. "Suddenly you want to involve God in this?"

Head down, Golden kept reeling off the names.

Ted Leo took up his rifle and nudged Golden with the barrel.

"Come on. I want you to see what's going to happen here. Look up. I want you to see this."

The dogs and the coyote were now only two or three hundred yards off in the draw just below them, circling and dodging, sometimes in a way that looked like play. Another coyote, this one smaller than the first with a reddish cast to its coat, had appeared on top of the rise. It paced nervously, sometimes coming down into the draw when it looked like there might be trouble, but always retreating to patrol the narrow ridgeline.

"That'd be the female," Ted Leo said. "A little more cautious than her mate, but I'm guessing not cautious enough."

The dogs, seeming to tire of the chase, began a loping zigzag up the rise toward the hunters, their tongues dangling. The male coyote charged after them, stopped suddenly, lifted its snout, and began a cautious, trotting retreat, checking back over its shoulder. Ted Leo made a barking call on his bugle and the coyote paused, looked around, sniffed again.

"You want to take him?" Nelson whispered.

"I'll take him." Ted Leo was already sighting through his scope. The taste of nausea Golden had woken up with began to fill the back of his mouth and thicken his tongue. His sinuses contracted, began to burn, and though he did everything to hold it back, he let loose one of his roaring, thunderclap sneezes. At the sound the coyote wheeled, flattening its body, and began a sprint up the draw toward its mate.

"Ah, shit," Ted Leo growled, and his gun went off in Golden's right ear. The coyote flinched and lifted a foreleg, stumbling a little, slowing, and then Nelson's gun went off in Golden's left ear, and the coyote was spun around, as if somebody had grabbed it by the tail. It began a horrific squealing that penetrated even Golden's stunned eardrums, biting at its hindquarters and turning in place like a puppy chasing its tail. Within a few seconds the dogs were on it, snarling and biting with a sudden bloodlust, and then the red female was there, leaping into the pile and slashing with her teeth, raising a great boil of dust.

Nelson yelled something that Golden couldn't make out. The dogs retreated, and when the female gave up following them to check on her mate, another gunshot concussed the side of Golden's head and the little rust-red coyote rose off the ground in a flexing convulsion and landed softly in the dirt, one hind leg still twitching.

Golden didn't know if the deep silence that followed was something real or a product of the gunshots, which had filled his head with wet cotton batting. He heard a kind of underwater murmuring, which turned out to be Ted Leo yelling at him, telling him to go down and retrieve the carcasses. Golden tried to play deaf and dumb, but Ted wasn't having any of it. He delivered a sharp jab to Golden's neck with his rifle barrel. "Bring the carcasses up. Or I'm going to set the dogs on *you*."

Golden made his way down the draw, his body numb except for the hot, tingling spot in the center of his back where he imagined Ted Leo's 30.06 was trained. He considered making a break for it, sprinting down the draw and out into the open desert just to see how far he could get. He clenched the muscles of his neck so he wouldn't look back, walking with the careful, overly dignified air of a drunkard asked to leave a party.

The two coyotes were laid out one next to the other in the sand, grinning and bloody. The dogs sniffed them, giving them little nips and dancing backward, as if coaxing them to continue the game a little longer. Golden risked a glance up the hill. Ted and Nelson were standing together, watching, and Golden felt a small swell of gratitude that neither had a gun pointed at him.

The task of dragging two dead coyotes uphill in the hot sun through tangles of brush turned out to be even less rewarding than Golden had anticipated: the dogs kept tugging on the coyotes' ears and digging in, playing tug-of-war with Golden all the way up the rise, while a caravan of refugee fleas began a full-scale evacuation of the coyotes' coats for the fertile, hairy fields of Golden's arms, back, and chest. Sweating and gulping for air, he said nothing to the dogs, made no move to slap away the fleas; he limped up the hill, a coyote leg in each hand, not stopping until he slumped with a sigh into Nelson's vast, planetary shadow.

"Bitch's got swollen teats," Nelson said. "Means she's got pups back up in them rocks. Hold on. Listen. You can hear 'em crying."

All three of them listened. Lying on his side, the sun in his eyes, Golden heard nothing except the ocean roar of his own lungs. His bad knee was killing him and his stomach churned. He gasped, "You going to leave them there?"

Ted Leo laughed. He laughed like this was the funniest thing he'd ever heard. "*We* going to leave them there? No, we're going to fetch them up and bottle-feed 'em and raise 'em as our own and one day, if they work hard and mind their manners, they'll go away to the Ivy Leagues and make us proud."

He shook his head, walked in a circle. Like the filament popping inside a lightbulb all the mirth drained out of him in an instant. His face went dark and he stiffened.

"You piece of shit," he said, and gave Golden a quick, hard kick in the ribs. "I should have known. You piece of fucking fuck." Though Golden gasped at the violence of it, the kick turned out not to hurt at all; it was like being kicked by an old lady wearing house slippers. "Maybe we'll leave you out here, too, with them poor little pups, what do you think? Maybe that'll teach you to make time with another man's wife. You piece of utter *shit*."

Ted Leo lifted his rifle and brought the butt of it down on the back of Golden's head. A red comet flared across his vision and his brain seemed to wobble inside his skull like a gyroscope. Now *that*, Golden had to admit, hurt. While he was busy writhing on the ground, ringing like a bell of pain, Ted Leo squatted next to him and spoke into his ear. "Now get those animals in the back of the truck so I can decide what to do with you."

Ted Leo got in the cab to deliberate and Golden took his time working his way to his feet, spending a good minute on all fours, drooling into the dust. Finally Nelson helped him up and together they swung the carcasses into the back of the pickup. He could hear the pups now, a faint mewling carried in on a gust of wind. Over-taken by a wave of dizziness, Golden pivoted, slumped against the rear tire, heaving in a way that sounded a little like sobbing, dripping with sweat, head bowed, exhausted beyond reason, ready to accept his fate, whatever it might be.

His immediate fate involved being forced to ride in back between the two dead coyotes like a trophy of the hunt. The dogs sat at the other end of the bed, wedged up against the tailgate, smiling at him shyly, their mouths rimmed with blood. Head lolling, he smiled back at them. Any of the fleas who had not jumped ship already did so now: they bounded in amazing little arcs off the dead coyotes onto Golden, crawling down his collar and up the cuffs of his pants, mak-ing themselves at home anywhere there was hair, which meant every part of him except his face and the no-man's-land around his groin.

They stopped behind the PussyCat Manor at the makeshift dock where the brothel accepted its bulk shipments of liquor, food, and dil-dos. Ted Leo went inside and came back holding an envelope and a sheet of paper. He said nothing to Golden, and they drove on, up the hill right through the construction site, where most of the men stopped to stare.

At Golden's trailer, Ted Leo did not get out of the cab. He rolled down the window and waited for Golden to climb down out of the bed and come to him.

"I don't make it a practice to trust anybody," he said in a low voice, staring out the windshield, "but you I trusted. I trusted you because I was dumb enough to think that a man who claims the title of Christian, a man married to four women, with a crowd of children to protect and feed, a man with all that to lose—why would a man like that do this to me? Last night when I found my wife out at the hot springs, I knew something was wrong. I went back, and followed your tracks—barefoot tracks, wandering all over the damn place—right back to this trailer, right to your front door there, and still I had trouble believing it. I made a few calls, and come to find out what a fool Ted Leo is. People around have seen you two together, taking romantic walks and carrying on on that couch, seems like I was the only one not to know. And I realized my mistake. Somebody like you, you have everything and you're not satisfied. You want more. You want what doesn't belong to you, you believe you're entitled to it all. You're exactly like your piece-of-shit father."

"I'm sorry, Mr. Leo," Golden said. "I don't know what else to say."

"I don't want you to say anything. I don't want to hear from you again. I considered putting you away forever, but you're not worth the trouble it would take to put a bullet in your head. Turn the other cheek, the Good Book says. Well, consider my cheek turned." He handed Golden an envelope with a check for three-quarters of the amount he owed him, and had him sign a cancellation of their contract, a document that permanently ended their business relationship henceforth and forever.

Golden touched the tender knot at the back of his head, checked his fingers for blood. He whispered, "And Huila?"

Something hardened in Ted Leo's eyes. His arm banged against the door as if he had a mind to step out of the truck and give Golden another beating. He said, "Don't you ever say that name again. Don't you ever think it. Now go away and don't come back." Before he rolled up his window he turned his head to address Nelson. "And Nelson'll have a little something to send you on your way."

Nelson got out of the truck and ambled around the front of the pickup. He gave Golden a small, apologetic smile and Golden opened his arms slightly as if to receive a farewell hug or a nice parting gift. With a short, brutal stroke, Nelson brought his fist up into Golden's diaphragm. He made a sharp, wheezing gasp, and collapsed to the ground, opening and closing his mouth and arching his back like a fish on the deck of a boat.

Nelson knelt on one knee and loosened Golden's belt. "There you go, okay, breathe, that's good, relax now."

Golden let his head fall back, looked up at the bleached-white sky, felt like he was suffocating.

Nelson put his head down close to Golden's. "Do what Ted Leo says, he means it, okay?"

"Okay," Golden wheezed.

"He knows people. A few worse than me."

"Thank you," Golden managed.

"Okay then," said Nelson. "You're welcome."

And they drove away, kicking up a column of dust that followed them down the hill to PussyCat Manor. Golden lay in the dirt for a long while, trying to learn how to breathe again, trying not to think about what would come next.

BELLY OF THE WHALE

After Ted Leo and Nelson had left him lying in the dirt in front of his trailer, he took fifteen minutes to gather himself and did the only thing left: collected his belongings from the work trailer, packed his things into the Airstream and drove away. With a pang of regret he left the Barge sitting alone in the yellow sand, an artifact for the ages, and drove past the work site, thinking it best not to say anything to anybody, to disappear and let gossip take care of the rest. But Leonard, who had a knack for being in the middle of everything, called out from the entrance of the new brothel where he was helping to install the great oak doors. He ran to intercept Golden's GMC.

"Where you going all loaded up?"

"I'm leaving, Leonard. Somebody else will take over for the last leg, maybe you. Tell the rest of the men goodbye for me. I'll try to get you on the next one."

It cheered him just a little to see how stricken Leonard looked by this news. He grabbed Golden's forearm. "What happened?"

"Ted Leo and I had a falling out. That's all. He gave me my walking papers."

Leonard nodded, closing his eyes with an air of profound intellec-
tual comprehension. "Because you was fucking his wife, ain't it."

Golden looked around at the men who had stopped their work
to watch. He settled his gaze on his hands gripping the steering
wheel. There was still coyote blood on one of his knuckles. He said, "I
didn't."

"Sure you did," Leonard said. He gave his boss an awkward half
hug through the pickup window and whispered gently into his ear.
"Don't worry, chief, happens to the best of us."

For a moment Golden stared blankly into Leonard's bright little
eyes. "Thank you so much, Leonard," he said, and put the truck into
gear.

Golden drove away then, Leonard in his rearview waving with his
whole arm as if from the rail of a departing steamer, and pulled out
onto the highway. He passed the PussyCat Manor going slowly, staring straight ahead as he went by. Up the hill he pulled onto the gravel
margins of the road for one last look. On the construction site they
were pinning up chicken wire for the stucco, and then it would be
mostly finish work, painting and carpet and trim. The whole thing
would be done in a month and he would not be there to see it. He was
proud of the work he'd put in—it was a well-constructed building,
the biggest he'd ever done, but he would be glad, he thought, not to
see it finished, not to have to think about it again.

He couldn't help it: he scanned the hills behind the site. He
couldn't see the pond from here, and he imagined Huila there, wading in the shallows, the water at her ankles. He tried not to think
about what might have happened between her and Ted Leo. A hot
breeze pushing his hair around, he scanned the landscape for any sign
of her. And then, feeling like a coward, like somebody running from
a fight, he drove away for good.

During the drive home, the midday light crowding the shadows
into the deepest fissures of the canyon walls, his thoughts began to
stir and chase themselves through the foggy depths of his exhaustion.
He experienced a series of impressions and images his jangled mind

presented to him at random: Huila's breasts suspended in the inky water of the hot springs, Trish's hand on his as she lay next to him in the dark, the coyote biting at its own hindquarters and spinning itself into the ground, one of Ted Leo's white loafers flashing in his peripheral vision before burying itself in his ribs, the black air of the cave pressing against his face, the sour smell of his own fear, on him even now.

His first coherent thought was that he had just escaped certain doom. Five years ago he had been hauling a load of cinder block on Highway 89 west out of Kanab in a sudden thunderstorm and had hit a pool of water, sending his truck out of control and into a slow roll down an embankment. The centrifugal force had wrenched open the driver's door and yanked him clear with such force he'd been separated from his hat and one of his shoes. He had no memory of hitting the ground, only of standing up covered with mud and finding himself—except for a sore shoulder and forearm embedded with bits of gravel—in perfect working order. He stood there weak-kneed and delirious in the rain, nothing to do but look around and palpate his bones, amazed.

And that was how he felt now: weightless, hollowed out, like an apple skinned and cored, but more than anything else lucky to be going home, his body and soul compromised but still intact. He had escaped not only Ted Leo's righteous anger, but the punishments, both earthly and eternal, if he'd made love to Huila. He shivered to think who he'd be if that had happened: not just a liar and a coward and a sneak, but an adulterer, someone unworthy of the sacred Principle, no longer fit to hold the sacred offices of husband and father. He would have had no future in the church or with his family, and none with Huila, that was for sure. For so long he had been dreaming of a release such as that, and now all he felt was relief that it hadn't happened. He would have lost everything and returned to where he had started: lonely, lost, with no one to love and nowhere to go.

He would have liked to believe it was God who had rescued him. He wondered: Could God have been responsible, somehow, for arranging the gum to end up in his pubic hair, which had prompted him to shave himself, the embarrassment of which had kept him from having intercourse with Huila? God was supposed to move in mysterious ways, but this seemed a little much. Still, it was comforting to think that, after everything, God might be looking out for him.

Something stung at the backs of his eyes and he began shaking his head and then he said it out loud, "No, no." No, it wasn't God—he was fooling himself even considering such a notion. It wasn't God or some divinely placed gum that had saved him. It was Glory, and nothing else. Since the day of her death, he had wanted to give up or let loose, to get drunk or throw some kind of existential tantrum as a way of showing what he thought of a God who allowed innocent children to come into the world to suffer and then die early and horrible deaths, but the possibility that all things might be restored to him, that the tragedies of this existence might be made right somehow, that Glory might be waiting on the other side, had kept him, as they said so often in church, holding fast to the iron rod. His faith in God and heaven had always been weak, but he believed in them now, if for no other reason than belief in them offered the possibility to be with his daughter again; he believed because to do otherwise would be to consign her to oblivion.

Last night, in the hot springs with Huila, when he was just about to throw away everything for a few minutes of bliss, something had stopped him, a chilly presence at the back of his mind, and he understood now that it was Glory who had come back to him for the briefest moment, it was Glory who had saved him.

The gospel taught that in the resurrection the diseased and broken would be made whole, but he didn't want to see her again in a perfect, glorified state, he wanted her as she was in his memory, her left arm folded up like the wing of a bird and her mouth full of small, crooked teeth, her lopsided face alive with sudden grins and sly glances. He wanted to smell the sour-milk tang of her breath and to hear her bright, shrieking squawks as he called to her from the front door. He wanted to hold her again and feel in the way she pressed her cheek against his chest her forgiveness, her sweet and uncomplicated love.

Here, alone in the cab of his truck, there was no reason to hold it all in, this grief which had become indistinguishable from every other part of his life, which had subsumed the stress and anticipation and terror of the last twelve hours, and he let go a few coughing sobs that came out in spasms. He sniffed and gave the steering wheel a hard shake. In his blubbering he must have taken his foot off the gas because he heard honking and looked in his rearview to see a line of cars backed up behind him. He was doing thirty-five in a no-passing zone on an interstate highway. He pressed down on the accelerator, but he was on an uphill grade and the engine seemed to gulp and then surrender when it engaged the extra weight of the trailer. The first to pass him was a woman in sunglasses driving a Mustang convertible. She bared her teeth and gave him the finger as she went by, but she must have gotten a look at his wet, ruined face because she turned her eyes away and sped by with the blinkered expression of someone who has just witnessed something intimate and shameful.

For no reason he could think of the story of Jonah and the Whale came into his head. He had first heard it one sticky fall morning at the Holiness Church of God in Jesus' Name, sitting in the rough cypress pew next to his mother. The Reverend Marvin J. Peete had been cycling through his weekly routine, which involved warbling snippets of gospel standards into the microphone with the husky whisper of a nightclub crooner and then suddenly barking out terrifying declamations of *Repentance!* and *Apocalypse!* and *Blood of the Lamb!* But on that day his voice lowered and he began to tell a story about Jonah, the man who had disobeyed God and as a result had been swallowed by a "great and terrible fish." Golden, his copper hair slicked back and his necktie arranged at the base of his Adam's apple in some overcomplicated sailor's knot, sat up and listened. According to the Bible the Lord had "prepared a large fish to swallow up Jonah"—the word "prepared" indicating the whale was not a *punishment* from God, but a gift, an *opportunity*. While Golden liked this idea, he liked even better the description of Jonah's time inside the whale, which was spent, according to the reverend, praying and singing canticles while perched on a giant kidney under festoons of intestines and trembling stalactites of whale mucus. Reverend Peete might not have had a solid grasp of marine mammal anatomy, but he made up for it with his descriptions of the glistening liver upon which Jonah made his bed at night and the wash of spiky and tentacled sea creatures, dead and alive, foaming around the prophet's legs while he implored the Almighty for mercy. It took three days, apparently, for the great fish to tire of having his kidney used as a bean bag, and when Jonah was vomited up on the beach, Reverend Peete nearly gave himself in to an apoplectic fit with the glory of this moment. He cried, "Oh Jonah! God's reluctant servant! Look at him there, washed up on that foreign shore! Half blind and tangled up in seaweed and whatnot. And that horrible smell? It's Jonah, people, covered with fish parts and digestive juices and so forth. It's pathetic old Jonah, pale and wrinkled like he's spent the weekend in a pickle barrel, blinking and looking around at the sand and the water and the tropical greenery and all that dazzling light after so much darkness. Imagine it, people! The ocean breeze in the nostrils, the sound of the surf and the wind in the palms. Imagine the *wonder*. The humble *gratitude*. *Oh praise be my king on high*, can you hear Jonah say it? Imagine the grace, the sweetness of that second chance."

Golden had felt it then, the beauty of that moment, and he felt it now, thirty-some years later, driving out of the deep river gorge and onto the wide face of a plateau shadowed by a field of brilliantly lit clouds. He had escaped the belly of the whale. He was bruised and battered, covered in dust and blood and infested with fleas, but he was returning home, where he allowed himself to imagine a bountiful and untroubled future, back in the bosom of his family.

For another thirty miles he did nothing but steer and look out into the glare of the day. At one point he reached up idly to investigate the goose egg on the back of his head and instead of his own fingers on the tender skin he felt Huila's—for a dislocating moment he sensed her next to him, felt the heat of her touch and got a whiff of her, a strong but pleasant smell like a new leather belt. As if it had been burned he pulled his hand away quickly, giving his head a hard shake to dislodge the very thought of her, realizing that he would be shaking off such thoughts for a long time to come.

By the time he made it to St. George, the fleas had begun to stir. They'd been laying low, like immigrants getting used to the neighborhood, but now that they'd acclimated, picked up on the local language and customs, they were on the move and causing trouble. Anywhere there was hair, they congregated: in the vast prairies of his chest and belly and the forests that covered his scalp. In particular they seemed to be making themselves comfortable in the crack of his ass.

His crotch, he noted with bitter satisfaction, was entirely flea-free.

They weren't biting him, thankfully, but they were, almost literally, making his skin crawl, but then, yes, no doubt about it, they were biting him. At some point he had himself going in a full body flex, craning his neck as he desperately ground his butt against the seat, digging into his belly with his fingers or attacking the soft spot behind his ear like a dog, but it was like trying to scratch a thousand small itches at once. For the last few miles he held on by sheer force of will, going a good twenty miles over the speed limit, and when he pulled up into the gravel drive, he skidded to a hard stop, ratcheted down the emergency brake and jumped out of the truck, scratching at himself in a spasm of delicious violence. When this didn't do the trick, he skipped around the side of the trailer facing the Spooners' pasture, away from the prying eyes of Old House, and yanked off his shirt, rubbing at the bare skin of his ribs with his fists and forearms and elbows. He had his pants unbuttoned, and was just sliding them down to have a go at his thighs and buttocks when he heard a soft thudding noise, like a turnip rolling in a bucket. The Airstream shifted slightly and he watched, mesmerized, as the trailer's doorknob, not three feet from his face, began to turn. He froze, and then—very slowly, very carefully—pulled up his pants. The latch clicked and the door creaked open. And there was Huila, in her pineapple dress with a bag slung over her shoulder, terrified and smiling.

]0.

. . . . .

TAMPON MAN

At night, he waited for the house to sleep. By nine-thirty Nephi and Parley were already making wheezy snuzzling noises, bushed after another long and exhausting day of being a-holes, and then the Big Girls in the room below would finally quit their dumb conversations about such fascinating topics as, *What are eyebrows for, exactly?* or *Which is the world's best shampoo and conditioner combination?* and then somewhere deep in the house Aunt Beverly would conclude her dastardly work for the day and the whole place would be quiet, except for Parley's all-night farting routine.

Since his mother had gone away to the hospital, Rusty couldn't sleep—not at night, anyway. At school, sitting in his desk, you can believe he slept just great. He slept so great he snored and drooled a big wet spot on the front of his shirt. And even though he heard the whole class laughing all at once like a bomb going off in his head, making him jerk awake and nearly fall out of his seat, he somehow did the exact same thing the next day, with the huge drool spot and everything, which made Mr. Van De Berg ask why did he always have to be such a distraction? as he hauled him by the arm toward the principal's office. Which was why they called Big House to see if there was trouble there, which was how they found out that his mother had had a nervous breakdown and was in the nervous breakdown hospital, which was why he had to talk to the counselor, a chubbo with green eye shadow.

Okay, then, Rusty. In your own words, why don't you tell me a little about life at home.

It's nice.

Nice?

Yeah.

And how do you feel about your mother being sick?

Fine.

Fine, Rusty?

Yeah. Do you want me to talk louder?

You're not worried about her? Your mother?

No.

And who takes care of you while your father is at work, Rusty?

My aunt.

Your mother's sister, or your father's?

I don't know. She's just my aunt. She's not my mother.

No. I see. Are you happy at home, Rusty? Do you feel comfortable there?

Yeah.

And how have you been sleeping?

On my back.

Okay. I feel like you're having a hard time opening up to me, Rusty. That you're not telling me everything on your mind. Can you tell me why that is, Rusty?

Yeah.

Well?

Because you keep saying my name like a thousand times and your breath smells like Lysol.

That shut her up for a few seconds. He could feel, from the way she looked at him, how much she wanted him to tell her everything. She wanted him to tell her that his father was a law-breaking polygamist wingnut with a Moses beard who never took a bath, who committed terrible actions against his wife and his children and didn't make enough money for all of them so they were forced to make their clothing out of gunnysacks and eat dog food for breakfast. She wanted to hear every little thing about their criminal lifestyle, so she could send the police out to their house to haul Sasquatch off to prison and break up their family forever.

"You be *careful* when you talk to people like that," Aunt Nola had told him. "They think they're doing the right thing, but all they really want to do is destroy our happy little dog-and-pony show, to tear it apart. It's because we're special."

Rusty had thought about telling the counselor everything she wanted to hear so she could do exactly what Aunt Nola said she would. But he decided he didn't need a chubbo who smelled like cough drops to help him. He could do it all by himself.

And that was why he couldn't sleep at night. He had some serious things to think about. He had some serious planning to do.

Of course, Aunt Beverly would do anything to stop him. She made him come home right home after school and let him outside only to do chores. And her spies were all over him, following him wherever he went, watching, waiting for him to slip up or make a break for it so they could sound the Rusty Alert. So he had started sneaking out after dinner, when nobody expected anything, when everyone else was downstairs doing their music lessons and homeschool projects. He was supposed to be upstairs in the Tower doing his homework— like it was some kind of terrible punishment not to be able to hang out with the jack-holes downstairs!—but all he had to do was crawl out his window and climb expertly all the way down to the garage roof and he was free to ride around for an hour or so, thinking his thoughts, figuring out how he was going to free himself of Old House once and for all.

When Aunt Beverly discovered he was sneaking out again, she ordered Nephi to nail the Tower's windows shut, which was turning out to be a punishment for everybody up here because of the lack of ventilation and Parley's night-farting. But it didn't matter. You could nail shut all the windows you wanted: Old House could not contain Rusty McCready Richards. Aunt Beverly and her spies and her witchy-woman intentions were helpless against him.

Instead of walking down the Tower stairs, which would have made a creaking racket all the way, he sat down on the top step, let himself go limp, and slithered down like a bag of jelly, the back of his head making a soft *bump-bump-bump* the whole way.

He was unstoppable. He could not be stopped.

At the bottom he did his silent-walking technique—*heel . . . toe . . . breath . . . heel . . . toe . . . breath*—all the way down the hall to the window without a screen. The night-light was on in the Black Hole of Calcutta and he could see his reflection in the hall mirror: a black form with a white rectangle on its head.

Here was the weird thing: the rectangle was, if you could believe it, a tampon. He'd gotten it on his birthday, when he had locked everyone out of Big House and Nephi and Parley had tackled him so hard his head smacked the edge of the windowsill. Because doctors cost too much and were not to be trusted, most people in the church went to Sister Sleigh. Sister Sleigh had once been a nurse in the army and everyone said she knew more about medical science than half the fancypants doctors in Europe and New York City put together. Rusty's head was bleeding everywhere, which was a good thing, because after he'd locked everyone out of the house and ruined the big party, wouldn't it be kind of like overkill to punish a kid who already had a major head wound and blood running down his face? Parley and Nephi had brought him out of the house with the little ones screaming, "Look! Blood! *Ahh!*" and Aunt Nola hollering, "Clear the way, let's get him to Sister Sleigh's, Sister Sleigh will take care of him!"

How did Sister Sleigh take care of him? By shaving a big patch out of his hair, stitching up his wound and taping an enormous tampon to his head. This, to Rusty, didn't seem like very good medical science. He didn't know there was a problem until he came home and some of the big girls started to whisper and giggle and Aunt Beverly said, "It's just a *sanitary napkin*, and it's serving a perfectly good purpose."

Did anyone ask him how he was doing? Did anyone wish him

a happy birthday? Did anyone even give him a look like, *Boy, we're sure sorry you have suffered a major head wound on your birthday and are forced to wear a sanitary napkin?* No. They all just stared at him. The only thing he could hope for now was that he would end up with a killer scar.

Within thirty seconds word had gotten around that Rusty was wearing a tampon on his head. Even the little kids, who had no idea what a tampon might be, stared at him and backed away if he got too close as if he had some kind of contagious tampon disease. Except for his father, who had already gone back to Nevada without waiting around to see if Rusty would survive the night, most of the family was still at Big House. It was getting dark, and they had finished off the birthday cake and torn Dwight Eisenhower limb from limb without him, and were all gathered around getting a load of the tampon on his head. Maybe it was the way he'd locked them all out of the house earlier, or how he'd come out with his face covered in blood, or maybe it was how the front of his new sweater was so bloodstained it looked like he'd had his throat slit by a homicidal murderer, but they appeared scared of him now, especially the little ones. He liked the way they backed away, their eyes wide. He made a little grunt and they cringed. He took a step at them and they flinched. Then he hunched his shoulders and tilted his neck with one eye scrunched up like the Hunchback of Notre Dame and yelled, "*Uhhh-wah-hah-hah-haaaaaaaah!*"

The girls shrieked and everybody jumped back and the Three Stooges knocked into each other trying to get away. He leapt forward like a cougar after a herd of frightened zebras, and of course he singled out the weak one, who in this case was Jame-o, who would not abandon his Hoover for anything and was trying to drag it like a wounded soldier toward the safety of the kitchen. At the last second Rusty changed directions and lunged at Naomi and Teague, who were trying to make it up the stairs, and he grabbed at their feet and they kicked and twisted, screaming till he let them go. His father was usually the one who came home from work and played the monster, Bob the Zombie, the Blind Octopus, the Man Without a Head, but his father was too busy to play with the kids these days or to pay attention to anyone at all, which made Rusty's face hot just thinking about what a gyp it all was, so when he growled and jabbered he did it extra loud, the kids scattering like tadpoles in a puddle, hiding behind furniture, screeching and tripping over each other while he ran around swinging his arms and showing his teeth and snatching at anyone who came too close. He had the Second Twins cornered at the back of the family room now and they looked up at him, covering their heads with their hands, and he howled, *Uhhh-hoooooooooo!* and they shrieked so long and high and with such fear that it sent a weird tingle of satisfaction down the back of his neck. He was Crazy Ape-Guy! He was Tampon Man! *Ah-huuuaaa-haaah-haaaaaaah!*

The little ones were shrieking too now, some of them crying and trying to roll themselves up in the curtains and begging for mercy, saying, *Stop! Stop! Stop!* Even Helaman, who wasn't scared of anything, looked like he was ready to make a break for it at any second. Rusty kept it up, monkey-legging though the kitchen, going, *Uh-hungh, uh-hungh*, until Aunt Beverly grabbed him from behind, and hugged him close, and said into his ear, "Stop this now, please stop, this can't go on, you can't do this anymore," and he looked up into her face and saw even she was scared of him, even the terrible Aunt Beverly, and he made a sort of laughing sob and let her hug him because it felt so good.

COUNT YOUR BLESSINGS

So why was he, Rusty Richards, riding down the middle of the road on a Big Wheel at midnight? Because he wanted to. Because he was the Tampon Man and nobody could stop him, because he was feeling g-g-goooood! Super-good, in fact, which was weird because for so long everything had been bad. And then, two days ago, they went to visit his mother at the hospital. The hospital was not a white place with white walls and white nurses wearing white dresses and white hats, as he thought it would be, but a brown building with green floors and greasy-haired creeps in pajamas wandering the halls talking to themselves or hunched in wheelchairs staring at their knees.

"This place smells like *poop!*" Ferris said, and Aunt Nola said, "I think what you're smelling is the cafeteria."

His mother was waiting for them in a room with orange plastic chairs. She wore a blue bathrobe he had never seen before, and then he realized he'd never seen her wearing a bathrobe, not once, which bothered him. At home she would never come out of her room unless she was all-the-way dressed, shoes on her feet, but here she was sitting around right out in the open in a bathrobe and paper slippers surrounded by maniacs with yellow toenails.

Her hair looked grayer than he remembered and she was wearing a paper bracelet with words typed on it. They walked up to her slowly. "Kids," she said, "oh kids," and opened her arms.

"Remember the rules," Aunt Nola said. "Line up. Single file and wait your turn."

On the drive over Aunt Nola had given them instructions, one of which was they were supposed to wait in line and approach her one at a time. "One of the reasons she's in the hospital is she can't take all the stimulation that you little darlings provide, what with everybody coming at her all the time. Believe me, I know how she feels. So you'll line up and go one at a time and *whisper*. You start yelling or acting up and it's outside you go."

Pauline asked why they all had to go at once, couldn't they go see their mother one or two at a time? This was the question every plyg kid was always asking: Can't we ever do *anything* alone? And Aunt Nola said what the mothers always said. "You think I don't have anything else to do? You think you're the center of the universe? You think your life is hard? Well, boo-hoo. Try thinking about somebody other than yourself for once."

If there's anything you learned as a plyg kid, it was that you were not the center of the universe. Rusty knew it better than any of them.

The monkey net was big and tangled and had no trouble holding them all at once. And the worst thing? The monkey net would never go away, it was forever. That was what they taught you in church. Because they were a special people, because they were living God's Principle, their families would live together in heaven for all time and eternity, which everybody seemed to think was a wonderfully fantastic idea. Was it wonderfully fantastic, Rusty wondered, to be stuck forever with a bunch of a-holes you didn't even like? Was it wonderfully fantastic to have to stand in line to talk to your own mother?

Because they went youngest to oldest, Rusty was fifth in line. Ferris gave their mother a pebble that was almost perfectly round and Fig Newton brought her report card which showed all S's, which meant Fig Newton was fantastically satisfactory. Wayne, who was mad at their mother for having a nervous breakdown and ending up in the loony bin, brought nothing and after giving her a fake hug stood out in the hall with a sour look on his face. Herschel the Buttkisser brought her favorite pillow, and her mug that she liked for drinking lemon tea, and Rusty quietly shook his fist, because why hadn't he thought of that? All he had was the picture of his birthday, with him sitting there cross-eyed next to his birthday cake and putting on the biggest, dumbest smile you have ever seen.

When it was his turn he didn't hug her because she looked like she was not at all interested in being hugged. He gave her the picture and she looked at it. "Yes," she said. "Yes."

"I'm wearing the sweater you made me," he whispered, very carefully. A lot of the blood hadn't come out of it in the wash, so he'd poured some bleach on it, which hadn't really helped. If you went to the cemetery in the middle of the night and dug up a grave and opened the coffin and the rotting skeleton inside was wearing a sweater, it would probably look a little better than the one he had on. If his mother noticed there was anything wrong with it, she wasn't saying. She smiled and patted his hand. He was glad she didn't ask about the tampon.

He sat down next to her, trying to think of something to talk about, hoping Aunt Nola wouldn't say, *Time's up!* and move him along. He let his shoulder touch hers. He said, really low so no one else could hear, "I'm starting to behave a lot better, I'm not going to get into trouble anymore." Which was a lie. Rusty understood that when you were talking to somebody in a place like this it was a good idea to lie to them as much as possible.

From down the hall came the kind of scream you hear in a horror movie where someone is being tortured with red-hot pliers in a dungeon. Fig Newton and Ferris looked around for someone to tell them that everything was all right, but no one did.

Before they left, Aunt Nola got them together and they sang their mother a song.

When upon life's billows you are tempest tossed,
When you are discouraged thinking all is lost,
Count your many blessings, name them one by one,
Count your many blessings, see what God has done.

It had to be the dumbest song in the world, if you wanted Rusty's opinion, but their mother, along with a crazy-eyed coot who'd butted in on the proceedings, smiled and politely clapped, and for about ten seconds they all pretended to be happy.

But when Rusty went home that night he was not happy. Up in the Tower by himself he tried to count his blessings, which was the easiest math problem ever, because the answer was a BIG FAT ZERO. And nobody cared, nobody would help him. He'd started to think he should just kill himself, stick a sharp pencil through his earhole or walk all the way to Iceland and float away on an iceberg. But last night, because his plans were ruined and he didn't know what to do, he decided to pray. He didn't like praying, because it never did any good. When they told him to say grace at supper or give the opening prayer in Sunday School, he just mumbled something that sounded like a prayer: *HeavenlyFatherthankeethisdaythefoodthehandspreparedittinnameaJesaChristamen*. But what else was there to do? He couldn't sleep at night, he was having bad thoughts in his head, so he might as well say a prayer.

When the prophet Joseph Smith was just a kid, not much older than Rusty, he'd given the most famous prayer ever. Joseph Smith was confused, he didn't know which church to join, so he went out into the forest to pray. Why he didn't just pray in the kitchen, or on his bed or somewhere comfortable like that, Rusty had no idea. He went out into the forest to pray and Jesus and God came to him in a bright ball of light and told him none of the churches were true, that Joseph Smith, even though he was just a kid, would be the new prophet and start his own church and become the most powerful person in the history of the universe.

Which was just great for Joseph Smith, but what about Rusty? There wasn't a forest nearby, not even two or three trees close together, so Rusty decided the bushes by the river would have to do. After everyone had gone to sleep he snuck out of the Tower and went down to the river. You were supposed to kneel down when you prayed, so God would know you were serious, but when Rusty knelt in the muddy grass the knees of his pajamas got covered with wet brown stains. What a gyp! He bowed his head and made a steeple with his hands, which looked kind of gay, but nobody was out here to see.

"Dearest Lord above," Rusty said, which was how he once heard a sexy nun pray in a movie, "hear Thee the desires of my heart."

He wanted to approach this the right way. That was a good start and the night was kind of beautiful, with a big moon, and the bushes looked sort of like a forest and he was in perfect prayer position, with his head down and doing the steeple-thing with his hands, and he started off by telling God that he was going to do his best to be a good person who wasn't such a pain in the behind, he was so sorry for all of his sins, and just as he was starting to get this nice holy feeling, everything started going wrong. He was asking God to bless his mother, to make her better, but he could feel an ant crawling up his leg. *Effing ant!* he thought. *Get the heck out of here!* which was probably not the holiest thing to be thinking during a prayer. Not to mention his underwear was riding up on him. And then who showed up but Raymond the Ostrich, watching from across the river with his glowing eyes, and Rusty couldn't concentrate, not with an ostrich staring at him and an ant crawling toward his privates. So he picked up a stick to throw at Raymond, to scare him off so he could have his privacy back and start feeling holy again, but the stick slipped and ended up hitting an old piece of tin on this side of the river and the *clang!* was so loud Rusty had to run like the wind to get back into the house before he was discovered.

Lying on his pad with a sweaty head and muddy knees, he was asking himself why he was such a buttfudge, what was wrong with him that he couldn't even say a prayer?—when something weird happened. He fell asleep for a little while. And then, even weirder, he had a dream. Normally his dreams were about friendly werewolves or giant chicks in bikinis who breathed molten fire, but this one was different. His mother came to him in a big ball of yellow light, just like God and Jesus came to Joseph Smith. She didn't say anything, but she was smiling and surrounded by bright sparks and little meteors that circled around her head and there was some kind of choir singing something holy-sounding in the background.

When he woke up this morning, he knew: his mother would be coming home. Rusty had prayed, and even though the prayer had gotten a little messed up, God had answered it. Take that, Joseph Smith! God would bless his mother, because Rusty had gone to a lot of trouble to kneel down in some muddy grass to pray for her and because she was a nice person who was never mean to anyone, and now that she would be getting stronger and thinking clearly she would say, *I am Rusty's true mother, let him come home.*

Which was why he was feeling so good riding down the middle of the road on a Big Wheel at midnight. He felt a cool air sensation and looked down and noticed he had forgotten to put on his pants. Oh well! He was silent as the wind, invisible as the Holy Ghost, and he could not be stopped.

Not that Aunt Beverly didn't try. After he'd crawled out the window at the end of the hall without a screen, he found she had locked up the garage with all the bikes inside. You should have seen it, he didn't even get mad. He just shook his head and said, *Nicely done, nicely done.* He looked around and sure enough, there was the Big Wheel at the side of the house, the one with the brake on the back wheel so if you felt like it you could do a cool spin-out when you pulled on the handle. He was too big for it and his knees kept hitting the handlebars, but anything was better than walking.

By the time he made it to Big House his knees felt like somebody had been banging on them with hammers and his feet were raw from the jagged pedals, but he hadn't seen a single car on the way and the night air was cool on his sweaty neck.

The doors of Big House were never locked. He crept upstairs and stood next to his mother's door, listening. *Any day now*, the grown-ups kept saying, *she'll be home any day now*, and Rusty was sure that if his mother did come home Aunt Beverly would keep that information to herself. He pictured her in her bed, without her earmuffs, sleeping peacefully in the dark with sparkles of light around her head.

He stepped inside the room and could hear breathing, definite breathing. His heart did a little flip and he snuck closer to the bed. What he found was *somebody*, but it was not his mother. It was Novella, and a second imposter, Gale, mumbling in her sleep. He looked around and could see they had brought in some of their things, clothes and books and a Lil' Strawberry Patch Girl lamp. Rusty's chest filled up with something hot and sour and he wanted to drag them out of the bed by the hair and take the Lord's name in vain right to their faces, because, what, did they think they could just move into his mother's room as if she was gone forever and not coming back? As if she'd never even been there at all? What did they think? And what did God think, sending him a dream and playing a trick on him like that?

He stood by the bed, breathing hard, grabbing his hair with both hands and giving it a good yank, telling himself to *calm down, calm down*.

He gave one big, shuddering snork, and then suddenly all his anger was gone and he was so tired. His knees and his feet and his head hurt and all he wanted to do was lie down in his mother's bed and smell her pillow. He crawled in next to his sister and she was soft and warm and didn't push him away.

When he woke up it was just getting light outside and the birds were singing like maniacs.

He got out of the bed and stood over Novella, putting his hand out over her face, and thought about pressing his palm down onto her mouth. Instead, he cocked his middle finger with his thumb, and flicked her across the tip of the nose, hard. Quick as lightning he did the same to Gale and then ducked down below the bed and crawled out the door before they could see anything.

Gale howled and Novella was screeching, "Who did that? Who's *there?*" By the time he'd sprinted down the stairs, out the side door, and was on his Big Wheel pedaling down the road, half the house was up and shouting, thrashing around like monkeys caught in a net.

31.
. . . . .

A MINOR PLAGUE

FOR SOME, THE PLAGUE CAME AS NO SURPRISE. SINCE THE CREATION
of the world God has visited plagues upon His children for many reasons: to test, to chastise, to invite them to repentance, but mostly to remind them, in a way that leaves little room for confusion, of the error
of their ways. And there was no doubt, in the minds of some of the
Richards clan, that they were in need of correction. As a family they
were adrift, lacking in obedience and low on faith: their father and
patriarch was absent in body and spirit and for too long had been of
little use to anyone; their mothers feuded and couldn't properly control their children, who in turn bickered and misbehaved and drove
their mothers (and in one recent case almost literally) crazy.

Unlike most plagues, which tend to kick off melodramatically
with rivers turning to blood or clouds of locusts boiling over distant
mountains to blot out the sun, this one started with . . . a mild itching.
Aunt Beverly, as always, was the first to note something amiss. Alvin,
idly digging at the skin of his hips and back, and a few minutes later
Martin pausing between bites of a sandwich to scratch at his ankles.
When Louise came into the kitchen and displayed the bites on her
belly—three tiny inflamed spots like the points of a triangle—Beverly
made the instant transition from guarded concern to no-holds-barred
crisis control. She shouted the alarm, ushered all of the kids out of
the house onto the front porch, counted heads and called Nola to
inform her there had been an outbreak of some kind, lice or bedbugs

or mites. Nola, of course, found this deliciously hilarious and figured this new development could keep her in a good mood for at least a week. But only a few hours later, after a quick late afternoon nap, she began to itch deep within the rolls of fat under her arms, locations difficult if not impossible to reach, and in a few minutes she was hopping on one foot in a throe of futile scratching, squirming, and swearing in high Aunt Nola fashion, "Dang potlickers! Ack! Little suck-egg sons-of-beekeepers!"

She pulled the sheets back on her bed, and sure enough, two black dots zinged in different directions, one landing in the carpet of the floor, the other on her pillow. Nola had grown up on a farm and was familiar with every class of vermin and pest in this part of the world. No doubt about it: the Richards family had fleas.

"Oh you little so and so's," she said. "Just you wait."

A strategy was formulated, debated, and implemented: everyone would be sent to Big House while Old House was washed, vacuumed, fumigated. At Big House the kids would be defleaed using Nola's tried and true home remedy, and then moved en masse to Old House so that Big House could be thoroughly cleansed.

Trish arrived from her afternoon visit with Rose to find the operation in full swing. While Beverly and the two oldest girls were cleaning Old House, Nola had been left to deal with the children. Most of the younger ones were aimlessly circling the racetrack, as if by force of habit alone, or standing around in the front room, despondently scratching themselves like bored baboons in a zoo. Trish went into the kitchen to find the rest of them arranged on chairs and stools, their heads hooded in black plastic bags. She thought she'd stumbled onto the scene of an execution.

"What's that *smell*?" she said.

"Kerosene!" called Nola, tugging a bag around the head of her last victim.

"You've soaked them in kerosene?"

"Only their hair."

"Are you *serious*? What about the fumes?"

"The fumes are the whole point, dear."

Now Trish could only stare at her.

"Oh, don't *worry*," Nola said. "I've cut everybody a mouth hole."

"Mama?" Faye called meekly from under one of the black bags. "Please help me."

Nola explained that kerosene was the most effective flea remedy there was. Showering would only encourage the fleas, who preferred heat and humidity, and the commercial products were spotty at best, not to mention expensive. "Fleas are hearty little scamps, you've got to hit 'em hard and fast. Three minutes sucking kerosene fumes, though, they don't stand a chance. There's not just the adults but the larvae and the eggs. You've got to get 'em all or the next thing you know you're infested."

"Aggh," someone cried from under one of the bags. "I can't breathe!"

"Oh please," Nola said.

"I'm getting dizzy," somebody said.

"I'm seeing spots," said somebody else.

"Maybe if you guys didn't live in such a dirty house," someone who sounded like Helaman shouted, "we wouldn't have to be doing this!"

"Who said that?" cried Clifton, easily identified by his barking monotone. "It's *you* guys who brought the fleas from Old House. It's *you* guys who are the dirty fleabag jerks."

"*You* guys are the jerks!" somebody shouted.

"Oh no we're not!" cried somebody else.

"At least we're not uptight buttholes," Clifton said.

There was some laughter, presumably from the Big House camp. Parley slipped off his stool and attempted to attack Clifton, but was limited in that his head was in a bag. He ended up bumping against one of the girls, who tipped forward, screaming, "Ahhh! I got some *in my eye*!" and everybody started shouting and jostling and trying to pull the bags off their heads. Nola went around slapping their hands away and saying, "Hey! Hey! No! Hey! Three minutes! Breathe through your mouth!," the kids shouted and complained, Darling, the family weeper, began to weep, and Cooter, who had become the scapegoat in this whole affair and been banished to the utility closet after the humiliation of a kerosene bath, put up a woebegone howl.

Trish spent the rest of the afternoon vacuuming carpets and scrubbing floors and refereeing skirmishes between the respective citizens of Big House and Old House, who seemed intent on teasing and aggravating each other to the point of all-out violence. She oversaw the washing of bed linens and lining up the younger children for their assembly-line baths and applications of calamine lotion. After a soup-kitchen dinner of canned stew and cheese sandwiches, she and Nola went out to sit on the back steps and take in a little fresh air. Trish had been spared the indignity of a plastic bag over her head, but the fumes inside the house were still strong enough to make her feel faint with nausea.

The evening air was warm and the western sky a thin wash of red and gold. Beverly had just called to say they hadn't gotten Old House thoroughly cleaned, and would it be all right if her children spent the night at Big House, just to be safe?

"She's got it all figured out, all arranged," Nola said. "By her way of thinking, these fleas have been sent from God to test us, to bring us closer together. Fleas from heaven, spare us all. I think she has it in her head that if we're truly faithful and pure of heart our kids are going to see past their differences and wake up tomorrow the best of friends, all of them singing 'Go Tell It on the Mountain' in three-part harmony and making each other breakfast. Let's just say I have my doubts."

"But she's not coming over?"

"Heavens, no! She wouldn't *dreeeeeeam* of spending a night in this house, not if she can help it. *She's* not the one who needs to come around to a different way of thinking, the Great Bev knows and understands all, she orchestrates from afar. No, she and Golden are going to spend a nice quiet night alone while I babysit the Revolutionary War."

"I can stay over and help," Trish said, trying not to let the surge of jealousy she felt alter her tone of voice, trying very hard not to entertain the idea that Golden had been home for over two days and had not come to see her, had only called her to say that things had changed and he would not be going back to Nevada. "It's not like one more thrilling night alone is going to make me any more beautiful and happier than I already am."

"Oh no, you go home and get your beauty rest, gorgeous, really. I think the kids'll be tired—they're worn out and most of 'em are loopy on fumes. Give 'em a pillow and they'll sleep like little drunken hobos. And it's not like there's going to be an available bed around here, anyway."

Inside, another shouting match had started up, this one a swelling and hotly contested debate that addressed the question of who was, and who was not, the boss.

"Here we are," Nola said, slumping even further so that her stomachs stacked up under her folded hands, pushing her mountainous bust right up under her chin. "Living the life."

Funny thing was, for Trish this *was* the life, the one she had envisioned when she first agreed to marry Golden. Years ago, when she called her mother to tell her the news, her mother clucked and sighed.

"I never should have sent you down there to stay with Aunt Daphne," she said, a wavering note of regret in her voice. "I can only blame myself."

Trish told her mother that for the first time in her adult life she was happy, that she'd found a good man who would treat her well.

"Oh, honey, that's what we all think, and then comes the truth."

"I really think I love him, Mom. The other wives, they're good women, we're already friends. This is what I need. Believe it or not, I'm happy."

"I know it won't do any good, but I won't be able to live with myself unless I remind you of a few things. Jealousy. Squabbling. Nastiness of every kind—if that sounds like your idea of happy, then by all means. Time to yourself? Out the window. The days will pass and you won't have any idea where they went. You'll have nothing to yourself anymore."

This did not sound at all bad to Trish—anything was better than being trapped in her own grief, bored out of her mind. After the tense emptiness of her life with Billy, this was exactly what appealed to her: a life shot through with conflicting, round-robin emotions and a thousand and one distractions, nights of exhausted sleep, and the clamor of children's voices upon waking. A life parceled out and sur-rendered, a life shared.

Even now Trish could not understand how such a life had been denied her. She did not know what was missing in her, where she had gone wrong.

"I'm lost, Nola," she said, just like that. "I don't know what's going to happen to me."

"No," Nola said, her voice rising, as if scolding a child. "Listen. You're going to be fine, honey. I know, I know how hard it is. Every-thing you've been through. You just have to stick it out."

Trish shook her head. "I'm not talking about what's already hap-pened. I'm talking about what's going to happen. It's hopeless for me. Do you know what Golden told me in Nevada? Do you know what I made him tell me?"

"I'd like very much to know," said Nola.

"I asked him . . ." The blood began to rise to her face and her eyes burned. "Why he wasn't *interested* in me. Why he's been avoiding me, physically."

"What did he say?"

"He said because he couldn't. He told me he was impotent, Nola."

At this, Trish had expected a joke, or one of Nola's grand, Mephis-tophelean laughs, the kind that had the power to obliterate anyone or anything unfortunate enough to wander into its path. But she only sat quietly, looking at her hands. "He said that?"

Trish nodded.

"I'm surprised he's never used that excuse with me," Nola said. Here a laugh did come: a flat, humorless chuckle. "With me, he's certainly had to make up his fair share."

The humiliation in Nola's voice—each word tender with some abiding pain—made Trish regret ever bringing up the subject. But she had come this far. There was only a little way left to go.

She put her hand on Nola's wrist. "So this is all I want to know. Was he telling me the truth, or was he just making another excuse?"

Nola shrugged, waited, as if hoping her good humor might return. "Hard to say, hard to say. It's been a long time with me, I can tell you that, but that's not too far out of the ordinary. Never has been. I'm not a young lady anymore and the Great Bev's more or less ancient, and Rose, who knows with Rose, really. You—I figured you, my sweet dear, were taking up the slack for the rest of us. I guess if he's acting that way around you, there's probably something to it."

Trish tried to accept this for the simple truth that it was. This was not the first time it had occurred to her that the only way to defeat her grief was with hope, even just a little, and everywhere she looked these days, hope was in short supply. She had survived the past year only because she could find it in herself to look forward to a better future, one in which Golden worked close by and found it within his means to offer the meager affection and commitment she required, one in which he could give her a child, or—hope of hopes!—two or three, children who could redeem (not replace, *never* replace) the children she had lost, the pain she had endured. Children who would give her a place in this big, ridiculous family.

The women looked at each other, both on the brink of tears, and something in this shared look, the self-pity so baldly displayed, made them sputter with sudden laughter.

"And all this time I was thinking you drove all the way out there to talk to him about Maureen Sinkfoyle," Nola said.

"I did," Trish said. "And he told me there was nothing to it. He said I was his last."

Though she tried to disguise it as another laugh, Nola let out a sigh of relief. Then she and her sister-wife shared a look, shaking their heads a little as if to say, *How did we ever get ourselves into something like this?*

"Come on," Nola said. "Right now. Come give this fat old lady a hug."

Trish leaned in, allowed herself to be taken in by Nola's immense softness, and immediately upon feeling the warmth of another's touch the laughter died in her throat and something welled up in her so strongly that, again, she had to fight back a sob.

"I'm a mess," she said, and gagged in a very unladylike way.

"Join the club, honey," Nola said. "But you're going to come out of this. God will provide a way. He always does."

A MOTHER, A SON

Before driving home, Trish carried the last load of washed bed linens up the stairs and found Rusty in his mother's bedroom, propped up on the bed, his legs under the covers. The bedside lamp illuminated little more than the circumference of its own shade, and the boy, cast in shadow and yellow light, looked carved out of wax. The skin around his eyes was stained with exhaustion and, though he'd taken a bath like everyone else, he still sported the smudged and tattered bandage, which Sister Sleigh had ordered not to be removed for two weeks, when the stitches would come out. He had a bright red scratch on his cheek and a series of flea bites, like footprints, tracking down his neck along the hairline.

"Hi there," she said.

He said, *"Buenos tarde, muchacho."*

"What are you up to?"

"Sitting here. Don't feel like dealing with the jerks out there."

"What happened to your face?"

"Gale."

Trish nodded in sympathy. "You say something to rub her the wrong way?"

"She and Novella think this is their bed now." He gave his head a slight shake. "This is my mom's room. She's coming back soon and I'm going to keep her place. This is where I'm sleeping tonight."

"Looks like you ran them off."

"For now." The boy shrugged. His eyes were liquid and dark and he blinked slowly. "They'll be back."

"I've got some clean sheets here," she said. "You want to help me make up the bed?"

Rusty rolled off the bare mattress and together they pulled away the bedcovers and laid out the sheets, pulled the corners tight. Rusty wore extra-snug-fitting pajamas with mismatched tops and bottoms that would properly fit someone two or three years his junior. Whenever his hands weren't busy with something else he kept one or both positioned over his groin.

"Visited your mom today," Trish said.

The boy looked at her and waited.

"She's doing really well," Trish said. Which was a lie. Since she'd told one already, she decided it couldn't hurt to throw in another. "She asked about you, how you're doing."

The truth of it was that Rose had improved since being admitted, but was still incapable of carrying on a normal conversation, as if the very act of speaking words, or committing the brainpower to call them up, were too much for her. She took little interest in the goings-on at home and repeatedly looked past Trish's face to watch a game show on the wall-mounted TV.

Trish thought of what Nola said after they admitted Rose: "Poor Rosie, just too sensitive to live in the world, much less this part of it. She can't stand for a *door* to slam because it might mean somebody is mad at her."

"What did you tell her?" Rusty said, taking a seat at the edge of the bed.

She sat down beside him. "I told her you were doing just great. I told her what a good piano player you are and what a fine time we had at your birthday party."

For just a moment, so fast you wouldn't have noticed if you weren't paying close attention, he gave her a pleased look, one that betrayed an innocence so touching her throat tightened. Then he glanced away, his features retreating into an expression of ragged world-weariness. He looked so pathetic sitting there, wounded and lonesome in his too-tight jury-rigged pajamas, not to mention the dirty sanitary napkin taped to his head. She put her arm around his shoulders and gave him a squeeze.

Slowly he let his head come to rest against her shoulder and snugged his arm around her middle to return the embrace. With her fingers she arranged his damp hair, smelled the residue of Ivory soap and kerosene still on him, and then she felt him shift a little, press his arm around her a little more tightly, and slowly roll his hips to press himself into her thigh.

"Okay," she said, "enough of that." But he didn't move; he had locked himself onto her like a ravenous tick. She could feel his hot breath on her collarbone and his arm had moved up so that it rested just below her breasts and she couldn't be sure, but it felt like, yes, definitely, he was grinding his groin against her hip.

"Hey!" she said. "Stop that. Come on." But still he held on until she levered her forearm between them and pried him loose. He released all at once and fell back onto the bed. He sat up quickly, turning his face away from her, shoulders hunched.

In a small voice he said, "I know you don't like me."

"Oh Rusty, you know I like you plenty. But you can't——" And here she fell speechless, unable to articulate in that moment, to this child, the difference between appropriate affection and forbidden, irrational desire. She wondered if she was to blame for this, wondered if in her own desperation—a desperation that was not altogether different from his—she had given him the idea that something like this might be what she wanted.

"It's okay," he said, shaking his head. Then he looked up at her, his face touched again with the flicker of innocence she'd seen a few minutes before. "I don't care if you don't like me." He shrugged, shook his head again. "I'm used to it. But I know who likes you."

"What?" she said. "Who likes *me*?"

"Yeah," Rusty said. "June. He likes you and he's, like, your age and everything."

"I know that, Rusty, but—"

"He thinks about you all the time. At night, when nobody else is around, he wishes he could be with you. He's in love with you. He thinks you're a fox."

Now she truly was speechless; she opened her mouth but nothing came out. She took a moment, made another try: "He told you this?"

"No," Rusty said. "I just know. People know things. Like I know that you like him, too."

"Now wait. I've had him over to fix a few things—at the house— you know that, but there's nothing else."

She added, "That's all there is to it."

"Don't worry," Rusty said. "I won't tell anybody. You don't have to worry."

And with that he crawled under the covers, laid down his bandaged head on the clean pillow and closed his eyes.

"There's nothing else," Trish said, but Rusty only pulled the blanket up to his chin and sighed. He began to snore in an odd, snuffling way that made her wonder if he was faking. Trish leaned forward, finally, and shut off the lamp; though it was barely after suppertime the boy looked like he needed his sleep.

She moved to the bedroom door, pausing to check on him one last time. His eyes were open now, watching her, and in the dull light from the hallway she could see in his chubby jowls and puffy lips the features of her own son, Jack, and she felt her heart catch and squeeze. She went to him, sat beside him on the bed, and when she gathered him into her arms there was nothing wrong or awkward in the way they grabbed each other and held on.

"I do like you, you know," she whispered. "You're not *nearly* as bad as everyone says."

She felt him soften, some rigidness leaving him, and when she let go of him he fell easily into his pillow. She arranged the covers on top of him, and by the time she closed the door behind her he was already asleep.

A NOTE IN THE DOOR

It was eight o'clock by the time she got away, exhausted and glad, for the first time in a long time, to be alone. Amazingly, Faye had asked to spend the night at Big House with all the others. When Trish had left her there with Nola to go to confront Golden, Faye had apparently struck up some kind of alliance or friendship with Fig Newton. When Nola reported this upon Trish's return, Trish dismissed it as wishful thinking, said she'd believe it when she saw it with her own eyes. Tonight, she had: the two girls sharing looks across the room, Faye at her spot on the divan being coy and unapproachable until Fig Newton drew her into a game involving secret messages written on folded gum wrappers and tossed across the room, and then they were following each other around the house, hatching plots and whispering in each other's ears and laughing behind their hands like best friends or, better yet, sisters.

In her warm little car with the radio playing, Trish thought she was happy to be alone until she pulled up into her driveway and was faced with the sight of the duplex, so starkly empty, the lawn so weedy, the windows so black. She was already mulling the idea of returning to Big House armed with a cheery excuse (sorry, forgot my jacket!), ready to lose herself again in the din, to witness her only child coming out of her very thick shell, to have the opportunity to tuck in two dozen bathed and sweet-smelling children, one by one— when something caught her eye. A white envelope tucked inside the screen door.

Dear Trish,

    Now that I've put new brackets on the gutters at the back of the house, I don't think there's anything left to fix, which is a shame, because now I don't really have a good excuse to stop by anymore. I've enjoyed getting to know you and Faye (not to mention the ever-present Lance/Rusty). It's been a long time since I felt so welcome, so comfortable around anybody. I know that you're married, and it's probably not a good idea for me to be stopping by anymore, but if you ever need anything, if something breaks or goes bad, please let me know and I'd be happy to pay a visit. Or, if you'd ever like to discuss romance novels or watch something burn to the ground, I'm your man! You and I may have more in common than you realize. But I'll leave it up to you. I'd love to have you stop by my place sometime (see below), but if not, thank you for the good meals and good conversation. Knowing you, even for such a little while, has brightened my life.

Yours,
June

Though the note had obviously been composed to affect a casual tone, each individual stroke of each individual letter seemed to have been designed with a jeweler's precision. The paper was heavy bond, creamy and thick, and every word, letter and line lay exactly equidistant from the one adjoining, as though the whole thing had been produced according to strict industrial standards, using protractors and slide rules. On the bottom half of the page was a map that depicted the route from her house to his, with to-scale buildings, roads and landmarks, along with comprehensive directions, penned in perfect miniature script, at every juncture or bend in the road.

The gentle sincerity of the words, the care with which they had been put on the page—the *hope* in them—constricted her chest with a sudden ache. She read the note twice more, folded the thick paper, and, feeling not a little self-consciously like a love-crossed heroine in a romance novel, touched it to her cheek.

32.

· · · · ·

JEALOUS IS THE RAGE OF MAN

THE CALL CAME JUST BEFORE BEDTIME. HE TOOK IT ON THE KITCHEN phone and, because he had some idea about who it might be, he wrapped the long cord around his forearm several times with the grim determination of someone about to rappel into a deep gorge, stepped into the walk-in pantry, and shut the door behind him.

"You read the Bible, Brother Richards?" Ted Leo said.

"Hello?" Golden said. "Who is this?"

"Please, this act you're putting on won't get you nowhere. Now I asked you a question. You ever read the Bible?"

Golden swallowed, said, "Parts."

"Parts? Well, that's nice. Parts. Maybe that explains something. Maybe you just haven't read the right *parts*, that's why you've gone and fucked up so bad. Me, I've been spending a little time with the Good Book here, trying to get my head straight. You know what parts I've been reading?"

"I wouldn't have any idea—"

"How 'bout I recite a couple of these parts for you?"

"Mr. Leo—"

Ted Leo cleared his throat. "Here's a part: Proverbs six twenty-nine. '*So he that goeth in to his neighbour's wife; whosoever touches her shall not be innocent.*' We can probably assume that's one of the parts you missed along the way, right? And you probably skipped the one comes just after, '*But whoso committeth adultery with a woman lacketh*

understanding; he that doeth it destroyeth his own soul. A wound and dis-
honour shall he get; and his reproach shall not be wiped away. For jealous
is the rage of a man: therefore he will not spare in the day of vengeance.'"
Breathing heavily through his nose, Ted Leo hummed a little tune of
outrage. "Which means, Brother Richards, that you are in for a world
of very bad things."

In the darkness of the pantry, Golden searched the dimly glinting
rows of canned peaches and bottled beets for some excuse or threat or
apology to make this go away. He considered the irony of having a
brothel owner reading biblical passages in condemnation of adultery,
but decided it wouldn't be in his interest to comment.

"You still there? I hope so, because this is something you'll want
to hear. This morning I was all ready to leave the vengeance part up
to the Almighty, turn the other cheek, like the Bible says. I let you go.
I let you deal with your own soul. But now my wife has disappeared,
along with money from my safe, and a reasonable person can only
come to the conclusion that you are responsible. Stealing, Brother
Richards. Apparently, that's another part of God's word you need to
catch up on."

"I haven't stolen anything, Mr. Leo," Golden said, his throat so
tight he had to force the words out. "I'm sorry that I was . . . *inappro-*
priate with your wife, but there was no adultery and no stealing. No
stealing and no adultery, that's for certain."

"You miss the parts about lying too, Mr. Richards? You ever *heard*
of the Ten Commandments? I'm starting to think you haven't read
the book at all, that's what I'm beginning to think."

"Please, just tell me what you want me to do."

"Well, that couldn't be more simple. I want you to return what's
mine, and I want you to do it in person, so you can apologize to me
face to face, for real this time. By four o'clock tomorrow afternoon. If
that doesn't happen, let's just say you'll be sorry."

"I don't have anything to return to you, Mr. Leo, I don't know
anything, I don't have anything."

"And when you come," Ted Leo said, as if Golden hadn't spoken, "bring your Bible along, maybe we'll sit down and underline some passages together."

BACK INTO THE WATER

Earlier that afternoon, when Huila had stepped out of the Airstream and tried to hug him, did he return her embrace with a lover's passion and whisper into her ear that he was so happy to see her, that he would protect her, that everything would be all right? Not hardly. When she put out her arms, ready to collapse into him, he took a step back and said, "I have fleas."

This confused her, of course, but there was no time to explain. They were shielded from view of Old House, but he could already hear the *whap* of the screen door and the voices of children come out to meet him. He hustled her back into the Airstream and jumped back into his pickup. Alvin was on the porch holding up a home-made contraption made of paper and sticks that might have been a kite, and the First Twins were already running across the lawn to ask for money or lodge a complaint. He cranked the ignition, threw the transmission into reverse, and gunned the engine. "Forgot something!" he called, the pickup and the rattling trailer hurtling backward through a cloud of dust. "Be right back!"

At considerable speed he drove east along Sand Creek Road until he realized he didn't know where he was going. He pulled off next to the river and killed the engine. He got out of the pickup and at a safe distance regarded the Airstream warily. Nothing moved or shifted or made a noise. Had he just hallucinated Huila coming out of the trailer? In his depleted state, it wasn't something he could rule out entirely. He waited for a few seconds, took a breath, yanked open the door.

There she was, sitting on the floor, her arms clasped around her knees, head down. She did not look up for a moment, and when she did he could see that her face was pale, her eyes bloodshot and wet.

She shook her head. "I'm sorry," she said. "I don't know what to do!"

"No," he said. "It's okay." He climbed into the trailer and sat on the floor in front of her. He put his hand out and she took it. He said, "Did he hurt you?"

She shook her head. When she was angry or excited, her English quickly went south and she tended to make up the difference with hand gestures and sound effects. "No. But he break everything. Window! Television! *Kish! Bwkish!* Crazy. Shouting,"—here she threw her arms around her head, miming a wild throwing motion and general craziness—"breaking, throwing everything, *loco, loco.*"

Golden nodded. "He is definitely not real happy."

She looked up at him. "He hurt *you?*"

"No," Golden said, but his hand immediately went to the twin knots at the back of his head. "A little."

"I'm sorry," she said plaintively, "I'm sorry." She took his hand and pressed it to her lips.

He said, "He didn't kill me, that's a plus."

She laughed and scooted closer to him, kissed his wrist and forearm, pulled herself even closer, swinging her legs over his so that she was straddling his waist. She shivered and put her cheek against his chest. He didn't bother to mention the fleas again—at this point they didn't seem all that relevant, even though it felt like they had successfully established an outpost in one of his armpits and were making a meal out of the tender flesh around his belly button. He put his nose into Huila's hair and inhaled deeply.

He said, "What are we going to do?"

She pushed back from his chest and leaned back so she could look him fully in the face. "Maybe . . ." she said, her eyes growing wide, "maybe we go away. We have a car. We have a house"—she gestured grandly at their present accommodations—"and I have money." Here she patted the leather bag at her hip. "Everything we need. No more bad things. We go away to be happy."

During all the time they had spent talking about their lives, about their respective sadnesses and frustrations and their desire for escape, this was a subject they had never quite breached—the question of running away together. For most affairs, this eventually becomes the most fundamental of questions, the only one that matters: *Do we love each other more than the lives we already have?* It is the question that hovers in the background of every secret phone call, flavors every tryst with the heady possibilities of apocalypse and renewal; and it is the answer to that question, or the lack thereof, that so often dooms an affair to failure. But Golden and Huila had been taking their sweet time working up to it, just as they had in every other aspect of their relationship; it is a generally accepted rule of modern affair-making that you must have sex once or twice before addressing the question of whether or not you will run away together. But now the process had been speeded up for them considerably, and Golden, less than two hours after acknowledging to himself and to his God the errors of his way, after rededicating himself to his family and his way of life, and after offering his deepest, most humble gratitude to the Almighty for rescuing him from the belly of the whale, was seriously considering wading right back into the water.

Maybe, he thought, they should have sex right here, right now, and then they could move on without delay to the question of running away together.

She looked up at him, waiting, smiling, hoping. Even with her bloodshot eyes, her lower lip swollen and a little raw from nervous biting, he found her beautiful. How could he say no to her?

He paused. He said, "I think it's something we should probably think about."

The smile didn't leave her face, but some of the hope did. She looked around. "Think? How much time do we have to think? Where are we going to think? Right here?"

A flea launched itself from the tip of his ear—*ping!*—and landed on the sleeve of her dress; luckily, she was too focused on him to notice. He reached out as if to place an affectionate hand on her shoulder and flicked it away with his finger. "No, I have an idea. I think I know where you can stay."

And so, with her tucked safely in the Airstream, he drove her the ten miles to Mexican Town.

THE TODD FREEBONE EPISODE

The following day he went about his business as if nothing were out of the ordinary. He checked in at the office, looked over some bid possibilities, had lunch with Nola, drove to St. George to visit Rose, who had very little to say to him except that she was feeling better and would be home soon. She did look a little better than last week, but not by much: her hair needed washing, the skin of her face and hands had gone strangely translucent, her eyes clouded with a wet fog. And this horrible place they had her in, with its damp cinder-block walls and strange odors and its corridors full of people who could have moonlighted as extras in a zombie film. It was no consolation to her or anybody else that this was the best he could afford.

Just before he left he told her, for some reason, that he loved her. He didn't know why he said it; it was something he had learned, from painful experience, never to voice out loud to any of the wives; as with everything else, they remembered, they compared, they kept score.

"Rose," he had said, getting up to leave, "you know I love you." And she had looked up at him and burst into tears.

When four o'clock came he was back at Old House, pretending to fix the sash on one of the upstairs windows. He was caught in a state of suspended animation, scraping the hard paint of the sash over and over until he was digging into bare wood, paying no attention to what he was doing, and it took so long in coming he wondered if he'd missed it, and then there it was: four chimes ringing throughout the house. He imagined Ted Leo at the PussyCat behind his desk or at the bar, himself watching the clock, getting angrier and angrier, thinking of all kinds of ways he was going to make Golden Richards sorry.

Yesterday, when he left Huila with Nestor, he'd told her he would come up with a plan, he would figure something out; he needed time to think, then he would know what to do. But he quickly realized there was little thinking to be done, and nothing for him to do. He could not take Huila back to Ted Leo; she was an adult who could come and go as she pleased. And running away—it was a wonderful thought in the abstract but the reality of it was that he did not think he had the will or the courage for it. What else was there? Telling the cops? Explaining everything to Beverly and begging for her protection? No, as far as he could figure there was nothing left to do but see what Ted Leo had in store for him.

So that's what he did the rest of the day: worry. He worried cleaning out the wood stove and going over the budget with Beverly after dinner and watching Helaman run the mile relay at a district tournament in Hurricane. Often, his worry seemed to have no content or substance; he idly scratched his flea bites and stared into the middle distance, his head full of choppy static, until somebody or something commanded his immediate attention. When menacing thoughts did intrude, he would banish them by taking up his habitual chant—*EmNephi HelamanNaomiJosephinePaulineNovellaParley GaleSybilDeeanneAlvinRustyCliftonHerschelGloryMartinBooWayne TeagueFayeLouiseFigNew-tonDarlingSariahJame-oFerrisPet*—until he could get through the list without making a mistake.

That night, he lay in Beverly's bed and did his best not to toss or roll over, which would set the old bedsprings to ringing. Beverly, of course, knew something was up, but she had never been the kind to jump in and start asking questions; she watched, she waited, she gathered her evidence, and when the time was right, she pounced. It seemed like hours until her breathing evened out and he was able to, with agonizing care and a cramp in his hamstring, roll off the bed and creep out of the room with all the stealth a man of his size could muster. In his red plaid pajamas and flopping work boots, he took a look outside, checked the locks on every door and drove out to Trish's duplex and then over to Big House, where he scanned the landscape for anything out of the ordinary. It was a windy night, the trees full of new leaves rattling on their branches. Down the road in front of the Pettigrews' sat an old blue Dodge he'd never seen before, but as he passed he could see it was a couple, maybe high schoolers, making out energetically in the front seat. He had told Nola to be sure to lock the place up tight, had made up some story about a rash of burglaries in the valley, but he found the front door unlocked and most of the windows open.

After securing the house, he sat in the lounge chair in the front room and gave in to another hour of stupefied worrying until sleep, which he'd seen precious little of in the past three days, pressed down on the top of his head like a huge, benevolent hand. He slept for four hours, his heavy chin pressing a divot into the flesh of his chest. The house woke, the kids readying themselves for school, Nola banging pans in the kitchen, a prolonged skirmish breaking out over what kind of sandwiches were going into today's bag lunches, and Golden did not wake. This was not out of the ordinary; the father of the house was known for prowling around at night and landing in armchairs or love seats or behind the wheel of his idling pickup, dead to the world. The phone rang, the kids tromped past him on their way to catch the bus, sometimes slamming the door behind them, and still he did not stir. Only when the house went completely quiet, a tensed hush that found its way into his dreams, did he startle himself awake, grabbing at the arms of the chair and saying, "Not the fingernails!"

He looked around in a panic before he remembered where he was. He listened, heard nothing. He slumped back into the chair and closed his eyes. Now he could hear something: water running through the pipes upstairs. Probably Nola, known to take epic showers that drained the water heaters and could last the better part of an afternoon. Underneath that sound he heard muffled, barely audible voices, the voice of a child and the voice, if he was not mistaken, of a man.

He felt a chill, like ice water trickling down the back of his neck. He got up and looked out the window. There, in the middle of the front lawn, not thirty feet away, sat the Barge. The Barge was facing away from the house, toward the road, but from this vantage point he could see there were two people sitting on it. A man with a tangle of bleached hair, and three-year-old Pet, whose spiky blond pigtails were all Golden could see of her over the back of the couch. He had to pause a moment to wonder if he was still asleep and dreaming, and then came to the oddly reasonable conclusion that it didn't matter. He took a breath and did not let it out again until he was standing in front of the Barge, staring at the strange man sitting on the couch with his daughter.

They were both licking lollipops, the kind of enormous, flapjack-sized multicolored lollipops found only in specialty candy stores and Shirley Temple movies.

"Daddy!" cried a deliriously happy Pet. She stared at her lollipop in wonder, and then back up at Golden, waiting for his take on this amazing turn of events. He snatched her up in his arms and took two steps back. The man smiled amiably and held up his own lollipop in salute. "Todd Freebone," he said. "At your service."

"What are you doing?" Golden breathed.

"Just sitting here, man. Enjoying the sunshine with this nice little girl. Right, little girl?"

Golden turned his whole body so this long-haired creep couldn't even *look* at his daughter. "I want you to tell me who you are."

"Didn't I already tell you that?" Todd Freebone looked confused for a moment. "Name's Todd Freebone." He held out his hand for a shake and Golden took another step back. Todd Freebone did not appear in the least offended by this rebuke. He took his time lighting a cigarette with an old brass Zippo.

Now that he was getting a good look at the man, Golden thought he recognized him as one of Ted Leo's lackeys who worked in various capacities around the PussyCat Manor. He wore a necklace of tiny white shells and a threadbare T-shirt with a multicolored sunset silk-screened on its front, and looked more like a surfer gone to seed than the usual overweight goombah Ted Leo tended to employ.

Todd Freebone said, "Mr. Ted Leo asked me to return your property to you." He patted the Barge, producing a small burst of dust. "And so"—he coughed, waving his hand—"I think you know where we're at here. You've got your couch, and Mr. Leo wants what's his. An exchange, that's what we should call this."

"I don't have anything," Golden said.

"Then you know where to find it," Todd said.

"No," Golden said. "I don't know anything."

"Well, fuck," Todd said, looking genuinely disappointed. He considered his lollipop, licked it, grimaced, then took a drag off his cigarette. "That's really too bad. I was hoping I could go home today and never have to see this hillbilly backwater again. Seriously, man. I didn't know there were still places like this left."

Golden looked around. It seemed the Barge, with Todd Freebone on board, had fallen out of the big blue desert sky; except for Golden's work truck and Nola's Country Squire station wagon, there were no other vehicles in sight. Golden turned in place, scanning the surrounding geography, until he spotted the back end of a blue pickup parked behind a clump of willows on the little two-track that followed the fence along the Pettigrews' alfalfa field.

"You stay right here," Golden told Todd. "You go anywhere near my house, I'm calling the cops."

Todd threw up his hands. "Oh shit, the cops! Please, man, take your time. I'll wait right here."

Golden started to set Pet down but had second thoughts and hefted her up onto his shoulder like a sack of corn. He crossed the expanse of grass and weeds, stepped over the old, leaning crosswire fence, and came up behind the pickup. Nelson sat behind the wheel staring straight ahead, looking sheepish. Even when Golden stuck his head in the driver's-side window and asked what was going on, Nelson would not look over.

"I ain't involved with this shit," he said. "I'm just the driver."

"You're not involved? You drove my couch all the way out here, put it out on my lawn, for some reason, and set loose this creep on my children?"

"Hey," Nelson said, turning to Golden. "I do what I'm told. Ted Leo sends his messages, you know, and now there's a couch on your lawn. This guy, this is how he takes care of his part of things, I guess. You think I'm enjoying myself? And that was one *heavy* motherfucking couch, if you want to know."

Golden positioned Pet in the open window, so Nelson could get a good look at her. Cute as a bug's ear, she was going at her lollipop with such gusto it appeared she was licking it with her entire face. "How would you like it if you came out of your house one morning and found some creep talking up that sweet little daughter of yours?"

"Wouldn't." Nelson gave Pet a shy smile and then turned his gaze quickly back to the windshield. "But then I wouldn't go running off with the boss man's wife, neither."

Even though he knew it would do no good, Golden swore to Nelson on his life that he didn't run off with Huila, that he had no idea where she was, that this was all an unfortunate misunderstanding.

Nelson shrugged. "Don't matter to me. But I was you, I'd tell Ted Leo what he wants to know. Then we can all be done with this. I don't need this any more'n you."

Just then came the *whap* of the front screen door, a sound that nearly stopped Golden's heart. He quickly ascertained that Todd Freebone was still safely on the Barge where he'd left him, and had to peer through a willow thicket to see who'd come out on the porch. It was Ferris, decked out in one of his customary outfits: sweater, jacket, ski hat, nothing below the waist. Staring intently at the huge anomaly on the lawn, he subtly rolled his naked hips counterclockwise as if test-

ing the air. Todd had turned around and was now waving his giant
lollipop in Ferris' direction and saying something Golden couldn't
hear.

Golden reached into the back of Nelson's pickup, grabbed the first
thing at hand—a rusted tire iron—and took off at a lope. Once he
climbed over the fence he put Pet down and sent her running for the
house. When Todd turned to see the giant man in pajamas bearing
down on him armed with some kind of rusty implement, he stood up,
the casual smile draining slowly from his face.

"Oh shit!" he chirped. He started in the direction of the house,
thought better of it, did a little juke, and, already grinning again,
headed down the driveway. He tossed the lollipop over his shoulder, either in an attempt to create a diversion or to lighten his load.
Golden, a reluctant sprinter in the first place and already getting
winded, pursued Todd down the gravel drive but was losing ground
by the step. Letting out a low, Cro-Magnon groan he heaved the tire
iron at Todd's retreating form, missing by a good thirty feet, the iron
gouging a divot into the hard-packed sand.

"Whoa-ho!" cried Todd.

"And don't ever come back here!" Golden shouted.

"Calm down, man!" Todd called from a safe spot on the other side
of the county road. "Violence ain't the answer!"

Golden bent down as if to pick up a rock, which sent Todd back-
pedaling into a thicket of wild rosebushes. Seizing the moment, Ferris dashed in front of Golden and snatched up the discarded lollipop
from the gravelly area at the edge of the lawn.

"Hey!" Golden shouted, but Ferris was already headed back to the
house, his pale little bottom flashing like a silver coin in the sun. In
the heat of the moment, Golden had not considered what might happen if one or, even worse, *two* of the kids entered the house in possession of an industrial-sized lollipop. And there it was: the shouting
and screaming had already started.

Stationed at the end of the driveway near the mailbox, Golden
stood watch while Nelson picked up Todd. As they drove past, Todd

grinned widely from the passenger-side window, and held up a nickel-plated pistol against his chest in a way that said, *Let this be our little secret.*

"Bye-bye, man!" he called as they pulled away. "By the way, *love* your jammies!"

LIES UPON LIES

He had spent a good portion of the last two days telling lies: lies about why the job in Nevada had ended early and suddenly; lies about the scratches and contusions on his hands and forehead; lies about why the Barge had suddenly appeared on the Big House lawn; lies about why the strange man who appeared with it had been handing out candy to the children before being summarily chased off the property. During his years in the church Golden had noticed that most of the polygamists he had come to know were honest, upright men. He had always believed this was because they lived according to their convictions, but now he was starting to suspect it was something else entirely: being a dishonest polygamist was an exceptionally difficult trick to pull off. If you told a lie to one wife, you were going to have to repeat it to all of them. And they all asked questions, of course, each of which had to be answered consistently and with the correct details in the correct order because you could be darn sure that afterward, like a bunch of dogged television police detectives investigating a capital murder case, they would get together and compare notes. It didn't take long to come to the conclusion that telling the truth—painful and inconvenient as it might be—was the only sensible option.

Which made Golden wonder: How had he managed to last this long? After all the lies of the past few days (not to mention the last year), he was now forced to tie them all together with one last (he hoped, he hoped) big one, which went something like this: Golden had not received the full sum he had been promised at this stage of the project and had threatened to shut down all work until he received payment, which ended up getting him fired. The Barge and the creep with the candy were nothing more than an attempt to threaten and intimidate him.

"These Nevada guys," Golden had already said more than once, chuckling with false humor, "they all think they're in the Mafia or something."

"Why are they threatening you?" Nola had asked. "Aren't you the one who hasn't been paid? Aren't you the one who should be threatening *them*?"

And so Golden had to, on the spot, create a new subplot to this story, one more lie, about how the man who'd hired him was worrying about getting sued, so he had lowered himself to threatening Golden and his family. This part of the story did not seem as likely, but there was no going back now—he would have to stick with it to the end.

"You going to call the police?" Nola said.

"Already have!" Golden lied, now with a certain doomed enthusiasm. "Going into town today to talk to Sheriff Fontana about this."

It was the fleas, of all things, that had saved him—temporarily, at least. When Beverly and Nola had discovered the little pests setting up shop in their beds and making meals of several of the children, he and his increasingly desperate explanations became, for the moment, an afterthought; he ducked out and drove to Mexican Town. When he pulled up onto the dead front lawn of the Old Lady, Nestor came out to greet him. Instead of hailing him with arms wide open and a loud *Jefe!* he curtly motioned for Golden to drive around back and park next to the old bread delivery truck that was occasionally pressed into service as a tour bus.

At this point Nestor gave Golden the customary, though somewhat subdued, embrace. Holding him by the arms, he said, "You look worse than before, Jefe, if such a thing is possible. Come in, I will make you some tea."

Putting a pot on the stove to boil, he explained that Huila was in one of the upstairs rooms sleeping, that she wasn't feeling well.

"She's been through a lot," Golden said, staring blankly at his hands on the vinyl tablecloth. It was hard not to come to the conclusion that everything she was now going through was his fault and his alone.

Nestor went to the front room, moved aside a dusty drape to peek outside. "Somebody follow you here?"

"I don't think so," Golden said. "I didn't really look for that."

"Next time, you look," Nestor said. "We have already had one *cabrón* coming around up here asking questions."

"I think I know the one you're talking about." Golden sighed. "He showed up at my place this morning giving my children candy."

Nestor sighed a commiseratory sigh. "I think somebody very much wants to find our little escaped *pajarito* upstairs." He gave Golden an appraising stare. "Honestly, Jefe, you look like shit. Combing your hair, sometimes it can make a man feel better."

"Have you talked to her?" Golden said.

"We talked much of the night. I helped her call home to *Wah-teh-mala*, to talk to her boy. She has money, so we can arrange to bring the boy across. It will take time, but I have talked to some people already."

"Thank you, Nestor." Golden reached out to give him a squeeze on the shoulder. "You've done me a great favor."

Nestor winced and pried Golden's fingers away. "A favor between friends is not a favor. But have you decided what to do? The husband, this guy sounds like a *buey*. She cannot hide forever."

"I don't know what to do, Nestor," Golden said, and it felt so good to admit this to someone that his voice cracked strangely. "Please tell me what to do."

"This is nice," Nestor said, taking a moment to sip his tea. Downstairs, a bass guitar began to play a polka beat. "A rich man, the man who owns the house where I live, a man with many wives and children, and he is asking Nestor the poor Mexican troubadour what to do. This is nice."

Golden waited; he wasn't interested in one of Nestor's offhand observations, he wanted answers—no, he wanted directions, detailed directions, direct orders. He wanted someone to explain to him exactly what to do and how, and in absence of that he would happily settle for some general advice. It would be reasonable to expect a man of Golden's age and circumstance to be experienced in resolving problems and refereeing disputes, but the truth was he was something of a naïf when it came to this sort of executive decision making. In his job, he almost always took the most convenient route, the option that offered the least complication, resistance and stress (a practice that had cost him vast amounts of money and time over the years) and in his family life, his wives, like corporate handlers or political advisors, jockeyed for position and battled it out among themselves, and when the time came he would be presented with a few limited options in a way that made it clear which option he was to choose. When it wasn't entirely clear to him which way the wind was blowing he had learned to stall, to withhold judgment until judgment, because it couldn't wait any longer, was made for him.

The most difficult decision he had made in his life was the one to take on the PussyCat Manor job. He had made it alone, with input from no one. And look where that had gotten him.

Golden let his head sink until his forehead rested on the cool table-cloth. He groaned.

"Come on, Jefe, I am only joking. You will find a solution, it's not so bad."

"You're always saying that, Nestor. This time, it's bad."

"I don't think so," Nestor said. "You love this lady, am I correct?"

Golden lifted his head and nodded.

"And she loves you?"

"Yes, I mean, I think so."

"Then you marry her, no? One more lady of the house, what's the difference? You tell the boss guy to suck his own *pinga*, she has found a new man in her life, someone to treat her like a woman should be treated. It won't be the first time this has ever happened, eh?"

Golden sighed. "It's not that simple. She doesn't even *know* I have more than one wife. She thinks I'm *normal*."

"Well"—Nestor laughed—"not no more."

"You *told* her?"

"How was I to know your secrets, Jefe? To me, four wives and too many children to count, that is something for boasting. I said something, you know, and she was confused, but I told her it's a common thing in this part of the world and not to worry about it too much. I think her worries are bigger than this anyway."

"But I lied to her," Golden said.

Nestor waved his hand. "Please. When it comes to love, everyone is a liar."

Golden sipped his tea and grimaced. This was why he liked Nestor so much; Nestor, who waved away sin and deceit as if they were nothing more than pesky houseflies.

"She wants to run away," Golden said quietly, as if he couldn't believe he was positing such a thing out loud. "She wants me to run away with her."

"Yes, that is the other option," Nestor said. "That is always an option for everyone, but not a good one. You disappear, you leave all your troubles behind, correct? I do not think it happens that way. I tell you from experience, I think it is better to try to keep all your troubles in one place."

After finishing his tea, which tasted like grass clippings boiled in water, Golden climbed the stairs to look in on Huila. In a warm upstairs bedroom she lay in the sunken center of a large, swaybacked bed, sleeping. The floor was littered with motorcycle magazines and engine parts, the bedposts wrapped in strings of glowing Christmas lights, and on the far table, displayed like a piece of industrial art, sat an unreasonably complicated bong, a contraption with so many levers and valves and curling glass tubes it was impossible to tell where the pot went in and the smoke came out. In the middle of this seamy still life was Huila, the essence of innocence, wrapped in an afghan, her dark hair like a frame around her face. Golden put a hand to her forehead, found it warm. In a bedside drawer he dug up a pencil and a notebook filled with scribbled lyrics. He tore a corner off one of the pages.

> *H,*
>
> *I came to see you. I shall be back soon. Don't worry. Nestor will take good care of you.*
>
> > *Besos,*
> >
> > *G*

He paused, wondering if *shall* was too formal and old-fashioned, but he decided to leave it, thinking this was a situation in which the old-fashioned, the formal, would be appropriate, and anyway, at this point there was nothing to lose. He folded the scrap of paper into a small, neat square and tucked it into her palm.

Downstairs he found Nestor backed into the corner of the kitchen next to the refrigerator, kissing a young woman and vigorously fondling her ample buttocks with both hands. When they disengaged at the sound of Golden's arrival, neither looked in the least bit sheepish.

"This is Juanita, she used to be my cousin's girlfriend," Nestor said by way of introduction. He took a bill from his wallet and handed it to her. "Some Marlboros and something for yourself. Thank you, my flower." With that, he gave her buttock one last squeeze and sent her on her way.

My flower. Golden liked that. He wished he had found a way to incorporate that into his note.

"So," Nestor said, wiping the lipstick from his mouth, "what were we conversing about?"

"Huila," Golden said. "I just went to check on her. I think she may have a bit of a fever."

"We have medicine of every kind," Nestor said. "But you, Jefe, I think you have some thinking to do."

Golden blew air out through his nose. "Yes, yes I do."

"But do not take too long. She cannot hide here forever. And I'm sorry, but I have to tell you that Friday we play the festival in Kingman. I don't think she should stay here alone. We will be back on Sunday, but maybe you can find another place for her? A motel, possibly. But be careful, if these *hijos de puta* are smart, and maybe they are, they will check the motels and they will be watching you, and if you are not careful they will follow you to her, you see?"

Golden nodded, rubbing his jaw. "I think I have an idea."

"Good, good." Nestor clapped his hands once, loudly, as if all were settled. "In the meantime we will protect her with our lives, like the knights of Camelot. Lardo is good with a switchblade and I have my chain saw."

Golden crossed the room, saying, "Thank you, Nestor, thank you for everything," and Nestor was backed into the corner he had occupied with Juanita, and taken in an awkward embrace. "Okay," he said, giving Golden a light pat on the hip, "yes, yes."

Golden straightened up, still holding Nestor by the shoulders. "Can I ask one more favor?"

"I am at your service," said Nestor.

"I was wondering," Golden said. "Do you have any more of that mescal?"

33.
· · · ·

THE BOY AT THE WINDOW

THE BOY WAITS AT THE WINDOW. HE HAS AWAKENED FROM A DREAM he can only dimly remember—the sensation of floating underwater and being nibbled at by a thousand tiny amphibian mouths—and has once again assumed his post on the radiator. After an hour's troubled sleep he is wide awake, eyes peeled, leg jiggling, his heart ratcheting inside his chest like an old-fashioned windup toy.

To pass the time, he is reading from one of his new favorite books, *Improvised Explosive and Incendiary Devices for the Guerrilla Fighter*. He holds the pages up so they catch the milky moonlight. He can read the words as clearly as if it were midafternoon.

Let guile and patience, the book says, *be your closest allies*.

Tonight is the first night in at least a week that he hasn't snuck out to haunt the empty roads on his younger brother's Big Wheel, hiding in roadside ditches when the odd car happens by, stopping off at darkened houses to creep through backyards and peer into windows and puzzle over the inventory of certain clotheslines, and finally pedaling madly onward to finish the mile-and-a-half trek to his house, the place of his true birthright and inheritance, to see if his mother has come home. It has become an obsession, this nightly checking, like the washing of hands or the inspecting of locks, a necessary chore that must be done before sleep can come.

He has decided his vigilance might be working against him, that ignoring the problem might be the best way to solve it. He half believes that in restraining himself from making his nightly rounds he is breaking an established pattern, altering certain cosmic inevitabilities, and thereby forcing a change that may just have him waking up tomorrow to find his mother restored to her rightful place, happy and improved.

He knows this is impossible and yet is still enough of a child to believe that it isn't.

One thing he knows for certain is that he must be careful. If he makes one mistake, and his night wanderings are discovered, he will be confined to this room every hour of the day except school and church and he knows he will not be able to stand it. Last night he was not being careful; he had parked his Big Wheel around back and entered Big House, sweaty and light-headed, thinking about his raw feet and smarting knees. He didn't notice the family dog falling in behind him as he crept up the stairs, and when the dog cut ahead of him, yipping and tossing his head in a way that meant he wanted to play, the boy was so surprised he jumped back and fell sideways against the wall with a thud. Above him two picture frames rattled and went silent. The boy waited. The dog stared at him and ran his tongue across his upper teeth. "Bad dog," the boy whispered to the dog with a mixture of annoyance and affection. "Bad, bad, ugly dog."

At the end of the hall a black form appeared. "Who is it?"

"The boogeyman," the boy said in his best Vincent Price boogeyman voice, "and I've come for your liver."

The shadow took a step back and shook its head. "You don't scare me one bit."

It was his little sister in her pink nightgown. The boy was now standing in front of his mother's bedroom doorway, peering into the darkness to confirm what he already knew: his mother was not there. He was joined by his little sister, six years old with a sugary crust of sleep around her eyes and bed-snaggled hair. When they were smaller, this particular sister had become attached to the boy, could not sleep at night unless he was next to her, singing "The Deep Blue Sea" in the quiet, husky way she liked. In a family such as this, the younger ones need a protector, an advocate, an ally, and she had chosen this boy. For a year or two she hovered near him the way a small, ice-bound moon attends a gaseous and unstable planet. The boy had mostly forgotten this; but not his sister. Though she was older now, feisty and independent (as children in such families can tend to become), she leaned in to him a little, let her arm touch his, to let him know she remembered.

Because the boy was the Bad Brother, a Weirdo, and reportedly a Pervert (which she took to mean a person who doesn't respect the privacy of others), and because she was now old enough to be conscious of her social standing both in the family and the world at large, she would never show him such affection in public, but here in this dark hallway there was no one to see.

"She's not coming back," said the sister.

"She will so," said the boy firmly. "But she won't if you keep saying things like that."

"I'm not going to tell on you for being here."

"You do, you'll live to regret it."

"Can I tell you something and you won't get mad?"

The boy shrugged.

"Maybe if you'd stop being such a jerk all the time you'd be happier and people would like you." With that she gave the dog a brisk head rub and retired to her bed.

Now, sitting on his radiator, the boy knows his sister is wrong; being nice, being a good person, doesn't make you any happier. Look at his mother. She is the nicest person he knows, and where is she now?

The guerrilla fighter should be ready and willing to suffer and, yes, die for his cause.

The boy likes this. He thinks about it and decides that if it's all the same he would rather not die for his cause, but suffering he can handle. Suffering he is used to.

The room is hot and the boy's skin itches. Right now his head wound is begging to be scratched with a special urgency, and after thirty seconds of excruciating self-denial, of pretending to read the book in his lap with grave interest like someone in a library, he digs savagely under the bandage, raking his fingers across the humped stitches until it hurts. Satisfied, he imagines the cool spring air outside, the slick grass under his feet, the hollow, granular sound of the Big Wheel tires on the chip-and-seal asphalt. Instead of going out on a reconnaissance mission or trying to stir something up like the guerrilla fighter he is, he waits and watches. There is tension in the house tonight, something charged in the atmosphere, and he's pretty sure it's not the ghosts who are rumored to live in the cellar or Jesus Christ the Eavesdropper who listens in on everyone's conversations and, like Santa Claus, knows who is sleeping and who is awake. It is something else, something dense that presses on the back of his neck. Something that makes his leg jiggle and his heart race.

For the first time tonight he notices movement outside. In his enclosure on the other side of the river the neighbors' ostrich, who usually dozes during the first half of the night so he can pace away the rest of it, is up hopping against his fence, thrusting his head out over the top wire. Then, on this side of the river, someone materializes out of the night-shadow of the house. The boy's father. On other nights he has seen his father get in his truck and drive off, sometimes in his pajamas, so this is nothing new. But this time he walks right past his pickup and down the driveway toward the road. Before he passes through the gate he stops, looks both ways, and then back toward the house.

He continues over the bridge, dragging his fingertips along the top of the guardrail, and then up the neighbors' driveway to their house. His father walks stiffly, with a slight limp the boy has never noticed before. The boy knows that the neighbors, boring old people who hate any children who aren't their grandkids, are spending the spring in Arizona. Two of the boy's sisters were specially chosen to water their plants and feed their mangy barn cats, and one of the neighbors' sons comes by every day to take care of the ostrich and the cows. But the boy's father, as far as the boy can tell, has no reason to be going over there, not in the middle of the night, not like this.

From where he is he can't see the front of the house, can't see his father enter. He wonders if he should climb out the hall window to investigate, to improve his vantage point, but he remembers: *Let guile and patience be your closest allies*. The silence of the room is of such density it is hard for him to breathe. He is not sure how much time passes, maybe three minutes, maybe an hour. No lights come on in the house, which the boy finds strange. He does not take his eyes from it, not once, until two figures walk out the back door. His father and a woman. A dark-skinned woman with long black hair.

The boy understands that this is why he has been waiting at the window so long, to see this. His father and the woman stand at the bottom of the steps and talk for a while. The image begins to blur and the boy doesn't understand what is happening until he realizes that his face is so close to the window his breath is fogging it up. He swipes away the condensation with his forearm and the image is clear again. The father looks back at his house, thinking he is blocked from view by the line of feed bins, but the boy can see him. From up here, the boy can see everything.

The boy can see the man and woman walking side by side, the backs of their hands touching. He can see the dim shapes of cows, their white faces like scraps of paper floating on dark water. He can see one of the barn cats creeping between the wheels of a tractor. He can see the black TV antenna jutting over the house and, in the far distance, the mountains still capped with snow. He can see the ostrich stamping its feet and straining against the fence as the humans pass by, and when they stop under the dwarf elm, its white blossoms vibrating in the breeze like agitated moths, he can see how they face each other. He can see the woman press her forehead into his father's chest. He can see the way he pulls her close.

34.

. . . . .

LETTERS MINGLE SOULS

SHE WOULD WRITE HIM A LETTER. NOT A *HI, HOW ARE YOU?* LETTER full of banal inquiries, but a letter of complaint, a cease-and-desist order, an argument, a shout, a baring of the soul in words, the kind of letter you could nail to a church door. Trish had returned from Nevada feeling strangely liberated, as if her talk with Golden had resolved something, as if she had asserted herself and was therefore in control of her own destiny and happiness, but that feeling hadn't lasted much longer than the drive home. Now the trip came to her as a distant and bitter memory, even though it had happened just a few days ago. And here she was again, alone, sitting at her kitchen table in her quiet little house feeling quietly desperate, as if she'd never taken a chance, as if she'd been here all her life.

This desperation, she was sure, had to do with the sudden spike of activity in the Richards family: Golden losing his job, the Barge appearing mysteriously on Big House's lawn, reportedly placed there by minions of his angry ex-boss for mysterious reasons, to make no mention of fleas and barn fires and birthday parties gone awry. There was something in the air, a sense of flux, or imminence, which left her feeling as she always felt at such times: that she was out of the mix, being left behind.

So: she was going to do something about it by . . . writing a letter. It was ridiculous, she knew. (*It can never hurt,* Uncle Chick always said, *to acknowledge your own foolishness*—which was one of the reasons she liked Uncle Chick so much.) What self-deluded saps letter-writers were, believing that by putting words on paper and sending them to the powers that be—the newspaper, the utility company, the local congressman—they were having an effect, making a difference. These kind of people, they were no different than she: helpless, irrelevant, and striving to feel less so.

Writing a letter, then, might or might not be better than sitting here in her profoundly sad nylon sweatpants and old cardigan, waiting while the world moved on without her, but it would give her something to do. She had gotten the idea this morning while visiting Rose at the hospital. She had come to enjoy those visits, not only because they filled a few hours, but because she had become fond of dumpy old Forest Glen; she was beginning to understand why Rose was in no hurry to leave the place. Sure, it smelled funny and was teeming with the deranged and suicidal, but its charms were undeniable: the I've-seen-it-all nurses in powder blue who approached cautiously and touched you with extreme care, the crisp white sheets on the beds, the murmuring televisions watching benevolently over every room, the tiny white paper cups full of pills floating by on trays, the staff asking each person they passed, residents and visitors alike, "How *are* you?" as if your feelings at that very moment were all that mattered in the universe.

She and Rose were sitting together in one of the visiting rooms watching *$10,000 Pyramid* with the sound off, clutching one another's hands for comfort like an elderly couple in a chaotic bus station, when some kind of therapy session started up in the room across the hall. A woman with a booming, mannish voice began talking to a group of patients about the transformative power of the written word. "The spoken word," she said, "is unreliable, let's face it, people! When you speak, you are speaking in the moment and prone to mistakes, and once the words come out of your mouth they are gone forever, or lodged in the memory of others, where they can be twisted or misconstrued. But the written word, it can be carefully fashioned, see, you can take your time with it, it *lasts*! Nobody is putting you on the spot.

You write something down, there is power in it exactly because you have taken the time and the effort to put it down."

With the easy solicitude of a first-grade teacher she asked the group what form of the written word they preferred. There was some mumbling Trish couldn't make out. Newspapers, somebody volunteered. Comic books. Suddenly there was shouting. Magazines! Novels! Crossword puzzles! Someone who may have been a joker hollered, "Movies with subtitles!"

"The question is," the woman said, "what are *you* going to write? You could write stories, you could write a poem, but honestly, who wants to read a poem?"

Everyone seemed to agree that nobody wanted to read a poem.

"That's what I thought," the woman said. "You could write in your diary, which is a perfectly good thing to do, but what about a letter? *More than kisses, letters mingle souls.* You know who said that? John Donne. You guessed it, a poet. Those kind of letters, the kind that mingle souls, those aren't the ones we're talking about today. We're talking about a less poetic kind of letter in which you clear the air or stake your claim or tell somebody off. So. Anybody here feel misunderstood or unappreciated or angry?"

I do, Trish thought, raising her hand just a little. *Me.*

"Maybe you need to clarify your life? Maybe you need to gain control over your emotions instead of giving them free rein in your mind and heart? Maybe you've got a bone to pick?"

Yes, yes and yes.

"Why not a letter, then. I bet there's somebody out there who needs to hear from you. Maybe it's somebody in your life right now, maybe it's a person you'll never see again. Who knows, it could be your old self, the self that got you in the mess you're in now. Maybe you need to write a letter to that whiskey bottle that's been on your mind all day. Maybe you need write a letter to your mean old father. I'm thinking maybe we all need to write a letter to our mean old fathers."

Trish, for the first time in a long time, thought of her mean old father. Who had not been mean at all, but patient and serene, almost saintly with his white beard and quivering hands. He was sixty-six years old when she was born, seventy-eight when he died, and in the time between he might have held her in his arms a few times or spoken to her in passing, but she had no recollection of any such thing.

What kind of letter would she write to him? It would probably be very short, something like:

> *Dear Dad,*
> *Remember me?*

A SIGN OF LIFE

So she got out her legal pad, her good pen and started writing.

> *Dear Golden,*
> *There are so many things I want to tell you, but I have never really known how.*

She slapped the pen onto the table and sighed. This was absolutely, without a doubt, the most idiotic idea she'd ever had. She tried another sentence, gave up immediately and tossed her pen across the room, hitting the ceramic cactus on the windowsill and knocking it onto the counter, where it broke into three pieces.

"Great," she said to herself, the broken cactus, the quiet house. "Look at us now."

She considered calling her mother, but she knew exactly what her mother would say. *Honey, I don't want to say I told you so, but damn it if I didn't. Do yourself a favor and get out while you still can.*

She thought she heard the faint, gravel-popping sound of a car pulling up out front. It was late and the house was so quiet she could hear the flipping numbers of the clock radio in the other room.

She went to the family room, stole a peek out the window. It was

Golden in his pickup, parked on the other side of the road, for some reason. He didn't get out, just sat there with the engine running and headlights off. She picked her way across the road in her bare feet, opened the passenger-side door, and got in.

"Hey there," he said, "I—"

"What are *you* doing *here?*" she said with piercing, antagonistic cheer. In the few days since he'd been back from Nevada—for good, apparently—there hadn't been time for the wives to get together to decide on Golden's new rotation schedule, so he was left to come and go at his leisure. Which bothered Trish only because his leisure did not seem to include her. Which, come to think of it, was one of the primary reasons she felt so compelled to write him the letter.

"Just checking up on things," he said. "Making sure everybody's safe."

"You look worried," she said, which was putting it mildly. He looked *distraught*, his features bunched in the middle of his face, his eyes tense with something very close to fright. He hadn't shaved in a few days and his silver whiskers glinted among the blond and red like flecks of mica in a bed of sand.

"Little bit," he said distractedly, staring out the window into the foggy dark. "Little bit . . . worried."

"You want to talk about it?"

He shrugged and shook his head; he *never* wanted to talk about it. And then he did something unexpected: he scooted toward her across the seat and with a meek sigh let his big head fall heavily into her lap. "I don't know," he mumbled into the fabric of her sweatpants. "I don't know what to do."

"Join the club, big guy."

"You know that hospital where Rose is? I think I need to check myself into that place."

"I'm already on the waiting list."

He released a deep, shuddering sigh and she could feel the heat of his breath on her legs.

She had already begun to stroke his hair and tell him everything would be all right when she remembered she was supposed to be so irate with him, so deeply and irretrievably vexed that she had resolved to take the drastic step of writing him a letter. She wanted to kick herself; she was so *easy*! *But what else is there to do*, she asked herself, *when your husband puts his head in your lap like a frightened child, except to stroke his hair and tell him everything will be all right?*

She might have carried on this argument with herself for quite some time if Golden had not begun to act even more strangely: he started to nuzzle her. While she'd been arguing with herself, her fingers had strayed from his hair down the collar of his shirt to the warm, fuzzy skin of his back, and in response he began to press his face into her inner thigh, then into her belly, and the next thing she knew that big head was slowly and erratically making its way up her torso, like a loosed balloon rising fitfully through the branches of a tree, grazing at her neck and chin as it went, and then, with a suddenness that made her mind go blank, he was kissing her on the mouth.

It had been so long since she'd been kissed, truly kissed, like she was being kissed now. She gave in to it, pressed herself against him, but something stopped her: there was a strange taste to his mouth, sweet and sharp, something she remembered from her high school days wrestling with boys in the cabs of pickups much like this one. She pulled away.

"Wait, wait," she said. "Have you been *drinking*?"

"What?" he said. "Drinking? Drinking what?"

"Alcohol," she said. "Booze. You taste like it. You smell like it."

He stared at her for a moment, his eyes wide and bloodshot. "I don't know. Maybe it's the mouthwash I've been using. Sorry if my mouth tastes bad."

He began to turn away but she wouldn't let him; she didn't care. She didn't care if he'd been drinking. She didn't care if he'd been shooting heroin. No, she didn't even care if he was distant and unavailable and possibly impotent. She cared only that he was with her, doing this, right now. She *was* easy, she realized. She required so very little, and when something good came her way, how glad she was! She grabbed him by the neck and pulled him toward her. Little by little she slid her body underneath his, grabbing the stick shift for leverage, and once she had one of her legs pressed between his she thought she felt something down *there*, a stirring, a sign of life and hope, and though it might only have been her imagination it gave her such a thrill she kissed him with a fierce, wet heat, squeezed him until he gasped, believing that it would be all right, all right for both of them, if she could just take him in the house with her and make love to him until he couldn't stand it anymore.

"The bedroom," she gasped. "No room in here. The bedroom will be better."

She led him stumbling into the house and deposited him on the bed. In a giddy panic she rushed into the hall to close Faye's bedroom door, made a detour into the bathroom for some deodorant—she hadn't showered in two days—and when she got back to the bedroom, panting and wild and nearly psychotic with hope, there was Golden, curled up in the middle of the bed, asleep. Though she'd left him alone for no more than thirty seconds he looked as if he'd been sleeping for hours: his mouth gone slack and his chest heaving with deep, even breaths.

"No!" she shouted, and clapped hard twice right over him as if he were a puppy about to soil a rug. "No, no!"

With a groan he fought to lift his head, eyes rolling and lips smacking, then relaxed, falling back into sleep with swift and enviable ease. She clapped her hands again, hard, just to feel the sting. For a moment she wished fervently that she owned a gun.

She went into the kitchen and retrieved the pen she had thrown earlier. She added a few sentences to the letter she had already started, slashing each word into the paper. Before she left, she propped the note between the sugar bowl and saltshaker so it could not be missed.

Dear Golden,
   There are so many things I want to tell you, but I have never
really known how. ONE OF THEM IS THAT YOU ARE
AN ASSHOLE! THE LITTLE GIRL SLEEPING IN THE
OTHER ROOM IS YOUR DAUGHTER, IN CASE YOU WERE
WONDERING. DON'T THINK ABOUT LEAVING UNTIL I
GET BACK.

T

P.S. this is bullSHIT!

PLYG KID

The directions, of course, were perfect. Even in the dark, in the fog,
she had made her way to June's place without a wrong turn or missed
landmark, as if he were sitting right next to her, pointing the way.
She had been expecting a small bachelor's house, maybe a single-wide
trailer, but not this: two Quonset huts, both lit from within, sitting
in the middle of a wonderland of sandstone buttes and pinnacles and
hoodoos turned eerie and animate in the slow churn of fog.

   She knocked on the door of the first. Under the bulb in a ceramic
socket that served as a porch light was hung a carefully hand-painted
sign in yellow and green: HOME SWEET HOME. The sight of which gave
her such a pang in her heart she had to pause to take a breath.

   When there was no answer she tried the next Quonset hut, flanked
on one side by an impressive display of rusted matériel: air tanks and
brush hogs and manual implements of every description, coils of
chain and wire and conduit stacked on wooden pallets and an old
yellow bulldozer napping under a blanket of khaki canvas. Coming
from inside the building was a rhythmic thumping and though she
gave the door a good knock she got no response. She peered through
the dusty window and could make out June sitting at a table next to
the back wall, operating what appeared to be an old-fashioned sewing
machine.

She opened the door, stuck her head in and called his name. He looked up, startled, and groped for his glasses on the table until he realized they were still strapped to his face. He stared uncomprehendingly for half a second, and when he broke into a wide, stunned grin she couldn't help but laugh.

"Just came to check up on you," she said with an air of mock authority. "Worried about you all alone out here in this nasty fog."

Now that he was standing she could see he was dressed in some kind of uniform, a charcoal waistcoat with brass buttons and blue-gray trousers piped in black satin. On his feet: bright green nylon running shoes. He seemed to realize what he was wearing the moment Trish did; he brought his hands up to his chest as if to cover himself, then sighed and let them fall back to his sides.

"This must look, uh, pretty weird," he said.

"I guess it depends whose side you're on."

"Confederate, of course. Because, you know, I'm a rebel."

"I'd say so, by the looks of those shoes."

He explained that collecting Civil War paraphernalia was one of his hobbies, and that because it was impossible to find shoes from the Civil War, he was attempting to make his own. He held up a flap of leather run through with heavy yellow thread. "Doesn't seem to be going too well, really, but, yeah, I hope that's a . . . a good enough explanation for why I'm out here at this time of night in a getup like this."

Which seemed to be an invitation for her to explain what she was doing here in the middle of the night in a getup such as hers; for the fifth time since leaving the house she berated herself for not having the presence of mind to change out of her sweatpants.

"I hope you don't mind me coming out here," she said. "I don't think I properly thanked you for all the nice things you've done, and I guess I felt like I needed to talk to somebody."

He shook his head. "I don't mind, not one bit." He waved the piece of leather in his hand. "Just out here making a mockery of history."

"For someone who doesn't know how to make shoes, you write very good directions," she said. "On a night like this I could have ended up in Canada."

He showed her around the shop, stuffed to the gills—very neatly, of course—with every sort of industrial tool, fabric, powder, and instrument imaginable. He pointed things out very generally, as if slightly embarrassed by the accumulated scale of it, and then showed her around his living quarters, quite homey, with plaid curtains and fruit in a bowl and a brown-and-white cowskin spread out in front of a cheerful little potbellied stove.

He tried to duck into his bedroom to remove the uniform and slip into something more comfortable but she asked him not to. "A man in uniform, you know," she said, and even though she wasn't entirely sure what she meant by this he blushed so hard you could see the glow through his beard. Once he'd recovered his composure he opened the front door and, like the officer and gentleman he was, showed her out.

"And last but not least there's the pièce de résistance," he said, in an accent that sounded vaguely German. "Or, you know, however you say it."

He helped her up a hill of sandstone scree that shifted and trickled under their feet, the fog now indistinguishable from the night itself. She had no idea where they might be going and could see almost nothing except the great mass of rock in front of them that looked like a giant hole scissored from the dark billowing fabric of the sky. Trish tripped and June turned to take her hand and pull her up.

"Should have brought a flashlight," he said. "Usually the light from the stars is enough out here."

She didn't let go of his hand until they were on solid ground. His fingers were so thin compared to Golden's, his skin papery and warm. He kicked around, searching for something, saying, *Just a second here, one second, where the heck is it*, and then the mechanical sound of a switch being flipped and light, in broad bolts and bands, shining out from *inside* the rock.

"Ha!" she said. "What is this?"

"It's the shelter I'm building," he said. "I thought maybe I mentioned it."

"You said a bomb shelter," she said. "I was thinking one of those concrete bunkers you put in your backyard, like everybody else around here has."

There were two arched entrances, both twelve feet high and one hundred feet apart from each other, each projecting a column of yellow, nearly opaque light deep into the fog. They stepped into the first chamber, skirting heaps of pulverized sandstone, while June explained in some detail the purposes each room would serve, his plans to drill two-hundred-foot boreholes from the top of the butte for ventilation, the challenges of wiring and plumbing, how the whole thing, once there were doors on it, would be a comfy sixty-eight degrees all year-round. But Trish was hardly listening. She was taken in by the negative shapes blasted and chiseled out of the rock, the ceiling vaulted and ribbed like a cathedral's. At the top, a lighter salmon color bled into a crimson painted with bands of ocher and brown near the floor. Even though it was a damp, cool night, the walls glowed with a sense of warmth and security. She put her hand on the stippled face of the stone and was surprised to find it cold.

"It's beautiful, June," she said, still looking up. "Calling it a shelter seems a bit modest, don't you think? Feels . . . safe in here, which I guess is the whole point."

"Well," he said, trying to hide a pleased smile and then, as if he just couldn't help himself, "it *will* withstand the fallout from a nuclear blast or direct strike by a five-ton ballistic missile."

"Which is good enough for me!" she chirped, sounding a little crazed, even to her own ears. He took her through a narrow unlit corridor and into the second chamber, this one more finished than the first, with all kinds of niches and shelves and cubbyholes hewn into one wall, as if he were planning to carve an entire kitchen, down to the sink and utensils, out of sheer stone. They sat on a bench June had cut into the far wall; Trish settled in and decided it was about as comfortable as one of the pews at church, which wasn't saying much.

"You said in your note that we may have more in common than we realize," Trish said. "I was wondering . . . I guess I was wondering what you meant by that."

"Ah, you know, just being a little mysterious, hoping you'd come out on a foggy night to ask me about it," he said.

"Took the bait, didn't I."

"No! No, really, it's wasn't bait. All I meant, yeah, is that I know a little about your . . . your lifestyle, you know, about the Principle. Because I've lived it."

Trish laughed. "You have?" She pretended to look around and wondered aloud: Where were all the wives? The screaming kids, the piles of dirty diapers and overdue utility bills?

"I grew up in it," he said. "In the Principle. Down in Short Creek, you know. Most of my family is still there."

"You're serious," she said, skeptically.

"I am," he said, seriously.

"Why didn't you say anything before?"

He shrugged, played with the brass buttons on his cuffs. "Never came up, I guess, just like you haven't told me anything about yourself, really. Anyway, I was nervous talking to you, you're the first woman I've had a regular conversation with in a long time. It was easier talking about swamp coolers."

So they talked. For two hours they sat on that hard shelf of rock and compared their personal stories of hardship and woe: he told her about being raised in Short Creek, the biggest polygamist community in the United States, and how at the age of seventeen he'd been exiled, torn from the bosom of his family for the crimes of listening to music and fraternizing with the opposite sex. She told him about the boxcar she'd grown up in, the nightly family dinners by the light of the hearth fire, her father's death, which put an abrupt end to the strange fairy tale of her first twelve years and landed her in Reno, Nevada. While Trish was in her senior year of high school June was doing construction work in Winslow, Arizona, getting drunk every night and living out of his car. While June was in Vietnam blowing up munitions dumps and collapsing Vietcong tunnels and smoking ungodly amounts of dope, Trish was losing her own little domestic war against depression and grief and her controlling ex-husband.

June turned out to be a champion listener; while she did most of the talking, backtracking and interrupting herself to make sure she shaded every nuance of biographical detail, he sat there in his uniform and old-timey spectacles, nodding encouragingly after every other sentence or so, which might have been a little excessive, but how Trish appreciated the effort.

"And would you look at us now," she said when she finally ran out of gas, feeling a strange, almost bitter elation at the symmetry of their stories, the way both seemed to have stalled in a kind of emptiness. "I'm right back where I started, living the plural life, and you're building the most beautiful bomb shelter in the world."

He smiled sadly. "Guess I couldn't think of anything better to do. Nowhere else to go. Pretty sad when you think about it."

"At least you have something to show for yourself, right? At least, when everything comes crashing down, you'll be safe."

"Nobody's safe," June said, his words echoing softly along the broken walls. "None of us are." He stared off into the darkness of the next chamber, a thick silence beginning to settle in around them, and Trish roused herself to ward it off.

"So! Okay then. I have just one question for you now. What music were you listening to?"

"Hmm?"

"The music you were listening to, that got you kicked out."

"You don't want to know."

"I do."

"You don't."

"Tell me now."

"Neil Sedaka."

She let go a laugh that turned into a cough. "Neil Sedaka? 'Breaking Up Is Hard to Do'? That guy?"

"'Breaking Up Is Hard to Do' is hardly his best work, I mean, really, but yeah, that guy. I found some old LPs and a turntable in my uncle's basement. I mean, I'd never even heard the *radio* before, and yeah, Neil Sedaka, I thought he was some kind of god among men, the way he sang. I listened to those records so many times sometimes the lyrics still come to me in my sleep. One of my uncle's wives reported me to the elders and a few months later I was seen talking to a girl who wasn't my sister. That was the last straw, I guess. With the boys, they're just looking for a reason to send you away; only the most obedient ones, the connected ones, get to stay—those elders, they aren't stupid, they know they have to thin out the competition a little, there can only be so many husbands with fifteen wives. Anyway, this girl, her name was Addie Barlow. I was caught giving her a little charm bracelet I'd made out of copper wire. I was seventeen, acting like a twelve-year-old. I didn't know she was going to be married to the prophet's brother. I didn't know anything about anything. The next day my father drove me to Cedar City, dropped me off with thirty dollars and a bag of clothes. I haven't seen him, my mother, any of my sisters or brothers since."

As he spoke, Trish could see in the hang of his jaw and the pleats at the corners of his eyes the deep hurt this had brought up in him. He took off his spectacles, which were fogged with condensation, and wiped them with what appeared to be, by the gray, tattered look of it, a genuine Civil War–era handkerchief. He said, "I was giving her a *charm bracelet.*"

"You haven't spoken to them?" she said. "Not a phone call?"

"Nothing. I don't know how many letters I've sent—they all come back unopened. I don't know if my mother's alive or dead. I've driven down there a few times but nobody answers the door, and then the sheriff always shows up to escort me to the town limits. As far as my own family is concerned I don't exist anymore."

What was there to say to that? What was there to say to any of it? *Letters mingle souls*, she thought. *But only when someone bothers to read them.* She considered, maybe for the first time, how lucky she was to be able to pick up the phone and call her mother whenever she needed some bad advice. She leaned her shoulder in to June's, waited until he leaned back. It was the best she could offer.

He rubbed his nose with the cuff of his sleeve. "The first time I saw Rusty, you know, I knew it right away, I thought: *Plyg kid*. Clear as day. The way he was dressed, all hand-me-downs and oddball haircut, how he just wanted somebody to notice him, to *look* at him. And I know he's going to end up like me, no family, lost, wondering who he's supposed to be with, what he's supposed to do."

She wanted to say no, it wasn't like that, that the church here wasn't like the Short Creek group or the one in Montana, they didn't just throw their children out. But there was truth in what he said: no matter how you looked at it, there was no place in this kind of life for boys like Rusty, boys who didn't know how to say and do the right things, boys who could not find their way beyond their boyhood urges and rages, boys who lived too much inside their own heads. This kind of life was for those with the conviction and discipline to obey without question, those who could make themselves believe that their suffering and uncertainty were for a reason yet to be fully revealed. And where, she wondered, did that leave her?

"Thanks for being nice to him," she said. "If anybody needs it, he does."

"I like him, even though he's kind of full of it. And besides, he introduced me to you."

She felt his weight shift against her, and she wondered if he was going to try to make some kind of move, to kiss her, to touch her, and she acknowledged to herself that she'd come here for that very reason, not only to talk, to be heard, but to be kissed and held by someone who merely had a little time and attention for her, who could find the reserves of will to stay awake in her presence. She turned into him, smelled the damp wool of his coat, the metal tang of his brass buttons, and she felt him stiffen and sit up. She looked up at his face and he was staring past her, into the foggy night. There was a sound, a drone she hadn't noticed before that suddenly turned into something much more high-pitched, and there was a squeal and a pop and everything went dark.

"Oh shit," June said. "The generator."

The darkness inside that mass of rock, with no visible light from the world outside, was heavy, primordial; it felt as if she were sinking into a vat of cold tar. Her heart seized and then kicked in hard, and though she instinctively clutched at June, she did not feel the romantic thrill of a movie theater gone dark. What she felt was terror, the sensation of tipping over a precipice, about to fall.

After a few sharp breaths, she managed to say, "Do you know what time it is?"

"Must be near midnight. Don't worry, it's just the belt, I can get it fixed right up."

"I need to go." She stood up, was overtaken by a swirl of vertigo, sat back down. "I'm worried about Faye. I need to go now."

With a calming word here and there, June helped her down the rock-littered slope, and though she could see nothing, not the sky, not a tree, not even the man whose hand she held in a bone-cracking and unladylike grip, he led her unerringly, without so much as a misstep or stubbed toe, to her Rabbit. She had to touch it with both hands, smell it, put her arms around it to make certain that it was, in fact, a car, and that it belonged to her.

She thanked him, and he told her he was sorry for the inconvenience of the broken generator, and even though her heart was still stuck in her throat and she was still sick with vertigo, she groped in the darkness for June and, with more than a little difficulty, found his mouth with hers. She hadn't really noticed his mouth before, partially hidden behind his beard as it was, but now she discovered that it was a little lopsided, his lips firm and full, and not at all unpleasant to kiss. There was something both numb and wild in her, and she might have dragged him into his HOME SWEET HOME and forced him to make love to her if they had not stumbled in their awkward embrace, their lips disengaging with a rather loud and unromantic *pop*. June gasped and Trish cried, "Okay then!" and jumped into her car, her heart a loosening fist, and drove home through the bright corridor of her headlights.

HER GOLDEN BOY

When she got home, Golden was sitting at the table, staring into space. He had a glass of water and the note she'd left him on the table in front of him. His hair was mashed against the side of his head and his eyes were so puffy and bloodshot they appeared bruised. He looked, if it was possible, even worse than when he'd shown up a few hours earlier.

She didn't speak or acknowledge him in any way. She went to check on Faye and when she came back to the kitchen he was out of his chair and putting on his jacket. He wouldn't look at her.

He said, finally, "You have every right to be mad at me."

"I was sure you were going to tell me you're sorry," she said. "Thanks for sparing me that, at least."

"I'm sor—" he began, and shook his head. "I can't stay, as much as I wish I could."

"Of course not," she said, with an emptiness in her voice that sounded alien—it was the voice of someone who no longer had the heart to make an effort. "You have so much to do."

He picked his way toward the door and opened it. Outside, a solid bank of fog had lifted halfway and stopped, like a faulty curtain in an elementary school play. He looked back at her, and over his shoulder and around his ribs she could see the brightness of stars. He paused there, her man, her Golden Boy, looking so sad and bewildered she could barely restrain herself from going to him.

"I love you," he said, and she realized, once he was gone, how much it sounded like a farewell.

35.

DOLL HOUSE

*I*n this house there is a smattering of just about everything: confusion, weariness, panic, exhilaration, doubt, and, of course, plain old gut-curdling fear. This house is, in fact, much too small to contain the Father or his wild, zigzag emotions, which he experiences in relentless succession and then in unprecedented and startling combinations that leave him hunched over and breathing hard, clutching the front of his shirt. For the last few days he has done his fatherly best to be strong, vigilant, and resourceful, to do the right thing by the Other Woman, to visit and comfort Mother #3, to assure Mother #4 he is not avoiding her, to convince wives #1 and #2 that the family will not end up broke because of the mismanagement of his latest project, to somehow assuage the Other Woman's irate husband, and, more than anything else, to keep his family safe. But it has become too much: the insomnia, the wracking worry, the paranoia that takes him by the throat and squeezes like a cold and steady hand. This unraveling he feels is a distinctly physical sensation, the cords and fibers that hold him together splitting under the pressure, occasionally breaking with a twang like the brittle strings on an old guitar.

And so he has made his final retreat. Look at him: crouching on a milk crate in this decrepit children's playhouse, scratching the flea bites in his armpit, and peering balefully out the small octagonal window, a jelly jar of homemade liquor tucked between his feet.

"Woe is me," the father says to himself, and for some reason finds this

*terrifically funny, but has only enough energy to squeeze out a small
laugh.*

*Of all his houses, this is the Father's favorite, the only one that can
truly be said to belong to him. Much like the children, the houses belong
in body and spirit to the wives; the father has no say in how they are managed or appointed, does not have in a single one a bed or a chair or an
out-of-the-way corner of his own. He wanders among the houses like a
vagrant or a ghost, easily forgotten and leaving no trace, his only companion a threadbare canvas overnight bag full of toiletries and a selection of
underwear.*

*For so long he has sensed that nothing in his life belongs to him, not
even his wives or his children, any of whom can be snatched away in an
instant, but this pathetic little shack, unfinished and being further dismantled by weather and pack rats and the vines of morning glory, is his
true inheritance, the only place in the world he can rightfully claim as his
own.*

*Outside, the day is overcast with the remnants of last night's fog, and
the river runs swift and silent, swollen over its banks with mountain
snowmelt and distant rains. From here he can see the neighbors' corrals,
the feed bins, the ever-present ostrich. To the north of the corrals, just
out of sight, is the neighbors' house, not three hundred yards from where
he sits. Which is not relevant in any way except for the fact that tonight
sometime the Other Woman will be delivered to that very house, where
she will stay for three days and nights.*

*The thought of this, and the possibilities it creates in his mind, both
terrifying and alluring, make him pick up the jar and take the tiniest
sip. And then, why not, one more. He groans, purses his lips, and lets the
fumes leak out through his nostrils. It is nine o'clock in the morning. (Not
being a drinker—or ever having been around drinkers except for construction workers who tend to drink like fish, but only during their off
hours—the Father has no idea drinking so early in the morning is a violation of the codes of respectable behavior. To him, this seems a perfectly
good time.)*

At first, the idea of temporarily stashing the Other Woman in the basement of the neighbors' empty house presented itself as a reasonable solution; the neighbors were in Tucson and would be none the wiser; the Father would not have to risk detection by driving back and forth to check on her. But now the Father is beset with second thoughts; he knows he is playing a dangerous game whose rules are beyond him, that bringing the Other Woman to within shouting distance of his family and Wife #1's fine-tuned radar is the plainest evidence yet of his willingness to tempt fate, to court oblivion, to pay his debts all at once and in the hardest way possible.

The Father is thinking about the Other Woman because thinking about her, despite everything that has happened, is the only thing — besides, maybe, this horrible Mexican liquor — keeping him from cracking at the seams. He went to visit her last night clinging to the idea that with some rigorous thinking and a well-defined plan (neither of which the Father has any real experience with) they could rescue themselves from this situation without anyone getting hurt. But when he saw her sitting at that old formica kitchen table, her hair tied up and her face glowing softly with fever, he forgot all about plans and the rational thinking. He wanted nothing but to go to her, to take refuge in the warmth of the simple affection she offered. And when she stood, smiling, apparently glad to see him, that's exactly what he did.

They talked about her health — she was fine, nothing more than a mild fever — and about her efforts to bring her son up from Guatemala, which made her eyes grow soft, her voice hushed. She asked if he had heard anything more from her husband, and he shook his head, though in these past two days he has seen much to indicate her husband has not forgotten about either of them. Twice more the Father has come across the sleazeball who trespassed on his property and plied his daughter with a lollipop: once at the IGA in town, buying beer and Swisher Sweets and Vienna sausages as if stocking up for a bachelors-only camping trip, and once more the following afternoon in the wide turnout just south of Big House, sitting in a white Buick Electra, looking up and waving happily at the Father as he drove by. The Father hopes it is nothing more than unchecked paranoia, but he has begun to notice all sorts of peculiar phe-

nomena: cars he'd never seen before driving past his houses, suspicious tire tracks in the gravel driveway of Big House, a strange man in a fringed suede jacket watching him from across the street while he took care of business at the bank. On his way to visit the Other Woman that very night he had been overcome with an icy certainty: someone was following him. The same pair of headlights had trailed him from the railroad crossing all the way onto the freeway, where he sped up—pushing the old engine on his GMC as far as it would go—and with a particularly graceless manipulation of the steering wheel nearly killed himself as he swerved off onto an exit ramp and down a dirt access road, where he stopped and turned off his lights, panting and light-headed with fright.

Telling her any of this, he realized, would do her no good. It would probably do her no good at all to know that he went out to his truck that very morning and found on the driver's-side seat a battered old Gideon's Bible left open to Psalms, with a single passage carefully underlined in blue ink: Happy shall he be that taketh and dasheth thy little ones against the stones.

He inquired off-handedly if she wouldn't be more comfortable staying in a motel for the next few days instead of in the basement of an empty house and she said she wanted to be able to see him, that she didn't want to be alone, and that was the end of it, because no matter how foolhardy a plan it may have been, there was this: he wanted to see her, to be near her, too. It was this feeling of swaddling contentment in her presence, and the prospect of living inside it forever, that had gotten him to seriously consider running away with her, disappearing into the misty and indistinct possibilities of a new existence. Of course, he had been entertaining fantasies of escape for a long time now, but they had always been just that: entertainments (simply thinking about escape had always been escape enough for him). But now that his world has been turned on its head he has begun, in his desperation, to force his imagination into unfamiliar territory: what would happen to his family if one day he disappeared, never to return? Most importantly, they would be protected, both from the Other Woman's husband and from their own bumbling father and husband who, despite his sporadically honorable intentions, did not seem to know how to keep them safe.

Each time he turns it over in his mind he finds his way to the conclusion—with considerably less resistance and more self-pity than he might like—that they would be better off without him.

Last night, in the overwarm kitchen that smelled of fried onions and marijuana smoke, he was entertaining out loud the notion of running away with the Other Woman—she was the one who had brought it up first, after all—when she asked him the question he'd been dreading. Was it true what she'd been told? Was he really married to more than one wife?

She wore an oddly noncommittal look, a look that said she was preparing herself to be amused or angry by his answer, she hadn't yet decided. He told her it was true, and that he was sorry for lying to her—he only did it because he was afraid of what she might think of him—and that yes, he had more than one wife. Four, in fact. Four wives who would be very angry if they knew where he was right now.

She did not laugh or hold up her hand to her mouth in abject horror, which he took as an encouraging sign. She simply continued staring at him expectantly, her face betraying nothing more than curiosity, and asked him if it was true that this was a normal thing for this part of the world, that the more wives a man had the more rich and important he was.

The Father blushed, said that it was normal for some, but not for others. Was he rich and important? Not, he said, in the way she might think.

When she asked how many children he had, and he answered her in a small, half-swallowed voice, the gasp she made in the back of her throat told him all he needed to know. He was simply confirming for her what she had already begun to suspect: that the bucktoothed lout sitting across from her was not anything close to the ordinary man of conventional tastes she thought she had taken up with, but a stranger of such odd and possibly dishonorable circumstances he had been lying to her about them all along.

Now, stuffed into the ground floor of this miniature house, sweating through his clothes at the armpits and with so little head room his neck is beginning to cramp, the Father tips his nose into the jelly jar and concedes that he has allowed himself, somewhere along the way, to be taken in by his own lies; playing the role of an average American breadwinner with the standard number of spouses and offspring has not only been strangely thrilling, but has made it easier, somehow, to betray his real family, to willfully discard their trust and faith in him. But of course he is not average in any way, he is the Father, everything in his life is magnified tenfold, including his sins, the worst of which just might be his willingness to give a moment's thought to the abandonment of his wives and children.

As long as he is being honest with himself, he might as well admit that hiding here is simply another form of desertion, one he has been practicing for a good long time.

From his pocket he extracts two pink antacid tablets, fumbles them into his mouth, and gnashes them into a gritty paste, which he washes down with a sip from his jar. He doesn't know whether it's the incessant worry or this battery acid he's been drinking, but for the past three days the flame in his stomach has only grown hotter. (Paranoia, the Father heard once, is having all the facts. He is sure he is in possession of only a very limited number of the facts, and can only guess at the gastrointestinal distress he will be experiencing once he has them all.)

The Father takes another greedy little sip—why not?—and slumps against the splintery plywood wall, sighing: he surrenders, he gives up completely and absolutely. God only knows what perils his family may be exposed to while he sits here, tucked out of sight. Though it's the last thing he wants to do, he begins to picture the possibilities, sees visions of bad men creeping in the bushes, peering into windows, testing the hone on their knives. His imagination gets away from him, as it so often does when he's alone like this, and eventually he is watching in the dark movie theater of his mind a detailed and brightly colored panorama of domestic destruction: houses set on fire and family pets hung from mailboxes with piano wire and wives assaulted and children stolen and stuffed into the trunks of cars.

Though it's absolutely the last thing he wants to do, he can't help it, he looks out the window, beyond the clumps of tamarisk and willow, and sees an empty wheelchair at the river's edge, the deep water moving swiftly past.

He puts his face into his hands and distracts himself with the filaments of pulsing red electricity behind his eyelids. After a while he hears a car coming at an even pace over the hill and then the whine of brakes, the rasp of tires turning off the hardtop, and it is as if all his immediate fears have brought themselves to bear in this single unassuming sound, the pop-and-crackle of a vehicle coming slowly up the gravel drive. The Father, who has spent many an hour in this spot with one ear to the wall, alert to the approach of those who would interrupt his seclusion, is versed in the distinctive rattles and creaks of his wives' cars, the well-oiled throb of farm trucks and old-fashioned sedans driven by neighbors and fellow church members. This vehicle, he is certain, belongs to nobody he knows. It emits a coughing, watery gurgle as it drags its broken tailpipe over the polished river rock with the faintest, almost imagined screech of finger-nails on a blackboard.

The engine idles for a moment, then hiccups into silence. A car door opens, shuts. There are voices, but another vehicle coming along the road—Gilbert Handrick's flatbed, by the sound of it—drowns them out. Straining, he hears nothing but the conspiratorial rustle of the dry grass under his window. At this moment his wife and children may be in mortal danger, subject to all the dire possibilities he has just imagined, but does he rush out to defend them, does he so much as steal a peek through a crack in the wall to see who has come calling? No, sir. He draws his knees and elbows in close, as if to will himself smaller, and concedes this simple truth: he is not capable of protecting them, he never has been.

Now there are footsteps on the gravel at the side of the house and then along the path of shattered lava rock edging the driveway. They come deliberately and ever so faintly, like footsteps echoing through an empty corridor in a bad dream. Amazingly, instead of following the path around the house to the backyard, they seem to be making their way across the muddy field toward him. He hears nothing for a few moments, and then there is the snapping of dead weeds not twenty feet away and he is *clutched with such a spasm of anxiety he nearly tips over his jelly jar and, in the scramble to keep it from spilling, rears up, ramming his head into the five-foot ceiling.*

In the silence that follows, he holds his head and counts his heartbeats, unable to breathe. There is a rustling and then boom . . . boom . . . boom someone is knocking on the door with all the casual malice of the big bad wolf. The Father waits, clinging to the child's hope that to be blind to danger is to be safe from it, believing that if he can wait long enough without moving or breathing, whoever is out there will disappear, that all of this will go away, forever.

The knocking comes again, and he can't stand it anymore, he takes a great, lung-rattling breath and pushes open the door.

36.

· · · · ·

A LITTLE HARMLESS COURTSHIP

HE FOUND HIMSELF STARING INTO CLEAVAGE. AT FIRST, IN HIS CON-
fusion, he could not make sense of what he was seeing, and so continued to stare, like a lizard in a trance, until the person to whom the
cleavage belonged called out, "Brother Richards?"

"Yes?" He did not duck his head under the lintel of the child-
sized doorway to find out who was speaking—he was too busy trying
to come to terms with the curious display in front of him: generously
freckled cleavage, polka-dot rayon shirt, and a plate of yellow cupcakes, all framed in the doorway like an art-student collage.

"Hello?" said the woman. "Everything okay out here?"

It took a moment for his addled mind to identify the distinctively
shrill voice of Maureen Sinkfoyle. For a year and a half he'd managed to sneak out here more or less undetected and now Maureen and
her cleavage, on the premises for the first time that he knew of, had
tracked him down in less than two minutes.

"One of your little girls said you might be back here somewhere,"
Maureen said. "I heard a noise and, well, I hope I'm not interrupting
anything."

"Not at all, not at all," Golden said, finally mobilized sufficiently
to bend himself at the waist so he could get a look at her face. "You
just startled me a little."

Maureen sported a beauty mark, which appeared to be natural,
and a great thundercloud of unconvincing auburn hair, which did

not. Golden couldn't be sure, but he thought he could detect on her upper lip the faint shadow of a mustache. She smiled at him with such expectancy, holding out the cupcakes, that he had to resist the urge to invite her in. With great care he set the jar of mescal behind the milk crate and proceeded to maneuver his bulk through the doorway, a complicated process that ended with him losing his balance and stumbling out onto the muddy ground. He gathered himself, suddenly dizzy, and stiffened his spine in an effort to keep from teetering.

"What's this?" Maureen said, nodding at the Doll House. "Some kind of project?"

Golden regarded the old playhouse as if he were laying eyes on it for the first time. With its half-shingled walls, its spidery, spray-painted *X*'s, its buckled plywood gone silver with age, it looked like a prop from a B-movie horror picture about homicidal dwarves.

"Yeah, a project," Golden said. "I've been working on it for a while now."

Maureen held up the plate of cupcakes. "Just a little token of my appreciation."

"For what?"

"For taking a look at my water heater."

Golden stared at her, not following, and suddenly he was teetering. In order to stay upright he had to take a quick step back, dipping at the waist like a flamenco dancer, and in an inspired move pretended he was doing so to swat away a particularly aggressive mosquito.

"My water heater?" Maureen said. "I know you haven't been able to make it out yet, but this is just to say thank you. In advance."

Golden remembered now: she had cornered him at church two weeks ago to complain about her failed water heater, which conveniently led to a rehearsal of complaints, both specific and general, about how difficult her life had become since her husband left her. In an effort to distance himself from the piercing feedback-whine of her voice, he had promised to swing by when he had a moment. He knew her pursuit of him was sanctioned by Uncle Chick, most likely with Beverly's blessing (she'd been mentioning Maureen in conversation with some regularity now, and even Trish had gotten word that something was afoot), but Golden was too distracted by his life sliding completely off the rails to give a damn. So he had made a promise out of cowardly convenience and, just like most of his promises these days, forgot it not ten seconds after it was made.

She turned her face toward the river. "Tried to get my boys to help, but their dad never taught them a thing, and anyway I can't control them anymore, now that I'm alone . . ." Her voice broke— a sound like a small rodent having its neck wrung—and when she looked back at him her eyes were moist. "I'm sorry," she said. "I didn't come here to do this."

Golden could hardly make himself look at her: in her thrift-store dress and muddy sling-back shoes, she was a textbook illustration of a cast-off, someone tossed aside in favor of the new, the fresh, the less complicated. She stood in his faint shadow, running on her last fumes of hope, nothing left to offer but cleavage and cupcakes.

In an attempt at comfort Golden put his hand on her forearm and with enterprising speed she stepped right up to him, nearly into his arms, squashing the cupcakes into his belly and pressing her cheek against his sternum to have herself a little cry. Lightly patting her back with both palms as if playing the bongos, he looked out over the swell of her hair and saw Naomi and Josephine watching from the back porch, Alvin spectating from behind the dusty glass of a bedroom window. Golden shrugged at them and wagged his head as if to say, *I have no idea what's going on here*, but they did not respond, just continued watching with looks of worry and fascination as he did his best to disengage himself from Maureen Sinkfoyle's soft but insistent grasp.

THE VILLAIN, THE VICTIM

For the rest of the morning and most of the afternoon, he drove around in a state of mild shock which eventually transformed into a

pleasant numbness as he stole a series of tiny sips from the jelly jar
under his seat. He stopped in at the office and the bank, pretending to work, pretending his life and its steady routines would carry
forward on their fixed and predictable trajectories. He had lunch at
the Rhino's Horn, spent twenty minutes talking gas prices and high
school football with DeLayne Woosley in front of the post office, and
in all that time did not notice anything out of the ordinary: no smiling Todd Freebone, no strange men in strange cars trailing him or
keeping watch from safe distances. As the day wore on he began to
tease himself with the hope that maybe Ted Leo had given up, that he
had made his point and had grown bored with this game, that instead
of spending his considerable time and resources looking for a disaf-
fected common-law wife he'd never cared much about anyway, he
was moving on to more profitable interests.

This feeble hope, like the doomed baby sparrow kept temporarily
alive on drops of sugar water, met its swift and brutal demise when
Golden pulled up into Old House's drive and found his way blocked
by Ted Leo's champagne Lincoln Continental with the spare tire
built into its trunk. Golden surprised himself by barking out a bitter,
cathartic laugh as he stared in wonder at the car's severely elongated
brake lights, the Nevada license plate, the bumper sticker that said
THE PUSSYCAT MANOR * WE'LL MAKE YOU PRRRRRRRRR. Ted Leo was sitting on Beverly's rocker, pushing himself back and forth, happy and
unmolested, on the shiny silver tips of his boots, smoking a cigar.

Golden's existential crisis in the Doll House must have purged all
the fear and anxiety right out of him, because other than a mild surprise, he felt almost nothing at the sight of Ted Leo grinning expectantly on his front porch, no panic or anger or high alarm, only the
wearied resignation of a man at the end of his rope, ready to be done
with it all, and the sooner the better.

He walked past the driver's side of the Continental, where Todd
Freebone sat behind the wheel, having himself a nap. As he climbed
the porch steps Golden noted that, beyond all reason, Ted Leo was in
one of his good moods. In what appeared to be a misguided attempt

to fit in with the local yokels, he wore, along with his high-buff cowboy boots, a brown western-style blazer with wide whip-stitched lapels, and a bolo tie made out of a polished hunk of petrified wood. He got to his feet, giving Golden a wide-eyed look of ersatz astonishment, and fairly shouted, "Well I'll be *darned*!"

Golden swallowed. "What can I do for you, Mr. Leo?"

Ted Leo practically gaped at Golden, sporting the self-satisfied cat-and-mouse grin of someone who had a secret but wasn't quite ready to let it out of the bag. "What can you—? What can you do for me? Ha! Now that's a good one."

Golden tried to make sense of what was happening here. Beverly's van was in the driveway, which meant she was home. There was no way Ted Leo could have come up the drive undetected—*nobody* approached Old House without being noticed by *somebody*—and yet there was a hush over everything, no noise or activity, as if the whole place were poised for something, holding its breath.

Golden peered through the screen door at the empty hallway and the fear that had failed to show moments before now roused itself, reaching from somewhere deep inside to give his heart a quick little squeeze.

Ted Leo seemed pleased by the change of expression on Golden's face. "Don't worry, Brother Richards! Everybody's safe and sound, for now. I was on my way up to Salt Lake to look at some flooring for the new place, and thought I'd stop by so we could bring an end to this nonsense once and for all—talk about it man to man—and what do you know? Knock on your door here and who, to my surprise, answers but sweet Jeannie with the light brown hair."

"Jeannie?"

"Your wife. One of 'em, I mean."

"You mean Beverly."

"So that's what she's calling herself these days. Back when I knew her, when she was working at Madam Pearl's, she was Jeannie. Oh but you shoulda seen her in her trick outfit! Little Shirley Temple chemise and bows on her shoes. All dimples and innocence until she got you into one of the back rooms, and then, *look out*! Mmm. We were all disappointed when she disappeared, me and half the male population of Las Vegas, but I should've known it was your dad who stole her away. Always took what he wanted, didn't he? Everybody else be damned. He brought her out here and before he died, I'm guessing, passed her right along to you, which is how you people do things, apparently."

Ted continued to study Golden's face as he spoke, growing more pleased with himself by the second. "Didn't know about any of this, did you? Oh this is *rich*. Who wouldn't keep such a secret if they could? Came out here to repent, wash away her sins, start a new life, probably said she was a virgin, right?—lots of whores-turned-virgins running around, I can tell you that—and who can blame her, we all have secrets, am I right, Brother Richards? I mean, your whole *existence* is a secret. But as for Jeannie-with-the-light-brown-hair, I'm getting it now. From working girl to polygamist wife, it kind of makes sense, don't it? Fucking for money, fucking for salvation, not a whole lot of difference."

Golden said, "You don't know what you're talking about."

Ted Leo got up on his tippy-toes, put his face as close to Golden's as he could manage. Through the haze of cigar smoke, Golden got a sharp whiff of alcohol, but he wasn't sure if it was coming from himself or Ted Leo.

Ted Leo wrinkled his nose, frowned. "Are you *drunk*?"

"No," Golden said. "Are you?"

For a moment they sniffed each other like two mutts, much too close for comfort, and Golden could see something like shame or uncertainty creased into the corners of the old man's eyes.

"Don't I wish!" roared Ted Leo, backing away, stubbing out his cigar on the arm of Beverly's chair with a distinct air of self-reproach. "And don't you wish that I had no idea what I'm talking about! If I'm an expert on anything, I guess it'd be whores, right? My wife's one, right? Right? And I can tell you, that wife of yours—and I'm not trying to flatter anybody here—*she was the best I ever fucked*." He waited a beat, jabbed a thumb toward the door and said, "Oh, sorry for the bawdy talk, I know there must be children there, hundreds of 'em, I'm guessing."

Suddenly Golden's mind was awash in red light and he saw himself taking Ted Leo firmly about the neck and shaking him like a doll. He looked away from the man's leering face and said, "You need to leave."

"Not before I get what I came for." The playful manner Ted Leo had arrived with was long gone. "I've given you a chance. The bozos I sent out here to do a simple job turned out to be useless"—he pointed out Todd Freebone, who was now awake and dazedly working his way through a large apple—"which has given you a window of opportunity, and you haven't taken advantage of it. I'm a busy man, and because of that I've been easy on you, but now it's time for you to tell me what I want to hear."

"I already told you. I don't know anything. You had your men creeping around here, harassing my family, and they haven't found anything. There's nothing to find. So you need to go."

"Or what? You going to get violent, Brother Richards? You going to stand up for yourself? Nah, didn't think so. Your little wife in there, you know, she seemed so *surprised* that you were working for me, I guess she was under the impression you've been spending all your time out in Nevada doing something *respectable*. Well, hasn't it been a day of surprises in the Richards family! She ran off before I could tell her about your extracurricular activities with my own wife; I thought maybe we could commiserate on the subject of unfaithful spouses . . ." His nostrils flared and his jaw tensed. He jabbed a finger into Golden's chest. "You tell me where she is. *Now*."

"I don't know."

"You do."

"Get off my porch or I'm calling the police."

Ted Leo didn't seem to hear this last remark. Something like doubt darkened his face and he looked away. "You really don't know where she is, do you? Is that it? A piece of shit like you, I'm wasting my time, right? She wouldn't really run out on me with somebody like you, is that what you're trying to sell me here?" He seemed to be arguing with himself now, and Golden took the opportunity to try to steer him down the steps, get him as far away as possible from his children, his house. Just as Golden grabbed hold of him, Ted Leo reared back and slapped Golden across the face. It was not the stinging slap one rival gives to another, but a blow heavy with weariness and disappointment, like a father might give a wayward son. The two faced each other, both red-faced and staggered, both a little drunk, and, feeling the give of the old man's flesh under his fingers, the soft fat and hardened tendons of his upper arm, Golden had to wonder: Who was the villain here, and who the victim? Who was wronging whom?

Unable to look into Ted Leo's watery, bloodshot eyes for one more second, Golden hung his head. "Please leave."

"I don't want to hurt anybody," Ted Leo said, jerking his arm away. "But I will if I have to."

"Please."

Ted Leo clapped down the porch steps in his ridiculous boots. He called over his shoulder, "You're only making this harder, you dumb son-of-a-bitch!"

Shrugging, Golden did not look up. He said, "I always do."

ROYAL TO THE END

Not yet ready to enter the house, he settled his bulk with tender care on the front steps to think. He knew, without needing any sort of confirmation, that what Ted Leo had told him about Beverly was true. In all the time he'd known her she had barely mentioned her own history, and Golden always assumed this was because she had no time for a past, rife as it was with inconveniences: the childhood hang-ups, the lingering insecurities of high school, the inevitable regrets—none of which serve any purpose except to cloud the mind and forestall the building of God's kingdom upon earth. She was someone who was so right, so deeply correct in everything she did, that it seemed impossible that anything belonging to her, even her distant past, could be wrong.

She had intimidated him with her icy rectitude since the first day they met. It was less than a week after Golden arrived in Virgin, and Royal had arranged for all of them to have dinner together at the Cattlemen's Club. Beverly, then in her mid-twenties and possessed of a taut Scandinavian beauty, had been dating his father for a few months and had only just been informed that Royal not only had a wife in Louisiana to whom he was still legally married, but a hulking, socially challenged son who happened to be sitting right across the table, hiding behind his menu.

Instead of taking out her anger on Golden, which some might have been inclined to do, she let Royal have it. For the rest of the night she did not speak a word to him. She was perfectly cordial toward Golden, asking him in solicitous tones how he was handling the dry desert air, about his hobbies and plans for the future, but as for Royal, who vied for her attention with snippets of Mel Tormé and questions about the quality of her food, she had only brief glances of such howling, arctic spite that even the waiter was rattled. Golden had never seen his father so thoroughly and aggressively ignored, and was surprised to find how much he was enjoying it.

It wasn't until Royal's final weeks in the hospital that Golden and Beverly spent any real time together. Before that, he saw her at church and occasionally at seminary study, where they took lessons on theology and church history in preparation for being baptized. Once, when Royal was out of town on business, she stopped by Big House to ask Golden if he'd noticed anything strange about his father's recent behavior. To Golden, this seemed like the oddest of questions. As far as he was concerned, *all* of his father's behavior was strange, recent or otherwise.

"He's got this *look* all the time now," she said, "and he's started forgetting where he is sometimes."

Golden knew the look she was talking about; he'd noticed it his first day in Virgin, and simply assumed that the manic glow in his father's eyes had everything to do with the transforming fire of the Holy Spirit. In fact, all of Royal's strange behavior—the sweaty, all-night prayer sessions, the spontaneous bouts of hugging and neck-kissing, the obsessive underlining of scripture with red pencil until there wasn't a single line of scripture *not* shaded in red—struck Golden as nothing more than the slightly overzealous eccentricities of a man who had come into the Truth a little late in life and was making up for lost time.

There were a few things, now that Beverly had mentioned it, that couldn't be easily connected to Royal's recent conversion. He had begun wearing military-issue aviator shades day and night, chewed aspirin by the handful, often lost his balance while doing nothing more than standing at the kitchen counter buttering a slice of toast. When Golden asked Royal how he was feeling healthwise, Royal explained that if weren't for the excruciating headaches, the jags of nausea, and the fact that the left half of his face had gone numb, he could honestly claim he'd never felt better in his life.

Golden suggested, in his mild way, that Royal see a doctor.

"*God* is my doctor," Royal said, in all apparent seriousness, smiling the slight, unnerving smile of a saint. "And He tells me every day I'm doing just fine."

When Royal passed out during a church social, going headfirst into the refreshment table, upsetting the punch bowl and having a leg-shaking seizure that terrified the children, everyone decided he could probably use a second opinion.

The tumor the doctors found in his brain was inoperable, as were the clusters of cancer that lined the walls of his lungs. Even through the pain, the delirium, the drug-induced cycle of diarrhea and constipation, he was Royal to the end. He wore his gray Stetson—the one with a medallion of uranium-rich pitchblende affixed to its headband—when the nurses weren't around, and sported his aviator shades because he couldn't take the light. When the young, ruddy-cheeked doctor—who Royal referred to as Little Doc Fauntleroy—suggested with some querulousness that wearing a lump of radioactive mineral on one's head might not be safe, and that long-term radiation exposure might in fact have been a contributing cause of Royal's cancer, Royal made a show of removing the hat and licking the hunk of pitchblende all over as if it were a piece of hard candy. Golden had seen his father make such a display many times, along with the parlor trick of passing a Geiger counter over his face so that it chattered and ticked like an irate dolphin, its needle pegging off the scale. This was how Royal demonstrated the wonder and harmlessness of radiation, which, he claimed, had never been proven to hurt a soul—except, of course, for a few hundred thousand Japs—*bada-bing!*—and was the only reliable means of keeping our great nation safe from the Reds and all the combined forces of Satan.

From the soapbox of his hospital bed he told anyone who would listen he had spent *years* breathing uranium dust in his own goddamn mine, had overseen the processing of yellowcake in the mills, had witnessed some of the biggest tests firsthand, and had breathed in the bouquet of radioactive fallout, which didn't smell much different, he claimed, than a rich woman's farts. And you didn't see anything wrong with him, did you? Shit, no! Look at him! Strong as a fucking ox! And then a childlike bewilderment would smooth out the sun-gouged lines of his face, a touch of doubt would dim those luminous eyes, and he would glance around, confused as to where he was, exactly, and where it was he was headed.

Even when he was too weak to lift his head from the pillow, and hat-wearing had become a luxury left to the hearty and spry, to spite the doctors and all the other doubting Thomases, he made sure his Stetson was displayed prominently on the hat rack in the corner, where it stayed until the day he died.

Together Golden and Beverly watched him go, inch by inch. From his bedside, they took turns reading to him from the Book of Mormon and *Prospector's Quarterly* and, when he could no longer take solid foods, fed him ice chips to keep him hydrated and soothe the sores in his mouth. At some point, when he was nearly blind and had lost so much weight the depressions and bony knobs of his body were hard to distinguish from the twist of bedsheets, he finally came to accept that he would not be spared. In his lucid moments, which seemed to come more frequently the worse he got, he made Golden promise, over and over again, that he would take care of Beverly, that they would live the Principle together, that he would make her his first wife and secure for her a place in the Celestial Kingdom.

Take care of her, boy, Royal would say, once or twice when Beverly was right there in the room with them, *and she'll take care of you.*

Golden, of course, never doubted this. In fact he had nothing but wary admiration for Beverly's resourcefulness, her stoic calm in the face of so much pain. Her Uncle Victor, her guardian and only living relative, had died after a long illness only a little more than a year before and now her fiancé was being taken from her in a similarly brutal fashion, and did she once curse God or beat her breast at the unfairness of it all? No. She just kept feeding Royal his ice chips and quietly doing battle with the nurses over his morphine dosages.

One bitter winter morning when Golden was on duty while Beverly was at her apartment sleeping off a long night-vigil, he found the will to bring up something that had been nagging him since Royal's diagnosis. "What about Mama?"

"Mama?" said his father.

"Malke. Your wife."

For a moment Royal's big, watery eyes went soft, as if he were remembering long-ago days bathed in golden light. He licked his lips. He said, "What about her?

"What should I tell her?"

This time, Royal didn't take too long to think. "Tell her about this," he said, with the slightest gesture of his head. "Tell her how I went. That ought to put her in a good mood for a while."

The rest of that morning and afternoon Golden spent watching his father suffer: wracking coughs and whole-body tremors and two watery bowel movements requiring a crack duo of cheerful orderlies to change the bedsheets out from under him while he wept and cursed as if under attack by ghouls. By nightfall Golden was heartsick, all but done in with boredom and dread, and, as always, Beverly showed up just in time, when he was certain he couldn't take another minute.

Go home, she told him, as she always did, squeezing his wrist in a way that brought a lump of gratitude to his throat, *get yourself some sleep*.

No, there was simply no way he could have managed it without her. It might as well have been the motto of his existence, tattooed on the billboard of his forehead: COULDN'T HAVE DONE IT WITHOUT BEVERLY! Not only had she seen him through his father's death and initiated their limited courtship and eventual marriage, she had helped him gain control of his father's finances and assets while he took a bruising crash course in the construction business. She suffered four miscarriages before having her first success and then gave birth to ten healthy children in a row, losing one along the way, even as she managed her day-to-day household down to the color of the hand towels in the bathrooms, almost single-handedly raising their children even as she brought her husband along slowly on the finer points of duty and fatherhood, talking him through sibling spats and IRS audits and client lawsuits and the tricky inner workings of the church, all the while overseeing the expansion of the greater empire, which involved arranging the courtships of and marriages to his three other wives as well as steering the whole hurly-burly crowd of them through privation and sickness and loss and every other conceivable sort of domestic weather, fair and foul.

And what had he ever done for her? Besides offering himself as a figurehead, a convenient mannequin she could dress and pose and move about as she saw fit? Not much. Unlike some others, she had never expected anything from him, he knew this. She understood better than anyone that he was not so much his father's son as a pale, off-brand imitation, a cheap replacement, a consolation prize who offered little in the way of consolation. Though she still occasionally pushed him to take the lead, to put more trust in his "patriarchal instincts," she seemed to have accepted that he would always need her steadying hand, that she would always have to be there to prop him up when the hard winds began to blow.

He was thinking about all this as he eased himself up from the porch steps and entered a queerly silent Old House. There were children inside, they were just being exceptionally careful not to make any noise: Nephi pretending to read a book, Louise and Sariah sandwiched between the couch and the wall, carrying on a cryptic conversation in sister-sign language, Em at the piano, staring at the sheet music like a mannequin in a music store window display.

"Your mother?" Golden put his hand on Em's shoulder and she whispered, hardly moving her lips, "Upstairs."

Beverly was seated on the cushioned stool at the side of the bureau. The late afternoon sun, partially blocked by a raft of clouds, filled the room with swirling motes. She was sitting straight-backed, as always, with her hands in her lap, looking shrunken, significantly smaller than the bigger-than-life woman who loomed in his imagination like a giantess. But mostly it was the look on her face that unnerved him. It was as if all the pins and clasps and fasteners that had been keeping her expression so securely in place for so many years had suddenly sprung loose, giving way to reveal an entirely different person, one who looked, despite the sharp cheekbones and wrinkles around the mouth, to be a lost and frightened girl.

He had seen her like this only one other time: the day his father died, driving home from the hospital in his dusty Thunderbird, the hard morning glare on the windshield. She sat next to him, her eyes dry but her face cracked open as it was now, Royal's last effects held tightly in her lap: his boots, his rings and wristwatch, his Stetson with its gaudy uranium brooch.

As they came around the big bend in the river she told him to stop the car. He pulled over near the bridge, and she got out, picked her way down the rocky slope, and, with a wild-animal screech and a surprisingly athletic throwing motion, slung the hat Frisbee-style toward the river. At first Golden didn't think it was going to make it, but the hat had stopped its end-over-end tumble and for a moment caught the air like a kite, spinning out into an elongated parabola and settling softly into the water, where it bobbed along shallow eddies between scrims of bank ice, listing to one side until the bowl filled with water and it sank from sight.

By the time she made it back to the car she had already recomposed her features into that famously impervious countenance, the one she would maintain dutifully and without variation until, as far as he knew, right now.

In their shadowed bedroom that smelled of stale sunshine, she looked up at him, eyes glimmering with an eerie vulnerability that made the bottom drop out of his stomach. She said, her voice airy and slight, "He's gone?"

Golden nodded. "He's not coming back."

"He told you, didn't he. About me."

Golden considered denying it—denial was his best and dearest friend these days—but this was a lie he knew he could not carry off just now; his own face, he was sure, had already revealed everything. "He told me, but Bev, listen to me, I don't care. I'm sure he told you what I've been doing—what I've been building this whole time."

Beverly shook her head. At the moment, Golden and his petty indiscretions weren't really registering with her. And while he should have felt some relief for this, as well as for the fact that Ted Leo had not revealed anything about Huila, what he was experiencing was a strange, lurching sense of vertigo. He had been relying for so long on Beverly as the only immediate source of stability in his life that seeing her like this—diminished and uncertain, ambushed by a past she thought she'd left forever—gave him the sense that there was nothing solid under his feet. Even in the midst of everything, he'd been operating, as he had for years, under a single, standing assumption: that if all else failed—and it probably would—Beverly would be there to save him. He would go to her and confess everything, prostrate himself before her and plead for mercy. Either she would go Old Testament on him, kick him out, banish him to someplace far away and unpleasant, or, as she had done any number of times before, she would swallow her anger and deep disappointment in him long enough to take care of everything. And then she would hold it over him for the rest of his living days.

He tried to sit, realized there was in fact nothing underneath him, and at the last moment shifted his weight to the side so that his wide behind landed with a *humpf* on the corner of the bed.

"Bev, don't worry about it, please, it doesn't matter, I myself, I've done some things—"

In a thin, toneless voice that seemed to belong to another person, she told him she had worked in "that place" only a few months. Her Uncle Victor had been injured working construction under the table, and to buy groceries and pay off his medical bills she had, in her desperation, gone for the quick money.

"Before that I'd always been a good girl," she said. "Mass every Sunday, daily rosary, all of it, but I was stupid. I thought I could cheat God, get us out of debt and then make it all disappear with confession and a few Hail Marys. But it was the worst thing . . ." Here she trailed off, her gaze falling to the floor. "And your father was the one who got me out of there. After Uncle passed I had nowhere else to go."

"No, please, you don't have to explain a thing," he said, desperate not to hear any more. Certainly there was a part of him that wanted to hear it all, every detail, to make a list of each man she'd been with—Ted Leo included—so he could track the bastards down and smother them in their sleep. And no, the irony of such a feeling at this moment in his life was not entirely lost on him. But mostly he stopped her because he didn't want to be responsible, didn't want to pity or second-guess her, didn't want the burden of her secrets and sins to be added to his own. It was selfish, of course it was, but then so were most all his thoughts and choices these days. Besides, he knew the rest of Beverly's story, because it was his story too. His father, with his money and influence and irresistible gonzo charisma, had saved her. He had invited her out to Virgin, where she would be offered a great gift: the chance to walk away from her previous life forever, to toss aside her stained and tattered self as if it were nothing more than an old sock meant for the rag box, to be cleansed and redeemed, to be chosen as one of God's special few.

"You don't have anything to be ashamed of," he said, worrying a loose thread on the hand-stitched bedcover with his big fingers. Unable to resist the urge to make his own confession, to relieve the pressure on his conscience just a little, he added, "I've been doing some things, you know, that I'm not so proud of lately."

At this, she looked up at him. "You were building one, not *working* in one." And he was heartened by the bit of steel that had come back into her voice. But it was only temporary. She coughed twice into her fist and seemed to go a shade paler. She whispered, "I'm sorry," and he said, "No. I don't care. It doesn't mean anything to me."

She sighed. "It should."

"Then it does," he said. "But I still love you." It felt good to say this—he couldn't remember the last time he'd made such a claim— eight, ten years ago, probably, before he knew any better. And it came to him that something peculiar was going on: *I love you.* What could have possessed him, especially during these uncertain times, to utter such potentially destabilizing words to three of his wives in as many days?

She did not respond, but seemed to relax a little, her shoulders dropping an inch or two. She would not look at him now. He noticed, as if for the first time, the mole under her left ear, the trace of down along the hinge of her jaw. She was the most familiar person in the world to him and therefore had always been that much harder to see.

Slowly she began removing the hardware from her hair, clips and barrettes and chopsticks and pins, placing each implement carefully on the top of the bureau, her springy iron-gray locks loosening, then falling around her face. She said, "I think I need to lie down for a while," and while Golden could not remember Beverly ever having taken a midafternoon siesta as long as he'd known her, he said, *Yes, of course, I'll take the children so you can have some quiet.* Unsteadily she rose to her feet. He stood and offered his hand and then she did an amazing thing: she accepted it. She grasped his wrist and leaned in to him, letting her weight rest against his, and for just a moment, before she pushed away, it felt very much as though he were holding her up.

—

37.
· · · · ·

IMPROVISED EXPLOSIVE AND INCENDIARY DEVICES
FOR THE GUERRILLA FIGHTER

FROM THE BUS STOP HE HUFFED ALL THE WAY HOME, DID ALL HIS chores as fast as he could, and wandered into the kitchen swaying around like somebody with a bad case of cancerous malaria. He had to do a little sick-person moaning and bump into a chair for Aunt Beverly, who was standing at the sink coughing, to notice him. She asked him if he was all right and he licked his lips and said in a weak prisoner-of-war voice that he couldn't hear her very well, that everything sounded far away. She touched his forehead, which was hot and sweaty because after chores he'd done like a hundred jumping jacks behind the chicken coop until it felt like he would faint or his arms would fly off his body into the weeds.

Aunt Beverly didn't even get suspicious. She gave him a cold washcloth to put on his forehead and said, "Why don't you go rest up in your room," and he climbed the stairs doing a version of the Honk Job, saying, *yes, yes, yes*, because he was Rusty the Guerrilla Fighter, and no one could stop him.

He spent the rest of the afternoon up in the Tower building an Improvised Explosive Device. He did not have a cardboard tube, but found—improvised!—an old Wilson tennis ball can that would work fine. Just like June had shown him, he took his time, spreading out all his items together on the closet floor—Safety First!—and then dumped in the plastic baggie of Potassium Nitrate and canisters of Red and Green Flash Powder into the can, nodding like an extremely intelligent scientist amazed at his own scientific advancements, and then to top it off he dropped in the two blasting caps, why not, he was going the distance. He cut out a circle of cardboard, punched a hole in the middle, slipped the fuse through the hole, and capped the can, sealing it up with half a bottle of rubber cement. To make sure he was doing it right he checked *Improvised Explosive and Incendiary Devices for the Guerrilla Fighter*, which was filled with complicated diagrams for things like the Whistle Trap, the Bangalore Torpedo, the Magnifying Glass Bomb, and the Exploding Pen, all of which would one day come in handy for a guerrilla fighter such as himself but right now were really not all that helpful.

In the section called "General Tips," it said, *Any glue can be useful to the guerrilla bomb-maker, but rubber cement, it must be said, is the bomb-maker's best friend. Use liberally but care must be taken at all times, because of extreme flammability.* Rusty liked that, *extreme flammability.* Just to be sure to achieve extreme flammability, he slobbed on another layer of rubber cement.

That night he went without his supper. He stayed up in the Tower, pretending to be sick, because if he sat downstairs with all the a-holes at the dinner table he might not be able to keep himself from smiling, and for once in their pathetic lives they might use their tiny rodent brains to figure out what he was up to. He didn't mind being hungry for one night because this was the end for him at Old House, he knew it, this was his last night in Alcatraz.

One more time he let himself imagine the incredible *BOOM,* the shooting colored lights, the whole sky lighting up like the Fourth of July and World War III and New Year's Eve put together, and everybody looking out the windows and running outside to see what the heck *that* was, and what would they find? You guessed it. His father the Sasquatch caught in the act, sneaking around the Spooner house hugging and holding hands with some black-haired lady who was very definitely not his wife.

Which made him think of his own mother, he couldn't help it, who was right now in a hospital surrounded by oldsters and lunatics, and here was his father walking around hugging some Mexican chick no one's ever seen before? He tried not to think about that part of it, because it made his stomach twist.

What a dickhead he'd been to think any of his other plans would work. Fighting Aunt Beverly or convincing his mother or Aunt Nola to let him come home would never work, who was he kidding. None of them, not even the all-powerful witchy-woman Aunt Beverly, could change anything, not really. His father was the only one. It was his father who had the power, who connected them all. You take his father out of the picture by showing everyone what a cheater and a liar he is? No more family. It was simple. You take away his father? No more monkey net.

He should have understood this because it had already happened to the Sinkfoyle brothers. Their father got excommunicated for running around with some hippie lady who wasn't even a Christian, and while everybody was saying, *Oh, those poor Sinkfoyle children, oh, those poor Sinkfoyle wives*, Chet and Dan, the redheaded Sinkfoyle brothers, were explaining to Rusty in Sunday School how effing great it was, how finally they got to live in their own house, have their own rooms and eat Corn Nuts and watch TV anytime they wanted because they were on their own now and their mother had other things on her mind. *It's the best!* they said. *We're having the time of our dang lives!* Sure, their new house was an old junky trailer out on the landfill road and their mother spent most of the day bawling into her pillow in her bedroom, but still.

And so Rusty waited up in the Tower hungry and happy, imagining a new life in which he had his own room and better underwear, in which his mother would come home from the hospital to take care of him and his sisters and brothers because they needed her more than ever, and they would become a regular family, a family in which no one would make fun of him or call him names anymore because he was a hero who had exposed the truth and destroyed the monkey net, a family in which he would be tolerated and maybe even loved.

So what the heck was taking everyone so long? It was forever

before Parley and Nephi came upstairs to go to sleep, but not before
they delivered a few more tampon jokes in his direction. Did Rusty
go crazy and try to hit them, which was the usual thing, did Rusty get
even the slightest bit mad? No, he just did some pleasant chuckling,
saying, *Good one, guys*, because right now, on this special night, he
was filled with kind thoughts toward all creatures of the earth, even
Nephi and Parley, especially now that he knew he wouldn't be seeing
much of them anymore.

When the house was quiet, when Nephi began to wheeze and Parley started releasing his *putt-putt-putt* sleep-farts into the atmosphere,
Rusty took his place at the window. He sat there for a long time. He
sat there and sat there and sat there and did not look away once, and
after what seemed like hours his head got heavy and he sometimes
didn't know if his eyes were opened or closed, and then there was the
crackle sound of his father's pickup pulling into the driveway with
its headlights off and suddenly his eyes were wide open watching
Sasquatch climb guiltily out of the truck and sneak off toward the
Spooners'.

From his top-secret location he retrieved a book of matches and
his Improvised Explosive Device, which looked like a giant yellow
firecracker. Down the stairs he went, out the window, and across the
roof, softly calling, *Geronimo!* as he jumped off the garage, and then
he was running barefoot down the driveway going, *Ouch! Ouch! Crap!
Ouch!* because once again he'd forgotten his shoes.

When he got to the Spooner driveway he began to creep like an
Apache who was one with the night, taking the form of fence posts
and dead shrubs and breathing only when he couldn't stand holding
his breath anymore. He was like the wind, but not like the wind at all
because the wind makes noise and he wasn't making any, you should
have seen him, nobody in the history of the world had ever walked
with such perfect silence.

He listened from the window at the side of the house and thought
he could hear voices. He crawled behind the big air-conditioning
unit to wait. It didn't take long. The back screen door whined and

when he could hear footsteps and whispering and they were walking around the other side of the house just like he knew they would, he took out his matchbook, got ready to light the fuse, but then there was a banging noise and Raymond was up against the gate of his pen, huffing and stomping his feet, staring at Rusty with those big yellow eyes.

Shhhh! Raymond! he whisper-shouted as loud as he dared. *Raymond! Stop it, dang it! Raymond!* But Raymond didn't listen, Raymond never listened to anyone, and now he was going crazy, butting the gate with his chest, and at any moment Sasquatch and the dark-haired lady would be coming around the house to see what was going on, so he lit the fuse, watched it burn for a minute, throwing off sparks so bright he could feel the heat of them on his neck, and then he ran out into the open and set the Improvised Explosive Device on the dirt next to the back steps and it was going to be so sweet, so very very sweet to see the look on Sasquatch's face when night turned to day and sudden supernatural thunder woke up everyone in Old House and worlds would collide and secrets would be revealed and life on earth would never be the same again.

He was creeping back to hide behind the air-conditioning unit with his hands over his ears when something fell on him from the sky. Or that's what it felt like, anyway. He hit the dirt, rolled over and saw feathers floating in the air above him and he realized it was Raymond, that idiot, who had jumped the gate and run over him, but he was not even hurt, he had survived, Raymond had just knocked him down and was now all tangled in the Spooner clothesline, flapping his wings and going, *urk, urk, urk*, which served him right. Rusty looked over at his Improvised Explosive Device, which should have gone off by now, but it just sat there, a little curl of smoke coming out of the top, and he ran to pick it up before Raymond untangled himself and attacked again. He was looking into the tiny black hole where the fuse had disappeared, wondering what had happened, *what a gyp, dang it what a big freaking gyp!* thinking how dark that hole was, how it seemed to be growing bigger and blacker, when his eyes filled with a white wall of light and inside his head bloomed huge flowers of fire that shot off red screaming meteors and fiery atoms exploding into green stars and shimmering sparkles of gold and blue and oh holy dear sweet jesus lord god it was so beautiful and bright and loud it was everything he could have ever hoped for.

38.

·····

SOMEONE NOT LIKE HIM

ONLY LATER WOULD GOLDEN REMEMBER MANY OF THE DETAILS. DURING the weeks and months afterward they would come to him at unexpected moments—in the middle of a conversation or the half sleep of early morning—bits of memory and disconnected sensation, broken images creeping into the dark corridors of his mind through back entrances and trapdoors: the swirl of feathers, the flash of light like a splinter lodged in his eye, the vibrating moon, the cold water of the river shocking his hands, the smell of burning hair.

It was the second night Huila had spent at the Spooner home. The first night they had both been too jittery to talk, to say or do anything in a coherent way, so they walked around the house holding hands and whispering awkward half phrases like AWOL teenagers sneaking around under a swollen moon. The second night, Golden decided, would be different. He planned to talk to her, really talk, to finally get down to business. They could not go on like this, he would tell her, trying hard to keep the whine out of his voice, he couldn't take it anymore, it was that simple, something bad was going to happen, it was only a matter of time. Either they were going to go through with it, they were going to run away together, or they would have to face up to everything they had done, stop sneaking around and accept the consequences. So this was his plan: they would talk, in a very serious and adult way, and once and for all she would tell him what to do.

They were walking around the west side of the house where Sister

Spooner kept her collection of birdbaths, bird feeders, birdhouses and
other bird-related paraphernalia, when Golden heard something. A
metallic rattle, a low grunting. His throat seized and he put his arm
in front of Huila to stop her. He imagined a shadowy figure waiting to ambush them, maybe more than one, maybe Todd Freebone
or the stranger from across the street at the bank, or Ted Leo himself. He waited, listened, heard nothing more. He peeked around the
corner of the house and what he saw confused him: a boy crouching
over something in the dirt, and behind him the ostrich, out of its pen
and bearing down on the unsuspecting child, its yellow eyes irate and
shining.

Golden stepped forward to shout, to try to intercept the bird or
ward it off, and it was here that his memory would falter. Afterward,
he wouldn't remember hearing anything: one moment he was reaching out, about to shout, and then he was on his knees, clutching the
side of his face, a burr of pain deep in his ear. He would not remember screaming at Huila to run, but later she would tell him that he
had done exactly that. He would remember the spangles of colored
light that dazzled his retinas—making it impossible for him to see
clearly—and imagining that he had been shot or clubbed over the
head or otherwise attacked. He scrambled to find the boy, blinking
hard, but his left eye registered only hazy red starbursts and the right
one didn't seem to be working at all until he saw, through a pall of
smoke, what he took to be a pile of garbage topped by a small gut-
tering flame. It was very close, nearly at his feet, and he was about to
step over it when he realized that it was the boy, that the boy's head
was on fire. He groaned—a sound of pain that came from somewhere
very deep—and the next thing he knew he was running with the boy,
who felt, gathered against his chest, like nothing more than a pile of
smoldering rags.

Later, one of the things that Golden would find hardest to forgive
himself for was the fact that he didn't know, as he stumbled toward
the river, exactly who he was cradling in his arms. It was his child, he
knew that much. He just didn't know which one.

Even after he'd doused the boy in the freezing water and gotten a look at his face, the top half of which was bloody and pitted beyond recognition, the skin charred, much of the hair on top of the head burned away, still he couldn't tell, and he would later wonder if he simply didn't *want* to know, if in its shocked state his mind had refused to speculate, to consider the names and possibilities, searching instead for some other, more acceptable outcome: that he was mistaken, that this was not his child at all but belonged to someone else entirely, someone stouthearted enough to withstand a blow such as this, someone wise and resolute and strong, a man of faith, a good father, someone not at all like him.

INTO THE DARK

Golden parked in the farthest corner of the PussyCat Manor parking lot, next to the dumpsters. The last time he was here, six or seven weeks ago—a period of time that now seemed like a span of years— he had claimed this very spot. It had been a sunny, clear morning, he remembered, and he had sat here slumped behind the wheel of his pickup, worrying, dithering, unable, as always, to come to a decision, wondering if he had the guts to walk though the brothel doors.

Tonight it was dark, blustery, an hour or two before sunrise, and he did not dither. He climbed out of the cab and rummaged through the bed of the pickup, looking for his axe handle, the one he'd bought ten years ago, shortly after the episode with Ervil LeBaron in which he'd broken out Ervil's taillights in front of the entire congregation and had become, briefly, a minor hero who some had already placed their bets on as the One Mighty and Strong, come to redeem the world and save them all. Heady days those had been, full of such hopes and expectations, and he hadn't thought twice about acquiring his own personal axe handle, to keep in the bed of his pickup, just in case. Of course, he had known he was not the One Mighty and Strong, or anything close to it, but that didn't stop him from driving over to Lamont Bros. Hardware and splurging on the deluxe model—a hickory Harvistall with a nice grain and heft to it—for the outlandish price of $5.99. He placed it in its special spot in the bed, right behind the rear window on the driver's side, and in those nine intervening years had never picked it up again.

It was still here in the truck somewhere, he was sure of it, prob-' ably buried under a pile of survey stakes or copper elbow joints. He cast around in the cumulus of broken tools and fast-food wrappers and snarls of baling wire, finally locating it by feel, snared in a tangle of a shorted-out extension cord. He held it up to the negligible light. It was nicked, dinged, weathered a splintery gray, and stained at the butt end with what looked to be spilled antifreeze, but it would do.

Walking across the parking lot, he felt weirdly clear-headed, charged and alert, which made little sense considering the night he'd had so far. It had been only a few hours ago that the two volunteer firefighters, twin brothers Ronnie and Donnie Gundersall, showed up within minutes of Beverly's emergency call, and with a deft competence belied by their scruffy facial hair and matching Lynyrd Skynyrd concert T-shirts, checked Rusty's vital signs, loaded him into the makeshift county rescue van and, with a spinning of tires and scattering of gravel that may have been excessive under the circumstances, headed off for the hospital in St. George. Before they'd gone, Ronnie told Golden that the sheriff had been called and suggested Golden wait around to talk to him, but Golden wasn't about to wait for anyone. He jumped into his pickup and, with Beverly and Nola in the station wagon not far behind, drove with his foot mashed on the gas, the only thought in his head that if he drove fast enough he might be able to beat Ronnie and Donnie to the emergency room.

At the hospital he was told Rusty was already being transferred to a Life Flight helicopter bound for University Medical in Las Vegas. Without waiting for his wives or speaking to anyone else, Golden got right back into his pickup and drove on, following I-15 through the winding gorges of Arizona and then across the moonlit desert plains of southern Nevada, his momentum stalled only by the old GMC's aversion to uphill grades, and the interminable fleets of sixteen-wheelers that seemed to clog the highway this time of night. Entering the great bowl of light that was Las Vegas in search of a sign that would point him in the direction of University Medical, he became disoriented, driving through intersections and over medians like someone who had never seen a stoplight or executed a left-hand turn in traffic. On the dark, humming highway he had been on a kind of autopilot, some part of his mind insisting on nothing but motion and progress, but now that progress had stalled he felt himself unmoored, swamped under by the tide of light and human noise, and in one black moment the horror of what had happened rose up in him with such force he heaved forward against the steering wheel, knocking the air out of his lungs. The pickup coasted for another twenty feet, hopped against the curb and stalled. Golden evacuated the cab for the sidewalk and, in front of an audience of singularly unimpressed bar-hoppers and motorists, vomited onto the base of a towering desert palm.

He would not remember getting back into his truck, or how he managed to find the hospital after what must have been another half hour of dazed wandering. He walked through the glass doors of the hospital and kept walking as if he didn't know how to do anything else, down one hall and then another, past people sleeping on plastic benches and small families carrying on their grim vigils and, finally, into a room full of desks and filing cabinets where a short Hispanic man was busy humming to himself and mopping the floor. The man looked up—he had a kind, generously creased face, and Golden went right to him. He tried to explain, to say, *I'm looking for my son*, but his voice was useless, ragged, as if he'd spent the last couple of hours screaming himself hoarse. The man smiled, seeming to understand perfectly, and then the room narrowed and darkened, and he felt himself toppling into the man's waiting arms.

He awoke on a gurney in the hall, a portly, freckled nurse looming above him. She said, "Back to the world of the living, are we?" With a nurse's cheerful competence she shone a penlight in his eye, fitted his arm with a blood pressure cuff, all the while asking what his name was, if he knew what day it was, if he had, in the last twenty-four hours, ingested alcohol or drugs. Again, he tried to speak, to make his identity and intentions known, but he seemed to have fallen mute: when he opened his mouth the only thing that came out was a wet, interrogative grunt.

The nurse noted this on her clipboard, and was pumping up the air-pressure cuff with forceful contractions of her meaty fist when a commotion down the hall drew her attention. She turned her back on him and proceeded to carry on a long-distance conversation—which consisted mostly of waving arms and dramatic shrugs—with another nurse on the other end of the long corridor trying to maneuver a large bleeding man in a wheelchair who was shouting about the mother-fucking bastards who'd stolen his Gold Toe socks. Golden thought about the friendly janitor he had apparently just fainted upon, and hoped he had not done the man any lasting harm. The nurse con-tinued ignoring him and Golden decided that, as comfortable as that gurney was, he couldn't wait around any longer. He sat up, tested his feet against the floor, and started in the opposite direction, taking the first left he came to, the blood-pressure apparatus still dangling from his arm. It wasn't long before he found Beverly and Nola, who shared a small, out-of-the-way alcove with a few plastic chairs and a coffee vending machine. They rushed to him, their hair wild and eyes bloodshot, clutching the necks of their nightgowns. The sight of these two women, their familiar smells, the weight of their palms on his wrists, brought him out of the fever dream he'd been having and fully into himself: he was suddenly aware of his own creaking mass, the smells of gunpowder and blood and river mud rising off him, the cold, clenched fist of his heart constricting with dread at the news he was about to receive. His wives asked him the same series of questions they'd been asking for years: What was wrong with him? Where had he been? What had taken him so long?

Even though he didn't speak or respond in any way, they must have been able to read the expression on his face, the single question

contained in it, because they both stopped at once and Beverly nodded. "He's alive."

Golden felt his equilibrium give. He pivoted and sat down hard.
For the moment, this was enough. His muscles and joints turned to
liquid and he thought he might slide right off the chair and onto the
floor.

But, of course, it wasn't that simple—nothing ever was. Nola sat
down next to him, and in hushed tones gave him the rest of the news,
which had been delivered by the lead surgeon only a few minutes
before.

Rusty had been rushed into emergency surgery the moment he
arrived, but once the doctors had opened up his head and had a look
around, they quickly put down their scalpels. There were too many
metal fragments embedded too deeply; if they tried to get at every one
they would end up doing more harm than good. So they had removed
several of the larger, more accessible fragments, and cut away a portion of his skull to accommodate the swelling of the brain. There
were other, less dire injuries. The boy's left eye had been destroyed,
as had most of his right hand. He had suffered third-degree burns to
his face and scalp. His chances of survival, the surgeon had told them,
were poor at best. Once he was transferred into the ICU they would
be allowed to see him.

The wives gave Golden a few seconds to let this sink in. They
watched him, waiting for a reaction, for some kind of explanation,
but he gave them none, simply sat there in the white hum of the waiting room, sporting the blood-pressure collar strapped around his
biceps and gripping his knees as if he might otherwise fly into pieces.

Nola, who was wearing a man's denim jacket over her nightgown,
along with a pair of mismatched rubber irrigation boots, carefully
removed the collar from his arm and placed it to the side. She gripped
one of his hands in hers. Normally, it was Beverly who would have
taken the lead in a situation like this, but Beverly sat across from
Golden looking strangely vacant and withdrawn, as she had for the

past couple of days. Nola hunkered down in front of Golden in an attempt to make eye contact, as if she were trying to induce a confession out of a grade-schooler, and asked the question Beverly had shouted at him from the porch as she watched him wade with Rusty across the swollen river, the question the Gundersall brothers had asked as they knelt down beside the boy to check his vital signs: "What *happened?*"

And Golden answered her now as he had answered them then, though he ended up only mouthing the words: *I don't know*.

I don't know. These three words composed the simplest, safest answer he could give; he was in no state to be offering explanations, to himself or anyone else. But he knew also that they were a denial, even a lie, a cheap and convenient way of absolving himself. Because if he was willing to give the whole thing even a little thought, if he backtracked even briefly along the lines of cause and effect, he was certain he would find himself, as he always did, the one to blame.

All he knew for sure was this: there had been some sort of explosion. Even though his memory had edited out this fundamental fact, the evidence was there in his still-buzzing left eardrum, in the way the sound of the blast had awakened all of Old House and some of the neighbors, in his son's ruined face. Who or what was responsible for the explosion was the more difficult problem, but as he puzzled it over, shuffling through the possibilities like a stack of paint chips, he could reach only one reasonable conclusion: Ted Leo. Somehow Ted Leo and his band of scuzzbuckets had discovered Huila's hiding place, and had set off some kind of explosion in an effort to scare or to harm. This made a certain kind of sense, especially taking into consideration Ted Leo's elaborate and often obtuse ways of making a point, but what had Rusty been doing there? And what about the ostrich? In his weakened, fuzzy-headed state, Golden was ready and willing to consider the possibility that the ostrich, with its smug air and cold yellow eyes, was itself responsible, that it was some kind of evil totem, the embodiment of a primordial curse that existed only to bring doom upon the Richards family, to steal away its children, to maim and mock and drown them, that it was, in fact, the source of all their suffering and strife, and he ground his teeth together in grim anticipation of what he would do to that ostrich when he got home.

He sat up, pressed his knuckles into his eyes. What was wrong with him? He shook his head in an effort to straighten out his thinking, and succeeded only in making himself more dizzy. No, the ostrich had had nothing to do with it. It could only have been Ted Leo. Ted Leo, who had already threatened him and his children in half a dozen ways, who had denigrated and belittled and bullied him, who had abused and exploited Huila for going on eight years, who had humiliated the seemingly invincible Beverly by dredging up the black mud of her past and throwing it in her face, and, worst of all by far, who had stolen the future and maimed the body of his innocent son.

Ted Leo. Golden mouthed these words, rolled them across his tongue like the medicinal, old-fashioned lozenges of his youth, tasted the bitter satisfaction of knowing that this time there really was someone else to be held to account, to be punished, that for once he would not have to shoulder the burden of responsibility alone.

A nurse came to tell them they could see Rusty. She took one look at Golden and asked if he needed something to calm him, a mild sedative, perhaps. He declined with a stiff shake of the head, but when he stood up and attempted a few steps, the muscles of his legs began to quiver, the edges of his vision darkened, and he wished he'd taken the nurse up on her offer. He put his hand on Nola's shoulder, as if to comfort or assure her, but if she had not been there to prop him up on the long trek down the hall to the ICU he would have fallen to the ground in a heap and stayed there.

They washed their hands in a steel basin, the nurse helped them don cotton surgical masks, and before Golden was ready, before he had a chance to try to convince himself that he was strong enough, that he could handle this, they were led into a room where Rusty lay propped up in a bed, splayed out as if caught like a spider's prey in the web of wires and tubes. It was worse than he could have imagined.

The upper half of the boy's head—including both eyes—was covered in bandages, while the skin of the lower half was so bruised and swollen it looked less like a face and more like an overripe melon left too long in the field, shiny and discolored and ready to split.

Golden shook his head, heard himself moan. In that dark room, with the IV bag filtering the light of the single lamp and throwing shimmering filaments across the ceiling, he gathered his shirt into both fists, rolling the fabric over his knuckles until it tore.

All the way down the hall, following Nola with his hand on her shoulder as if lame or blind, Golden had prayed. Lifted by a moment of desperate hope, a lurch of faith he didn't know he was still capable of, he had pleaded with God to wipe away everything the doctor had told Nola and Beverly, to make all of this a misunderstanding, a horrible mistake. He prayed in a way he never had before, without the formal constructions he had learned in church, without the *thees* and *thous* and *Our Heavenly Fathers,* and as he stood at the door, unwilling to cross the threshold just yet, he begged, letting the words rise out of him without sound: *Please, I will do anything, I will give anything, let him live, let him get better, make him better, I will give anything, my own life, everything I have, please, please.*

But, of course, it had been too little too late, and whatever scraps of hope and faith he had carried into that room crumbled instantly to ash. If there was an answer to his prayer, here it was, in the form of this burned and broken child who, as anyone could see, would not be getting better, would not go on to live any sort of life, would probably not survive the night.

Beverly and Nola did not hesitate, they went right to him, murmuring over him and stroking the bare skin of his arms, ignoring the nurse when she told them not to touch or get too close, while Golden hovered near the door, his face turned toward the wall, trembling with fury.

He set his jaw against it, tried to fight it off, but it had him now, the old childhood rage, come to claim him once again. It had been stalking him for years, ever since his days of sitting at the attic window in Louisiana, listening to his mother run through her repertoire of moans and sighs, waiting for his father to come home. The anger always took him by surprise, welling up suddenly from some fissure that reached all the way to the core of him, and he always did his best to resist, to run from it or tamp it down or wait it out until it dissipated into useless vapors. But now he did not fight it; he let himself fill with its heat until every cell and corpuscle had turned brittle and he was nothing more than a body of hot glass, poised to shatter at the slightest touch.

He jerked open the door and fell into the hall, joints locked stiff, struggling to breathe. After a while Nola and Beverly emerged, fixing him with their standard looks of resignation and pity. Once more he had given them reason to be disappointed: in his faint heart, his frailty in the face of crisis. Back in the waiting room, they embarked on a subdued discussion over when and how to give Rose-of-Sharon the bad news, and Golden was not once consulted or asked for his input; they seemed to have forgotten he was there. So they didn't notice when he walked away, his head and shoulders held so still he seemed to be floating, down the hall and through the automatic doors and into the early morning dark.

THE PUSSYCAT MANOR

It was very late, even for a brothel, and there were only four girls working the parlor: three sitting at the bar, chatting with the graveyard bartender, and the fourth dozing on the crushed velvet davenport in the center of the room. The bartender, bald as a seal except for a pair of lamb-chop sideburns, was busy blending the girls a celebratory end-of-shift margarita, which was why none of them heard the electric chime indicating a visitor had walked through the double-glass doors.

Letting his feet settle into the ultra-shag carpeting, Golden took a moment to consider his options. Nothing had changed since the last

time he was here: the place still glowed with the soft, burnished light
of a Buddhist shrine, still smelled like cigarette smoke, hair spray,
and overhandled dollar bills. What first caught his eye was the long
row of liquor bottles, three or four ranks deep and gleaming like
organ pipes, arranged on the shelf above the mirror. Only when he
had started forward across the expanse of crimson carpet did the bartender look up.

"Whoa, buddy," he said as he shut off the blender, the color draining from his face. "Wait a second, now."

Golden paused, not at the bartender's warning, but at the sudden flash of movement to his left. There was someone else behind the
bar he hadn't yet noticed, someone large and rumpled and dirty who
seemed to be brandishing an axe handle. . . . Golden peered suspiciously at this obviously deranged person for several seconds before
realizing that he was looking into his own reflection. On another
night, under different circumstances, he might have chuckled at his
routine gullibility, but tonight he greeted himself with an expression
of such seething reproach he felt a chill go through him. No wonder,
he thought, the girls at the bar were scooting away from him in horror. He looked like a shambling, humpbacked minotaur, eyes bright
with suffering, encrusted with mud up to his waist, shirt streaked
with blood, and hair matted at the sides of his head in a way that suggested horns. He skirted the far end of the bar and, with something
like pleasure, raised the axe handle and delivered a blow to the center
of his own face.

Sounding a single clamorous note, the mirror leapt off the wall
in several large pieces and hundreds of smaller ones. The girls
screamed, the bartender yelped and dove for cover. Golden moved
on to the glassware, then the glittering column of liquor bottles, and
for a moment it was like a small thunderstorm was blowing through,
chunks of glass raining down like hail, running cloudbursts of whiskey and rye and rum leaving in their wakes a rising alcoholic mist
that burned the nostrils and stung the eyes. Temporarily blinded and
swiping expensive bourbon from his eyebrows, Golden stumbled

toward the most obvious source of light in the room: the jukebox, from whose depths rose the moaning baritone of Teddy Pendergrass. Golden took a wild swing, missed the jukebox entirely, then connected on his second try, the tip of the axe handle lodging in the wire mesh that covered the speakers. Teddy Pendergrass chirped, his voice warping, and when Golden yanked the axe handle free the needle skipped, condemning Teddy to some R&B purgatory to wonder, over and over again, why he was alone again tonight, all because of some silly fight.

Golden heard yelling now, more women screaming, several voices calling out in alarm, "Bruno! Bruno!" which was either a code word for danger or the name of someone who they believed might come to their rescue. But it didn't matter to Golden; nothing was going to stop him as long as he had this angry, burning hurt in the middle of his chest and there were still items belonging to Ted Leo to be broken. After he'd kicked over the jukebox, putting Teddy Pendergrass out of his misery, he attacked the grand piano. He couldn't have said why, but he hated this piano more than he hated anything or anyone in his life. He raked the axe handle across the keyboard twice, chipping the keys and producing two clanging, gothic chords that made the windows rattle. He was about to knock aside the prop that held up the piano's lid, already savoring the great whooping clap it would make, when someone grabbed his elbow, yanking hard, and then the weight of another body landed on his back, an arm grappling his neck. He struggled and spun, lost his balance, veered into a wall, but they held on, breathing gusts of steam into his ear. He staggered forward, despite the two men hanging off him, one of whom seemed to be trying to choke him to death, the other who had found a way to reach around and punch him repeatedly in the face, and went on with his business, managing to free his right arm long enough to take out the ceramic statue of Venus de Milo with one swing and put a cleft, and one more for good measure, in the four-by-six oil painting of the wide-bottomed lady of the evening with a grape between her teeth.

As Golden lurched past the doorway hung with strings of glass beads, Todd Freebone burst through it in nothing but tube socks and a towel clutched around his waist. He shouted, "What the fu—" but was interrupted when Golden, with a lucky sideways chop of the axe handle, caught him full in the mouth. Todd Freebone dropped his towel and slumped against the wall, groaning, "Shit, man!" One by one he spit several bloody teeth into his cupped palm.

It was Miss Alberta, finally, who put an end to it all. Golden saw her out of the corner of his eye, her head full of fat pink curlers, holding in front of her what looked to be a long yellow cattle prod. "Stop this nonsense right now!" she scolded, as if she'd caught a classroom of third-graders misbehaving, and without further ado pressed the tip of the prod into his ribs. A hot electric spasm jerked him upright, he dropped the axe handle, and the men fell off him. He bent at the knees to retrieve his weapon but his arm had gone numb, his fingers stiff. Golden sensed a presence behind him and as he started to turn, Miss Alberta said, "Anytime now, Ernest, Jesus Christ," and something crashed into the back of his head and he pitched forward, his vision filled with starbursts and blazing sparks.

He lay facedown in the shag, splayed like someone floating in the middle of a warm summer pond, feeling quite comfortable except for the seam of pain at the back of his skull. Somewhere a door slammed, the sound of footsteps making the floor vibrate lightly against his chin, and as he slowly began to sink into deeper, darker waters, he heard Ted Leo's voice: "Well look at this. Put down that phone, Coral, put it down. We don't need to involve the police, go back to your rooms, girls, just a drunken customer, nothing to worry about, I think we can take care of him ourselves."

A DREAM OF ESCAPE

Golden came to on his back, staring up in vacant wonder at the tilted dome of a star-blown sky. He had never truly noticed the night sky this way, seeing as if for the first time the individual bodies themselves, their particular hues and intensities, and beyond them whole galaxies like ghostly blooms of dust layered one on top of the other, the distances between them vast and growing as he watched. Only after several minutes of rapt astronomical observation, accompanied by a gentle rocking that made him feel as if he were laid out on the deck of some creaking old boat, did he think to wonder where he was. His hands were secured behind his back—this fact suggested gradually by the sharpening throb in his shoulders and wrists—and the familiar smells of dog and oil and dried blood told him he had been in this place before, and not all that long ago. His concussed brain took its sweet time circling around to the conclusion that he was in the bed of a moving pickup. Nelson Norman's pickup, he decided, finally. And just like that he understood how he'd gotten here, and where it was he was being taken.

He rolled onto his side to take the pressure off his arms, rested his head on the bald treads of a spare tire; there was nothing to do now, he decided, but enjoy the ride.

This grew increasingly difficult as the road grew rougher and his mind cleared, allowing his body to assert its various pains and infirmities. A hard wind had begun to howl, tossing the occasional handful of sand into his face. Soon his arms were cramping, the edges of his vision sparkled with nausea, and the lurching of the pickup kept his swollen and tender head bouncing in rhythm against the spare tire. He was given thirty seconds of relief when the pickup eased to a standstill, someone got out of the driver's side to conduct some mysterious business, and then they were moving again, the sound of dead vegetation screeching against the pickup's sides and the chain-link fence of the Test Site passing slowly a few feet above his head.

When they stopped ten minutes later, Golden was in agony; the bones of his arms felt like they might pop from their sockets, his stomach sloshed with hot bile, and an old steel toolbox had managed to clatter inch by inch across the pickup's bed and lodge itself against his hipbone.

"Nice ride?" Ted Leo shouted as he jerked open the tailgate. He grabbed one of Golden's ankles, Nelson came around and grabbed the other, and with the well-timed teamwork of a magician and his trusted assistant, they yanked him from the bed in a single smooth motion so that the first thing to hit the ground was the back of his neck. Ted Leo told him to get up, and he rolled around, moaning, trying to find his breath, until Nelson hooked him under the armpits and hauled him to his feet.

Ted Leo, decked out for this late-night adventure in track pants and a gold silk kimono, reached into the glove box and came out with the long-barreled Luger that Golden had seen before. The pistol had reputedly been owned by Al Capone, and Ted Leo was fond of brandishing it when he was angry, or if he was in a good mood, showing it off to guests and friends as one of his most cherished possessions. He made a show of checking the clip and then slamming it back home with a loud *ka-chick*. He accepted a shovel from Nelson, told him to stay with the pickup, and gave Golden a stiff jab in the spine with its blade. "March, soldier. Double-time. We don't got all night."

It did not occur to Golden to fight or run. Even if his hands had not been secured snugly behind his back, he wouldn't have had the focus or energy to use them; even if his legs were not weak to the point of shaking, his bad knee grinding with every step, there was nowhere for him to go. The fury that earlier had filled him so completely, that had carried him from Las Vegas on its combustible fumes and released itself upon the unsuspecting furnishings of the PussyCat Manor, had now burned off, leaving him flattened and spent, a hollow man walking meekly to his fate, leaking smoke and ashes at the seams, nothing left in him but surrender.

The wind came at them hard, pushing down out of the atmosphere in rhythmic bursts, raising walls of sand the two men walked through like spirits or ghosts. A startling patch of crystalline night sky would reveal itself for a moment, then disappear behind a black sheet of dust. Almost instantly Golden's eyes and throat were caked with grit, his ears filled with hissing particles. Feeling nothing but the occasional jab from Ted Leo's shovel when the wind blew him off course, he bowed his head and walked.

Just when Golden thought they had been separated, that he was walking alone into the roaring darkness, Ted Leo shouted for him to stop. Ted had a penlight, which he clenched in his teeth, and he scraped around in the dirt with his shovel, the dragon stitched into the back of his kimono whipping and writhing in the indefinite light. Even in the midst of a windstorm in the bitter hours of night, Ted went about this business with a kind of top-of-the-morning enthusiasm, as if everything were going perfectly according to some master plan. When the shovel rang out against metal, Ted Leo looked up and grinned like a jack-o'-lantern around the glow of his penlight.

He shouted something, but the wind swallowed every word. He was attempting to make some kind of speech, his eyes aglow, the black stalks of his lacquered hair lifting stiffly from his scalp. He kept on, gesturing with the shovel, but Golden could make out none of it; his head was filled with a crackling static that rose and fell. At some point Ted Leo realized his message, probably something cribbed from an old Jimmy Cagney movie—or maybe it was another lecture about the government's atomic testing program—was not getting across. He stepped up and shouted into Golden's face, "First off, okay, you're going to tell me where she is! That's what's gonna happen first!"

She. All this time, and Golden had not given a single thought to Huila. For a moment he saw her face, got a whiff of sandalwood in his nose, and felt a pang. He was glad to know she'd gotten away, that Ted had not yet found her. Now all he could do was hope she had found somewhere safe to hide.

Ted Leo waited for a response, but Golden simply stood in the swirling dust, the cuff of his pants caught in the spines of a fat little barrel cactus, mute. He wasn't sure if it was in some kind of protest against the horror of what had happened tonight, or if it was nothing but simple shock, but he had found himself unable or unwilling to speak, and in this silence, this refusal of words and their potential for harm, he had provided himself some small but necessary shelter.

"What's this?" Ted Leo shouted, his voice straining. The wind blew his kimono out with a crack, reversed, snapped it tightly around him again. "You just going to stand there, you big dumb Mormon jackass, and let me shoot you and put you in this hole?" He pointed the penlight into Golden's face. "Did you think you'd come all the way out here, after all you've done to *me*, the embarrassment you've caused *me*, thinking you're going to break up my place, you're going to hurt *me*, and then you're just going to stand there looking at me like that?"

Golden gave a slight shrug; Ted Leo seemed to have summed up the situation quite nicely. Grasping the handle of the shovel with both hands, Ted Leo let the penlight drop, and in its residual glow Golden could see that Ted Leo's cheerful mood was well on its way to abandoning him; his face had gone dark, his neck pulsing against its delicate gold chain. His big plan, apparently, was not working out as he'd hoped; he figured they would come out to this ominous location, he would give some kind of show-stopping speech made of equal parts Mafioso bromides and obscure scriptural references, and Golden would tell him everything he wanted to know before falling on his knees and, in a most pathetic and satisfying way, begging the great Ted Leo to spare his life. But Golden was not cooperating and this windstorm was turning out to be a problem; Ted kept having to blink sand from his eyes and spit it from the corners of his mouth as he spoke. For Golden, it felt like small victory to be able to see, and have a part in, Ted Leo being angered to the point of apoplexy one last time.

Because he caught a stinging gust of wind to the face at just the right moment, he did not see the blow coming. Luckily, the head of the shovel glanced off his shoulder before it rang against his left temple, sending a hard rattle through his skull and pitching him sideways. He staggered, but did not go down. If the tone of his voice was any indication, this made Ted Leo even angrier.

"You think this is funny?" he shouted, his voice cracking and singing in two different pitches. He was gripping the shovel as if he might take another swing. "You think any of this is funny?"

Golden straightened, his head still chiming. Strangely, the blow seemed to have cleared his mind a little, as if counteracting the effects of the coldcocking that had been administered to him earlier. He felt something sharpen in his chest, a quickening of the lungs, and when he looked into the purple shadows of Ted's contorted face, he remembered why he had come out here, and what he had failed so far to do: make this man pay for the harm that had been done to his boy, to his family. He had a harsh, metallic taste in the back of his mouth like a memory of the smell of Rusty's blood, his burning hair and flesh, and something at the center of him wobbled and tipped, spilling the last dregs of anger into his veins. He lurched forward, jerking wildly at the cords holding his wrists, and even as he shuddered through one final spasm of grief and rage he realized he *did* have something to say, though he wasn't sure what, exactly, and when he tried to speak what came out was nothing but mangled noise, something raw and shredded and torn up by the roots.

Ted Leo's eyes widened and he took a step back, shielding himself with the shovel, his expression changing in a second from angry, to frightened, to mocking.

"What's this?" he shouted, cupping his hand to his ear. "The man speaks. Say again, please?"

With this last bit of exertion Golden had drained himself thoroughly. He was tied up, wrung out, impotent in the truest sense of the word, and the only thing left to him now was to lodge a complaint, to let Ted Leo understand the suffering he'd caused. When he spoke, the pain in his throat made him dizzy: "You hurt my boy. My *son*."

"Oh, I haven't hurt anybody," Ted Leo said brightly, "and I've had no reason to hurt anybody until you came along." In illustration of his point he flipped the shovel around and with an awkward overhand motion drove the handle-end deep into Golden's solar plexus. While Golden was doubled over, gasping to recover his breath, Ted

Leo busied himself—nearly at Golden's feet—opening the bunker's metal hatch. The first breath Golden was able to negotiate into his lungs was so full of the spoiled, dead air of the bunker that he gagged and launched into a new fit of choking.

"Get used to it," Ted Leo said. He stood over Golden and gave him a paternal pat on the back. "You're going to be down there a long time."

When Ted Leo removed his pistol from the sash of his kimono and pressed the cold tip of the barrel against the side of his head, Golden experienced no panic or fear, but a spreading numbness, something close to peace. Bent over at the waist and unable to raise the necessary reserves to stand up straight and face his comeuppance, he stared into the perfect black hole in the ground that represented his oblivion, mesmerized by the notion that maybe he hadn't, after all, come out here for justice or vengeance or plain, pleasurable spite, but to realize, finally and in the most complete way possible, his desire for release, his dream of escape.

He closed his eyes and waited. But oblivion seemed to be taking a while. Ted Leo, always one for dramatics, was letting the moment play out, and now it seemed he was talking again, standing directly over Golden's doubled-over form and making some final pronouncement, though Golden could hear very little over the wind and the ocean sounds of his own lungs and heart. Something rose in him, some echo or vibration, and before he realized what he was doing he was already mumbling under his breath, his old habitual chant, *Emma-NephiHelamanNaomiJosephinePaulineNovellaParleySybilDeeanne* . . . and as the names made their way past his lips he felt, as if for the first time, the peculiar shape of each one, their particular syllables attended in his mind by some token to whom each name belonged, a dragonfly barrette, a smile full of missing teeth, a pair of orthopedic shoes, the dusty scent of sun-warmed hair, a nightmare cry from down the hall, an infant's tart breath, and here they came, his children, one after the other—not as a hopelessly long and tangled strand of DNA nonsense-letters, or as a single, pulsing organism (as he had come to think of them lately), ever-growing and demanding to be fed, but as individual bodies and faces appearing behind the glass of windows and the screens of front doors, waiting, eyes bright, wondering where he was, what was taking him so long to come home.

The names came faster now . . . *GaleAlvinRustyClifton* . . . bringing with them the memories of evenings, not so long ago, when they would squeeze together on the Barge, their heads still wet and soap-scented from their baths, and listen to him recite the made-up adventures of the Flatulent Astronaut or Johnny the Car-Driving Raccoon. Sweet, soft evenings when he could, if he tried hard enough, still hold them in the circumference of his arms. When he was still safe from the knowledge of how easily one of them might be lost.

Pierced by a fierce, sudden longing, he reached for them now . . . *HerschelGloryBooMartinWayneTeagueLouise* . . . believing if he could gather them one more time, before it was too late, they might be able to save him.

But, of course, he was too late, he would forever be too late, one step behind, apologies already in hand. He began to stumble over the names, mixing up the order and backtracking to get it right, straining to reach the list's end, to do this one thing right, at least, this one simple, last thing . . . *FigNewtonDarlingJame-o* . . . and now he was no longer speaking the names so much as inhaling them, swallowing them into his lungs and holding them there, his tongue thickening in his mouth, his rib cage creaking as it swelled, unable to withstand the mounting pressures of anxiety and sorrow and regret, and all at once the muscles of his neck tensed so painfully his eyes watered, and with a single great roar of release, he sneezed.

The sneeze jerked him upright and he felt a sharp impact at the top of his head, a moment of luminous weightlessness, and then nothing. It took him some time to understand that his eyes were closed, and that with some effort he could open them. He found himself standing, apparently still alive, in the middle of a great, black silence, his vision full of dying phosphorescence. He looked around: the mouth of the bunker at his feet, the hunkering forms of sagebrush, and to his right, a small triangle of ozone-blue light, which turned out to be the penlight abandoned in the dirt.

By the fresh new pain at the crown of his skull and the sensation of cold as the wind passed over it, he was fairly certain that part of his head had been blown off. But he was still standing, still thinking, which meant either the missing portion of his head was not strictly necessary, or that some alternate explanation was in order.

Behind him a moan rose up—a slow, devastated sound—and there was his alternate explanation, in the form of a half-conscious Ted Leo laid out on the ground wearing a bib of blood, his nose burst all over his face. At this sight the back of Golden's head began to sting more intensely, as if in sympathy for the damage it had caused. Ted moaned again, shifted one leg and, seized by a sudden, almost childish energy, Golden began to dance on his heels, working at his wrists; all along he thought he'd been tied up with some kind of cord, nylon or cotton, but he soon realized that it was nothing more than a few loops of electrical tape. With a sustained application of force he could get it to stretch just a little, a little more, and then he was free.

He cast around until he found the pistol. With a sudden black willingness he stood over Ted Leo and leveled it at his chest. He sighed, swallowed, decided he had a better idea. His hands clumsy and numb, he managed to drag Ted Leo the five feet to the bunker and feed him, headfirst, into its mouth. The folds of Ted's soft belly caught the steel edges, the fine silk of his kimono snagged and tore; it was like trying to force a Q-tip into a keyhole. It took more than a little nudging and tucking, then some outright shoving and tamping before something gave way and Ted Leo disappeared into the inky shadows with such a suddenness it was as if he'd fallen through to another dimension. Golden thought he heard a thud and the echoing word "No" but did not hesitate; he clanged the lid down and cranked the rusted latch.

In the moments he took to gather himself, to work the blood back into his hands and catch his breath, he sensed a vibration beneath his feet, a mournful lowing that quickly rose in pitch, spiking into pleading shouts, formless words that boomed and echoed and were slowly lost to the wind as he limped off into the swirling dark.

TWO BIG MEN, ONE LITTLE GIRL

When Golden opened the door and settled into the passenger-side seat, Nelson Norman did not so much as look his way. For a while they stared out the windshield at the granular light of predawn, an awkward silence between them like two strangers waiting at a bus stop. The cab smelled like stale beer and cinnamon gum, and the only sound besides the scudding wind was the comforting whir of the truck's heater.

"So it's just you then?" Nelson said finally.

Golden gave a slight movement of the head that might have been a nod.

Nelson eyed the pistol that Golden held in his lap. He let a good ten seconds pass. "You shoot him?"

"Thought about it."

Ten more seconds. "He's still out there?"

"In the bunker."

"Huh," said Nelson. He nodded once. "You going to leave him there?"

"Haven't decided."

"Just to tell you?" Nelson said. "I ain't going to mention none of this to nobody. And I'm not just saying that because you got that gun."

They made eye contact and Golden surprised himself by nearly laughing, a bubble of noise rising in his throat that had no business making it into the open. He swallowed it down and let himself sink into the seat springs, shuddering with relief, and then the feeling turned on him and his throat closed up again, a black fluttering passed through his chest, and he had to brace his hand against the dashboard. He said, "He hurt my son."

"Your who?"

Golden gave a brief, poor explanation of the events of that night, asked Nelson what he knew.

Nelson shook his head. "That wasn't Ted Leo, no. He's done some things, but a bomb or something, no, that don't make no sense. I'd know."

"He was going to shoot me, with this gun."

"Nuh-uh. He was just scaring you, hey? The whole thing, the coyotes and the bunker, that damn couch, all this. He'd never shoot nobody. No guts, all show, that's Ted Leo. And you ain't the first one. Crazy as he is, the man's a fucking kitty cat. And now somebody's called his bluff."

"He thinks I stole his wife."

Nelson grunted, sighed. "You think he did all this 'cause he cared about her? You think? You embarrassed him, that's all, and you ain't the first. She's been working out how to leave for a long time. He treated her terrible. I'm glad she got away. You hadn't come out here and busted up his place, he'd a gotten bored with you sooner than later."

Golden considered for a moment the depths of his misapprehensions about the world he thought he knew. Could it be that for Huila he had been nothing more than just a way out, a means of escape? Before he finished asking himself the question it occurred to him how easily she could be asking the same about him.

For a time they watched the paling sky. One by one the clumps of sage revealed themselves like puffs of smoke rising out of the earth, everything one distinct shade of gray against another. Wind whistled around the pickup's antenna, rattled against the windows, but in here it was a distant, comforting sound.

"Looks like you're bleeding out of your ear there."

"A lot?" Golden touched his ear.

"Not too bad," Nelson said. "Damn. You really leave him in that hole?"

Golden nodded in disbelief. "I did."

Nelson sniffed, smiled. He sat there for a while, cupping his giant belly like a Buddha statue in somebody's garden. He said, "Your boy, he's gonna be all right?"

Golden remained motionless, as if he hadn't heard the question. Then, almost imperceptibly, he shook his head.

"I'm sorry," Nelson said. He listened to the wind. "What I could tell, you got a nice family."

"I do," Golden whispered.

"Big family," Nelson said.

Golden nodded.

"Don't know how you do it."

"Neither do I."

Something in Golden's vision shifted, the stark world beyond the windshield going fuzzy and indistinct as the picture hanging from the rearview mirror came into focus. He found himself looking at the bright, hopeful face of Nelson's daughter—what was her name? Mary? Marlene?—and Nelson followed his gaze and they were both staring at the picture as if mesmerized, two big men looking into the eyes of one little girl. Something welled in Golden so strongly his voice failed when he spoke: "Don't ever let her out of your sight."

"No," Nelson whispered.

"Don't ever," Golden said.

"No."

They were quiet a long time. Nelson asked what they should do. There would be a patrol along in the next few minutes. Golden asked if Nelson would mind driving him back to his pickup.

"And Ted Leo?" Nelson set one big paw on the vibrating bakelite shift knob.

"You can let him out or leave him down there to rot, it's up to you," he said. "But you do let him out, tell him I'm keeping this gun of his, just in case."

THE CONFESSIONS OF GOLDEN RICHARDS

EARLY THE MORNING AFTER IT HAD HAPPENED TRISH DROVE OVER TO Forest Glen to pick up Rose to take her to the hospital in Las Vegas. They did not speak the entire trip, crammed together into that small car like astronauts, the sun breaching the horizon behind them, the pink, dawn-washed desert floating by. Of course, there was great concern over how Rose would handle this new shock, but she walked with a certain hunched purposefulness across the hospital's parking lot, resisting Trish's offer of a steadying hand. At the nurses' station, she was the one to ask for directions. In the room, where Rusty lay hidden beneath a webwork of bandages and wires and tubes, she addressed the sight of her maimed son with a calm that Trish, who stood behind her weeping, on the verge of hysteria, could never have managed.

This was all more than enough—too much—for any one morning, but when Trish came out into the hall Nola took her aside and told her that Golden was MIA. He had been acting strangely, she said, not speaking, something wild in his eyes. She and Beverly had decided he was in shock, nothing more than that, and under the circumstances there were bigger things to worry about. But now he had been gone almost five hours. Sheriff Fontana, who had driven down from St. George to conduct interviews and gather information, made little effort to hide his concern over Golden's disappearance.

"Something's not right here," the sheriff had said, sipping at a paper coffee cup from the machine, "and maybe we oughta figure it out sooner rather than later."

Golden showed up not long afterward, proving the sheriff correct: something was, most definitely, wrong. As he limped down the corridor, people stared or turned away as if they had stumbled on something intensely private; a mother and her two children fled before him and an old lady stepping out of her room called upon Jesus as he passed. Dusty from head to toe, trailing sand from the rolled cuffs of his jeans and sporting a carnation of bloody hair at the back of his head, he looked like someone who had been beaten up, buried in a shallow grave, and unearthed only to be roughed up some more. His eye sockets were bruised, his bottom lip swollen and split neatly down the middle, his left ear caked with blood. If you looked closely you could see a shard of glass glinting like a half-buried diamond in the side of his neck.

Before they could ask him what had happened, he was intercepted by a fat orderly, who called for a wheelchair and a nurse.

"Sir!" shouted the orderly, as if Golden were a foreigner or a senior citizen, or some infernal combination of both. "Sir! Stop, please, sir! Right there, we've got a chair here for you, have a seat and we'll take care of you, sir!" Another orderly slipped behind Golden with the chair and together, as if they were all in on the same vaudeville routine, they executed a maneuver that had Golden falling backward in the chair and being wheeled off toward the emergency room, head lolling.

After some X-rays, a few stitches, and the setting of a broken pinky finger, he was installed in a semiprivate room where Trish and Nola were allowed to visit. They arrived just before the attending physician, who wore his silver hair pulled back in a neat little pigtail, entered the room waving an X-ray exposure around as if it were a Polaroid he was trying to hurry along. His name tag said FULDHEIM, and he was, Trish noted, wearing clogs.

"Well, Mr. Richards," he said. "We've been involved in some kind of altercation, have we?"

"Looks like it," Golden said. In his light blue smock he was laid out on the white expanse of the bed like a halibut on ice. A perfect tonsure had been shaved in the crown of his head, his wound sewn up with thirteen sutures and swabbed with Betadine. His nose looked a half-size too big and had gone a dusky purple around the bridge. Along with the eclectic collection of facial welts and bruises he now wore several bandages of various shapes and sizes.

"And you've already spoken to law enforcement, I take it?"

"That comes next, I think," Golden said.

"Your injuries are mostly superficial, Mr. Richards, except one." He held up the X-ray to the overhead light and Trish and Nola gathered in to look. Dr. Fuldheim traced something with his finger, but all Trish could make out was a ghostly opalescence. "That dark line? That's a hairline fracture to the skull. You were struck with something, Mr. Richards? Some blunt object?"

"A shovel?" said Golden.

"A shovel," said Dr. Fuldheim.

"Or an axe handle. Could've been any number of things."

The doctor made a sour face and gave his pigtail a tug as if to confirm it was still attached to his head. "Whatever it was, you are now the proud owner of a grade-three concussion, which will entail your taking it easy for the next while. We'll keep you here overnight for observation. You're also dehydrated, possibly malnourished, with a couple of cracked ribs, and the ER nurse noted that you have some kind of burn on your left side. May I take a peek?"

Golden lifted his arm and the doctor spread open the gap in the smock to reveal a shiny raised welt a few inches above the hip.

"Dare I ask where this came from?"

"A cattle prod?" Golden said.

"A cattle prod," said the doctor.

"Give a pretty good jolt, those things."

"A cattle prod," the doctor repeated.

"I think that's what it was."

The doctor cast an accusatory glance toward Nola and Trish. "And you're family, I take it?"

"We're his *wives*," Nola said, showing her teeth. "Half of 'em, anyway. The other two are upstairs."

The doctor forced a thin smile, looked at Golden and back to the two women, to see if there was a joke he was missing out on. Clearly, he was dealing with crazy people.

When Sheriff Fontana arrived, Dr. Fuldheim seized the opportunity to escape into the hall. What relief Trish felt at the sight of the sheriff, who brought with him an Aqua Velva–scented familiarity to this surreal morning, the calming influence of a man in uniform, one who made daily scrutiny of life's strife and ugliness while managing to hold a steady gaze. If there was anyone who could sort this out, tell them exactly what was happening and why, he could.

"Ladies," he said, removing his hat and placing one hand gently inside its crown. His thin face bore all the pits and facets of a roughly napped arrowhead. "I'll need a few minutes alone with your husband. After that, you can feel free to do with him as you see fit."

They went out in the hall to wait, and the only thing Nola had to say was, "A *cattle prod*?"

Beverly had come down from Rusty's room to wait with them when the sheriff emerged. He inquired about Rusty's condition and Beverly told him that nothing had changed, that they could only wait to see which way he would go. The sheriff nodded, turned his watery eyes on each one of them in turn. He explained that Golden wanted to talk to them one at a time, alone.

"It's not my place to say so," he said, before making his way to the exit, "but I hope you'll give him the benefit of the doubt. I think there's a good chance he's gonna need it."

One by one they went in to him. Later, they would compare notes, and find that what he told each of them was remarkably consistent. First, he made his confessions: the PussyCat Manor, Ted Leo, Huila, all of it. He explained that, though he had not technically committed adultery and thereby broken his sacred marital covenants, he had carried on a secret relationship with a woman who was not his wife. He had lied, he had coveted, he had lusted in his heart. He had betrayed his wives and his children and, maybe worst of all, had put them in harm's way; what had happened to Rusty, he believed, was a result of the selfish and shortsighted choices he had made.

He would understand if they left him, he told each of them, he deserved no less. If they did leave, he would do everything he could to support each wife and her children until she found a better situation. And then he told them how sorry he was.

The *sorrys*, when they started, fairly boiled out of him. He had held up well, if a little stiffly, under the stress of open confession, but when it came to contrition, it was as if he were letting down his defenses and getting comfortable in the presence of an old and beloved friend; he let the *sorrys* fly. He was sorry for his complacency, his chronic boneheadedness, his propensity for worry and gloom. He apologized for his abdications of duty and authority, his bland and deferential ways, his flaws of character and lapses in judgment too many and comically varied to name. He was ashamed of his financial failings and romantic shortcomings, his jags and silences, sorry for all the lost and forgotten details, the sorrows gone unattended, for his willingness to concede everything and anything for one blessed moment's peace. But mostly he was sorry, so sorry, for Glory, for losing her and, once she was gone, for not being able to let her go; for Jack, for not properly mourning him; and for Rusty—here his voice faltered, and a look of sharp and crippling pain flashed across his face—for the boy he had never really gotten to know, and never would.

He gritted his teeth, shook his head. He was sorry, above all else, for how very sorry he was, sorry enough that he would do everything he could not to be sorry for anything ever again.

When he was finished he looked at Trish and waited. As was customary, she had been the last to take her turn, which meant he had given a version of this address four times now, and though he looked depleted by the effort, pale and shrunken on the white expanse of hospital linen, there was a flat resolve in his eyes she had never seen before; he held her stare and did not look away. Whether this was merely a symptom of his concussion or something more lasting was hard to say.

Outside, it was a bright morning, the sky a high flawless blue, but here, within the circumference of the pleated privacy curtain, they were caught in a pocket of dim air that smelled of floor wax. He kept quiet, waiting, the bruises around his eyes dark as seawater. Clearly, he wanted a reaction or a response, something, but she had only one question: Who was this person she had married? This man who courted strange women and built brothels in secret and went out to get himself roughed up by the shady elements of the world only to be back in time for breakfast?

They gazed in speculation at each other, holding the stare until Trish couldn't stand it any longer. "And what's her name?"

"Who?"

"This girlfriend of yours." Such a petty thing to say under the circumstances, but in her shock she couldn't decide if the question came out of anger or spite or simple, plain old curiosity.

"Huila," he said.

"Huila." She nodded, thinking, *How could you* not *fall for a woman with such a name?*

"And she's beautiful?"

Golden nodded. "No," he said.

"And you love her?"

This got him, finally; he looked away, down at the scraped knuckles of his hands, turning them over in his lap as if he'd never seen them before. Much more quickly than she would have expected, he said, "I don't know. I guess I do, or did. But that doesn't mean I've ever loved you any less."

At this, she could only smile; he couldn't have given her a more perfect, watertight answer. Because this, after all, was the basic truth they all chose to live by: that love was no finite commodity. That it was not subject to the cruel reckoning of addition and subtraction, that to give to one did not necessarily mean to take from another; that the heart, in its infinite capacity—even the confused and cheating heart of the man in front of her, even the paltry thing now clenched and faltering inside her own chest—could open itself to all who would enter, like a house with windows and doors thrown wide, like the heart of God itself, vast and accommodating and holy, a mansion of rooms without number, full of multitudes without end.

JUST A MIXED-UP BOY

The days that followed were an exercise in controlled chaos; the wives circulated from Las Vegas to Virgin and back again, trying to keep the houses running, the children washed and fed and on top of their schoolwork, while in the meantime shuttling them back and forth to Las Vegas, in groups of threes and fours, so they could have the chance to visit their brother while he still lived. The doctors, and there seemed to be more of them than anyone could keep track of, agreed on one basic point: Rusty could go at any time. Though they had been able to stop most of the bleeding, and the swelling was under control, the metal fragments still embedded in his brain had done too much damage already and threatened to do more. One of them could drift or shift, causing a new hemmorhage, damaging a part of the brain that controlled a vital function or inducing a cata-strophic stroke. As one doctor—a tall, craggy sort who prided himself on his western-style plainspokenness—had explained to Trish: they could do further surgery now, which would almost certainly end the boy's life or leave him in a permanent vegetative state, or they could wait for the end to come in its own good time.

Of the wives, only Rose stayed in Las Vegas for the long haul, unwilling to leave her son's bedside except to use the bathroom and occasionally take a quick meal in the cafeteria; if her child was going to pass on, she intended to be there to see him off. The worry that the shock of this tragedy might push her, once and for all, over the slippery edge of her sanity had quickly vanished; if anything, the opposite had happened. Within hours of arriving at the hospital a bit of color returned to her cheeks, a clarity to her eyes. She asked the doctors about EKG readouts, kept an eye on the heart monitor and IV, and in her quiet way quizzed the nurses over antibiotics and morphine dosages. It turned out that at the age of nineteen she had defied her parents by going off to a nursing school in Colorado, where she spent two years before coming back to Utah to attend to her ailing mother, who refused to see a doctor or set foot in a hospital, who would put her fate in no hands but God's. By the time her mother died—of a liver condition that could have been easily treated with medication— Rose had lost her scholarship and burned through most of her mea- ger savings. As if it had been prearranged by those mysterious and unpredictable hands of the Almighty, she ended up, just like her sis- ters and her mother and her mother's mother before her, a woman of the Principle, a plural wife.

Rose was not the only one who seemed to have been fundamen- tally altered by the events of the past few days; what to make of Bev- erly, sitting in the waiting room with a lost, almost bovine cast to her eyes, some sternness in her broken, watching *One Life to Live* in the company of a large Filipino family? Or of Golden, who came and went with his fearfully puffy face and raccoon mask, the cords of his neck pulled tight with anger or irritation, slamming doors and mak- ing gruff noises like a shambling revenant who had left his old mild and deferential self behind?

No, very little made sense anymore. On her way back to the hospi- tal from Virgin Trish had stopped off at a used book store to pick up a few Harlequins for Rose, thinking she could use a little distraction, something to lose herself in for a few hours. She left the stack of books on the bedside table, hoping it wouldn't bother Rose that Trish knew her badly kept secret, and when she came back she found Rose on one side of Rusty's bed and Beverly on the other, both so absorbed in their books—*No Place for a Lady* and *The Bride Wore Spurs*, respectively— that neither could be bothered to look up when Trish entered the room.

Through all of this only Nola seemed to have managed to keep a grip on herself. She gave back rubs and pep talks to children and adults alike, handed out loose change for the vending machine and reminded them all, with her bursts of high-octane chatter and her ability to cry and laugh with equal vigor, that while all the moping and mournful whispering was understandable, it sure as heck wasn't doing anybody any good.

It was Nola who called Trish into Golden's room the morning after he had been admitted. With the encouragement of some pain medication, he had slept through the rest of the day and the following night. Once up, he groaned and stumbled around half blind like a bear just out of his winter den. There was a tiny nurse shouting at him to lie back down, he could not leave without being given clearance by a doctor, and Nola was doing her best to direct him back to his bed, but he was having none of it, crackling loudly in his paper smock and tangling himself in the IV tube, letting it be known that he wanted to be left alone. He wanted to go see his son. He wanted to know where his pants were.

Even when Sheriff Fontana arrived carrying a canvas knapsack, Golden did not calm down. He ripped the IV needle out of his hand and complained to the sheriff that someone had absconded with his shoes. The sight of her husband shocked Trish; in his severely undersized gown, with his ripening face and pathetically pale and mottled limbs, he looked like he had aged twenty years and lost as many pounds.

"Maybe you'd like to rest easy for a minute," the sheriff suggested. "I've come to talk to you about your boy."

Immediately Golden quit agitating. He slumped back onto the bed and waited for the news.

Sheriff Fontana, creaking like an old wooden bridge, explained that their search of Old House and the grounds of the Spooner place had turned up a few things. He opened his sack and displayed the items they'd found hidden in the closet of the boy's bedroom: three battered homemade notebooks, stapled together from stacks of cheap composition paper, a spool of fuse cord, several canisters of black powders—a couple of them nearly empty—a Luden's tin full of magnetized iron filings, a few comic books, a magazine called *Ukrainian Lovelies*, a partially gnawed Bit-O-Honey, some loose rocks and rusty nails, a paperback copy of *Improvised Explosive and Incendiary Devices for the Guerrilla Fighter*, and a few items that had gone missing from the various houses in the last couple of months: a small quartzite Mayan figure from Trish's mantel, one of Rose's embroidered pillowcases, a silver serving spoon that had once belonged to Beverly's grandmother, and several bras of various colors and sizes.

"Bit of a pack rat, this one," said the sheriff dryly. "Among a whole lot of other things, what you're looking at is the ingredients for a pretty serious firecracker and pointers on how to build it."

Golden gave one of the canisters an idle shake. "He did this . . . himself?"

The sheriff nodded. "Looks like it. You read those notebooks, it comes pretty clear. What we got here, I think, is just a mixed-up boy wanting a little attention."

Golden rifled through one of the notebooks, scanning page after scribble-filled page. Later, Trish would read every word of them herself, something spiking through her chest at seeing her own name written so often and fondly in the boy's fierce hand, wondering at the level of detail and invention, the spectacularly long and angry lists, the crude but loving doodles of naked eyeballs and swirling explosions and daggers dribbling blood, the plots and schemes of such impressive unlikelihood they revealed a kind of brave and dogged faith. Stung by guilt, she would remember the sheriff's words—*just a mixed-up boy wanting a little attention*—and she would realize how culpable all of them were, the whole family, how they had stood by, doing nothing, while Rusty slid away into the abyss. But what would stay with her for a long time to come was the fallen look on Golden's face as he read, the way his eyes lost focus and his cheeks sagged with the unbearable weight of his failure to preserve and protect his son from his own failures as a father, from failures of genetics and circumstance and fate, from failure itself.

"What we'll need now," said the sheriff quietly, "is to figure out where he got his hands on these things. You don't have"—he tipped back one of the canisters—"red magnesium flash powder just laying around the house, do you?"

Golden did not respond, still lost in the notebooks, but Trish and Nola shook their heads.

"I'm pretty sure I know most of the names in here—family members, kids from school—but there's one that shows up a few times that I don't recognize. Any of you know somebody named June?"

Trish flushed at the sound of the name, at the recognition that June was almost certainly the source of the bomb-making ingredients, but when the sheriff fixed her with his watery gaze she found herself shaking her head again.

After the sheriff left, she counted to twenty, excused herself, and ran down the hall, catching him just as he'd donned his felt hat and was pushing through the glass doors into the unreasonably bright Las Vegas morning.

"I think—" she began, but her throat closed on her and suddenly she wasn't sure what she'd come to say; it occurred to her that she no longer had a clear impression of who she was or where her allegiances lay.

The sheriff removed his hat again, tucked it gently against his belly as if it were a sleeping kitten. "Anything you could tell me, that'd be fine. But don't go rushing to say something you'll regret."

To her, this didn't sound at all like the kind of thing an officer of the law should say to a potential witness or informant, but, strangely, it was what gave her the encouragement she needed to tell him what she knew. She told him about June: where he lived, about his relationship with Rusty, and that she was certain he had not knowingly supplied the boy with explosives.

"He's a good man," she said.

"Course he is," said the sheriff, glancing up at the sun. "I don't doubt it a bit."

A NEW PLAN

Rusty lasted longer than anyone expected. The doctors had been pessimistic about his chances to survive the night, much less a week, and after ten days they decided he'd stabilized well enough to be transferred to St. George, where the family could carry on their vigil with much less in the way of inconvenience.

It was the day before this relocation that Golden called a special family meeting at Big House. Nobody could remember a special family meeting being called for a very long time; the family gathered twice a week for the Summit of the Wives and for Family Home Evening—to attempt to muster them all into one place at any other time or for any other reason would have been an act of senseless self-punishment. But this was a new dispensation in the Richards family; everyone was acting weirdly, stepping cautiously and speaking in altered voices, every day arriving empty and strange like an alien craft lowering itself out of the sky.

They assembled in the family room, the little ones, as had become their habit, standing on the hearth or scaling the rock fireplace a few feet so they could get a better view. The only ones not in attendance were Rusty, of course, and Rose, who was still in Las Vegas arranging the final details of Rusty's transfer to St. George. Golden stood at the margin where the carpet met the linoleum of the kitchen, looking over the room and running through the list of names to make sure everyone was present; you could see his lips move as he whispered each name, could almost hear the singsong tune echo inside his head. And then he went quiet, as if waiting for the chatter to die down, though no one had made a peep.

Most of his bruises had faded by now, but he still bore the drained and slightly puckered look of a corpse. His pants did not seem to fit

him anymore—his belt bunched his pants at the waist—and his normally expressive mouth, with its large teeth always ready to reveal
themselves, had fallen into a straight, grim line. He had spent the last
week either sitting at Rusty's bedside or speaking on the phone and
going on long, mysterious errands that no one dared ask him about.

Today, in the family room filled with expectant bodies, he did
not hem and haw and purse his lips, as was his usual practice when
speaking in front of a group. He simply nodded once and gave them
the news.

He had a new plan for the family, he said, a plan he had already
put in motion, and he thought it was about time they all heard about
it. Earlier that day he had finalized the sale of Old House to that nice
little snowbird couple from Canada who had been offering to buy it
for years with the idea of turning it into a bed and breakfast. The pro-
ceeds of the sale would be used pay off his business debts—to save
Big Indian Construction from bankruptcy, essentially—but mostly to
fund the large-scale renovation of Big House, which would begin as
soon as possible. The plan was to build a three-thousand-square-foot
addition onto the south portion of Big House, making it large enough
to fit them all under its single roof. He'd done a lot of praying and
soul-searching since Rusty's accident, and decided that if they were
going to be a family, a real family who loved and watched out for
each other, this was the only way.

He cleared his throat. He wondered if there were any questions.

Everyone, of course, was already looking at Beverly, who had been
making the plans and decisions around here before most of them
were born, who was the source and matrix of every policy and agenda
that had ever remotely affected the family's interests. On some level
even the little ones understood this, but it was immediately clear to
them, as it was to everyone else, that this new plan, and all that it
implied, came as a surprise to Beverly. Just like the rest of them she
sat speechless, looking around as if hoping for some kind of clarification, wearing an expression of puzzled shock.

"You mean," said Naomi, her voice rising with dismay, "we're going to be living *together*?"

Golden nodded.

"*All* of us?" cried Jame-o.

"All," said Golden.

If, as it appeared, Golden had assumed this announcement would be greeted with a sober acceptance befitting the situation, he was sorely mistaken. A squall of murmuring and moaning raced through the room, and then some of the kids began to cry outright. Only the Three Stooges, who jostled and gave each other five, seemed at all pleased.

"Mom!" wailed Sybil, the tears already starting. "Say something!"

For once, Nola was caught speechless. She shrugged, an uncertain grin wavering on her face. Finally, she said, "And we're all supposed to live *where* while this renovation is taking place?"

"Right here, in Big House," Golden said. "It's going to be cramped, and we're going to have to be patient with each other, work around each other, but it'll be good for us, it's exactly what we need."

Trish, who was standing behind the couch and trying to console a weeping and inconsolable Josephine, made eye contact with Nola, who then shot a look at Beverly. This was entirely new territory for the sister-wives; they had never, as a group, been taken off guard in quite this way; if they were going to protest or make some kind of last-ditch play, it would have to happen now. But they were caught, Trish realized, in a bind of their own making. Long before she had ever come onto the scene, the wives had been pleading with Golden to take control, to embrace his God-given patriarchal authority, to please, for the love of heaven and earth, make a *decision* once in a while. And now that he had gone and embraced his God-given patriarchal authority in the fullest and most audacious of ways, what was there for any of them to say?

And what's more, this new situation might actually work to their benefit, Trish decided, at least for some. Despite the grand bother of it all, the inevitable squabbles and turf wars, the further loss of privacy and individual identity, Nola and Rose would almost surely come out ahead; according to the indisputable bylaws of domestic provenance, Big House was *their* house, *their* domain—no matter how many additions were made to it or who came to live under its roof—and if the house was the body and the family its soul, then Nola and Rose would be exercising much more control over the body—and therefore the soul—of the Richards clan in the years to come.

And if she was willing to look at it in the right way, Trish, too, would be gaining something: a place at the bright center of things to which she could return from the exile of her loneliness and grief, where Faye could learn to be a friend, a sister, maybe even a normal little girl.

Only Beverly would be losing on every account. Not only would her beloved Old House be taken from her, but many of the perks and privileges she enjoyed as the first and only lawfully wedded wife; in a single stroke she would become a refugee, stripped of all of the entitlements of home, forced to start over in a strange and hostile land. So did she protest, did she fume, did she bring to bear all her legendary powers of persuasion and resolve? Hardly. She sat stiff-backed and mute in her chair like a defendant under the echo of a guilty verdict, hands folded meekly in her lap, as if this were the outcome she expected all along.

Wisely, Golden did not allow more time for his audience to formulate additional questions or commentary; he excused them all, and they scattered into the warm afternoon with wailing and gnashing of teeth, to face the prospect of an uncertain and very crowded future.

ONLY THE BODY

Another night, and she couldn't find her way into sleep. Strangely, her insomnia had nothing to do with the fact that she was sleeping on an army surplus cot that squeaked and groaned pitifully every time she moved; or that her new quarters—Big House's utility closet—smelled of bleach and old mop and something vaguely mineral and sharp that may have been urine; or that at this moment Cooter, who was used to having the room to himself, was now tucked snugly into her ribs, occasionally stretching to dig his hind paws into her sensitive flesh, snoring and sighing his way through a heedless sleep that made her grind her molars with jealousy. No, what was keeping her awake was her own mind—spinning with the possibilities and decisions of her new situation—and her own body, which felt like a piece of fruit left too long on the vine, swollen with the carefully hoarded juices of a hundred sunny days, wanting only to be plucked and eaten, ready to burst.

When, in a fit of insomniac exasperation, she threw off her blanket and planted her feet on the cold concrete floor, Cooter groaned and rolled onto his back, making little growls of annoyance at having his slumber disturbed.

"Keep it to yourself," she advised, and not for the first time wondered how, after everything, all the strife and sorrow of her life, she had been given this reward: bunking in a utility closet with a flatulent dog.

As had become her nightly habit, she padded out into the hall to make her tour of the house. She was met first, as always, by the strange sight of her husband, stretched out on the Barge at the edge of the dim dining room. In the chaos and rancor that accompanied the mass relocation to Big House, nobody had given much thought to where Golden would sleep. That first night he had the good sense to spend in the cab of his pickup, where he wouldn't have to listen to the squabbling and backbiting and on-the-hour outbursts caused by twenty-six irritable children crammed into a space barely adequate for half as many. The second night, after coming home to find the house in a free-for-all, the children madly circling the racetrack, trying to burn off the stress of their new circumstance, he stepped into the flow of bodies and shouted for them to stop. He decreed that from that day hence there would be no more running on the racetrack. "No more!" he croaked, and because he had spent the entire day long bargaining with subs and crew bosses and haggling with the boneheads at the county offices, calling in every favor he could think of to get this renovation up and running as soon as possible, his voice had gone hoarse, with a raspy bass undertone. He sounded, Nola commented, a little like Johnny Cash. "No more!" he boomed again in his Johnny Cash voice, and the children, frozen in their tracks, stared at him in wonder.

He gave an order for the older boys to retrieve the Barge from where it had been stashed behind the toolshed after the Todd Freebone episode. He had them place it directly in the entryway to the dining room—where it would serve to block racetrack traffic as well as make the passage from family room to dining room one giant inconvenience—and, after a spartan dinner of cube steak and cold peas, wrapped himself in a scratchy, brightly striped Mexican blanket and fell immediately unconscious in its lumpy embrace.

The ploy worked for a couple of days until the racetrack's primeval call proved too strong to resist. By Friday of that week the children were already back to their laps, charged with the pure joy that comes with performing a strictly forbidden act in the company of others, bounding off the Barge's cushions and arms, doing the Flying Dutchman and the Fosbury Flop, the little ones swarming over the back of it like lemmings off a cliff.

Their father would never again make so much as a peep about the racetrack. Some mornings, if he did not vacate the Barge quickly enough, the early risers, usually the young ones in footsie pajamas, would clamber over him as if he were nothing but a part of the furniture, and with an expression of pained tolerance he would submit himself to the abuse of their sharp knees or badly groomed toenails as they hauled themselves up by an ear or a handful of belly fat, occasionally using his big head for a stepping-stone.

Upstairs, she walked the long hall, keyed in to the house's audible frequencies, the collective drone of sleeping bodies, the sighing vents, the rasp of skin against sheets. On Golden's orders the children had been divided randomly among the rooms, separated only by gender. Amazingly, after those first few difficult nights, things had calmed down considerably. Here was Alvin sharing a bed with both Herschel and Clifton, here were sworn enemies Novella and Josephine wrapped in the same blanket, the lion lying down with the lamb if Trish had ever seen it. And here was Faye, one arm thrown over the hip of her sister and new best friend Fig Newton; when Trish had given Faye the option of sleeping with her in the utility closet or braving one of the upstairs bedrooms, she had chosen the latter without so much as an attempt at sparing her mother's feelings.

Back in the closet, Trish fished the envelope from the secret pocket inside her suitcase, and for the thirtieth or fortieth time read the letter it contained.

> *Dear Trish,*
>
> *If only I was brave enough to talk to you in person, but you should know that writing this letter is taking every scrap of courage I have. I can't tell you how terrible I feel about Rusty. Of course I am largely responsible for what happened and while I would do anything, give anything to make it right, all I can offer is my deepest regret and sorrow.*
>
> *I wanted to tell you that I've decided to move away. To where, I haven't really decided yet, but I can't stay here. (Even though the sheriff's office has cleared me of wrongdoing, it won't stop the people here from blaming me, and rightfully so. You've probably seen the story in the paper. Whenever I go out now, people point and stare.) So I'll be leaving in the next couple of weeks after I sell my equipment. Which is why I'm writing. I'd like to invite you to come with me. I don't know where I'm going or what I'm going to do, and I know how absurd it must sound, especially under the circumstances. You already have a life and a family and you're probably laughing as you read this, but I can't get over the idea that I may never see or speak to you again. So I decided, for once in my life, to take a chance. Would it sound like something out of your favorite romance novel if I said that I would do*

everything I could to give you the happiness you deserve? Yes, it prob-
ably would. So I will stop before I embarrass myself anymore. I won't
even pretend to hope that you'll consider my offer, so I'll just say that the
hours I've spent with you are the most precious and happy of my life.

>   *Your friend always,*
>   *June*

One week ago today that she had found the letter stuck in her
screen door. She had pulled up in front of the duplex, intending, after
moving her possessions to Big House, to make one final sweep of the
place. She had been thinking about how the same drive she had taken
hundreds, maybe thousands of times, with the same evening sun dipping behind the same broken mountains, could turn, in the wake
of catastrophe, beautifully strange: frogs calling out from some wet
ditch, the scent of cooling tar, the violet light of dusk caught in the
bowl of a lost hubcap, a troupe of quail sprinting single-file down the
middle of the road.

She was also thinking—marveling, really—about how her life
could be so easily picked up and moved, how the collected sum of her
shrinking existence could fit into a Volkswagen Rabbit with room to
spare.

June's pickup had been pulling away just as she arrived. Though
she waved, he seemed to turn his head away and hide under the bill
of his cap. She'd thought about it many times, but had not found the
right time to visit him since the accident; she figured he might have
difficulty understanding why she'd sold him out to the sheriff. And
then she read the letter, standing in the empty living room of a shabby
house for which she was already nostalgic, and hadn't slept more than
an hour at a time since.

It helped to lose herself in the new routine of her days: a morning and afternoon of babysitting and domestic duty at Big House,
her four-hour shift at the hospital, and then back to her utility closet,
where she would spend another restless night. Her evenings at the

hospital she liked the most: the quiet order of the place, the squeak and clatter of gurneys and carts, the sweet chemical smell of X-ray exposures, the rustle of sensible nurse hosiery, the predictable disturbances quickly and efficiently resolved. They'd installed Rusty at the far end of the old ward—which in a bygone era had served as the region's only cotton mill—in a room with high ceilings hung with coils of painted ductwork, a single narrow window, and one wall still showing some of its original hand-thrown brick.

Rose had arranged it so that along with her daily eight-to-four shift, Beverly, Nola, Trish and even Golden would each be responsible for a four-hour block and Rusty would be attended to around the clock. With the blessing of the nursing staff, many of whom had family ties to the Virgin polygamists, she showed them how to keep his tongue and lips moist with ice chips, how to change his diapers and give him his sponge baths and swab his gums with lemon glycerine, the proper way to work his muscles and joints to stave off atrophy, the whole while being sure to speak or sing to him, to hold his hand, as if he could be tied down, by the cords of voice and touch alone, to the world of the living.

It was quite something to watch Rose care for her son. She worked with a focus Trish had never seen her bring to anything else in her life; to concentrate on one child to the exclusion of everything else, this she could do. Her eyes shone, her neck rigid in constant surveillance, her movements deliberate and sure even as she lifted bandages to check for infection, the body of the boy beneath her administering hands so pale and flawless it seemed to give off a light of its own.

She did not seem to dwell for a second on the idea, as Trish was inclined to, that Rusty had only a minimal chance of survival, that even if he managed to hold on for weeks or months, he would never again be the boy they had known.

Though Rose gave him a sponge bath every morning, Trish made it a point to do the same at the beginning of her shift; there was not much they could do for him now, she decided, except keep him company and keep him clean. Nurse Pickless, a wry, thin-as-a-nail ranch widow who had worked battlefield hospitals in Italy and Korea, was there to supervise her first attempt. Trish prepared the soapy solution in a washbasin, removed Rusty's gown, and by the time she had his diaper undone was finding it hard to ignore the rigid and insistent erection contained therein.

"Well, howdy-*do*," said Nurse Pickless to the erection. And then, to Trish, "Usually it'll take quite a bit of advanced sponging to get one worked up as this. The male of the species, my laws. Once in a while we'll get a comatose ninety-year-old whose body seems to think it's eighteen again, all pumped and primed for a Saturday night."

Having already taken a step back, Trish asked what she should do.

"Oh, just work around it, dear, it won't last forever and it ain't gonna bite."

She gave it a wide berth anyway, doing her best to focus on the other extremities. But during the entire process it did not show any intention of retreating, even after she had finished the bath and massaged the straining joints and limbs, which felt held together by wires ratcheted tight, and had settled down in the bedside chair to read out loud from a battered hospital copy of *Harrowing Tales of the High Seas*. The following afternoon, before she had the diaper off there was already a definite bulging under way, and when Nurse Pickless arrived to get a look at things, she said, "I've worked three twelve-hour shifts around this youngster and he's never *once* given me a salute like that. Maybe you oughta take it as a compliment."

Trish blushed and Nurse Pickless flashed a quick sideways grin. "Dear, if it'll make you more comfortable I'll show you an old nurse's trick. Sometimes we have to resort to certain measures for a catheter insertion or what have you."

She tossed the diaper into the rolling hamper and then sized up the erection. It was about the length and width of a man's thumb, uniformly white with a tinge of pink at the head (unlike the variegated and strangely hued adult penises Trish had laid eyes on) and canted slightly toward the southeast. Nurse Pickless cocked her middle finger against her thumb, said, "Sometimes you've just got to show it who's boss," and gave the penis a quick little thump.

Trish startled and the nurse waved her hand. "No need to worry, he can't feel a thing. We're just trying to discourage it a little. Case you're wondering, this'll also work on your husband when he gets too enthusiastic."

They both kept an eye on the erection for any signs of discouragement, but it was holding firm.

"My husband," Trish said, not caring to hide the resentment in her voice, "hasn't been this enthusiastic for a very long time."

The old nurse put her hand on Trish's shoulder. "Take it from someone who knows, dear, there'll come a time when you'll thank the good Lord for small favors." She was already preparing to give the erection another finger-flick, saying, "Just a titch harder should do the trick," when Trish stopped her: "It doesn't bother me, really, please, I'll be fine."

"Sure?"

"Certain."

"Just one more pop and it'll be down for the count, I promise you."

"No, please. Really. Thank you so much."

"It's only the body, remember," said Nurse Pickless, already heading out the door to continue her rounds. "It comes and it goes. Nothing to be afraid of."

For a time, Trish did nothing but study Rusty's face, or the part of it, at least, that was not covered with bandages: the freckled nose and fuzzy round ears, the single exposed eye that occasionally opened, seeming to focus on something for a moment before swiveling back under its half-drawn lid. All of which, according to the doctors, could sense nothing, were shut down or short-circuited by the boy's irredeemably damaged brain. As she often had in the past two weeks, to keep herself from crying or otherwise falling into hysterics, she bent down and gave him a light kiss on both smooth cheeks and, imagining he could hear her, told him that she loved him, and always would.

She stood up, gasping a little at the way the bones of her chest ached. She decided Nurse Pickless had a point: What *was* there to be afraid of? Why should the body be discouraged—Rusty's or hers or anyone else's? She dipped her washcloth in the basin and gave his chest some brisk business with it, moving to his stomach and then his groin, putting a thorough, workmanlike polish on the stiff penis as if it were the hood ornament of an expensive car. Just as she was about to move on to the thighs she sensed a deep rippling under the skin and Rusty's hips twitched once, twice, and with only that much warning he ejaculated a thin, glistening string across the inside of his leg. Trish made a surprised noise in her throat—something like a laugh—but after the merest pause went right on soaping and rinsing as if nothing out of the ordinary had occurred, feeling with some pride the tension go out of boy's legs like the air from a tire, the bones loosening, the muscles going soft, the whole body, with a single grateful exhale, pooling like spilled water in the hollows of the bed.

DON'T LOOK BACK

A few days later, she was sitting with Rose in the same hospital room in the late morning sunshine. There had been a lull at Big House, and as had become her custom lately she had driven over to keep Rose company for an hour or two. Sometimes they did nothing but read or do crossword puzzles, but mostly they talked. In the two years since they had become sister-wives they had not talked half as much as they had in the past weeks; with all the recent upheavals they had been released, somehow, to speak about their pasts, their doubts, pretty much anything at all—what did they have to lose? This morning they were discussing the possibility of Golden's taking another wife, which in different times had never been a topic for open discussion, especially in a public place such as this. Last night he had gathered his current wives around the dining room table to get their approval on the blueprints of the new addition: three new bathrooms, a small kitchen, a large recreation room, and seven new bedrooms, three in the basement, four on the second floor. He explained the room configurations and sleeping arrangements, but by the time he was finished it was clear he had left two bedrooms unaccounted for, an oversight Nola immediately pointed out.

"This one," Golden said, resting his fingertip on the smallest bedroom, a tiny ten-by-eleven tucked between a linen closet and Bathroom #3, "this one's for me, I guess. You know, to have my own place once in a while. Or we could use it for something else, if you don't think . . ."

He searched his wives' faces for approval. No one, of course, had ever heard of a plural husband having his own bedroom—in theory it was ludicrous, almost sacrilegious; in a house full of clamoring children and demanding wives, how could a godly husband justifiably keep anything—even a night here or there—to himself? But this was a new time; the old rules didn't apply. The wives looked at each other and seemed to agree: *Why not?*

"And this one?" Beverly said, pointing to the last bedroom, the tone in her voice suggesting she already knew the answer, that she herself had scripted it.

Golden said, "This one is for, you know, future possibilities."

It wasn't hard for the other wives to guess the room's purpose: in the next few months they would almost certainly be welcoming a new sister-wife to the family. Golden had already been under heavy pressure from Uncle Chick to take a fifth wife, and now that his recent indiscretions had become common knowledge, the pressure had only increased; if he wanted to maintain his standing in the church, prove his faithfulness and good intentions, he would be bringing another wife into the fold as quickly as possible. The only question now was who the lucky lady might be.

The obvious answer was Maureen Sinkfoyle, mostly because she had been available the longest, and because Beverly favored her. Though something had clearly happened to Beverly around the time of Rusty's accident, and there were still days when she walked with a slight slump to her shoulders and a pallor to her skin, some-times retreating to her bedroom to cough herself hoarse, she seemed to be regaining her old form. She had roused herself to begin taking on more responsibilities and dictating tasks, and lately had started to engage in milder sorts of Beverly-style maneuvering: agitating on behalf of her children for better sleeping arrangements, making sure each design element of the new addition met her approval. Until now, she and Nola had been coexisting in Big House under a stay of remarkable calm, but any fool could see that trouble was on its way.

Maureen Sinkfoyle was not the only candidate in the running. There was the recently widowed LaDonna Ence and the twenty-year-old, scared-of-her-own-shadow Tanya Belieu, who Nola and Rose favored. And now, rather amazingly, a dark horse seemed to have entered the race: the beautifully named Huila, of all people. Not long ago Golden had asked permission from his wives to pay her a visit; she had taken out a restraining order on her husband and was living temporarily in one of the rentals in Mexican Town. He prom-ised there would be no funny business—he was long past that—he simply felt responsible for her plight and wanted only to make sure she was safe. Though Nola made a few comments under her breath and Beverly was clearly less than enthusiastic about it, they all relented. It seemed harmless, but Nola was convinced something was afoot. There'd been a rumor that Uncle Chick had gone out to Mexi-can Town to see Huila as well, which meant he might be testing her interest in joining the church. This kind of missionary work was an Uncle Chick specialty—bringing in the wayward and lost, extend-ing the hand of fellowship to the last person anyone would expect. It was how Golden's father had come into the church, and by extension Golden and Beverly as well.

"Do you think it's possible?" Trish asked Rose. They had been chatting aimlessly for a half hour, Rose in the easy chair next to Rusty's bed, skimming the final chapter of *A Gentleman in My Bed-room*, and Trish making a sorry attempt at knitting some wool booties for Rusty's cold feet.

Rose shrugged. "Could be. Crazier things have happened."

"I can't see it, not if Beverly has a say."

"Beverly's not really in charge anymore, is she?"

"Then who is?"

Rose glanced up from her book, blinking. "I don't have any idea."

Here was the thing: though Golden was giving it all he had, nobody was really in charge. They were all in separate holding patterns, looking for guidance, waiting for the haze to clear.

For a while they said nothing. A cart with a squeaky wheel passed in the hall and Rusty's heart monitor beeped with its stubborn regularity.

"If you had the chance," Trish said, trying her best to affect an idle tone, "do you think you could just pick up and go away somewhere new, leave everything behind?" She glanced up to see if Rose had heard her, but Rose murmured something and kept her gaze on the pages of her book.

Until she'd asked it, Trish hadn't realized how much she needed to air this question, to let it out into the open, even if nobody would hear it. "I mean, if you had somebody to go with, to be with, do you think you could just leave?"

Rose looked up at her then; obviously, she *had* been listening. Her eyes shone and her lips parted slightly to show her teeth. "Do it, Trish. You might never get another chance."

"No, see . . ." Trish shook her head and tried to go back to her knitting, which now seemed like nothing more than a big mess of knots. "I'm just asking hypothetically—"

"Go," Rose said. Her eyes were as sharp and clear as Trish had ever seen them, her voice an urgent whisper. "Don't even think about it. Go, Trish. Go and don't look back."

40.

- - · · ·

THE BOY AT THE WINDOW

THE BOY WAITS AT THE WINDOW. IT IS WIDE, UNCURTAINED, A SINGLE pane of dusty glass that looks over a parking lot filled with cars. But when the boy's good eye swivels spastically toward the block of light, a parking lot is not what he sees. On the other side of the glass are small still lifes and huge panoramas, all of them strangely familiar: alleyways and backyards and prehistoric swamps full of long-necked dinosaurs, the contents of a kitchen junk drawer, a wave taking shape on the horizon, a steaming garbage dump, the remains of a rabbit flattened in the middle of the road, a barbed-wire fence made soft with a fur of snow, the bleak red surface of Mars. Every time it has been something different, but lately, as he emerges from the grainy drift of unconsciousness, he is confronted with the same heavenly tableau: clouds stacked into towering ramparts packed with teeming masses of bodies, each one vaguely outlined and imbued with light, clamoring in voices the boy can barely hear, millions of them, billions, rank after rank of nameless souls, terrifying in their numbers, the great family of the dead.

The boy closes his eye and sinks back into himself, but there's no escaping it: the dead are everywhere, and they are waiting for him.

But he's not ready to go, not yet, especially now that he has everything he ever wanted: his own room, his own bed with sheets clean and crisp, his mother all to himself. His mother, who dotes on him, who sings to him while she swabs out his ears and brushes what's left of his hair, who reads to him every day from *Johnny Tremain* or *I Was There at the Alamo*, who has come back to him, as he always knew she would. The details of his old life are sifting away like the finest powder, but he hasn't yet forgotten how hard he planned and worked, how he suffered for this reward.

When his father comes to visit, he is quiet, but the boy can sense him there, a presence at the foot of the bed. He can hear the breath whistling through his nostrils, can smell the minty bite of his mouthwash. Unlike the other visitors, his father doesn't speak, doesn't nervously chatter or coo over the boy, or stroke his arms. He stands at the foot of the bed or sits in the easy chair next to it, doing nothing, saying nothing, so quietly that the boy becomes charged with the silence as if it were an electrical current, his body poised and straining for some word or touch. And then one morning the boy wakes and his father is there, quiet as always, the light in the room gray and somber and cool. For a long time there is nothing but the wet sound of breathing, the creaking of work boots, and then the boy feels his father's rough palm settle gently on his neck. He says the boy's name, *Rusty*, and it is the first time in the boy's fractured memory that his father has ever spoken it without at least a tinge of anger or bewilderment or exasperation, and if the boy could have he would have asked only one question: *Was that so hard? Was that really so hard?*

Most of the boy's other visitors, he can take or leave them. Sometimes he listens to what they have to say, sometimes prefers to tune them out and float through the warm and sparkling waters of his mind. So many people come, schoolmates and relatives and church members, most of them strangers. At first, when his siblings came, they were brought in bunches, which was a mistake: buttons were pushed, tubes yanked, dials turned, a stethoscope went missing, and the nurses threatened to ban all family visits until the children learned some manners. The mothers decided that each of the older children would be given five minutes alone with the boy, and though a few might have acted inappropriately (one brother pinched the boy's arm just to make absolutely sure he wasn't faking, and one sister threw herself weeping across the boy's body as if she were Mary Magdalene and he the crucified Lord), most did exactly what was expected of them, which was to tell the boy they were praying for him, they were so very sorry for how they'd treated him, ignored him, ditched and mocked and teased him, how sorry they were for ganging up on him and hurting his feelings. They told him what a good person he was, what a wonderful brother. Like a thirsty sponge the boy absorbed every word, and if he could have he would have told them how wrong they were. He had been Wrong his whole life and he wanted them to know how Wrong they were, too, because he was not a good person or a wonderful brother, he was Wrong, he was the Bad Brother, he was Ree-Pul-Seevo!, the Weirdo and the Pervert. And who were they? They were liars and a-holes, all of them, to be treating him like this now, what a gyp, what a gyp to be saying such things now, to be touching him with such kindness and care.

But they have kept coming, saying nice things and praying over him and bringing him cards which they tape to the walls. Every day his mothers sit with him, massage his limbs and wash and powder his skin. And of course there is the special mother, his secret crush, the one who smells like oranges and glows with a warm light. Somehow he has forgotten her name—like so many other details it has been lost to the gaping crevasses in his head, but it doesn't matter, she comes to visit every day. The moment she steps into the room he can sense her presence, can smell the citrusy conditioner she uses in her hair, which brings him back into his body so completely he feels the full pain of his broken head and shattered hand, the burns on his face and arms, the corporal poisons of anger and stifled lust seeping from his glands. When she is there next to him, when she rests her hand on his, his whole body aches with something like knowledge for all he has lost, the chances he will never have, to return such a touch, to fall off a horse or eat Chinese food or shoot a crossbow (which has always been one of his most dear wishes), to receive a letter in the mail, to be kissed with longing or punched in the jaw. And though none of this comes to him as conscious thought he brims with the injustice of it, with every unmet need and carefully savored resentment and thwarted desire, every dirty thought and dearest wish, the whole of his childish optimism and loneliness boiling to the surface until he is a straining vessel, ready to burst.

One night she puts her hands on him, as if she knows this, as if she alone can understand. She touches him just the right way, coaxing him along until the pressure is released with a rush of such pleasure and hurt that everything goes white and for a moment it all pours out of him, his past and future, his very soul, and still he comes back, not yet ready to go, and as he sinks into the dark, mica-specked depths of himself he calls out to her, *Thank you Thank you Thank you.*

Yes, they keep coming, his sisters and brothers and mothers, the nurses who call him *Hon* and *Baby Doll*, who rub lotion into his sweet-smelling feet. They keep coming, the church members and neighbor ladies who bring fresh-cut flowers from their gardens, the elders who anoint his ruined head with holy oil and sanctify him with their healing power; his seventh-grade class, which tromps into his room single file, sings one rousing chorus of "For He's a Jolly Good Fellow," and hangs a crooked banner above the window:

GETWELLSOONRUSTY!!! WELOVEYOU!!!

Is it any wonder the boy slowly loses all trace of himself, gradually becomes the person he never, in his most ardent imaginings, hoped he could be: a good boy, a special child, a beloved brother and son.

On a perfect late spring morning in May the boy suffers a massive stroke, which cleaves him neatly down the middle. During the following week, unbeknownst to the doctors, undetected by their machines, he suffers a series of smaller strokes, each further dividing him from himself until he is little more than a scattering of thoughts and impressions held together by filaments of will. He seems to have lost access to his own body, which lies twisted and strange on the bed, bathed in the copper light of late afternoon, but still he is unwilling to let go, he wants to stay just a little while longer, to smell the flowers and read the handmade cards, to look out the bright window where the dead, in their billions, wait for him, to watch his visitors come and go, sometimes laughing, sometimes crying and shaking their heads and whispering sweet, doubtful things only he can hear.

It is a warm day, the sky empty, the heat rippling over the surface of the parking lot like water. The boy waits at the window. He won't be waiting long.

41.

•••••

THE MIDDLE PAIN

AT NIGHT, AFTER HER SHIFT AT THE HOSPITAL, SHE WOULD DRIVE home, the stars aligning haphazardly in the eastern sky, the shadows of dusk soaking into the fields and foothills. She often sat for long stretches in her idling car in Big House's driveway, considering the prospect of another night with the illustrious Cooter in the swanky confines of the utility closet. Because there were no longer enough parking spots to accommodate Golden's work vehicles and the wives' cars, and because all rules of order and common sense seemed to have been suspended until further notice, she had taken to parking in the middle of the lawn.

Her mornings and afternoons were filled with a noisy amplitude, with the piping clamor of children calling her name, demanding her presence. But nights were a different story. Nights were a long slog of the mind, her thoughts sliding past one another but never catching, the gears of her brain stripped smooth. Sometimes she would reach that point in the early morning when all the birds of the world went quiet, that perfect half hour when even the most psychotic starlings slept, and the silence would reach such a pitch she would find herself singing half-forgotten Beach Boys lyrics to ward it off.

And it wasn't helping at all that her body was sending her messages—the pangs in her uterus, the swelling of her breasts—trying to convince her, dumb beast that it was, that it had the power to conceive a bit of joy amid so much uncertainty and grief, that anything was possible. At times it was hard not to feel like the butt of a cosmic joke, lying alone in her dark little cave, wide awake, the owner of a body so hopeful and full of yearning, while not thirty feet away slept her strapping husband, sad and impotent as an old shoe.

Every night she would venture into the dusky atmosphere of the dining room and stare into his sleeping face, searching for some change, a glimmer in which she could read a future for herself, but all she could see there were crosshatchings of exhaustion and bewilderment, a trace of pain around the eyes. Each evening he arrived home well after dinnertime, beleaguered and spent, and, after a quick meal, family prayer, and a good-night kiss for each child and wife, dived headfirst into the Barge's questionable comforts. Besides the new mantle of authority he seemed to be fitfully trying on for size, the only real change in him was in his attitude toward the children; he had always been sweet with them, mild and forgiving, but now his tenderness had a custodial quality to it. He no longer tried to hide or to escape them, to find a quiet corner where, his back to the wall, he could ward them off with his rolls of blueprints or the phone receiver pressed to his ear. During those first days at Big House, she came upon him more than once holding one of the younger ones, Jame-o or Sariah or Pet, clutching them with such an intensity he seemed to be trying to beam a promise or a prayer of forgiveness into their damp foreheads.

Each night, after making a circuit of the house, and checking in on Faye, who had taken to the new family situation with an enthusiasm rivaled only by that of the Three Stooges, Trish would retire to the utility closet. Each night by the blue glow of the water heater's pilot light she would reread June's letter, and then spend much of the early morning hours trying to chase down the possibilities it set loose in her head.

And then one late Friday she dozed off only to be wakened by the sharp, needling pain of ovulation—the charmingly named *Mittelschmerz*, the middle pain. This time it lasted only an hour or so and ended with that almost pleasurable sensation, deep in her abdomen, of a nickel dropping through a slot. Afterward, she would try to remember what was going through her head as she pulled on her tennis shoes, walked past Golden's sleeping form to the front door, where she took her keys off the hook. But there was nothing there, as far as she could tell, except a buzzing mental static. She emerged into a crisp, late spring night and settled into the driver's seat of the Rabbit without a thought in her head.

Only when she turned onto Water Socket Road did she realize where she was headed. She drove fast with her window open, the turbulence tangling her hair, and when she got to the mailbox with the name HAYMAKER painted on the side, she pulled onto the rough two-track without touching the brakes. She bumped over potholes and clattering tablets of sandstone, letting the car roll to a stop as she crested the shallow rise. Down below it was dark except for a single lit window at the back of the first Quonset hut. And there it was: June's Ford parked in the night shadows out front. She let out a hard, shuddering breath.

But she did not go down. She stayed in her seat, listening to the lowing of a train passing somewhere to the south. She got out and paced around the car under an impossible net of stars, seized by a black flash of confusion. What was she about to do? Where was Faye? With a burst of relief she realized she had forgotten something. She got back in the car.

The hospital parking lot was nearly empty. She walked down the long corridors, past the darkened rooms and the abandoned nurses' station. Nola had the eight-to-twelve shift tonight, and Trish found her in the soft easy chair next to Rusty's bed, head thrown back and snoring in rhythm like a well-oiled machine. Trish woke her, told her as long as she couldn't sleep she might as well take the rest of Nola's shift, and Nola wandered off, stretching, smacking her lips, saying, "Thanks, Trishy dear, you're a doll."

Earlier today, Rusty had spent most of Trish's shift down in Radiology getting a few more X-rays at Rose's request, in hopes the doctors would find a miracle: the metal fragments in his brain suddenly

accessible and therefore removable or, better yet, disappeared altogether, spirited away by the hand of God. The family had been fasting
and praying for such an outcome, gathering each night to say a special
prayer on Rusty's behalf, and Rose in particular seemed convinced that
faith, exercised with staunch vigilance, could bring back her son.

And so today Trish had not given Rusty his bath, which was why
she was here now. His body was slowly transforming itself into an
expression of the trauma visited upon his brain; head craned to the
left and into his shoulder, his neck held rigid, his knees drawing up
under the sheets, his left hand clenched and beginning to curl inward
at the wrist, as if his body were trying to fold itself around the last
mote of life at its center. Even the simple task of taking off the gown
had become difficult—the joints stiff, the tendons like sun-hardened
leather—but once she had removed the diaper and quickly swabbed
the genitals, bringing the straining body to a quick, shuddering
release, she felt it relax, the flesh softening, the neck going slack, the
head easing into the pillow.

She'd always rushed through bath duty in the perfunctory manner she'd learned from the nurses, but here, now, in the deep hush
of night, with no one to see or to judge, she took her time. First the
feet, cold and bone-white and decidedly feminine—the nails carefully
tended, she knew, by the boy's mother—and then on to the calves and
thighs, the full hips and soft belly, the chest with its nipples so faint
and vestigial they were hardly there at all, and then the smooth arms,
limp and wet in her hands. Except for a scattering of freckles and the
few faint curling hairs on the groin and in the armpits it was still very
much the body of a child, pale and sweet and untouched by time.

With great care she soaped and rinsed the pleats of his neck, the
shallow sockets behind the ears, and for a moment, in that dim room,
she could not help but see the face of her own son in the features of
this boy, in the cupped chin with its off-center dimple, in the low
cheekbones and full, fleshy lips, each a shared inheritance from their
father. Bending close, anointing every crease and crevice of that face
with the tip of her damp cloth, she felt the entirety of her loss as both

love and emptiness—for her, two strands of the same cord—a deep, pained mourning for this child, for the children she had lost, for the children she might never have.

In a daze, and feeling suddenly exhausted, she climbed onto the bed, breathing in the soapy scent of the boy's neck, pulling him close, feeling the heat and weight of him against her chest, and as she dozed off she thought she could sense him lifting, releasing, taking her with him into some bright place—heaven, she hoped—where the souls of children pulsed like sparks, lighting up the dark.

She was awakened by a noise in the hall—a nurse making her rounds, or maybe Beverly come to start her shift—but she did not move. She stared at the cracks in the plaster ceiling, feeling the knowledge rise in her, stirred by this breathing child in her arms, that despite everything that had been taken from her, despite all she had lost and could never have back, this emptiness inside her could be filled again.

She took the long way back, slowing as she passed the little cemetery on the ridge where Jack was buried. Though she did not stop—visiting a cemetery in the dead of night struck even her as a bit morbid and inappropriate—in her mind she called out to him and to her other two lost ones, told them no matter what happened she would not abandon them, they would always be loved, they could never be replaced.

When she pulled up in front of June's the place was dark. She got out of the car, looked up for a second at the deep sky layered thick with stars and galaxies, tasted the dust of the road on her tongue. Before she could knock, the porch light came on. And there was June, one hand on the doorknob, the other holding his glasses, dressed in jeans and a T-shirt, freshly shaven, as if he had been waiting for her all along. The look of open expectation on his face nearly broke her heart.

"I can't go with you," she told him. "But I'd like to stay the night if you'd let me."

Something flared in his eyes and went out. He nodded, letting out a single, sharp breath, and opened the door wide.

After that night, she returned four times over the course of the next ten days. Each time he begged her to come with him, showed her maps of the places they might go: Mexico, British Columbia, California, anywhere she wanted. She listened, dreamed a little along with him, but made no commitments. At every visit she noticed more material and equipment missing, compressors and arc welders sold at auction, piles of lumber and rebar hauled off their piers. The house grew progressively emptier and more cave-like until it contained nothing but a bed, a refrigerator and a small chair and card table in the front room. The last time she went, a warm breezy night at the beginning of June, the place was abandoned, the Quonset huts dismantled and gone, nothing but two concrete pads and a few scraps sifted over with red dust, the desert already come to reclaim its own.

42.

. . . . .

A FUNERAL

THOUGH RUSTY MCCREADY RICHARDS WAS NOBODY SPECIAL, JUST a kid, his funeral drew the largest congregation the Living Church of God had ever seen. Not only had the strange story of his accident, his miraculous five weeks of survival, and eventual death been featured in the *Dixie Weekly*, but the superintendent of schools had decreed that any student who attended the funeral would be given an excused absence for the day. It was standing room only, then, the multitudes spilling out well into the cinder parking lot.

After the service, Golden stepped out of the church and was immediately pulled into the gears of the crowd, the mourners and well-wishers and malingerers, eventually finding himself spit out on the other side. He scooted past a local family he vaguely knew, gave quick handshakes, fended off hugs and, desperate for a few moments alone, ducked into the driver's side of the hearse, pulling the door shut behind him.

The pallbearers had already placed the casket in the back, and the red velvet curtains were drawn, lending the car's interior a warm Martian glow. Golden held on to the steering wheel for a while, then gave it a single desultory shake. He had promised himself he wouldn't cry; for the past month he'd been swallowing tears and now seemed to have a permanent ache in the hinge of his jaw. He had managed to hold himself together for most of the service, even while around him his wives and children sniffled and wept. It was when Uncle Chick gave the final prayer and closed the lid of the casket that he lost himself, just for a moment, and let out a short, breathless shout through his teeth.

Be strong, he told himself one more time. *You've got to be strong.*

He remembered the mess he had been at Glory's funeral more than three years ago, so much weeping and carrying on, as if he alone had lost something. He had insisted on making the drive from the church to the cemetery by himself, just the two of them, and it seemed to him now that all his mistakes as a husband and father could be summed up in that single gesture.

He rolled down the window and called out to Em, who was being consoled by a clutch of girls doing an admirable job of pretending to be distraught. Em, radiant in a dark navy dress, her hair done up in a duenna's bun, came right away. She bent down a little so she could look in his eyes, and when she put her hand on his neck and said, "Daddy," in a soft voice, he had to turn away and clench his jaw to hold back a sob.

He swallowed, nodding to buy a little time. Then told her to gather up the children, that they would all be riding to the cemetery together.

"All of us?" she said, and he said, "Everyone."

It was five and a half miles from the church to the cemetery. The procession moved slowly, never more than ten miles an hour, with the sheriff and his new deputy taking the lead, lights flashing feebly in the summer sun. Traffic was stopped at the county cutoff, and all along the way cars and pickups and flatbeds with heeler dogs in the back pulled over and waited for the procession, more than a quarter mile long, to pass. Housewives and their youngsters stepped out onto porches, men paused in their work, calling to each other to shut down their machines. A crew of Mexican laborers cutting the first alfalfa of the season gathered in a ragged line, the field green and brilliant beneath them, each one removing his hat to make the sign of the cross.

If any of those people noticed the long Cadillac hearse was packed floor to ceiling with a seething mass of bodies, feet jutting up at odd angles, arms and faces and whole torsos hanging out the windows, they had the good decency not to gawk or point.

The first mile or so was the worst. The kids were heaped all over each other, having dog-piled into the car as if they were going for a joyride. To accommodate the casket, Golden had had to remove the three homemade bench seats, so only the front and rear seats remained, upon which fourteen of them, including Golden with Pet on his lap doing much of the steering, were now haphazardly stacked, while the back bay was crammed full with the other thirteen, including Rusty in his casket. Even before they pulled out of the parking lot the wailing and carping had started. Ferris hollered at no one in particular, Alvin claimed in a muffled voice he was being asphyxiated by someone's butt, and Darling, because she had lost her shoe, wept louder and longer than she had during the funeral service. Smuggled in from Nola's station wagon by Clifton and lost somewhere deep within the pile, Cooter howled and whined as if he were being boiled in a pot.

There were a dozen minor scuffles as they grappled for position, the bass-drum thump of someone's head landing on the lid of the casket, a shouting match over whose foot was being jammed into whose back. And the heat inside the car was a punishment (though Golden had the AC cranked and all the windows open, the tight knit of bodies stymied any kind of airflow and radiated a sweatshop heat of its own). But eventually they began to sort themselves out. In their badly knotted neckties and wrinkled funeral dresses they negotiated for space, wiggling into niches and voids, the older ones taking the brunt of the weight, stiffening their arms and spines to protect those underneath, bracing their legs against seat backs and door handles, managing a quickly engineered scaffolding of limbs held in a trembling balance, bodies leveraged against one another until they seemed to be holding each other aloft.

Now the procession crested the cambered incline of Grover's Hill, filed past the remains of the old rodeo arena, the wooden corrals and chutes silvered with age, and onward to the north past a group of Herefords who could not be bothered to lift their heads.

"Doing good, kids," Golden called out to them, his voice thick, "it won't be long."

He let Pet steer the downslope straightaway and swiveled around to make sure no one was suffocating or succumbing to heatstroke. From the dregs of the rear seat came a weakened, desolate whine and from the farthest back somebody—possibly Naomi—said in the most matter-of-fact of voices, "I think my whole body is starting to cramp."

"Okay then, all right," Golden said. "Just hold on, you're all doing great, all of you, just hold on."

For a while there was nothing but the subterranean gurgle of the car's engine and the children's collective breathing, a noise like the gentle crash of surf that lulled Golden into a moment of heavy-lidded torpor—which was interrupted when Pet discovered the Cadillac's horn. She pressed the shiny chrome button at the center of the steering wheel, giving it one short blast and one long, like a medieval call to arms, making everyone jump, causing the sheriff to crane his neck out the window to see what was the matter and Golden to raise both arms in demonstration of his innocence. It was at this moment that Pet gave it one more good blast and from behind there was a wheeze and a giggle and then the children were all laughing at once, a swelling, cackling cheer that was one of the sweetest sounds Golden had ever heard.

The cemetery in view now, they rattled over the last cattle guard on the way up the hill. There was a full minute of peace before an agitation started in the rear seat, a ripple of an argument that crescendoed in a burst of complaint and backbiting, which triggered a structural collapse in the far back, setting off a general howl of woe, and then the last straw, a sharp, bitter stench that quickly filled the car. Novella, sitting next to Golden with Louise on her lap, covered her mouth with her hand and said, "Oh, *dear*," and that was when it hit him. At first he thought it had to be something wrong with the engine, a melted hose or failed radiator, but then he realized that Cooter, spooked by the commotion or moved by simple spite, had relieved himself under the seat. Those who could pressed their noses toward an open window and those who couldn't cursed the day Cooter was ever born.

Finally, they rolled through the cemetery gates and everyone, including Cooter, bailed out in a slipstream of tumbling bodies before Golden could bring the hearse to a stop.

Only Golden took his time getting out. For a few moments he was alone again, just him and the boy, and there under the outstretched arms of an old locust, the other cars filing slowly past, he let himself have his cry.

ONE MORE CHILD OF GOD

In the sharp heat of noon, the graveside ceremony was mercifully short. Uncle Chick dedicated the grave, said a few final words, and that was all. The mourners offered their condolences and went back to their lives. Soon it was only the Richards family, the funeral director, Mr. Baugh, who sat sulking in his Buick because, once again, he had not been allowed to drive the company hearse to transport the body, which was only customary and proper and part of the *comprehensive funeral package*, and, of course, Tellis Blackmore, the county grave digger, waiting patiently to finish his job.

The Richards family plots took up most of the northwest corner of the cemetery. There were sixteen of them, an area of nearly seven hundred square feet bisected by a three-foot-wide walkway. Royal was buried just southwest of the center, Glory three plots over to the east, and Jack's small headstone stood at the far southeast corner next to a red currant bush. Rusty's grave, dug with meticulous care by Tellis Blackmore and his backhoe, lay just kitty-corner to his grandfather's. Golden stood in the expanse of all that pristine red dirt and realized it would never be sufficient, never close to enough.

Later that afternoon, during the funeral luncheon, he would get a
call from a Mr. Edward Pinsker, one half of the snowbird couple who
had purchased Old House with the intention of transforming it into
the Jewel of the Desert Bed and Breakfast, who, having been back
and forth to Minneapolis for the past month and not terribly interested in the local media, would have no idea that Golden had just
buried his third child in as many years. For the sixth time, according
to his records, Mr. Pinkser would be calling to complain that some of
the house's old outbuildings that were supposed to have been razed,
per the purchase agreement, were still very much standing, and he
would wonder when he might expect to see them gone. Golden
would not respond except to hang up the phone, go out back where
the old Case front loader was parked among all the other machines
currently being put to use in the Big House renovation and, still
in his funeral clothes, the knot of his tie thick as a fist at his throat,
drive the mile and a half to Old House, where he would chug up the
driveway at full speed, lowering the big bucket as he came, and plow
through the old chicken coops, flattening them in a hail of splinters,
as if they had never been there at all. He would continue along the
side of the house, his necktie slapping him in the face, Mr. and Mrs.
Edward Pinsker watching from behind the safety of the screen door,
and under a black haze of diesel fumes push Doll House, with a great
shrieking of nails and snapping timbers, thirty yards across the grassy
banks and into the river.

(All of this would be reported later by Nephi, who had been
enlisted by Beverly to follow Golden in the work truck, to make sure
he didn't do anything extreme; she had heard his end of the phone
conversation and had seen the look in his eyes.)

Sitting stiffly in the rusted spring seat, the exhaust pipe clattering
and belching smoke, Golden would watch the remains of Doll House
float out of sight, debris spreading out and disappearing along the
big bend in the river, and then would spend a minute or two considering Raymond, loitering near the fence to watch the proceedings.
Raymond, of course, had survived the accident that had taken Rusty's

life. His breast feathers had been singed and he'd taken shrapnel to one of his legs, but other than a mild limp was no worse for wear; he stood at the fence with his head held high, blinking his girlish lashes. After a time Golden would back up the loader and pull up next to his work truck in which Nephi sat wondering how, exactly, he was supposed to have stopped his father from doing, as his mother put it, "anything extreme." Nephi would later report the look on his father's face as "kind of weird and freaky" as he told Nephi to move aside, casting around under the bench seat and coming up with a strange, old-fashioned long-barreled pistol. Carrying the pistol close to his leg, he would walk down the driveway, across the bridge and up to the ostrich pen, which he would open, letting the gate swing wide. Nephi was sure, he would later say, that his father was going to shoot the thing, the way he brought the gun up at it, but would end up pointing a few feet over its head, the echoing *crack* sending it charging from the pen, around the house and into the road, where it would pause on the double yellow line, looking around as if wondering how it had managed to end up there. Golden would discharge the gun once more, and with his memory now refreshed, Raymond would sprint through the Pettigrews' south pasture, scrabble wildly over a sagging barbed-wire fence and strike out across the raw desert, growing smaller and less distinct as he weaved and bobbed through the brush, dissolving and reappearing under the lip of the horizon until he seemed to have vanished into the sky.

All of this would happen a few hours from now, in a final tide of anger that, after everything, Golden would not have believed he had left in him. But here, surrounded by his wives and children, he was merely exhausted, aching, sapped by the heat of the day. It was all he could do to stand in place in front of the casket mounded with flowers and let Rose lean in to him.

The other mourners were long gone, the children getting restless, the younger ones beginning to wander out among the stones and monuments, their shoes and pant cuffs powdered with red dust, but Rose showed no signs of being ready to leave; she stared at the casket almost without blinking, as if trying to memorize the pattern of its grain. Mr. Baugh got out of his Buick and started toward them slowly, professionally, both hands clasped behind his back in a way that suggested *all things must come to an end*, but a cold look from Golden stopped him in his tracks.

At some point Trish stepped away from the graveside to help Beverly and Em gather wayward children; a few of the girls were collecting beauty-pageant armfuls of dried-out wreaths and bleached plastic flowers, Herschel and the Three Stooges were climbing all over Tellis Blackmore's backhoe and Ferris already had his pants down and was pressing himself into the cool, polished marker of one MRS. ONEITA TORGERSON, 1901–1959, CHERISHED SISTER AND AUNT.

After getting Ferris back in his pants and calling the boys away from the machinery, Trish stopped near Jack's headstone. She was here, of course, to mourn Rusty, to support and comfort Rose, but could not help pausing for a moment, standing a little off to the side as if she were doing nothing more than scanning the cemetery for additional troublemakers. She resisted the urge to reach out and touch the small marker, to pull the weeds growing at its base, to swab with the hem of her dress the dust that had gathered in the carved letters of her son's name.

Out of the corner of her eye she saw Golden look back at her and then he and Rose were stepping forward to gather several bouquets off the casket. With Golden beside her, Beverly laid a mixed wreath at Glory's grave, and eventually Golden stepped away to rest a bouquet of carnations against his father's stone. Trish did not know how long they maintained those positions, mourning alone in their separate corners, only Rose comforted by the soft weight of her sister's arm. Freed of any pretense, Trish bent on one knee to wrestle a few clutches of chickweed from the ground, and when she rose Golden was next to her, holding a bouquet of chrysanthemums. He arranged it carefully on the small grave, and when he stepped back he was so close the buttons of his jacket cuff grazed her arm. He wiped his mouth and whispered, so low she almost couldn't hear, "He was a beautiful boy." His hand drifted sideways and, just for a moment, touched hers.

For some time they stood that way, without moving or speaking, the sun so high they stood perfectly inside their own shadows. Mr. Baugh checked his watch and the younger kids chased each other through the stones, their shouts carrying on the warm air, and Tellis Blackmore sat in his preferred spot under the shade of a gnarled juniper, finishing up his lunch and waiting patiently to lower one more child of God into the earth.

43.

. . . . .

A FUNDAMENTAL TRUTH

THE MONSOONS CAME EARLY THAT YEAR. EVERY AFTERNOON THE clouds would build to the south, darkening the far horizon and throwing down the occasional thunderbolt. The dry grass along the ditches would stir, the cottonwood leaves clatter like loose coins, the clouds swell and fold and spread, blocking the sun and pushing great walls of water-cooled air in front of them, bending trees and making laundry jump on the line, the temperature dropping fifteen degrees in twenty minutes. During the average monsoon season it didn't rain every afternoon, but this year it seemed to, storms lining up like causeway traffic, pushing up from Mexico by way of Arizona one after the other, sometimes well into the night.

Though almost everyone was grateful for the moisture, the relief from the heat, the beauty and distraction of such big weather, for Golden, trying to complete the Big House renovation as quickly as possible, it was a nightmare. Luckily he'd dug out and poured the new walls of the expanded basement before the rains came, but the entire south side of the house had been torn away to accept the new addition, and though the opening was draped with twenty-foot lengths of clear plastic, the rain gusted in, soaking into the subfloors and drywall. Part of every day was lost to channel-making and dam construction to keep the water from flowing into the kitchen and the basement, and everywhere you walked it was mud and slop and branching tributaries of brown water spanned by bridges of plywood scrap or warped two-by-sixes. Even worse, his crews balked at working in the rain, even the Mexican framers and roofers who wouldn't have thought twice about hammering right through a dust storm or logging a twelve-hour day in one-hundred-degree heat. Some were terrified by lightning and others seemed to believe that a rainstorm was nothing less than a memo from God reminding them to take the day off or risk the consequences.

Golden worked every day except Sunday, with or without his crew. On a given afternoon you might have found him trying to put up plywood sheeting alone or straddling a high truss in the middle of a squall, pounding away with his oversized framing hammer, soaked through, buck teeth exposed and hair plastered to his head in a way that brought to mind an irritable muskrat. He got so used to slipping in the thick clay gumbo that he would go down on his back or side, smeared all the way to the shoulders, and be right up and moving on to the next thing as if nothing had happened. Some evenings he'd come in for dinner nearly encased in dried mud, his eyes and teeth flashing white like some Aborigine on a vision quest.

Every night he would take a long shower, go to church meetings, or play with the kids upstairs, and every night at the chime of the clock he would show up for his ten-thirty appointment with the Barge. For weeks he'd been falling into a desperate, lost sleep, but sometime in late June he began waking in the early hours, stirred by an ache he at first took for sorrow, before realizing what he was feeling was desire. The kind of rich bodily pangs he was sure had abandoned him for good. More than once he awakened to discover Trish standing over him, a pale shadow in a long white T-shirt, a vision created out of the moist vapors of his longing. By the time he could rub the crust from his eyes and rouse himself completely she would be gone.

Sometimes, unable to get back to sleep, he'd creep down the hall and stand in the doorway of the utility closet, noting how the blue radiance of the water heater's pilot light played over her sleeping form. He allowed himself to go no further, only to look.

Trish, feigning sleep, would watch through the blur of her eye-lashes, keeping perfectly still. But Golden only stood at the door, a stark black cutout backlit by the dim light of the hall. In the days after Rusty's funeral, acutely aware of the two weeks since her missed period, the tenderness in her breasts, the growing tightness at her waist, Trish had convinced herself that this new child would be enough, that—especially considering the illicit way in which it had been acquired—she should be grateful for what she had, with the life she had made for herself. But Golden's dark form in the doorway had imprinted something new and painful on the hard plates of her chest: that old devil, hope. The kind of hope that abandons you in your worst moments and is suddenly there again, weeks later, trailing you like the stubborn, slinking dog who will not take no for an answer. The kind of greedy hope that tricks you into believing that at least some of the things taken from you might be restored, that after every-thing, you might find your way back to something like happiness.

So Trish lay in her cot, Cooter's hot little head wedged into her stomach, hoping, trying not to hope. When Golden appeared in the doorway she would attempt to lure him in like a hunter lures a bear: with a silence and stillness too delicious to resist. She knew how broken with sadness he was, how uncertain around his wives, how unworthy he felt, how nearly impossible he found it to look any one of them in the eye. There was part of her that still wanted to pun-ish and hurt him, to meet his reticence with hers. But since her own betrayal—for which she continued to place, unfairly or not, a large portion of the blame at his feet—she had found herself less and less able to work up anything like anger or jealousy. She wanted only what she had wanted all along: a loving touch once in a while, the companionship of family, to belong.

One night, a steady procession of thunder skipping through dis-tant canyons, she awoke from a fitful half sleep to find Golden in the doorway and without thinking opened her eyes to look right at him. He disappeared into the hall but, spurred by a sudden, reckless clarity, she followed. He was already sinking back into the Barge, trying to wrestle himself under his Mexican blanket. When she approached he closed his eyes and froze in place like a lizard playing dead. She shook her head and sighed, wondering why they had continued with this silly game for so long.

She said, "Having trouble sleeping?"

Blanket clutched under chin, Golden seemed to conduct a quick debate with himself over whether or not to continue the ruse. Without opening his eyes he said, "A little."

"Me too," she said. "A lot."

"The thunder," he said, "it's kind of loud."

"I was thinking maybe it's this crappy old couch you're sleeping on. I was also noticing how big it is. How it might be big enough for one more."

He looked at her for the first time, and together they confronted two possibilities: he could stay as he was, protecting himself, pretending he hadn't heard her, and she could go back to her cot in the closet, her independence and pride intact. Or something could be risked, a new reality seeded with the promise of pain and disappointment that attends every act of love. Damp air gusted through the plastic curtains that shielded the gaping breach in the house. In the half-light the whites of her husband's eyes were luminous, the sides of his mouth pinched, his nostrils flaring with what might have been excitement or fear. He lifted the blanket to let her in.

This time, she did not rush. She did not smother or clutch at him, as had always been her inclination. She let her body ease into his. This is what she had always loved most about him: his body, his movement and shape, his smell. It was a smell that, when mixed with the rich, percolating odors of the couch, produced in her something like yearning or nostalgia; there were the bodily perfumes of thousands of children in their various ages and incarnations, baby lotion and wet diapers and shampooed hair, the faint metallic tang of old pennies and autumn leaves stuck to the bottoms of shoes, the residue of smoky winter nights and summer dust. For her, it was a smell that meant family and memory and time. It was the smell—and she could find no better word for it—of home.

Together they listened to a line of heavy rain pass over the house and move on. He put his hand on her hip and from that point of contact radiated a warm, tingling current. Lifting her chin, she searched the shadows of his face, and a question rose in her mind that she was not quick enough to beat back: "All this time, you weren't really *impotent*"—she took special care with the word's pronunciation— "were you?"

He stiffened, pulled away a little, and just like that the spell was broken. What had gotten into her, to ask this question, at this moment? Slowly it came to her, with some satisfaction, that maybe she *did* still have her pride, that this *was* the perfect moment, maybe the only one they would have, to clear the air in a lasting way, to start fresh.

"Not," he said, searching for the proper diplomatic construction, "in a manner of speaking."

She almost laughed but sighed instead, with only the barest hint of bitterness. "I should have known, I really should have. You'd think I'd have you figured out by now."

"Trish, I'm sor—" and he caught himself. "It's just, I didn't know what to do or how to act. I still don't. I don't know that I ever will."

"You're getting better," she said. "This is a start."

"I'm trying," he said. "For you and the others."

"And there's going to be a new one? For sure?" *Why not?* she thought. Here they were, about to make love for the first time in nearly a year, and who does she invite to the party but the new wife, the one who will one day compete with her for nearly everything that matters, who will just as likely come to view her as an enemy as a friend, who could even turn out to be the raven-haired mistress with the beautiful name who Golden had been courting and cuddling these past several months while she sat at home alone in her sad sweatpants trying not to lose her mind? *Why not, really?* On this crowded couch, in this crowded house, here it was: the crowded life she had chosen, in all its glory, a life that had to be, by its very definition, divided and shared and shared again.

"It looks like it, but I don't want to think about that right now. Do you?"

"Not really. I guess I kind of like knowing what you're up to."

After this interruption it took them a while to find a way forward. There was a hovering indecisiveness that quickly turned into urgency. Beginning to kiss, they shifted to find a better angle, nearly dumping Trish over the edge of the couch in the process. Golden was quick to throw his arms around her and pull her back, squeezing with such force her breath left her and her joints popped. Trish kissed him hard, grasping his collarbone as if it were the rung of a ladder, and in one motion hoisted herself on top of him. Quickly she shed her own T-shirt and then spent a dozen precious seconds working his over his inconveniently enormous head. Distant lightning ignited the windows twice, three times. He began to strain against her, bearing her up as a wave lifts a boat, a muggy heat rising off him, making her sweat. Centered high on his hipbone, she pressed down, searching for leverage, her vision pulsing with the beat of her heart. Thunder sounded against the walls of the house and she heard him saying something, what she thought might be an expression of pleasure, but then he was grabbing her arms and she heard the word, "Wait."

"Trish," he gasped. "Please."

"What?" she said, still moving against him. "What is it?"

"I don't think—" He began to sit up. "I don't think I can."

Her body weak, shuddering with desire, she could barely keep from shouting. "Don't start that again, I *know* you can! We just talked about it!"

"No," he pleaded, shaking his head. "It's not that. Please, I have an idea. Can you give me just a minute? One second?"

With his free hand he cast around the living room floor for his jeans, from which he extracted his overstuffed leather wallet. He rifled through it contents and removed a square of gold foil with the words *A PleasurePlus Prophylactic* printed across it in cursive.

"What is *that*?" she said, though she knew exactly what it was.

"It's—"

"I know what it is, Golden. Where did you get it?"

"I'm thinking you probably don't want to know."

"Then why are you showing it to me?"

He was giving her a strange look, one of equal parts expectation and embarrassment, hoping the square of gold foil might communicate everything that he could not.

"And what?" she said. "You want us to use that? *Now*?"

He nodded, but with such an air of uncertainty he might as well have been shaking his head. He said, "You don't understand?"

"What?" she said. "What am I supposed to understand?"

The words came out with an edge of hostility she hadn't entirely intended and he looked away, the muscles of his neck clenching in a way that suggested he was trying to hold back tears.

"Golden, no, don't do this, not now." She felt a surge of nausea at the base of her throat and wondered, not for the first time, if there was simply too much that had happened to them—could their relationship be so irretrievably damaged that they could not manage even a simple act of lovemaking? Old folks, invalids, dumb teenagers, complete strangers did it all the time; monkeys, she read somewhere, were known to do it thirty times a day. So what was wrong with her and Golden? The only good answer she could come to was that the chasm that had opened between them over the past year and a half was too wide to breach, and that in deciding to stay, she had made a terrible mistake.

"See?" he said, turning back to her. His face was soft, his eyes bright but without tears. "It's just that, right now, I have to take care of the ones I already have."

The air seemed to go out of her then, leaving a feeling of empty calm. "I see," she said. "I do." Yes, she did. She understood that her greatest wish had turned into his greatest fear, and that if there was going to be a compromise, she, of course, would have to be the one to make it. And yet she'd already taken what she wanted, hadn't she, stolen it for herself with a boldness that surprised her still? And why not, she wondered, why not allow him to believe, at least for a little while, that he could exercise some power over life and how it was given? He would learn soon enough that when it came to children, there was no way to control how they came and went. They arrived as miracles and were snatched away again without meaning, without the least reason or sense, and she and this sweet, sad man were going to have to help each other accept this as the most fundamental truth of their lives.

So she set about kissing him again, and as she did she pried open his fist and removed the condom crumpled inside it.

Coming up for air, he said, "I have to tell you, I don't have any idea how to use that thing."

"Oh," she said, "don't worry, hon, I do."

In one quick motion she pulled down his sweatpants and underwear, and while she was busy noticing how very *un*impotent he was—a rather difficult fact to miss from her vantage point—something else caught her eye. It appeared as if the hair around his genitals had been trimmed back in an almost perfectly round circle, half an inch long or so, like the green on a golf course cut from the surrounding rough.

"What," she said, "is *this*?"

He looked down at himself. "Yeah," he said, "this. I don't know. A while back I got some *gum* caught there somehow. I guess I got carried away cutting it out."

In a few moments Trish and her husband would make love for the first time in nearly a year, with such vigor and abandon that they would have to bite their lips and hold their hands over each other's mouths to keep from waking the house. But right now, slipping the condom from its little golden pouch, she laughed longer and louder than she had in a very long time.

44.

. . . . .

A WEDDING

A SATURDAY AFTERNOON IN LATE SEPTEMBER, THE SKY A CHECKER-board of clouds, the air soft with the coming fall. The Big House renovation is winding down, and none too soon; the work, as always, has been plagued by mishaps and delays, broken sewer pipes and code violations, bureaucratic snafus at the county office, nasty weather of all kinds. The crew, offered a handsome bonus to finish the job by the end of the month, lay shingles and set windows and paint trim with uncommon industry, the entire rear of the house so jumbled with ladders and scaffolding and scrambling men that the whole enterprise brings to mind the Tower of Babel.

Occasionally, the roofers pause in their hammerivng to watch the spectacle below. On the broad, weedy lawn a couple hundred people have gathered for a wedding: rows of folding chairs, banquet tables spread with desserts and finger food, and up front, at the outer edge of the milling crowd, the happy couple, the handsome groom and lovely bride.

The ceremony doesn't take long. A thin silver cloud passes in front of the sun, casting everything a deeper shade of itself, and as if this is his cue Uncle Chick asks the crowd to be seated. There is a brief bout of musical chairs that leaves at least thirty disappointed stragglers searching for a place to stand. Mostly, this is a typical fundamentalist crowd, comprised of the usual mob of children, the men in polyester suits and bolo ties, the women with their long hair brushed and shimmering in the glassy light. But there are a few who obviously don't belong (invited here by Golden unbeknownst to Uncle Chick or anyone else): Nelson Norman, settled in next to the banquet tables, having already sampled three kinds of cake and two flavors of punch; Leonard Odlum, looking sorely out of place in a rented maroon tuxedo and trying in vain to make meaningful eye contact with some of the young ladies in the audience; and near the back, Nestor, flanked on one side by a few of his hungover bandmates, and on the other by Huila, her son Fredy, and her silver-haired uncle Esteban, who accompanied the boy on the journey from Guatemala.

Clearing his throat, Uncle Chick takes his place before the groom (who sweats despite the cool air, as if at the tail end of a forced march) and the beaming bride in the pale chiffon dress she wore for her first wedding nearly seventeen years ago, altered to show a hint of cleavage. She lifts a hand to keep her complicated and newly dyed hairdo in proper alignment, and the sudden movement causes the dress, already showing signs of considerable strain, to make a sharp tearing noise at one of its seams.

An hour or so ago, to prepare himself for this moment, Golden snuck out to his work truck while the older boys were busy setting up chairs and fished out his jelly jar from under the bench seat. Though tempted on more occasions than he could count, he had not partaken of it since Rusty's accident. He held it up to the light: less than an inch of amber liquid at its bottom. *One sip for comfort, two for courage*, he thought, and took one exceptionally long and very deep sip until the jar was emptied. He shuddered, gave himself an exhortatory slap on the face, and tossed the jar into his neighbor's trash heap on the other side of the fence.

Now, while Uncle Chick cracks his oversized Bible-and-Book-of-Mormon combination to a random page and without looking at it begins to recite a series of wedding-related scriptures, Golden concentrates, making sure not to teeter or sway. Speaking at a good clip, as if he's trying to get this over with as soon as possible, Uncle Chick explains to the couple that they will be required, from this day hence, to love and support each other, that it is the sacred duty of the wife to submit herself to her husband in all things and in return he must protect and provide for her, to cleave unto her as if she were his own body, that they must share all things in love and righteousness and always keep their marriage bed pure—here he pauses to give Golden a less-than-enigmatic look through the smoked lenses of his glasses—and if they will heed this counsel and keep God's commandments they shall forever be as one mind, one flesh.

The sun slides free of the silver clouds and Golden is dazzled for a moment, he has to close his eyes and turn his head, and when he opens them again he is looking at his four wives, seated side by side in the front row just to his right, wearing identical cream-colored dresses. They are holding hands and in each of their eyes, even Beverly's, is the evidence of tears.

For a moment he experiences that familiar, almost thrilling sense of dislocation—*How did I get here? How did this happen?*—and then the web of phosphenes and colored dots clears from his vision and he is struck by the beauty of these women, their generous mouths and graceful arms, their backs held straight as if in defiance or pride. His own body, compressed for so long under the weight of sadness and doubt, creaks at this sudden and irregular expansion of feeling, with the swelling of belief that he *can* do this, that he has the capacity to love and care for these women—his wives!—that his heart is spacious enough to accommodate them all, even this strange woman at his side who nudges him a little to direct his attention back to the matter at hand, her hair crackling in his ear.

In this single bright moment, surrounded by his loved ones, his new home being raised in a racket of hammering and shouts, the air imprinted with the scent of hot sawdust, he is ready to believe that anything is possible.

He can't help himself; before he turns back he steals a look across the heads of family and friends, finds Huila near the back standing by the propane tank. He can't be sure, but she appears to be holding Nestor's hand. They both smile broadly, her son clutching his mother's leg, the weathered old uncle looking around, an expression on his face that says, *These are some very strange people.* Huila is wearing the peasant dress he first saw her in, the one decorated with yellow pineapples and bananas in rough yarn, and he knows that for all the undeserved bounty of his life, she will always be there, at the edge of his vision, to remind him of all the things he can never have.

Uncle Chick asks the wives to come forward and take their place next to the bride: Trish closest to Maureen, then Rose-of-Sharon, Nola, and Beverly at the end.

Now that Trish is standing, the slight rounding of her belly is obvious. After that first night months ago, until her morning sickness (which seemed to peak during evening hours) got the better of her, they'd had sex with some regularity on the Barge's smelly decks, healing sex, tired sex, sex whose only purpose, it seemed, was to make the world and everything in it disappear. Though she was never enthusiastic about it, Golden insisted they use the condoms he had purchased, in a moment of abject embarrassment, from the old bald druggist in St. George. Now the sight of his young wife, flushed at the cheeks, radiant with the new life inside her, he can only accept as a miracle, a divine rebuke to his selfish desires.

Both Rose and Nola have a different look to them as well, Rose with her hair in a simple bun, her skin tanned from a summer spent mostly outside, away from the hubbub of construction, herding kids and working in the family garden, and Nola, who has shed a good fifteen pounds since finding out that it would be Maureen Sinkfoyle joining the family (she has let it be known that her new life's goal is to be "only the second tubbiest wife in the Richards clan"). And there is Beverly, at the end of the line, a flash of new gray at her temples, coughing quietly into her fist. A month ago, after she had succeeded in her campaign to ensure that Maureen would be Golden's fifth wife, she informed him in the most matter-of-fact way that she had been to see the doctor, who told her what she had suspected for quite a while: she had inoperable lung cancer, almost certainly contracted from exposure to radioactive fallout. She would not seek treatment, which had little chance of helping anyway, and her only request of him was that he keep this news a secret for as long as she asked. She would spend the rest of her time tutoring Maureen and making peace with the other wives, to ensure that once she was gone the Richards family would soldier forward in harmony and righteousness until the promised day, on the other side of the veil, when they would be joined together again.

From the back of the house there is the sharp whine of a power saw followed by some good-natured cursing in Spanish, and one of the redheaded Sinkfoyle brothers (both of whom will be adding their number to the ranks of the Richards family any moment now) makes an off-color joke under his breath that draws a few titters from the crowd. Uncle Chick barks out a cough of warning and turns to address the wives. He asks them if they are ready to stand as Sarah of old and sacrifice their personal desires to the greater glory of God and His kingdom. To each one in turn he asks, "Do you, willingly and of your own accord, give this good sister to this man in marriage for time and all eternity?" and each one, with only a slight hesitation, nods, says, "I do."

At this point of the ceremony, it is up to Trish, as the last wife, to deliver the bride. She takes Maureen's wrist, but doesn't seem to possess the strength to lift it. A muscle in her jaw flares and, in a single, insistent motion, she places Maureen's right hand in Golden's and covers them both with her own. The other wives step forward to do the same and as they huddle close, breathing the same air, Golden hopes to meet their eyes, to assure them of his love for them, his good intentions, but he can see only a series of wet, flesh-colored blurs, and the moment is lost when Uncle Chick, by the power vested in him by no one but the true and living God, pronounces them man and wives. They step back, and for those in attendance it is difficult to say if the tears they discreetly knuckle from their eyes are tears of sorrow or joy.

The groom is instructed to kiss the bride, and Maureen tugs Golden down by his tie and mashes her face into his. The crowd exhales a sigh of relief and the Richards children, prodded by the several old church ladies who value politeness and decorum above all else, step uncertainly forward to offer their congratulations. Under a wide western sky they gather round, father, mothers and children, the whole mob of them shaking hands, giving kisses and exaggerated hugs, as if hoping to convince themselves, once and for all, that they are that most wondrous and impossible of things: one big happy family.

AUTHOR'S NOTE

While I tried to defer to geography and history whenever possible, in this book they have been employed opportunistically; where they didn't serve the story, they were blissfully ignored.

I'd like to offer my thanks to these people and organizations:

The families in Utah and Arizona for their generosity and insight, for allowing me into their lives.

My editor, Jill Bialosky, for taking on this book and under difficult circumstances, and to all the good people at Norton who have helped along the way.

Francis Geffard, editor at Albin Michel, for his knowledge and appreciation of the American West, and his support of my work.

Peter Rudy and Aaron Cohen, friends and first readers, whose advice and criticism made this a better book.

Matt Crosby, whose sharp eye and editorial instincts saved the day.

Colorado Art Ranch and the Retreat at Railroad Ranch, for providing time and beautiful places in which to write.

Raye C. Ringholz, author of *Uranium Frenzy: Saga of the Nuclear West*, and Carole Gallagher, author of *American Ground Zero: The Secret Nuclear War*, for their work on American nuclear testing and its victims.

Dorothy Allred Solomon, whose memoir, *Daughter of the Saints*, is the best account of polygamy ever written.

And to three people in particular, my deepest gratitude:

Carol Houck Smith, who didn't get to see this book into print, but whose influence lives on every page.

Nicole Aragi, for so many things: advice, humor, perspective, friendship, support.

Kate, for strength and sweetness, for being there every step of the way.